Famous FANTASTIC Mysteries ™

30 Great Tales of Fantasy and Horror
from the Classic Pulp Magazines
Famous Fantastic Mysteries & Fantastic Novels
Edited by Stefan R. Dziemianowicz, Robert Weinberg
& Martin H. Greenberg

GRAMERCY BOOKS
NEW YORK

First published in 1991 by Gramercy Books, distributed by
Outlet Book Company, Inc., a Random House Company,
225 Park Avenue South, New York, New York 10003.

Famous Fantastic Mysteries is a trademark co-owned by Argosy Communications.

FISHHEAD is a trademark owned by Argosy Communications, Inc.
All rights reserved.

Interior illustration by Virgil Finlay

Printed and bound in the United States of America

Library of Congress Cataloging-in-Publication Data

Famous fantastic mysteries : 30 great tales of fantasy and horror from
the classic pulp magazines Famous fantastic mysteries & Fantastic
novels / edited by Stefan R. Dziemianowicz, Robert Weinberg &
Martin H. Greenberg.
p.   cm.
ISBN 0-517-05577-5
1. Fantastic fiction, American.   2. Horror tales, American.
I. Dziemianowicz, Stefan R.   II. Weinberg, Robert E.
III. Greenberg, Martin Harry.   IV. Famous fantastic mysteries.
V. Fantastic novels.
PS648.F3F34   1991
813'.0873808—dc20
91-10646
CIP

8 7 6 5 4 3 2 1

Acknowledgments

Grateful acknowledgment for permission to reprint material is hereby given to the following:

Pegasus by Henry Kuttner—Copyright 1940 by Popular Fiction Publishing Co.; renewed © 1968 by C. L. Moore. Reprinted by permission of Don Congdon Associates, Inc.

The Face in the Abyss by A. Merritt—Copyright 1923; renewed 1941 by A. Merritt. Reprinted by permission of Forrest J. Ackerman, 2495 Glendower Ave., Los Angeles, CA 90027.

Fungus Isle by Philip M. Fisher—Copyright 1923 by Frank A. Munsey Publications. Reprinted by permission of Argosy Communications, Inc.

John Ovington Returns by Max Brand—Copyright 1941 by Frank A. Munsey Publications. Reprinted by permission of Brandt & Brandt Literary Agents, Inc.

Fishhead by Irvin S. Cobb—*The Cavalier,* January, 1913. FISHHEAD is a trademark of Argosy Communications, Inc. Copyright © 1913 by The Frank A. Munsey Company. Copyright renewed © 1941 and assigned to Argosy Communications, Inc. All rights reserved. Reprinted by arrangement with Argosy Communications, Inc.

The Outcast by E. F. Benson—Reprinted by permission of A. P. Watt Limited on behalf of the Executors of the Estate of K. S. P. McDowell.

The Novel of the White Powder by Arthur Machen—appears by arrangement with The Estate of the late Arthur Machen and the publisher, and A. M. Heath & Company Limited, London.

Daemon by C. L. Moore—Copyright 1946; renewed © 1974 by C. L. Moore. Reprinted by permission of Don Congdon Associates, Inc.

The Day of the Deepies by Murray Leinster—Copyright 1947 by Popular Fiction Publishing Co. Reprinted by permission of the agents for the author's Estate, the Scott Meredith Literary Agency, Inc., 845 Third Ave., New York, NY 10022.

The Lonesome Place by August Derleth—Copyright 1948 by Popular Publishing Co. Reprinted by permission of the agents for the author's Estate, the Scott Meredith Literary Agency, Inc., 845 Third Ave., New York, NY 10022.

That Low by Theodore Sturgeon—Copyright 1948; renewed © 1976 by Theodore Sturgeon. Reprinted by permission of Kirby McCauley, Ltd.

CONTENTS

Introduction

The first issue of *Famous Fantastic Mysteries* appeared at newsstands in the fall of 1939, and the first issue of *Fantastic Novels* the following summer. Although neither could lay claim to being the first or the most famous fantasy fiction magazine, at the time of their debuts they were probably the most distinguished. Both *Famous Fantastic Mysteries* and *Fantastic Novels* were published by the Frank A. Munsey Company, and so had a heritage extending back to the nineteenth century and the beginning of the pulp magazine phenomenon. Indeed, to understand how the magazines came into being and why they appealed to readers, one must go back almost a half century.

In 1896, publishing mogul Frank A. Munsey converted his children's magazine, *The Argosy,* to an all-fiction monthly for adults printed on inexpensive pulp paper stock. Though not appreciated at the time, Munsey's money-saving innovation created the first pulp magazine—and a legacy that continues to affect the contemporary fiction market. Over the next half-century, it encouraged numerous imitators, who produced thousands of popular fiction periodicals. It was in the pages of these magazines that genres such as science fiction, detective fiction, weird fiction, the western, the sports story, and the love story were to achieve their greatest popularity, and a number of today's bestselling authors see their first efforts published.

Initially, though, no pulp magazine was devoted exclusively to a particular literary genre. *The Argosy* and its companion publications, *The All-Story Magazine* and *The Cavalier,* were non-specialized fiction magazines designed to appeal to the broadest possible audience. Readers of fantasy and science fiction in search of the most recent Edgar Rice Burroughs story would buy them, but so would fans of adventure writer Theodore Roscoe, devotees of Zane Gray's western novels, lovers of Jack London's tales of the Yukon, and enthusiasts of the short fiction of William Sidney Porter (who would later sign his name "O. Henry"). Not until the 1920s would the general fiction magazines be outnumbered be the genre pulps.

Though the Munsey magazines eventually had to contend with a number of competitors, such as *The Blue Book Magazine, The Popular Magazine,* and *The Thrill Book,* they were a formidable publishing presence in the first two decades of the century. Then the Great Depression of 1929 changed the whole outlook of the pulp fiction market, killing off scores of magazines which suddenly found themselves insolvent or unable to coax a dime out of the pockets of their readers on a monthly (or, in some cases, weekly) basis. The Munsey chain survived these years, but not without losing a significant number of readers to the genre pulps, many of which supplied more thrilling escapism than a middle-class oriented magazine like *The Argosy* could offer.

By 1939, with America beginning to recover from its financial hardships and entertaining hope of future prosperity, an explosion of pulp magazines hit the newsstands. Publications catering to every taste imaginable proliferated, but science fiction and fantasy in particular enjoyed a phenomenal growth spurt as publishers tested the waters with a dazzling array of titles like *Unknown, Strange Stories, Fantastic Adventures, Planet Stories,* and *Startling Stories.* Among these were two new Munsey pulps, *Famous Fantastic Mysteries* and *Fantastic Novels.*

Actually, *Famous Fantastic Mysteries* was only *somewhat* new. Realizing that it had published a considerable amount of fantasy and science fiction in *Argosy, All-Story,* and *Cavalier,* and that some of these stories—like Burroughs' *Tarzan of the Apes* and A. Merritt's *The Ship of Ishtar*—ranked among the most popular to have appeared in those publications, the Munsey Company decided to create a genre pulp of its own, the contents of which would be culled from the first forty years of its general fiction magazines. The reasoning behind this decision was simple: readers of the genre pulps who were too young or too exclusive in their tastes to have picked up copies of the original magazines might take a chance on the second go-round of stories selected with genre interests in mind. And because in most instances Munsey still owned the magazine publication rights to these stories, the overhead for turning out the new magazine would amount to little more than production costs.

So what exactly is a "famous fantastic mystery?" The variety of fiction published in the magazine's eighty-one issues was such that it is nearly impossible to define this term. Initially, though, the type of story being published by the top weird and science fiction magazines of the day was a good example of what a famous fantastic mystery was *not.* In comparison to the stories appearing in *Weird Tales, Amazing Stories,* and *Astounding Science-Fiction,* those published by the Munsey magazines were more innocent: the science fiction was less hardware- or concept-oriented, and the fantasy less grim and Gothic. *Argosy* and its brethren had enjoyed their heyday during the years of World War I, when success at the newsstand was determined by the amount of escape a periodical could offer from the real world. The stories they carried, no matter how well written, had been selected largely to appeal to the daydreamer in their readers.

The Munsey magazines served as a showcase for a particular type of fantasy known as the scientific romance. Acknowledged as a prototype of science fiction, the scientific romance usually set a love story of brave men and women battling evil adversaries against an exotic or futuristic backdrop of pseudoscientific gizmos and strange and wondrous creatures. The heroes were always rugged and intelligent, the heroines spunky and beautiful, and the villains (often supernatural in origin) hissable. Although the basic boy-meets-girl scenario varied little from story to story, settings for the scientific romances ranged from the parallel world of Austin Hall and Homer Eon Flint's *The Blind Spot,* to the post-apocalyptic future of George Allan England's *Darkness and Dawn* trilogy, the subatomic world of Ray Cummings' *The Girl in the Golden Atom,* the submerged continent of Atlantis in Cutcliffe Hyne's *The Lost Continent,* the distant Venus of Ralph Milne Farley's *Radio Planet,* and the lost world beneath the Ponape Islands in A. Merritt's *Conquest of the Moon Pool.* And no matter how short on logic, or duty-bound to uphold the eternal verities of love and honor, the scientific romance was always suffused with an invigorating sense of wonder.

Where the scientific romances tended to run to novel length and share a number of common features, the many short fantasies in the Munsey magazines offered a cornucopia of styles and subject matter. Among some of the better stories were Irvin S. Cobb's revenge fantasy "Fishhead," E. F. Benson's ghost tale "The Outcast," Philip Fisher's high seas horror story "Fungus Isle," J. U. Giesy's gadget tale "The Gravity Experiment," Tod Robbins' whimsical fantasies "Who Wants a Green Bottle?" and "Wild Wullie the Waster," and A. Merritt's sentimental war story "Three Lines of Old French."

The predominance of A. Merritt's name among all types of fantastic fiction in the Munsey magazines is worth noting, for without his stories it is doubtful that *Famous Fantastic Mysteries* and *Fantastic Novels* would have succeeded. Although largely forgotten today, Merritt was one of the most influential fantasy authors of his time (his work inspired science fiction greats Edmond Hamilton, Jack Williamson, C. L. Moore, and Henry Kuttner) and Edgar Rice Burroughs' greatest rival for reader acclaim. Burroughs departed from the Munsey pulps soon after he became famous, and took the reprint rights to his stories with him, but Merritt published almost exclusively in *Argosy* and *All-Story* until 1934. As a result, he became the most published author in both *Famous Fantastic Mysteries* and *Fantastic Novels.*

Not surprisingly, Merritt's novella "The Moon Pool" was chosen as the lead story for the first issue of *Famous Fantastic Mysteries* with the idea that it would whet reader appetites for the serialization of the novel-length sequel, *The Conquest of the Moon Pool,* over the next six issues. The strategy appears to have worked, since Munsey's turned the magazine into a monthly beginning with the second issue. And so it went for the first eight issues, with editor Mary Gnaedinger offering readers a mix of classic short fiction, novellas, and novels, the latter serialized and run in overlapping sequences to ensure that readers always would anticipate—and buy—the next issue.

Famous Fantastic Mysteries attempted several experiments to enhance its appeal, including publication of an occasional original story or non-Munsey reprint. But the most successful innovation was the decision to use cover art beginning in March 1940 and to commission new interior illustrations for the stories. It was in the pages of *Famous Fantastic Mysteries* that Virgil Finlay (whose work is reproduced on the dustjacket and in the interior of this book) raised the craft of pulp illustration to the level of art. When Finlay's work began appearing in *Weird Tales* in the late thirties, illustrations for the pulps were, with a few notable exceptions, crude and unmemorable; the purpose of cover art was to attract attention and interiors simply to break up the text. But Finlay's eye for detail and use of classic imagery gave any magazine in which his work appeared a look of sophistication and professionalism. Although his work already had graced the pages of several weird fiction pulps, he seemed born to his task at *Famous Fantastic Mysteries,* where his talent for evoking the wondrous rather than the gruesome perfectly matched the content of the fiction. When he enlisted in the armed services in 1943 another fine artist, Lawrence Sterne Stevens, took on the bulk of the illustrating duties. Late in the magazine's life Finlay and Stevens were joined by *Weird Tales* alumnus Hannes Bok, and the work produced by this trio was so outstanding that many readers who already owned books or magazines in which the stories had appeared bought *Famous Fantastic Mysteries* solely for the illustrations.

By early 1940, it had become clear to the editor and publisher of *Famous Fantastic Mysteries* that even with concurrently running serials it would take years to satisfy reader demands for novel-length reprints. Thus, in the issue dated May/June 1940, readers were informed of the creation of a new Munsey reprint magazine, *Fantastic Novels. Famous Fantastic Mysteries* was to change back to bi-monthly publication; *Fantastic Novels* also would publish bi-monthly, but during the alternate months. The intended result was that readers would buy both magazines and, in twelve issues per year, get their fill of both novels *and* short fiction. Although this must have seemed like an innovative idea, it ended up producing essentially the same magazine under two different titles, since soon afterward *Famous Fantastic Mysteries* also began publishing a full novel per issue and filling out the remaining space with two or three shorter works.

For almost a year, Munsey's gambit was successful. But World War II had begun in Europe almost the same time that the first issue of *Famous Fantastic Mysteries* reached the newsstands, and America had already begun to feel its effects in the form of dwindling overseas markets and evaporating paper supplies. After only five issues, *Fantastic Novels* was absorbed into *Famous Fantastic Mysteries,* which continued on a bi-monthly schedule.

The magazine returned to a monthly schedule with the June 1942 issue, only to be confronted with a problem of a different sort. *Argosy,* still the flagship pulp for Munsey's, was ailing, and in an effort to boost its circulation, the publisher had tried to modernize its look. But some of the photos used to punch up its appearance met with objections from the Postmaster General, and as a result, *Argosy* was banned from the mails in July. The pulps depended on their ability to take advantage of low second-class postage rates, and the revoking of such privileges meant almost certain death for the magazine. Before the year was out, Munsey decided to cut its losses. *Argosy* and a number of other pulp titles were sold to Popular Publications, among these *Famous Fantastic Mysteries* and (the suspended) *Fantastic Novels*.

At that time, Popular Publications was probably the most successful pulp publisher in the country. Through its early thirties experiments *Horror Stories, Terror Tales,* and *Dime-Mystery Magazine,* Popular had pioneered the "shudder pulp," a magazine filled with lurid and often sadistic stories of weird menaces. A bit later came a series of gritty hero pulps, including *G-8 and Battle Aces* and *The Spider,* that gave the squeaky clean heroes in market leaders *Doc Savage* and *The Shadow* a run for their money. Indeed, Popular made enough profit from these magazines that it was in a position to buy up several pulp lines weakened by the wartime paper shortages and the loss of readers to comic books.

The acquisition of a venerable magazine like *Famous Fantastic Mysteries* should have been a feather in Popular's cap, but it created a problem almost immediately. It was Popular's policy to run a cover line on all of its magazines proclaiming "All stories in this issue are either new or have never appeared before in a magazine"—but here was a magazine whose readers expected nothing but reprints!

What could have been a fiasco resulted instead in one of the most felicitous developments in pulp fantasy publishing. To find a happy medium that would neither compromise its editorial policy nor dissatisfy its readers, Popular began reprinting fantasy stories that never had appeared before in *American* magazines. As good as much of Munsey's fantasy had been, it couldn't match the breadth and variety of stories that Popular now could reprint from books and non-American periodicals.

Popular published only fourteen issues of *Famous Fantastic Mysteries* before dropping its "all new" disclaimer, but the fiction in those issues was telling. There were two supernatural horror novels by renowned British fantasist William Hope Hodgson; G. K. Chesterton's brilliant metaphysical nightmare *The Man Who Was Thursday;* a short novel by H. Rider Haggard (author of the ever-popular *She* and *King Solomon's Mines*); and short stories recognized today as fantasy classics by Arthur Machen, Lord Dunsany, Algernon Blackwood, and Robert W. Chambers. In addition, Popular revived the idea of printing an occasional original story, such as Ray Bradbury's "King of the Gray Spaces" (later to be renamed as the title story of his collection *S is for Space*) and C. L. Moore's exquisite "Daemon." Through a simple bending of the rules, *Famous Fantastic Mysteries* became almost overnight one of the most literate pulp magazines.

Reader reception to the new editorial policy was positive, and this convinced Popular to follow up on the earlier dream of the Munsey chain and resume publishing *Fantastic Novels* on an alternate bi-monthly basis starting in 1948. Popular did a much better job of keeping the two magazines distinct, publishing more short fiction in *Famous Fantastic Mysteries,* and using *Fantastic Novels* as a showcase for the Munsey reprints. It was in the latter that the remainder of A. Merritt's fantasy novels, Garrett P. Serviss's science fiction disaster novel *The Second Deluge,* scientific romances by Ray Cummings and Otis Adelbert Kline, and the underappreciated short fiction of Tod Robbins were given another chance.

By this time, *Famous Fantastic Mysteries* had dropped all pretense of only reprinting stories from unfamiliar sources. A typical issue of the magazine might include a classic novel like H. G. Wells' *The War of the Worlds* or a reprint of a pulp favorite like Thomas Calvert McClary's *Rebirth.* There were short stories such as Theodore Sturgeon's "Killdozer" and Robert A. Heinlein's "—And He Built a Crooked House," which had appeared previously in *Astounding Science-Fiction,* and completely new stories like August Derleth's "The Lonesome Place," Henry Henry Kuttner's "Before I Wake" and Robert Bloch's "The Man Who Collected Poe." By the time *Famous Fantastic Mysteries* and *Fantastic Novels* ceased publication, the short fiction measured up to the quality of that in other fantasy and science fiction pulps (in part because much of it had come from them). And their novel-length features, a nearly extinct concept among magazines trying to survive on tight paper rations, were unique attractions for readers.

When *Fantastic Novels* suspended publication with its twenty-fifth issue in June, 1951, and *Famous Fantastic Mysteries* followed exactly two years later, it wasn't for want of readers. Both magazines succumbed to the rise in publishing costs, the onslaught of comic books and television, and the growing paperback book market that they had helped pave the way for. But at least *Famous Fantastic Mysteries* went out with a bang. Its final issue mixed reprints of stories by Robert E. Howard and Ray Bradbury with the first and only pulp appearances of Franz Kafka's "The Metamorphosis" and Ayn Rand's first novel, *Anthem.* One can only speculate how the nature of weird fiction reading in America—and perhaps popular fiction publishing in general—might have changed had so eclectic an editorial policy been allowed to evolve into a trend.

It is difficult to evaluate the impact that *Famous Fantastic Mysteries* and *Fantastic Novels* had upon modern fantasy fiction. In some ways, the editorial policy of printing stories that were already proven winners foreshadowed the rise of popular theme and "best-of" fiction antholo-gies. More important, it is possible that the publication of work by British authors like Arthur Machen, William Hope Hodgson, Arthur Conan Doyle, H. G. Wells, John Benyon (a.k.a. John Wyndham), and Lord Dunsany, and stories by Sax Rohmer, E. Charles Vivian, and Fitz-James O'Brien (which hitherto had been available only in hard-covers too expensive for most pulp buyers) helped to expand the literary horizons of readers. It is especially interesting to note that a number of classic authors published in *Famous Fantastic Mysteries* and *Fantastic Novels* received their first book publication in the United States only after appearing in the magazines.

It was not easy to make the selections for this anthology for any number of reasons, but there are two in particular. First, approximately eighty percent of the fiction published in both *Famous Fantastic Mysteries* and *Fantastic Novels* ran to novel length. The choice of A. Merritt's short novel "The Face in the Abyss" meant passing up Jesse Douglas Kerruish's fine werewolf novel *The Undying Monster,* William Hope Hodgson's rarely reprinted *The Boats of the Glen Carrig,* Sax Rohmer's occult thriller *Brood of the Witch Queen,* or even an outstanding full-length A. Merritt novel like *Burn, Witch, Burn!* But the more important reason is that the contents of both magazines originally were compiled from stories that already had withstood the test of time, and were considered among the best of their type. It is difficult to choose the best of the best. But we feel that these stories give a fair representation of the very best that *Famous Fantastic Mysteries* and *Fantastic Novels* had to offer, and that they will permit readers to determine for themselves exactly what a "famous fantastic mystery" is.

STEFAN DZIEMIANOWICZ

New York,
1991

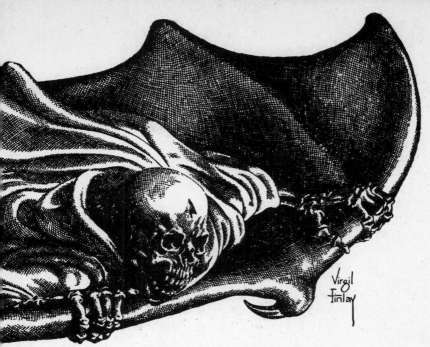

Behind the Curtain

FRANCIS STEVENS

Although men wrote most of the fantasy and science fiction published in the pulps, Francis Stevens (a pseudonym for Gertrude Bennett) was one of the best fantasy writers to emerge from the pages of the Munsey magazines. Famous Fantastic Mysteries *reprinted her popular novel of Atlantis,* Claimed, *and devoted the entire February 1942 issue of the magazine to her lost race novel* The Citadel of Fear *(one of only two novels so honored). Between them,* Famous Fantastic Mysteries *and* Fantastic Novels *reprinted six of the eleven fantasies Stevens is known to have authored, including the grim revenge story "Behind the Curtain."*

IT WAS after nine o'clock when the bell rang, and descending to the dimly lighted hall I opened the front door, at first on the chain to be sure of my visitor. Seeing, as I had hoped, the face of our friend, Ralph Quentin, I took off the chain and he entered with a blast of sharp November air for company. I had to throw my weight upon the door to close it against the wind.

As he removed his hat and cloak he laughed good-humoredly.

"You're very cautious, Santallos. I thought you were about to demand a password before admitting me."

"It is well to be cautious," I retorted. "This house stands somewhat alone, and thieves are everywhere."

"It would require a thief of considerable muscle to make off with

1

some of your treasures. That stone tomb-thing, for instance; what do you call it?"

"The Beni Hassan sarcophagus. Yes. But what of the gilded inner case, and what of the woman it contains? A thief of judgment and intelligence might covet that treasure and strive to deprive me of it. Don't you agree?"

He only laughed again, and counterfeited a shudder.

"The woman! Don't remind me that such a brown, shriveled, mummy-horror was ever a woman!"

"But she was. Doubtless in her day my poor Princess of Naam was soft, appealing; a creature of red, moist lips and eyes like stars in the black Egyptian sky. 'The Songstress of the House' she was called, ere she became Ta-Nezem the Osirian. But I keep you standing here in the cold hall. Come upstairs with me. Did I tell you that Beatrice is not here tonight?"

"No?" His intonation expressed surprise and frank disappointment. "Then I can't say good-by to her? Didn't you receive my note? I'm to take Sanderson's place as manager of the sales department in Chicago, and I'm off tomorrow morning."

"Congratulations. Yes, we had your note, but Beatrice was given an opportunity to join some friends on a Southern trip. The notice was short, but of late she has not been so well and I urged her to go. This November air is cruelly damp and bitter."

"What was it—a yachting cruise?"

"A long cruise. She left this afternoon. I have been sitting in her boudoir, Quentin, thinking of her, and I'll tell you about it there—if you don't mind?"

"Wherever you like," he conceded, though in a tone of some surprise. I suppose he had not credited me with so much sentiment, or thought it odd that I should wish to share it with another, even so good a friend as he. "You must find it fearfully lonesome here without Bee," he continued.

"A trifle." We were ascending the dark stairs now. "After tonight, however, things will be quite different. Do you know that I have sold the house?"

"No! Why, you are full of astonishments, old chap. Found a better place with more space for your tear-jars and tombstones?"

He meant, I assumed, a witty reference to my collection of Coptic and Egyptian treasures, well and dearly bought, but so much trash to a man of Quentin's youth and temperament.

I opened the door of my wife's boudoir, and it was pleasant to pass into such rosy light and warmth out of the stern, dark cold of the hall. Yet it was an old house, full of unexpected drafts. Even here there was a draft so strong that a heavy velour curtain at the far side of the room continually rippled and billowed out, like a loose rose-colored sail. Never far enough, though, to show what was behind it.

My friend settled himself on the frail little chair that stood before my wife's dressing-table. It was the kind of chair that women love and most men loathe, but Quentin, for all his weight and stature, had a touch of the feminine about him, or perhaps of the feline. Like a cat, he moved delicately. He was blond and tall, with fine, regular features, a ready laugh, and the clean charm of youth about him—also its occasional blundering candor.

As I looked at him sitting there, graceful, at ease, I wished that his mind might have shared the litheness of his body. He could have understood me so much better.

"I have indeed found a place for my collections," I observed, seating myself near by. "In fact, with a single exception—the Ta-Nezem sarcophagus—the entire lot is going to the dealers." Seeing his expression of astonished disbelief I continued: "The truth is, my dear Quentin, that I have been guilty of gross injustice to our Beatrice. I have been too good a collector and too neglectful a husband. My 'tear-jars and tombstones,' in fact, have enjoyed an attention that might better have been elsewhere bestowed. Yes, Beatrice has left me alone, but the instant that some few last affairs are settled I intend rejoining her. And you yourself are leaving. At least, none of us three will be left to miss the others' friendship."

"You are quite surprising tonight, Santallos. But, by Jove, I'm not sorry to hear any of it! It's not my place to criticize, and Bee's not the sort to complain. But living here in this lonely old barn of a house, doing all her own work, practically deserted by her friends, must have been—"

"Hard, very hard," I interrupted him softly, "for one so young and lovely as our Beatrice. But if I have been blind, at least the awakening has come. You should have seen her face when she heard the news. It was wonderful. We were standing, just she and I, in the midst of my tear-jars and tombstones—my 'chamber of horrors' she named it. You are so apt at amusing phrases, both of you. We stood beside the great stone sarcophagus from the Necropolis of Beni Hassan. Across the trestles beneath it lay the gilded inner case wherein Ta-Nezem the Osirian had slept out so many centuries. You know its appearance. A thing of beautiful, gleaming lines, like the quaint, smiling image of a golden woman.

"Then I lifted the lid and showed Beatrice that the one-time song-stress, the handmaiden of Amen, slept there no more, and the case was empty. You know, too, that Beatrice never liked my princess. For a jest she used to declare that she was jealous. Jealous of a woman dead and ugly so many thousand years! Or—but that was only in anger—that I had bought Ta-Nezem with what would have given her, Beatrice, all the pleasure she lacked in life. Oh, she was not too patient to reproach me, Quentin, but only in anger and hot blood.

"So I showed her the empty case, and I said, 'Beloved wife, never again need you be jealous of Ta-Nezem. All that is in this room save her and her belongings I have sold, but her I could not bear to sell.

That which I love, no man else shall share or own. So I have destroyed her. I have rent her body to brown, aromatic shreds. I have burned her; it is as if she had never been. And now, dearest of the dear, you shall take for your own all the care, all the keeping that heretofore I have lavished upon the Princess of Naam.'

"Beatrice turned from the empty case as if she could scarcely believe her hearing, but when she saw by the look in my eyes that I meant exactly what I said, neither more nor less, you should have seen her face, my dear Quentin—you should have seen her face!"

"I can imagine." He laughed, rather shortly. For some reason my guest seemed increasingly ill at ease, and glanced continually about the little rose-and-white room that was the one luxurious, thoroughly feminine corner—that and the cold, dark room behind the curtain—in what he had justly called my "barn of a house."

"Santallos," he continued abruptly, and I thought rather rudely, "you should have a portrait done as you look tonight. You might have posed for one of those stern old *hidalgos* of—which painter was it who did so many Spanish dons and donesses?"

"You perhaps mean Velasquez," I answered with mild courtesy, though secretly and as always his crude personalities displeased me. "My father, you may recall, was of Cordova in southern Spain. But—must you go so soon? First drink one glass with me to our missing Beatrice. See how I was warming my blood against the wind that blows in, even here. The wine is Amontillado, some that was sent me by a friend of my father's from the very vineyards where the grapes were grown and pressed. And for many years it has ripened since it came here. Before she went, Beatrice drank of it from one of these same glasses. True wine of Montilla! See how it lives—like fire in amber, with a glimmer of blood behind it."

I held high the decanter and the light gleamed through it upon his face.

"Amontillado! Isn't that a kind of sherry? I'm no connoisseur of wines, as you know. But—Amontillado."

For a moment he studied the wine I had given him, liquid flame in the crystal glass. Then his face cleared.

"I remember the association now. 'The Cask of Amontillado.' Ever read the story?"

"I seem to recall it dimly."

"Horrible, fascinating sort of a yarn. A fellow takes his trustful friend down into the cellars to sample some wine, traps him and walls him up in a niche. Buries him alive, you understand. Read it when I was a youngster, and it made a deep impression, partly, I think, because I couldn't for the life of me comprehend a nature—even an Italian nature—desiring so horrible a form of vengeance. You're half Latin yourself, Santallos. Can you elucidate?"

"I doubt if you would ever understand," I responded slowly, wondering how even Quentin could be so crude, so tactless. "Such a revenge might have its merits, since the offender would be a long time dying. But merely to kill seems to me so pitifully inadequate. Now I, if I were driven to revenge, should never be contented by killing. I should wish to follow."

"What—beyond the grave?"

I laughed. "Why not? Wouldn't that be the very apotheosis of hatred? I'm trying to interpret the Latin nature, as you asked me to do."

"Confound you, for an instant I thought you were serious. The way you said it made me actually shiver!"

"Yes," I observed, "or perhaps it was the draft. See, Quentin, how that curtain billows out."

His eyes followed my glance. Continually the heavy, rose-colored curtain that was hung before the door of my wife's bedroom bulged outward, shook and quivered like a bellying sail, as draperies will with a wind behind them.

His eyes strayed from the curtain, met mine and fell again to the wine in his glass. Suddenly he drained it, not as would a man who was a judge of wines, but hastily, indifferently, without thought for its flavor or bouquet. I raised my glass in the toast he had forgotten.

"To our Beatrice," I said, and drained mine also, though with more appreciation.

"To Beatrice—of course." He looked at the bottom of his empty glass, then before I could offer to refill it, rose from his chair.

"I must go, old man. When you write to Bee, tell her I'm sorry to have missed her."

"Before she could receive a letter from me I shall be with her—I hope. How cold the house is tonight, and the wind breathes everywhere. See how the curtain blows, Quentin."

"So it does." He set his glass on the tray beside the decanter. Upon first entering the room he had been smiling, but now his straight, fine brows were drawn in a perpetual, troubled frown, his eyes looked here and there, and would never meet mine—which were steady. "There's a wind," he added, "that blows along this wall—curious. One can't notice any draft there, either. But it must blow there, and of course the curtain billows out."

"Yes," I said. "Of course it billows out."

"Or is there another door behind that curtain?"

His careful ignorance of what any fool might infer from mere appearance brought an involuntary smile to my lips. Nevertheless, I answered him.

"Yes, of course there is a door. An open door."

His frown deepened. My true and simple replies appeared to cause him a certain irritation.

"As I feel now," I added, "even to cross the room would be an effort. I am tired and weak tonight. As Beatrice once said, my strength beside yours is as a child's to that of a grown man. Won't you close that door for me, dear friend?"

"Why—yes, I will. I didn't know you were ill. If that's the case, you shouldn't be alone in this empty house. Shall I stay with you for a while?"

As he spoke he walked across the room. His hand was on the curtain, but before it could be drawn aside my voice checked him.

"Quentin," I said, "are even you quite strong enough to close that door?"

Looking back at me, chin on shoulder, his face appeared scarcely familiar, so drawn was it in lines of bewilderment and half-suspicion.

"What do you mean? You are very—odd tonight. Is the door so heavy then? What door is it?"

I made no reply.

As if against their owner's will his eyes fled from mine, he turned and hastily pushed aside the heavy drapery.

Behind it my wife's bedroom lay dark and cold, with windows open to the invading winds.

And erect in the doorway, uncovered, stood an ancient gilded coffin-case. It was the golden casket of Ta-Nezem, but its occupant was more beautiful than the poor, shriveled Songstress of Naam.

Bound across her bosom were the strange, quaint jewels which had been found in the sarcophagus. Ta-Nezem's amulets—heads of Hathor and Horus, the sacred eye, the uræus, even the heavy dull-green scarab, the amulet for purity of heart—there they rested upon the bosom of her who had been mistress of my house, now Beatrice the Osirian. Beneath them her white, stiff body was enwrapped in the same crackling dry, brown linen bands, impregnated with the gums and resins of embalmers dead these many thousand years, which had been about the body of Ta-Nezem.

Above the white translucence of her brow appeared the winged disk, emblem of Ra. The twining golden bodies of its supporting uraeii, its cobras of Egypt, were lost in the dusk of her hair, whose soft fineness yet lived and would live so much longer than the flesh of any of us three.

Yes, I had kept my word and given to Beatrice all that had been Ta-Nezem's, even to the sarcophagus itself, for in my will it was written that she be placed in it for final burial.

Like the fool he was, Quentin stood there, staring at the unclosed, frozen eyes of my Beatrice—and his. Stood till that which had been in the wine began to make itself felt. He faced me then, but with so absurd and childish a look of surprise that, despite the courtesy due a guest, I laughed and laughed.

I, too, felt warning throes, but to me the pain was no more than a gage—a measure of his suffering—a stimulus to point the phrases in which I told him all I knew and had guessed of him and Beatrice, and thus drive home the jest.

But I had never thought that a man of Quentin's youth and strength could die so easily. Beatrice, frail though she was, had taken longer to die.

He could not even cross the room to stop my laughter, but at the first step stumbled, fell, and in a very little while lay at the foot of the gilded case.

After all, he was not so strong as I. Beatrice had seen. Her still, cold eyes saw all. How he lay there, his fine, lithe body contorted, worthless for any use till its substance should have been cast again in the melting-pot of dissolution, while I who had drunk of the same draft, suffered the same pangs, yet stood and found breath for mockery.

So I poured myself another glass of that good Cordovan wine, and I raised it to both of them and drained it, laughing.

"Quentin," I cried, "you asked *what door,* though your thought was that you had passed that way before, and feared that I guessed your knowledge. But there are doors and doors, dear, charming friend, and one that is heavier than any other. Close it if you can. Close it now in my face, who otherwise will follow even whither you have gone— the heavy, heavy door of the Osiris, Keeper of the House of Death!"

Thus I dreamed of doing and speaking. It was so vivid, the dream, that awakening in the darkness of my room I could scarcely believe that it had been other than reality. True, I lived, while in my dream I had shared the avenging poison. Yet my veins were still hot with the keen passion of triumph, and my eyes filled with the vision of Beatrice, dead—*dead in Ta-Nezem's casket.*

Unreasonably frightened, I sprang from bed, flung on a dressing-gown, and hurried out. Down the hallway I sped, swiftly and silently, at the end of it unlocked heavy doors with a tremulous hand, switched on lights, lights and more lights, till the great room of my collection was ablaze with them, and as my treasures sprang into view I sighed, like a man reaching home from a perilous journey.

The dream was a lie.

There, fronting me, stood the heavy empty sarcophagus; there on the trestles before it lay the gilded case, a thing of beautiful, gleaming lines, like the smiling image of a golden woman.

I stole across the room and softly, very softly, lifted the upper half of the beautiful lid, peering within. The dream indeed was a lie.

Happy as a comforted child I went to my room again. Across the hall the door of my wife's boudoir stood partly open. In the room beyond a faint light was burning, and I could see the rose-colored curtain sway slightly to a draft from some open window.

Yesterday she had come to me and asked for her freedom. I had refused, knowing to whom she would turn, and hating him for his youth, and his crudeness and his secret scorn of me.

But had I done well? They were children, those two, and despite my dream I was certain that their foolish, youthful ideals had kept them from actual sin against my honor. But what if, time passing, they might change? Or, Quentin gone, my lovely Beatrice might favor another, young as he and not so scrupulous?

Everyone, they say, has a streak of incipient madness. I recalled the frenzied act to which my dream jealousy had driven me. Perhaps it was a warning, the dream. What if my father's jealous blood should some day betray me, drive me to the insane destruction of her I held most dear and sacred?

I shuddered, then smiled at the swaying curtain. Beatrice was too beautiful for safety. She should have her freedom.

Let her mate with Ralph Quentin or whom she would, Ta-Nezem must rest secure in her gilded house of death. My brown, perfect, shriveled Princess of the Nile! Destroyed—rent to brown, aromatic shreds—burned—destroyed—and her beautiful coffin-case desecrated as I had seen it in my vision!

Again I shuddered, smiled and shook my head sadly at the swaying, rosy curtain.

"You are too lovely, Beatrice," I said, "and my father was a Spaniard. You shall have your freedom!"

I entered my room and lay down to sleep again, at peace and content. The dream, thank God, was a lie.

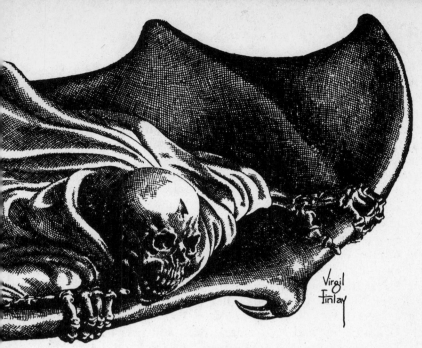

Pegasus

HENRY KUTTNER

It was a rare fantasy or science fiction pulp that the prolific Henry Kuttner did not write for. Although remembered mostly for the stories he wrote for Astounding Science-Fiction *(many under the pseudonym Lewis Padgett) and for a series of novels co-authored with his wife C. L. Moore for* Startling Stories, *Kuttner was able to adapt his writing to the needs of most fiction markets of his day. "Pegasus," his first contribution to* Famous Fantastic Mysteries, *was one of only four non-reprint stories published by the magazine during its first three years. Like his later submission, "Before I Wake," it deals with a clash between the fantastic and the rude reality of modern times.*

I WANT to tell you about Jim Harry Worth and the nag with wings. Now a lot of people think myths are just lying stories, sort of fairy tales that have grown big in the telling by old folks to young ones. And every country has its legends; in China I've heard about dragon ladies—But that's beside the point and I was going to tell you about Jim Harry and the magic horse he got for himself.

He was a tall, lanky, thin-faced youngster, brown as a nut, adolescently awkward when he stood still, but graceful as a colt when he moved. The Worths had a farm in Imperial, and Jim Harry was raised there, taught to do the chores and sent to school when he was old enough. He loved horse-flesh. The boy could ride, and he did, a lot.

It's open country here, and it's big. A kid can lie on his back out in the yellow slopes and look up at a sky that's bigger than all the world. He can lie there and watch the clouds drift till he feels that the earth is moving under him, till he feels the rush of a planet through the universe, and he has time to think. Jim Harry did, I know. The boy had a dream in his brown eyes, and his feet were touched with wanderlust. At first he didn't know what it was. He used to ride helter-skelter all over the place, and hike when he couldn't ride. Then at school he learned to read, and the Valley became a prison that was worse because it had no boundaries.

A dream in the eyes and restless feet—ah, but they are hell for a man, and heaven, too. That I know. You go wandering, and worse, for you go seeking as well, and what you seek you don't know and can never find.

You're trying to answer a question; you don't know what the question is; and in the end it's not answered. When you're tired at last you're ready to sit in the sun and think, but not when you're young. So young Jim Harry thought a lot, and read a great deal, and in a bad day he asked a question about Breadloaf Mountain that towered up to the south, barren and waterless and old.

"Nobody goes up there," said Andy Worth, Jim Harry's dad.

"But hasn't anybody ever gone?"

Andy didn't think so, but he had to go to town to buy some new saddles, so there wasn't much more conversation. Jim Harry's mother, Sarah, didn't know any more, and she told the boy not to bother about it. So Jim Harry went out with his older brother Tom, who was setting traps, and only got laughed at for his pains.

But he got the truth of it from Tante Rush. Some said she was a *paisano* and others said she was once a great woman and had been in Europe. Now she lived in a ramshackle frame building by a spring and kept pigs and chickens, a hag with a withered walnut of a face and eyes bright as garnets. People said she ate loco weed, and maybe she did. Anyway, she was a lonely old woman and because she liked company, she'd learned to listen and agree. The kids would come and talk to her by the hour, and she'd try to bribe them with her poor food to stay longer. Jim Harry went to see Tante Rush often, because she let him talk and didn't laugh at him, except in a kindly way.

Tante Rush said there might be anything on top of Breadloaf Mountain.

"Nobody's ever been there, I guess," the crone said. "Pooty hard to climb, ain't it, Jim Harry? You never been and climbed it?"

"Probably nothing up there. Except it's the highest spot for miles. You can see way over the Valley." The boy thrust away a hen that came pecking at his worn shoe. "Maybe you can see out to the Pacific."

"They're mountains in the way, youngster. Ain't you never see the ocean?"

"I went to Frisco once with Pop. I got whacked, too. Ran away and went over to Sausalito—climbed up Tamalpais."

"You like to climb, heh?"

"Yeah," he said. "I like high places. Say, you ever heard of Pegasus?" He pronounced the word wrongly, staring up at Breadloaf.

"Nope. What is it?"

"Just a story. About a horse with wings. It was supposed to live on a mountain, or come down there once in a while, anyway."

"I heard of unicorns," Tante Rush said doubtfully, wriggling a loose incisor back and forth. "Horses might grow horns, but hardly wings, I guess. What good would they do?"

"I dunno." Jim Harry rolled over on his back and lay in the weeds, watching the clouds move toward Breadloaf. He was silent for a time; then, half asleep, he mused, "Wonder if maybe Pegasus is up on Breadloaf."

"Shouldn't wonder," Tante Rush mumbled agreeably. "Ain't nobody to say no."

"I think—maybe—" Jim Harry sat up. "I got nothing to do today except fix the barn, and that'll wait a bit. I guess I'll go climb Breadloaf."

"It's too hot," the old woman objected, sighing. "I'll fix some corn bread if you wait a bit."

"Nope." He stood up, started off, and then came back. "Got any sugar?"

Tante Rush found a few bits, which Jim Harry dropped in the pocket of his overalls. Then he went up the trail. When he was hidden from sight, the crone suddenly laughed the high, whinnying laughter of age. "Kids," she said. "Kids!" A bit of sugar remained in her hand, and she popped it into her mouth, munching slowly. "A horse with wings! Kids!"

But Jim Harry went up Breadloaf, and after a while he met a funny, gnarled, humpbacked dwarf of a man hobbling along on a crooked stick. The manling looked at Jim Harry steadily and said, "I hear that you're going after the winged horse, boy."

Jim Harry got a queer uneasy feeling, and wanted to run away. But the dwarf reached out his crooked staff and barred the path.

"Don't be afraid of me, youngster," he said. "Why you're almost twice as big as I am. And you haven't got your full growth yet."

Jim Harry tried to broaden his chest, though he knew he was skinny for his age. "I don't know you," he said.

"I've seen you in town, though. So you're after Pegasus."

"Is that the way to say it?" Jim Harry blushed, for he thought the dwarf was making fun of him. "Nope. I'm just hiking."

The other's deep-set eyes were a little sad. "You're learning fast, boy. Already you fear laughter. Ah, go on up Breadloaf; you'll find Pegasus. But how the devil do you expect to ride him? He won't take a saddle, but you'll need a bridle."

Jim Harry looked sullen and traced designs in the dust with his toe-cap.

"Well, you go on up, and I shouldn't be surprised if you found a bridle on a rock somewhere. But don't forget that Pegasus belongs to the sky. He'll be your feet and take you away and away; he'll be your eyes and see wonderful things. But don't let him stay on the ground long."

The last words sighed out like the rustle of the wind. When Jim Harry looked up the little man was gone, though the tap-tap of the staff drifted up from below.

The boy was tempted to go down and retrace his steps, for he was sensitive to mockery. But then he looked up and saw the top of Breadloaf, and he couldn't help himself after that. And it was a funny thing, but about half a mile further Jim Harry saw a grand bridle lying on a rock just beside the trail. He was a little frightened at first. Then he went on up, carrying the bridle and wondering about the dwarf.

It was hard to reach the summit. Jim Harry was bleeding in several places, and his overalls were sadly torn, when at last he scrambled over the lip of the rock and rolled down a grassy slope. He got up and looked around. The summit wasn't very large; it was saucer-shaped, covered with fine pasturage, and there was a little pool of rain-water in the depressed center. There were a few bushes, but no sign of any horse, winged or otherwise.

So Jim Harry went up to the rim and looked way out at all the world spread underneath him. The Imperial Valley lay little and unreal to the blue western mountains. In back of him the white-capped Sierras towered. And the winds that blew upon him had never been breathed by earthly being.

Jim Harry's feet started to itch, and he wanted to walk right out into the air and away off to the west beyond those shadowy dim ranges, and he wanted to go in the other direction over the Sierras. And north were the snow-lands, and south was Mexico and Panama, and it was a wonder Jim Harry didn't just fall over the edge in his excitement and kill himself. But something made him look up, and there was a speck in the sky, getting larger.

Maybe it was the dream in the boy's eyes that made him recognize Pegasus. Anyway, he ran down to the pool and dropped a few bits of sugar there, and then made a trail of it to the nearest bush. He hid himself in that bush and waited. And Pegasus came.

Ah, but that horse was God's own wonder! A stallion, with high-arched neck, and fine withers, and a white coat that glistened like the stars themselves, and a mane that flew like the borealis, and eyes that could be red as mad flame, and soft and melting as a baby's. Lord, but a man could die after having seen Pegasus, and reckon himself very lucky. And the wings on the stallion! White as an egret's feathers, the powerful pinions spread from the shoulders and glistened in the sun.

Wheeling he came. White against the blue he circled and dropped, and started up in affright, and landed gently as any sparrow beside the pool, and the great wings were furled, and the hoofs of Pegasus spurned the earth. He drank, daintily, and cropped the grass, and fell to playing, kicking up his heels like a colt, and laughing as horses do, and turning back his lovely head to nip at the feathered wings, and all the while Jim Harry watched in a dream.

Pegasus fell to cropping again, and discovered the sugar. Perhaps he mistook it for ambrosia. At any rate, he savored the sweet and followed the trail up to the bush where Jim Harry crouched hidden. There he started back, but too late. The boy clapped on the bridle, and as Pegasus spread his wings for flight Jim Harry leaped on his back and was off!

And like a rocket the great stallion fled up, his muscles shuddering against the boy's thighs. The wings beat the air with a noise of thunder. Pegasus threw back his head and screamed; he trumpeted his amazement and wrath; and the mane struck Jim Harry's face and made his nose bleed. But the reins were coiled tight around brown fists. The strong thighs were tensed. And only Gabriel with his flaming sword could have knocked Jim Harry from his seat then.

The winds were a gale. Pegasus somersaulted in the air. Jim Harry threw his arms around the neck and clung. Somehow he stuck on. Looking down he could see Breadloaf incredibly far below; he could see beyond the Sierras and out to the Pacific.

Now a funny thing happened. Pegasus, being a horse, loved sugar, and being something more than a horse, he was more than ordinarily smart. So what did he do but reach his head around, sailing along at an even keel with the wings spread horizontally, and nudge Jim Harry's pocket where he smelled the sugar.

At first the boy didn't understand. Then he took out the sweet and fed his mount. He stroked the velvet muzzle, felt the lip of the horse against his palm, and loved the steed. And when the sugar was gone, Pegasus seemed tame enough. He let Jim Harry guide him as though he'd been broken to harness all his life. And I have no words nor heart to tell of that flight through the blue, and of what Jim Harry thought and felt I should not like to say.

But at last the sun was westering and Jim Harry decided to go home. He was late anyway, and he wanted to show Pegasus to his father and mother and his brother. So down they went past Breadloaf till the farm lay spread beneath them.

But nobody was home. The family had gone to town because it was Saturday night, and the hired man was with them. Jim Harry didn't quite know what to do with Pegasus, and he wouldn't put him in the stable; Pegasus couldn't have stood the smell. Finally he put the winged horse in the pasture, tying him with a long rope. Then he went into the house.

That night he took a short ride on Pegasus, getting home about ten o'clock and going to bed right away, for he was tired and fagged. He didn't hear the family come in, and they didn't notice Pegasus in the darkness.

So, anyway, Jim Harry woke up in the dawn to find his father shaking him, looking pretty white and sick. Old Andy Worth knew horse-flesh, and he knew Pegasus couldn't exist. Yet a stallion with wings was in the north pasture, and every time Andy tried to get close the beast would sail up like a bird.

"He's mine," Jim Harry said. "I caught him up on Breadloaf yesterday."

"Gosh A'mighty," said Andy. "A freak like that must belong to somebody. Pull on your pants and come on."

So they went down to the pasture, and Pegasus, who had broken his rope in the night, shot up, trailing it like a tail. Jim Harry felt awful. It was like losing his right arm.

"Yell at him," Andy said. "Maybe he'll come to you."

Jim Harry did. Pegasus came down and skitted around nervously, with a wary eye on Andy.

"Grab the reins," said the older man. "That's it. Now—hey, hold on!" For Pegasus lunged away, dragging Jim Harry after him. "Won't let me get near him, hey? Well, he'll learn." Andy scrutinized the horse closely. "They're real, all right. I never heard the like. Now just what happened yesterday, Jim Harry, and don't give me no lies."

So Jim Harry told his dad all about it. Andy believed what he wanted to. "They's no brand on the beast. Get him in the stable. I'll go get some sugar."

"I don't want to put him in the stable," Jim Harry started to say, but only got a box on the ear for his trouble.

Anyhow, they put Pegasus in the stable, and had a hard time quieting him. He kept bruising his wings against the stalls, fluttering around for a while like a caged chicken. Andy made Jim Harry tie him up pretty carefully, with leather and rawhide, and the boy got quite a few swats for objecting. Then they went back to the house to get Sarah, Tom, and Buck, the hired man.

Jim Harry should have been excited at the prospect of showing off Pegasus, but he wasn't. The horse looked different in the stable. He kept jerking up his head, his nostrils twitching in disgust at the foul odors. The other horses were afraid of him, too.

"I'm going to get Doc West," Andy said, rubbing his stubbled lean chin. "He can tell if it's fake or not. Though I don't see how it can be, rightly."

Doc West, the vet, said Pegasus was a sport. He'd never heard the like, either, but he'd seen two-headed calves, and there'd been a baby with a goat's head born to a woman in the next county, once. Doc West leered at Andy and talked in an undertone, casting quick glances at Sarah, who stood self-consciously aside, watching Pegasus. Jim Harry listened, but some of the things he heard made him feel sick. Tom, his brother, stood with open mouth, breathing hard. And the smell of the stable was everywhere. This wasn't like riding the skies with Pegasus. It was pretty awful.

Nobody seemed to realize that Pegasus belonged to Jim Harry, or that Jim Harry belonged to Pegasus. His ears still smarted from his father's calloused palm. There was no help from his mother, either; she'd nearly fainted when she learned that Jim Harry had been riding through the air on the winged horse. It wasn't natural, she said.

"But a thing like that has to belong to somebody," Andy said.

"If it does, you'll hear about it. You got a mint of money in that nag," said Doc West, casting a greedy glance at Pegasus. "You wouldn't think of selling him, now, would you?"

"Gosh, no. I'm going to—I dunno. Maybe rent him out to a zoo, or something. He's worth plenty, I bet."

Jim Harry ran over to Pegasus and stood in front of the stall. "He's mine. You can't have him—"

"Don't use that tone of voice to me," Andy grunted. "What would you do with him? Break your fool neck, and it's a wonder you didn't do it already. Leaving the horse out in the pasture all night with a broke rope. Miracle he didn't go off for good."

"Can he honest to gosh fly?" Tom wanted to know. Doc West, too, looked an inquiry.

"Sure can. I saw him." Andy went toward the stall, but changed his mind when Pegasus flung back and reared, snorting. "Doc, I want you should send some telegrams for me when you get back to town."

"You're sure you don't want to sell him—"

But Andy wouldn't sell, and wires were sent to various people. There weren't many answers. Nobody believed in a winged horse. It looked like just another fake—another Barnum mermaid. One man came from Los Angeles to check up, but even he wouldn't buy or rent Pegasus for his circus.

"Yeah, I know it's real," he said, looking puzzled. "But, ye gods, who'd believe it? Everybody'd yell fake. If we advertised a winged horse and showed 'em a colt with bumps on his shoulders, they'd be satisfied. But this—it's too real. People'd never believe it. They'd think we glued the wings on. It's too good to be true."

"You could let him fly around," Andy suggested. "That'd show he was real."

"Will he fly with a rope on him?"

Andy had already made Jim Harry try this, without success. "Nope. But he can be ridden—he's broken pretty well."

"Catch me riding him! Not even a trapeze artist would do it. It'd be suicide, man. I'll talk to the boss about it, but it isn't much use. Not unless we clipped all the feathers off the wings. People might swallow it then."

Jim Harry was listening through a knothole, and he started to shake. When the man was gone he accosted his father.

"You wouldn't do that, would you? Pluck Pegasus' feathers off—"

"Nah," Andy said absent-mindedly. "Listen, Jim Harry, I want you should see how that horse can run. Not fly—just run. You let him get off the ground and I'll skin you."

Jim Harry was only too glad to seize the opportunity of getting on Pegasus' back again. The horse was fast. He went around the north pasture like greased lightning, his wings folded back and his hoofs spurning the ground. Andy, watching from the rail fence, took off his straw hat and fanned himself. "Okay," he called at last. "Rub him down and stable him."

The next day Andy sent more telegrams, and got a man out to time Pegasus with a stop-watch. The two conferred for some time after that.

Jim Harry caught snatches of the conversation. "More money in it, anyway . . . circuses are dead now . . . faster than Man o' War ever was . . . but you can't . . ."

The two looked stealthily at Jim Harry and moved further away.

All this worried the boy. He went to the stable, where Tom was trying to get near Pegasus, with no success at all.

"He's ornery," Tom said. "Needs breaking. I could do it, too."

Jim Harry thought of spurs and whips, and went white. He squabbled a bit with Tom, till the older boy left. Then Jim Harry fed Pegasus sugar and rubbed him down carefully, afterwards mixing him a bran mash and getting fresh rain-water.

The winged horse was drooping. His eye had lost its fire, and the proud neck was no longer arched. Pegasus nudged his nose under Jim Harry's arm and pushed at him, as though inviting the boy to take a ride.

"Gee, I'd like to. But I can't. Pop'd skin me. I wish I'd never brought you back here, Pegasus. I'd let you go now, if—" But that was no good. Andy would make Jim Harry call the winged horse back, and Pegasus would probably obey his adopted master. Jim Harry remembered Breadloaf and the flight down the winds, and then he sat down in the stall and bawled like a baby. But that did no good, either.

Some weeks passed, and Andy began to look more and more sullen and angry. Tom kept begging him for permission to break Pegasus, till he was sent sprawling under the blow of a hard palm. Sarah didn't say much, but she made every excuse to keep Jim Harry away from the horse. She knew Pegasus wasn't good for him. The horse was a freak, and dangerous, and it put ideas into the boy's head. He was queer enough already.

So one day Andy sent Jim Harry to town with Buck, and for some reason they took a back road that wound through the mountains. The old Ford wheezed and chugged, its worn tires screeching on sharp curves. Buck, a big-shouldered, bad-tempered lout, talked little.

"We got plenty of saddles," Jim Harry said, squirming about on the broken springs. "Why get another now? And why do I have to go along?"

"You do what your old man says," Buck grunted, trying to push the brake through the floorboards. To the right the cliff dropped into a sheer abyss. On the left a steep slope mounted. The motor started to boil, and just then they rounded a bend and came in sight of a gnarled dwarf standing beside the road, gripping a twisted stick in his big hands.

Jim Harry recognized the little man. He told Buck to stop, but the hired man just cursed hitch-hikers and went right past. He didn't go far, though, because the engine went dead and the brakes locked. The dwarf called to Jim Harry.

"It's a bad thing they're doing to Pegasus, boy," he said. "They sent you to town to get you out of the way."

Jim Harry's heart went down in his boots. "What are they doing?" he asked.

"Your father's going to make Pegasus into a race-horse. He's fast, you know, and there's more money in that than in circuses. But nobody would let a winged horse run, so Doc West is with your father, and they're going to operate and take off Pegasus' wings. That's why they sent you to town. It'll kill Pegasus, boy—"

"Shut your trap!" Buck roared, and cursed the dwarf obscenely. He jumped out of the car and ran toward the other, his fist lifted. Jim Harry had seen Buck knock men out with that dangerous hand, and he cried out and tried to scramble out of the Ford. But his overalls had caught on the broken springs.

Jim Harry's help wasn't needed, though. The dwarf just lifted his crooked stick and hit Buck with it. It didn't look like a hard blow; yet Buck collapsed in a heap, knocked cold as an iceberg.

"He isn't dead," the dwarf said. "Just stunned. But you'd better be getting back home, boy. The car will work now, I guess. I told you not to let Pegasus stay on the ground long. He belongs to the sky."

Jim Harry had slid over under the wheel and was trying to start the motor. It caught easily enough. The brakes weren't locked any more, either. Jim Harry turned the car around with some difficulty on the narrow road, and went kiting back home hell-for-leather.

It was a wonder he didn't kill himself. The funny part was that he got through the mountains all right, and nothing happened till he was home. A crude plank bridge lay across the irrigation ditch that bounded the road; at the best of times it was pretty shaky. Jim Harry swerved too quickly, and the left front tire hit something and blew out. The Ford turned and went right over the edge of the bridge. It wasn't much of a drop, and there was only a trickle of water in the ditch, but somehow the car seemed to turn over and fold up like an accordion. Jim Harry was knocked out for a minute or so. Agony brought him back to life.

He was lying in the wreck, and his right foot was one throbbing bundle of pain. It seemed to be pinned under the car, and, in fact, it had been mashed between metal and a rock that lay buried in the mud. If the car hadn't settled and slid away a bit Jim Harry might have stayed there till help came. And apparently nobody had heard the crash, because a horse was screaming in the stable.

Jim Harry smelled something burning. His foot was free now, and he tried to get up. But he couldn't, so he squirmed along in the mud and somehow scrambled up the sloping side of the ditch. Then he looked at his foot, trailing along behind him.

Well, it wasn't a foot any more. No surgeon could help it. Jim Harry might eventually learn to use a crutch pretty well, though. But you'll remember the wanderlust that was in his feet, and it's no great wonder that Jim Harry felt like going back into the ditch and smashing his skull open against a bit of jagged metal that was sticking up there.

Instead, he screamed.

The outcry from the barn ceased suddenly. Then there was a trumpeting, furious noise. Have you ever heard a horse shriek? It's like nothing else on God's earth. Pegasus shrieked, and the men within the barn began to yell, too. There was the sound of wood being smashed, and the trample of swift hoofs. The stable's door burst open; for a second the rearing figure of the winged horse was outlined, white and rampant, hoofs flying, nostrils red and inflamed.

A man was yelling in agony; another was cursing luridly.

Pegasus, trailing broken thongs and a snapped chain, thundered down the meadow. His wings spread, and he cried out in pain. Blood dappled one mighty pinion.

He rose, circled, and swept down toward Jim Harry. Lightly as a feather he alighted beside the prostrate boy. His neck arched; he nudged Jim Harry's face with his velvety muzzle. The youngster reached up to put his arms around the strong neck.

Men came running. "Hold him! . . . What's happened? . . . Hold on to him!"

Jim Harry looked into the eyes of Pegasus, and man and horse understood each other. The boy rose, lifting himself by gripping the long mane; he gritted his teeth to keep from crying in agony. And Pegasus knelt, so that Jim Harry could mount upon the broad back. There was no rein, but it was not needed.

The running men were very close when Pegasus spurned the earth. Up he went, favoring one wing a little, but seeming to find new strength as he mounted. Jim Harry held on to the mane. He looked down and saw the farm getting smaller and smaller. And he saw Breadloaf to the east, and the Sierras to the east beyond it.

"Higher," he whispered. "Higher, Pegasus."

He could see beyond the Sierras. He could see the Pacific. The sharp wind cooled his burning, crushed foot. On each side the great wings rose and fell steadily, rhythmically.

"Higher—"

Pegasus threw back his head and answered. Up they went, riding the winds, and now the farm was invisible and Breadloaf was dwindling, and the Valley no longer seemed immense.

Then, queerly enough, the gnarled old dwarf was talking, though Jim Harry couldn't see him anywhere.

"Remember what I told you, boy. Pegasus will be your feet and take you away and away; he'll be your eyes and see wonderful things. But don't let him stay long on the ground."

"I won't," Jim Harry promised.

"Never come down again, Pegasus. Go on up—"

The wind was bitterly cold. The sky was darkening to purple. Faintly a few stars appeared. The earth revolved, with a slow and majestic motion, incredibly far beneath the hoofs of Pegasus.

The fingers of Jim Harry tightened on the horse's mane. Then, slowly, gradually, they began to loosen their grip.

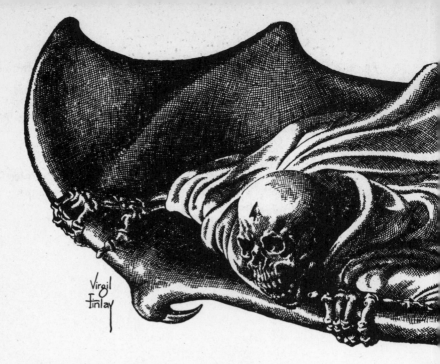

The Face in the Abyss

A. MERRITT

"The Face in the Abyss" was first published in 1923, and it marked A. Merritt's return to his trademark brand of scientific romance after a brief dalliance with radical scientific concepts in The Metal Monster (1920). Acclaim for this novella of a lost race in the Andes mountains gave Merritt the confidence to write a novel-length sequel, The Snake Mother, seven years later. Although Merritt had written the novella to stand on its own, he revised it extensively and incorporated it into the sequel for book publication in 1931. The original version of "The Face in the Abyss" reprinted here marks one of the few times the work has appeared in this form since it was published in the October 1940 Famous Fantastic Mysteries.

CHAPTER I

OUT OF THE HAUNTED HILLS

IT HAS been just three years since I met Nicholas Graydon in the little Andean village of Chupan, high on the eastern slopes of the Peruvian uplands. I had stopped there to renew my supplies, expecting to stay not more than a day or two. But after my *arrieros* had unlimbered my luggage from the two burros, and I entered the unusually clean and commodious *posada,* its keeper told me that another North American was stopping there.

He would be very glad to see me, said the innkeeper, since he was very ill and there was no other *Americanos* in the hamlet. Yes, he was so ill that he was, to tell me all the truth, certain to die, and it would beyond doubt comfort him much to have a fellow countryman with him when that sad moment came. That is, he added, if he were able to recognize a fellow countryman, since all the time the *señor* had been at the *posada* he had been out of his mind with fever, and would probably pass away so.

Then with a curiously intense anxiety he implored me to stay on until death did come; a matter, he assured me, that could be one of only a few days—maybe hours.

I bluntly asked him whether his desire for me to remain was through solicitude for my ailing countryman or through fear for himself. And after a little hesitation he answered that it was both. The *señor* had come to the village a week before, with one burro and neither guides nor *arrieros.* He had been very weak, as though from privations and long journeying. But weaker far from a wound on his neck which had become badly infected. The wound seemed to have been made by either an arrow or a spear. The *señor* had been taken care of as well as the limited knowledge of the *cura* and himself permitted. His burro had been looked after and his saddlebags kept scrupulously closed. But I could understand that questions might be raised after the *señor's* death. If I remained I could report to the authorities that everything possible had been done for the *señor's* comfort and testify that none in Chupan was responsible for his injuries.

This did not sound very convincing to me, and I said so. Then the worthy innkeeper revealed what actually was in his mind. The *señor,* he said, had spoken in his ravings, of dreadful things, things both accursed and devilish. What were they? Well—he crossed himself—if I remained I would no doubt hear for myself. But they had even greatly disturbed the good *cura,* despite that he was under the direct protection of God. The *señor* had come, so his ravings indicated, from a haunted place. No less a place, the innkeeper whispered crossing himself again, than the shunned Cordillera de Carabaya, which every one knew was filled with evil spirits. Yes, evil spirits which would not lightly give up any one who had once been in their power!

And, in fine, the idea seemed to be that some of these demons of the Cordillera—about which, as a matter of fact, I had heard some strange tales—might come at any time for the sick man. If they did, they would be more apt to wreak their fury on one of the *señor's* own countrymen—especially if he was in the same room. The keeper of the *posada* did not put it that way, of course; he said that one of his own people was better qualified to protect the *señor* in such case than any strangers were. Nevertheless the theory plainly was that if I stayed I would act as a lightning rod for any levin of hell that might strike!

I went to the room of the sick man. At first glance I could see that here was no *andreine,* no mountain vagabond. Neither fever nor scrub beard could hide the fineness, the sensitivity, the intelligence of the face on which I looked. He was, I judged, about thirty, and he was in ill case indeed. His temperature showed 105 point 6. At the moment he was in delirium.

My first shock of surprise came when I examined his wound. It seemed to me more like the stab of some great bird beak than the work of spear or arrow. It was a puncture—or better, perhaps, a punch— clear through the muscles of the back and left shoulder and base of the neck. It had missed the arteries of the last by the narrowest of margins. I knew of no bird which could make such a wound as this, yet the closer I looked and probed the more sure I was that it had been inflicted by no weapon of man.

That night, after I had arranged my own matters and had him sleeping under a hypodermic, I opened up his saddlebags. Papers in them showed his name to be Nicholas Graydon, a mining engineer, a graduate of the Harvard School of Mines, his birthplace, Philadelphia. There was a diary that revealed so much of him truly likable that had I not already made up my mind to stop on with him it would have impelled me to do so. Its last entry was about a month before and ran:

Two weeks now since our *arrieros* deserted us and we seem to be pretty thoroughly lost. Effects upon the three are curious. Sterrett manages to keep himself evenly drunk all the time. That spare burro of his must be loaded with nothing but that Indian hell-brew.

Dancre is moody and sullen. Soames seems to have developed a morbid suspicion of all of us. Strange how the wilderness, the jungle, the desert, bring out the latent man in all of us.

In Quito none of the three was half bad. But now—well, the luckiest thing for me will be for us to find no treasure. If we do, my throat will probably be the first to be cut.

Further down in the bag were two parcels, each most carefully and securely wrapped. Opening the first I found a long black feather oddly marked with white. I did not recognize the plume as belonging to any bird I knew. Its shaft was inlaid with little bands of gold, altogether a curiously delicate bit of goldsmith's work.

But the contents of the second package made me gasp with amazement. It was a golden bracelet, clearly exceedingly ancient, the band an inch broad and expanding into an oval disk perhaps three inches long by two wide. That disk held in high relief the most extraordinary bit of carving I had ever seen. Four monsters held on uplifted paws, a bowl on which lay coiled a serpent with a woman's face and woman's breasts. Nor had I ever beheld such suggestion of united wisdom and weirdness as the maker had stamped upon the snake woman's face.

Yet it was not that which called forth the full measure of my wonder; no. There are certain pictures, certain sculptures, certain works of art which carry to their beholders conviction that no fantasy, no imagination, went into their making and that they are careful, accurate copies of something seen by those who made them. This bit of golden carving carried that conviction.

The four monsters which held up the snake woman were—dinosaurs!

There was no mistaking them. I had examined too many of the reconstructions made by scientists from the fossil bones of these gigantic, monstrous reptilian creatures to be in error. But these giants were supposed to have died off millions of years before man first appeared on earth! Yet here they were, carved with such fidelity to detail, such impress of photographic accuracy, that it was impossible to believe that the ancient goldsmith who made this thing had not before him living models!

Marveling, I held the bracelet closer to the light and as I did so I thought I heard far away in the blackness of the mountains and high in the air a sound like a tiny bugle. In that note was something profoundly, alienly weird. I went to the window and listened, but the sound did not come again. I turned to find the eyes of Graydon opened and regarding me. For a moment he had slipped from the thrall of the fever—and the thought came to me that it had been that elfin bugling which had awakened him.

It was six weeks before I had Graydon well out of danger. And in that time he had told me bit by bit that well nigh incredible experience of his in the haunted hills of the Cordillera de Carabaya and what it was that had sent him so far down into the valley of the shadow.

Three years it has been since then. Three years and I have heard nothing of him. Three years and he has not returned from his journey back to the Cordillera de Carabaya where he went to seek mystery, ancient beyond all memory of man, he believed was hidden there. But more than that—to seek Suarra.

"If you don't hear from me in three years, tell the story and let the people who knew me know what became of me," he said, as I left him at the beginning of that strange trail he had determined to retrace.

And so I tell it, reconstructing it from his reticences as well as his confidences, since only so may a full measure of judgment of that story be gained.

CHAPTER II

SUARRA OF THE GOLDEN SPEARS

GRAYDON HAD run into Sterrett in Quito. Or, rather, Sterrett sought him out there. Graydon had often heard of the giant West Coast adventurer, but their trails had never crossed. It was with a lively curiosity, then, that he opened the door of his room to this visitor.

And he had rather liked Sterrett. There was a bluff directness about the big man that made him overlook a certain cruelty of eye and a touch of brutality about mouth and jaw.

Sterrett came to the point at once. Graydon had no doubt heard the story of the treasure train which had been bringing to Pizarro the ransom of the Inca Atahualpa? And learning of the murder of that monarch had turned back and buried that treasure somewhere in the Peruvian wilderness? Graydon had heard of it, hundreds of times. And, like every other adventurer in the Andes, spent a little time himself searching for those countless millions in jewels and gold.

Sterrett nodded.

"I know how to find it," he said.

And Graydon had laughed. How many had told him that they, too, knew where lay hidden the hoard of Atahualpa the Inca!

But in the end Sterrett convinced him; convinced him at least that there was something more solid than usual in his story, something decidedly worth looking into.

There would be two others in the expedition, Sterrett told him, both men long associated with him. One was Dancre, a Frenchman, the other an American named Soames. These two had been with Sterrett when he had got hold of the old parchment with its alleged map of the treasure trail, and with its carefully drawn signs that purported to be copies of those along that trail; signs cut by its makers to guide those who one day, when the Spaniard was gone, would set out to recover the hidden hoard.

Graydon asked why they wanted him. Sterrett bluntly enough told him—because he was an American; because they knew he could be trusted; because he could afford to pay half the expenses of the ex-pedition. He, Dancre and Soames would pay the other half. They would all share equally if the treasure was found. Still another reason, Graydon was a mining engineer and his special knowledge might be essential when it came to recovering the stuff. Furthermore, if the treasure was not found, the region where they were going was full of minerals. He might make some valuable discoveries. In which event all would share equally as before.

There were no calls on Graydon at the time. It was true that he could well afford the cost. At the worst there would be adventure and some pleasant excitement. He met Dancre and Soames, the first a cynical, but amusing, little bunch of wires and nerves, the second a lanky, saturnine, hard-bitten Yankee. They had gone down by rail to Cerro de Pasco for their outfit, that being the town of any size closest to where, according to the map, their trail into the wilderness began. A week later, with eight burros and six *arrieros* or packmen, they were well within the welter of peaks through which the old map indicated their road lay.

They found the signs cut in the rocks exactly as the parchment had promised. Gay, spirits high with anticipation, three of them at least spending in advance their share of the treasure, they followed the symbols. Steadily they were led into the uncharted wilderness.

At last the *arrieros* began to murmur. They were approaching, they said, a region that was accursed, the Cordillera de Carabaya, where demons dwelt and only fierce Aymaras, their servants, lived. Promises of more money, threats, pleadings, took them along a little farther.

Then one morning the four awoke to find the *arrieros* gone—and with them half the burros and a portion of their supplies.

They pressed on. Then suddenly, the signs had failed them. Either they had lost the trail, or there were no more carven symbols and the parchment which had led them truthfully so far had lied at the last. Or was it possible that the signs had been obliterated—cut away?

The country into which they had penetrated was a strangely deserted one. They saw no sign of Indians—had seen none indeed since when, more than a week before, they had stopped at a Quicha village and Sterrett had got mad drunk on that fiery spirit the Quichas distil. Food, too, was curiously hard to find; there were few animals and fewer birds.

But worst of all was the change that had come over his companions. As high as they had been lifted by their certainty of success, just so deep were they now cast into despair. The wilderness, the loneliness of it, their disappointment, had brought out the real man that lies hidden beneath the veneer we all of us carry. Sterrett kept himself at a steady level of drunkenness, alternately quarrelsome and noisy or sunk in a sullen mood of brooding, brutal rage.

Dancre had become silent and irritable. Soames seemed to have reached the conclusion that Graydon, Sterrett and the Frenchman had combined against him; that they had either deliberately missed the trail or had erased the signs. Only when the two of them joined Sterrett and drank with him the Quicha hell-brew did either of them relax. At such times Graydon had the uneasy feeling that they were holding the failure against him and that his life might be hanging on a thin thread.

On the day that his adventure really began—that strange adventure to which all that had passed before had been prelude—Graydon was coming back to the camp. He had been hunting since morning. Dancre and Soames had gone off together on another desperate search for the missing symbols that would lead them to the treasure trail again.

Cut off in mid-flight, the girl's cry came to him as the answer to all his apprehensions; materialization of the menace toward which his vague fears had been groping ever since he had left Sterrett alone at the camp hours ago. He had sensed some culminating misfortune close, and here it was! He knew it; how, he did not stop himself to ask; he was sure. He broke into a run, stumbling up the slope to the group of gray green *algarroba* trees where the tent was pitched.

What had the drunken fool done? Graydon had warned them all that their situation was perilous; that if Indians came they must try to make friends with them—that they must be superlatively careful in their treatment of any Indian woman.

He reached the *algarrobas;* crashed through the light undergrowth to the little clearing. Why didn't the girl cry out again? he wondered. There was a sickness at his heart. A low chuckle reached him, thick, satyr-toned. Then Sterrett's voice, cruel, mocking!

"No more fight in you, eh? Well, which'll it be, pretty lady—the way to the gold or you? And, by Heaven—I guess it'll be you—first!"

For an instant Graydon paused. He saw that Sterrett, half crouching, was holding the girl bow fashion over one knee. A thick arm was clinched about her neck, the fingers clutching her mouth brutally, silencing her; his right hand fettered her slender wrists; her knees were caught in the vise of his bent right leg.

She was helpless, but as Graydon sprang forward he caught a flash of wide black eyes, wrath-filled and defiant, staring fearlessly into those leering so close.

He caught Sterrett by the hair, locked an arm under his chin, drawing his head sharply back.

"Drop her!" he ordered.

Sterrett hurled himself to his feet, dropping the girl as he rose.

"What the devil are you butting in for?" he snarled. His hand struck down toward his pistol. But even while the fingers were tightening around the butt, Graydon's fist shot out and caught him on the point of the hairy jaw. The clutching fingers loosened, the half drawn pistol slipped to the ground, the great body quivered and toppled over. Long before it fell the girl had leaped up and away.

Graydon did not look after her. She had gone no doubt to bring down upon them her people, some tribe of those fierce Aymaras that even the Incas of old had never quite conquered and who would avenge her, in ways that Graydon did not like to visualize.

He bent down over Sterrett. His heart was beating; feebly it was true—but beating. The reek of drink was sickening. Graydon's hand touched the fallen pistol. He picked it up and looked speculatively at the fallen man's rifle. Sterrett, between the blow and the drink, would probably be out of the running for hours. Graydon wished that Dancre and Soames would get back soon to camp. The three of them could put up a good fight at any rate; might even have a chance for escape. So ran his thoughts. But Dancre and Soames would have to return quickly. The girl would soon be there, with the avengers; no doubt at this very moment she was telling them of her wrongs. He turned.

She stood there, looking at him.

And drinking in her loveliness, Graydon forgot the man at his feet; forgot all, and was content to let his soul sit undisturbed within his eyes and take its delight to her.

Her skin was palest ivory. It gleamed translucent through the rents of the soft amber fabric like the thickest silk that swathed her. Her eyes were deep velvety pools, oval, a little tilted; Egyptian in the wide midnight of their irises. But the features were classic, cameo; the nose small and straight, the brows level and black, almost meeting above it. And her hair was cloudy, jet, misty and shadowed, and a narrow fillet of gold bound the broad, low forehead. In it like a diamond were entwined the sable and silver feathers of the *caraquenque,* that bird whose plumage in lost centuries was sacred to the princesses of the Incas alone. Above her dimpled elbows golden bracelets twined, reaching to the slender shoulders. The little high arched feet were shod with high buskins of deerskin.

She was light and slender as the Willow Maid who waits on Kwannon when she passes into the World of Trees to pour into them new fire of green life. And like the Willow Maid green fire of tree and jungle and flame of woman gleamed within her.

Nothing so exquisite, so beautiful had ever Graydon beheld. Here was no Aymara, no daughter of any tribe of the Cordilleras, no descendant of Incas. Nor was she Spanish. There were bruises on her cheeks—the marks of Sterrett's cruel fingers. Her long, slim hands touched them. The red lips opened. She spoke in the Aymara tongue.

"Is he dead?" she asked. Her voice was low, a faint chime as of little bells ringing through it.

"No," Graydon answered.

In the depths of the midnight eyes a small hot flame flared, he could have sworn it was of gladness; it vanished swiftly as it had come.

"That is well," she said. "I would not have him die—" the voice became meditative—*"so!"*

"Who are you?" Graydon asked wonderingly. She looked at him for a long moment, enigmatically.

"Call me—Suarra," she answered at last.

Sterrett stirred; groaned. The girl gazed down upon him. The slim hand touched once more the bruises on her cheek.

"He is very strong," she murmured.

Graydon thought there was admiration in the voice; wondered whether all that delectable beauty was after all but a mask for the primitive woman, worshipping brute strength; looked into the eyes scanning Sterrett's bulk, noted the curious speculation within them, and knew that whatever the reason for her comment it was not that which his fleeting thought had whispered. She looked at him, questioningly.

"Are you his enemy?" she asked.

"No," said Graydon, "we travel together."

"Then why," she pointed to the outstretched figure, "why did you do this to him? Why did you not let him have his way with me?"

Graydon flushed, uncomfortably. The question, with all its subtle implications, cut. What kind of a beast did she think him? His defense of her had been elementary—as well be asked to explain why he did not stand by and watch idly while a child was being murdered!

"What do you think I am?" His voice shook with half shamed wrath. "No man stands by and lets a thing like that go on."

She looked at him, curiously; but her eyes had softened.

"No?" she asked. "No man does? Then what is he?"

Graydon found no answer. She took a step closer to him, her slim finger again touching the bruises on her cheek.

"Do you not wonder," she said—"now do you not wonder why I do not call my people to deal him the punishment he has earned?"

"I do wonder." Graydon's perplexity was frank. "I wonder indeed. Why do you not call them, if they are close enough to hear?"

"And what would you do were they to come?" she whispered.

"I would not let them have him—alive," he answered. "Nor me!"

"Perhaps," she said, slowly, "perhaps—knowing that—is why—I do not call them!"

Suddenly she smiled upon him, and it was as though a draft of wild sweet wine had been lifted to his lips. He took a swift step toward her. She drew up to her slim lithe height, thrust out a warning hand.

"I am—Suarra," she said; then, "and I am—Death!"

An odd chill passed through Graydon. Again he realized the unfamiliar, the alien beauty of her. Was there truth after all in those legends of the haunted Cordilleras? He had never doubted that there was something behind the terror of the Indians, the desertion of the *arrieros*. Was she one of its spirits, its—demons? For an instant the fantasy seemed no fantasy. Then reason returned. This girl a demon! He laughed.

She frowned at that laughter.

"Do not laugh," she said. "The death I mean is not such as you who live beyond the high rim of our land may know. It is death that blots out not alone the body, but that lord whose castle is the body; that which looks out through the windows of your eyes—that presence, that flame, you believe can never die. That, too, our death blots out; makes as though it never had been. Or letting it live, changes it in—dreadful—ways. Yet, because you came to me in my need—nay, more because of something I sense within you—something that calls out to me and to which I must listen and do desire to listen—because of this I would not have that death come to you."

Strange as were her words, Graydon hardly heard them; certainly did not then realize fully their meaning, lost still as he was in wonder.

What was this girl doing here in these wild mountains with her bracelets of gold and the royal Inca feathers on her lovely little head?

No demon of the wilderness, she! Absurd! She was living, desirable, all human.

Yet she was of no race he knew. Despite the *carquenque* plumes, not of the Incas.

But she was of pure blood. The blood of kings. Yes, that was it— a princess of some proud empire, immemoriably ancient, long lost! But what empire?

"How you came by the watchers, I do not know. How you passed unseen by them I do not know. Nor how you came so far within this forbidden land. Tell me," her voice was imperious, "why came you here at all?"

Graydon stirred. It was a command.

"We came from afar," he said, "on the track of a great treasure of gold and gems; the treasure of Atahualpa, the Inca. There were certain signs that led us. They brought us here. And here we lost them. And found soon that we, too, were lost."

"Atahualpa," she nodded. "Yes, his people did come here. We took them, and their treasure."

Graydon stared at her, jaw dropping in amazement.

"You—you took them—and the treasure!" he gasped.

"Yes." She nodded, indifferently. "It lies somewhere in one of the thirteen caves. It was nothing to us—to us of Yu-Atlanchi where treasures are as the sands in the stream bed. A grain of sand, it was, among many. But the people of Atahualpa were welcome, since we needed new folks to care for the Xinli and to feed the wisdom of the Snake Mother."

"The Snake Mother!" exclaimed Graydon.

The girl touched the bracelet on her right arm. And Graydon, looking close, saw that this bracelet held a disk on which was carved a serpent with a woman's head and woman's breasts and arms. It lay coiled upon a great dish held high on the paws of four animals. The shapes of these did not at once register upon his consciousness, so absorbed was he in that coiled figure.

And now he saw that this face was not really that of a woman. It was reptilian. But so strongly had the maker feminized it, so great was the suggestion of womanhood modeled into every line of it, that constantly the eyes saw it was woman, forgetting all that was of the serpent.

Her eyes were of some small, glittering, intensely purple stone. And as Graydon looked he felt that those eyes were alive—that far, far away some living thing was looking at him through them. That they were, in fact, prolongations of some one's—some *thing's*—vision!

And suddenly the figure seemed to swell, the coils to move, the eyes come closer.

He tore his gaze away; drew back, dizzily.

The girl was touching one of the animals that held up the bowl or shield or whatever it was that held the snake woman.

"The Xinli," she said.

Graydon looked; looked and felt increase of bewilderment. For he knew what those animals were. And, knowing, knew that he looked upon the incredible.

They were dinosaurs! Those gigantic, monstrous grotesques that ruled earth millions upon millions of years ago, and but for whose extinction, so he had been taught, man could never have developed.

Who in this Andean wilderness could have known the dinosaur? Who here could have carved the monsters with such life-like detail as these possessed? Why, it was only yesterday that science had learned what really were their huge bones, buried so long that the rocks had molded themselves around them in adamantine matrix. And laboriously, with every modern resource still haltingly and laboriously, science had set those bones together as a perplexed child a picture puzzle, and timidly put forth what it believed to be reconstructions of these long vanished chimeras of earth's nightmare youth.

Yet here, far from all science it must surely be, some one had modeled those same monsters for a woman's bracelet. Why then, it followed that whoever had done this must have had before him the living forms from which to work. Or, if not, copies of those forms set down accurately by ancient men who had seen them. And either or both these things were incredible.

What were these people to whom this girl belonged? People who— what was it she had said?—could blot out both body and soul or change the soul to some dreadful thing? There had been a name— Yu-Atlanchi.

"Suarra," he said, "where is Yu-Atlanchi? Is it this place where we are now?"

"This?" She laughed. "No! Yu-Atlanchi is the ancient land. The hidden land where the Five Lords and the Lord of Lords once ruled, and where now rules only the Lord of Fate and the Lord of Folly and the Snake Mother. This place Yu-Atlanchi!" Again she laughed. "Now and then we hunt here, with the Xinli and the—the—" She hesitated, looking at him oddly; then went on. "So it was that he," she pointed to Sterrett, "caught me. I was hunting. I had slipped away from my— my—" again she hesitated, as oddly as before—"my followers, for sometimes I would hunt alone, wander alone. I came through these trees and saw your *tetuane,* your lodge. I came face to face with—him. And I was amazed. Too amazed to strike with one of these." She pointed to a low knoll a few feet away. "So, before I could conquer that amaze he seized me, choked me. And then you came."

Graydon stared at the place where she had pointed. There upon the ground lay three slender shining spears. Their slim shafts were of gold; the arrow-shaped heads of two of them were of fine opal.

But the third—the third was a single emerald, translucent and flawless, all of six inches long and three at its widest and ground to keenest point and cutting edge!

There it lay, a priceless jewel tipping a spear of gold—and a swift panic shook Graydon. He had forgotten Soames and Dancre! Suppose they should return while this girl was there! The girl with her ornaments of gold, her gem tipped golden spears, and her—beauty! Well, he knew what they could do. And while now he knew, too, how with all his wit and strength he would fight for her, still they were two and armed and cunning, and he only one.

Suddenly he discounted all that tale of hers of a hidden land with its Lords and Snake Mother and its people who dealt out mysterious unfamiliar deaths. If this were all so, why had she come alone into the *algarrobas?* Why was she still alone? As suddenly he saw her only a girl, speaking fantasy, and helpless.

"Suarra," he said, "you must go and go quickly. This man and I are not all. There are two more and even now they may be close. Take your spears, and go. Else I may not be able to save you."

"You think I am—" she began.

"I tell you to go," he answered. "Whoever you are, whatever you are, go now and keep away from this place. Tomorrow I will try to lead them back. If you have people to fight for you—well, let them come and fight if you so desire. But take this instant your spears and go."

She crossed to the little knoll and slowly picked them up. She held one out to him, the one that bore the emerald point.

"This," she said, "to remember—Suarra."

"No," he thrust it back. "No!"

Once the others saw that jewel, never, he knew, would he be able to start them on the back trail—if they could find it. Sterrett had seen it, of course, but that was not like having it in the camp, a constant reminder to Soames and Dancre of what might be unlimited riches within their reach. And he might be able to convince those others that Sterrett's story was but a drunken dream.

The girl regarded him meditatively, a quickened interest in the velvety eyes. She slipped the golden bracelets from her arms, held them out to him with the three spears.

"Will you take all of them, and leave your comrades?" she asked. "Here are gold and gems. They are treasures. They are what you have been seeking. Take them. Take them and go, leaving that man there and those other two. Consent, and I will not only give you these, but show you a way out of this forbidden land."

For a moment Graydon hesitated. The great emerald alone was worth a fortune. What loyalty did he owe after all, to Sterrett and Soames and Dancre? And Sterrett had brought this thing upon himself.

Nevertheless, they were his comrades. Open-eyed he had gone into this venture with them.

He had a swift vision of himself skulking away with this glittering, golden booty. Creeping off to safety while he left them, unwarned, unprepared to meet—what? Peril, certainly; nay, almost as certainly—

death. For whatever the present danger of this girl might be at the hands of his comrades, subconsciously Graydon knew that it must be but a brief one; that she could not be all alone; that although through some chance she had strayed upon the camp, somewhere close were those who would seek for her when they missed her. That somewhere were forces on which she could call and against which it was unlikely three men, even well armed as they were, could prevail.

Very definitely he did not like that picture of himself skulking away from the peril, whatever it might be.

"No," he said. "These men are of my race, my comrades. Whatever is to come—I will meet it with them and help them fight it. Now go."

"Yet you would have fought them for my sake—indeed did fight," she said, as though perplexed. "Why then do you cling to them when you can save yourself; go free, with treasure? And why, if you will not do this, do you let me go, knowing that if you kept me prisoner, or— slew me, I could not bring my people down upon you?"

Graydon laughed.

"I couldn't let them hurt you, of course," he said, "and I'm afraid to make you prisoner, because I might not be able to keep you free from hurt. And I won't run away. So talk no more, but go—go!"

She thrust the gleaming spears into the ground, slipped the golden bracelets back on her arms, held white hands out to him.

"Now," she cried, "now, by the Wisdom of the Snake Mother, by the Five Lords and by the Lord of Lords, I will save you if I can. All that I have tempted you with was but to test that truth which I had hoped was in you and now know is within you. Now you may not go back, nor may they. Here is Yu-Atlanchi and Yu-Atlanchi's power. Into that power you have strayed. Nor have those who have ever so strayed ever escaped. Yet you I will save—if I can!"

Before he could answer her he heard a horn sound; far away and high in air it seemed. Faintly it was answered by others closer by; mellow, questing notes—yet with weirdly alien beat in them that subtly checked the pulse of Graydon's heart!

"They come," she said. "My followers! Light your fire tonight. Sleep without fear. But do not wander beyond these trees!"

"Suarra—" he cried.

"Silence now," she warned. "Silence, until I am gone!"

The mellow horns sounded closer. She sprang from his side; darted through the trees.

From the little ridge above the camp he heard her voice raised in one clear, ringing shout. There was a tumult of the horns about her, elfinly troubling. Then silence.

Graydon stood listening. The sun touched the high snowfields of the majestic peaks toward which he faced; touched them and turned them into robes of molten gold. The amethyst shadows that draped their sides thickened, wavered and marched swiftly forward. Still he listened, scarce breathing.

Far, far away the horns sounded again; faint echoing of the tumult that had swept about Suarra—faint, faint and faerie sweet.

The sun dropped behind the peaks; the edges of their frozen mantles glittered as though sewn with diamonds; darkened into a fringe of gleaming rubies. The golden fields dulled, grew amber and then blushed forth a glowing rose. They changed to pearl and faded into a ghostly silver, shining like cloud wraiths in the highest heavens. Down upon the *algarroba* clump the quick Andean dusk fell.

And not till then did Graydon, shivering with sudden, inexplicable dread, realize that beyond the calling horns and the girl's clear shouting he had heard no other sound. No noise either of man or beast, no sweeping through of brush or grass, no fall of running feet nor clamor of the chase.

Nothing but that mellow chorus of the horns!

From infinite distances, it seemed to him, he heard one single note, sustained and insistent. It detached itself from the silence. It swept toward him with the speed of light. It circled overhead, hovered and darted; arose and sped away; a winged sound bearing some message, carrying some warning—where?

CHAPTER III

THE EYES OF THE SNAKE MOTHER

GRAYDON TURNED back. He bent over Sterrett who had drifted out of the paralysis of the blow into a drunken stupor. There were deep scratches on the giant's cheeks—the marks of Suarra's nails. The jaw was badly swollen where Graydon had hit it. Graydon dragged the other man over to the tent, thrust a knapsack under his head and threw a blanket over him. Then he went out and built up the fire.

Hardly had he begun to prepare the supper when he heard a trampling through the underbrush. Soon Soames and Dancre came up through the trees.

"Find any signs?" he asked them.

"Signs? Hell—no!" snarled the New Englander. "Say, Graydon, did you hear something like a lot of horns? Damned queer horns, too. They seemed to be over here."

Graydon nodded, abstractedly. Then he realized that he must tell these men what had happened, must warn them and urge them to prepare for defense. But how much should he tell? All?

Tell them of Suarra's beauty, of her golden ornaments and her gem-tipped spears of gold? Tell them what she had said of Atahualpa's treasure and of that ancient Yu-Atlanchi where priceless gems were "thick as the sands upon the bed of a stream"?

Well he knew that if he did there would be no further reasoning with them; that they would go berserk with greed. Yet something of it he must tell them if they were to be ready for that assault which he was certain would come with the dawn.

And of Suarra they would learn soon enough from Sterrett when he awakened.

He heard an exclamation from Dancre who had passed on into the tent; heard him come out; stood up and faced the wiry little Frenchman.

"What's the matter wit' Sterrett, eh?" Dancre snapped. "First I thought he's drunk. Then I see he's scratched like wild cat and wit' a lump on his jaw as big as one orange. What you do to Sterrett, eh?"

Graydon had made up his mind; was ready to answer.

"Dancre," he said, "Soames—we're in a bad box. I came in from hunting less than an hour ago and found Sterrett wrestling with a girl. That's bad medicine down here—the worst, and you two know it. I had to knock Sterrett out before I could get the girl away from him. Her people will probably be after us in the morning. There's no use trying to get away. They'll soon enough find us in this wilderness of which we know nothing and they presumably know all. This place is as good as any other to meet them. And it's a better place than any if we have to fight. We'd better spend the night getting it ready so we can put up a good one, if we have to."

"A girl, eh?" said Dancre. "What she look like? Where she come from? How she get away?"

Graydon chose the last question to answer.

"I let her go," he said.

"You let her go!" snarled Soames. "What the hell did you do that for, man? Why didn't you tie her up? We could have held her as a hostage, Graydon—had something to do some trading with when her damned bunch of Indians came."

"She wasn't an Indian, Soames," began Graydon, then hesitated.

"You mean she was white—Spanish?" broke in Dancre, incredulously.

"No, not Spanish either. She was white. Yes, white as any of us. I don't know what she was," answered Graydon.

The pair stared at him, then at each other.

"There's something damned funny about this," growled Soames, at last. "But what I want to know is why you let her go, whatever the hell she was."

"Because I thought we'd have a better chance if I did than if I didn't." Graydon's own wrath was rising. "I want to tell you two that we're up against something mighty bad; something none of us knows anything about. And we've got just one chance of getting out of the mess. If I'd kept her here we wouldn't have even that chance."

He halted. Dancre had stooped; had picked up something from the ground, something that gleamed yellow in the firelight. And now the Frenchman nudged the lank New Englander.

"Somet'ing funny is right, Soames," he said. "Look at this."

He handed the gleaming object over. Graydon saw that it was a thin golden bracelet, and as Soames turned it over in his hand he caught the green glitter of emeralds. It had been torn from Suarra's arm, he realized, in her struggle with Sterrett.

"Yes, somet'ing funny!" repeated Dancre. He glared at Graydon venomously, through slitted lids. "What that girl give you to let her go, Graydon, eh?" he spat. "What she tell you, eh?"

Soames's hand dropped to his automatic.

"She gave me nothing, I took nothing," answered Graydon.

"I t'ink you damned liar!" said Dancre, viciously. "We get Sterrett awake." He turned to Soames. "We get him awake quick. I t'ink he tell us more about this, *oui*. A girl who wears stuff like this, and he lets her go! Lets her go when he knows there must be more where this come from, eh, Soames? Damned funny is right, eh? Come, now, we see what Sterrett tell us."

Graydon watched them go into the tent. Soon Soames came out, went to a spring that bubbled up from among the trees; returned, with water.

Well, let them waken Sterrett; let him tell them whatever he would. They would not kill him that night, of that he was sure. They believed that he knew too much. And in the morning—

What was hidden in the morning for them all?

That even now they were prisoners, Graydon did not doubt. Suarra's warning not to leave the camp had been too explicit. And since that tumult of the elfin horns, her swift vanishing and the silence that had followed he had no longer doubt that they had strayed as she had said within the grasp of some power, formidable as it was mysterious.

The silence? Suddenly it came to him that the night had become strangely still. There was no sound either of insect or bird nor any stirring of the familiar after-twilight life of the wilderness.

The camp was ringed with silence.

He strode away, through the *algarroba* clump. There was a scant score of trees. They stood up like a little leafy island peak within the brush-covered savannah. They were great trees, every one of them, and set with a curious regularity as though they had not sprung up by chance; as though indeed they had been carefully planted.

Graydon reached the last of them, rested a hand against the bole that looked like myriads of tiny grubs turned to soft brown wood. He peered out. The slope that lay before him was flooded with moonlight; the yellow blooms of the *chilca* shrubs that pressed to the very feet of the trees shone wanly in the silver flood. The faintly aromatic fragrance of the *quenuar* stole around him. Movement or sign of life there was none.

And yet—

The spaces seemed filled with watchers; he felt their gaze upon him; knew with an absolute certainty that some hidden host girdled the camp. He scanned every bush and shadow; saw nothing. Nevertheless the certainty of a hidden, unseen multitude persisted. A wave of nervous irritation passed through him. He would force them, whatever they were, to show themselves.

He stepped boldly into the full moonlight.

On the instant the silence intensified; seemed to draw taut; to lift itself up whole octaves of stillnesses; to become alert, expectant—as though poised to spring upon him should he take one step further!

A coldness wrapped him, a shudder shook him. He drew swiftly back to the shadow of the trees; stood there, his heart beating furiously. The silence lost its poignancy, dropped back upon its haunches—but watchful and alert!

What had frightened him? What was there in that tightening of the stillness that had touched him with finger of nightmare terror?

Trembling, he groped back, foot by foot, afraid to turn his back to the silence. Behind him the fire flared. And suddenly his fear dropped from him.

His reaction from the panic was a heady recklessness. He threw a log upon the fire and laughed as the sparks shot up among the leaves. Soames, coming out of the tent for more water, stopped as he heard that laughter and scowled at him malevolently.

"Laugh," he said. "Laugh while you can, you damned traitor. You'll laugh on the other side of your mouth when we get Sterrett up and he tells us what he knows."

"That was a sound sleep I gave him, anyway," jeered Graydon.

"There are sounder sleeps! Don't forget it." It was Dancre's voice, cold and menacing from within the tent. He heard Sterrett groan.

Graydon turned his back to the tent and deliberately faced that silence from which he had just fled. How long he sat thus he did not know. It could not have been for long. But all at once he was aware that he was staring straight into two little points of vivid light that seemed at once far, far away and very close. They were odd, he thought. What was it so odd about them? Was it their color? They were purple, a curiously intense purple. As he stared, it seemed to him that they grew larger, but the puzzling double aspect of distance and nearness did not alter.

It was very curious, he thought. He had seen two eyes—yes, they were eyes—of that peculiar purple, somewhere, not long ago. But he could not remember just where. There was a drowsiness clouding his thought. He would look at them no more. He raised his gaze, slowly and with perceptible effort, to the leafy screen above him. Unwinkingly the brilliant orbs stared back at him from it. He forced his gaze downward. There, too, they were.

And now he knew them—the eyes that had glittered from Suarra's bracelet of the dinosaurs! The eyes of that mingled serpent and woman she had called the Snake Mother!

They were drawing him—drawing him—

He realized that his lids had closed; yet, closing, they had not shut out the globes of vivid purple. His lethargy increased, but it was of the body, not of the mind. All his consciousness had concentrated, been gathered, into the focus of the weird, invading eyes.

Abruptly they retreated. And like line streaming out of a reel the consciousness of Graydon streamed out of him and after them—out of his body, out of the camp, through the grove and out into the land beyond!

It seemed to him that he passed swiftly over the moonlit wastes. They flashed beneath him, unrolling like panorama under racing plane. Ahead of him frowned a black barrier. It shrouded him and was gone. He had a glimpse of a wide circular valley rimmed by sky-piercing peaks; towering scarps of rock. There was the silver glint of a lake, the liquid silver of a mighty torrent pouring out of the heart of a precipice. He caught wheeling sight of carved colossi, gigantic shapes that sat bathed in the milky flood of the moon guarding each the mouth of a cavern.

A city rushed up to meet him, a city ruby-roofed and opal-turreted and fantastic as though built by jinn out of the stuff of dreams.

And then it seemed to him that he came to rest within a vast and columned hall from whose high roof fell beams of soft and dimly azure light. High arose those columns, unfolding far above into wide wonderous petalings of opal and of emerald and turquoise flecked with gold.

Before him were the eyes that in this dream, if dream it were, had drawn him to this place. And as the consciousness which was he and yet had, he knew, neither visible shape nor shadow, beheld it; it recoiled, filled with terror of the unknown; struggled to make its way back to the body from which it had been lured; fluttered like a serpent-trapped bird; at last, like the bird, gave itself up to the serpent fascination.

For Graydon looked upon—the Snake Mother!

She lay just beyond the lip of a wide alcove set high above the pillared floor. Between her and him the azure beams fell, curtaining the great niche with a misty radiance that half-shadowed, half-revealed her.

Her face was ageless, neither young nor old; it came to him that it was free from time forever, free from the etching acid of the years. She might have been born yesterday or a million years ago. Her eyes, set wide apart, were round and luminous; they were living jewels filled with purple fires. Above them rose her forehead, wide and high and sloping sharply back. The nose was long and delicate, the nostrils dilated; the chin small and pointed.

The mouth was small, too, and heart-shaped and the lips a scarlet flame.

Down her narrow childlike shoulders flowed hair that gleamed like spun silver. The shining argent strands arrow-headed into a point upon her forehead; coifed, they gave to her face that same heart shape in which her lips were molded, a heart of which the chin was the tip.

She had high little breasts, uptilted. And face and neck, shoulders and breasts were the hue of pearls suffused faintly with rose; and like rosy pearls they glistened.

Below her breasts began her—coils!

Mistily Graydon saw them, half buried in a nest of silken cushions— thick coils and many, circle upon circle of them, covered with great heart shaped scales; glimmering and palely gleaming; each scale as exquisitely wrought as though by elfin jeweler; each opaline, nacreous; mother-of-pearl.

Her pointed chin was cupped in hands tiny as a baby's; like a babe's were her slender arms, their dimpled elbows resting on her top-most coil.

And on that face which was neither woman's nor serpent's but subtly both—and more, far more than either—on that ageless face sat side by side and hand in hand a spirit of wisdom that was awesome and a spirit weary beyond thought!

Graydon forgot his terror. He paid homage to her beauty; for beautiful she was though terrible—this serpent woman with hair of spun silver, her face and breasts of rosy pearls, her jeweled and shimmering coils, her eyes of purple fire and her lips of living flame. A lesser homage he paid her wisdom. And he pitied her for her burden of weariness.

Fear of her he had none.

Instantly he knew that she had read all his thoughts; knew, too, that he had pleased her. The scarlet lips half parted in a smile—almost she preened herself! A slender red and pointed tongue flicked out and touched her scarlet lips. The tiny hands fell; she raised her head; up from her circled coils lifted and swayed a pearled pillar bearing that head aloft, slowly, sinuously, foot by foot until it paused twice the height of a tall man above the floor; twisting, it turned its face to the alcove.

Graydon, following the movement, saw that the alcove was tenanted. Within it was a throne—a throne that was as though carved from the heart of a colossal sapphire. It was oval, ten feet or more in height, and hollowed like a shrine. It rested upon or was set within the cupped end of a thick pillar of some substance resembling milky rock crystal. It was empty, so far as he could see, but around it clung a faint radiance. At its foot were five lesser thrones, low and with broad table-like seats. They were arranged in a semi-circle. The throne at the right end of this semi-circle was red as though carved from ruby; the throne at the left was black as though cut from jet; the three central thrones were red gold.

Black throne and ruby throne and middle throne of red gold were empty. In each of the other two a figure sat, cross-legged and squatting and swathed from feet to chin in silken robes of blue and gold. Incredibly old were the faces of the pair, the stamp of lost aeons deep upon them—except their eyes.

Their eyes were young; as incredibly young as their settings were ancient. And incredibly alive! And those vital, youthful eyes were reading him; the minds behind them were weighing him; judging him. Judging him with what purpose?

Floated through Graydon's mind—or whatever it was of him that hovered there in dream or in spell or in obedience to laws unknown to the science of his world—the memory of Suarra's vow. By the Wisdom of the Snake Mother, and by the Five Lords and by the Lord of Lords she had sworn to save him if she could.

Why, these must be they, the two Lords she had told him still lived in Yu-Atlanchi! Certainly there was the Snake Mother. And that sapphire throne of luminous mystery must be the seat of the Lord of Lords, whatever he might be.

That fantastic city that had raced upward to enfold him was—Yu-Atlanchi!

Yu-Atlanchi! Where death—where death—

The Snake Mother had turned her head; the eyes of the two Lords no longer dwelt on his. They were looking, the three of them, beyond him. The serpent woman was speaking. He heard her voice like faint, far off music. Graydon thought that she glanced behind him.

He saw—Suarra.

So close to him she stood that he could have touched her with his hand. Slender feet bare, her cloudy hair unbound, clothed only in a single scanty robe that hid no curve nor lithesome line of her, no ornament but the bracelet of the dinosaurs, she stood. If she saw him, she gave no sign.

And it came to him that she did not see him; did not know that he was there!

On her face was the light of a great gladness, as of one who has made a prayer and knows that prayer has been granted. He reached out a hand to touch her; make her aware of him. He felt nothing, nor did she move.

And suddenly he realized once more that he had no hands!

As he labored to understand this, he saw the Snake Mother's swaying column grow rigid, her purple eyes fix themselves upon some point, it seemed, far, far beyond the walls of that mysterious temple.

Swift as a blow they returned to him. They smote him; they hurled him away. The hall disintegrated, vanished. He had vertiginous sensation of nightmare speed, as though the earth had spun from under him and let him drop through space. The flight ended; a shock ran through him.

Dazed, he raised his lids. He lay beside the crackling camp fire. And half way between him and the tent was Sterrett charging down on him like a madman and bellowing red rage and vengeance as he came.

Graydon leaped to his feet, but before he could guard himself the giant was upon him. The next moment he was down, over-borne by sheer weight. The big adventurer crunched a knee into his arm and gripped his throat. Sterrett's bloodshot eyes blazed into his, his teeth were bared as though to rend him.

"Let her go, did you!" he roared. "Knocked me out and then let
her go! Well, damn you, Graydon, here's where you go, too!"

Frantically Graydon tried to break that grip on his throat. His lungs
labored; there was a deafening roaring in his ears; flecks of crimson
began to dance across his vision. Sterrett was strangling him. Through
fast dimming sight he saw two black shadows leap through the firelight
glare and throw themselves on his strangler; clutch the swaying hands.

The fingers relaxed. Graydon, drawing in great sobbing breaths,
staggered up. A dozen paces away stood Sterrett, still cursing him,
vilely; quivering, straining to leap again upon him. Dancre, arms around
his knees, was hanging to him like a little terrier. Beside him was
Soames, the barrel of his automatic pressed against the giant's stomach.

"Why don't you let me kill him?" raved Sterrett. "Didn't I tell you
the wench had enough on her to set us up the rest of our lives? Didn't
I tell you she had an emerald that would have made us all rich? And
there's more where that one came from. And he let her go! Let her
go, the—"

"Now look here, Sterrett." Soames's voice was deliberate, cold. "You
be quiet or I'll do for you. We ain't goin' to let this thing get by us,
me and Dancre. We ain't goin' to let this double-crossing whelp do
us, and we ain't goin' to let you spill the beans by killing him. We've
struck something big. All right, we're goin' to cash in on it. We're
goin' to sit down peaceable and Mr. Graydon is goin' to tell us what
happened after he put you out, what dicker he made with the girl and
all of that. If he won't do it peaceable, then Mr. Graydon is goin' to
have things done to him that'll make him give up. That's all, Danc',
let go his legs. Sterrett, if you kick up any more trouble until I give
the word I'm goin' to shoot you. From now on I boss this crowd—
me and Danc'. You get me, Sterrett?"

Graydon, head once more clear, slid a cautious hand down toward
his pistol holster. It was empty. Soames grinned, sardonically.

"We got it, Graydon," he said. "Yours, too, Sterrett. Fair enough.
Sit down, everybody."

He squatted by the fire, still keeping Sterrett covered. And after a
moment the latter, grumbling, followed suit. Dancre dropped beside
him.

"Come over here, Mr. Graydon," snarled Soames. "Come over and
cough up. What're you holdin' out on us? Did you make a date with
her to meet you after you got rid of us? If so, where is it—because
we'll all go together."

"Where'd you hide those gold spears?" growled Sterrett. "You never
let her get away with them, that's sure."

"Shut up, Sterrett," ordered Soames. "I'm holdin' this inquest. Still,
there's something in that. Was that it, Graydon? Did she give you the
spears and her jewelry to let her go?"

"I've told you," answered Graydon. "I asked for nothing, but I took
nothing. Sterrett's drunken folly had put us all in jeopardy. Letting the

girl go free was the first vital step toward our own safety. I thought it was the best thing to do. I still think so."

"Yes?" sneered the lank New Englander, "is that so? Well, I'll tell you, Graydon, if she'd been an Indian maybe I'd agree with you. But not when she was the kind of lady Sterrett says she was. No sir, it ain't natural. You know damned well that if you'd been straight you'd have kept her here till Danc' and I got back. Then we could all have got together and figured what was the best thing to do. Hold her until her folks came along and paid up to get her back undamaged. Or give her the third degree till she gave up where all that gold and stuff she was carrying came from. That's what you would have done, Mr. Graydon, if you weren't a dirty, lyin', double-crossin' hound."

Graydon's temper awakened under the insult, his anger flared up.

"All right, Soames," he said. "I'll tell you. What I've said about freeing her for our own safety is true. But outside of that I would as soon have thought of trusting a child to a bunch of hyenas as I would of trusting that girl to you three. I let her go a damned sight more for her sake than I did for our own. Does that satisfy you?"

"Aha!" jeered Dancre. "Now I see. Here is this strange lady of so much wealth and beauty. She is too pure and good for us to behold. He tell her so and bids her fly. 'My hero,' she say, 'take all I have and give up this bad company.' 'No, no,' he tell her, t'inking all the time if he play his cards right he get much more, and us out of the way so he need not divide, 'no, no,' he tell her. 'But long as these bad men stay here you will not be safe.' 'My hero,' say she, 'I will go and bring back my family and they shall dispose of your bad company. But you they shall reward, my hero, *oui!*' Aha, so that is what it was!"

Graydon flushed; the little Frenchman's malicious travesty shot uncomfortably close. After all, Suarra's unsought promise to save him if she could might be construed as Dancre had suggested. What if he told them that he had warned her that, whatever the fate in store for them, he was determined to share it and that he would stand by them to the last? They would not believe him.

Soames had been watching him closely.

"By Heaven, Danc'," he said. "I guess you've hit it. He changed color. He's sold us out."

For a moment he raised his automatic, held it on Graydon. Sterrett touched his hand.

"Don't shoot him, Soames," he begged. "Give him to me. I want to break his neck."

Soames pushed him away, lowered the gun.

"No," he said, deliberately. "This is too big a thing to let slip by bein' too quick on the trigger. If your dope is right, Danc', and I guess it is, the lady was mighty grateful. All right—we ain't got her, but we have got him. As I figure it, bein' grateful, she won't want him to get killed. Well, we'll trade him for what they got that we want. Tie him up!"

He pointed the pistol at Graydon, Sterrett and Dancre went into the tent, returned with ropes from the pack saddles. Unresisting, Graydon let them bind his wrists. They pushed him over to one of the trees and sat him on the ground with his back against its bole. They passed a rope under his arms and hitched it securely around the trunk. Then they tied his feet.

"Now," said Soames, "if her gang show up in the morning, we'll let 'em see you and find out how much you're worth. They won't rush us; there's bound to be a palaver. And if they don't come to terms, well, Graydon, the first bullet out of this gun goes through your guts. That'll give you time to see what goes on before you die!"

Graydon did not answer him. Nothing that he might say, he knew, would change them from their purpose. He closed his eyes, reviewing that strange dream of his—for dream he now believed it, thrust back among the realities of the camp. A dream borne of Suarra's words and that weird bracelet of the dinosaurs from which gleamed the purple orbs of the serpent woman.

Once or twice he opened his eyes and looked at the others. They sat beside the fire, heads close together, talking in whispers, their faces tense, and eyes a-glitter with greed, feverish with the gold lust.

And after a while Graydon's head dropped forward. He slept.

Chapter IV

THE WHITE LLAMA

IT WAS dawn when Graydon awakened. Some one had thrown a blanket over him during the night, but he was, nevertheless, cold and stiff. He drew his legs up and down painfully, trying to start the sluggish blood. He heard the others stirring in the tent. He wondered which of them had thought of the blanket, and why he had been moved to that kindness.

Sterrett lifted the tent flap, passed by him without a word and went on to the spring. Graydon heard him drinking, thirstily. He returned and busied himself about the fire. There was an oddly furtive air about the big man. Now and then he looked at the prisoner, but with neither anger nor resentment. Rather were his glances apologetic, ingratiating. He slipped at last to the tent, listened, then trod softly over to Graydon.

"Sorry about this," he muttered. "But I can't do anything with Soames or Dancre. Had a hard time persuading 'em even to let you have that blanket. Here take a drink of this."

He pressed a flask to Graydon's lips. He took a swallow; it warmed him.

"Sh-h," warned Sterrett. "Don't bear any grudge. Drunk last night. I'll help you—" He broke off, abruptly; busied himself with the burning logs. Out of the tent came Soames. He scanned Sterrett suspiciously, then strode over to Graydon.

"I'm goin' to give you one last chance, Graydon," he began without preliminary. "Come through clean with us on your dicker with the girl and we'll take you back with us and all work together and all share together. You had the edge on us yesterday and I don't know that I blame you. But it's three to one now and the plain truth is you can't get away with it. So why not be reasonable?"

"What's the use of going over all that again, Soames?" Graydon asked wearily. "I've told you everything. If you're wise, you'll let me loose, give me my guns and I'll fight for you when the trouble comes. For trouble is coming man, sure—big trouble."

"Yeh?" snarled the New Englander. "Tryin' to scare us, are you? All right, there's a nice little trick of drivin' a wedge under each of your finger nails and a-keepin' drivin' 'em in. It makes 'most anybody talk after a while. And if it don't there's the good old fire dodge. Rollin' your feet up to it, closer and closer and closer. Yes, anybody'll talk when their toes begin to crisp up and toast."

Suddenly he bent over and sniffed at Graydon's lips.

"So that's it!" He faced Sterrett, tense, gun leveled from his hip pocket straight at the giant. "Been feedin' him liquor, have you? Been talkin' to him, have you? After we'd settled it last night that I was to do all the talkin'. All right, that settles you, Sterrett. Dancre! Danc'! Come here, quick!" he roared.

The Frenchman came running out of the tent.

"Tie him up." Soames nodded toward Sterrett. "Another damned double-crosser in the camp. Gave him liquor. Got their heads together while we were inside. Tie him."

"But Soames," the Frenchman was hesitant, "if we have to fight the Indians it is not well to have half of us helpless, no. Perhaps Sterrett he did nothing—"

"If we have to fight, two men will do as well as three," said Soames. "I ain't goin' to let this thing slip through my fingers, Danc'. I don't think we'll have to do any fightin'. If they come, I think it's goin' to be a tradin' job. Sterrett's turnin' traitor, too. Tie him, I say."

"Well, I don't like it—" began Dancre; Soames made an impatient motion with his automatic; the little Frenchman went to the tent, returned with a coil of rope, sidled up to Sterrett.

"Put up your hands," ordered Soames. Sterrett swung them up. But in mid swing they closed on Dancre, lifted him like a doll and held him between himself and the gaunt New Englander.

"Now shoot, damn you," he cried, and bore down on Soames, meeting every move of his pistol arm with Dancre's wriggling body. Then his own right hand swept down to the Frenchman's belt, drew from the holster his automatic, leveled it over the twisting shoulder at Soames.

"Drop your gun, Yank," grinned Sterrett triumphantly. "Or shoot if you want. But before your bullet's half through Dancre here, by Heaven I'll have *you* drilled clean!"

There was a momentary, sinister silence. It was broken by a sudden

pealing of tiny golden bells. Their chiming cleft through the murk of
murder that had fallen on the camp; lightened it; dissolved it as the
sunshine does a cloud. Graydon saw Soames's pistol drop from a hand
turned nerveless; saw Sterrett's iron grip relax and let Dancre fall to
the ground; saw the heads of Dancre and Sterrett and Soames stiffen
and point to the source of that aureate music like hounds to a huddling
covey.

His own eyes followed.

Through the trees, not a hundred yards away, was Suarra!

And there was no warrior host around her. She had brought with
her neither avengers nor executioners. With her were but two followers.
Yet even at his first glimpse it came to Graydon that if these were
servants, they were two strange, strange servants indeed!

A cloak of soft green swathed the girl from neck almost to slender
feet. In the misty midnight hair gleamed a coronal of emeralds set in
red gold, and bandlets of gold studded with the same virescent gems
circled her wrists and ankles. Behind her paced sedately a snow white
llama; there was a broad golden collar around its neck from which
dropped the strands of golden bells that shook out the tinkling harmonies. Its eyes were blue and between them swayed a pendant of
some gem, rosy as the fruit of rubies mated to white pearls. From each
of its silvery silken sides a pannier hung, woven, it seemed, from
shining yellow rushes.

And at the snow white llama's flanks were two figures, bodies covered
by voluminous robes whose goods covered their faces. One was draped
in darkest blue; he carried a staff of ebony and strode beside the llama
soberly, something disconcertingly mathematical in each step he took.
The other was in yellow; he carried a staff of vermilion and he fluttered
and danced beside the beast, taking little steps backward and forward;
movements that carried the weird suggestion that his robes clothed not
a man but some huge bird.

Save for the tinkling of the bells there was no sound as they came
on. Graydon's three jailers stared at the caravan, struck immobile with
amazement, incredulous, like dreaming men. Graydon himself strained
at his bonds, a sick horror in his heart. Why had Suarra returned
deliberately back to this peril? He had warned her; she could not be
so innocent as not to know what dangers threatened her at the hands
of these men. And why had she come decked out with a queen's ransom
in jewels and gold? Almost it seemed that she had done this deliberately;
had deliberately arrayed herself to arouse to the full the very passions
from which she had most to fear!

"Dieu!" It was Dancre, whispering. "The emeralds!"

"God—what a girl!" It was Sterrett, muttering; his thick nostrils
distended, a red flicker in his eyes.

Only Soames said nothing, perplexity, suspicion struggling through
the blank astonishment on his bleak and crafty face. Nor did he speak
as the girl and her attendants halted close beside him. But the doubt,

the suspicion, in his eyes grew as he scanned her and the hooded pair, then sent his gaze along the path up which they had come searching every tree, every bush. There was no sign of movement there, no sound.

"Suarra!" cried Graydon, despairingly. "Suarra, why did you come back?"

Quietly, she stepped over to him, drew a dagger from beneath her cloak, cut the thong that bound him to the tree, slipped the blade under the cords about his wrists and ankles; freed him. He staggered to his feet.

"Was it not well for you that I did come?" she asked sweetly.

Before he could answer, Soames strode forward. And Graydon saw that he had come to some decision, had resolved upon some course of action. He made a low, awkward, half mocking, half respectful bow to the girl; then spoke to Graydon.

"All right," he said, "you can stay loose, as long as you do what I want you to. The girl's back and that's the main thing. She seems to favor you quite a lot, Graydon, an' maybe that's goin' to be damned useful. I reckon that gives us a way to persuade her to talk if how happens it she turns quiet like when I get to askin' her certain things— like where those emeralds come from an' how to get there an' the likes of that.

"Yes, sir, and you favor her. That's useful, too. I reckon you won't want to be tied up an' watch certain things happen to her, eh?" He leered at Graydon who curbed with difficulty the impulse to send his fist crashing into the cynical face. "But there's just one thing you've got to do if you want things to go along peaceable," Soames continued. "Don't do any talkin' to her when I ain't close by. Remember, I know the Aymara as well as you do. And I want to be right alongside listenin' in all the time, do you see? That's all."

He turned to Suarra, bowed again.

"Your visit has brought great happiness, maiden," he spoke in the Aymara. "It will not be a short one, if we have our way, and I think we *will* have our way." There was covert, but unmistakable menace in the phrase, yet if she noted it she gave no heed. "You are strange to us, as we must be to you. There is much for us each to learn, one of the other."

"That is true, stranger," she answered, tranquilly. "I think, though, that your desire to learn of me is much greater than mine to learn of you—since, as you surely know, I have had one not too pleasant lesson." She glanced at Sterrett."

"The lessons, sister," he told her bluntly, indeed brutally, "shall be pleasant or—not pleasant even as you choose to teach us or not to teach us—what we would learn."

This time there was no mistaking the covert menace in the words, nor did Suarra again let it pass. Her eyes blazed sudden wrath.

"Better not to threaten," she warned, her proud little head thrown haughtily back. "I, Suarra, am not used to threats, and if you will take my counsel you will keep them to yourself hereafter."

"Yes, is that so?" Soames took a step toward her, face grown grim and ugly; instantly Graydon thrust himself between him and the girl. There came a curious, dry chuckling from the hooded figure in yellow. Suarra started; her wrath, her hauteur vanished; she became once more naïve, friendly. She pushed Graydon aside.

"I was hasty," she said to Soames. "Nevertheless it is never wise to threaten unless you know the strength of what it is you menace. Yet I know all that you wish to learn. You wish to know how I came by this—and this—and this—" She touched her coronal, her bracelets, her anklets. "You wish to know where they came from, and if there are more of them there, and if so how you may possess yourself of as much as you can carry. Well, you shall know all that. I have come to tell you."

At this astonishing announcement, apparently so frank and open, all the doubt and suspicion returned to Soames. Again his gaze narrowed and searched the trail up which Suarra and her caravan had come. It returned and rested on the girl; then scrutinized the two servitors who, Graydon now realized, had stood like images ever since that caravan had come to rest within the camp; motionless, and except for that one dry, admonitory chuckling, soundless.

And as Graydon stood thus, considering, Dancre came up and gripped his arm.

"Soames," he said, and his voice and his hand were both shaking, "the baskets on the llama! They're not rushes—they're gold, pure gold, pure soft gold, woven like straw! *Dieu,* Soames, what have we struck!"

Soames's eyes glittered.

"Better go over and watch where they came up, Danc," he answered. "I don't quite get this. It looks too cursed easy to be right. Take your rifle and squint out from the edge of the trees while I try to get down to what's what."

As though she had understood the words, Suarra struck in:

"There is nothing to fear. No harm will come to you from me. If there is any evil in store for you, you yourselves shall summon it— not us. I have come to show you the way to treasure. Only that. Come with me and you shall see where jewels like these"—she touched the gems meshed in her hair—"grow like flowers in a garden. You shall see the gold come streaming forth, living, from"—she hesitated; then went on—"come streaming forth like water. You may bathe in that stream, drink from it if you will, carry away all that you can bear. Or if it causes you too much sorrow to leave it, why—you may stay with it forever; nay, become a part of it, even. Men of gold!"

She laughed; turned from them; walked toward the llama.

The men stared at her and at each other; on the faces of three, greed and suspicion; bewilderment on Graydon's, for beneath the mockery of those last words he had sensed the pulse of the sinister.

"It is a long journey," she faced them, one hand on the llama's head. "You are strangers here; indeed, my guests—in a sense. Therefore a little I have brought for your entertainment before we start."

She began to unbuckle the panniers. And Graydon was again aware that these two attendants of hers were strange servants—if servants, indeed, they were. They made no move to help her. Silent they still stood, motionless, faces covered. In their immobility he felt something implacable, ominous, dread. A little shiver shook him.

He stepped forward to help the girl. She smiled up at him, half shyly. In the midnight depths of her eyes was a glow warmer far than friendliness; his hands leaped to touch hers.

Instantly Soames stepped between them.

"Better remember what I told you," he snapped; then ran his hand over the side of the pannier. And Graydon realized that Dancre had spoken truth. The panniers were of gold; soft gold, gold that had been shaped into willow-like withes and plaited.

"Help me," came Suarra's voice. Graydon lifted the basket and set it down beside her. She slipped a hasp; bent back the soft metal withes; drew out a shimmering packet. She shook it and it floated out on the dawn wind, a cloth of silver. She let it float to the ground where it lay like a great web of gossamer spun by silver spiders.

Then from the hamper she brought forth cups of gold and deep, boat-shaped golden dishes, two tall ewers whose handles were slender carved dragons, their scales made, it seemed, from molten rubies. After them small golden-withed baskets. She set the silver cloth with the dishes and the cups. She opened the little baskets. In them were unfamiliar, fragrant fruits and loaves and oddly colored cakes. All these Suarra placed upon the plates. She dropped to her knees at the head of the cloth, took up one of the ewers, snapped open its lid and from it poured into the cups clear amber wine.

She raised her eyes to them; waved a white hand, graciously.

"Sit," she said. "Eat and drink."

She beckoned to Graydon; pointed to the place beside her. Silently, gaze fixed on the glittering board, Sterrett and Dancre and Soames squatted before the other plates. Soames thrust out a hand, took up one of these and weighed it, scattering what it held upon the ground.

"Gold!" he breathed.

Sterrett laughed, crazily; raised his wine-filled goblet to his lips.

"Wait!" Dancre caught his wrist. "Eat and drink, she said, eh? Eat, drink and be merry—for tomorrow we die, eh—is that it, Soames?"

The New Englander started, face once more dark with doubt.

"You think it's poisoned?" he snarled.

"Maybe so—maybe no." The little Frenchman shrugged. "But I think it better we say 'After you' to her."

"They are afraid. They think it is—that you have—" Graydon stumbled.

"That I have put sleep—or death in it?" Suarra smiled. "And you?" she asked.

For answer Graydon raised his cup and drank it. For a moment she contemplated him, approval in her gaze.

"Yet it is natural." She turned to Soames. "Yes, it is natural that you three should fear this, since, is it not so—it is what you would do if you were we and we were you? But you are wrong. I tell you again that you have nothing to fear from me—who comes only to show you a way. I tell you again that what there is to fear as we go on that way is that which is in yourselves."

She poured wine into her own cup, drank it; broke off a bit of Sterrett's bread and ate it; took a cake from Dancre's plate and ate that, set white teeth in one of the fragrant fruits.

"Are you satisfied?" she asked them. "Oh, be very sure that if it were in my wish to bring death to you it would be in no such form as this."

For a moment Soames glared at her. Then he sprang to his feet, strode over to the hooded, watching figures and snatched aside the cowl of the blue-robed one. Graydon with a cry of anger leaped up and after him—then stood, turned to stone.

For the face that Soames had unmasked was like old ivory and it was seamed with a million lines; a face stamped with unbelievable antiquity, but whose eyes were bright and as incredibly youthful as their setting was ancient.

The face of one of those two draped figures that had crouched upon the throne in that mystic temple of his dream!

The face of one of those mysterious Lords who with that being of coiled beauty Suarra had named the Snake Mother, had listened to, and as he then had thought had granted, Suarra's unknown prayer!

A dozen heart beats it may be the gaunt New Englander stared into that inscrutable, ancient face and its unwinking brilliant eyes. Then he let the hood drop and walked slowly back to the silver cloth. And as he passed him, Graydon saw that his face was white and his gaze was fixed as though he had looked into some unnamable terror. And as he threw himself down at his place and raised his wine cup to his lips, his hand was shaking.

The spell that had held Graydon relaxed. He looked at the black-robed figure; it stood as before, motionless and silent. He dropped beside Suarra. Soames, hand still shaking, held out to her his empty goblet. She filled it; he drained it and she filled it again. And Graydon saw now that Sterrett's ruddy color had fled and that Dancre's lips were twitching and had grown gray.

What was it that they had seen in that seamed ivory face, that had been invisible to him? What warning? What vision of horror?

They drank thirstily of the wine. And soon it had taken effect; had banished their terror—whatever it had been. They ate hungrily of the loaves, the little cakes, the fruit. At last the plates were empty—the tall ewer, too.

"And now," Suarra said as she arose, "it is time for us to go, if you desire still to be led to that treasure house."

"We're going, sister, never fear." Soames grinned half drunkenly, and lurched to his feet. "Danc', stay right here and watch things. Come on, Sterrett." He slapped the giant on the back, all distrust, for the moment at least, vanished. "Come on, Graydon, let by-gones be by-gones."

Sterrett laughed vacantly, scrambled up and linked his arms in the New Englander's. Together they made their way to the tent. Dancre, rifle ready, settled down on a boulder just beyond the fire and began his watch.

Graydon lingered behind. Soames had forgotten him, for a little time at least; he meant to make the best of that time with this strange maid whose beauty and sweetness had netted heart and brain as no other woman ever had. He came close to her, so close that the subtle fragrance of her cloudy hair rocked his heart, so close that her shoulder touching his sent through him little racing, maddening flames.

"Suarra—" he began hoarsely. Swiftly she turned and silenced him with slender fingers on his lips.

"Not now," she whispered. "You must not tell me what is in your heart, O man to whom my own heart is eager to speak. Not now— nor, it may be, ever." There was sorrow in her eyes, longing, too; quickly she veiled them. "I promised you that I would save you, if I could. And of that vow was born another promise." His glance sought the two silent, quiet shapes in blue and in yellow, meaningly. "So speak to me not again," she went on hurriedly, "or if you must, let it be of commonplace things. Not of that which is in your heart, or mine!"

Stupidly he looked at her. What did she mean by a promise born of that she had made to him? A vow to these—Lords; to the mystery of the serpent's coils and woman's face and breasts—the Snake Mother? A vow in exchange for his life? Had they seen deeper into her heart than he, and found there in very truth what he had half dreamed might be? Had she vowed to them to hold him apart from her if they would grant him protection, his comrades, too—if they would have it?

Suddenly it came to him that for him, at least, the life she would save by such a barter would not be worth living.

She was packing away the golden cups and dishes. Mechanically he set about helping her. And, save for what he handled, he thought with grim humor, this was a commonplace thing enough surely to satisfy her. She accepted his aid without comment, looked at him no more. And after a while the fever in his blood cooled, his hot revolt crystallized into cold determination. For the moment he would accept the situation. He would let matters develop. His time would come. He could afford to wait.

Without a word when the last shining cup was in the pannier and the mouth of the latter closed he turned and strode to the tent to get together his duffle, pack his burro. The voices of Sterrett and Soames came to him; he hesitated; listened.

"What it was when I looked into his damned wrinkled old face I don't know," he heard Soames say. "But something came over me, Sterrett. I can't remember, only that it was like looking over the edge of the world into hell!"

"I know." Sterrett's voice was hoarse. "I felt the same way."

"Hypnotism," said Soames, "that's what it was. The Indian priests down here know how to work it. But he won't catch me again with that trick. I'll shoot. You can't hypnotize a gun."

"But they're not Indians, Soames," came Sterrett's voice. "They're whiter than you and me. What are they? And the girl—Heavens—"

"What they are we'll find out, never fear," grunted the New Englander. "To hell with the girl. Take her if you can get her. But I'd go through a dozen hells to get to the place where that stuff they're carryin' samples of comes from. Man, with what we could carry out on the burros and the llama and come back for—man, we could buy the world!"

"Yes—unless there's a trap somewhere," said Sterrett, dubiously.

"We've got the cards in our hands." Plainly the drink was wearing off Soames; all his old confidence and cunning were returning. "What's against us? Two old men and a girl. Now I'll tell you what I think. I don't know who or what they are, but whoever or whatever, you can bet there ain't many of 'em. If there was, they'd be landin' on us hard. No—they're damned anxious to get us away and they're willin' to let us get out with what we can to get us away. Poor boobs, they think if they give us what we want now we'll slip right off and never come back. And as for what they are, well, I'll tell you what I think—half-breeds. The Spanish were down here; maybe they bred in with the Incas. There's probably about a handful left. They know we could wipe 'em out in no time. They want to get rid of us, quick and cheap as possible. And the three of us could wipe 'em out."

"Three of us?" asked Sterrett. "Four you mean. There's Graydon."

"Graydon don't count, the damned crook. Thought he'd sold us out, didn't he? All right, we'll fix Mr. Graydon when the time comes. Just now he's useful to us on account of the girl. She's stuck on him. But when the time comes to divide, there'll only be three of us. And there'll only be two of us if you do anything like you did this morning."

"Cut that out, Soames," growled the giant. "I told you it was the drink. I'm through with that now that we've seen this stuff. I'm with you to the limit. Do what you want with Graydon. But save the girl for me. I'd be willing to make a bargain with you on that—give up a part of my share."

"Oh, hell," drawled Soames. "We've been together a good many years, Bill. There's enough and plenty for the three of us. You can have the girl for nothing."

Little flecks of red danced before Graydon's eyes. With his hand stretched to tear open the tent flap and grapple with these two who could talk so callously and evilly of Suarra's disposal, he checked himself. That was no way to help her. Unarmed, what could he do against these armed adventurers? Nothing. Some way he must get back his own weapons. And the danger was not imminent. They would do nothing before they reached that place of treasure to which Suarra had promised to lead them.

There had been much of reason in Soames's explanation of the mystery.

That vision of his—what was it after all but an illusion? He remembered the sensation that had caught him when he had first seen those brilliant purple jewels in Suarra's bracelet. The feeling that he looked along them for great distances back to actual eyes of which the purple jewels were but prolongations. That vision of his—was it not but a dream induced by those jewels? A fantasy of the subconsciousness whipped out of it by some hypnotic quality they possessed? Science, he knew, admits that some gems hold this quality—though why they do science cannot tell. Dimly he remembered that he had once read a learned article that had tried to explain the power. Something about the magnetic force in light; a force within those vibrations we call color. Something about this force being taken up by the curious mechanism of rods and cones in the retina which flashes the sensations we call color along the optic nerves to the brain.

These flashes, he recalled the article had said, were actual though minute discharges of electricity. And since the optic nerves are not in reality nerves at all, but prolongations of the brain, this unknown force within the gems impinged directly upon the brain, stimulating some cells, depressing others, affecting memory and judgment, creating visions, disturbing all that secret world until the consciousness became dazzled, bewildered, unable to distinguish between reality and illusion.

So much for his vision. That the face of the figure in blue seemed to be one of those Lords he had seen in that vision—well, was not that but another illusion?

Soames might well be right, too, he thought, in his interpretation of Suarra's visit to the camp. If she had power behind her would she not have brought it? Was it not more reasonable to accept the New Englander's version of the thing?

And if that were so, then Suarra was but a girl with only two old men to help her. For Graydon had no doubt that the figure in yellow like that in blue was an old man, too.

And all that meant that he, Graydon, was all of strength that Suarra could really count on to protect her.

He had spun his web of reasoning with the swiftness of a dream. When he had arrived at its last strand he stole silently back a score of paces; waited for a moment or two; then went noisily to the tent. For the first time in many hours he felt in full command of himself; thought he saw his way clear before him. Faintly he recognized that he had glossed over, set aside arbitrarily, many things. No matter—it was good to get his feet on earth again, to brush aside all these cobwebs of mystery, to take the common sense view. It was good and it was—safer.

He thrust aside the tent flap and entered.

"Been a long while comin'," snarled Soames, again his old, suspicious self. "Been talkin', after what I told you?"

"Not a word," answered Graydon cheerfully. He busied himself with his belongings. "By the way, Soames," he said casually, "don't you think it's time to stop this nonsense and give me back my guns?"

Soames made no answer.

"Oh, all right then," Graydon went on. "I only thought that they would come in handy when the pinch comes. But if you want me to look on while you do the scrapping—well, I don't mind."

"You'd better mind." Soames did not turn around, but his voice was deadly. "You'd better mind, Graydon. If a pinch comes, we're takin' no chances of a bullet in our backs. That's why you got no guns. And if the pinch does come—well, we'll take no chances on you anyway. Do you get me?"

Graydon shrugged his shoulders. In silence the packing was completed; the tent struck; the burros loaded.

Suarra stood awaiting them at the side of the white llama. Soames walked up to her, drew from its holster his automatic, balanced it in outstretched hand.

"You know what this is?" he asked her.

"Why, yes," she answered. "It is the death weapon of your kind."

"Right," said Soames. "And it deals death quickly, quicker than spears or arrows." He raised his voice so there could be no doubt that blue cowl and yellow cowl must also hear. "Now, sister, I and these two men here," he indicated Sterrett and Dancre, "carry these and others still more deadly. This man's weapons we have taken from him." He pointed to Graydon. "Your words may be clearest truth. I hope they are, for your sake and this man's and the two who came with you—him and him—" He wagged a long finger at Graydon, at blue cowl, at yellow cowl. "Quick death! We'll get them out of the way first. And we'll attend to you later, as it seems best to me."

He scanned her through slitted eyes that gleamed coldly.

"You understand me?" he asked, and grinned like a hungry wolf.

"I understand." Suarra's eyes and face were calm, but there was more than a touch of scorn in her golden voice. "You need fear nothing from us."

"We don't," said Soames. "But you have much to fear—from us."

Another moment he regarded her, menacingly; then shoved his pistol back into its holster.

"Go first," he ordered. "Your two attendants behind you. And then you." He pointed to Graydon. "We three march in the rear, with guns ready."

Without a word Suarra swung away at the white llama's head; behind her paced blue cowl and yellow. And a dozen paces behind them walked Graydon. Behind the file of burros strode giant Sterrett, lank Soames, little Dancre—rifles ready, eyes watchful.

And so they passed through the giant *algarrobas;* out into the oddly parklike spaces beyond.

CHAPTER V

THE THING THAT FLED

THEY HAD traveled over the savanna for perhaps an hour when Suarra abruptly turned to the left, entering the forest that covered the flanks of a great mountain. Soon the trees closed in on them. Graydon could see no trail, yet the girl went on surely, without pause. He knew there must be signs to guide her since her course took them now to one side, now to another; once he was certain that they had almost circled.

Yes, trail there must be, unless Suarra was purposely trying to confuse them to prevent them from return. He could see nothing around him but the immense tree trunks, while the thick roof of leaves shut out all sight of the sun and so hid this means of discovering direction.

Another hour went by and the way began to climb, the shade to grow denser. Deeper it became and deeper until the girl was but a flitting shadow. Blue robe he could hardly see at all, but yellow robe stood out sharply, his bird suggestion suddenly accentuated—as though he had been a monstrous yellow parrot.

Once or twice Graydon had glanced at the three men behind him. The darkness was making them more and more uneasy. They walked close together, eyes and ears obviously strained to catch first faint stirrings of ambush. And now, as the green gloom grew denser still, Soames strode forward and curtly ordered him to join Dancre and Sterrett. For an instant he hesitated; read murder in the New Englander's eyes; realized the futility of resistance and dropped back. Soames pressed forward until he was close behind blue cowl and yellow. They did not turn their heads nor did the girl.

Dancre motioned him in between himself and Sterrett, grinning wickedly.

"Soames has changed his plan," he whispered. "If there is trouble he shoot the old devils—quick. He keep the girl to make trade wit' her people. He keep you to make trade wit' the girl. Eh?"

Graydon did not answer. He had already realized what the maneuver meant. But a wave of jubilation swept over him. When the Frenchman had pressed close to him he had felt an automatic in his side pocket. If an attack did come, he thought; he would leap upon Dancre, snatch the pistol and gain for himself at least a fighting chance. He kept as close to him as he dared without arousing suspicion.

Darker grew the woods until the figures in front of him were only a moving blur. Then swiftly the gloom began to lighten. It came to him that they had been passing through some ravine, some gorge whose unseen walls had been pressing in upon them and that had now begun to retreat.

A few minutes longer and he knew he was right. Ahead of them loomed a prodigious doorway, a cleft whose sides reached up for thousands of feet. Beyond was a flood of sunshine, dazzling. Suarra stopped at the rocky threshold with a gesture of warning; peered through; beckoned them on.

Blinking, Graydon walked through the portal. Behind and on each side towered the mountain. He looked out over a broad grass-covered plain strewn with huge, isolated rocks rising from the green like menhirs of the Druids. There were no trees. The plain was dish-shaped; an enormous oval as symmetrical as though it had been molded by the thumb of Cyclopean potter. Straight across it, five miles or more away, the forests began again. They clothed the base of another gigantic mountain whose walls arose perpendicularly a mile at least in air. The smooth scarps described, he saw, an arc of a tremendous circle, as round as Fujiyama's sacred cone, but hundreds of times its girth.

Rushed back on Graydon the picture of that hidden circular valley with its wheeling, moon-bathed colossi and uprushing city of djinns into which last night he had dreamed the purple eyes of the Snake Mother had drawn him! Had it after all been no dream, but true vision? Were these rounded precipices the outer shell of that incredible place? Suarra's story—true?

Shaken, he glanced toward her. She stood a dozen paces away, hand on the white llama's neck and gazing intently over the plain. There was anxiety in her gaze, but there was none in the attitude of those two strange servitors of hers. As silent, as unconcerned, as detached as ever, they seemed to await the girl's next move.

And now Graydon noted that they were on a wide ledge that bordered this vast oval bowl. This shelf was a full hundred feet higher than the bottom of the valley whose sides sloped up to it like the sides of a saucer. And, again carrying out that suggestion of huge dish, the ledge jutted out like a rim.

He guessed that there was a concavity under his feet, and that if one should fall over the side it would be well nigh impossible to climb back because of that overhang. The surface was about twelve feet wide, and more like road carefully leveled by human hands than work of nature. Its nearer boundary was a tree-covered wall of rock, unscalable. On one side the curving bowl of the valley with its weird monoliths and the circular scarp of the mysterious mountain; on the other the wooded cliff.

There was a stirring in the undergrowth where the trees ended their abrupt descent. A goatlike animal slipped out of the covert and paused, head high, nostrils testing the air.

"Meat!" exclaimed Sterrett. His rifle cracked. The beast sank to the path, twitched and lay still. Suarra leaped from the llama's side and faced the giant, eyes blazing wrath and behind that anger, or so it seemed to Graydon, fear.

"Fool!" she cried, and stamped her foot. "You fool! Get back to the cleft. Quick! All of you."

She ran to the llama; caught it by the bridle; drove it, the burros and the four men back to the shelter of the ravine mouth.

"You—" She spoke to Soames. "If you desire to reach that gold for which you thirst, see that this man uses no more that death weapon of his while we are on this path. Nor any of you. Now stay here, and be quiet until I bid you come forth."

She did not wait for reply. She ran to the cleft's opening and Graydon followed. She paused there, scanning the distant forest edge. And once more—and with greater force than ever before—the tranquillity, the inhuman immobility, the indifference of those two enigmatic servitors assailed him.

They had not moved from the path. Suarra took a step toward them, and half held out helpless, beseeching hands. They made no movement, and with a little helpless sigh she dropped her hands and resumed her scrutiny of the plain.

There flickered through Graydon a thought, a vague realization. In these two cloaked and hooded figures dwelt—power. He had not been wrong in recognizing them as the Two Lords of the luminous temple. But the power they owned would not be spent to save him or the three from any consequences of their own acts, would not be interposed between any peril that they themselves should invite.

Yes, that was it! There had been some vow—some bargain—even as Suarra had said. She had promised to save him, Graydon—if she could. She had promised the others treasures and freedom, if they could win them. Very well, the hooded pair would not interfere. But neither would they help. They were judges, watching a game. They had given Suarra permission to play that game, but left the playing of it rigidly up to her.

That nevertheless they would protect her he also believed. And with that conviction a great burden lifted from his mind. Her anxiety now he understood. It was not for herself, but for—him!

"Suarra," he whispered. She did not turn, but she quivered at his voice.

"Go back," she said. "Those for whom I watch have sharp eyes. Stay with the others—"

Suddenly he could have sworn that he heard the whirling beat of great wings over her head. He saw—nothing. Yet she lifted her arms in an oddly summoning gesture, spoke in words whose sounds were strange to him, all alien liquid labials and soft sibilants. Once more he heard the wing beats and then not far away but faint, so faint, a note of the elfin horn!

She dropped her arms, motioned him back to the others. From the dimness of the cleft he watched her. Slow minutes passed. Again he heard the horn note, the faint whirring as of swiftly beating pinions above her. And again could see nothing!

But as though she had received some message Suarra turned, the anxiety, the trouble gone from her face. She beckoned.

"Come out," she said. "None has heard. We can be on our way. But remember what I have said. Not a second time may you escape."

She marched on with the llama. When she reached the animal that had fallen to Sterrett's aim she paused.

"Take that," she ordered. "Throw it back among the trees as far as you can from this path."

"Hell, Soames," cried Sterrett. "Don't fall for that. It's good meat. I'll slip it in on one of the burros."

But Soames was staring at the girl.

"Afraid something'll track us by it?" he asked. She nodded. Some of the cynic evil fled from the New Englander's face.

"She's right." He spoke curtly to Sterrett. "Pick it up and throw it away. And do as she says. I think she's goin' to play square with us. No more shootin', d'you hear?"

Sterrett picked up the little animal and hurled it viciously among the trees.

The caravan set forth along the rimlike way. Noon came and in another ravine that opened upon the strange road they snatched from saddle bags a hasty lunch. They did not waste time in unpacking the burros. There was a little brook singing in the pass and from it they refilled their canteens, then watered the animals. This time Suarra did not join them, sitting aloof with blue cowl and yellow.

By mid-afternoon they were nearing the northern end of the bowl. All through the day the circular mountain across the plain had unrolled its vast arc of cliff. And through the day Suarra's watch of its forest-clothed base had never slackened. A wind had arisen, sweeping toward them from those wooded slopes, bending the tall heads of the grass so far below them.

Suddenly, deep within that wind, Graydon heard a faint, far off clamor, an eerie hissing, shrill and avid, as of some onrushing army of snakes. The girl heard it, too, for she halted and stood tense, face turned toward the sounds. They came again—and louder. And now her face whitened, but her voice when she spoke was steady.

"Danger is abroad," she said. "Deadly danger for you. It may pass and—it may not. Until we know what to expect you must hide. Take your animals and tether them in the underbrush there." She pointed to the mountainside which here was broken enough for cover. "The four of you take trees and hide behind them. Tie the mouths of your animals that they may make no noise."

"So?" snarled Soames. "So here's the trap, is it? All right, sister, you know what I told you. We'll go into the trees, but—you go with us where we can keep our hands on you."

"I will go with you," she answered indifferently. "If those who come have not been summoned by the noise of that fool's death weapon"—she pointed at Sterrett—"you can be saved. If they have been summoned by it, none can save you."

Soames glared at her, then turned abruptly.

"Danc'," he ordered, "Sterrett—get the burros in. And Graydon, you'll stay with the burros and see they make no noise. We'll be right close, with the guns. And we'll have the girl."

Again the wind shrilled with the hissing.

"Be quick," cried Suarra.

Swiftly they hid themselves. When trees and underbrush had closed in upon them it flashed on Graydon, crouching behind the burros, that he had not seen the two cloaked familiars of Suarra join the hurried retreat and seek the shelter of the woods. He was at the edge of the path and cautiously he parted the bushes; peered through.

The two were not upon the rim!

Simultaneously, the same thought had come to Dancre. His voice came from a near-by bole.

"Soames—where those two old devils wit' the girl go?"

"Where'd they go?" Soames repeated blankly. "Why, they came in with us, of course."

"I did not see them," persisted Dancre. "I t'ink not, Soames. If they did, then where are they?"

"You see those two fellows out on the path, Graydon?" called Soames, anxiety in his tones.

"No," answered Graydon curtly.

Soames cursed wickedly.

"So that's the game, eh?" he grunted. "It's a trap! And they've cut out and run to bring 'em here!"

He dropped into the Aymara and spoke to Suarra.

"You know where those men of yours are?" he asked menacingly.

Graydon heard her laugh and knew that she was close beside the New Englander with Dancre and Sterrett flanking her.

"They come and go as they will," she answered serenely.

"They'll come and go as I will," he snarled. "Call them."

"I call them," again Suarra laughed. "Why, they do not my bidding. Nay, I must do theirs—"

"Don't do that, Soames!" Dancre's cry was sharp, and Graydon knew that Soames must have made some threatening movement. "If they're gone, you cannot bring them back. We have the girl. Stop, I say!"

Graydon jumped to his feet. Bullets or no bullets, he would fight for her. As he poised to leap a sudden gust of wind tore at the trees. It brought with it a burst of the weird hissing, closer, strident, in it a devilish undertone that filled him with unfamiliar nightmarish terror.

Instantly came Suarra's voice.

"Down! Down, Graydon!"

Then Dancre's, quivering Graydon knew, with the same fear that gripped him:

"Down! Soames won't hurt her. For God's sake, hide yourself, Graydon, till we know what's coming!"

Graydon turned; looked out over the plain before he sank again behind the burros. And at that moment, from the forests which at this point of the narrowing bowl were not more than half a mile away, he saw dart out a streak of vivid scarlet. It hurled itself into the grass and scuttled with incredible speed straight toward one of the monoliths that stood, black and sheer a good three quarters of the distance across the disk-shaped valley and its top fifty feet or more above the green. From Graydon's own height he could see the scarlet thing's swift rush through the grasses. As he sank down it came to him that whatever it was, it must be of an amazing length to be visible so plainly at that distance. And what was it? It ran like some gigantic insect!

He parted the bushes, peered out again. The scarlet thing had reached the monolith's base. And as he watched, it raised itself against the rock and swarmed up its side to the top. At the edge it paused, seemed to raise its head cautiously and scan the forest from which it had come.

The air was clear, and against the black background of the stone, the vividly colored body stood out. Graydon traced six long, slender legs by which it clung to the rocky surface. There was something about the body that was monstrous, strangely revolting. In its listening, reconnoitering attitude and the shape of its head was something more monstrous still, since it carried with it a vague, incredible suggestion of humanness.

Suddenly the scarlet shape slipped down the rock breast and raced with that same amazing speed through the grasses toward where Graydon watched. An instant later there burst out of the forest what at first glance he took for a pack of immense hunting dogs—then realized that whatever they might be, dogs they certainly were not. They came forward in great leaps that reminded him of the motion of kangaroos. And as they leaped they glittered in the sun with flashes of green and blue as though armored in mail made of emeralds and sapphires.

Nor did ever dogs give tongue as they did. They hissed as they ran, shrilly, stridently, the devilish undertones accentuated. A monstrous, ear-piercing sibilation that drowned all other sounds and struck across the nerves with fingers of unfamiliar primeval terror.

The scarlet thing darted to right, to left, frantically; then crouched at the base of another monolith, motionless.

And now, out of the forest, burst another shape. Like the questing creatures, this glittered, too, but with sparkles of black as though its body was cased in polished jet. Its bulk was that of a giant draft horse, but its neck was long and reptilian. At the base of that neck, astride it, he saw plainly the figure of—a man!

A dozen leaps and it was close behind the glittering pack, now nosing and circling between the first monolith and the woods.

"The Xinli," came Suarra's voice from above him.

The Xinli? It was the name she had given the beasts of the bracelet that held in their paws the disk of the Snake Mother!

The dinosaurs!

His own burro lay close beside him. With trembling hand he reached into a saddlebag and drew out his field glasses. He focused them upon the pack. They swam mistily in the lenses, then sharpened into clear outline. Directly in his line of vision, in the center of the lens, was one of the creatures that had come to gaze, that stood rigidly, its side toward him, pointing like a hunting dog. The excellent glasses brought it so closely to him that he could stretch out a hand it seemed, and touch it.

And it was—a dinosaur!

Dwarfed to the size of a Great Dane dog, still there was no mistaking its breed—one of those leaping, upright-walking monstrous lizards that millions of years ago had ruled earth and without whose extinction, so science taught, man could never have arisen ages later to take possession of this planet. Graydon could see its blunt and spade shaped tail which, with its powerful, pillarlike hind legs, made the tripod upon which it squatted.

Its body was nearly erect. It had two forelegs or arms, absurdly short, but muscled as powerfully as those upon which it sat. It held these half curved as though about to clutch. And at their ends were—no paws; no—but broad hands, each ending in four merciless talons, of which one thrust outward like a huge thumb and each of them armed with chisel-like claws, whose edges, he knew, were sharp as scimitars.

What he had taken for mail of sapphire and emerald were the scales of this dwarfed dinosaur. They overlapped one another like the scales upon an armadillo and it was from their burnished blue and green surfaces and edges that the sun rays struck out the jewel glints.

The creature turned its head upon its short, bull-like neck; it seemed to stare straight at Graydon. He glimpsed little fiery red eyes set in a sloping, bony arch of narrow forehead. Its muzzle was shaped like that of a crocodile, but smaller; truncated. Its jaws were closely studded with long, white and pointed fangs. The jaws slavered.

In a split second of time the mind of Graydon took in these details. Then beside the pointing dinosaur leaped the beast of the rider. Swiftly his eyes took it in—true dinosaur this one, too, but ebon scaled, longer tailed, the hind legs more slender and its neck a cylindrical rod five times thicker than the central coil of the giant boa. His eyes flashed from it to the rider.

Instantly Graydon knew him for a man of Suarra's own race, whatever that might be. There was the same ivory whiteness of skin, the same more than classic regularity of feature. The face, like hers, was beautiful, but on it was stamped an inhuman pride and a relentless, indifferent

cruelty—equally as inhuman. He wore a close fitting suit of green that
clung to him like a glove. His hair was a shining golden that gleamed
in the sun with almost the brilliancy of the hunting dinosaurs' scales.
He sat upon a light saddle fastened to the neck of his incredible steed
just where the shoulders met it. There were heavy reins that ran to
the mouth of the snake-slender, snake-long head of the jetty dinosaur.

Graydon's glasses dropped from a nerveless hand. What manner of
people were these who hunted with dinosaurs for dogs and dinosaur
for steed!

His eyes fell to the base of the monolith where had crouched the
scarlet thing. It was no longer there. He caught a gleam of crimson in
the high grass not a thousand feet from him where he watched. Cautiously the thing was creeping on and on toward the rim. He wondered
whether those spider legs could climb it, carry it over the outjutting
of the ledge. He shuddered. A deeper dread grew. Could the dinosaur
pack scramble or leap over that edge in pursuit? If so—

There came a shrieking clamor like a thousand fumaroles out of
which hissed the hate of hell. The pack had found the scent and were
leaping down in a glittering green and blue wave.

As they raced the scarlet thing itself leaped up out of the grasses not
a hundred yards away.

And Graydon glared at it with a numbing, sick horror at his heart.
He heard behind him an incredulous oath from Soames; heard Dancre
groan with, he knew, the same horror that held him.

The scarlet thing swayed upon two long and slender legs, its head a
full fifteen feet above the ground. High on these stilts of legs was its
body, almost round and no larger than a child's. From its shoulders
waved four arms, as long and as slender as the legs, eight feet or more
in length. They were human arms, but human arms that had been
stretched like rubber to thrice their normal length. The hands, or claws,
were gleaming white. Body, arms, and legs were covered with a glistening, scarlet silken down.

The head was a human head!

A man's head and a man's face, brown skinned, hawk nosed, the
forehead broad and intelligent, the eyes inordinately large, unwinking
and filled with soul destroying terror.

A man-spider!

A man who by some infernal art had been remodeled into the
mechanical semblance of the spinning Arachnidae, without the stamp
of his essential human origin having been wiped away in the process!

Only for a moment the man-spider stood thus revealed. The pack
was rushing down upon it like a cloud of dragons. It screamed, one
shrill, high pitched note that wailed like the voice of ultimate agony
above the hissing clamor of the pack. It hurled itself, a thunderbolt of
scarlet fear, straight toward the rim.

Beneath him, Graydon heard the sounds of frantic scrambling and
a scratching. Two hands a full foot long, pallidly shining, shot over

the rim of the ledge, gripping it with long fingers that were like blunt needles of bone, horn covered. They clutched and shot forward, behind them a length of spindling scarlet-downed arm.

It was the man-spider, drawing himself over—and the wave of dinosaurs was now almost at the spot from which it had hurled itself at the ledge!

The spell of terror upon Graydon broke.

"A gun," he gasped. "For God's sake, Soames, throw me a gun!"

Against his will, his gaze swept back to those weird, clutching hands. He thought he saw a rod dart out of the air and touch them—the long blue rod he had last seen carried by Suarra's hooded attendant in blue.

Whether he saw it, whether he did not, the needle-fingered claws opened convulsively; released their hold; slid off.

Glittering pack and ebon dinosaur steed alike were hidden from him by the overhang of the shelf-like road. But up from that hidden slope came a fiendish, triumphant screaming. An instant later and out into the range of his sight bounded the great black dinosaur, its golden haired rider shouting; behind it leaped the jewel scaled horde. They crossed the plain like a thunder cloud pursued by emerald and sapphire lightnings. They vanished into the forest.

"That danger is over," he heard Suarra say coolly. "Come. We must go on more quickly now."

She stepped out of the tree shadows and came tranquilly to him. Soames and Dancre and Sterrett, white faced and shaking, huddled close behind her. Graydon arose; managed to muster something of his old reckless air. She smiled at him, that half shy approval of him again in her eyes.

"It was just a weaver," she said gently. "We have many such. He tried to escape, or maybe Lantlu opened the door that he might try to escape, so he could hunt him. Lantlu loves to hunt with the Xinli. Or it may be that his weaving went wrong and this was his punishment. At any rate, it is fortunate that he did not gain this road, since if he had, the Xinli and Lantlu would surely have followed. And then—"

She did not end the sentence, but the shrug of her shoulders was eloquent.

"Just a weaver!" Soames broke in, hoarsely. "What do you mean? God in heaven, it had a man's head!"

"It was a man!" gasped Dancre.

"No." She paid no heed to him, speaking still to Graydon. "No, it was no man. At least no man as you are. Long, long ago, it is true, his ancestors were men like you. But not he. He was just—a weaver."

She stepped out upon the path. And Graydon, following, saw waiting there, as quietly, as silently, as tranquilly as though they had not stirred since first he and his companions had fled—the blue cowled and yellow cowled familiars of Suarra. Immobile, they waited while she led forth the white llama. And as she passed Graydon she whispered to him.

"The weaver had no soul. Yu-Atlanchi fashioned him as he was. But remember him, Graydon, when you come to our journey's end!"

She took her place at the head of the little caravan. Blue cowl and yellow paced behind her. Soames touched Graydon, woke him from the stark amaze into which those last words of hers had thrown him.

"Take your old place," said Soames. "We'll follow. Later, we want to talk to you, Graydon. Maybe you can get your guns back, if you're reasonable."

Suarra turned.

"Hurry," she urged; "the sun sinks and we must go quickly. Before tomorrow's noon you shall see your garden of jewels and the living gold streaming for you to do with it—or the gold to do with you—as you yourselves shall will it."

They set forth along the rimmed trail.

The plain was silent, deserted. From the far forests came no sound. Graydon, as he walked, strove to fit together in his mind all that swift tragedy he had just beheld and what the girl had told him. A weaver she had called the scarlet thing, and soulless and no man. Once more she had warned him of the power of that hidden, mysterious Yu-Atlanchi. What was it she had told him once before of that power? That it slew souls—or changed them!

A weaver? A man-spider who was soulless but whose ancestors ages ago had been men like himself—so she had said. Did she mean that in that place she called Yu-Atlanchi dwelt those who could reshape not only that unseen dweller in our bodies that we name the soul, but change at will the house of the soul?

A weaver? A spider-man whose arms and legs were slender and long and spiderlike—whose hands were like horn-covered needles of bone— whose body was like the round ball of a spider!

And she had said that the scarlet thing might have offended Lantlu by its weaving. Lantlu? The rider of the jetty dinosaur, of course.

A weaver! A picture flashed in his brain, clean cut as though his eyes beheld it. A picture of the scarlet thing in a great web, moving over it with his long and slender legs, clicking his needled hands, a human brain in a superspider's body, weaving, weaving—the very clothing that Suarra herself wore.

A vast ball of giant webs, each with its weaver—man headed, man faced, spider bodied!

Was that true picturing? Suddenly he was sure of it. Nor was it impossible. He knew that Roux, that great French scientist, had taken the eggs of frogs and by manipulating them had produced giant frogs and dwarfs, frogs with two heads and one body, frogs with one head and eight legs, three-headed frogs with legs like centipedes.

And other monsters still he had molded from the very stuff of life— monstrous things that were like nothing this earth had ever seen, nightmare things that he had been forced to slay—and quickly.

If Roux had done all this—and he had done it, Graydon knew—

then was it not possible for greater scientists to take men and women and by similar means breed—such creatures as the scarlet thing? A man-spider?

Nature herself had given the French scientist the hint upon which his experiments had been based. Nature herself produced from time to time such abnormalities—human monsters marked outwardly and inwardly with the stigmata of the beast, the fish—even of the insect.

In man's long ascent from the speck of primeval jelly on the shallow shores of the first seas, he had worn myriad shapes. And as he moved higher from one shape to another his cousins kept them, becoming during the ages the fish he caught today, the horses he rode, the apes he brought from the jungles to amuse him in his cages. Even the spiders that spun in his gardens, the scorpion that scuttled from the tread of his feet, were abysmally distant blood brothers of his, sprung from the ancient Trilobite that in its turn had sprung from forms through which at last man himself had come.

Yes, had not all life on earth a common origin? Divergent now and myriad formed—man and beast, fish and serpent, lizard and bird, ant and bee and spider—all had once been in those little specks of jelly adrift in the shallow littorals of seas on an earth still warm and pulsating with the first throbs of life. *Protalbion,* he remembered Gregory of Edinburgh had named it—the first stuff of life from which all life was to emerge.

Could the germs of all those shapes that he had worn in his progress to humanity be dormant in man? Waiting for some master hand of science to awaken them, and having awakened, blend them with the shape of man?

Yes! Nature had produced such monstrosities, and unless these shapes had lain dormant and been capable of awakening, even Nature could not have accomplished it. For even Nature cannot build something out of nothing. Roux had studied that work of hers, dipped down into the crucible of birth and molded there his monsters from these dormant forms, even as had Nature.

Might it not be then that in Yu-Atlanchi dwelt those who knew so well the secrets of evolution that in the laboratories of birth they could create men and women things of any shape desired?

A loom is but a dead machine on which fingers work more or less clumsily. The spider is both machine and living artisan, spinning, weaving, more surely, more exquisitely than could any dead mechanism worked by man. Who had approached the delicacy, the beauty, of the spider's web?

Suddenly Graydon seemed to look into a whole new world of appalling grotesquerie; soulless spider-men and spider-women spread out over great webs and weaving with needled fingers wondrous fabrics. Gigantic soulless ant-men and ant-women digging, burrowing, mazes of subterranean passages, conduits, *cloaca* for those who had wrought them into

being. Strange soulless amphibian folk busy about that lake that in his
vision had circled up to him before he saw the djinn city.

Phantasmagoria of humanity twinned with Nature's perfect machines
while still plastic in the egg!

Came to him remembrance of Suarra's warning of what might await
him at journey's end. Had she meant to prepare him for change
like this?

Shuddering, he thrust away that nightmare vision!

CHAPTER VI

THE ELFIN HORNS

THE SUN was halfway down the west when they reached the far
end of the plain. Here another ravine cut through the rocky wall,
and into it they filed. The trees closed in behind them, shutting out
all sight of the bowl and the great circular mountain.

The new trail ran always upward, although at an almost imperceptible
grade. Once, looking backward through a rift in the trees, Graydon
caught a glimpse of the grassy slopes far beneath. For the rest the tree
screened, tree bordered way gave no hint of what lay behind.

It was close to dusk when they passed out of the trees once more
and stood at the edge of a little moor. A barren it was indeed, more
than a moor. Its floor was clean white sand and dotted with hillocks,
mounds flat topped as though swept by constant brooms of wind. Upon
the rounded slopes of these mounds a tall grass grew sparsely. The
mounds arose about a hundred feet apart with curious regularity; almost,
the fancy came to him, as though they were graves in a cemetery of
giants. The little barren covered, he estimated roughly, about five acres.
Around its sides the forest clustered. Near by he heard the gurgling of
a brook.

Straight across the sands Suarra led them until she had reached a
mound close to the center of the barren. Here she halted.

"You will camp here," she said. "Water is close by for you and your
animals. You may light a fire. And sleep without fear. By dawn we
must be away."

She turned and walked toward another knoll a hundred feet or more
away. The white llama followed her. Behind it stalked the silent pair.
Graydon had expected Soames to halt her, but he did not. Instead his
eyes flashed some crafty message to Dancre and Sterrett. It seemed to
Graydon that they were pleased that the girl was not to share their
camp; that they welcomed the distance she had put between them.

And their manner to him had changed. They were comradely once
more.

"Mind taking the burros over to water?" asked Soames. "We'll get
the fire going and chow ready."

He nodded and led the little beasts over to the noisy stream. Taking them back after they had drunk their fill he looked over at the mound to which Suarra had gone. There at its base stood a small square tent, glimmering in the twilight like silk and fastened to the ground at each corner by a golden peg. Tethered close to it was the white llama, placidly munching grass and grain. Its hampers of woven golden withes were gone. Nor were Suarra or the hooded men visible. They were in the little tent, he supposed, when they had carried the precious cargo off the llama.

At his own hillock a fire was crackling and supper being prepared. Sterrett jerked a thumb over toward the little tent.

"Got it out of the saddlebags," he said. "Looked like a folded up umbrella and went up like one. Who'd ever think to find anything like that in this wilderness!"

"Lots of things I t'ink in those saddlebags we have not yet seen maybe," whispered Dancre, an eager, covetous light in his eyes.

"You bet," said Soames. "And the loot we have seen's enough to set us all up for life, eh, Graydon?"

"She has promised you much more," answered Graydon. There was an undercurrent of sinister meaning in the New Englander's voice that troubled him.

"Yeah," said Soames, absently. "Yeah. I guess so. But—well, let's eat."

The four sat around the burning sticks as they had done many nights before his quarrel with Sterrett. And to Graydon's perplexity they ignored that weird tragedy of the plain. They pushed it aside, passed it by, seemed to avoid it. Their talk was all of treasure, and of what they would do with it when out of these mountains and back in their own world. Piece by piece they went over the golden hoard in the white llama's pack; gloatingly they discussed Suarra's emeralds and their worth.

"Hell! With just those emeralds none of us'd have to worry!" exclaimed Sterrett.

Graydon listened to them with increasing disquiet. They were mad with the gold lust—but there was something more behind their studied avoidance of the dragging down of the scarlet thing by the dinosaurs, this constant reference to the llama's treasure, the harking back to what ease and comfort and luxury it would bring them all. Something lurking unsaid in the minds of the three of them of which all this was but the preliminary.

At last Soames looked at his watch.

"Nearly eight," he said, abruptly. "Dawn breaks about five. Time to talk turkey. Graydon, come up close."

Graydon obeyed, wondering. The four drew into a cluster in the shelter of the knoll. From where they crouched Suarra's tent was hidden—as they were hidden to any watchers in that little silken pavilion looking now like a great golden moth at rest under the moonlight.

"Graydon," began the New Englander, "we've made up our minds on this thing. We're goin' to do it a little different. We're willin' and glad to let by-gones be by-gones. Hell! Here we are, four white men in a bunch of God knows what. White men ought to stick together. Ain't that so?"

Graydon nodded, waiting.

"All right," went on Soames. "Now here's the situation. I don't deny we're up against somethin' I don't know much about. We ain't equipped to go up against anything like that pack of hissin' devils we saw today. But—we can come back!"

Again Graydon nodded. They had decided then to go no farther. The lesson of the afternoon had not been lost. Soames would ask Suarra to lead them out of the haunted Cordillera. As for coming back—that was another matter. He would return. But he would come back alone—seek Suarra. Since well he knew no mysterious peril either to life or soul could keep him from her. But first he must see these men safe, wipe off the debt that he believed as one man of his race to another he owed them. He was glad, but the gladness was tempered with sudden doubt. Could the game be finished thus? Would Suarra and that pair of strange old men let them go?

Soames's next words brought him back to reality.

"There's enough stuff on that llama and the girl to set us all up right, yeah. But there's also enough to finance the greatest little expedition that ever struck the trail for treasure," he was saying. "And that's what we plan doin', Graydon. Get those hampers and all that's in 'em. Get the stuff on the girl. Beat it. An' come back. I'll bet those hissin' devils wouldn't stand up long under a couple of machine guns and some gas bombs! And when the smoke's cleared away we can lift all we want and go back and sit on top of the world. What you say to that?"

Graydon fenced.

"How will you get it?" he asked. "How will you get away with it?"

"Easy." Soames bent his head closer. "We got it all planned. There ain't any watch bein' kept in that tent, you can bet on that. They're too sure of us. All right, if you're with us, we'll just slip quietly down there. Sterrett and Danc' they'll take care of the old devils. No shootin'. Just slip their knives into their ribs. Me and you'll attend to the girl. We won't hurt her. Just tie her up and gag her. Then we'll stow the stuff on a couple of the burros, get rid of the rest and that damned white beast and beat it quick."

"Beat it where?" asked Graydon, striving to cover the hot anger that welled up in him. He slipped a little closer to Dancre, hand alert to seize the automatic in his pocket.

"We'll get out," replied Soames, confidently. "I've been figurin' out where we are and I saw a peak to the west there both Sterrett and me recognized. Looked like pretty open forest country between us, too. Once we're there I know where we are. And travelin' light and all night we can be well on our way to it by this time tomorrow."

Graydon thrust out a cautious hand, touched Dancre's pocket. The automatic was still there. He would try one last appeal—to fear.

"But, Soames," he urged. "There would be pursuit. What would we do with those brutes you saw today on our track? Why, man, they'd be after us in no time. You can't get away with anything like that." Instantly he realized the weakness of that argument.

"Not a bit of it," Soames grinned evilly. "That's just the point. Nobody's worryin' about that girl. Nobody knows where she is. She was damned anxious not to be seen this afternoon. No, Graydon, I figure she slipped away from her folks to help you out. I take my hat off to you—you got her sure hooked. Nobody knows where she is, and she don't want anybody to know where she is.

"The only ones that might raise trouble is the two old devils. And a quick knife in their ribs'll put them out of the runnin' soon enough. Then there's only the girl. She'll be damned glad to show us the way out if chance we do get lost again. But me and Sterrett know that peak. We'll carry her along and when we get where we know we are we'll turn her loose to go home. None the worse off, eh, boys?"

Sterrett and Dancre nodded.

Graydon seemed to consider, fighting still for time. He knew exactly what was in Soames's mind—to use him in the cold blooded murder the three had planned and, once beyond the reach of pursuit, to murder him, too. Nor would they ever allow Suarra to return to tell what they had done. She too, would be slain—after they had done as they willed with her.

"Come on, Graydon," whispered Soames impatiently. "It's a good scheme and we can work it. Are you with us? If you ain't—well—"

His knife glittered in his hand. Simultaneously Sterrett and Dancre pressed close to him, knife, too, in readiness, awaiting his answer.

Their movement had given him the one advantage he needed. He swept his hand down into the Frenchman's pocket, drew out the gun and as he did so, landed a sidewise kick that caught Sterrett squarely in the groin. The giant reeled back.

But before Graydon could cover Soames, Dancre's arms were around his knees, his feet torn from beneath him.

"Suar—" Graydon cried before he was down. At least his shout might waken and warn her. The cry was choked in mid-utterance. Soames's bony hand was at his throat. Down they crashed together.

Graydon reached up, tried to break the strangling clutch. It gave a little, enough to let him gasp in one breath. Instantly he dropped his hold on the New Englander's wrists, hooked the fingers of one hand in the corner of his mouth, pulling with all his strength. There was a sputtering curse from Soames and his hands let go. Graydon tried to spring to his feet, but one arm of the gaunt man slipped over the back of his head held his neck in the vise of bent elbow against his shoulder.

"Knife him, Danc'," growled Soames.

Graydon suddenly twisted, bringing the New Englander on top of

him. He was only in time, for as he did so he saw Dancre strike, the
blade barely missing Soames. The latter locked his legs around his,
tried to jerk him over in range of the little Frenchman. Graydon sank
his teeth in the shoulder so close to him. Soames roared with pain
and wrath; threshed and rolled, trying to shake off the agonizing grip.
Around them danced Dancre, awaiting a chance to thrust.

There came a bellow from Sterrett:

"The llama! It's running away! The llama!"

Involuntarily, Graydon loosed his jaws. Soames sprang to his feet.
Graydon followed on the instant, shoulder up to meet the blow he
expected from Dancre.

"Look, Soames, look!" The little Frenchman was pointing. "They
have put the hampers back and turned him loose. There he goes—wit'
the gold—wit' the jewels!"

Graydon followed the pointing finger. The moon had gathered strength
and under its flood the white sands had turned into a silver lake in
which the tufted hillocks stood up like tiny islands. Golden hampers
on its sides, the llama was flitting across that lake of silver a hundred
paces away and headed, apparently, for the trail along which they had
come.

"Stop it!" shouted Soames, all else forgotten. "After it, Sterrett! That
way, Danc'! I'll head it off!"

They raced out over the shining barren. The llama changed its pace;
trotted leisurely to one of the mounds and bounded up to its top.

"Close in! We've got it now," he heard Soames cry. The three ran
to the hillock on which the white beast stood looking calmly around.
They swarmed up the mound from three sides. Soames and Sterrett
he could see; Dancre was hidden by the slope.

As their feet touched the sparse grass a mellow sound rang out, one
of those elfin horns Graydon had heard chorusing so joyously about
Suarra that first day. It was answered by others, close, all about. Again
the single note. And then the answering chorus swirled toward the
hillock of the llama, hovered over it and darted like a shower of winged
sounds upon it.

He saw Sterrett stagger as though under some swift shock; whirl
knotted arms around him as though to ward off attack!

A moment the giant stood thus, flailing with his arms. Then he cast
himself to the ground and rolled down to the sands. Instantly the notes
of the elfin horns seemed to swarm away from him, to concentrate
around Soames. He had staggered, too, under the unseen attack. But
he had thrown himself face downward on the slope of the mound and
was doggedly crawling to its top. He held one arm shielding his face.

But shielding against what?

All that Graydon could see was the hillock top, and on it the llama
bathed in the moonlight, the giant prone at the foot of the mound and
Soames now nearly at its crest. And the horn sounds were ringing,
scores upon scores of them, like the horns of a fairy hunt. But what

it was that made those sounds he could not see. They were not visible; they cast no shadow.

Yet once he thought he heard a whirring as of hundreds of feathery wings.

Soames had reached the edge of the mound's flat summit. The llama bent its head, contemplating him. Then as he scrambled over that edge, thrust out a hand to grasp its bridle, it flicked about, sprang to the opposite side and leaped down to the sands.

And all that time the clamor of the elfin horns about Soames had never stilled. Graydon saw him wince, strike out, bend his head and guard his eyes as though from a shower of blows. Still he could see nothing. Whatever that attack of the invisible, it did not daunt the New Englander. He sprang across the mound and slid down its side close behind the llama. As he touched the ground Sterrett arose slowly to his feet. The giant stood swaying, half drunkenly, dazed.

The horn notes ceased, abruptly, as though they had been candlelights blown out by a sudden blast.

Dancre came running around the slope of the hillock. The three stood for a second or two, arguing, gesticulating. And Graydon saw that their shirts were ragged and torn and, as Soames shifted and the moonlight fell upon him, that his face was streaked with blood.

The llama was walking leisurely across the sands, as slowly as though it were tempting them to further pursuit. Strange, too, he thought, how its shape seemed now to stand forth sharply and now to fade almost to a ghostly tenuity. And when it reappeared it was as though the moonbeams thickened, whirled and wove swiftly and spun it from themselves. The llama faded, and then grew again on the silvery warp and woof of the rays like a pattern on an enchanted loom.

Sterrett's hand swept down to his belt. Before he could cover the white beast with the automatic, Soames caught his wrist. The New Englander spoke fiercely, wrathfully. Graydon knew that he was warning the giant of the danger of the pistol crack; urging silence.

Then the three scattered, Dancre and Sterrett to the left and right to flank the llama, Soames approaching it with what speed he might without startling it into a run. As he neared it, the animal broke into a gentle lope, heading for another hillock. And, as before, it bounded up through the sparse grass to the top. The three pursued, but as their feet touched the base of the mound once more the mellow horn sounded—menacingly, mockingly. They hesitated. And then Sterrett, breaking from Soames's control, lifted his pistol and fired. The silver llama fell.

"The fool! The damned fool!" groaned Graydon.

The stunned silence that had followed on the heels of the pistol shot was broken by a hurricane of the elfin horns. They swept down upon the three like a tempest. Dancre shrieked and ran toward the camp fire, beating the air wildly as he came. Halfway he fell, writhed and lay still. And Soames and the giant—they, too, were buffeting the air with great blows, ducking, dodging. The elfin horns were now a ringing, raging tumult—and death was in their notes!

Sterrett dropped to his knees, arose and lurched away. He fell again close to Dancre's body, covered his head with a last despairing gesture and lay—as still as the little Frenchman. And now Soames went down, fighting desperately to the last.

There on the sands lay the three of them, motionless, struck down by the invisible!

Graydon shook himself into action; leaped forward. He felt a touch upon his shoulder; a tingling numbness ran through every muscle. With difficulty he turned his head. Beside him was the old man in the blue robe, and it had been the touch of his staff that had sent the paralysis through Graydon. The picture of the clutching talons of the spider-man upon the edge of the rimmed road flashed before him. That same rod had then, as he had thought, sent the weird weaver to its death.

Simultaneously, as though at some command, the clamor of the elfin horns lifted from the sands, swirled upward and hung high in air—whimpering, whining, protesting.

He felt a soft hand close around his wrist. Suarra's hand. Again he forced his reluctant head to turn. She was at his right, and pointing.

On the top of the hillock the white llama was struggling to its feet. A band of crimson ran across its silvery flank, the mark of Sterrett's bullet. The animal swayed for a moment, then limped down the hill.

As it passed Soames it nosed him. The New Englander's head lifted. He tried to rise; fell back. Then with eyes fastened upon the golden panniers he squirmed up on hands and knees and began to crawl on the white llama's tracks.

The beast went slowly, stiffly. It came to Sterrett's body and paused again. And Sterrett's massive head lifted, and he tried to rise, and, failing even as had Soames, began, like him, to crawl behind the animal.

The white llama passed Dancre. He stirred and moved and followed it on knees and hands.

Over the moon-soaked sands, back to the camp they trailed—the limping llama, with the blood dripping drop by drop from its wounded side. Behind it three crawling men, their haggard, burning eyes riveted upon the golden withed panniers, three men who crawled, gasping like fish drawn up to shore.

Three broken men, from whose grim drawn faces glared that soul of greed which was all that gave them strength to drag their bodies over the shining sands.

Chapter VII

"COME BACK—GRAYDON!"

NOW LLAMA and crawling men had reached the camp. The elfin horn notes were still. Graydon's muscles suddenly relaxed; power of movement returned to him.

With a little cry of pity Suarra ran to the white llama's side; caressed it, strove to stanch its blood.

Graydon bent down over the three men. They had collapsed as they had come within the circle of the camp fire. They lay now, huddled, breathing heavily, eyes fast closed. Their clothes had been ripped to ribbons.

And over all their faces, their breasts, their bodies, were scores of small punctures, not deep, their edges clean cut, as though they had been pecked out. Some were still bleeding; in others the blood had dried.

He ran to the rushing brook. Suarra was beside her tent, the llama's head in her arms. He stopped, unbuckled the panniers; let them slip away; probed the animal's wound. The bullet had plowed through the upper left flank without touching the bone, and had come out. He went back to his own camp, drew forth from his bags some medical supplies, returned and bathed and dressed the wound as best he could. He did it all silently, and Suarra was silent, too.

Her eyes were eloquent enough.

This finished, he went again to the other camp. The three men were lying as he left them. They seemed to be in a stupor. He washed their faces of the blood, bathed their strained bodies. He spread blankets and dragged the three up on them. They did not awaken. He wondered at their sleep—or was it coma?

The strange punctures were bad enough, of course, yet it did not seem to him that these could account for the conditions of the men. Certainly they had not lost enough blood to cause unconsciousness. Nor had any arteries been opened, nor was one of the wounds deep enough to have disturbed any vital organ.

He gave up conjecturing, wearily. After all, what was it but one more of the mysteries among which he had been moving? And he had done all he could for the three of them.

Graydon walked away from the fire, threw himself down on the edge of the white sands. There was a foreboding upon him, a sense of doom.

And as he sat there, fighting against the blackness gathering around his spirit, he heard light footsteps and Suarra sank beside him. Her cloudy hair caressed his own. His hand dropped upon hers, covering it. And after a shy moment her fingers moved, then interlaced with his.

"It is the last night—Graydon," she whispered, tremulously. "The last night! And so—they—have let me talk with you a while."

"No!" He caught her to him—fiercely. "There is nothing that can keep me from you now, Suarra, except—death."

"Yes," she said, and thrust him gently away. "Yes—it is the last night. There was a promise—Graydon. A promise that I made. I said that I would save you if I could. I asked the Two Lords. They were amused. They told me that if you could conquer the Face you would be allowed to go. I told them that you would conquer it. And I promised them that after that you would go. And they were more amused, asking me what manner of man you were who had made me believe you could conquer the Face."

"The Face?" questioned Graydon.

"The great Face," she said. "The Face in the Abyss. But of that I may say no more. You must—meet it."

"And these men, too?" he asked. "The men who lie there?"

"They are as already dead," she answered, indifferently. "Dead—and worse. They are already eaten!"

"Eaten!" he cried incredulously.

"Eaten," she repeated. "Eaten—body and soul!"

For a moment she was silent.

"I do not think," she began again. "I did not really think—that even you could conquer the Face. So I went to the Snake Mother, and she, too, laughed. But at the end, as woman to woman—since, after all, she *is* woman she promised me to aid you. And then I knew you would be saved, since the Snake Mother far excels the Two Lords in craft and guile. And she promised me, as woman to woman. The Two Lords know nothing of that," she added naively.

Of this, Graydon, remembering the youthful eyes in the old, old face that had weighed him in the temple of the shifting rays, had his doubts.

"So," she said, "was the bargain made. And so its terms must be fulfilled. You shall escape the Face, Graydon. But you must go."

To that he answered nothing. And after another silence she spoke again, wistfully:

"Is there any maid who loves you—or whom you love—in your own land, Graydon?"

"There is none, Suarra," he answered.

"I believe you," she said simply. "And I would go away with you, if I might. But—they—would not allow it. And if I tried, they would slay you. Yes, even if we should escape—they—would slay you and bring me back. So it cannot be."

He thrilled to that, innocently self-revelant as it was.

"I am weary of Yu-Atlanchi," she went on somberly. "Yes, I am weary of its ancient wisdom and of its treasures and its people who are eternal—eternal at least as the world. I am one of them—and yet I long to go out into the new world—the world where there are babes, and many of them, and the laughter of children, and where life streams passionately, strong and shouting and swiftly, even though it is through the opened doors of Death that it flows. In Yu-Atlanchi those doors are closed, except to those who choose to open them. And life is a still stream, without movement. And there are few babes—and of the laughter of children—little."

"What are your people, Suarra?" he asked.

"The ancient people," she told him. "The most ancient. Ages upon ages ago they came down from the north where they had dwelt for other ages still. They were driven away by the great cold. One day the earth rocked and swung. It was then the great cold came down and the darkness and icy tempests and even the warm seas began to freeze. Their cities, so the legends run, are hidden now under mountains of ice. They journeyed south in their ships, bearing with them the Serpent people who had taught them most of their wisdom—and the Snake Mother is the last daughter of that people. They came to rest here. At that time the sea was close and the mountains had not yet been born. They found here hordes of the Xinli. They were larger, far larger than now. My people subdued them and tamed and bred them to their uses. And here for another age they practiced their arts and their wisdom, and learned more.

"Then there were great earth shakings and the mountains began to lift. Although all their wisdom was not great enough to keep the mountains from being born, it could control their growth around that ancient city and its plain that were Yu-Atlanchi. Slowly, steadily through another age the mountains arose. Until at last they girdled Yu-Atlanchi like a vast wall—a wall that could never be scaled. Nor did my people care; indeed, it gladdened them, since by then they had closed the doors of death and cared no more to go into the outer world. And so they have dwelt—for other ages more."

Again she was silent, musing. Graydon struggled against his incredulity. A people who had conquered death? A people so old that their birthplace was buried deep beneath eternal ice? And yet, as to the last, at least—why not? Did not science teach that the frozen poles had once basked beneath a tropical sun? Expeditions had found at both of them the fossil forms of gigantic palms, strange animals, a flora and a fauna that could only have lived under tropical conditions.

And did not science believe that long, long ago the earth had tipped and that thus the frozen poles had come to be?

An inexplicable irritation filled him, instinctive revolt of the young against the very old.

"If your people are so wise," he questioned, "why do they not come forth and rule this world?"

"But why should they?" she asked in turn. "They have nothing more to learn. If they came forth what could they do but build the rest of the earth into likeness of that part in which they dwell? What use in that, Graydon? None. So they let the years stream by while they dream—the most of them. For they have conquered dream. Through dream they create their own worlds; do therein as they will; live life upon life as they will it. In their dreams they shape world upon world upon world, and each of their worlds is a real world to them. And so they let the years stream by while they live in dream! Why should they go out into this one world when they can create myriads of their own at will?"

Again she was silent.

"But they are barren, the dream makers," she whispered. "Barren! That is why there are few babes and little laughter of children in Yu-Atlanchi. Why should they mate with their kind, these women and men who have lived so long that they have grown weary of all their kind can give them? Why should they mate with their kind when they can create new lovers in dream, new loves and hates! Yea, new emotions, and forms utterly unknown to earth, each as he or she may will. And so they are—barren. Not alone the doors of death, but the doors of life are closed to them, the dream makers!"

"But you—" he began.

"I?" She turned a wistful face to him. "Did I not say that when they closed the doors of death the doors of life closed, too? For these are not really two, but only the two sides of the one door. Some there are always who elect to keep that door open, to live the life that is their own, to have no dealing with—dreams. My father and mother were of these. They took the hazard of death that they might love.

"Ancient arts, ancient wisdom," she went on. "Wisdom that perhaps you have rediscovered and call new. Wisdom you yet may gain. Wisdom that may never be yours—and thank whatever gods you worship that you have not."

"Such wisdom as shaped the weaver?" he asked.

"That! He was child's play," she answered. "A useful toy. There are far, far stranger things than the weaver in Yu-Atlanchi, Graydon."

"Suarra," he asked abruptly. "Why do you want to save me?"

A moment she hesitated; then:

"Because you make me feel as I have never felt before!" she whispered slowly. "Because you make me happy; because you make me sorrowful. When I think of you it is like warm wine in my veins. I want both to sing—and to weep. I want your touch—to be close to you. When you go, the world will be darkened. Life will be drab."

"Suarra!" he cried, and drew her, unresisting now, to him. His lips sought hers and her lips clung to his. A flame leaped through him. She quivered in his arms; was still.

"I will come back," he whispered. "I will come back, Suarra!"

"Come!" she sobbed. "Come back, Graydon!"

She thrust him from her, leaped to her feet.

"No! No!" she cried. "No, Graydon. I am wicked! No—it would be death for you!"

"As God lives, Suarra," he said, "I will come back to you!"

She trembled; leaned forward, pressed her lips to his, slipped through his arms and ran to the silken pavilion. For an instant she paused there, stretched wistful arms to him; entered and was hidden within its folds.

"There seemed to come to him, faintly, heard only by heart—

"Come back! Come back to me!"

He threw himself down where their hands had clasped, where their lips had met. Hour after hour he lay there, thinking, thinking. His head dropped forward at last.

He carried her into his dreams.

Chapter VIII

THE FACE IN THE ABYSS

THE WHITE sands of the barren were wan in the first gleaming of the dawn when Graydon awakened. He arose with the thought of Suarra warm around his heart. Chilling that warmth, swift upon him like a pall fell that bleak consciousness of doom against which he had struggled before he slept; and bleaker, heavier now; not to be denied.

A wind was sweeping down from the heights. Beneath it he shivered. He walked to the hidden brook; doffed clothing; dipped beneath its icy flow. Strength poured back into him at the touch of the chill current.

Returning, he saw Suarra, less than half clad, slip out of the silken tent. Clearly, she too, was bound for the brook. He waved a hand. She smiled; then long silken lashes covered the midnight eyes; rose-pearl grew her face, her throat, her breasts. She slipped back behind the silken folds.

He turned his head from her; passed on to the camp.

He looked down upon the three—gaunt Soames, little Dancre, giant Sterrett. He stopped and plucked from Soame's belt an automatic—his own. He satisfied himself that it was properly loaded, and thrust it into his pocket. Under Soames's left arm pit was another. He took it out and put it in the holster from which he had withdrawn his. He slipped into Sterrett's a new magazine of cartridges. Dancre's gun was ready for use.

"They'll have their chance, anyway," he said to himself.

He stood over them for a moment; scanned them. The scores of tiny punctures had closed. Their breathing was normal. They seemed to be asleep. And yet they looked like dead men. Like dead men, livid and wan and bloodless as the pallid sands beneath the growing dawn.

Graydon shuddered; turned his back upon them.

He made coffee; threw together a breakfast; went back to rouse the three. He found Soames sitting up, looking around him, dazedly.

"Come get something to eat, Soames," he said, and gently, for there was a helplessness about the gaunt man that roused his pity—black hearted even as the New Englander had shown himself. Soames looked at him, blankly; then stumbled up and stood staring, as though waiting for further command. Graydon leaned down and shook Sterrett by the shoulder. The giant mumbled, opened dull eyes; lurched to his feet. Dancre awakened, whimpering.

As they stood before him—gaunt man, little man, giant—a wonder, a fearful wonder, seized him. For these were not the men he had known. No! What was it that had changed these men so, sapped the life from them until they seemed, even as Suarra had said, already dead?

A verse from the Rime of the Ancient Mariner rang in his ears—

> *"They groaned, they stirred, they all uprose,*
> *Nor spake, nor moved their eyes;*
> *It had been strange, even in a dream,*
> *To have seen those dead men rise."*

Shuddering again, he led the way to the fire. They followed him, stiffly, mechanically, like automatons. And like automatons they took the steaming coffee from him and drank it; the food and swallowed it. Their eyes blank, devoid of all expression, followed his every movement.

Graydon studied them, the fear-filled wonder growing. They seemed to hear nothing, see nothing—save for their recognition of himself— to be cut off from all the world. Suddenly he became conscious of others near him; turned his head and saw close behind him Suarra and the hooded pair. The eyes of Soames, of Sterrett and of Dancre turned with his own. And now he knew that not even memory had been left them! Blankly, with no recognition—unseeing—they stared at Suarra.

"It is time to start, Graydon," she said softly, her own eyes averted from their dead gaze. "We leave the llama here. It cannot walk. Take with you only your own animal, your weapons and what belongs to you. The other animals will stay here."

He chilled, for under her words he read both sentence of death and of banishment. Death of all of them perhaps—banishment for him even if he escaped death. In his face she read his heart, accurately; tried to soften his sorrow.

"They may escape," she continued hastily. "And if they do, the animals will be here awaiting them. And it is well for you to have your own with you, in case—in case—"

She faltered. He shook his head.

"No use, Suarra," he smiled. "I understand."

"Oh, trust me, trust me," she half sobbed. "Do as I say, Graydon."

He said no more. He unhobbled his burro; fixed the saddlebags; took his own rifle and strapped it to them. He picked up the rifles of the others and put them in their hands. They took them, as mechanically as they had the coffee and the food.

Now blue cowl and yellow swung into the lead, Suarra at their heels.

"Come on, Soames," he said. "Come, Sterrett. It's time to start, Dancre."

Obediently they swung upon the trail, marching side by side—gaunt man at left, giant in the center, little man at right. Like marionettes they marched, obediently, unquestioning, without word. If they knew the llama and its treasures were no longer with them, they gave no sign. If they knew Graydon again carried his guns, they give no sign, either.

Another line of the "Rime" echoed in his memory—

"They raised their limbs like lifeless tools—"

Graydon swung in behind them, the patient burro trotting at his side.

They crossed the white sands, entering a broad way stretching through close growing, enormous trees, as though it had once been a road of stone upon whose long deserted surface the leaves had rotted for centuries; upon which turf had formed, but in which no trees had been able to get root hold. And as they went on, he had evidence that it had been actually such a road, for where there had been washouts the faces of gigantic cut and squared granite blocks were exposed.

For an hour they passed along this ancient buried trail. They emerged from it, abruptly, out upon a broad platform of bare rock. Before them were the walls of a split mountain. Its precipices towered thousands of feet. Between them, like a titanic sword cut, was a rift, a prodigious cleavage which widened as it reached upward as though each side had shrunk away from the splitting blade as it had struck downward. The platform was the threshold of this rift. Fifty feet wide from edge to edge it ran. At each edge stood a small, conical-shaped building— temple or guard house—whose crumbling stones were covered with a gray lichen so ancient looking that it might have been withered old Time's own flower.

The cowled figures neither turned nor stopped. They crossed the threshold between the ruined cones; behind them Suarra; and after her, never hesitating, the stiffly marching three. Then over it went Graydon and the burro.

The way led downward at an angle barely saved from difficult steepness. No trees, no vegetation of any kind, could he see—unless the ancient, gray and dry lichen that covered the road and whispered under their feet could be called vegetation. But it gave resistance, that lichen; made the descent easier. It covered the straight rock walls that arose on each side.

The gorge was dark, as he had expected. The light that fell through its rim thousands of feet overhead was faint. But the gray lichens seemed to take it up and diffuse it. It was not darker than an early northern twilight. Every object was plainly visibly.

Down they went and ever down; for half an hour; an hour. Always

straight ahead the road stretched, never varying in its width and growing
no darker, even the gray lichens lightened it. He estimated its drop
was about fifteen feet in the hundred. He looked back and upward
along its narrowing vista. They must be, he thought, half a mile or
more below the level of the rift threshold.

The road angled. A breast of rock jutted abruptly out of the cliff,
stretching from side to side like a barrier. The new road was narrowed,
barely wide enough for the three marionettes in front to walk on side
by side. As they wheeled into it Graydon again felt a pang of pity.
They were like doomed men marching to execution; hopeless; helpless
and—drugged. Nay, they were men who had once been slain and drawn
inexorably on to a second death!

Never speaking, never turning, with mechanical swing of feet, rifles
held slack in limp arms, their march was a *grotesquerie* tinged with
horror.

The new road was darker than the old. He had an uneasy feeling
that the rocks were closing high over his head; that what they were
entering was a tunnel. The gray lichens rapidly dwindled on walls and
underfoot. As they dwindled, so did the light.

At last the gray lichens ceased to be. He moved through a half
darkness in which barely could he see, save as shadows, those who
went before.

And now he was sure that the rocks had closed overhead, burying
them. He fought against a choking oppression that came with the
knowledge.

And yet—it was not so dark, after all. Strange, he thought, strange
that there should be light at all in this covered way—and stranger still
was that light itself. It seemed to be in the air—to be of the air. It
came neither from walls nor roof. It seemed to filter in, creeping, along
the tunnel from some source far ahead. A light that was as though it
came from radiant atoms, infinitely small, that shed their rays as they
floated slowly by.

Thicker grew these luminous atoms whose radiance only, and not
their bodies, could be perceived by the eye. Lighter and lighter grew
the way.

Again, and as abruptly as before, it turned.

They stood within a cavern that was like a great square auditorium
to some gigantic stage; the interior of a cube of rock whose four sides,
whose roof a hundred feet overhead, and whose floor were smooth and
straight as though trued by giant spirit level and by plane.

And at his right dropped a vast curtain. A curtain of solid rock lifted
a foot above the floor and drawn aside at the far end for a quarter of
its sweep. From beneath it and from the side, streamed the radiant
atoms whose slow drift down the tunnel had filled it with its ever
increasing luminosity.

They streamed from beneath it and around the side, swiftly now, like countless swarms of fireflies, each carrying a lamp of diamond light.

"There"—Suarra pointed to the rocky curtain's edge—"there lies your way. Beyond it is that place I promised I would show you. The place where the jewels grow like fruit in a garden and the living gold flows forth. Here we will wait you. Now go."

Long Graydon looked at that curtain and at the streaming radiant atoms pouring from beyond it. Gaunt man, little man, giant man stood, beside him, soulless faces staring at him—awaiting his command, his movement.

In the hooded pair he sensed a cynical amusement—in yellow cowl, at least. For blue cowl seemed but to wait—as though—as though even now he knew what the issue must be. Were they baiting him, he wondered; playing him for their amusement? What would happen if he were to refuse to go farther; refuse to walk around the edge of that lifted curtain; summon the three and march them back to the little camp in the barren? Would they go? Would they be allowed to go?

He looked at Suarra. In her eyes of midnight velvet was sorrow, a sorrow unutterable; despair and agony—and love!

Whatever moved that pair she called the Two Lords—in her, at least, was no cynical gaming with human souls. And he remembered her promise, that he could look upon the Face and conquer it.

Well, he would not retreat now, even if they would let him. He would accept no largess at the hands of this pair who, or so it now seemed to him, looked upon her as a child who must be taught what futile thing it was that she had picked for chosen toy. He would not shame himself, nor her.

"Wait here," he spoke to the three staring ones. "Wait here—do you understand? Soames—Dance—Sterrett! Do not move! Wait here until I come back."

They only stared on at him; unanswering either with tongue or face.

He walked up to the hooded pair.

"To hell with you!" he said clearly and as coldly as he felt they themselves might speak were they to open those silent lips of theirs. "Do you understand that? I said to hell with you!"

They did not move. He caught Suarra in his arms; kissed her; suddenly reckless of them. He felt her lips cling to his.

"Remember!" he whispered. "I will come back to you!"

He strode over to the curtain's edge, swinging his automatic as he went. He strode past the edge and full into the rush of the radiance. For perhaps a dozen heart beats he stood there, motionless, turned to stone, blank incredulity stamped deep upon his face. And then the revolver dropped from nerveless hand; clattered upon floor of stone.

For Graydon looked into a vast cavern filled with the diamonded atoms, throbbing with a dazzling light that yet was crystalline clear. The cavern was like a gigantic hollow globe that had been cut in two, and one half cast away. It was from its curving walls that the luminosity streamed, and these walls were jetty black and polished like mirrors, and the rays that issued from them seemed to come from infinite depths within them, darting through them with prodigious speed— like rays shot up through inconceivable depths of black water, beneath which in some unknown firmament, blazed a sun of diamond incandescence.

And out of these curving walls, hanging to them like the grapes of precious jewels in the enchanted vineyards of the Paradise of El-Shiraz, like flowers in a garden of the King of the Djinn, grew clustered gems!

Great crystals, *cabochon* and edged, globular and angled, alive under that jubilant light with the very soul of fire that is the lure of jewel. Rubies that glowed with every rubrous tint from that clear scarlet that is sunlight streaming through the finger tips of delicate maids to deepest sullen reds of bruised hearts; sapphires that shone with blues as rare as that beneath the bluebird's wings and blues as deep as those which darken beneath the creamy crest of the Gulf Stream's crisping waves; huge emeralds that gleamed now with the peacock verdancies of tropic shallows, and now were green as the depths of a jungle glade; diamonds that glittered with irised fires or shot forth showers of rainbowed rays; great burning opals; gems burning with amethystine flames; unknown jewels whose unfamiliar beauty checked the heart with wonder.

But it was not the clustered jewels within this chamber of radiance that had released the grip of his hand upon the automatic; turned him into stone.

It was—the Face!

From where he stood a flight of Cyclopean steps ran down a hundred feet or more into the heart of the cavern. At their left was the semiglobe of gemmed and glittering rock. At their right was—space!

An abyss, whose other side he could not see, but which fell sheer away from the stairway in bottomless depth upon depth.

The Face looked at him from the far side of this cavern. Its eyes were level with his. Bodiless, its chin rested upon the floor a little beyond the last monolithic step. It was carved out of the same black rock as the walls, but within it was no faintest sparkle of the darting luminescences.

It was man's face and devil's face in one; Luciferean; arrogant; ruthless. Colossal, thirty yards or more in width from ear to ear, it bent a little over the abyss, as though listening. Upon the broad brow power was throned, an evil and imperial power. Power that could have been godlike in beneficence had it so willed, but which had chosen instead the lot of Satan. The nose was harpy curved, vulture bridged and cruel. Merciless was the huge mouth, the lips full and lecherous; the corners cynically drooping.

Upon all its carved features was stamped the very secret soul of humanity's insatiable, eternal hunger for gold. Greed and avarice were graven there, and spendthrift recklessness and callous waste. It was the golden lust given voice of stone. It promised, it lured, it threatened, it cajoled—summoned!

He looked into the eyes of the Face, a hundred feet above the chin. They were made of pale blue crystals, cold as the glint of the Polar ice. Within them was centered all the Face's demoniac strength.

And as Graydon glared into their chill depths swift visions passed from them to his own. Ravishing of cities and looting of ships; men drunk with greed wresting great golden nuggets from the breast of earth; men crouching like spiders in the hearts of shining yellow webs and gloating over hordes of golden flies.

He heard the shouts of loot-crazed legions sacking golden capitols; the shouting of all Argonauts since first gold and men were born. And he thrilled to their clamor; answered it with shoutings of his own!

Poured into him from the cold eyes other visions—visions of what gold, gold without end, could do for him. Flaming lures of power over men and nations, power limitless and ruthless as that which sat upon the Face's own brow—fair women—earthly Paradises—Fata Morganas of the senses.

There was a fire in his blood, a Satanic ecstasy, a flaming recklessness. Why, the Face was not of stone! The eyes were not cold jewels!

The Face was living!

And it was promising him this world and dominion over all this world, if he would but come to it!

He took a step down the stairway. There came to him Suarra's heartbroken cry!

It checked him.

He looked again at the colossal Face.

And now he saw that all the darting ominous atoms from the curving walls were concentrated upon it. It threw them back, into the chamber and under and past the curtain of rock, and out into the abyss. And that there was a great circlet of gold around the Face's brow—a wide, deep crown almost like a cap. From that crown, like drops of yellow blood, great globes of gold fell slowly! They crept sluggishly down the cheeks.

From the eyes ran slowly other huge golden drops, like tears.

And out of each downturned corner of the mouth the gold dripped like slaver!

The drops of golden sweat, the golden tears, the golden slaver rolled and joined a rivulet of gold that crept out from behind the Face, crawled sluggishly to the verge of the abyss and over its lip into the unfathomable depth—

"Look into my eyes! Look into my eyes!"

The command came to him—imperious, not to be disobeyed. It seemed to him that the Face had spoken it. He stared again straight into the cold blue crystals. And forgotten now was its horror. All that he knew was—its promise!

Graydon dropped to the second step, then to the third. He wanted to run on, straight to that gigantic mask of black rock that sweated, wept and slavered gold, take from it what it had offered—give it whatever it should demand in return—

He was thrust aside. Reeled and caught himself at the very edge of the stairway.

Past him rushed the three—gaunt man, giant man and little man.

He caught a glimpse of their faces. There was no blankness in them now, no vagueness. No, they were as men reborn. Their eyes were burning bright. And upon the face of each was set the stamp of the Face. Its arrogance, its avarice, its recklessness and its cruelty.

Faster, faster they ran down the steps, rushing to the gigantic Face and what it had promised them. As it had promised—him!

Rage, murderous and confusing, shook him. By Heaven, they couldn't get away with that! Earth and the dominion of earth! They were his own for the taking. The Face had promised them to him first. He would kill them.

He leaped down behind them.

Something caught his feet, pinioned them, wrapped itself around his knees, brought him to an abrupt halt. He heard a sharp hissing. Raging, cursing, he looked down. Around his ankles, around his knees, were the coils of a white serpent. It bound him tightly, like a rope. Its head was level with his heart and its eyes looked unwinkingly into his.

For a breathless moment revulsion shook him, an instinctive and panic terror. He forgot the Face—forgot the three. The white serpent's head swayed; then shot forward, its gaze fastened upon something beyond him. Graydon's gaze followed its own.

He saw—the Snake Mother!

At one and the same time real and unreal, she lay stretched out upon the radiant air, her shining lengths half coiled. She lay within the air directly between him and the Face. He saw her, and yet plainly through her he could see all that weird cavern and all it held. Her purple eyes were intent upon him.

And instantly his rage and all that fiery poison of golden lust that had poured into him were wiped away. In their place flowed contrition, shame, a vast thankfulness.

He remembered—Suarra!

Through this phantom of the Snake Mother, if phantom it was, he stared full and fearlessly into the eyes of the Face. And their spell was broken. All that Graydon saw now was its rapacity, its ruthlessness and its horror.

The white serpent loosed its coils; released him! Slipped away. The phantom of the Snake Mother vanished.

Trembling, he looked down the stairway. The three men were at its end. They were running—running toward the Face. In the crystalline luminosity they stood out like moving figures cut from black cardboard. They were flattened by it—three outlines, sharp as silhouettes cut from black paper. Lank and gaunt silhouette, giant silhouette and little one, they ran side by side. And now they were at the point of the huge chin. He watched them pause there for an instant, striking at each other, each trying to push the others away. Then as one, and as though answering some summons irresistible, they began to climb up the cliffed chin of the Face. Climbing, Graydon knew, up to the cold blue eyes and what those eyes had seemed to promise.

Now they were in the full focus of the driving rays, the storm of the luminous atoms. For an instant they stood out, still like three men cut from cardboard a little darker than the black stone.

Then they seemed to gray, their outlines to grow misty—nebulous. They ceased their climbing. They writhed as though in sudden intolerable agony.

They faded out! Where they had been there hovered for a breath something like three wisps of stained cloud.

The wisps dissolved—like mist.

In their place stood out three glistening droplets of gold!

Sluggishly the three droplets began to roll down the Face. They drew together and became one. They dripped slowly down to the crawling golden stream, were merged with it—were carried to the lip of the abyss—

And over into the gulf!

From high over the gulf came a burst of the elfin horns. And now, in that strange light, Graydon saw at last what it was that sent forth these notes. What it was that had beaten out on the moonlit barren the souls of the three; breaking them; turning them into dead men walking.

Their bodies were serpents, sinuous, writhing and coiling, silver scaled. But they were serpents—winged. They dipped and drifted and eddied on snowy long feathered wings, blanched, phosphorescent plumes fringed like the tails of ghostly Birds of Paradise.

Large and small, some the size of the great python, some no longer than the little *fer-de-lance,* they writhed and coiled and spun through the sparkling air above the abyss, trumpeting triumphantly, calling to each other with their voices like elfin horns.

Fencing joyously with each other with bills that were like thin, straight swords!

Winged serpents, Paradise plumed, whose bills were sharp rapiers. Winged serpents sending forth their paeans of faery trumpets while that crawling stream of which Soames—Dancre—Sterrett—were now a part dripped, dripped, slowly, so slowly, down into the unfathomable void.

Graydon fell upon the great step, sick in every nerve and fiber of his being. He crept up the next, and the next—rolled over the last, past the edge of the rocky curtain, out of the brilliancy of the diamonded light and the sight of the Face and that trumpet clamor of the flying serpents.

He saw Suarra, flying to him, eyes wild with gladness.

Then he seemed to sink through wave after wave of darkness into oblivion.

CHAPTER IX

"I AM GOING BACK TO HER!"

GRAYDON AWAKENED. "Suarra! Beloved!" he whispered, and stretched out eager arms.

Memory rushed back to him; he leaped to his feet, stared around him. He was in a dim forest glade. Beside him his burro nibbled placidly the grass.

"Suarra!" he cried again loudly.

A figure stirred in the shadow; came toward him. It was an Indian, but one of a type Graydon had never seen before. His features were delicate, fine. He wore a corselet and kilt of padded yellow silk. There was a circlet of gold upon his head and bracelets of the same metal on his upper arms.

The Indian held out a package wrapped in silk. He opened it. Within it was Suarra's bracelet of the dinosaurs and the *caraquenque* feather she wore when first he had seen her.

Graydon restored the feather in its covering, thrust it into his pocket over his heart. The bracelet, and why he did it he never knew, he slipped over his own wrist.

He spoke to the Indian in the Aymara. He smiled; shook his head. Nor did he seem to understand any of the half dozen other dialects that Graydon tried. He pointed to the burro and then ahead. Graydon knew that he was telling him that he must go, and that he would show him the way.

They set forth. He tried to etch every foot of the path upon his memory, planning already for return. In a little while they came to the edge of a steep hill. Here the Indian paused pointing down. Fifty feet or so below him Graydon saw a well-marked trail. There was an easy descent, zigzagging down the hillside to it. Again the Indian pointed, and he realized that he was indicating which way to take upon the lower trail.

The Indian stood aside, bowed low and waited for him to pass down with the burro. He began the downward climb. The Indian stood watching him; and as Graydon reached a turn in the trail, he waved his hand in farewell and slipped back into his forest.

Graydon plodded slowly on for perhaps a mile farther. There he waited for an hour. Then he turned resolutely back; retraced his way to the hillside and driving his burro before him, quietly reclimbed it.

In his brain and in his heart were but one thought and one desire, to return to Suarra. No matter what the peril, to go back to her.

He slipped over the edge of the hill and stood there for a moment, listening. He heard nothing. He pushed ahead of the burro; softly bade it follow; strode forward.

Instantly close above his head he heard a horn note sound, menacing, angry. There was a whirring of great wings.

Instinctively he threw up his arm. It was the one upon which he had slipped Suarra's bracelet. As he raised it, the purple stones that were the eyes of the Snake Mother carved upon it, flashed in the sun.

He heard the horn note again, protesting; curiously—startled. There was a whistling flurry in the air close beside him as of some unseen winged creature striving to check its flight.

Something struck the bracelet a glancing blow. He felt another sharp blow against his shoulder. A searing pain darted through the muscles. He felt blood gush from shoulder and neck. The buffet threw him backward. He fell and rolled over the edge of the hill and down its side.

In that fall his head struck a stone, stunning him. When he came to his senses he was lying at the foot of the slope, with the burro standing beside him. He must have lain there unconscious for considerable time, for the stained ground showed that he had lost much blood. The wound was in an awkward place for examination, but so far as he could see it was a clean puncture that had passed like a rapier thrust through the upper shoulder and out at the neck. It must have missed the artery by a hair.

And well he knew what had made that sound. One of the feathered serpents of the abyss.

The cliff or mill marked no doubt the limits of Yu-Atlanchi at that point. Had the strange Indian placed the creature there in anticipation of his return, or had it been one of those "Watchers" of whom Suarra had spoken and this frontier one of its regular points of observation? The latter, he was inclined to think, for the Indian had unquestionably been friendly.

And did not the bracelet and the *caraquenque* feather show that he had been Suarra's own messenger?

But Graydon could not go back, into the unknown perils, with such a wound. He must find help. That night the fever took him. The next day he met some friendly Indians. They ministered to him as best they could. But the fever grew worse and the wound a torment. He made up his mind to press on to Chupan, the nearest village where he might find better help than the Indians could give him.

He had stumbled on to Chupan, reached it on his last strength.

*   *   *

Such was Graydon's story. If you ask me whether I believe it, or whether I think it the vagaries of a fever-stricken wanderer, I answer— I do believe it. Yes, from the first to the last, I believe it true. For remember, I saw his wound, I saw the bracelet of the dinosaurs and

I listened to Graydon in his delirium. A man does not tell precisely the same things in the cool blood of health that he raves of in delirium, not at least if these things are but fancies born of that delirium. He cannot. He forgets.

There was one thing that I found it hard to explain by any normal process.

"You say you saw this—well, Being—you call the Snake Mother as a phantom in that cavern of the Face?" I asked. "But are you sure of that, Graydon? Are you sure that this was not hallucination, or some vision of your fever that you carried into waking?"

"No," he said, "No. I am very sure. I would not call what I saw a phantom. I only used that word to describe it. It was more—a projection of her image. You forget, don't you, that other exercise of this inexplicable power of projection that night I was drawn into Yu-Atlanchi by her eyes? Well, of the reality of that first experience there cannot be the slightest doubt. I do not find the other more unbelievable than it.

"The cavern of the Face," he went on, thoughtfully. "That I think was a laboratory of Nature, a gigantic crucible where under certain rays of light a natural transmutation of one element into another took place.

"Within the rock, out of which the Face was carved, was some mineral which under these rays was transformed into gold. A purely chemical process of which our race itself is not far from learning the secret, as you know.

"The Face! I think that it was an afterthought of some genius of Yu-Atlanchi. He had taken the rock, worked upon it and symbolized so accurately man's universal hunger for gold, that inevitably he who looked upon it responded to its call. The sub-consciousness, the consciousness, too, leaped out in response to what the Face portrayed with such tremendous power. In proportion to the strength of that hunger, so was the strength of the response. Like calls to like the world over."

"But do you think that Soames and Sterrett and little Dancre really turned into gold?" I asked him.

"Frankly, of that I have my doubts," he answered. "It looked so. But the whole scene was so—well, so damnably devilish—that I can't quite trust to my impression of that. It is possible that something else occurred. Unquestionably the concentration of the rays on the region about the Face was terrific. Beneath the bombardment of those radiant particles of force, whatever they were, the bodies of the three may simply have disintegrated. The droplets of gold may have been oozing from the rock behind them and their position in the exact place where the three disappeared may also have been only a vivid coincidence."

"That the flying serpents were visible in that light and not in normal light shows, I should think, that it must have been extraordinarily rich in the ultraviolet vibrations," I suggested.

He nodded.

"Of course that was it," he said. "Invisible in day or night light, it took the violet rays to record their outlines. They are probably a development of some form of flying saurian such as the ancient pterodactyls."

He mused for a moment.

"But they must have possessed a high degree of intelligence," he went on at last; "those serpents. Intelligence higher even than the dog—intelligence perhaps on a par with that of the elephant. The creature that struck me certainly recognized Suarra's bracelet. It was that recognition which checked it, I am sure. It tried to stop its thrust, but it was too late to do more than divert it.

"And that is why I think I am going to find her," he whispered.

"She wanted me to come back. She knew that I would. I think the bracelet is a talisman—or better still, a passport to carry me by the watchers, as she called them. It was not just as a remembrance that she gave the ornament to me. No!

"I will come back—and with her," he told me on that day we clasped hands in farewell.

I stood watching him until he and the little burro were hidden by the trees of the trail he must follow until he had reached the frontier of the haunted Cordillera, the gateway of those mysteries with which he had determined to grapple to wrest from them the maid he named Suarra.

But he has not come back.

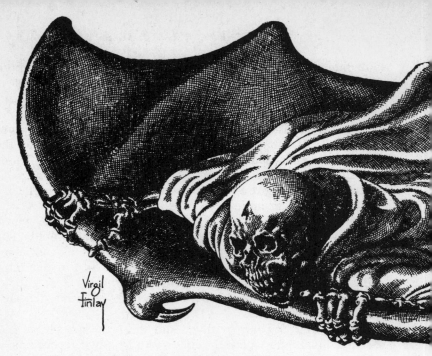

Virgil Finlay

Fungus Isle

PHILIP M. FISHER

The voyage to lands unknown is a favorite theme of fantasy and horror writers that lends itself to the invention of bizarre and menacing environments. Four of the five stories by Philip M. Fisher reprinted in Famous Fantastic Mysteries *were weird sea tales in which ocean voyages led to the discovery of strange new worlds and their terrifying inhabitants. It's not likely that Fisher had the opportunity to read the work of William Hope Hodgson, but "Fungus Isle" can be read as a companion piece to Hodgson's classic high-seas horror story, "The Voice in the Night."*

CHAPTER I

EVEN AS I crawled up the gently sloping beach, gasping and sobbing with half strangled lungs seeking to retch out the burning water and gulp in some life-giving air, I sensed something uncanny in the low-lying hedge of scrub before. It did not give me fear—my fears had come with the first roaring swoop of the typhoon, had vanished when the schooner struck the barrier reef and time for action came. Even the wandering thought of sharks had not restored them. And now, with solid land beneath me, fear was the emotion furthest away.

As I toiled on I admit I gave the feeling but little actual attention. My voluntary thought was of other things: My shipmates, the loss of the Emerald Spray. I found myself, in choking, water-quenched anathema, cursing the fate that had so malevolently pursued us ever since our discovery, months back in the scorching barrens of West Australia, of the petrified log whose heart had glowed with the pulsing greens, crimsons, and blues of fire opal. I looked bitterly back on shattered dreams of wealth, revenge, and of recovery from the blackguards who had fled with our treasure through these ill-known waters for their haven in degenerate Macao.

Yet, still would this subtle sense persist. And soon, it seemed, I must regard it. Something must be above me there, something. Else why to my unusually blunt perceptions should come such sense of eerie menace?

I scrutinized the black fringe before me intently as I crept on. My salt burning eyes could make out no movement there. And besides what moving thing, animate or inanimate, could compel that atmosphere of vague distrust? I knew where we were just before the typhoon had blown up. There were islands by the hundreds scattered under the southern coast of New Guinea; many of them unexplored. But all known were the same, all of coral origin, protected by barrier reefs, and crowned with wind-bent coconuts. All were the same with nothing on them to fear but loneliness; no serpents, no beasts, no human beings. And this—this land was but another islet in the chain.

I found myself striving to put aside this peculiar unease that was growing on me. I insisted now that it was foolishness; that there were other and more important questions. Douglas Gordon, whose tortures and canteen I had shared in our search for the block of crystallized fire that had promised life comfort to us all. He had been in the bows, clinging to the stay, and his was the first cry just before the hope-ending crash. Had the smothering torrent of solid green that roared over us then swept him to his death? The leader of our little party, skipper of the crushed schooner that the dying storm must now be mercilessly battering out there on the coral heads, Jim Dowell, what of him? And the Kanaka boy, faithful slave. Once in the quieter lagoon they had been safe; all could swim, and well. But had they fought down the outward seas and broken through?

These were the questions, these were the important things just now. Not the disquieting sense that beyond that nearing black mass of vegetation, and within it—yes, and of it—there lay a strange and waiting menace. Not that, I did persist. My friends. Water. Food. A boat—for continuing our chase. Revenge. To glory again in the mystic beauty of the stone—to touch again, in full possession, our fortune.

I dragged my eyes away, and scanned the wide spreading beach. Even under the black and cloud-flung sky its ghostly surface would betray another man. But the pale sands showed not a single darker object, no moving thing. I crawled on.

Then, quite suddenly, I stopped.

I repeat that I do not know why. I have read of charging soldiery coming to sudden involuntary halt—then, after a screaming shell had all but burned their faces with its wind, press on. They had been brought to a full stop warned by some unconscious perception of danger—and so, I must suppose, had I.

I stared before me. Crept a dozen yards forward. Paused again.

I did not fear. I repeat: there was nothing to fear. Common sense insisted that there could be nothing to fear. And yet I stopped there on my knees, and stared.

In the back of my mind began a whisper. It tried to explain a simple cause for part, at least, of the feeling that was on me. I groped to catch the words, to understand it. It was so simple, so obvious. Yet strain though I might, I could not comprehend. And in exasperation I cursed a dumbness I could not overcome.

Then, as I stared, I heard myself speak, with a kind of half laugh.

"Funny. Where are the coconuts?"

I gave a grunt of humor again—it did sound idiotic. Yet now a more discerning eye swept up and down the black fringe before me, to right and left. Not a palm in sight. The voice at last—clearly.

"Every coral islet in the South Pacific is fringed with coconut palms. Why isn't this? Every one of them. Why not this?"

The impenetrable blackness above me, the smooth, warm sand beneath, the sea at my back, and before me—mystery. The shadowed hedgelike growth, but not one single towering palm. And the storm from the sea fiercely determined to push me on. The wind?

Came another whisper. Another interpretation for my feeling, another solution based on common sense. This wind, trying to urge me forward—yet up there, but a dozen steps, not a sound. No thrashing rustle of torn foliage, no screaming rub of branch. Yet there was vegetation. I could see differences in it now; shapes, pillarlike. But not a sound of swishing leaf.

"That *is* funny," I said aloud. "Damn funny."

I started to crawl on, but the impulse died as I put out a hand. I cursed my folly, yet decided to hang the wind, anyway, and sleep the night out where I was.

First, though, another look up and down the sands.

My heart gave a great leap. I rose to my feet unsteadily and wildly whooped. Answer shrilled at once, and a figure lifted and came slowly to me. A welling of thanksgiving tore at my throat.

"Doug! You came through."

Silently he gripped my hand. Then his eyes left mine and he glanced to the shelter of the growth. Then back at me.

"I've crawled along that stuff for a quarter mile," he said in a low voice. "I wanted to get somewhere out of this wind."

My fingers clenched about his arm.

"Why didn't you go behind the trees, Doug?" I demanded in a whisper.

He turned and stared again. Then shrugged his shoulders, gave a short, dry laugh.

"I—I don't know. Just didn't, I suppose." He paused a moment, then quickly countered: "Why didn't you?"

I pointed, stiff armed, and even to me my words still sounded like those of a child.

"Where are the coconuts? Where are the palms? And why doesn't the wind make a noise of some kind among that stuff?"

He grunted again. And this time did not laugh.

"I move we camp right here," he said. "Right here. We both need sleep."

CHAPTER II

BUT I found that I could not sleep. And despite the fact that I had but just been shipwrecked, my body was not by any means exhausted. The typhoon had come up with hardly any barometric warning, had caught us beating through Torres Straits, that broad, though treacherous, channel between the great island continent of Australia, and that last unexplored land of mystery, the steaming man-killing green of New Guinea.

The three of us, with the Kanaka lad, had done our best to take in the canvas, but the rushing madness of the storm had won out. Two hours perhaps had we scudded, under bare poles, swept ever and ever to the north. Then, even as Douglas Gordon, clinging in the bows, had cried his warning of land ahead, we had struck. Came the short struggle with great avalanching seas, the comparative peace of the lagoon, then the beach.

No, I could not sleep. I was not weary enough for that.

I lay there in the smooth coral sand, and stared up at the clearing skies, and wondered about things. And most of all, I wondered now about this sense of uncanniness that had sifted into me as I crept up toward the black line of vegetation that was ahead. That growth had called me so at first—called me when I waded through the shallows; there, just ahead, I would find shelter from the stinging wind. And then, as I neared—it repelled. As I lay there I felt working into me, body and soul, the feeling that it would not be shelter. Something—I could not name it—menaced there. A voice within me warned against seeking its refuge. Insisted that it would not give refuge, but something else.

The wind died, and but for an occasional swift sand-scattering ruffle, left a growing peace in which the eeriness somewhat dimmed. I began again to call myself a fool. It had been the blackness of the night, the desolation of shipwreck and loneliness, and the simple fact that this island was not adapted to the natural growth of palms. That latter was exceptional, true, yet it had worked upon my imagination. And that the wind made no noise in rushing through the low scrub, but added to the natural unease of a black and stormy night. It was all nonsense. I was a fool.

And yet, how about Doug?

He certainly had sensed something. What had he said: that he had crawled along the stuff for a quarter mile, looking for shelter? Why had he not entered the stuff? Wasn't that shelter?

This was not like him. Long had I roamed the seven seas with Douglas Gordon, many the tight hole in which we had found ourselves; yet never had I seen him in a predicament which he had feared, or, discovering doubt within himself, given that doubt voice. But now— why had he glanced askance at the black fringe above us? Had he not sensed, too, that which I had felt?

If he had, then the thing was not the result of my own environment-stimulated imagination. No, then there was something else.

Suddenly I found myself stiffening, my body quite tense.

An odor—a dank, peculiarly pungent odor—was in the now quiet air. A strange odor, thick, almost tangible, and heavy, as though of a miasmic gas settling close to the ground because of its own damp weight.

This could not possibly come from the sea. It could not drift down upon us from the clouds above, nor yet percolate up through the coral sands. It could have but one source. The vegetation that crowned the low-rising land above us.

And yet, if this were a coral island—I seized a handful of the sand beneath me. Yes, its rounded, slick-coated grains were of disintegrated coral, unmixed with the sharp silicate particles from a rock-bound coast. The sudden newer doubt as to the land upon which we had been thrown left me; the storm had not driven us so far to northward as the mainland of savage New Guinea. We were on a coral island without doubt.

Yet coral islands do not ordinarily contain marshy land. And only from a dank, steaming morass could such a peculiar odor emanate. The belief that something here was far from the usual began again to strengthen.

I glanced at my old companion. He was limp in the sand, arms thrown wide, eyes closed. I wondered if he slept, yet hesitated to whisper to him. If he were finding peace in unconsciousness after his trial of the last few hours it were the last thing to do to awaken him. No, I must at present keep my thoughts to myself.

The odor persisted.

And now, too, with even the fitful puffs of the passed storm exhausted, it took on a certain warmth.

This, in itself, was not unusual.

In these equatorial seas, the heat of the sun is literally soaked into the land areas as it is into the blue waters themselves, and by night as by day the earth gives forth soothing comfort to one's recumbent form.

And to the stimulation of this warmth, as well as to the torrential downpour, the fertile land responds, giving birth to that lush and overwhelming tropical vegetation so astonishing to men of more temperate climes. Man, white man, quickly falls beneath its rhythmic impulse. Heat and moisture first forced life itself in times primeval. And tropical heat and tropical moisture, now that man is man, double his every bodily process. He comes to early maturity, his own seed bursts forth into bloom with results alarming even to the accustomed mind. Seasons are blended into one ebullient springtime, and before he is aware of it, he has come to manhood, the fruit of his own flesh is matured about him, his own decay brings him back to elemental disintegration. Heat, moisture, the tropics are a forcing house for living organisms.

Yet, the sand was warm beneath me. This miasmic odor was warm and moist to my nostrils. And lush, alive, it tasted to me. Alive, and— I felt an involuntary thrill pass through me—it, too, seemed to menace. It smelled of growing things, but of things growing too quickly. Of life developing in its highest intensity, of animate things that, with their own life force, their own will to grow and mature and decay, threatened with almost a premeditated malignancy all other animate things, all other forms of slower developing life than their own.

All this I sensed. And the sensing of it had no calming effect. The very fact beyond all others, perhaps, that this warm, moist odor had a lulling effect upon my nerves and body, did most to expand my growing apprehension until it tingled in every fiber.

Why had the wind made no sound in the vegetation up there? The eternal silence of it, the *waiting* silence, the silence that was so sure of its own power that in its very silence lay its threat!

I was becoming vastly uneasy, I had to admit. I did not like it. I dared not sleep.

The sky was sweeping clear, and the brilliants with which it was bespangled were outthrust ready for a plucking hand. The lagoon, peaceful now, glowed with a superphosphorescence lately lashed into being by the elements in conflict. The moon had risen behind me and the beach spread to the water's edge like a sheet of ghostly silver, though I myself yet lay in shadow.

I was still prone upon my back, with hands beneath my head, struggling to keep awake despite the influence of the strangely drugging odor, when my restless eye was arrested by a movement above the gleaming coral far down the strand to my right. I watched it at first rather absorbedly, and with a feeling of relief, wondering what it might be. Some sea fowl, I decided, preying on other living things lately cast upon the beach. I grunted and relaxed.

Quickly, as in answer to my movement, came a grip, hard upon my arm. Then Doug's voice, tense with wonder.

"Clarke! What—what do you make of it?"

I swung about upon my stomach—and felt again the strength of menacing mystery.

The full moon was peering over the island at us, yet had not cleared completely the fringe of growing stuff above. And the shapes it blackly lined were shapes such as I had never dreamed of before.

No—there were no gaunt rising, gracefully bending, palms! No sharp crested tangle of tropical grasses, no wreathing tendrils of vine, against the silver glowing face of the curious satellite.

Instead, upon the sand itself, sharp outlined, lay a solid wall of black. And from this wall soared strange, unheard-of forms; rounded trunklike forms that ended not in branch or leaf, but in egg-shaped, caplike heads, black, too, against the brilliant sky. Some of these, where the moon cut low, were but a few feet above the dense thicket below, others rose to perhaps three times the height of a man. Some were body thick; others, and these sometimes bent as by the weight of the bulbous tops, appeared no larger though than my own right arm. Some, also, stretched clean cut against the moon. Others seemed distorted with nodular swellings that presented the appearance of horrid plant disease.

But all—all, rising more or less pillarlike, swelled out at last into a heavier top, grotesquely shaped: the heads of gigantic asparagi, the semblance of an ovate sphere, others of an umbrella shape that, in its significance, brought my heart leaping.

The rays of the moon were luminously dissipated just where these forms broke from the black beneath. And ever and ever again wraithlike ghosts would tear away from this heavy lying mist and, clinging for a moment as though reluctant to sever themselves from the dense mass of it, drift vanishing away like the shrouded spirits of a seance.

Then would come, with renewed strength, the warm, moist odor, stealing down upon us as we stared in unbelief.

I sniffed again, almost without thought. Musty it was, as if a warning, pregnant, fallow, a thing vital and fecund with a staggering regenerative force. And overwhelming in its impression; yet held as in waiting. As though, suddenly released, this power to grow would submerge even us in its life force, suck us dry for its own sustenance, rush our own bodies into some devastating supermaturity that could only end in decay and horrid death. The odor of it sank into my senses, and for the first time I really feared.

The pressure of Doug's clenched hand upon my arm had not been lessened as we lay thus upon the sand, rigid, eyes hypnotically held on those weird black silhouettes against the silver moon and the glittering sky. And I believe that at least ten minutes passed before either of us thought to speak—or could. The sight was so utterly unbelievable. It stupefied. I know that I myself had no consecutive thought. I could not think. I could only wonder and stare, with something like the prickling of primeval fear proceeding up and down my spine.

"What—what do you make of that?"

Thus came Douglas's first words, and almost in exact repetition of the exclamation with which he had startled me from my contemplation of the fluttering thing down the strand. I suddenly found loose tongue.

"Heaven knows," I whispered back. "Nothing like anything I've ever seen before."

"You—you notice that peculiar smell—kind of heavy; like mold?"

"And warm? Damp? Steamy—"

"Like a drug?" he whispered. "Yes. I've been lying here trying to think what it was. I still don't know. But it certainly has something to do with that stuff above there, and the mist that is beneath. Clarke, I confess it, the thing doesn't appeal to me at all. I've been in some funny places—but—" His hand tightened, and rising to his knees he pointed toward the face of the moon. "There's something else."

Well above the peculiar vegetation, and at some distance from us, had suddenly risen a flock of flopping, batlike creatures. They were flying about with no apparent motive or destination, weaving in and out among themselves with slowly beating wings, dipping, swooping, fluttering high again, now in compact body, then in scattering disorder, almost as though in aimless play. Not a cry came from them. They winged against the face of the moon in absolute silence, a silence as uncanny as the grimly waiting growth just before us, and from whose depths they had come.

Then, as though by command, they suddenly dropped from our sight.

Recollection of things I had seen in other South Sea lands flashed before me.

"Flying foxes!"

But Douglas shook his head, though his hand now left my arm.

"No. I've seen them flying almost like that; but once in a while at least they'd let out a chirruping squeak. It's something else." His whisper came tense again: "I tell you, Clarke, I don't like this place at all. Not even a coc' palm! What the devil'll we eat, or drink? And this sickening smell, thick. Why, it almost seems alive! Like a living thing that's seeking us out to do us harm.

I felt again the pricklings run over my skin. He had sensed the menace of the thing as surely as had I.

A gentle puff of wind came to us then, and the odor, doubly strong, swept mist-clad upon us. I had just raised a hand to cover my mouth and nose, when I felt, rather than heard, a gentle swishing behind me. Almost immediately something seemed to alight and creep clingingly upon the back of my neck.

With an oath which I heard echoed from Douglas, I swung about and struck with my open hand.

Whatever it was fluttered beneath, then fell away.

And on the sands beside me, twisting and turning in vain attempt to take to the air, was what seemed at first glance to be a strangely shaped bird. I scrambled to seize it, and my very touch apparently spelled its death. For a handsize sector of the unbroken wing came off between my fingers, and the mutilated body shivered, wilted, and lay inert.

Then again I felt the weird sense of uncanny things about me. The piece of wing at which Douglas and I stared was not feathered, nor was it the leathery membrane of a bat. No; it was thin and smooth, and covered with an almost microscopically furry substance. And the foot-long body on the moonlit sand was not that of any bird or animal I knew. Feelers—the body of an insect. And my companion's own startled whisper gave the thing its name.

"A giant moth!"

Then we stared again into each other's eyes in silent question.

That fluttering swarm of things we had seen against the moon—had they not been the same? And the creature I had noted slowly beating along the sand—that must have been this very one.

A peculiar thought took hold of me as I again examined the wing in my hands. It had broken off so easily. That were hardly natural. The wing of a moth fresh struck down does not crumple at a touch; it is of more substantial material, has more strength. Yet this—I took the edge of it between my finger and thumb. It broke off at my least effort. I raised my eyes to Douglas Gordon.

He was watching me intently, and now he took the thing from me and with his own hands deliberately broke off a corner of it. Then his glance sought the fantastically shaped growth rearing up to the spangled sky—he sniffed at the thick air again—dropped his gaze upon the wing stuff he held.

"Breaks up at a touch," he whispered uneasily. "At the lightest touch. Like—like—that's it, like a thin rolled sheet of yeast. In Heaven's name, how does it live? How—"

He broke off sharply, mouth open, swung back staring to the shadows above. And though he had asked a question, I did not answer. I could not.

From the black depths of the island had arisen a cry that made my blood run cold. The first sound. Low at first, then rising higher, higher, higher, the cry reached a point where its vibration seemed to become rhythmic with that which I felt in my own body. Then, quite suddenly, it turned to a sobbing diminuendo moan, as of hopelessness and despair. Down, down, down it fell, until we strained to hear. We strained, every nerve, but the hidden shadows were become as silent as before, as darkly mysterious, as menacing, as evil with the now even doubled feel of malignant life force that with deadly will and diabolic artifice was reaching out for us, and ever drawing, drawing us in.

CHAPTER III

THE CRY was not repeated. And to tell the truth, although I, too, with Doug, stared into the tangle of strange black shapes beneath the rising moon, and strained every nerve to listen, something within me was saying over and over again, insisting that I did not want to hear that cry again. Had it been clear call of anything normal in our lives, this peculiar insistence would have had no effect. I would have wanted then to hear it so as to place it in its proper category of known things. It would have been the call of some night bird; or of a startled monkey, perhaps, or of a man himself, on some nocturnal hunt.

Of course, I must admit, I was still filled with the uncanny feel of this lonely bit of land. The silence of it, the misshapen vegetation, the soporific odor of the warm, heavy mist, the great moth to which death and decay had so quickly come at our veriest touch, the flutter of a myriad of its fellows, black against the moon—and then, this cry. Of utter woe, despair, and of horror, too. A cry not more of the fear of death than of dread of a living death from which there could be no escape. Yet it was not so much the hopelessness in it that struck me, as the peculiar lack of real vibration in its wavering notes. It was, in a certain sense, rhythmically harmonious with the taut vibration then in my own body, and yet it did not present to my mind, as well it must have to the mere mechanism of my ear, the sense of a physical impact. Furry. That was it. As though the sound had come from an organ pipe that was lined with fur. At once the logical answer leaped before me: a pipe lined with fur, or a throat with—mold.

The train of conjecture following this idea so filled me that when Douglas suddenly again gripped my shoulder and pointed down the silvered beach to a dark object moving there, I felt no further apprehension. I watched the thing approach. It seemed to stagger, wabble in its gait—fall—then rise and continue on. Its distance prevented even vague surmise as to its shape, yet on it came in that oddly awkward stumbling.

Then suddenly the grip on my shoulder relaxed, and with a muttered cry Doug left me and ran toward the thing. And I, in a spasm of fear, and with a glance at the silent rising stuff above me, took to my heels after him.

And a moment later I found myself with an arm about the skipper of the little schooner, Jim Dowell, half fainting as he recognized us.

We must have slept. I know that the sun was well above us when first I perceived in that gentle struggle for consciousness that precedes awakening, that something was wrong. The perception gradually became two. The first of these was the natural one—there was no motion about me; the sea was not underfoot; something had happened to it, for the schooner's motion was gone. Then I remembered. I was on solid earth. With a rush came the second feeling—distinct, clear, as I opened my eyes. Something—I could not tell what, nor whence came the sense of it—something was watching me.

I flung myself about, and caught a fleeting glimpse of movement in the vegetation above us. Just a glimpse, and so vague a one that I almost doubted. Then, for the first time, I saw what manner of vegetation that was, and my involuntary exclamation of wonder and disbelief brought my two companions to their knees.

The blackness of the night before had given no idea of the color of the growth above us. Yet deep rooted within all mankind, I suppose, is the firm belief that all growing things must necessarily be green. Or at least, if not inevitably green in the individual plant, at least verdant in the general aspect of growing things in the mass.

Yet here—it was perhaps the lack of fresh green life that so astounded me, so bewildered. Fresh green betokens normal life. It means clean life. It gives the appearance of everyday life under a beneficient Nature. Secure life—and a right one.

But here there was no such green.

The panorama before us was a horrid futuristic conception in ugly splotched colors—purples, yellows, browns, vermilions, and hideously mottled green grays. The mass of it repelled. The eye was tormented, the senses appalled. The colors were monstrous, loathsome—as though reeking with the deadly poison of an unclean and obscene living malignance.

And the shapes of these horrid growths were now in the light of day familiar, awfully familiar, staggeringly so.

The lower hedgelike mass of the stuff, stretching from one curve of the upper beach to the other, had been a black wall under the shadows cast by the moon. Now it showed itself the edge of an earth-covering bloat, consistently of one hideously painted purple, a purple that seemed slowly to pulsate, to watch the three of us human beings as we stiffened on the sands and stared.

Just above the oily looking smoothness of its upper line it was spined and folded and serrated with masses of splotched vermilion and poison orange, slick-surfaced crimsons, and dull brick reds. And above this soared greasy-coated trunks of leprous, gray-spotted yellows. These trunks rose to various heights, the greatest of them arising to perhaps three times the height of the tallest man of us. And they terminated in the nodular caps we had seen silhouetted against the moon the night before.

Deeper in the island, we could make out huge fanlike objects, fluted like deepsea shells, and whose brownish purple was as repulsive to the eye as their size was stupendous. To the right, also, and creeping toward us over the creamy cleanness of the coral sands, stretched long tendril-like things that seemed like the leathery feelers of gigantic starfish, vermilion, and spotted with the yellow grays again—unclean. Dipping down toward our staring trio, leaning to us on its attenuated stalk of streaked and greasy yellow, one great egg-shaped head peered at us not a dozen feet away, its purple-spotted surface a great all-seeing eye, an eye that thought, that calculated, that menaced.

I glanced at the white sun above us, and to the pure coral sands beneath our feet. They were the only natural elements about us, the only clean things. That growth—no wonder I had sensed the uncanny when I had crawled up the beach in the blackness of the night before. No wonder I had felt repelled when I would have sought shelter from the dying typhoon. No wonder Doug had crawled for a quarter mile, not daring to enter the black growth at his very side because something deeper in him than voluntary thought had warned him.

The warm, damp odors of the night, the wraithy mist under the rising moon, the sense of a life that menaced, of living things of such swift growth, such absorbent vitality, such relentless devotion to that teeming vitality—no wonder we had felt it as a presence. These haunting shapes, by their very gigantic familiarity becoming each second more awful, lived, and the life in them was so strong that they seemed to think and to threaten all other life that their own might be the more secure. I found myself shuddering at what might have happened had we entered its depths—and at that moment Douglas Gordon's voice broke the silence, hoarse, choked, unbelieving.

"Fungus! A forest of giant fungus growth. Good Heavens!"

Captain Jim's muttered oath followed.

And I turned to find him rubbing his forehead with the back of one hairy hand. I do not know what started my heart to beating then. Yet beat it did, indeed, and a surge of genuine alarm rushed to my throat for the first time since the wreck of the Emerald Spray on the jagged coral head of the outer reef.

Then my eyes flashed to the face of Douglas Gordon. Paused there a moment. Then back to Captain Jim.

And my own hand went uncertainly to my own forehead, furtively rubbed. My heart beat again, as I held my hand before my eyes. The palm of it was slightly browned from contact with my face.

I stared at it, then to the faces of my companions. And I saw that their eyes had followed my own, their glances slowly bending first upon my own face, then upon the others'.

"Covered with the stuff," I gasped. "Covered with it. What can it be?"

My eyes went over Doug's shoulder to the fungus growth behind him. Then to the green-brown scum on my hand. I lifted my hand to my nose.

"The same smell," I muttered. "The same."

Doug was the first to recover himself.

"And that fungus growth! Humph! I don't think we need be alarmed, fellows. Toadstools, puff-balls, any fungus, you know. During the night, while we slept and the wind fell, it drifted out and settled upon us. Spores from that fungus. Like from a mushroom, you know. Spores, that's all."

Gradually I felt my apprehension depart. Well I recalled certain grammar school experiments. The head of the toadstool, or the mushroom, cut off from the stem, set down upon a sheet of glass or white paper. And in the morning the delicate print of its gill-like under part traced in the fallen spores.

"Naturally," I nodded. "But it got me for a moment. This heathenish place—uncanny. Never can tell what might happen, you know. I thought—"

I came to an abrupt halt. I really did not know what I thought, or had thought. The alarm had made itself felt. That was sure enough. It had come upon me with a heart-jolting sense of danger. Impressed itself upon me even as the uncanny feel of the dark fringe of growth before me had impressed itself upon my consciousness as I crawled toward it in the night.

Jim Dowell dipped his head toward me, his wide blue eyes staring into mine.

"Just what did you think?" he demanded in a low tone.

I shook my head.

"I don't know," I muttered again.

For a moment Captain Jim stared, then slowly turned toward that mammoth and horrid colored fungus growth above the sands.

Then with a grunt gave word to the first practical suggestion since our casting upon this strange bit of land.

"Last night," he said, "I saw something flying about in the moonlight. And I'm hungry and thirsty. The first thing we must find is water. I move we explore a bit."

Chapter IV

REACTION CAME then to us all. It was quite evident to me that the soporific exhalations from the giant fungus, warm, damp, insinuating, had had much to do with the sleep that had gripped us until the sun, risen high toward tropic noon, scorched our nerves into wakefulness. And I knew that I was very thirsty and hungry as well. Yet there was, however, something unaccountable about this thirst. I had taken in some salt water while in the crashing breakers of the reef, and later during my swim to the ghostly line of the beach. I had experienced thirst, too, on the semidesert regions of West Australia, when we had searched for, and found, the fabled block of fire opal. Yet now there were none of the torturing symptoms of thirst.

I needed water badly, but my lips were not cracked; they were smooth to my tongue—almost feeling as though spread with camphor ice. And my tongue itself, and the roof of my mouth, had nothing of dryness. Yet my body craved water, overpoweringly demanded it.

I do not believe that I was wakefully conscious of my mouth and lips being in this condition. Yet I do recall now that thus they felt— as though oiled with some tasteless oleate fluid or rubbed with some tasteless theatrical grease. But I could not have explained this then. I thirsted, but something about even that thirst was not normal.

The call of my stomach for food, however, was the call of old.

We decided to go together and explore the beach for any depression through which water might flow to the sea. We knew, of course, that

the ordinary coral atoll has no flowing streams. But with the uncanny vegetation of the land only too present, other peculiarities might
easily be.

"So profuse and gigantic growth of fungus can only argue plenty of
fresh water," declared Douglas. "And with such an amount of fresh
water in the place we ought surely to come upon some of it flowing
into the sea."

We had grunted that our sentiments were the same, and plodded
down the beach to our left.

Not a dozen steps away we came upon a brownish object lying in
the sands. We paused a moment, looking at it, for nothing dark had
been upon them during the night. Then I saw the two depressions
made by Doug's body and my own, and at once the things came to
us.

"The body of the moth!" exclaimed Doug.

Jim Dowell looked at us quickly, blue eyes wide again.

"The moth?"

I told him of our visitor of the night before, and stooped for the
body. But even as my hand was about to touch it, Doug seized
my arm.

"Don't!"

I straightened up in some surprise.

"I wouldn't touch the thing, Clarke," Doug said. "It was gray last
night, remember. Even in the moonlight there could be no mistake; it
was gray. But now—look at it."

The foot-long body was hardly gray now. Brown it had appeared as
we approached it, but upon closer examination the brown was slightly
greened, and blotched here and there with leprous yellow. I shuddered.
Thank Heaven, I hadn't touched the thing! It was covered with a
scumlike mold.

Furtively my hand went to my forehead and face again, and as we
plodded on I rubbed the skin until, in the white hot rays of the
overhead sun, it tingled and drew.

The beach curved ever to our right, and still we came upon no
running dip in the glistening sands. And the thirst was growing upon
us. I licked my lips again, and found them still as though lately rubbed
with grease paint. Yet my body demanded water, water—and my throat
was getting dry. Yet, strangely enough, my tongue did not thicken, and
the roof of my mouth was smooth.

"What's that?"

Jim was pointing down to the water's edge, where there appeared a
great mound of brownish green, set off clearly against the emerald
crystal of the water of the lagoon.

"Rock! Seaweed!"

The words came from all three of us, and unmindful of the beating
of the sun, we raced down to it. For seaweed meant crabs in these
latitudes, and crabs were food, and food was life.

Yet disappointment met us with her hard, rebuffing hand.

"Fungus!" exclaimed Doug disgustedly. "Just a great mass of fungus. Hell!"

"It's water I want," grunted Captain Jim. "If I don't find it soon on the beach, I move we break through the stuff and look for it inside."

For some reason neither Douglas nor I made answer to that last suggestion. And something bade me hasten my step to keep abreast of the others. Break through that stuff and look for water inside? I wasn't so sure that I wanted to crash through that low-crawling mass of purple bloat. The idea of my bare foot crunching through up to my knee into the hidden flesh of it made me shudder. No, until absolute necessity demanded it, I would place these feet of mine where I could see.

Then Captain Jim gave a whoop.

He had led us straight up the sands from the mass we had examined at the water's edge, and between the weird fungoid forms was a break in the purplish ground mass. The ground dipped slightly, too, and in the tiny depression crept a lichenlike growth, too brilliantly orange in color for beauty, and seeming to my rather stimulated imagination to be the tentatively outthrown pickets of the strange life behind it.

For a moment we looked at each other, standing in that dip beneath the soaring forms. I think each of us well knew what was in the others' minds, yet we knew too that if we would live we must go within.

Doug coughed slightly, then, with his eyes on mine, nodded.

"Jim ought to know," he said quietly. "Last night, cap'n, just before we were put to sleep by this stuff, something from inside here made its call. I can't tell you what the cry was like, except that I never heard anything just like it before. It didn't exactly frighten us, either, Cap'n Jim. But there was something to it that"—Doug shrugged his shoulders—"that made us feel that something had gone wrong with the thing that made it. I don't know if you get me, but that's the way it sounded. Something had gone wrong—hopelessly wrong."

Doug turned and his eyes sought the horrid colored depths. "Just thought you ought to know, that's all."

Jim Dowell made no answer.

Yet we stood there some moments before any of us made a move.

Beneath our feet was the lichenous mat of glaring orange, vermilion, running from beneath that purple, crimson mottled, bloated mass that, knee high, lay like a spreading quilt, covering the ground itself in all directions as far as the eye could carry. To our right, within hand reach, stretched a brown mottled trunk of dirty yellow. This rose to the height of perhaps fifteen feet, and there spread out into the umbrella-shaped head of a giant toadstool. The gills on the under part of this head were close tightened, and but for the fine radial lines tracing the contracted lips might have been a smooth uncut surface, of a light and greasy green, like the underside of a fish.

To the left was a widespread fan, as wide as the stretch of a tall man's arms, and as high as a man might reach—purple at its base, shading to a green-spotted purplish-brown at its rounded edge. Where it burst through the bloated cover at our side, small tongues of the orange stuff ran out, as though eager for the light, avidly, lustfully, pursuing its own desire for unhindered life.

Before us ran the depression itself, crowded upon all sides by the purple undercarpet with its oily, leather-appearing surface, and overbent by huge, heavy-topped forms of musty toadstools. More fanlike growths, strange shapes noduled in uncouth cactus form, queer mounds of grayish white, some of a single leprous hue, others mottled with the greenish brown of mold. Perhaps a dozen paces up the depression the sun broke through upon a large, waist-high boulder—gray green.

The scene was not one to give confidence to men in love with life, clean life of clean sea and clean air. And I confess I did not care to follow up between the purple bloatings bordering the vermilion-tongued depression. But we must have water, and surely such a dip in the ground and such a break in the growth could but argue that in times of storm the water drained thither from the interior of the island.

Douglas himself gave an oath, and started forward.

Then before we knew it something swooped overhead, and we were drenched with a suffocating mass that had fallen upon us from above.

Coughing and choking, we broke out to the beach for air. And looking back, I saw that the great toadstool had bent its head almost upon our own, and discharged a cloud of brownish spores from its suddenly opened gills. My heart had almost stopped beating, and the sense of uncanny menace seized me again with greater strength as I saw the great umbrella head suddenly raise back to its full height, and watched the gills themselves slowly, lap by lap, close until the underside of the thing again was like the belly of a fish, oily smooth.

We found our breath at last, and cleared our throats and eyes and ears of the clinging spores. Then Doug looked again into our eyes.

"Fellows," he said slowly, and as though weighing his words, "the thing did that deliberately."

For a moment there was silence.

Then Captain Jim guffawed—a bit too loudly.

"Nothing but a damned overgrown toadstool! Faugh! Coincidence. We just happened to be there when it burst with ripeness. Come on!"

CHAPTER V

WATER WE must have. But as I looked up at that motionless giant fungus, hardly daring to believe that but the moment before it had bent to us and let go its choking cloud of seed upon our heads, I felt that, once discovering that water, we must make all haste to take our fill and return to the sun-swept beach again. And Jim Dowell gave voice to my thoughts.

"Rush it, fellows. Up the creek bed."

Rush we did.

And I, in my greater desperation—or, perhaps, more tumultuous imagination—took the lead. A dozen paces up the depression I came upon the boulderlike thing, and, not thinking, dropped a hand upon it and vaulted.

The next moment I had crushed through the thin crust of what had seemed solid stone, and head and shoulders deep, was choking in a mass of damp, clabberlike substance. Doug and Jim dragged me forth and cursed me for my foolhardiness, sympathizing the while for the accident. I shook off the clinging pulp of the giant puffball and followed on.

The depression twisted and turned, and each bend gave glimpses of newer and stranger forms of fungus life. Each moment, too, the warmth increased, and the steamy dankness of the heavy exhalations of the strange life surrounding us settled deeper and deeper in our lungs.

Great man-thick trunks soared fifty feet into the air here, trunks warted and noduled with masses of parasitical fungi. Huge fluted fangs of leather-surfaced brown spread on either side of us. Giant puffballs loomed beside us like gray scum-surfaced balloons at anchor on the purple bloated earth. Things spread out in poison-splotched yellow greens like enormous fungoid octopi, lying in wait with their thousand warted suckers to trap the unwary and take his life that their own might rush on to completion. But the path itself, save for that first obstacle, was smooth spread before us with its carpet of brilliant vermilion and orange.

Here and there the sun glared through and the colors would clash in hideous contrast, the vapors disappearing and now again would come the slow, silent burst of a vast umbrella head, and the thick air would cloud with suffocating brown.

On we rushed. And at last came a half strangled cry from Doug, who now led, and Captain Jim and I flung ourselves upon our knees beside him and plunged our heads beneath the clear waters of a fungus surrounded pool.

The risk we took in doing that!

When I think of it now, I can see how men of usual good sense may needlessly throw away their lives. We made no test of that water. We thought of nothing else but that it was water. We believed it must be fresh; and even the poisonous looking growth teeming about the pool did not give us thought that the waters, even if fresh, might be polluted. We threw ourselves upon our knees, dipped our burning faces into the clear fluid of that tepid pool in a fungus forest, and drank.

It was Jim, I think, who gave the first cry.

I looked up and saw him, still kneeling, slap at something upon his neck; saw him dip his face again and drink. Then felt something light, yet clinging, touch my own neck. Reached back one hand and brushed. The feeling departed. I dropped my hand again to the lukewarm waters that were so grateful—the sense of something touching my skin came again. Tingling, yet coldly so, coldly—like back there on the vermilion trail—the giant puffball.

With a loud yell of alarm I started up, and flung my hands back to my shoulders and neck. Tore them away, and my hands were full of a grayish fungus growth. A mass of the stuff seemed to be enveloping me. I gave another yell, and saw with horror that Jim and Doug were struggling with a foggy cloud of it even as I was.

Jim's cursing began to rend the silent air, and I heard Doug muttering as he strove to fling the suffocating frondlike stuff from about him.

"The trail! The trail!"

Jim this time.

I looked frantically about me. The trail! "Where the devil is the trail out?" Jim's voice rose to almost a shriek.

And I felt my own heart misgive me as I seized a mass of the now warming, puttylike stuff that seemed to grow even as I tore it from my eyes, my face. Warm, warmer now—with the quickening chemistry of life!

The trail—the entrance to the pool! Where—

The fungus walls had closed in about the place, were slowly thickening before my eyes—growing, sending out new shoots, pulsating with avid, eager life—life begotten of the white hot sun and steaming tropic rains. A life that rushed forth, madly demanding more life; life that thought, that sensed, that knew, that menaced—

A shadow cast over us, and raising my eyes I beheld three great umbrella heads bending over. Even as my eyes were cast up upon them, their great gill lips opened as if by concerted action, and again came the drench of suffocating brown spores.

I heard Doug's voice, half choked, desperate.

"To your right, Clarke. To your right, Jim. Break, break now—or you never will."

It rose to a crescendo of horror at the end—Douglas Gordon crying out with horror—with fear. I fell, tripped by a great spongy mass that seemed to grow out of the very earth. I stamped it down, and other stuff grew, unfolded, shot upward to and about me in putty-like fronds, clinging, warmly now, thrilling my skin with the feel of their resistless life energy, their will, their *will* to live, and their determination to add our lives to their own.

Another shadow above. Another silent descent of a great spore cloud. Another gasping curse from Jim or Doug, I could not tell which.

"To your right!"

Soft, clammy warm, so easily pulled off, destroyed, torn asunder—yet growing, growing, enveloping us, throbbing with life, determination—another cloud above, overshadowing all. With a last desperate effort I struggled to my feet, tore away the gray stuff that clung, ever growing, to my face, eyes, nose—and crashed with all my remaining strength through the thick of the walled mass to my right. One great sobbing moment, and the sun shone down again on a hideous motley of poisonous color and giant forms. I was free.

But Doug. And the captain.

Back there. And I—I alone. I plunged back, only to be thrown against the purple bloating that walled the little depression as two gray-shrouded, uncouth figures broke through into the clear.

"Clarke! Clarke!"

One of the figures turned as if to go back, and I caught it by its horrid arm.

"Doug! I'm Clarke. I'm all right, Jim!"

"Thank God! All here. To the beach."

Ah, the cleansing action of the clear salt water of that beautiful emerald lagoon!

I cannot tell you how we rushed into it, threw ourselves down into its limpid cleanness. The stuff broke up, dissolved to mere shreds of itself. Salt, salt water—it seemed that the fungus stuff found a sole life-destroying element in the salt water of the sea. We bathed in it frantically, rubbing the last bits of the foul growth from our skins.

We breathed deep, but found ourselves choking with gray froth in our nasal passages, our lungs, our mouths. Desperately, one by one, we plunged into the deeper part of the lagoon, and, despite the spasmodic effort of a reluctant nature, deliberately breathed in the cleansing fluid. Then would a companion, gasping for breath against the choking fungus developing in his very lungs, haul us out and cast us strangling and gagging upon the glistening coral strand. Then he would fling himself into the sea, and in turn be dragged out, and belly down, drain himself of the cleaner element and gulp, in great convulsive heavings the pure, life-giving air.

In another fear now we threw ourselves back into the lagoon and even as we had gulped of the fresh waters of the treacherous pond far up that twisting color-clashed glade, gulped now of the salt. But at last we deemed our bodies saved, and we relaxed in the scorching sun, forgetful of the burning that was sure to follow, only grateful for its purging warmth and light.

A dread weakness took us, and in that weakness we cared not what might come against us from out of the sea. It at least was clean. That hot, lustful, fungoid life was not. Here, we knew we might have a chance for life, a fighting chance, and if death were our lot at least we might expect that it, too, would be clean. But back there—

Two things, however, must be spoken of. First—it was Doug who brought up that.

The Kanaka boy—what of him?

"He jumped with me," volunteered Captain Jim. "Jumped with me in the ruck of it out there. I hollered to him to keep close to me, but the little devil could swim like a fish and I've no doubt he reached the beach long before I did. Lord knows I was slow enough."

For a moment there was silence. Then Doug again: "Good God!"

The words were not a profanation. They were more a prayer, and I think Jim and I both knew well enough what Douglas Gordon feared. No lashing sea could have beaten the brown lad down. He must have reached the lagoon; he must have reached these very sands. Yet we had not seen him, nor any trace. What else then might we expect?

Minutes passed in which we drew in the grateful air which now with the coming of the night stirred in gentle motion.

Then Captain Jim spoke again.

"We must get off this island. But to get off we must have two things, something that will bear us up in the water, and something to eat and drink."

"Heaven forbid drinking at that pool again," I muttered.

Captain Jim raised himself on one elbow.

"Yet water we must have, my boy. And, food. But what to eat— what to drink—"

He raised himself again, inquiringly, his face grave in the moonlight.

"Coming down the beach this morning, did either of you see any drift from the schooner? Wood? Oars? Chests? One of those little pontoon rafts we got in Sydney? Anything?"

Slowly we shook our heads.

The only things upon the beach had been the body of the giant moth lying near where Doug and I had slept in the sands, and the huge mound of fungus not a hundred yards from where we now lay. Nothing else.

And Captain Jim echoed again our thoughts in monotonous repetition.

"We must get off this island. We must get off."

Then we stiffened, staring at each other in suspense and question.

From far in the interior of the fungoid forest above us had come again that strange unearthly cry. Again, the lonely, hopeless, sheer horror of it quickened our hearts, yet chilled the leaping blood in our veins.

Low at first, then ever rising higher, higher, higher, the weird cry came to a crescendo pitch that cut every nerve. Then, with disconcerting suddenness, it droned away in a sobbing diminuendo moan, a dying echo of hopelessness and utter despair.

Down, down, down it fell—until we strained to hear.

Then the black depths, with the moonlit monster silhouettes ranging above, became as silent as before, as darkly mysterious, as menacing, as deadly with its waiting malignant life force as we had found it when we fought that very life force by the pool.

CHAPTER VI

DESPITE OUR weakness we could not think of sleep. We lay there in the sands staring back upon black forest, from the depths of which had come that cry. Twice now we had heard it, Doug and I.

We knew now that the first had been no nightmare, no horrid fiction of our imaginations. Something lived within those horrid depths, something besides the giant gray moths, something other than the silently waiting and diabolic fungus.

"Animal?"

Doug's wondering voice questioned the stars above. And I found that I could say neither yes nor no. We were animals, we humans, and the strenuous demands of that life within the island—and island it surely must be—had all but made our animal bodies its own. How could that cry have come then from anything of the animal kingdom? But could it be of vegetable origin? Of fungoid? That, too, could not be answered with a simple yes or no.

Captain Jim's words, coming in answer, and yet not in answer, to Doug's query, brought again the desperateness of our situation.

"It cried out, at any rate. It must be different from anything we've seen so far. And anything different might mean something that will save us."

"How do you mean?" I demanded, rolling over so as to face him.

His answer came in one word.

"Food."

Again we relapsed into silence.

Food, indeed—and water.

Without thought my tongue ran along my lips, and then came the consciousness that now they were dry and cracked. And I was thirsty. I recalled that earlier in the day when first we had set out to search for water the call for fluid had been just as strong, but my lips, my mouth, my throat, had not been dried. No. Instead they had felt as though smoothed with grease paint, camphor ice. Now—now that sensation was gone.

I started—the salt water I had drunk to kill the crowding fungus growth that would have choked me! It had cut the greasy feel, and it had cut, later, the fungus itself. Had that first smoothness been but a result of the spores drifted upon us during the night? Had it? If it had, then—

I found myself repeating, too, in dulled monotony:

"Fellows, we must get off this island. We must get off this island. We—we're threatened. Our lives, our bodies—we must get off this island."

"How do you feel now?" demanded Captain Jim.

I shook my head.

"Like a rag, eh? Well, my boy, no one wants to get off this filthy spot any more'n I do. But we've got to find something to get off on, don't we? And we've got to have some strength before we can even search. Sleep now, that's the dope. Come morning, we'll search for some wreckage from the Emerald Spray—go clean around the cursed island. Something'll show up, sure. But now, take it easy and sleep."

The advice was good.

I grinned weakly at him, and murmured a response.

But no sooner had I settled myself for sleep than my skin prickled once more as that weird call came again from the depths of the island.

I sat up instantly, turning my face to the interior. And Doug and Jim, I noticed, were not behind me in apprehensive movement.

Again came the call. And even before it dropped to the final sobbing wail there arose above the forest a veritable cloud of the great flapping moths. Once more under the moon they waved in and out, up and down, in inexplicable play in the now breathless night. Perhaps ten minutes passed as we watched, eyes hypnotically held upon the moon-touched gray of them. Then, as if by preconcerted order, they dropped back into the black mass from which they had arisen.

With another grunt Captain Jim turned back and wriggled to a more comfortable position in the coral bed.

But Doug himself was the one who mentioned the fear they had suddenly brought to me.

"May they have a pleasant night's rest," he said; then added with undue emphasis: "And stay right there for the rest of the night."

"Right!" The ejaculation burst with vehemence from Jim.

Somewhere in the night I began to dream.

A great cloud of those huge gray things had winged their way from the center of the island. Their horrid-eyed leader saw us, indeed they seemed to have risen again from their black retreat for the very purpose of seeking us out, and steered the mass of them our way. Over our recumbent sleeping forms they fluttered and dipped and rose and dipped again, watching us, making sure, gaining strength in numbers, and in will. Then, as one, they had descended upon us, covering our bodies completely with their yeasty wings, crawling over our skins, seeking, feeling, rubbing.

We struggled against the suffocation of their mass. The musty smell of dank mold choked our lungs. It became insufferable. We began to struggle. To fight even as we had fought back there by the pool. And like that devilish fungus, leaping forth into hot breathed life even as we ripped and tore and fought, they broke beneath our effort, crumbled to nothing, vanished—only to be replaced by countless hordes of newer things, leaping up in full life and body from the broken remnants of the old.

The weight of them. The overpowering odor of their moldy foot-long bodies. . . .

I flung out my arms in a last frantic effort to throw them off—and found myself lying on the open sands of the beach, with the glittering diamond points of the blue-black sky staring in cold wonder down upon me. I glanced over to my companions. Beneath the white light of the moon their chests rose and fell to the deep breathing of sleep. I was a fool. I had been dreaming.

And yet—something, something was now right about us.

Something was close upon us. Watching us. Had even noted my

wakening movements, and retreated somewhat. Yet, retreating, still watched—and thought. Watched and thought, and—I felt it uncannily—did *not* fear.

I sat bolt upright with a jerk. And would have cried out but that my tongue cleaved to the roof of my mouth.

Between us and the great mound near the water's edge a hundred steps away stood a group of figures. Upright they stood, even as men, and I found myself counting them as I stared. Five—five; yes, certainly, there were five of them.

Not twenty paces away from us they stood, and though the moon gave no hint of white upon the faces of them, I knew that they were intently watching us.

For some minutes I sat thus, petrified, staring at the five figures and feeling their own stare upon me. A gentle breeze had again arisen, and the lulling *lap-lap* of waters on the beach brought me finally to a sense of reality. This was no dream. Here was the beach, spreading silver to right and to left. Above was the dense black of the fungus forest. Below, not a step away, the flashing waters of the clean lagoon. Overhead were the same old stars, and at my side Douglas Gordon and Captain Jim.

And these things that watched—no, certainly they did not fear; but neither did they menace. Just stood and watched. Pity? Was it *pity* I sensed in their distant regard?

I whispered softly. "Doug. Jim."

My companions did not show by word or movement that they had heard me. Evenly their deep respirations showed their sleep.

I called again, a bit louder, and from the tail of my eye saw the five figures retreat a step toward the dark mass behind them.

"Doug. Jim!"

Had they not awakened then, I believe I should have given a veritable bellow. The feeling that I was alone with that staring quintet out there was not calming in its effect.

Silently then I pointed.

And Doug and Jim froze even as had I.

Then, slowly, came a gasp from Jim.

"Whew-w-w! What the devil—"

He started to his feet, and Doug and I were instantly at his side. All the exhaustion of the earlier night slipped from me. If this were to be the end, I was ready for it. These things before us were alive, and alive with animal life, not fungoid. And if fight we must now, the odds were not so bad, and the struggle would at least be clean. Blood against blood.

Yet, these things did not menace.

The five of them retreated another step, then gathered together, heads close bent.

"Show 'em we're peaceful. Raise your arms up and hold 'em so," whispered Doug tensely.

At our motion the figures seemed to stiffen once more. Then the heads went closer. Thus a moment, and now one of the figures stepped a half dozen paces nearer to us.

Grotesque, that figure was. Upright like a man, and yet in the moonlight surely no man had so appeared before. The face should have stood out milk-pale in the silver light, and its features clear. Some grace, too, there would have been, some trimness of form. But this creature had none of these. The face turned upon us was of the same weirdly mottled cast as the rest of the body, and the latter itself was neither trim nor shapely. It seemed peculiarly broken in outline. Distorted. Uncouth. Broken. Things—things hung upon it, dangled from it, crusted over it, like a thing unclean.

Unclean! The thought rushed to me, and I felt my raised arms tremble. Unclean, even as the fungoid stuff had been upon us when we had torn from its menacing life force in there by the pool.

"Quiet," cautioned Doug.

The creature came closer.

It, too, raised one arm, and slowly waved it to and fro.

But a couple of fair leaps' distance from us, it came to a halt, half turned as though ready to flee at our slightest hostile move. And then we could see the full horror of its body, and I knew that the mold I had smelled in my dream of the cloud of great gray moths had come veritably from these.

Legs, body, and arms were ridged and mottled and fringed with fungus-like growths—ghastly, splotched green and gray in the moonlight. The head itself was a huge modular mass of the same gruesome hues. And of features it seemed to have none, though from somewhere in the fungus crusted face of the thing shone two deep-set eyes, the only part of the creature that appeared alive.

I heard Jim's quick, indrawn hiss as we stared.

Then came a movement in the lower part of the face of the thing, and in a low, monotonous, furry-soft voice it spoke. We shook our heads. It spoke again, and the same sounds seemed repeated.

In startling contrast boomed Captain Jim's voice.

"No *sabe*. Say it again."

The creature took one step back, and repeated. Then raised its arms again in a beckoning movement.

Jim turned to us. "Does it want us to follow? Shall we go?"

Doug's voiced sentiments were my own.

"I certainly am not going to lie here in the sand while those things are around. Yes. Go ahead."

We took a step forward. And the creature nodded its awful head, and turned away, stepping slowly and silently toward his fellows and the hill-like mound of fungus near the lagoon. Shortly he turned and glanced at us, raised his arm, still beckoning, and went on.

In wondering silence we followed. The others joined him, and walked on in a compact group until in the very shade of the mound.

There the first creature raised his arm, and signaled us to stop. Then he pointed to the great mass, then to himself, and then to us. Back to the mass of fungus again. And began to talk once more in his peculiar, furry-throated, monotonous tones.

"What does it mean?" demanded Captain Jim, turning to us, his wrinkled brow contrasting oddly with the light of half fear in his eyes.

We shrugged our shoulders.

Doug stepped forward toward the stuff. He raised his arm and elaborately pointed at it.

"You mean that?"

The great mottled head of the thing nodded eagerly.

"What about it, then? What's it to us?"

The peculiar voice came again, pointing once more to the fungus mound, to us, to his fellows, back to the mound.

"Hanged if I know what he wants," exclaimed Jim. "Something about that stuff there."

With a sudden thought coming to me, I stepped quickly toward the mound to examine it. But no sooner was I close upon it than all five creatures leaped in a line between it and me and began to claw eagerly at the fungus growth on the surface. I jumped to them to help. Instantly one of them emitted a short cry and seized me by the arm.

The damp, clinging touch of the creature filled me with a spasm of fear. I swept at the arm that had reached to me, and to my horror it seemed to break beneath my blow—break and a crustlike bit of ridgelike excrescence upon it fell to my feet.

At once the five of them turned and fled toward the blackness of the forest and disappeared within its shadows.

Then, once more, came that awful call.

CHAPTER VII

WATCH AND watch we stood for the rest of the night, judging the hours by the passage of the moon.

But before falling back into my hollowed resting place I went to the lapping waters and scrubbed my hands and arms and face. Rubbed and rubbed, in feverish regard for thoroughness, my left hand and forearm, for with it I had touched the creature. That contact had been unclean.

The others watched a moment in silence, then one by one, and without word or explanation, they also laved themselves in the purifying salt water of the lagoon.

Toward morning Doug awakened me with a touch. The moon was overcast with a single black cloud, and we were soaked in the drenching downpour of a tropical squall. He nodded as I lay back, for a moment, arms spread wide, mouth open.

"Take your time, Clarke. Let it soak in. This rain may save our lives."

We awakened Captain Jim. He, too, stretched so that every part of his body might be cleansed now from the sticky salt. He, too, lay face to the storm, mouth open, drinking in hungrily the great heavy drops of fresh water. Then the beach was flooded with silver again, and the silence fell like a pall.

From the fungus growth above us came a breath of the warm, mold-rank mist, drifting along the sands, spreading out, all seeking. Thus it covered the strand for a moment, then, with a counterwhip of breeze from seaward, disappeared.

So the others lay them down again, and I took over the watch.

Clear thought came to me as I paced the smooth coral sands, and traced again the events that had put us in this predicament.

The long search in the semi-desert land of western Australia, the search impelled by that whispering hearsay drifting so tentatively, yet so persistently, through the public houses of Melbourne. The half jocular suggestion that Doug had made.

"Let's get the stuff, Clarke."

Then, with the romance of the thing covering all doubt with its veil of glamour, a serious desire to follow up the insistently recurring rumor. Then the search, and finally the discovery of the great petrified log in the heart of which we had come upon the solid block of glowing fire opal. How we had clasped hands over it—the light of fortune in our eyes.

Then the long, careful, conveying of the precious stone. The report that our success was known at Melbourne. Our decision to change our point of destination to Sydney. The ambuscade when not twenty miles from that port, and the theft of our fortune.

Our search for clues. Then the certainty that the half-caste, Point-Five Markleigh, with his company of cronies in crime, had sailed with the opal in the stolen schooner, Black Moth, for that haven of all thieves, all treachery, all degenerate vice, Macao.

Two weeks later our own schooner, owned by Captain Jim, shoving off through the twisted harbor of Sydney in pursuit.

And now—this.

My thirst had departed, but I was filled now with a great hunger. I recalled my boyhood days, mushroom hunting in the pasture land of the hills behind our town. And I found myself staring up at the fungus of the island—somewhere I had read that there were nearly eight hundred known varieties of mushroom, the greater proportion of them edible. Surely, somewhere in that fecund growth would be some fungoid that we could eat. Its sustaining powers might be weak, yes. But anything was better than nothing, and a filled stomach gives at least the feel of coming strength.

Those great moths—must eat. The horrid manlike creatures—must eat. Both lived; both must be sustained by some kind of food that grew in that weird and fearsome forest.

My pacing drew me closer to the long, narrow hill of the fungus stuff on the beach. The things had led us to it; obviously that had been their intention. Intention argues the power to think. And they had spoken. I shuddered. Were they men, or were they, like the moths, half fungoid? The way that fringing ridge had sloughed off the thing's arm at my first slight violence!

But why had they come to us? Come with such obviously peaceful intentions? Pointed out the mound there? Torn at its lower surface with their moldy, handlike paws? Then, at my touch, fled for the shelter of their uncanny retreat?

The stars were retiring now, and the silhouetted forms peering above the island clear cut against a flushing dawn.

Near the fungus mound I saw the broken lump of stuff that I had knocked from the creature's arm. I knew now that salt water would cleanse, and an irresistible curiosity drew me closer to the thing. I stooped and picked it up. It crumbled in my hands, like the yeasty wings of the giant moth that first night. One part, however, seemed of stronger texture. I rubbed it, placed it in the palm of one hand, and smote it with the other.

Then, in sudden comprehension, leaped to the water's edge and scrubbed it in the crystal fluid. Then stood long and quietly, with heart heavily pumping, staring first at the grotesque and poisonously colored fungus of the fast lighting forest, then to the incomprehensible, yet in a way horribly illuminating, thing I held in my palm.

I raised a hand to my forehead, and jerked it down again with a sudden cry. My skin had felt as though incrusted with a bubbled grease. My hand was covered again with greenish brown mold. I raised it to my nostrils, cried out again and dashed down the beach to my companions.

One look, and I dared not touch them with my hands. I cried wildly to them to awaken. They came jerkily to a sitting position, wild-eyed in alarm. Then with cries of horror stared upon each other. Faces, necks, hands, exposed feet and wrists were covered with a finger-thick moldy crust. And Mack's hair was a mass of feathery gray.

Madly we dashed again into the salt lagoon. And came from it many, many minutes later, clean, but with skin strangely drawing and tingling. And on Doug's left cheek was a whitish spot, which, as the natural flood of life fluid rushed to the place to rebuild the broken tissue, rapidly became veined with crimson.

Silence then, for there was no need to speak what we now felt was certainty.

Without a word I showed them what I had come upon beneath the crust broken from the creature's arm. Then, at last, Douglas spoke, and his voice throbbed not so much with fear as with deep pity.

"Cloth! Part of a shirt! The things were men."

But Captain Jim amended the statement, with a fear in his voice that doubled the tingling on my skin.

"You mean," he whispered—"you mean they *had* been men."

His eyes seemed to center hypnotically upon the blotch upon Doug's cheek, and slowly my old friend flushed; then turned away.

There is but little use in recounting our search for drift from the wreck. Suffice it to say that before noon time arrived we had made our way completely around the island, only to come at last upon the long mound near which we had spent the night. We held a short consultation, and decided that we must try the material the island afforded.

It was with loathing that we approached the vermilion-carpeted glen upon which we had made our search for water the day before. And at once I caught sight of a flitting figure in the depths, a figure whose gray-mottled dull green and erect posture showed that the manlike things were watching our every move.

The giant trunk of the towering fungus that had first drenched us with its brown cloud of spores was easily pushed over by our combined effort. And the flat head of the thing, its diameter as great as our arms could stretch, twisted off and fell limply flat at our feet.

We dragged the leprous trunk to the water's edge, and, with hope beating high, out into the deeper waters of the lagoon. Then again did our hearts drop, for the fungoid log sank like a plummet to the bottom.

We returned and dragged down the great fluted fan whose hideous green speckled purple brown was so greasy to the touch. It, too, sank.

It was then that Captain Jim began to curse the fire opal that had brought us to this place of horrible and deathly existence.

"Unlucky!" he cried suddenly. "Opals—always unlucky. The curse of the ages is on them, and misfortune they bring to man. I'm through. I'm going back there to find something to eat. I don't care if it kills me now, I'm through. The cursed things are unlucky. We're going to die here, anyway, horribly, and I'm going to eat. Anything! Anything! Those man-things must eat. And I'm going to. I'm *through*. I'm going to eat."

And before Doug or I could stop him, he had dashed up the beach and disappeared.

Go in after him? Doug made a move to follow, and I held him back with all the desperate strength I had left.

"No," I cried. "No, no, *no!* Doug, in God's name, don't follow! Don't. He'll come to his senses when the—the things in there get after him. He'll come to his senses after their first touch. He can get out again. No; no."

Doug slumped to the creamy, clean sands.

"We must get off this island. We must."

Then without a word he jumped to his feet, and tearing off his shirt, dropping his trousers, he started for the lagoon.

"Wait!" I cried. "What are you going to do? You can't swim to safety."

"No," he returned calmly. "But I can swim out to the reef and bring back some parts of the Emerald Spray from which we can make a raft."

In my desperation I followed him to the strand. Then gripped his arm again.

"You can't," I whispered. "Look."

The great triangular dorsal fins of sharks cruised in the quiet waters.

"You can't," I repeated. "They're surer death than Jim has gone to. You must not go."

"We must get off this island," he muttered, staring out at the green combers battering the distant reef.

From behind us came the rising wail we knew so well. At once came an answering call.

Spellbound, we turned and watched, expectant of I know not what.

Closer and closer came the calls. Rising in hopeless wail, falling again with that shuddering sob of hopelessness and despair.

Then suddenly rose a cry that was different, a scream of fear.

As one we started for the vermilion trail.

Yet before we had gone ten steps a figure broke through the purple bloating undergrowth and rushed down to us, howling with fear. At our feet it fell to its knees, raising arms trailing with leprous growth— a face on which was sprouted the moldy, green-brown nodular excrescences we had seen the night before.

But the voice was different. Clearer. Somehow familiar. It pleaded with us, and a word or two of blurred English came to our startled ears.

The trailing arms gesticulated. Pointed back at the forest. Then to us. To the sea. Back to the fungus.

With a sudden oath Doug seized the mold-odored creature by the arm and dragged it toward the water.

"Doug!" I cried.

"Help me!" he snapped. "Help me! He knows something. To the water—to the water! Maybe then he can speak."

CHAPTER VIII

THE CREATURE was—or, I should say, had been—the Kanaka boy.

In terror he came to us, terror of something that had come upon him in the midst of the island's haunting growth. But it was with cries of desperate fear that he tried to fight Doug and me off when we dragged him to the waters.

I know now why this was.

I know now that the fungus stuff had so worked into his very flesh that the action of the salt water was nothing less than torture. I know now that while the fringing crust of the stuff sloughed off his skin almost instantly under the decomposing action of the saline fluid's chemistry, the growth had already, in these two days upon the island, worked in its horrid development so as to penetrate the skin and spread out into the living red flesh beneath. And I know that, though we saved the lad from the living death that would have been his upon this fearful bit of land, nevertheless we almost took away that life in the process of salvage.

At last his frantic strength gave way to exhaustion, and when we finally bore him from the lagoon and laid him upon the glistening sand, he collapsed in a wilted, sobbing heap.

And Doug and I looked at each other now with a full comprehension of the doom that was ours with horrible certainty, were we to sojourn longer in this place. There was but one kind of life upon the island—fungoid. The only creatures natural to the island, the giant moths, were all but fungoid. The things that had visited us during the night had once been men even as we—but they, too, were now all but fungoid. During the nighttime, when we slept and our own resistance was at the ebb, we ourselves had fallen beneath the power of that malignant life. And this Kanaka lad, with but two days in the midst of that hotly teeming life, had all but succumbed.

And Jim, Captain Jim—he had fallen to the cries of his body for food, and even now was somewhere, somewhere—we stared into the violently poison color of the stuff—in there.

We recalled the battle we had had with the living stuff that, even as we tramped it down and tore off its clinging growth, had leaped up with renewed vigor, with relentless persistency, diabolic menace.

Doug, wide eyed, took his eyes off the exhausted boy for a moment, and voiced my own thought.

"The damned stuff all but beat us down, Clarke. Filled our throats, our lungs, our bodies. It would have killed. But this lad here—is still alive. And those other poor devils—they're still alive. Is there something that—that kills the human in a man, kills the clean animal of him, and yet allows his body, in its form at least, to still keep on? To still, in its ghastly way, live on?"

I shook my head. How did I know? It was unbelievable, and yet in that creature of the night, and in the Kanaka, did we not have something of proof? And on our own bodies, the same? That grayish blotch on Doug's own cheek. I found myself staring at it, and dropped my eyes guiltily only when the sudden flush rushed to it, and my partner covered it with a quick flash of his hand.

"But why," I demanded, speaking more to myself than to him—"why, when these other—men—found themselves falling beneath the influence of the stuff, did they not get off the island?"

Doug stared out into the placid emerald crystal of the lagoon. My own eyes followed his as they watched the tacking dorsal fins of the great sharks.

Then he gave a short cough.

"I choose the water and the sharks first," he suddenly cried.

"I, too."

Yet, why, if they had been men, had these others not chosen the quick, clean death themselves? Did they take the chance here because of hope—hope for a rescue?

Then, if that were true, I argued, why had they not come to us at once, as soon as they discovered the presence of clean men upon the shores, and on their mold crusted knees pleaded for deliverance?

"They didn't do it," I insisted; "they didn't do it."

Doug watched the slow breathing of the brown lad, the blotched leprous discoloring of his once sleek skin.

"They came to us last night," he suggested. "They tried to speak to us. They wanted to tell us something; and, fools that we were, we scared them off."

"I know that," I cried. "But if they really feared the life here, if they really wanted to get off this devilish place, they must have known that we were their best bet. Why did they run from us, back to—back to that?"

Then in Doug's eye, steadily fixed upon mine, I saw his answer. And it was even as I feared. The horror of it, the pity! It was the only answer that could be, the only answer that could clear these things that had been men from the charge of mental and physical cowardice. A great rush of emotion rose to my throat, and I choked back a gulping sob. Captain Jim—in there—now—even now—in the beginning of his—

"The boy here had been in there two days," he cried. "He rushed out from it to us in some great fear. Yet he had been in there two whole days—eating—drinking. Yet, in sudden fear, with those cries behind him—rushed out to us—"

I touched the lad with my foot. He did not stir. His long, labored breathing told the story of a complete exhaustion.

"He will stay here for some time," I said. "Come, friend. We must follow Captain Jim. We must save him. We must get him, and then the four of us, while we are men, must get away. Away, Doug. You hear me—we must get away. We—"

And suddenly I came to a full halt, my face hot with the rush of shame. For my own voice had wailed in my ears with a note of hysteria.

Then Doug seized my arm again, and we walked steadily up the sands, over the vermilion carpet of the tiny glade.

An involuntary shudder shook me from head to foot as we passed the giant puffball into which I had crunched and all but buried myself when first we had sought for water. And the feeling came strong upon me again that the bloated purple that covered the ground as far as the eye could see was watching us, creeping out to enclose us, and I came to fear a glance to our rear lest—I should find we were already cut off from the haven of the beach.

The huge gaunt stalks of the fungus soared again about us, and the sickening stench of the hotly palpitant life force of the stuff steamed in our nostrils once more.

Twice there came a sudden, shadowy movement over our heads,

and each time followed the drenching discharge of a suffocating cloud of brown spores.

But on we marched, Douglas and I, in the vain hope that before we succumbed we might find Captain Jim, and drag him, even if it be against his will, back to the clean chemistry of the waters of the blessed life-saving lagoon.

Chapter IX

HOW LONG we tramped through the silent fungus I do not know. Hours, I suppose, and not a second of the time were we free of the feeling that the stuff was watching our every move, waiting for us to get deeper within its hot heart, breathing upon us its dankly soporific breath, gathering to itself an overwhelming potential of life strength that this battle might be our last. Then, quite suddenly, and almost upon us, it seemed, came the wailing cry of the man-creatures.

Instantly a deep guttural curse.

We wheeled about, and there, squatting on his hams beneath a great fluted fan—specked with a thousand eyes of arsenic green on its leathery brown surface—was Captain Jim. In his hands he held a broken chunk of the stuff, and over this he peered with glaring eyes at our intrusion. Glared, then ducked his head into the horrid mass of the thing he held and ate. Raised his face again, chewing voraciously.

"Jim!"

The word burst from both of us.

With an oath he leaped to his feet.

"Get away! Get out!"

The voice was hardly his. The eyes were hardly his. The action was that of a maniac.

Before we could say a word, he had dropped to a squatting position again, and with his eyes gleaming balefully over his crust of fungus began to feed once more.

My partner's grip on my arm again.

I looked where he silently indicated, and started. But a step from where Captain Jim squatted lay one of the man-creatures, sprawled awkwardly, motionless, silent. And I knew in my heart that the thing was dead. Dead—and Captain Jim—

Doug whispered in my ear.

"Those cries just before the Kanaka boy rushed out to us—Had they—those things—attacked Jim?"

Hardly had he spoken when again came the sobbing wail, from close at hand. And just beyond Captain Jim we made out four of the grotesque fungoid figures. Their own coloring was that of the lower growth, and it was only their sudden movement that made us aware of their presence. They were not watching us, however. Their eyes, half hidden in the horrid nodular and befringed growth on their faces, were on Jim.

"They don't mean any harm to us or him, Doug!" I whispered. "They want to help. And yet—yet he's killed one of them, killed one."

"Come on!"

And we leaped upon Captain Jim.

He seemed to have gathered a triple strength from the food he had eaten. Down the three of us went, with the fungus stuff crunching beneath. I sensed a shadow pass over us again, and even as I fought awaited the downpour of brown spores. Then wondered that it did not come.

For a moment then my eyes were held by the glaring orbs of Captain Jim as he cursed and struggled to throw us off. Then a movement beyond us caught my glance again, and I saw that the four man-creatures had approached in a group, and were watching intently, hopping, in uncanny watching of the battle, from one foot to another. And above the cursing came the furry calls again and again.

"Fools!"

The word came in a veritable shriek from Jim.

"Fools! Eat the stuff, eat it. God! You've never eaten the like before. Stop this. Cut it. There, damn you, take that! Will you let me alone? Will you try to stop me from eating this—"

And his voice trailed off in a sobbing curse.

Doug, struggling with the madman's right arm as was I with his left, cried above the mêlée:

"The stuff's got him, too, Clarke. Fight for his life now. For his life and ours."

Ah, I cannot tell of the battle there in that ungodly place, with the feel of the utterly damned about us. The sense of a life force holding itself in until the most propitious moment for onslaught, watching us, menacing—The hellish coloring, the nightmare forms. The warm vapor, life-laden, sodden. And those four pitiful things that had been men, grouped there, hopping about in excitement as they watched, calling with their furry voices as we fought.

Twice my bare foot broke through the leathery surface of the purple bloat beneath us, and the tiny vermilion tongues of the palpitant fungoid beneath leaped forth, flickered, spread in a living mat under our heaving forms—warmly, dankly, horribly alive.

Again and again the shadows crossed and recrossed over us, as the giant umbrella heads of towering stools peered down, as though watching the progress of the struggle. And my fears ebbed and flowed each time, yet each time the shadows passed and the dread drench of spores did not come. What are the things holding off for, I wonder? Did they know? Were they certain now that their turbulent, though silent, life force would in the end have its way? Did they know that Captain Jim already had partially succumbed, and that if he defeated my partner and me, we, too, would become as those man-creatures peering at us there? Did this fungus life know? Could it reason?

Strange thoughts, you may say. Aye, they were strange thoughts. Yet

had you been there—Had you been struggling in that warmly steaming
hell, feeling with every resistant sense of you that that steaming hell
itself was alive with evil purpose and malignant desire—ah!

"*Eat!*" screamed Jim again. "Stop. Eat it yourselves. Then—damn
you!—then, you'll know. Then, *then,* you'll stop. *Eat*—"

"You fool!" stormed Douglas. "Be a man—a *man,* Captain Jim!"

The words seemed to penetrate some undrugged part of Jim's mind.
His eyes slowly changed. His struggles ceased. He lay back in our arms,
and gasped in great gulps of the warm, throbbing, sodden air. Then,
quickly, he brushed his eyes with his arm.

"Doug! Clarke! In Heaven's name—where—what—" He stared about
him. He covered his face with his hands, and sobbed. "Take me out,
take me out. Before it comes on me again. You don't know. You can't
know—"

We held him between us, and taking our bearing by the sun, dipped
in the west, started for the distant beach.

A furry cry came then from the pitiful man creatures, and I swung
about with a knotted fist ready to fend off their attack. But they took
the lead before us, and hopped on in their peculiar gait, turning now
and again to beckon us on.

And Captain Jim groaned aloud.

"One of them—back there—the Kanaka boy was eating the stuff.
Said it was good. So I tried it—was coming back to you. Forgot. I—
forgot. Then they came—and one of them—tried to stop me. The boy
was with them. They seemed to know—tried to stop me. I went mad.
The boy ran, screaming. I didn't think—I ate, *ate*—"

"We know, Jim," Doug whispered. "We know."

Then the sun was suddenly blotted out. The purple bloat beneath
our feet arose, furrowed, and broke. The stream of released living vapor
enveloped us. And with a silent, but palpitating rush, the living fungus
leaped again to hot, lustful life.

The weird hopeless call came distantly.

"*Keep together!*" cried Jim. "Fight! Fight! Fight!"

CHAPTER X

THE TRAILING tatters of gray stuff grew on the beach where we
flung them. Spread. Carpeted the coral sands with a shroud of
spongy fungus that filled the air with the warm stream of its diabolically
effervescent rush into life, and more life, and yet more. Reached out,
arose in great cloudlike masses until, overtopped with its own weight,
it fell with a sickening crunch and a puff of steaming spores that brought
forth new masses.

Shapes arose in it, nodular, spherical, huge soaring forms that burst
into great umbrella heads, matured, and drenched the lower masses of
stuff with the brown clouds of their fertilizing dust. Huge fan-shapes
of the hideous green-specked brown leaped up in our very path. The

gray underfoot took on the purplish tinge of the bloated quilting of the main forest.

Our lungs were filling. Great masses of the gray stuff choked my very throat, the warmth of its generation burning the membranes, the steamy mold of it dulling my senses.

But one thought—the lagoon—

We plunged in.

To the very water's edge that tremendous life energy beat its way— gray masses of it, huge stalks of leprous yellow, pale purples and fishbelly greens—slowly, as we fought there in the salt waters for life, changing to the deeper colors of the more hideous shade. Sickening miasmic steam spread low and seeking.

Spore heads burst—giant puffballs—great roached mounds—and all ebullient with the terrific life force of a malignant fungus that owed its supergenerative powers to the torrid tropical sun and the steaming tropical downpours. And perhaps to some strange seed fetched out of the depths of the sea from a prehistoric continent long submerged— brought to the fertilizing heat and moisture of the equatorial belt by the tiny coral insect that builds great lands. And here—rushing at us, great things peering out over the very water upon us, bursting in a brown stench of spores—then, one of them, overbalanced in horrid eagerness, fell into the sea.

With the speed of its growth it disintegrated, dissolved, disappeared. We gave a feeble shout. The salt lagoon was our refuge—in the water we were safe.

Then a sudden cry from the Kanaka boy, who had come to life again during our absence. And sailing in upon us, tacking to right, tacking to left but approaching with relentless certainty, was the great dorsal fin of a shark.

We stared at the baffled fungus, and out to that white and gray messenger of quick doom. If death were to come, the latter were the better way.

Came a cry from the beach, far down to our left—the shrill sobbing cry of the man creatures, of the things this teeming life had resolved to make of us. We had come out of the forest far to the southward of the vermilion-carpeted glade—the great mound of growth near which we had slept the night before was close to the western curve of the beach. The cry came from it, and high upon it we could make out the figures of the fungoid men.

"By Heaven, they're calling to us!" cried Doug. "They can't mean us any harm. They didn't harm you there in the island, Jim. They must mean something. That shark—jump!"

The great fin had veered from its angular course and the water seethed before it. Madly we tore into the fringing rot of the fungus and splashed through the lapping shallows down the beach. The force of the growing stuff seemed momentarily to have spent itself, and a clear sweep of the clean sands spread before us.

The man creatures leaped up and down in their excitement as we approached the great mound near the water's edge.

Once more they began to tear at the stuff on the lower surface and to beckon us to do the same.

And in sudden comprehension as I stared at the peculiar shape of the hill-like mass, I started to tear the stuff away myself. Then, though quivering with the thought of the thing, the terror of land and sea forced me, and I plunged my hand arm-length into the mass. Abruptly, not an elbow's depth beneath the crusted surface, it crashed against something hard. I gave a cry of excitement, and dashed to the lagoon. Coming back I showered a cupped handful of salt water against the hole I had made. Another and another, then finally, when the light of day penetrated, gave a whoop of half hysterical joy.

"*Wood!* It's wood, fellows, it's wood—a ship—a ship!"

With what cries then did Doug and Captain Jim and the Kanaka boy dash water upon the enshrouding fungus. And how the man creatures hopped awkwardly about, ever dodging the falling spray themselves, but ever tearing at other parts of the mound, disclosing more and more that what we had all at first taken for a huge mass of fungoid material was but a fungus hidden wreck.

Then came a curious call from Captain Jim, who had been working at the vessel's stern.

"Fellows! Look at this."

One glance at the exposed transom of the schooner, and we turned our eyes upon the man creatures hopping behind us.

"God pity them!" breathed Douglas Gordon. "Punishment they deserved, but never this."

The name of the wrecked schooner was still apparent, gleaming dirty white against the molded teak of the vessel's transom. It spelled the fate that had come to these unfortunate creatures, it spelled the end of our chase, it spelled too, hope that we might evade the horror that had come to these men who had stolen our great fire opal and fled before our vengeance in the schooner Black Moth.

Truly had their punishment been a dreadful one. Yet, truly, too, did they realize their own condition, and that that same condition would be ours did we dally overlong upon the Fungus Isle. They had seen us, they must have recognized us as men at least, even if their brains were too far gone to know us as the rightful owners of the treasure stone. And as best they could, though fearing our very touch, they had conveyed to us the information that in this molded mound lay our salvation, and our only one.

The moon rose, and still the things worked with us as we cleaned the wreck. And toward dawn, Captain Jim came upon the hatchway aft, and despite our remonstrances declared he was going down below decks.

Evidently during the storm the hatchway had been closed. It took our united effort to slide the door forward in its swollen grooves, but our hearts beat gladly again when we saw that the necessities imposed by the storm that had brought the Black Moth to the coral sands had also kept her cabin clear of the island's horrid growth.

The schooner was canted over on her side as though beached for a cleanup of her bottom, but we scrambled madly down the short ladder, slipping and falling over each other in our efforts each to be first to find the thing that had suddenly again become uppermost in our minds. Water, and food—of which we had had none for forty-eight hours and more—were things for the future. Fear of the fungus was gone—the planks were here about us wherewith to build a raft and sail for a cleaner, saner land. And a shark was naught but a fish in the sea.

But now—at last, with a whoop of joy, we came upon a small blackwood chest. Caught it up, bore it topside, set it down in the angle of deck and cabin bulkhead, opened it—and the slanting rays of the sun just peering over the eastern horizon, over the mad, soaring forms of the fungus forest, were broken into the thousand and one gleaming flames of the great block of fire opal.

Water beakers we discovered in the hold, and tinned food. Sparingly we ate, with the hopeless, but nodding things that had been the rapers of our treasure, silently watching. We called them to us. But they shook their heads quickly, and with their peculiar hopping movement, turned as one, and disappeared up the vermilion-carpeted trail.

And Captain Jim, turning to us, told us why they would never again come out.

"I ate some of the fan stuff," he said. "In the first days here they must have sampled it, too, perhaps in curiosity. You saw how the stuff affected me—drugged, gentle swaying joy—bliss beyond words; more, and more, and more—they *cannot* leave. They lost all that made them man, they took on the life of the fungus—and God help them, they became half fungoid themselves. Yet—"

And Douglas Gordon finished for him.

"Yet they knew somehow what their fate must be, and ours. And somehow, heaven alone knows, they knew they must warn us. Whatever they were, and whatever they have become, there still is something in them that makes them men."

I stared from the growing warmth of our returned mass of opal up the vermilion-carpeted trail, at the silently waiting forms of poison color, at the gray mass of stuff that had pursued us in our last flight to the cleansing water of the lagoon—and in my mind I saw with full clarity the fate that, but for them, must also have been ours. And I dropped my head.

"God help them!" I muttered as had Doug and Captain Jim. "God help them. And may they soon pass to a cleaner, sweeter life than that of Fungus Isle."

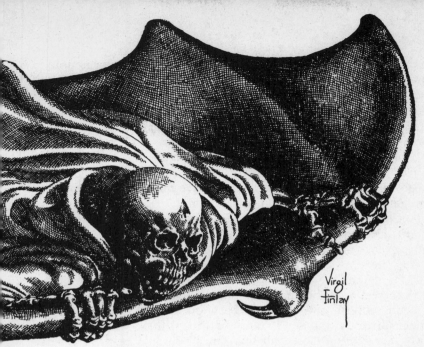

John Ovington Returns

MAX BRAND

Before he became one of the best-known writers of western fiction and created the character of Dr. Kildare, Max Brand (one of several aliases for Frederick Faust) wrote a number of fantasy stories for the Munsey pulps. Under the pseudonym of George Challis, he contributed the scientific romance The Smoking Land, *and under the Max Brand pen name he wrote four shorter fantasies, the best-known of which is "That Receding Brow." Like Brand's other* Famous Fantastic Mysteries *reprint, "The Lost Garden," "John Ovington Returns" deals with reincarnation, one of the most popular fantasy themes of the early twentieth century.*

CHAPTER I

THE OLD servant stopped and faced him. The light from the candle he carried flickered across his bald head as he nodded wonderingly, and John Ovington hardly repressed a smile.

"You are quite sure you were never in the house before?" asked Hillton.

"No," said Ovington, "I was never here before, but somehow it seems to me that a big amber-colored vase with black figures tracing down the sides should stand by that window. It's just a fancy, but rather unusual in its clearness."

"The Ovingtons are an unusual family, sir," said Hillton, and he raised his candle so that its light fell more fully on the sternly graven

125

face of his new master. After his moment's scrutiny he shook his head
as one who gives up a problem.

"A vase like the one you speak of stood there ever since the house
was built, but last week Mrs. Worth broke it while she was cleaning
the room. Every week I have the rooms cleaned, sir, but for the past
year they have never been used, none except the kitchen and Mr.
Ovington's bedroom where he lay sick for so long."

"And died?" said Ovington.

"And died, sir. He wouldn't trust any one save me. I wrote the letter
which brought you here, and I signed it for him."

"I shall never forget that letter," said Ovington. "And that is the
room where I sleep now?"

"The master has always slept in that room since the family came
here to live," he answered. "Now I think you have seen the whole
house, Mr. Ovington."

"But isn't there a room behind those folding doors?" asked Ovington.

"That is the library, and it hasn't been opened these past fifteen
years. Fifteen dreary years, sir. It must be fearful thick with dust."

"And why has it been closed all this time?"

"That was the time when young Master Ovington died, and since
then the master couldn't bear to go into that room. For the family
pictures hang there, and he couldn't stand to look on them, he having
lost his heir. The family name ended with him, as he thought. It was
only through the lawyers that we traced the line to you, sir, through
your great-grandfather, John Ovington, the man who disappeared."

"So I understand," said Ovington. "But let's have a look at the
room."

Hillton drew in his wrinkled lips anxiously.

"Tonight, sir?"

"Why not?"

"It's a fearsome place to go into at night with all the great, stern
old Ovingtons painted and hanging on the wall. It's most like a
graveyard, sir, with the ghosts up and sitting on their tombs. I'm sure
you will not like it to be there at night, Mr. Ovington."

"Tut!" smiled Ovington, and he laid a reassuring hand on the old
man's shoulder. "We'll risk the dust and the family pictures."

It was only after much reluctant fumbling and many sidewise glances
as if in hope that Ovington's resolution would die away that Hillton
finally produced the key. The lock had set so fast that it required a
great effort for Ovington to send it gritting back. He swung the door
wide and stepped into the high, dark room. The wavering of the light
behind him made him turn to Hillton, who stood outside the door,
the candle fairly shaking in his hand.

"Come, come!" laughed Ovington. "After all, it's only a room with
nothing more dangerous in it than shadows."

"No, sir," said Hillton, "I'm not afraid. But it's a strange house and
a strange people."

He entered slowly, the candle held high above his head, and he peered about at every step.

Into the highest shadows of the raftered ceiling the wavering candle-light hardly reached, but it shone on the ponderous table, thickly dusted, and into the black throat of the fireplace, and picked out the long row of portraits receding dimly on either side of the room. Among them were a few dressed in the ruffs of the Tudor period. Others appeared in somber Puritan gray, straight faces under tall hats. Among these one caught Ovington's eye. He took the candle from Hillton and held it close to the portrait.

He almost thought for a moment that he was dressed for a fancy ball and stood before a mirror, for it was his own face which returned his gaze with a half scowl and a half sneer, the same strong nose, thin cheeks, and unflinching eyes. He blinded himself with his hand and looked again, but the resemblance persisted. He felt that his forehead had grown very cold.

"And who is this, Hillton?" he asked, wondering if the servant would notice the resemblance.

"That is your great-grandfather, whose name was John Ovington, like your name," said Hillton, forgetting his uneasiness as he talked. "He was the strangest of all the Ovingtons, for he rode away one day and never came back, and that is the last people ever heard of him. And all that was many and many years ago. So long that my father could not remember."

He led the way to the window and drew aside the curtain, loosing a cloud of choking dust. Outside the moon glimmered on the garden terraces, which stepped down to a tree-covered hollow, but the other side of the valley rose dark and steep, with a great square housing topping it.

"That is the Jervan house," said Hillton, and his pointing hand trembled in the moonlight. "That is the house where Beatrice Jervan lived, who was the sweetheart of our John Ovington in those old days, but John Ovington went across the seas and fought in France. So when he came back Beatrice Jervan loved him no longer, and they say that he would have forced her to marry him, for he was a stark fierce man; but she fled away in the night with another man. And John Ovington waited for them at a forking of the Newbury Road as they fled on their horses. He stopped them and would have made them turn back, but the man drew a horse-pistol and shot him through the shoulder and rode on with Beatrice Jervan, and God knows what became of them both. We only know that a granddaughter of that couple married back into the Jervan family, and now there is a Beatrice Jervan over there again in that house; and over here"—he laughed tremulously in the moonlight—"is a John Ovington again.

"Well, when the man rode on with Beatrice that other John Ovington rose up from the road where he had fallen and called after them: 'I have failed this time, but I shall not fail twice. I shall come again. I shall wait for you in this place, Beatrice Jervan, and carry you away with me forever.'

"But that he never did, for shortly afterward he went and took ship in Boston Harbor and went across the sea to other countries. And he was your great-grandfather. All that he left was this picture on the wall and a little cedar chest of his papers which sits on that shelf next to the brass-bound Bible. He was the last of the old family, for after him his cousin took the name and the inheritance."

Through a long moment Ovington stood staring at the opposite house.

"I am going to stay here and read some of those papers," said he at last, "so you can leave the candle, Hillton."

"Will you sit here all alone, sir, on your first night?"

He folded his hands in his anxiety, and when Ovington nodded he turned and went falteringly from the room, shaking his head solemnly as he walked.

CHAPTER II

ON TOP of the papers in the small chest lay a miniature of a girl. It had evidently at one time been a bust painted by an artist of some skill, but the lower part of the picture was rubbed and faded beyond recognition of any form. Only the face remained clear. The hair drew back from the forehead in the severe lines which pleased those grim old New Englanders, and the eyes drooped demurely downward, but no moral preceptor could lessen the curve and the lure of the red lips. It seemed to Ovington that the eyes might at any moment flash up and yield him unknown depths of light and mockery.

He dropped the miniature to his knee and sat for a long time looking straight before him. When he had rallied his thoughts he commenced to turn over the papers. They were all letters written in a woman's hand, and despite the yellowing of time and the fading of the ink, he could make out the words with little effort. Arranged in the order of their receipt the letters told their own story of the love between Beatrice Jervan and John Ovington.

There was a long group covering the period of the wooing, and then came the time when Ovington decided to go to the war, and her letter:

I could not say it last night. I needed quiet so that I could think it all out clearly, and now I know what I wanted to say. You must not go to the war, John dear.

I know that glory is a wonderful thing, but a good wife is a wonderful thing, too, John, and would you care to win glory and lose a wife? Not that I am sure you would lose me; but I love happiness, dear, and I am afraid of pain; and if you were thousands and thousands of miles away, what would I have to remember you by? It is so hard to remember a man by his silences, John!

Dear, will you try to please me in this? And then I will try to please you all the days of my life. But the sea is so broad, and the French shoot so straight — and I do so love laughter, John! Come to me tonight, and I know I can change your mind.

He rose and walked with the candle until he faced the picture of John Ovington. Yes, that was the face of a man able to defy the charm of sudden glances and slow smiles. He went back to the letters. They diminished rapidly in length, and then came this:

If you want me, you must come and fight for me, Captain John Ovington. There may be dreadful fighting on the plains of France, but I think you will find enough war here on the hills of Connecticut. He has yellow, curling hair, John, and wide, blue eyes, and a gentle voice and a ringing laugh, and he's as much of a man as you are, almost. If you want me, you must come for me. It may be too late. I can't tell.

Then came a short note:

You need not come. It is too late!

But John Ovington had decided to come back and try, and after his return were two letters, the last:

If you will not come to see me, John Ovington, I shall come to see you; though if I do that I know that mother will faint.

I think I have never seen so grave a man as the John Ovington I met on the bridge the other day. Have you truly forgotten me? All grave men are not silent, John Ovington. I have a plan to discover if you can really smile.

I will be by the fountain in the garden tonight if it is not too cold.

And John Ovington had evidently changed his mind that night and gone to the garden and made desperate love, hoping against hope, for the last letter said:

Vincent Colvin has been with me all this morning. I am going to ride away with him tonight. I have not forgotten, but I promised myself to him long ago, and now I shall keep the promise. My father objects, so we are going to go out for a ride from which we shall never come back, and we will take the Newbury Road. Oh, my dear, it breaks my heart to ride out of your life. It has all been so strange, so maddeningly dear and painful. Must this be good-by?

He read no more that night, but he sat a long time at the window watching the night mist creep up the valley, tangling among the trees, and at last setting a gray veil across the window pane.

The next morning the challenge of the keen October air drew him out into the open. In the stables he found a great black charger and had him saddled. The groom eyed him dubiously as he lengthened his stirrups to suit his western fashion of riding, but when he swung into the saddle and started down the path with his broad hat curling up in front to the wind and his cloak fluttering behind him, while his powerful pull on the reins held down the horse to an uneasy prance, the groom grinned with open admiration.

"I reckon an Ovington," he said, "is always an Ovington."

But as he took the road down the valley Ovington could not forget the adventure of the previous evening, for the Connecticut hills rolled up on either side, a remembered beauty of yellowing browns, gold, and crimson running riotously together, and all the trees still shining with the touch of the night mist. And the great lift and sway of the gallop set his heart singing in unison with the hoof-beats. He could not tell how far he had ridden, for every bend invited him on and on down flaming vistas.

He passed from the main road on to a narrow path which, after a quarter of a mile, surged to the left, and around a quick turn he thundered across a stream on a narrow foot-bridge, a frail structure which tottered and shook under him. At the same time he heard the clatter of hoofs coming toward him down the same path and in a moment a racing brown horse flashed about the curve and dashed onto the bridge.

It was far too narrow for two horses to edge by each other. He brought his mount to a rearing stop.

When he looked again the brown horse stood head to head with his black, and he was face to face with the loveliest girl he had ever seen, but a remembered beauty—yes, the face of the miniature, a spray of autumn leaves at her breast stirring as she panted.

"This is a real escape, isn't it?" she cried, and her voice carried more mirth than fear.

"I guess it's an escape," he said quietly, after another moment of staring. "Here, there is not room for two to pass. I'll back off the bridge."

But when he drew on the reins the black horse reared straight up, and when he came down stiff-legged the little bridge wavered and groaned.

"Don't do that!" she cried, truly frightened by this time. "I'll back off."

She moved her horse back cautiously, step and step, and he followed, but when they came onto the path again he still blocked the way and the puzzled searching of the eyes made her flush slightly.

"Your name is Beatrice Jervan," he stated.

"Yes," she said.

"And mine is John Ovington."

She clapped her hands in delighted discovery.

"Are you really the new John Ovington? Let's shake hands and be friends. We're neighbors, you know."

He rode beside her and took her hand. He knew that she was saying: "But you are a stranger here. How did you know my name?"

He smiled vaguely on her. "Can you tell me how old this bridge is?"

"Yes," she said, wondering. "It is said to be a hundred and fifty years old. But I doubt it."

"Well," he said, "I feel as if I had known you for one hundred and fifty years."

"With that soft hat and that riding-cloak," she laughed, "you look as if you might be a bandit of that period."

"With that smile," he said, "you look as if you might be a woman of almost any period. May I ride with you?" he continued. "If I may I'll try not to say any more foolish things like that last one."

"It doesn't matter," she said; "it's the October air that makes one happy without knowing just why. Of course you may ride with me if you care to."

They made back across the bridge again and up onto the road. As they broke into a canter he fell back a little to watch the lilt of her perfect horsemanship.

"If you ride so far back I can't talk to you," she complained, "and then you'll think I'm stupid."

"You don't have to talk," he said. "I'm quite perfectly entertained, and besides—"

But she spurred her horse to a wild gallop and the rest of his sentence was jolted from his mind as he pursued. The long stride of the black brought him beside her in a few seconds.

"You ride well," he shouted as he reined in to her pace, "but you see you can't escape me."

She slowed down rather sullenly.

"I have never been passed before on these roads," she said.

"Not passed," he corrected; "merely caught."

She accepted the comment with a cold glance. He rode a little behind her, perfectly happy and perfectly silent. A keen wind rose and whirled down the valley to meet them. Sometimes the force of the gust seemed to sway her back in her saddle. From stirrup to head she gave the graceful lines to the sway and lunge of the gallop, and Ovington ground his teeth to keep from singing aloud. It seemed hardly a moment before she checked her horse.

"Our ways part here," she said, then smiling: "Are you always silent, Mr. Ovington?"

He raised his hat without replying, wheeled, and spurred up the hill, and she remained for a breathing space watching the play of his broad shoulders as he rode.

CHAPTER III

THROUGH THE next ten days he wandered about the place uneasily. He could hardly define his own mood. He felt vaguely that he was waiting, but he had not the slightest idea for what. But on the tenth day a letter came and he knew. He recognized the handwriting, but before he dared to tear it open he went first to the little cedar chest and compared the two scripts.

They were identical.

The letter began without prelude just as that other letter came to that other John Ovington a hundred and fifty years before:

> If you will not come to see me, John Ovington, I shall come to see you.

A red mist came before him. He felt himself trembling like a child, and it was some time before he could resume the reading. Without a single variation the letter repeated the time-yellowed manuscript of the cedar chest.

> I think I have never seen so grave a man. All grave men are not silent, John Ovington. I have a plan to discover if you can really smile. I will be in the garden tonight if it is not too 'cold.

"I will not go," he said aloud, as if to convince himself against himself. "I will not let this damned riddle ruin me as it ruined a John Ovington four generations before me."

He commenced to pace up and down the room. According to the old story he should go to that garden tonight and make desperate love to her. And according to that story he was lost in the end, fate played against him.

Ovington tried to rally his reason. He tried to convince himself that this was all a weird dream, but the two letters lay convincingly side by side. Had the spirit of the old John Ovington truly come back to try the old task again? Would there be for him the same agony of heart and mind? He covered his face with his hands and groaned aloud, for he saw again the spray of autumn leaves stirring at her breast.

After supper he went into the library to fight out the night there, but the old portraits leered down at him, the little cedar chest loomed like a silent oracle of sorrow. He rose at last and went out to pace the terraces of the garden.

His foot sounded hollowly over the little bridge across the river, but he did not notice it. Unconsciously he wandered up the path on the other side of the valley, through the opening of the hedge of evergreen, and onto the velvet lawns of the Jervan estate.

A light laugh only a few feet away startled him. He found that he stood near a circle of shrubbery, in the center of which a fountain splashed and showered, and through the light falling of the spray he heard the thrilling velvet of Beatrice Jervan's voice:

"Go away now, Vincent. I so want to be alone."

And a pleasant voice answered:

"Have I wearied you, dear?"

"No," she answered, "but I am tired of saying pretty things and hearing them, just for a little while. I am hungry for the quiet and the chill of this air. Please go back to the house and tell them that I am taking a walk through the garden. They will understand."

"And I shall see you later? And you are not cold?"

"You will see me later. I am not the least cold."

"Au revoir a little while. Dear, I am full of strange thoughts to-night. It is almost as if you were slipping away from me. I have reached out to you a hundred times, and my heart has closed on nothing. What does it mean?"

"Fantasy!" she said, and as she laughed the sound broke and ran trilling down like the musical chuckle of a bird. "Adieu. You need not fear. I shall stay true to our plan. Adieu."

Ovington heard the man's lightly treading step pass away over the lawn, the shrubbery brushed against him noisily, and then the silence slipped back over the place and the faintly moving air shook the fountain into light showerings of spray, felt rather than heard, like the pulse of a heart. And a great yellow moon floated up through the branches of the eastern trees, took the changing tracery of the black limbs, and now drifted abroad into the pathless heaven, so her light, peering aslant over the shrubbery, looked on the silver nodding head of the fountain.

And deeper and deeper slanted the light until he saw it glimmer like a dark star in the hair of Beatrice.

She raised her head up to meet that light. It fell upon her face like a sculptured smile, and Ovington stood breathless watching, waiting, with a musical dread in his heart. Then the dark fur which clung against her throat shifted and the shadow of the lifted eyes changed. He stepped into the circle of the shrubbery and stood before her, and she, looking up, saw the black outline of his head against the rolling moon.

"You are for all the world like a man come down from the moon," she said, and her voice was so low that she seemed to be talking to herself rather than to him.

He stood for a long moment before he could speak.

"And who," he asked, "is dear Vincent?"

"Vincent is a very nice boy," she answered, "who has yellow curling hair and wide blue eyes and is as much of a man as you are, John Ovington."

He dropped into the stone seat beside her and leaned forward, his hands clasped and his eyes on the ground. He was so perilously near her that she could make out the tensed lips, the frowning forehead of his profile, but the wide brim of his hat put all the rest of his face in shadow. She watched his strongly interlaced fingers.

"So you are a silent man, John Ovington?"

"I am thinking very hard," he answered.

"Yes, you are troubled about something?" He felt the perfume and the touch of her breath as she leaned swiftly toward him. And as she leaned she saw the interlacing fingers grind together. A tremor shook her that was half fear and half delight.

"I suppose," he began at last, "that you have watched the sun glinting in Vincent's yellow hair?"

"Of course," she said.

"And your fingers have touched it where the sun has fallen?"

"That," she said, "is a secret."

"I am quite sure I have no use for Vincent," he said.

In the pause the wind went rushing past them and ran on through the far-off tree-tops, whispering and muttering.

"And I suppose," he went on, "that you could not begin to count the moments you have spent looking into Vincent's wide, blue eyes?"

"I am sure that would be hard to reckon," she said gravely.

"I think I could hate Vincent," he mused. "Do you like him a great deal?"

"I'm sure I dislike confessionals."

"It is rather hard," he said at last.

"What is hard?"

"To play against fate, and to come into the play with the stage set against me."

"I don't understand!"

But watching those gripping fingers she did understand, and the shaking of the fountain counted out the waiting seconds until he spoke again.

"It would have been so easy in any other setting," he said. "For instance I might have seen you first at a tea-table, saying the silly things that go with tea."

"I hate tea," she said feverently.

"Or I might have seen you at the end of a long ride instead of the beginning. I might have seen you with your hair tumbling roughly and your hat askew, and your figure slumping wearily at every stride of the horse. You would not have mattered then, very much."

She looked up to the moon, but it seemed too bright, too searching, now, and she dropped her eyes hastily back to his hands.

"But even as it was," he said, "I could have stood out against you if it had not been for the spray of autumn leaves at your breast." He nodded solemnly. "That was what did the harm. It was hardly fair, do you think?"

"They were only autumn leaves," she said, "and anyway I don't understand why you are so solemn."

"That is fibbing," he remarked unemotionally, "and it is not even a white fib. You know perfectly well that the stage was set, and that I had not a chance when I came blundering on to the boards, a mere supernumerary in the last act. But, knowing all this, why did you send me the note? I don't like bear-baiting when I am the bear."

She looked away from him suddenly into the shadows of the shrubbery. Then, almost desperately:

"Is this mere neighborliness, John Ovington? Can a man meet a girl once and then talk as you are talking?"

"Does it seem impossible to you, Beatrice?" he muttered. "Does it really seem so strange to you? Tell me frankly."

"I don't know," her lips framed, but without sound.

"Your face is so in the shadow," she said in a very low voice, "that I cannot tell whether or not you are smiling to yourself."

"I don't dare to look up to you for fear that you would understand too clearly. But tell me truly, why did you write that note?"

"I cannot tell. I sat down before a piece of paper and the words came of themselves. I don't know what I wrote. I am sorry if I hurt you."

"And I cannot tell why I came here tonight," he answered, "for I determined to stay away, but my steps guided themselves. Here I am. It is not you or I who speak here tonight, Beatrice, but old forces greater than we. We are puppets in the game. We are the guests of chance. Do you not feel it?"

"I cannot say," she said, "but everything seems changed. It is as if I knew you for a long time. When you speak I remember your words from long ago. And my heart is cold and strange. And—and—I wish you would go, John Ovington. I am afraid of you."

"I cannot go yet," he answered bitterly, "for I sit here and see as plainly as if I were looking at you, the stir of your breast, and the moonlight white and cold along your throat, and the unconscious smiling of your lips, and the unsearchable shadows of your eyes."

He turned to her fiercely and his left hand gripped the back of the stone seat as he leaned over her.

"Can't you make them clear and plain and readable? Can't you make me feel that I have no hope? That you are completely lost to me? That I have no share in your soul? Why do you torment me with this damnable ghost of hope, Beatrice?"

She made no answer to the compelling whisper, but through a long moment she met his eyes and into the silence once more the shaking of the fountain beat like a pulse. Then she shrank a little away with a musical tremor of sound, and her hand fell palm up across her eyes. He drew her to him, rich with the soft warmth of her body.

His lips touched her throat. A sob formed there. He kissed the tremulous hollow of her hand. At once it fell away helplessly. He crushed the parted lips. At once her breath came brokenly and moaning to his ear, and while the thunder of his heart shook both their spirits, she whispered:

"God help me! God help me!"

Thereat he rose suddenly and turned away with bowed head, for at the moan of her voice the thought of the yellow, rustling papers of the cedar box came upon him like a drift of the last leaves of dead autumn. Then he knew that she was by his side.

"It is not ended yet," she was saying. "If we are the guests of chance now, oh, be strong and become the master of it all! Find out the way. There is always one road home. John, I trust in you."

When he was able to raise his head she was gone, and a mist that drew across the moon made all the play gray and cold.

He reached his house again and stood a long time before the picture of John Ovington until it seemed that the hard half sneer of the pictured smile was meant for him, and when he slept that night the mockery of the smile followed him.

CHAPTER IV

BUT WHEN he rose the next morning and looked over the shimmer of color running on the hills, a new hope swelled in him and a confidence of power. But as the day drew on the thought of the papers in the cedar box depressed him.

In the middle of the afternoon Hillton brought him a letter. Once more he knew the contents before he broke the seal, but as he read the expected words a sick feeling of suspense came over him.

Vincent Colvin has been with me all this morning. I am going to ride away with him tonight. I have not forgotten, but I promised myself to him long ago, and now I shall keep the promise. My father objects, so we are going out for a ride from which we shall never come back. We will take the Newbury Road. Oh, my dear, it breaks my heart to ride out of your life! It has all been so strange, so maddingly dear and painful. Must this be good-by?

After that he rode the black horse down the Newbury Road.

"And John Ovington waited for them at a forking of the Newbury Road."

He would have ridden out and found some other waiting-place as he remembered, but a grim determination came up in him and he sat his horse motionless. He remained there for perhaps an hour. The moon came up and ran white along the road. Then a clatter of hoofs beat far away.

Colvin came first as they rounded the last run, a large man riding strongly on a gray horse. They were a hundred yards away when Ovington rode out from beneath the tree, his hand raised.

Colvin brought his horse to a stop on grinding hoofs.

"Who the devil are you, sir?" he shouted. "What do you mean by stopping me?"

"I haven't the least wish to stop you," said Ovington calmly, "but I intend to stop Beatrice Jervan tonight. As for you, you may ride to hell, for all of me."

He could see Colvin's face set with fury as he shouted:

"What authority have you for this?"

"The authority of good sense," smiled Ovington, "which says that it is both too late and far too cold for a girl to be out riding."

"Damn your impertinence," cried Colvin. "Get out of the road or I'll ride you down like a dog!"

"Ah," said Ovington, "you talk well, Colvin. But there is an older score to settle between us than you dream of. You must ride this way alone tonight."

"You fool," shouted Colvin, "if you must have it, take it!"

As he spoke a revolver flashed in his hand, but as it dropped to the level Ovington spurred his black suddenly forward.

With his left hand he struck up Colvin's arm, and the revolver roared past his ear. With his right arm he seized Colvin about the waist and drew him bodily from the saddle.

As he swayed a moment struggling on the saddle-bow, Ovington swung his right hand free and struck. The blow fell behind Colvin's ear and he collapsed without a sound.

Ovington flung his limp body to the ground.

"You have killed him!" whispered Beatrice. "Flee! Flee!"

"He is merely stunned," said Ovington. "Turn your horse. We ride another way this night."

She reined her horse away and raised her riding-crop.

"Keep away," she cried in a choked voice. "I am afraid! Keep away. He has my promise—I shall never leave him!"

He laughed short and hard.

"Promise?" he said. "Do you think that words will stop me tonight after I have conquered destiny at last? Do you dream that words will stop me? Then one way with both!"

As he spoke he rode upon her. The riding-crop fell upon his shoulder, but he did not notice it. He swept her from the saddle into his arms and crushed the parted lips fiercely against his own.

"Dearest," he said, "after four generations of waiting, I have returned for you and won you away from fate."

Suddenly her straining body gave to him; he heard a murmuring and changed voice in his ear:

"Ride! Ride! He is stirring on the road. He is awakening!"

And as they spurred up the road he turned his head and saw the gray horse and the brown fleeing side by side far away with loose shaken bridle-reins and empty saddles.

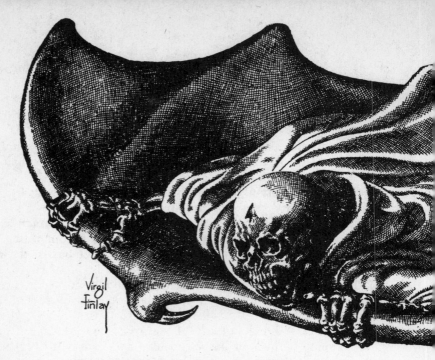

Virgil Finlay

Fishhead

IRVIN S. COBB

Like E. F. Benson, Jerome K. Jerome, and several other authors represented in this book, Irvin S. Cobb was best known in his time as a humorist. So it is ironic that Cobb is remembered almost exclusively today for the horrifying "Fishhead," a story considered so controversial for its time— as much for its racial content as its gruesome climax—that it was rejected by a number of magazines. "Fishhead" appeared in a 1913 issue of Munsey's The Cavalier, *and H. P. Lovecraft, who was notoriously finicky in his tastes, singled it out as a personal favorite in his groundbreaking* Supernatural Horror in Literature.

IT GOES past the powers of my pen to try to describe Reelfoot Lake for you so that you, reading this, will get the picture of it in your mind as I have it in mine.

For Reelfoot Lake is like no other lake that I know anything about. It is an after-thought of Creation.

The rest of this continent was made and had dried in the sun for thousands of years—millions of years, for all I know—before Reelfoot came to be. It's the newest big thing in nature on this hemisphere, probably, for it was formed by the great earthquake of 1811.

That earthquake of 1811 surely altered the face of the earth on the then far frontier of this country.

It changed the course of rivers, it converted hills into what are now the sunk lands of three states, and it turned the solid ground to jelly and made it roll in waves like the sea.

And in the midst of the retching of the land and the vomiting of the waters it depressed to varying depths a section of the earth crust sixty miles long, taking it down—trees, hills, hollows, and all; and a crack broke through to the Mississippi River so that for three days the river ran up stream, filling the hole.

The result was the largest lake south of the Ohio, lying mostly in Tennessee, but extending up across what is now the Kentucky line, and taking its name from a fancied resemblance in its outline to the splay, reeled foot of a cornfield negro. Niggerwool Swamp, not so far away, may have got its name from the same man who christened Reelfoot; at least so it sounds.

Reelfoot is, and has always been, a lake of mystery.

In places it is bottomless. Other places the skeletons of the cypress-trees that went down when the earth sank, still stand upright so that if the sun shines from the right quarter, and the water is less muddy than common, a man, peering face downward into its depths, sees, or thinks he sees, down below him the bare top-limbs upstretching like drowned men's fingers, all coated with the mud of years and bandaged with pennons of the green lake slime.

In still other places the lake is shallow for long stretches, no deeper than breast high to a man, but dangerous because of the weed growths and the sunken drifts which entangle a swimmer's limbs. Its banks are mainly mud, its waters are muddied, too, being a rich coffee color in the spring and a copperish yellow in the summer, and the trees along its shore are mud colored clear up their lower limbs after the spring floods, when the dried sediment covers their trunks with a thick, scrofulous-looking coat.

There are stretches of unbroken woodland around it, and slashes where the cypress knees rise countlessly like headstones and footstones for the dead snags that rot in the soft ooze.

There are deadenings with the lowland corn growing high and rank below and the bleached, fire-blackened girdled trees rising above, barren of leaf and limb.

There are long, dismal flats where in the spring the clotted frog-spawn cling like patches of white mucus among the weed-stalks, and at night the turtles crawl out to lay clutches of perfectly round, white eggs with tough, rubbery shells in the sand.

There are bayous leading off to nowhere, and sloughs that wind aimlessly, like great, blind worms, to finally join the big river that rolls its semi-liquid torrents a few miles to the westward.

So Reelfoot lies there, flat in the bottoms, freezing lightly in the winter, steaming torridly in the summer, swollen in the spring when the woods have turned a vivid green and the buffalo-gnats by the million and the billion fill the flooded hollows with their pestilential buzzing, and in the fall, ringed about gloriously with all the colors which the first frost brings—gold of hickory, yellow-russet of sycamore, red of dogwood and ash, and purple-black of sweet-gum.

But the Reelfoot country has its uses. It is the best game and fish country, natural or artificial, that is left in the South today.

In their appointed seasons the duck and the geese flock in, and even semi-tropical birds, like the brown pelican and the Florida snake-bird, have been known to come there to nest.

Pigs, gone back to wildness, range the ridges, each razor-backed drove captained by a gaunt, savage, slab-sided old boar. By night the bullfrogs, inconceivably big and tremendously vocal, bellow under the banks.

It is a wonderful place for fish—bass and crappie, and perch, and the snouted buffalo fish.

How these edible sorts live to spawn, and how their spawn in turn live to spawn again is a marvel, seeing how many of the big fish-eating cannibal-fish there are in Reelfoot.

Here, bigger than anywhere else, you find the garfish, all bones and appetite and horny plates, with a snout like an alligator, the nearest link, naturalists say, between the animal life of today and the animal life of the Reptilian Period.

The shovel-nose cat, really a deformed kind of fresh-water sturgeon, with a great fan-shaped membranous plate jutting out from his nose like a bowsprit, jumps all day in the quiet places with mighty splashing sounds, as though a horse had fallen into the water.

On every stranded log the huge snapping turtles lie on sunny days in groups of four and six, baking their shells black in the sun, with their little snaky heads raised watchfully, ready to slip noiselessly off at the first sound of oars grating in the row-locks. But the biggest of them all are the catfish!

These are monstrous creatures, these catfish of Reelfoot—scaleless, slick things, with corpsy, dead eyes and poisonous fins, like javelins, and huge whiskers dangling from the sides of their cavernous heads.

Six and seven feet long they grow to be, and weigh 200 pounds or more, and they have mouths wide enough to take in a man's foot or a man's fist, and strong enough to break any hook save the strongest, and greedy enough to eat anything, living or dead or putrid, that the horny jaws can master.

Oh, but they are wicked things, and they tell wicked tales of them down there. They call them man-eaters, and compare them, in certain of their habits, to sharks.

Fishhead was of a piece with this setting.

He fitted into it as an acorn fits its cup. All his life he had lived on Reelfoot, always in the one place, at the mouth of a certain slough.

He had been born there, of a negro father and a half-breed Indian mother, both of them now dead, and the story was that before his birth his mother was frightened by one of the big fish, so that the child came into the world most hideously marked.

Anyhow, Fishhead was a human monstrosity, the veritable embodiment of nightmare!

He had the body of a man—a short, stocky, sinewy body—but his face was as near to being the face of a great fish as any face could be and yet retain some trace of human aspect.

His skull sloped back so abruptly that he could hardly be said to have a forehead at all; his chin slanted off right into nothing. His eyes were small and round with shallow, glazed, pale-yellow pupils, and they were set wide apart in his head, and they were unwinking and staring, like a fish's eyes.

His nose was no more than a pair of tiny slits in the middle of the yellow mask. His mouth was the worst of all. It was the awful mouth of a catfish, lipless and almost inconceivably wide, stretching from side to side.

Also when Fishhead became a man grown his likeness to a fish increased, for the hair upon his face grew out into two tightly kinked slender pendants that drooped down either side of the mouth like the beards of a fish!

If he had any other name than Fishhead, none excepting he knew it. As Fishhead he was known, and as Fishhead he answered. Because he knew the waters and the woods of Reelfoot better than any other man there, he was valued as a guide by the city men who came every year to hunt or fish; but there were few such jobs that Fishhead would take.

Mainly he kept to himself, tending his corn patch, netting the lake, trapping a little, and in season pot hunting for the city markets. His neighbors, ague-bitten whites and malaria-proof negroes alike, left him to himself.

Indeed, for the most part they had a superstitious fear of him. So he lived alone, with no kith nor kin, nor even a friend, shunning his kind and shunned by them.

His cabin stood just below the State line, where Mud Slough runs into the lake. It was a shack of logs, the only human habitation for four miles up or down.

Behind it the thick timber came shouldering right up to the edge of Fishhead's small truck patch, enclosing it in thick shade except when the sun stood just overhead.

He cooked his food in a primitive fashion, outdoors, over a hole in the soggy earth or upon the rusted red ruin of an old cookstove, and he drank the saffron water of the lake out of a dipper made of a gourd, faring and fending for himself, a master hand at skiff and net, competent with duck gun and fishspear, yet a creature of affliction and loneliness, part savage, almost amphibious, set apart from his fellows, silent and suspicious.

In front of his cabin jutted out a long fallen cottonwood trunk, lying half in and half out of the water, its top side burnt by the sun and worn by the friction of Fishhead's bare feet until it showed countless patterns of tiny scrolled lines, its underside black and rotted, and lapped at unceasingly by little waves like tiny licking tongues.

Its farther end reached deep water. And it was a part of Fishhead, for no matter how far his fishing and trapping might take him in the daytime, sunset would find him back there, his boat drawn up on the bank, and he on the other end of this log.

From a distance men had seen him there many times, sometimes squatted motionless as the big turtles that would crawl upon its dipping tip in his absence, sometimes erect and motionless like a creek crane, his misshapen yellow form outlined against the yellow sun, the yellow water, the yellow banks—all of them yellow together.

If the Reelfooters shunned Fishhead by day they feared him by night and avoided him as a plague, dreading even the chance of a casual meeting. For there were ugly stories about Fishhead—stories which all the negroes and some of the whites believed.

They said that a cry which had been heard just before dusk and just after, skittering across the darkened waters, was his calling cry to the big cats, and at his bidding they came trooping in, and that in their company he swam in the lake on moonlight nights, sporting with them, diving with them, even feeding with them on what manner of unclean things they fed.

The cry had been heard many times, that much was certain, and it was certain also that the big fish were noticeably thick at the mouth of Fishhead's slough. No native Reelfooter, white or black, would willingly wet a leg or an arm there.

Here Fishhead had lived, and here he was going to die. The Baxters were going to kill him, and this day in late summer was to be the time of the killing.

The two Baxters—Jake and Joel—were coming in their dugout to do it!

This murder had been a long time in the making. The Baxters had to brew their hate over a slow fire for months before it reached the pitch of action.

They were poor whites, poor in everything, repute, and wordly goods, and standing—a pair of fever-ridden squatters who lived on whiskey and tobacco when they could get it, and on fish and cornbread when they couldn't.

The feud itself was of months' standing.

Meeting Fishhead one day in the spring on the spindly scaffolding of the skiff landing at Walnut Log, and being themselves far overtaken in liquor and vainglorious with a bogus alcoholic substitute for courage, the brothers had accused him, wantonly and without proof, of running their trout-line and stripping it of the hooked catch—an unforgivable sin among the water dwellers and the shanty boaters of the South.

Seeing that he bore this accusation in silence, only eyeing them steadfastly, they had been emboldened then to slap his face, whereupon he turned and gave them both the beating of their lives—bloodying their noses and bruising their lips with hard blows against their front teeth, and finally leaving them, mauled and prone, in the dirt.

Moreover, in the onlookers a sense of the everlasting fitness of things had triumphed over race prejudice and allowed them—two freeborn, sovereign whites—to be licked by a nigger! Therefore they were going to get the nigger!

The whole thing had been planned out amply. They were going to kill him on his log at sundown. There would be no witnesses to see it, no retribution to follow after it. The very ease of the undertaking made them forget even their inborn fear of the place of Fishhead's habitation.

For more than an hour they had been coming from their shack across a deeply indented arm of the lake.

Their dugout, fashioned by fire and adz and draw-knife from the bole of a gum-tree, moved through the water as noiselessly as a swimming mallard, leaving behind it a long, wavy trail on the stilled waters.

Jake, the better oarsman, sat flat in the stern of the round-bottomed craft, paddling with quick, splashless strokes. Joel, the better shot, was squatted forward. There was a heavy, rusted duck gun between his knees.

Though their spying upon the victim had made them certain sure he would not be about the shore for hours, a doubled sense of caution led them to hug closely the weedy banks. They slid along the shore like shadows, moving so swiftly and in such silence that the watchful mudturtles barely turned their snaky heads as they passed.

So, a full hour before the time, they came slipping around the mouth of the slough and made for a natural ambuscade which the mixed-breed had left within a stone's jerk of his cabin to his own undoing.

Where the slough's flow joined deeper water a partly uprooted tree was stretched, prone from shore, at the top still thick and green with leaves that drew nourishment from the earth in which the half uncovered roots yet held, and twined about with an exuberance of trumpet vines and wild fox-grapes. All about was a huddle of drift—last year's corn-stalks, shreddy strips of bark, chunks of rotted weed, all the riffle and dunnage of a quiet eddy.

Straight into this green clump glided the dugout and swung, broadside on, against the protecting trunk of the tree, hidden from the inner side by the intervening curtains of rank growth, just as the Baxters had intended it should be hidden, when days before in their scouting they marked this masked place of waiting and included it, then and there, in the scope of their plans.

There had been no hitch or mishap. No one had been abroad in the late afternoon to mark their movements—and in a little while Fishhead ought to be due. Jake's woodman's eye followed the downward swing of the sun speculatively.

The shadows, thrown shoreward, lengthened and slithered on the small ripples. The small noises of the day died out; the small noises of the coming night began to multiply.

The green-bodied flies went away and big mosquitoes, with speckled gray legs, came to take the places of the flies.

The sleepy lake sucked at the mud banks with small mouthing sounds, as though it found the taste of the raw mud agreeable. A monster crawfish, big as a chicken lobster, crawled out of the top of his dried mud chimney and perched himself there, an armored sentinel on the watchtower.

Bull bats began to flitter back and forth, above the tops of the trees. A pudgy muskrat, swimming with head up, was moved to sidle off briskly as he met a cotton-mouth moccasin snake, so fat and swollen with summer poison that it looked almost like a legless lizard as it moved along the surface of the water in a series of slow torpid *s's*. Directly above the head of either of the waiting assassins a compact little swarm of midges hung, holding to a sort of kite-shaped formation.

A little more time passed and Fishhead came out of the woods at the back, walking swiftly, with a sack over his shoulder.

For a few seconds his deformities showed in the clearing, then the black inside of the cabin swallowed him up.

By now the sun was almost down. Only the red nub of it showed above the timber line across the lake, and the shadows lay inland a long way. Out beyond, the big cats were stirring, and the great smacking sounds as their twisting bodies leaped clear and fell back in the water, came shoreward in a chorus.

But the two brothers, in their green covert, gave heed to nothing except the one thing upon which their hearts were set and their nerves tensed. Joel gently shoved his gun barrels across the log, cuddling the stock to his shoulder and slipping two fingers caressingly back and forth upon the triggers. Jake held the narrow dugout steady by a grip upon a fox-grape tendril.

A little wait and then the finish came!

Fishhead emerged from the cabin door and came down the narrow footpath to the water and out upon the water on his log.

He was barefooted and bareheaded, his cotton shirt open down the front to show his yellow neck and breast, his dungaree trousers held about his waist by a twisted tow string.

His broad splay feet, with the prehensile toes outspread, gripped the polished curve of the log as he moved along its swaying, dipping surface until he came to its outer end, and stood there erect, his chest filling, his chinless face lifted up, and something of mastership and dominion in his poise.

And then—his eye caught what another's eyes might have missed— the round, twin ends of the gun barrels, the fixed gleam of Joel's eyes, aimed at him through the green tracery!

In that swift passage of time, too swift almost to be measured by seconds, realization flashed all through him, and he threw his head still higher and opened wide his shapeless trap of a mouth, and out across the lake he sent skittering and rolling his cry.

And in his cry was the laugh of a loon, and the croaking bellow of a frog, and the bay of a hound, all the compounded night noises of the lake. And in it, too, was a farewell, and a defiance, and an appeal!

The heavy roar of the duck gun came!

At twenty yards the double charge tore the throat out of him. He came down, face forward, upon the log and clung there, his trunk twisting distortedly, his legs twitching and kicking like the legs of a speared frog; his shoulders hunching and lifting spasmodically as the life ran out of him all in one swift coursing flow.

His head canted up between the heaving shoulders, his eyes looked full on the staring face of his murderer, and then the blood came out of his mouth, and Fishhead, in death still as much fish as man, slid, flopping, head first, off the end of the log, and sank, face downward slowly, his limbs all extended out.

One after another a string of big bubbles came up to burst in the middle of a widening reddish stain on the coffee-colored water.

The brothers watched this, held by the horror of the thing they had done, and the cranky dugout, having been tipped far over by the recoil of the gun, took water steadily across its gunwale; and now there was a sudden stroke from below upon its careening bottom and it went over and they were in the lake.

But shore was only twenty feet away, the trunk of the uprooted tree only five. Joel, still holding fast to his shot gun, made for the log, gaining it with one stroke. He threw his free arm over it and clung there, treading water, as he shook his eyes free.

Something gripped him—some great, sinewy, unseen thing gripped him fast by the thigh, crushing down on his flesh!

He uttered no cry, but his eyes popped out, and his mouth set in a square shape of agony, and his fingers gripped into the bark of the tree like grapples. He was pulled down and down, by steady jerks, not rapidly but steadily, so steadily, and as he went his fingernails tore four little white strips in the tree-bark. His mouth went under, next his popping eyes, then his erect hair, and finally his clawing, clutching hand, and that was the end of him.

Jake's fate was harder still, for he lived longer—long enough to see Joel's finish. He saw it through the water that ran down his face, and with a great surge of his whole body, he literally flung himself across the log and jerked his legs up high into the air to save them. He flung himself too far, though, for his face and chest hit the water on the far side.

And out of this water rose the head of a great fish, with the lake slime of years on its flat, black head, its whiskers bristling, its corpsy eyes alight. Its horny jaws closed and clamped in the front of Jake's flannel shirt. His hand struck out wildly and was speared on a poisoned fin, and, unlike Joel, he went from sight with a great yell, and a whirling and churning of the water that made the cornstalks circle on the edges of a small whirlpool.

But the whirlpool soon thinned away into widening rings of ripples, and the corn stalks quit circling and became still again, and only the multiplying night noises sounded about the mouth of the slough.

The bodies of all three came ashore on the same day near the same place. Except for the gaping gunshot wound where the neck met the chest, Fishhead's body was unmarked.

But the bodies of the two Baxters were so marred and mauled that the Reelfooters buried them together on the bank without ever knowing which might be Jake's and which might be Joel's.

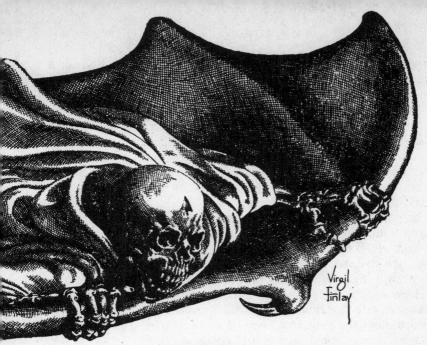

Virgil Finlay

The Outcast

E. F. BENSON

Edward Frederick Benson's popular first novel Dodo *established his reputation as a social satirist when it was published in 1913. This image of Benson has been reinforced for contemporary television audiences who have watched dramatizations of his humorous Mapp and Lucia novels. Yet readers of supernatural fiction know Benson as the author of four collections of fantastic stories that appeared between 1912 and 1934, and that contain some of the most powerful horror fiction written in this century.* Famous Fantastic Mysteries *reprinted five of Benson's tales of the supernatural, among them "The Outcast."*

WHEN MRS. ACRES bought the Gatehouse at Tarleton, which had stood so long without a tenant, and appeared in that very agreeable and lively little town as a resident; sufficient was already known about her past history to entitle her to friendliness and sympathy. Hers had been a tragic story, and the account of the inquest held on her husband's body, when, within a month after their marriage, he had shot himself before her eyes, was recent enough, and of as full a report in the papers to enable our little community at Tarleton to remember and run over the salient grimness of the case without the need of inventing any further details (which, otherwise, it would have been quite capable of doing).

Briefly, then, the facts had been as follows:

Horace Acres appeared to have been a heartless fortune hunter; a handsome, plausible wretch, ten years younger than his wife. He had made no secret to his friends of not being in love with her, but of having a considerable regard for her more than considerable fortune. But hardly had he married her than his indifference developed into violent dislike, accompanied by a mysterious, inexplicable dread of her.

He hated and feared her, and on the morning of the very day when he had put an end to himself he had begged her to allow him, by the commission of some technical cruelty, followed by desertion, to obtain his divorce. It was, of course, in his power to commit this cruelty and to leave her; but for some reason which did not come out at the inquest, and which his widow averred was quite inexplicable to her, the mere fact of leaving her would not be enough for him; what he desired was the dissolution of the marriage.

She, poor soul, had refused to grant him this, for, as corroborated by the evidence of friends and servants, she was utterly devoted to him, and stated, with that quiet dignity which distinguished her throughout this ordeal, that she hoped that he was the victim of some miserable and temporary derangement, and would come to his right mind again.

He had dined that night at his club, leaving his month-old bride to pass the evening alone, and had returned between eleven and twelve that night in a state of vile intoxication. He had gone up to her bedroom, pistol in hand; had locked the door, and his voice was heard screaming and yelling at her. Then followed the sound of one shot.

On the table in his dressing room was found a half sheet of paper, dated that day, and this was read out in court. "The horror of my position," he had written, "is beyond description and endurance. I can bear it no longer; my soul sickens."

The jury, without leaving the court, returned the verdict that he had committed suicide while temporarily insane; and the coroner, at their request, expressed their sympathy and his own with the poor lady, who, as testified on all hands, had treated her husband with the utmost tenderness and affection.

For six months Bertha Acres had traveled abroad, and then in the autumn she had bought the Gatehouse at Tarleton, and settled down to the pleasant and absorbing trifles which make life in a small country town so busy and strenuous.

Our modest little dwelling is within a stone's throw of the Gatehouse, and when, on the return of my wife and myself from two months in Scotland, we found that Mrs. Acres was installed as a neighbor, Madge lost no time in going to call on her. She returned with a series of pleasant impressions.

Mrs. Acres, still on the sunny slope that leads up to the table-land of life which begins at forty years, was extremely handsome, cordial and charming in manner, witty and agreeable, and wonderfully well-dressed. Before the conclusion of her call Madge, in country fashion, had begged her to dispense with formalities, and instead of a frigid return of the call, to dine with us quietly next day. Did she play bridge? That being so, we would be a party of four, for her brother, Charles Alington, had proposed himself for a visit.

I listened to this with sufficient attention to grasp what Madge was saying, but what I was really thinking about was a chess problem which I was attempting to solve. But at this point I became acutely aware that her stream of pleasant impressions dried up suddenly, and Madge became stonily silent.

She shut speech off, as by the turn of a tap, and glowered at the fire, rubbing the back of one hand with the fingers of another, as is her habit in perplexity.

"Go on," I said.

She got up, suddenly restless.

"All I have been telling you is literally and soberly true," she said. "I thought Mrs. Acres charming and witty and goodlooking and friendly. What more could you ask from a new acquaintance? And then, after I had asked her to dinner, I suddenly found, for no earthly reason, that I very much disliked her. I couldn't bear her."

"You said she was wonderfully well-dressed," I permitted myself to remark. "If the queen took the knight—"

"Don't be silly," said Madge. "I am wonderfully well-dressed, too. But behind all her agreeableness and charm and good looks I suddenly felt there was something else, which I detested and dreaded. It's no use asking me what it was, because I haven't the slightest idea. If I knew what it was, the thing would explain itself. But I felt a horror, nothing vivid, nothing close, you understand, but somewhere in the background.

"Can the mind have a 'turn,' do you think, just as the body can, when, for a second or two, you suddenly feel giddy? I think it must have been that. Oh, I'm sure it was that. But I'm glad I asked her to dine. I mean to like her. I shan't have a 'turn' again, shall I?"

"No, certainly not," I said. "If the queen refrained from taking the knight—"

"Oh, do stop your silly chess problem," said Madge. "Bite him, Fungus."

Fungus, so called because he is the son of Humor and Gustavus Adolphus, rose from his place on the hearth rug, and, with a hoarse laugh, nuzzled against my leg, which is his way of biting those he loves. Then the most amiable of bulldogs, who has a passion for the human race, lay down on my foot and sighed heavily. But Madge evidently wanted to talk, and I pushed the chessboard away.

"Tell me more about the horror," I said.

"It was just horror," she said; "a sort of sickness of the soul—"

I found my brain puzzling over some vague reminiscence, surely connected with Mrs. Acres, which those words mistily evoked. But next moment that train of thought was cut short, for the old and sinister legend about the Gatehouse came into my mind as accounting for the horror of which Madge spoke. In the days of Elizabethan religious persecutions it had, then newly built, been inhabited by two brothers, the elder of whom, to whom it belonged, had mass said there every Sunday. Betrayed by the younger, he was arrested and racked to death.

Subsequently the younger, in a fit of remorse, hanged himself in the paneled parlor. Certainly there was a story that the house was haunted by his strangled apparition dangling from the beams, and the late tenants of the house—which now had stood vacant for over three years—had quitted it after a month's occupation in consequence, so it was commonly said of unaccountable and horrible sights.

What was more likely, then, than that Madge, who from childhood has been intensely sensitive to occult and psychic phenomena, that atmosphere that lies so close about our common material life that often we breathe it unawares, should have caught, on that strange wireless receiver which is characteristic of "sensitives," some whispered message?

"But you know the story of the house," I said. "Isn't it quite possible that something of that may have reached you? Where did you sit, for instance—in the paneled parlor?"

She brightened at that.

"Ah, you wise man!" she said. "I never thought of that. That may account for it all. I hope it does. You shall be left in peace with your chess for being so awfully brilliant."

I had occasion, half an hour later, to go to the post office, a hundred yards up High Street, on the matter of a registered letter which I wanted to dispatch that evening. Dusk was gathering, but the red glow of sunset still smoldered in the west, sufficient to enable me to recognize familiar forms and features of passers-by.

Just as I came opposite the post office there approached from the other direction a tall, finely built woman, whom, I felt sure, I had never seen before. Her destination was the same as mine, and I hung on my step a moment to let her pass in first. Simultaneously I felt that I knew, in some vague, faint manner, what Madge had meant when she talked about a "sickness of the soul."

It was no nearer realization to me than in the running of a tune in the head to the audible external hearing of it, and I attributed my sudden recognition of her feeling to the fact that, in all probability, my mind had subconsciously been dwelling on what she had said, and not for a moment did I connect it with any external cause. And then it occurred to me who, possibly, this woman was.

She finished the transaction of her errand a few seconds before me, and when I got out into the street again she was a dozen yards down the pavement, walking in the direction of my house and of the Gatehouse. Opposite my own door I deliberately lingered, and saw her pass down the steps that led from the road to the entrance of the Gatehouse.

Even as I turned into my own door the unbidden reminiscence which had eluded me before came out into the open, and I cast my net over it. It was her husband who, in the inexplicable communication he had left on his dressing-room table, just before he shot himself, had written "my soul sickens."

It was odd, though scarcely more than that, for Madge to have used those identical words.

Charles Alington, my wife's brother, who arrived next afternoon, is quite the happiest man whom I have ever come across. The material world, that perennial spring of thwarted ambition, physical desire and perpetual disappointment, is practically unknown to him. Envy, malice, and all uncharitableness are equally alien, because he does not want to obtain what anybody else has got, and has no sense of possession, which is queer, since he is enormously rich. He fears nothing, he hopes for nothing, he has no abhorrences or affections, for all physical and nervous functions are in him in the service of an intense infinitiveness.

He never passed a moral judgment in his life; he only wants to explore and to know. Knowledge, in fact, is his entire preoccupation; and since chemists and medical scientists probe and mine in the world of tinctures and microbes far more efficiently than he could do, since he has so little care for anything that can be weighed or propagated, he devotes himself absorbed and ecstatically to that world that lies about the confines of conscious existence.

Anything not yet certainly determined appeals to him with a call of a trumpet; he ceases to take an interest in a subject as soon as it shows signs of assuming a practical and definite status. He was intensely concerned, for instance, in wireless transmission, until Signor Marconi proved that it came within the scope of practical science, and then Charles abandoned it as dull.

I had seen him last two months before, when he was in great perturbation, since he was speaking at a meeting of Anglo-Israelites in the morning to show that the Scone Stone, which is now in the coronation chair at Westminster, was for certain the pillow on which Jacob's head had rested when he saw the vision at Bethel; was addressing the Psychical Research Society in the afternoon on the subject of messages received from the dead through automatic script; and in the evening was—by way of a holiday—only listening to a lecture on reincarnation.

None of these things could, as yet, be definitely proved, and that was why he loved them. The intervals when the occult and the fantastic does not occupy him he is, in spite of his fifty years and wizened mien, exactly like a schoolboy of eighteen, back on his holidays and brimming with superfluous energy.

I found Charles already arrived when I got home next afternoon, after a round of golf. He was betwixt and between the serious and the holiday mood, for he had evidently been reading to Madge from a journal concerning reincarnation, and was rather severe to me.

"Golf!" he said, with insulting scorn. "What is there to know about golf? You hit a ball into the air—"

I was a little sore over the events of the afternoon.

"That's just what I don't do," I said. "I hit it along the ground."

"Well, it doesn't matter where you hit it," said he. "It's all subject to known laws. But the guess, the conjecture—there is the thrill and the excitement of life. The charlatan with his new cure for cancer, the automatic writer with his messages from the dead, the reincarnationist with his positive assertions that he was Napoleon or a Christian slave—they are the people who advance knowledge. You have to guess before you know. Even Darwin saw that when he said you could not investigate without a hypothesis."

"So what's your hypothesis this minute?" I asked.

"Why, that we've all lived before, and that we're going to live again here on this same old earth. Any other conception of a future life is impossible. Are all the people who have been born and have died since the world emerged from chaos going to become inhabitants of some future world? What a squash, you know, my dear Madge!

"Now, I know what you will ask me. If we've all lived before, why can't we remember it? But that's so simple! If you remembered being Cleopatra, you would go on behaving like Cleopatra, and what would Tarleton say? Judas Iscariot, too! Fancy knowing you had been Judas Iscariot! You couldn't get over it; you would commit suicide, or cause everybody who was connected with you to commit suicide from their horror of you.

"Or imagine being a grocer's boy who knew he had been Julius Caesar! Of course sex doesn't matter; souls, as far as I understand, are sexless—just sparks of life, which are put into physical envelopes, some male, some female. You might have been King David, and poor Tony here one of his wives."

"That would be wonderfully neat," said I.

Charles broke out into a loud laugh.

"It would, indeed," he said. "But I won't talk sense any more to you scoffers. I'm absolutely tired out, I will confess, with thinking. I want to have a pretty lady to come to dinner and talk to her as if she was just herself and I myself, and nobody else. I want to win two and sixpence at bridge with the expenditure of enormous thought. I want to have a large breakfast tomorrow and read the *Times* afterward, and go to Tony's club and talk about crops or golf or Irish affairs and peace conferences, and all the things that don't matter one straw!"

"You're going to begin your program tonight, dear," said Madge. "A very pretty lady is coming to dinner, and we're going to play bridge afterward."

Madge and I were ready for Mrs. Acres when she arrived, but Charles was not yet down. Fungus, who has a wild adoration for Charles, quite unaccountable, since Charles has no feeling for dogs, was helping him to dress; and Madge, Mrs. Acres and I waited for his appearance.

It was certainly Mrs. Acres whom I had met last night at the door of the post office, but the dim light of sunset had not enabled me to see how wonderfully handsome she was. There was something slightly Jewish about her profile; the high forehead, the very full-lipped mouth, the bridged nose, the prominent chin, all suggested rather than exemplified an Eastern origin. And when she spoke she had that rich softness of utterance, not quite hoarseness, but not quite of the clear-cut distinctiveness of tone which characterizes northern nations. Something Southern, something Eastern.

"I am bound to ask one thing," she said when, after the usual greetings, we stood round the fireplace, waiting for Charles. "Have you got a dog?"

Madge moved toward the bell.

"Yes, but he shan't come down if you dislike dogs," she said. "He's wonderfully kind, but I know—"

"Ah, it's not that," said Mrs. Acres. "I adore dogs. But I only wished to spare your dog's feelings. Though I adore them, they hate me and they're terribly frightened of me. There's something anti-canine about me."

It was too late to say more. Charles's step clattered in the little hall outside, and Fungus was hoarse and amused. Next moment the door opened, and the two came in. Fungus came in first.

He lolloped in a festive manner into the middle of the room, sniffed and snorted in greeting, and then turned tail. He slipped and skidded on the parquet outside, and we heard him bundling down the kitchen stairs.

"Rude dog," said Madge. "Charles, let me introduce you to our neighbor, Mrs. Acres. My brother, Mrs. Acres—Sir Charles Alington!"

Our little dinner table of four would not permit of separate conversations, and general topics, springing up like mushrooms, wilted and died at their very inception. What mood possessed the others I did not at that time know, but for myself I was only conscious of some fundamental distaste of the handsome, clever woman who sat on my right hand and seemed quite unaffected by the withering atmosphere. She was charming to the eye, she was witty to the ear, she had grace and gracefulness, and all the time she was something terrible.

But by degrees, as I found my own distaste increasing, I saw that my brother-in-law's interest was growing correspondingly keen. The "pretty lady" whose presence at dinner he had desired and obtained was enchaining him. Not, so I began to guess, for her charm and her prettiness, but for some purpose of study, and I wondered whether it was her beautiful Jewish profile that was confirming to his mind some Anglo-Israelitish theory, whether he saw in her fine brown eyes the glance of the seer and the clairvoyant, or whether he divined in her some reincarnation of one of the famous or the infamous dead.

Certainly she had for him some fascination beyond that of the legitimate charm of a very handsome woman. He was studying her with intense curiosity.

"And you are comfortable in the Gatehouse?" he suddenly rapped out at her, as if asking some question of which the answer was crucial.

"Ah, but so comfortable," she said. "Such a delightful atmosphere. I have never known a house that *felt* so peaceful and homelike. Or is it merely fanciful to imagine that some houses have a sense of tranquillity about them and others are uneasy and even terrible?"

Charles stared at her a moment in silence before he recollected his manners.

"No, there may easily be something in it, I should say," he answered. "One can imagine long centuries of tranquillity actually investing a home with some sort of psychical aura perceptible to those who are sensitive."

She turned to Madge.

"And yet I have heard a ridiculous story that the house is supposed to be haunted," she said. "If it is, it is surely haunted by delightful, contented spirits."

Dinner was over; Madge rose.

"Come in very soon, Tony," she said to me, "and let's get to our bridge."

But her eyes said: "Don't leave me long alone with her."

Charles turned briskly round when the door had shut.

"An extremely interesting woman," he said.

"Very handsome," said I.

"Is she? I didn't notice. Her mind, her spirit, that's what intrigued me. What is she? What's behind? Why did Fungus turn tail like that? Queer, too, about her finding the atmosphere of the Gatehouse so tranquil. The late tenants, I remember, didn't find that soothing touch about it!"

"How do you account for that?" I asked.

"There might be several explanations. You might say that the late tenants were fanciful imaginative people, and that the present tenant is a sensible, matter-of-fact woman. Certainly she seemed to be."

"Or?" I suggested.

He laughed.

"Well, you might say—mind, I didn't say so—but you might say that the—the spiritual tenants of the house find Mrs. Acres a congenial companion, and want to retain her. So they keep quiet, and don't upset the cook's nerves!"

Somehow this answer exasperated and jarred on me.

"What do you mean?" I said. "The spiritual tenant of the house, I suppose, is the man who betrayed his brother and hanged himself. Why should he find a charming woman like Mrs. Acres a congenial companion?"

Charles got up briskly. Usually he is more than ready to discuss such topics, but tonight it seemed that he had no such inclination.

"Didn't Madge tell us not to be long?" he asked. "You know how

I run on if I once get on that subject, Tony, so don't give me the opportunity."

"But why did you say that?" I persisted.

"Because I was talking nonsense. You know me well enough to be aware that I am an habitual criminal in that respect."

It was indeed strange to find how completely both the first impression that Madge had formed of Mrs. Acres, and the feeling that followed so quickly on its heels was endorsed by those who, during the next week or two, did a neighbor's duty to the newcomer. All were loud in praise of her charm, her pleasant, kindly wit, her good looks, her beautiful clothes, but even while this Lob-gesang was in full chorus, it would suddenly die away, and an uneasy silence descended, which, somehow, was more eloquent than all the appreciative speech.

Odd, unaccountable little incidents had occurred, which were whispered from mouth to mouth till they became common property. The same fear that Fungus had shown of her was exhibited by another dog. A parallel case occurred when she returned the call of our parson's wife. Mrs. Dowlett had a cage of canaries in the window of her drawing-room. These birds had manifested symptoms of extreme terror when Mrs. Acres entered the room, beating themselves against the wires of their cage, and uttering the alarm note. She inspired some sort of inexplicable fear, over which we, as trained and civilized human beings, had control so that we behaved ourselves. But animals, without that check, gave way altogether to it, even as Fungus had done.

Mrs. Acres entertained. She gave charming little dinner parties of eight, with a couple of tables at bridge to follow, but over these evenings there hung a blight and a blackness. No doubt the sinister story of the paneled parlor contributed to this.

This curious secret dread of her, of which, as on that first evening at my house, she appeared to be completely unconscious, differed very widely in degree. Most people, like myself, were conscious of it, but only very remotely so, and we found ourselves at the Gatehouse behaving quite as usual, though with this uneasiness in the background. But with a few, and most of all with Madge, this uneasiness by degrees grew into a sort of obsession. She made every effort to combat it, her will was entirely set against it, but her struggle seemed only to establish its power over her.

The pathetic and pitiful part was that Mrs. Acres from the first had taken a tremendous liking to her, and used to drop in continually, calling first to Madge at the window, in that pleasant, serene voice of hers, to tell Fungus that the hated one was imminent. Then came a day when Madge and I were bidden to a party at the Gatehouse on Christmas evening. This was to be the last of Mrs. Acres's hospitalities for the present, since she was leaving immediately afterward for a couple of months in Egypt. So, with this remission ahead, Madge almost gleefully accepted the bidding.

But when the evening came she was seized with so violent an attack of sickness and shivering that she was utterly unable to fulfill her engagement. Her doctor could find no physical trouble to account for this; it seemed that the anticipation of her evening alone caused it, and here was the culmination of her shrinking from our kindly and pleasant neighbor. She could only tell me that her sensations, as she began to dress for the party, were like those of that moment in sleep when somewhere in the drowsy brain nightmare is ripening. Something independent of her will revolted at what lay before her.

Spring had begun to stretch herself in the lap of winter when next the curtain rose on this veiled drama of forces, but dimly comprehended and shudderingly conjectured, but then, indeed, nightmare ripened swiftly in broad noon.

Charles Alington had again come to stay with us five days before Easter, and expressed himself as humorously disappointed to find that the subject of his curiosity was still absent from the Gatehouse. On the Saturday morning before Easter he appeared very late for breakfast, and Madge had already gone her ways. I rang for a fresh teapot, and while this was on its way, he took up the *Times*.

"I only read the outside page of it," he said. "The rest is too full of mere materialistic dullness—politics, sports, money market—" He stopped, and passed the paper over to me.

"There, where I'm pointing," he said. "Among the deaths. The first one."

What I read was this:

ACRES, BERTHA. Died at sea Thursday night, March 30, and by her own request, buried at sea. Received by wireless from P. and O. steamer Peshawar.

He held out his hand for the paper again, and turned over the leaves.

"Lloyd's," he said. "The Peshawar arrived at Tilbury yesterday afternoon. The burial must have taken place somewhere in the English Channel."

On the afternoon of Easter Sunday Madge and I motored out to the golf links three miles away. She proposed to walk along the beach just outside the dunes, while I had my round, and return to the clubhouse for tea in two hours' time. The day was one of most lucid spring: a warm southwest wind bowled white clouds along the sky, and their shadows jovially scudded over the sand hills. We had told her of Mrs. Acres's death, and from that moment something dark and vague which had been lying over her mind since the autumn seemed to join this fleet of the shadows of clouds, and leave her in sunlight. We parted at the door of the clubhouse, and she set out on her walk.

Half an hour later, as my opponent and I were waiting on the fifth tee, where the road crosses the links, for the couple in front of us to move on, a servant from the clubhouse scudding along the road caught sight of us, and, jumping from his bicycle, came to where we stood.

"You're wanted at the clubhouse, sir," he said to me. "Mrs. Garford was walking along the shore, and she found something left by the tide. A body, sir. 'Twas in a sack, but the sack was torn, and she saw—It's upset her very much, sir. We thought it best to come for you."

I took the boy's bicycle and went back to the clubhouse as fast as I could turn the wheel. I felt sure I knew what Madge had found, and knowing that, realized the shock. Three minutes later she was telling me her story in gasps and whispers.

"The tide was going down," she said, "and I walked along the high-water mark. There were pretty shells. I was picking them up. And then I saw it in front of me. Just shapeless, just a sack—and then, as I came nearer, it took shape; there were knees and elbows. It moved, it rolled over, and where the head was, the sack was torn, and I saw her face.

"Her eyes were open, Tony, and I fled. All the time I felt it was rolling along after me. Oh, Tony, she's dead, isn't she? She won't come back to the Gatehouse? Do you promise me? There's something awful! I wonder if I guess. The sea gives her up. The sea won't suffer her to rest in it—"

The news of the finding had already been telephoned to Tarleton, and soon a party of four men with a stretcher arrived. There was no doubt as to the identity of the body, for though it had been in the water for three days, no corruption had come to it. The weights with which, at burial, it had been laden, must, by some strange chance, have been detached from it, and by a chance, stranger yet, it had floated and drifted to the shore closest to her home.

That night it lay in the mortuary, and the inquest was held on it next day though that was a bank holiday. From there it was taken to the Gatehouse and coffined, and it lay that next night in the paneled parlor for the funeral.

Madge, after that one hysterical outburst, had completely recovered herself and on Monday evening she made a nice little wreath of the spring flowers which the early warmth had called into blossom in the garden, and I went across with it to the Gatehouse. Though the news of Mrs. Acres's death and the subsequent finding of the body had been widely advertised, there had been no response from relations or friends, and as I laid the solitary wreath on the coffin, a sense of the utter loneliness of what lay within seized and encompassed me.

And then a portent, no less, took place before my eyes. Hardly had the freshly gathered flowers been laid on the coffin than they drooped and wilted. The stalks of the daffodils bent, and their bright chalices closed. The odor of the wallflowers died, and they withered as I watched. What did it mean, that even the petals of spring shrank and were moribund?

I told Madge nothing of this and she, as if through some pang of remorse, was determined to be present next day at the funeral. No arrival of friends or relations had taken place, and from the Gatehouse there came none of the servants. They stood in the porch as the coffin was brought out of the house and, even before it was put into the hearse, had gone back again and closed the door. So, at the cemetery on the hill above Tarleton, Madge and her brother and I were the only mourners.

The afternoon was densely overcast, though we got no rainfall, and it was with thick clouds above, and a sea mist drifting between the gravestones, that we came, after the service in the cemetery chapel, to the place of interment. And then—I can hardly write of it now—when it came for the coffin to be lowered into the grave, it was found that by some faulty measurement, it could not descend, for the excavation was not long enough to hold it.

Madge was standing close to us, and at this moment I heard her sob.

"And the kindly earth will not receive her," she whispered.

There was awful delay: the diggers must be sent for again, and meantime the rain had begun to fall thick and tepid. For some reason—perhaps some outlying feeler of Madge's obsession had wound a tenacle round me—I felt that I must know that earth had gone to earth, but I could not suffer Madge to wait. So, in this miserable frame, I got Charles to take her home, and then returned.

Pick and shovel were busy, and soon the resting place was ready. The interrupted service continued, the handful of wet earth splashed on the coffin lid, and when all was over, I left the cemetery, still feeling, I knew not why, that all was *not over*. Some restlessness and want of certainty possessed me, and instead of going home, I fared forth into the rolling, wooded country inland, with the intention of walking off these batlike terrors that flapped around me. The rain had ceased, and a blurred sunlight penetrated the sea mist which still blanketed the fields and woods, and for half an hour, moving briskly, I endeavored to fight down some fantastic conviction that had gripped my mind in its claws. I refused to look straight at that conviction, telling myself how fantastic, how unreasonable it was, but as often as I put out a hand to throttle it, there came the echo of Madge's words: "The sea will not suffer her; the kindly earth will not receive her."

And if I could shut my ears to that, there came some remembrance of the day she died, and of half forgotten fragments of Charles's superstitious belief in reincarnation. The whole thing, incredible though its component parts were, hung together with a terrible tenacity.

Before long the rain began again, and I turned, meaning to go by the main road into Tarleton, which passes in a wide-flung curve some half mile outside the cemetery. But as I approached the path through the fields, which, leaving the less direct route, passes close to the cemetery and brings you by a steeper and shorter descent into the town, I felt myself irresistibly impelled to take it. I told myself, of course, that I wished to make my wet walk as short as possible, but at the back of my mind was the half-conscious, but none the less imperative, need to know by ocular evidence that the grave by which I had stood that afternoon had been filled in, and that the body of Mrs. Acres now lay tranquil beneath the soil.

My path would be even shorter if I passed through the graveyard, and so presently I was fumbling in the gloom for the latch of the gate, and closed it again behind me. Rain was falling now thick and sullenly, and in the blurred twilight, I picked my way among the mounds, and slipped in the dripping grass, and there in front of me was the newly turned earth. All was finished, the grave diggers had done their work and departed, and earth had gone back again into the keeping of the earth.

It brought me some great lightening of the spirit to know that, and I was on the point of turning away when a sound or stir from the heaped soil caught my ear, and I saw a little stream of pebbles mixed with clay trickle down the side of the mound above the grave; the heavy rain, no doubt, had loosened the earth. And then came another, and yet another, and with terror gripping at my heart, I perceived that this was no loosening from without, but from within, for to right and left the piled soil was falling away with the press of something from below. Faster and faster it poured off the grave, and even higher at the head of it rose a mound of earth pushed upward from beneath.

Somewhere out of sight there came the sound as of creaking and breaking wood, and then through that mound of earth there protruded the end of the coffin. The lid was shattered: loose pieces of the boards fell off it, and within the cavity there faced me white features and wide eyes. All this I saw, while sheer terror held me motionless; then, I suppose, came the breaking point, and with such panic as surely man never felt before, I was stumbling away among the graves, and racing toward the kindly human lights of the town below.

I went to the parson who had conducted the service that afternoon with my incredible tale, and an hour later, he, Charles Alington, and two or three men from the undertaker's were on the spot. They found the coffin, completely disinterred, lying on the ground by the grave, which was now three-quarters full of the earth which had fallen back into it. After what had happened, it was decided to make no further attempt to bury it; and next day the body was cremated.

Now it is open to any one who may read this tale to reject the incident of this emergence of the coffin altogether, and account for the other strange happenings by the comfortable theory of coincidence. He can certainly satisfy himself that one Bertha Acres did die at sea on this particular Thursday, and was buried at sea; there is nothing extraordinary about that. Nor is it the least impossible that the weights should have slipped from the canvas shroud, and that the body should have been washed ashore on the coast by Tarleton—why not Tarleton, as well as any other little town near the coast?—nor is there anything inherently impossible in the fact that the grave, as originally dug, was not of sufficient dimensions to receive the coffin.

That all these incidents should have happened to the body of a single individual is odd, but then the nature of coincidence is to be odd. They form a startling series, but unless coincidences are startling, they escape observation altogether. So, if you reject the last incident here recorded, or account for it by some local disturbance, an earthquake, or the breaking of a spring just below the grave, you can comfortably recline on the cushion of coincidence.

For myself, I give no explanation of these events, though my brother-in-law brought forward one with which he himself is perfectly satisfied. Only the other day he sent me, with considerable jubilation, a copy of some extracts from a medieval book on the subject of reincarnation which sufficiently indicates his theory. The original work was in Latin, which, mistrusting my scholarship, he kindly translated for me. I transcribe them exactly as he sent them to me. The reader will probably guess whom the word "he" refers to. This is the translation:

Gnostic literature gives us two certain instances of his reincarnation. In one his spirit was incarnated in the body of a man, in the other, in that of a woman, fair of outward aspect, and of a pleasant conversation, but held in dread and in horror by those who came into more than casual intercourse with her. She, it is said, died on the anniversary of his death, but of this I have no certain information. What is sure is that when the time came for her burial, the kindly earth would receive her not, but though the grave was dug deep and well it spewed her forth again. Of the man in whom his cursed spirit was reincarnated, it is said that being on a voyage when he died, he was cast overboard with stones to sink him, but the sea would not suffer him to rest in her bosom, but slipped the weights from him, and cast him forth again on to the coast. How be it when the full time of his expiation shall have come and his deadly sin forgiven, the corporal body, which is the cursed receptacle of his spirit, shall at length be purged with fire, and so he shall, in the infinite mercy of the Almighty, have rest, and shall wander no more.

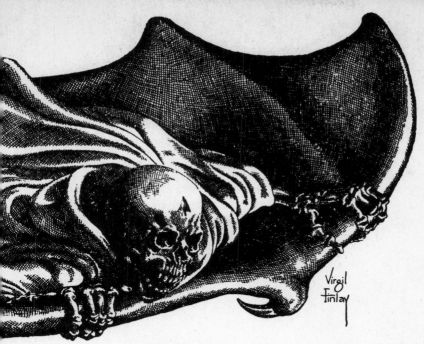

The Yellow Sign

ROBERT W. CHAMBERS

Were it possible to purge "The Yellow Sign" of its fantasy elements, one would have left the sort of pleasant but undistinguished romantic fiction Robert W. Chambers was best known for. But Chambers imbued even the most innocent elements of this tale with such an overwhelming sense of dread that the story is recognized as a horror fiction classic. Chambers had originally tried to make a career as an artist, but the success of his 1898 fantasy collection, The King in Yellow, *convinced him to take up writing as a full-time profession.* Famous Fantastic Mysteries *reprinted two other stories from that volume, along with several more fantasies Chambers wrote over his very prolific lifetime, but none of them match the power of "The Yellow Sign."*

> *Along the shore the cloud waves break,*
> *The twin suns sink behind the lake,*
> > *The shadows lengthen*
> > > *In Carcosa.*

> *Strange is the night where black stars rise*
> *And strange moons circle through the skies,*
> > *But stranger still is*
> > > *Lost Carcosa.*

Songs that the Hyades shall sing,
Where flap the tatters of the King,
Must die unheard in
Dim Carcosa.

Song of my soul, my voice is dead,
Die thou, unsung, as tears unshed
Shall dry and die in
Lost Carcosa.

—Cassilda's song in "The King in Yellow,"
ACT I SCENE 2

CHAPTER I

THERE ARE so many things which are impossible to explain! Why should certain chords in music make me think of the brown and golden tints of autumn foliage? Why should the Mass of Sainte-Cécile send my thoughts wandering among caverns whose walls blaze with ragged masses of virgin silver? What was it in the roar and turmoil of Broadway at six o'clock that flashed before my eyes the picture of a still Breton forest where sunlight filtered through spring foliage, and Sylvia bent, half curiously, half tenderly, over a small, green lizard, murmuring, "To think that this also is a little ward of God"?

When I first saw the watchman his back was toward me, I looked at him indifferently, until he went into the church. I paid no more attention to him than I had to any other man who lounged through Washington Square that morning, and when I shut my window and turned back into my studio I had forgotten him. Late in the afternoon, the day being warm, I raised the window again and leaned out to get a sniff of air. A man was standing in the courtyard of the church, and I noticed him again with as little interest as I had that morning. I looked across the square to where the fountain was playing, and then, with my mind filled with vague impressions of trees, asphalt drives, and the moving groups of nursemaids and holiday-makers, I started to walk back to my easel.

As I turned, my listless glance included the man below in the church-yard. His face was towards me now, and with a perfectly involuntary movement I bent to see it. At the same moment he raised his head and looked at me. Instantly I thought of a coffin-worm. Whatever it was about the man that repelled me, I did not know, but the impression of a plump, white grave-worm was so intense and nauseating that I must have shown it in my expression, for he turned his puffy face away with a movement which made me think of a disturbed grub in a chestnut.

I went back to my easel and motioned the model to resume her pose. After working awhile, I was satisfied that I was spoiling what I had done as rapidly as possible, and I took up a palette-knife and scraped the color out again. The flesh tones were sallow and unhealthy, and I did not understand how I could have painted such sickly color into a study which before that had glowed with healthy tones.

I looked at Tessie. She had not changed, and the clear flush of health dyed her neck and cheeks as I frowned.

"Is it something I've done?" she asked.

"No; I've made a mess of this arm, and for the life of me I can't see how I came to paint such mud as that into the canvas," I replied.

"Don't I pose well?" she insisted.

"Of course, perfectly."

"Then it's not my fault?"

"No. It's my own."

"I'm very sorry," she said.

I told her she could rest while I applied rag and turpentine to the plague-spot on my canvas, and she went off to smoke a cigarette and look over the illustrations in the *Courier Français*.

I did not know whether it was something in the turpentine or a defect in the canvas, but the more I scrubbed the more that gangrene seemed to spread. I worked like a beaver to get it out, and yet the disease appeared to creep from limb to limb of the study before me. Alarmed, I strove to arrest it, but now the color of the flesh changed and the whole figure seemed to absorb the infection as a sponge soaks up water. Vigorously I plied palette-knife, turpentine, and scraper, thinking all the time what a séance I should hold with Duval, who had sold me the canvas; but soon I noticed that it was not the canvas which was defective, nor yet the colors of Edward.

"It must be the turpentine," I thought, angrily, "or else my eyes have become so blurred and confused by the afternoon light that I can't see straight." I called Tessie, the model. She came and leaned over my chair, blowing rings of smoke into the air.

"What *have* you been doing to it?" she exclaimed.

"Nothing," I growled; "it must be this turpentine!"

"What a horrible color it is now," she continued. "Do you think my flesh resembles green cheese?"

"No, I don't," I said, angrily, "did you ever know me to paint like that before?"

"No, indeed!"

"Well, then!"

"It must be the turpentine, or something," she admitted.

She walked to the window. I scraped and rubbed until I was tired, and finally picked up my brushes and hurled them through the canvas with a forcible expression, the tone alone of which reached Tessie's ears.

Hearing this she promptly began: "That's it! Swear and act silly and ruin your brushes! You have been three weeks on that study, and now look! What's the good of ripping the canvas? What creatures artists are!"

I felt about as much ashamed as I usually did after such an outbreak, and I turned the ruined canvas to the wall. Tessie helped me clean my brushes, and then danced away to get ready to go home. Then she regaled me with bits of advice concerning whole or partial loss of temper, until thinking perhaps I had been tormented sufficiently, she suddenly changed the subject.

"Everything went wrong from the time you came back from the window and talked about that horrid-looking man you saw in the church-yard," she announced.

"Yes, he probably bewitched the picture," I said, yawning. I looked at my watch.

"It's after six, I know," said Tessie, adjusting her hat before the mirror.

"Yes," I replied. "I didn't mean to keep you so long." I leaned out of the window, but recoiled with disgust, for the young man with the pasty face stood below in the church-yard. Tessie saw my gesture of disapproval, and leaned from the window.

"Is that the man you don't like?" she whispered.

I nodded.

"I can't see his face, but he does look fat and soft. Some way or other," she continued, turning to look at me, "he reminds me of a dream—an awful dream—I once had. Or," she mused, looking down at her shapely shoes, "was it a dream after all?"

"How should I know?" I smiled.

Tessie smiled in reply.

"You were in it," she said, "so perhaps you might know something about it."

"Tessie! Tessie!" I protested, "don't you dare flatter by saying that you dream about me!"

"But I did," she insisted. "Shall I tell you about it?"

"Go ahead," I replied, lighting a cigarette.

Tessie leaned back on the open window-sill and began, very seriously:

"One night last winter I was lying in bed thinking about nothing at all in particular. I had been posing for you and I was tired out, yet it seemed impossible for me to sleep. I heard the bells in the city ring ten, eleven, and midnight. I must have fallen asleep about midnight, because I don't remember hearing the bells after that. It seemed to me that I had scarcely closed my eyes when I dreamed that something impelled me to go to the window. I rose, and, raising the sash, leaned out. Twenty-fifth Street was deserted as far as I could see. I began to be afraid; everything outside seemed so—so black and uncomfortable. Then the sound of wheels in the distance came to my ears, and it seemed to me as though that was what I must wait for.

"Very slowly the wheels approached, and, finally, I could make out a vehicle moving along the street. It came nearer and nearer, and when it passed beneath my window I saw it was a hearse. Then, as I trembled with fear, the driver turned and looked straight at me. When I awoke I was standing by the open window shivering with cold, but the black-plumed hearse and the driver were gone. I dreamed this dream again in March last, and again awoke beside the open window. Last night the dream came again. You remember how it was raining; when I awoke, standing at the open window, my night-dress was soaked."

"But where did I come into the dream?" I asked.

"You—you were in the coffin; but you were not dead."

"In the coffin?"

"Yes."

"How did you know? Could you see me?"

"No; I only knew you were there."

"Had you been eating Welsh rarebits, or lobster salad?" I began to laugh, but the girl interrupted me with a frightened cry.

"Hello! What's up?" I said, as she shrank into the embrasure by the window.

"The—the man below in the church-yard; he drove the hearse."

"Nonsense," I said; but Tessie's eyes were wide with terror. I went to the window, and looked out. The man was gone. "Come, Tessie," I urged, "don't be foolish. You have posed too long; you are nervous."

"Do you think I could forget that face?" she murmured. "Three times I saw the hearse pass below my window, and every time the driver turned and looked up at me. Oh, his face was so white and—and soft! It looked dead—it looked as if it had been dead a long time."

I induced the girl to sit down and swallow a glass of Marsala. Then I sat down beside her and tried to give her some advice.

"Look here, Tessie," I said, "you go to the country for a week or two, and you'll have no more dreams about hearses. You pose all day, and when night comes your nerves are upset. You can't keep this up. Then again, instead of going to bed when your day's work is done, you run off to picnics at Sulzer's Park, or go to the Eldorado or Coney Island, and when you come down here next morning you are fagged out. There was no real hearse. That was a soft-shell-crab dream."

She smiled faintly.

"What about the man in the church-yard?"

"Oh, he's only an ordinary, unhealthy, every-day creature."

"As true as my name is Tessie Reardon, I swear to you, Mr. Scott, that the face of the man below in the church-yard is the face of the man who drove the hearse!"

"What of it?" I said. "It's an honest trade."

"Then you think I *did* see the hearse?"

"Oh," I said, diplomatically, "if you really did, it might not be unlikely that the man below drove it. There is nothing in that."

Tessie rose, unrolled her scented handkerchief, and, taking a bit of gum from a knot in the hem, placed it in her mouth. Then, drawing on her gloves, she offered me her hand with a frank "Good-night Mr. Scott," and walked out.

CHAPTER II

THE NEXT morning, Thomas, the bellboy, brought me the *Herald* and a bit of news. The church next door had been sold. I thanked Heaven for it, not that I, being a Catholic, had any repugnance for the congregation next door, but because my nerves were shattered by a blatant exhorter, whose every word echoed through the aisles of the church as if it had been my own rooms, and who insisted on his r's with a nasal persistence which revolted my every instinct.

Then, too, there was a fiend in human shape, an organist, who reeled off some of the grand old hymns with an interpretation of his own, and I longed for the blood of a creature who could play the "Doxology" with an amendment of minor chords which one hears only in a quartet of very young undergraduates. I believe the minister was a good man, but when he bellowed, "And the Lorrd said unto Moses, the Lorrd is a man of war; the Lorrd is his name. My wrath shall wax hot, and I will kill you with the sworrd!" I wondered how many centuries of purgatory it would take to atone for such a sin.

"Who bought the property?" I asked Thomas.

"Nobody that I knows, sir. They do say the gent wot owns this 'ere 'Amilton flats was lookin' at it. 'E might be a bildin' more studios."

I walked to the window. The young man with the unhealthy face stood by the church-yard gate, and at the mere sight of him the same overwhelming repugnance took possession of me.

"By-the-way, Thomas," I said, "who is that fellow down there?"

Thomas sniffed. "That there worm, sir? 'E's night-watchman of the church, sir. 'E makes me tired a-sittin' out all night on them steps and lookin' at you insultin' like. I'd 'a' punched 'is 'ed, sir—beg pardon, sir—"

"Go on, Thomas."

"One night a comin' 'ome with 'Arry, the other English boy, I sees 'im a sittin' there on them steps. We 'ad Molly and Jen with us, sir, the two girls on the tray service, an' 'e looks so insultin' at us that I up and sez, 'Wat you lookin' hat, you fat slug?'—beg pardon, sir, but that's 'ow I sez, sir. Then 'e don't say nothin', and I sez, 'Come out and I'll punch that puddin' 'ed.' Then I hopens the gate an' goes in, but 'e don't say nothin', only looks insultin' like. Then I 'its 'im one; but, ugh! 'is 'ed was that cold and mushy it ud sicken you to touch 'im."

"What did he do then?" I asked curiously.

"'Im? Nawthin'."

"And you, Thomas?"

The young fellow flushed with embarrassment, and smiled uneasily.

"Mr. Scott, sir, I ain't no coward, an' I can't make it out at all why I run. I was in the Fifth Lawncers, sir, at Tel-el-Kebir, an' was shot by the wells."

"You don't mean to say you ran away?"

"Yes, sir; I run."

"Why?"

"That's just what I want to know, sir. I grabbed Molly an' run, an' the rest was as frightened as I."

"But what were they frightened at?"

Thomas refused to answer for a while; but now my curiosity was aroused about the repulsive young man below, and I pressed him. Three years' sojourn in America had modified Thomas's cockney dialect but he was still "close."

"You won't believe me, Mr. Scott, sir!"

"Yes, I will."

"You will lawf at me, sir?"

"Nonsense!"

He hesitated. "Well, sir, it's Gawd's truth, that when I 'it 'im, 'e grabbed me wrists, sir, and when I twisted 'is soft, mushy fist one of 'is fingers come off in me 'and."

The utter loathing and horror of Thomas's face must have been reflected in my own, for he added:

"It's orful, an' now when I see 'im I just go away. 'E maikes me hill."

When Thomas had gone I went to the window. The man stood beside the church railing, with both hands on the gate; but I hastily retreated to my easel again, sickened and horrified, for I saw that the middle finger of his right hand was missing.

At nine o'clock Tessie appeared, with a merry "Good-morning, Mr. Scott." When she had taken her pose upon the model-stand I started a new canvas, much to her delight. She remained silent as long as I was on the drawing, but as soon as the scrape of the charcoal ceased, and I took up my fixative, she began to chatter.

"Oh, I had such a lovely time last night. We went to Tony Pastor's."

"Who are 'we'?" I demanded.

"Oh, Maggie—you know, Mr. Whyte's model—and Pinkie McCormick—we call her Pinkie because she's got that beautiful red hair you artists like so much—and Lizzie Burke."

I sent a shower of spray from the fixative over the canvas, and said, "Well, go on."

"We saw Kelly, and Baby Barnes, the skirt-dancer, and—and all the rest. I made friends with a new fellow."

"Then you have gone back on me, Tessie?"

She laughed and shook her head.

"He's Lizzie Burke's brother, Ed. He's a perfect gen'l'man."

Then she related how Ed had come back from the stocking-mill in Lowell, Massachusetts, to find her and Lizzie grown up—and what an accomplished young man he was—and how he thought nothing of squandering half a dollar for ice-cream and oysters to celebrate his entry as clerk into the woollen department of Macy's. Before she finished I began to paint, and she resumed the pose, smiling and chattering like a sparrow. By noon I had the study fairly well rubbed in and Tessie came to look at it.

"That's better," she said.

I thought so, too, and ate my lunch with a satisfied feeling that all was going well. Tessie spread her lunch on a drawing-table opposite me, and we drank our claret from the same bottle and lighted our cigarettes from the same match. I was much attached to Tessie. I had watched her shoot up into a slender but exquisitely formed woman from a frail, awkward child. She had posed for me during the last three years, and among all my models she was my favorite.

I knew she would do what she liked, still I did hope she would steer clear of complications, because I wished her well, and then also I had a selfish desire to retain the best model I had.

I am a Catholic. When I listen to high mass, when I sign myself, I feel that everything, including myself, is more cheerful; and when I confess, it does me good. A man who lives as much alone as I do must confess to somebody. Then, again, Sylvia was Catholic, and it was reason enough for me. But I was speaking of Tessie, which is very different. Tessie also was Catholic, and much more devout than I, so, taking it all in all, I had little fear for my pretty model until she should fall in love. But *then* I knew that fate alone would decide her future for her, and I prayed inwardly that fate would throw into her path nothing but Ed Burkes and Jimmy McCormicks, bless her sweet face!

Tessie sat blowing rings of smoke up to the ceiling and tinkling the ice in her tumbler.

"Do you know that I also had a dream last night?" I observed.

"Not about that man?" she asked, laughing.

"Exactly. A dream similar to yours, only much worse."

It was foolish and thoughtless of me to say this, but you know how little tact the average painter has.

"I must have fallen asleep about ten o'clock," I continued, "and after a while I dreamed that I awoke. So plainly did I hear the midnight bells, the wind in the tree-branches, and the whistle of steamers from the bay, that even now I can scarcely believe I was not awake. I seemed to be lying in a box which had a glass cover. Dimly I saw the street lamps as I passed, for I must tell you, Tessie, the box in which I reclined appeared to lie in a cushioned wagon which jolted me over a stony pavement.

"After a while I became impatient and tried to move, but the box was too narrow. My hands were crossed on my breast so I could not raise them to help myself. I listened and then tried to call. My voice was gone. I could hear the trample of the horses attached to the wagon, and even the breathing of the driver. Then another sound broke upon my ears like the raising of a window-sash.

"I managed to turn my head a little, and found I could look, not only through the glass cover of my box, but also through the glass panes in the side of the covered vehicle. I saw houses, empty and silent, with neither light nor life about any of them excepting one. In that house a window was open on the first floor and a figure all in white stood looking down into the street. It was you."

Tessie had turned her face away from me and leaned on the table with her elbow.

"I could see your face," I resumed, "and it seemed to me to be very sorrowful. Then we passed on and turned into a narrow, black lane. Presently the horses stopped. I waited and waited, closing my eyes with fear and impatience, but all was silent as the grave. After what seemed to me hours, I began to feel uncomfortable. A sense that somebody was close to me made me unclose my eyes. Then I saw the white face of the hearse-driver looking at me through the coffin-lid—"

A sob from Tessie interrupted me. She was trembling like a leaf. I saw I had made a fool of myself, and attempted to repair the damage.

"Why, Tess," I said, "I only told you to show you what influence your story might have on another person's dreams. You don't suppose I really lay in a coffin, do you? What are you trembling for? Don't you see that your dream and my unreasonable dislike for that inoffensive watchman of the church simply set my brain working as soon as I fell asleep?"

She laid her head between her arms and sobbed as if her heart would break. What a precious triple donkey I had made of myself! But I was about to break my record. I went over and put my arm about her.

"Tessie, dear, forgive me," I said; "I had no business to frighten you with such nonsense. You are too sensible a girl, too good a Catholic to believe in dreams."

Her hand tightened on mine and her head fell back upon my shoulder, but she still trembled and I petted her and comforted her.

"Come, Tess, open your eyes and smile."

Her eyes opened with a slow, languid movement and met mine, but their expression was so queer that I hastened to reassure her again.

"It's all humbug, Tessie. You surely are not afraid that any harm will come to you because of that?"

"No," she said, but her scarlet lips quivered.

"Then what's the matter? Are you afraid?"

"Yes. Not for myself."

"For me, then?" I demanded, gayly.

"For you," she murmured, in a voice almost inaudible. "I—I care for you."

At first I started to laugh, but when I understood her a shock passed through me, and I sat like one turned to stone. This was the crowning bit of idiocy I had committed. During the moment which elapsed between her reply and my answer I thought of a thousand responses to that innocent confession. I could pass it by with a laugh, I could misunderstand her and reassure her as to my health, I could simply point out that it was impossible she could love me. But my reply was quicker than my thoughts, and I might think and think now when it was too late, for I had kissed her on the mouth.

That evening I took my usual walk in Washington Park, pondering over the occurrences of the day. I was thoroughly committed. There was no back-out now, and I stared the future straight in the face. I was not good, not even scrupulous, but I had no idea of deceiving either myself or Tessie. The one passion of my life lay buried in the sunlit forests of Brittany. Was it buried forever? Hope cried "No!" For three years I had been listening to the voice of Hope, and for three years I had waited for a footstep on my threshold. Had Sylvia forgotten? "No!" cried Hope.

I said that I was not good. That is true, but still I was not exactly a comic-opera villain. I had led an easy-going, reckless life, taking what invited me of pleasure, deploring and sometimes bitterly regretting consequences. In one thing alone, except my painting, was I serious, and that was something which lay hidden if not lost in the Breton forests.

It was too late now for me to regret what had occurred during the day. Whatever it had been, pity, a sudden tenderness for sorrow, or the more brutal instinct of gratified vanity, it was all the same now, and unless I wished to bruise an innocent heart my path lay marked before me. The fire and the strength, the depth of a love which I had never even suspected, with all my imagined experience in the world, left me no alternative but to respond or send her away.

Whether because I am so cowardly about giving pain to others, or whether it was that I have little of the gloomy Puritan in me, I do not know, but I shrank from disclaiming responsibility for that thought-less kiss, and, in fact, had not time to do so before the gates of her heart opened and the flood poured forth. Others who habitually do their duty and find a sullen satisfaction in making themselves and everybody else unhappy, might have withstood it. I did not. I dared not.

After the storm had abated I did tell her that she might better have loved Ed Burke and worn a plain gold ring, but she would not hear of it, and I thought perhaps that as long as she had decided to love somebody she could not marry, it had better be me. I at least could treat her with an intelligent affection, and she could go none the worse for it. For I was decided on that point, although I knew how hard it would be.

She would either tire of the whole thing, or become so unhappy that I should have either to marry her or go away. If I married her we would be unhappy. I with a wife unsuited to me, and she with a husband unsuitable for any woman. If I went away she might either fall ill, recover, and marry some Eddie Burke, or she might recklessly or deliberately go and do something foolish. On the other hand, if she tired of my friendship, then her whole life would be before her with beautiful vistas of Eddie Burkes and marriage rings, and twins, and Harlem flats, and Heaven knows what.

As I strolled along through the trees by the Washington Arch, I decided that she should find a substantial friend in me anyway, and the future could take care of itself. Then I went into the house and put on my evening dress, for the little, faintly perfumed note on my dresser said, "Have a cab at the stage door at eleven," and the note was signed, "Edith Carmichel, Metropolitan Theater."

I took supper that night, or, rather, we took supper, Miss Carmichel and I, at Solari's, and the dawn was just beginning to gild the cross on the Memorial Church as I entered Washington Square after leaving Edith at the Brunswick. There was not a soul in the park, as I passed among the trees and took the walk which leads from the Garibaldi statue to the Hamilton apartment house, but as I passed the church-yard I saw a figure sitting on the stone steps. In spite of myself a chill crept over me at the sight of the white, puffy face, and I hastened to pass. Then he said something which might have been addressed to me or might merely have been a mutter to himself, but a sudden furious anger flamed up within me that such a creature should address me.

For an instant I felt like wheeling about and smashing my stick over his head, but I walked on, and, entering the Hamilton, went to my apartment. For some time I tossed about the bed trying to get the sound of his voice out of my ears, but could not. It filled my head, that muttering sound, like thick, oily smoke from a fat-rendering vat or an odor of noisome decay. And as I lay and tossed about, the voice in my ears seemed more distinct, and I began to understand the words he muttered. They came to me slowly, as if I had forgotten them, and at last I could make some sense out of the sounds. It was this:

"Have you found the Yellow Sign?

"Have you found the Yellow Sign?

"Have you found the Yellow Sign?"

I was furious. What did he mean by that? Then with a curse upon him and his I rolled over and went to sleep, but when I awoke later I looked pale and haggard, for I had dreamed the dream of the night before, and it troubled me more than I cared to think.

I dressed and went down into my studio. Tessie sat by the window, but as I came in she rose and put both arms around my neck for an innocent kiss. She looked so sweet and dainty that I kissed her again.

I said, "We will begin something new"; and I went into my wardrobe and picked out a Moorish costume which fairly blazed with tinsel. It was a genuine costume, and Tessie retired to the screen with it, enchanted. When she came forth again I was astonished. Her long, black hair was bound above her forehead with a circlet of turquoise. Her feet were encased in the embroidered, pointed slippers, and the skirt of her costumé, curiously wrought with arabesques in silver, and held with a glittering girdle, fell to her ankles. The deep metallic blue vest, embroidered with silver, and the short Mauresque jacket, spangled and sewn with turquoises, became her wonderfully. She came up to me and held up her face, smiling. I slipped my hand into my pocket, and, drawing out a gold chain with a cross attached, dropped it over her head.

"It's yours, Tessie."

"Mine?" she faltered.

"Yours. Now go and pose." Then with a radiant smile she ran behind the screen, and presently reappeared with a little box on which was written my name.

"I had intended to give it to you when I went home tonight," she said, "but I can't wait now."

I opened the box. On the pink cotton inside lay a clasp of black onyx, on which was inlaid a curious symbol or letter in gold. It was neither Arabic nor Chinese, nor, as I found afterwards, did it belong to any human script.

"It's all I had to give you for a keepsake," she said, timidly.

I was annoyed, but I told her how much I should prize it, and promised to wear it always. She fastened it on my coat beneath the lapel.

"How foolish, Tess, to go and buy me such a beautiful thing as this," I said.

"I did not buy it," she laughed.

"Where did you get it?"

Then she told me how she had found it one day while coming from the aquarium in the Battery, how she had advertised it and watched the papers, but at last gave up all hopes of finding the owner.

"That was last winter," she said, "the very day I had the first horrid dream about the hearse."

I remembered my dream of the previous night but said nothing, and presently my charcoal was flying over a new canvas, and Tessie stood motionless on the model-stand.

Chapter III

THE DAY following was a disastrous one for me. While moving a framed canvas from one easel to another my foot slipped on the polished floor and I fell heavily on both wrists. They were so badly sprained that it was useless to attempt to hold a brush, and I was obliged to wander about the studio, glaring at unfinished drawings and sketches, until despair seized me and I sat down to smoke and twiddle my thumbs with rage. The rain blew against the windows and rattled on the roof of the church, driving me into a nervous fit with its interminable patter.

Tessie sat sewing by the window, and every now and then raised her head and looked at me with such innocent compassion that I began to feel ashamed of my irritation and looked about for something to occupy me. I had read all the papers and all the books in the library, but for the sake of something to do I went to the bookcases and shoved them open with my elbow. I knew every volume by its color and examined them all, passing slowly around the library and whistling to keep up my spirits.

I was turning to go into the dining room when my eye fell upon a book bound in serpent-skin standing in a corner of the top shelf of the last bookcase. I did not remember it, and from the floor could not decipher the pale lettering on the back, so I went to the smoking-room and called Tessie. She came in from the studio and climbed up to reach the book.

"What is it?" I asked.

"The King in Yellow."

I was dumbfounded. Who had placed it there? How came it in my rooms? I had long ago decided that I should never open that book, and nothing on earth could have persuaded me to buy it. Fearful lest curiosity might tempt me to open it, I had never even looked at it in bookstores. If I ever had had any curiosity to read it, the awful tragedy of young Castaigne, whom I knew, prevented me from exploring its wicked pages. I had always refused to listen to any description of it, and, indeed, nobody ever ventured to discuss the second part aloud, so I had absolutely no knowledge of what those leaves might reveal. I stared at the poisonous, mottled binding as I would at a snake.

"Don't touch it, Tessie," I said; "come down."

Of course my admonition was enough to arouse her curiosity, and before I could prevent it she took the book, and, laughing, danced off into the studio with it. I called her, but she slipped away with a tormenting smile at my helpless hands, and I followed her with some impatience.

"Tessie!" I cried, entering the library, "listen; I am serious. Put that book away. I do not wish you to open it!" The library was empty. I went into both drawing-rooms, then into the bedrooms, laundry, kitchen, and finally returned to the library and began a systematic search. She had hidden herself so well that it was half an hour later when I discovered her crouching white and silent by the latticed window in the storeroom above. At the first glance I saw she had been punished for her foolishness. "The King in Yellow" lay at her feet; but the book was open at the second part.

I looked at Tessie and saw it was too late. She had opened "The King in Yellow." Then I took her by the hand and led her into the studio. She seemed dazed, and when I told her to lie down on the sofa she obeyed me without a word. After a while she closed her eyes and her breathing became regular and deep; but I could not determine whether or not she slept. For a long while I sat silently beside her, but she neither stirred nor spoke, and at last I rose and, entering the unused store-room, took the book in my least injured hand. It seemed heavy as lead; but I carried it into the studio again, and, sitting down on the rug beside the sofa, opened it and read it through from beginning to end.

When, faint with the excess of my emotions, I dropped the volume and leaned wearily back against the sofa, Tessie opened her eyes and looked at me.

We had been speaking for some time in a dull, monotonous strain before I realized that we were discussing "The King in Yellow." Oh, the sin of writing such words—words which are clear as crystal, limpid and musical as bubbling springs, words which sparkle and glow like the poisoned diamonds of the Medicis! Oh the wickedness, the hopeless damnation, of a soul who could fascinate and paralyze human creatures with such words—words understood by the ignorant and wise alike, words which are more precious than jewels, more soothing than music, more awful than death!

We talked on, unmindful of the gathering shadows, and she was begging me to throw away the clasp of black onyx quaintly inlaid with what we now knew to be the Yellow Sign. I shall never know why I refused, though even at this hour, here in my bedroom as I write this confession, I should be glad to know *what* it was that prevented me from tearing the Yellow Sign from my breast and casting it into the fire. I am sure I wished to do so, and yet Tessie pleaded with me in vain.

Night fell, and the hours dragged on, but still we murmured to each other of the King and the Pallid Mask, and midnight sounded from the misty spires in the fog-wrapped city. We spoke of Hatur and of Cassilda, while outside the fog rolled against the blank window-panes as the cloud waves roll and break on the shores of Hali.

The house was very silent now, and not a sound came up from the misty streets. Tessie lay among the cushions, her face a gray blot in the gloom, but her hands were clasped in mine, and I knew that she knew and read my thoughts as I read hers, for we had understood the mystery of the Hyades, and the Phantom of Truth was laid. Then, as we answered each other, swiftly, silently, thought on thought, the shadows stirred in the gloom about us, and far in the distant streets we heard a sound.

Nearer and nearer it came—the dull crunching of wheels, nearer and yet nearer, and now, outside, before the door, it ceased, and I dragged myself to the window and saw a black-plumed hearse. The gate below opened and shut, and I crept, shaking, to my door, and bolted it, but I knew no bolts, no locks, could keep that creature out who was coming for the Yellow Sign. And now I heard him moving very softly along the hall. Now he was at the door, and the bolts rotted at his touch. Now he had entered. With eyes starting from my head I peered into the darkness, but when he came into the room I did not see him. It was only when I felt him envelop me in his cold, soft grasp that I cried out and struggled with deadly fury, but my hands were useless, and he tore the onyx clasp from my coat and struck me full in the face.

Then, as I fell, I heard Tessie's soft cry and her spirit fled; and even while falling I longed to follow her, for I knew that the King in Yellow had opened his tattered mantle and there was only God to cry to now.

I could tell more, but I cannot see what help it will be to the world. As for me, I am past human help or hope. As I lie here, writing, careless even whether or not I die before I finish, I can see the doctor gathering up his powders and phials with a vague gesture to the good priest beside me, which I understand.

They will be very curious to know the tragedy—they of the outside world who write books and print millions of newspapers, but I shall write no more, and the father confessor will seal my last words with the seal of sanctity when his holy office is done. They of the outside world may send their creatures into wrecked homes and death-smitten firesides, and their newspapers will batten on blood and tears, but with me their spies must halt before the confessional.

They know that Tessie is dead, and that I am dying. They know how the people in the house, aroused by an infernal scream, rushed into my room, and found one living and two dead, but they do not know what I shall tell them now; they do not know that the doctor said, as he pointed to a horrible, decomposed heap on the floor—the livid corpse of the watchman from the church: "I have no theory, no explanation. That man must have been dead for months!"

I think I am dying. I wish the priest would—

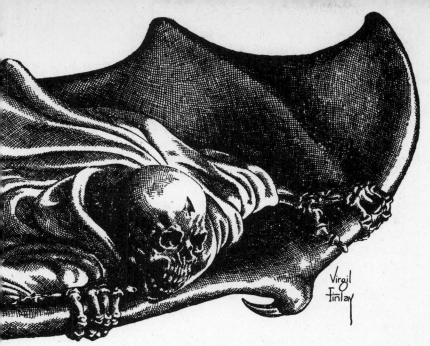

The Derelict

WILLIAM HOPE HODGSON

William Hope Hodgson has been compared to Joseph Conrad and Herman Melville for the body of sea fiction he produced. In his two powerful fantasy novels, The Ghost Pirates *and* The Boats of the Glen Carrig *(both reprinted in* Famous Fantastic Mysteries*), he portrayed the ocean as terra incognita, and the sailor's life as a never-ending series of encounters with the unknown and inexplicable. Hodgson also showed himself adept at capturing the awe and mystery of the sea in a number of atmospheric short stories, one of the best of which is "The Derelict."*

I T'S THE *Material,*" said the old ship's doctor. . . . "The *Material,* plus the conditions; and, maybe," he added slowly, "a third factor— yes, a third factor; but there, there. . . ." He broke off his half-meditative sentence, and began to charge his pipe.

"Go on, Doctor," we said encouragingly, and with more than a little expectancy. We were in the smoke-room of the *Sand-a-lea,* running across the North Atlantic; and the doctor was a character. He concluded the charging of his pipe, and lit it; then settled himself, and began to express himself more fully.

"The *Material,*" he said, with conviction, "is inevitably the medium of expression of the Life-Force—the fulcrum, as it were; lacking which, it is unable to exert itself, or, indeed, to express itself in any form or fashion that would be intelligible or evident to us.

177

"So potent is the share of the *Material* in the production of that thing which we name Life, and so eager the Life-Force to express itself, that I am convinced it would, if given the right conditions, make itself manifest even through so hopeless-seeming a medium as a simple block of sawn wood; for I tell you, gentlemen, the Life-Force is both as fiercely urgent and as indiscriminate as Fire—the Destructor; yet which some are now growing to consider the very essence of Life rampant. . . . There is a quaint seeming paradox there," he concluded, nodding his old gray head.

"Yes, Doctor," I said. "In brief, your argument is that Life is a thing, state, fact, or element, call-it-what-you-like, which requires the *Material* through which to manifest itself, and that given the *Material,* plus the conditions, the result is Life. In other words, that Life is an evolved product, manifested through Matter and bred of conditions—eh?"

"As we understand the word," said the old doctor. "Though, mind you, there *may* be a third factor. But, in my heart, I believe that it is a matter of chemistry; conditions and a suitable medium; but given the conditions, the Brute is so almighty that it will seize upon anything through which to manifest itself. It is a force generated by conditions; but nevertheless this does not bring us one iota nearer to its *explanation,* any more than to the explanation of electricity or fire. They are, all three, of the Outer Forces—Monsters of the Void. Nothing we can do will *create* any one of them; our power is merely to be able, by providing the conditions, to make each one of them manifest to our physical senses. Am I clear?"

"Yes, Doctor, in a way you are," I said. "But I don't agree with you; though I think I understand you. Electricity and fire are both what I might call natural things; but life is an abstract something—a kind of all-permeating wakefulness. Oh, I can't explain it; who could? But it's spiritual; not just a thing bred out of a condition, like fire, as you say, or electricity. It's a horrible thought of yours. Life's a kind of spiritual mystery. . . ."

"Easy, my boy!" said the old doctor, laughing gently to himself; "or else I may be asking you to demonstrate the spiritual mystery of life of the limpet, or the crab, shall we say?"

He grinned at me, with ineffable perverseness. "Anyway," he continued, "as I suppose you've guessed, I've a yarn to tell you in support of my impression that life is no more a mystery or a miracle than fire or electricity. But, please to remember, gentlemen, that because you've succeeded in naming and making good use of these two forces, they're just as much mysteries, fundamentally, as ever.

"And, anyway, the thing I'm going to tell you, won't explain the mystery of life; but only give you one of my pegs on which I hang my feeling that life is, as I have said, a force made manifest through conditions (that is to say, natural chemistry), and that it can take for its purpose and need, the most incredible and unlikely matter; for without matter, it cannot come into existence—it cannot become manifest. . . ."

"I don't agree with you, Doctor," I interrupted. "Your theory would destroy all belief in life after death. It would. . . ."

"Hush, sonny," said the old man, with a quiet little smile of comprehension. "Hark to what I have to say first; and, anyway, what objection have you to material life, after death? And if you object to a material framework, I would still have you remember that I am speaking of life, as we understand the word in this our life. Now do be a quiet lad, or I'll never be done.

"It was when I was a young man, and that is a good many years ago, gentlemen. I had passed my examination; but was so run down with overwork, that it was decided that I had better take a trip to sea. I was by no means well off, and very glad, in the end, to secure a nominal post as a doctor in a sailing passenger-clipper, running out to China.

"The name of the ship was the *Bheotpte,* and soon after I had got all my gear aboard, she cast off, and we dropped down the Thames, and next day were well away out in the Channel.

"The captain's name was Gannington, a very decent man; though quite illiterate. The first mate, Mr. Berlies, was a quiet, sternish, reserved man, very well read. The second mate, Mr. Selvern, was, perhaps, by birth and upbringing, the most socially cultured of the three; but he lacked the stamina and indomitable pluck of the other two. He was more of a sensitive; and emotionally and even mentally, the most alert man of the three.

"On our way out, we called at Madagascar, where we landed some of our passengers; then we ran eastward, meaning to call at North-West Cape; but about a hundred degrees east, we encountered a very dreadful weather, which carried away all our sails and sprung the jibboom and fore t'gallant mast.

"The storm carried us northward for several hundred miles, and when it dropped us finally, we found ourselves in a very bad state. The ship had been strained, and had taken some three feet of water through her seams; the main topmast had been sprung, in addition to the jibboom and fore t'gallant mast; two of our boats had gone, as also one of the pigsties (with three fine pigs), this latter having been washed overboard but some half hour before the wind began to ease, which it did quickly; though a very ugly sea ran for some hours after.

"The wind left us just before dark, and when morning came, it brought splendid weather; a calm, mildly undulating sea, and a brilliant sun, with no wind. It showed us also that we were not alone; for about two miles away to the westward was another vessel, which Mr. Selvern, the second mate, pointed out to me.

" 'That's a pretty rum-looking packet, Doctor,' he said, and handed me his glass. I looked through it, at the other vessel, and saw what he meant; at least, I thought I did.

" 'Yes, Mr. Selvern,' I said, 'she's got a pretty old-fashioned look about her.'

"He laughed at me, in his pleasant way.

" 'It's easy to see you're not a sailor, Doctor,' he remarked. 'There's a dozen rum things about her. She's a derelict, and has been floating round, by the look of her, for many a score of years. Look at the shape of her counter, and the bows and cut-water. She's as old as the hills, as you might say, and ought to have gone down to Davy Jones a long time ago.

" 'Look at the growths on her, and the thickness of her standing rigging; that's all salt encrustations, I fancy, if you notice the white color. She's been a small barque; but don't you see she's not a yard left aloft? They've all dropped out of the slings; everything rotted away; wonder the standing rigging hasn't gone too. I wish the Old Man would let us take the boat, and have a look at her; she's well worth it.'

"There seemed very little chance of this, however, for all hands were turned to and kept hard at it all day long, repairing the damage to the masts and gear, and this took a long while, as you may think. Part of the time I gave a hand, heaving on one of the deck-capstans; for the exercise was good for my liver. Old Captain Gannington approved, and I persuaded him to come along and try some of the medicine, which he did; and we grew very chummy over the job.

"We got talking about the derelict, and he remarked how lucky we were not to have run full tilt on to her, in the darkness; for she lay right away to leeward of us, according to the way that we had been drifting in the storm. He also was of the opinion that she had a strange look about her, and that she was pretty old, but on this latter point he plainly had far less knowledge than the second mate; for he was, as I have said, an illiterate man, and he knew nothing of seacraft beyond what experience had taught him. He lacked the book knowledge, which the second mate had, of vessels previous to his day, which it appeared, the derelict was.

" 'She's an old 'un, Doctor,' was the extent of his observations in this direction.

"Yet, when I mentioned to him that it would be interesting to go aboard, and give her a bit of an overhaul, he nodded his head, as if the idea had already been in his mind.

" 'When the work's over, Doctor,' he said. 'Can't spare the men now, ye know. Got to get all shipshape an' ready as smart as we can. But we'll take my gig, an' go off in the Second Dog Watch. The glass is steady, an' it'll be a bit of jam for us.'

"That evening, after tea, the captain gave orders to clear the gig and get overboard. The second mate was to come with us, and the skipper gave him word to see that two or three lamps were put into the boat, as it would soon fall dark. A little later, we were pulling across the calmness of the sea with a crew of six at the oars, and making very good speed of it.

"Now, gentlemen, I have detailed to you, with great exactness, all the facts, both big and little, so that you can follow step by step each incident in this extraordinary affair; and I want you now to pay the closest attention.

"I was sitting in the stern-sheets, with the second mate and the captain, who was steering; and as we drew nearer and nearer to the stranger, I studied her with an ever-growing attention, as, indeed, did the captain and the second mate. She was, as you know, the westward of us, and the sunset was making a great flame of red light to the back of her, so that she showed a little blurred and indistinct by reason of the halation of the light, which almost defeated the eye in any attempt to see her rotting spars and standing rigging, submerged as they were in the fiery glory of the sunset.

"It was because of the effect of the sunset that we had come quite close, comparatively, to the derelict before we saw that she was sur- rounded by a sort of curious scum, the color of which was difficult to decide upon, by reason of the red light that was in the atmosphere; but which afterwards we discovered to be brown. This scum spread all about the old vessel for many hundreds of yards, in a huge, irregular patch, a great stretch of which reached out to the eastward, upon our starboard side, some score, or so, fathoms away.

"'Queer stuff,' said Captain Gannington, leaning to the side, and looking over. 'Something in the cargo as 'as gone rotten an' worked out through 'er seams.'

"'Look at her bows and stern,' said the second mate; 'just look at the growth of her.'

"There were, as he said, great clumpings of strange-looking sea-fungi under the bows and the short counter astern. From the stump of her jibboom and her cutwater, great beards of rime and marine growths hung downward into the scum that held her in. Her blank starboard side was presented to us, all a dead, dirtyish white, streaked and mottled vaguely with dull masses of heavier color.

"'There's a steam of haze rising off her,' said the second mate, speaking again; 'you can see it against the light. It keeps coming and going. Look!'

"I saw then what he meant—a faint haze or steam, either suspended above the old vessel, or rising from her; and Captain Gannington saw it also.

"'Spontaneous combustion!' he exclaimed. 'We'll 'ave to watch w'en we lift the 'atches; 'nless it's some poor devil that's got aboard her; but that ain't likely.'

"We were now within a couple of hundred yards of the old derelict, and had entered into the brown scum. As it poured off the lifted oars, I heard one of the men mutter to himself: 'Damn treacle!' and indeed, it was something like it.

"As the boat continued to forge nearer and nearer to the old ship, the scum grew thicker and thicker; so that, at last, it perceptibly slowed us.

" 'Give way, lads! Put some beef to it!' sung out the captain; and thereafter there was no sound, except the panting of the men, and the faint, reiterated *suck, suck* of the sullen brown scum upon the oars, as the boat was forced ahead. As we went, I was conscious of a peculiar smell in the evening air, and whilst I had no doubt that the puddling of the scum, by the oars, made it rise, I felt that in some way, it was vaguely familiar; yet I could give it no name.

"We were now very close to the old vessel, and presently she was high above us, against the dying light. The captain called out then to 'in with the bow oars, and stand-by with the boat-hook,' which was done.

" 'Aboard there! Ahoy! Aboard there! Ahoy!' shouted Captain Gannington, but there came no answer, only the flat sound of his voice going lost into the open sea, each time he sang out.

" 'Ahoy! Aboard there! Ahoy!' he shouted, time after time; but there was only the weary silence of the old hulk that answered us; and, somehow as he shouted, the while that I stared up half expectantly at her, a queer little sense of oppression, that amounted almost to nervousness came upon me. It passed, but I remember how I was suddenly aware that it was growing dark. Darkness comes fairly rapidly in the tropics, though not so quickly as many fiction-writers seem to think; but it was not that the coming dusk had perceptibly deepened in that brief time, of only a few moments, but rather that my nerves had made me suddenly a little hypersensitive. I mention my state particularly; for I am not a nervy man, normally; and my abrupt touch of nerves is significant, in the light of what happened.

" 'There's no one aboard there!' said Captain Gannington. 'Give way, men!' For the boat's crew had instinctively rested on their oars, as the captain hailed the old craft. The men gave way again; and then the second mate called out excitedly: 'Why, look there, there's our pigsty! See, it's got *Bheotpte* painted on the end. It's drifted down here, and the scum's caught it. What a blessed wonder!'

"It was as he had said, our pigsty that had been washed overboard in the storm, and it was most extraordinary to come across it there.

" 'We'll tow it off with us, when we go,' remarked the captain, and shouted to the crew to get down to their oars; for they were hardly moving the boat, because the scum was so thick, close in around the old ship, that it literally clogged the boat from going ahead. I remember that it struck me in a half-conscious sort of way, as curious that the pigsty, containing our three dead pigs, had managed to drift so far, unaided, whilst we could scarcely manage to *force* the boat in now that we had come right into the scum. But the thought passed from my mind; for so many things happened within the next few minutes.

"The men managed to bring the boat alongside, within a couple of feet of the derelict, and the man with the boathook hooked on.

" ''Ave you got 'old there, forrard?' asked the captain. 'Yessir!' said the bow man; and as he spoke there came a queer noise of tearing.

" 'What's that?' asked the captain.

" 'It's tore, sir. Tore clean away!' said the man; and his tone showed that he had received something of a shock.

" 'Get a hold again, then!' said Captain Gannington, irritably. 'You don't s'pose this packet was built yesterday! Shove the hook into the main chains.' The man did so gingerly, as you might say; for it seemed to me, in the growing dusk, that he put no strain on the hook, though, of course, there was no need; you see the boat could not go very far, of herself, in the stuff in which she was embedded. I remember thinking this, also, as I looked up at the bulging side of the old vessel. Then I heard Captain Gannington's voice:

" 'Lord, but she's old! An' what a color, Doctor! She don't half want paint, do she! . . . Now then, somebody—one of them oars.'

"An oar was passed to him, and he leaned it up against the ancient, bulging side, then he paused, and called to the second mate to light a couple of lamps, and stand by to pass them up; for the darkness had settled down now upon the sea.

"The second mate lit two of the lamps and told one of the men to light a third, and keep it handy in the boat; then he stepped across, with a lamp in each hand, to where Captain Gannington stood by the oar against the side of the ship.

" 'Now, my lad,' said the captain, to the man who had pulled stroke, 'up with you, an' we'll pass ye the lamps.'

"The man jumped to obey; caught the oar, and put his weight upon it, and as he did so, something seemed to give a little.

" 'Look!' cried the second mate, and pointed, lamp in hand. . . . 'It's sunk in!'

"This was true. The oar had made quite an indentation into the bulging, somewhat slimy side of the old vessel.

" 'Mould, I reckon,' said Captain Gannington, bending towards the derelict, to look. Then to the man:

" 'Up you go, my lad, and be smart. . . . Don't stand there waitin'!'

"At that, the man, who had paused a moment as he felt the oar give beneath his weight, began to shin up, and in a few seconds he was aboard, and leaned over the rail for the lamps. These were passed up to him, and the captain called to him to steady the oar. Then Captain Gannington went, calling me to follow, and after me the second mate.

"As the captain put his face over the rail, he gave a cry of astonishment:

" 'Mould, by gum! Mould. . . . Tons of it! . . . Good Lord!'

"As I heard him shout that, I scrambled the more eagerly after him, and in a moment or two, I was able to see what he meant—everywhere that the light from the two lamps struck, there was nothing but smooth, great masses and surfaces of a dirty-white mould.

"I climbed over the rail, with the second mate close behind, and stood upon the mould-covered decks. There might have been no planking beneath the mould, for all that our feet could feel. It gave under our tread, with a spongy, puddingy feel. It covered the deck-furniture of the old ship, so that the shape of each article and fitment was often no more than suggested through it.

"Captain Gannington snatched a lamp from the other man, and the second mate reached for the other. They held the lamps high, and we all stared. It was most extraordinary, and, somehow, most abominable. I can think of no other word, gentlemen, that so much describes the predominant feeling that effected me at the moment.

" 'Good Lord!' said Captain Gannington, several times. 'Good Lord!' But neither the second mate nor the man said anything, and for my part I just stared, and at the same time began to smell a little at the air, for there was again a vague odor of something half familiar, that somehow brought to me a sense of half-known fright.

"I turned this way and that, staring, as I have said. Here and there, the mould was so heavy as to entirely disguise what lay beneath, converting the deck-fittings into indistinguishable mounds of mould, all dirty-white, and blotched and veined with irregular, dull purplish markings.

"There was a strange thing about the mould, which Captain Gannington drew attention to—it was that our feet did not crush into it and break the surface, as might have been expected, but merely indented it.

" 'Never seen nothin' like it before! . . . Never!' said the captain, after having stooped with his lamp to examine the mould under our feet. He stamped with his heel, and the stuff gave out a dull, puddingy sound. He stooped again, with a quick movement, and stared, holding the lamp close to the deck. 'Blest if it ain't a reg'lar skin to it!' he said.

"The second mate and the man and I all stooped, and looked at it. The second mate prodded it with his forefinger, and I remember I rapped it several times with my knuckles, listening to the dead sound it gave out, and noticing the close, firm texture of the mould.

" 'Dough!' said the second mate. 'It's just like blessed dough! . . . Pouf!' He stood up with a quick movement. 'I could fancy it stinks a bit,' he said.

"As he said this, I knew suddenly what the familiar thing was in the vague odor that hung about us—it was that the smell had something animal-like in it; something of the same smell only *heavier,* that you smell in any place that is infested with mice. I began to look about with a sudden, very real uneasiness. . . . There might be vast numbers of hungry rats aboard. . . . They might prove exceedingly dangerous, if in a starving condition, yet, as you will understand, somehow I hesitated to put forward my idea as a reason for caution. It was too fanciful.

"Captain Gannington had begun to go aft, along the mould-covered main-deck, with the second mate; each of them holding his lamp high up, so as to cast a good light about the vessel. I turned quickly and followed them, the man with me keeping close to my heels, and plainly uneasy. As we went, I became aware that there was a feeling of moisture in the air, and I remembered the slight mist, or smoke, above the hulk, which had made Captain Gannington suggest spontaneous combustion in explanation.

"And always, as we went, there was that vague animal smell; and suddenly I found myself wishing we were well away from the old vessel.

"Abruptly, after a few paces, the captain stopped and pointed at a row of mould-hidden shapes on either side of the main-deck. . . . 'Guns,' he said. 'Been a privateer in the old days, I guess; maybe worse! We'll 'ave a look below, Doctor; there may be something worth touchin'. She's older than I thought. Mr. Selvern thinks she's about three hundred years old; but I scarce think it.'

"We continued our way aft, and I remember that I found myself walking as lightly and gingerly as possible; as if I were subconsciously afraid of treading through the rotten, mould-hid decks. I think the others had a touch of the same feeling, from the way that they walked. Occasionally the soft mould would grip our heels, releasing them with a little, sullen suck.

"The captain forged somewhat ahead of the second mate, and I know that the suggestion he had made himself, that perhaps there might be something below, worth the carrying away, had stimulated his imagination. The second mate was, however, beginning to feel somewhat the same way that I did; at least, I have that impression. I think if it had not been for what I might truly describe as Captain Gannington's sturdy courage, we should all of us have just gone back over the side very soon; for there was most certainly an unwholesome feeling aboard that made one feel queerly lacking in pluck, and you will soon perceive that this feeling was justified.

"Just as the captain reached the few, mould-covered steps, leading up on to the short half-poop, I was suddenly aware that the feeling of moisture in the air had grown very much more definite. It was perceptible now, intermittently, as a sort of thin, moist, foglike vapor, that came and went oddly, and seemed to make the decks a little indistinct to the view, this time and that. Once, an odd puff of it beat up suddenly from somewhere, and caught me in the face, carrying a queer, sickly, heavy odor with it, that somehow frightened me strangely, with a suggestion of a waiting and half-comprehended danger.

"We had followed Captain Gannington up the three mould-covered steps, and now went slowly aft along the raised after-deck.

"By the mizen-mast, Captain Gannington paused, and held his lantern near it. . . .

" 'My word, mister,' he said to the second mate, 'it's fair thickened up with the mould; why, I'll g'antee it's close on four foot thick.' He shone the light down to where it met the deck. 'Good Lord!' he said. 'Look at the sea-lice on it!' I stepped up; and it was as he had said; the sea-lice were thick upon it, some of them huge, not less than the size of large beetles, and all a clear, colorless shade, like water except where there were little spots of gray in them—evidently their internal organisms.

" 'I've never seen the like of them, 'cept on a live cod!' said Captain Gannington, in an extremely puzzled voice. 'My word, but they're whoppers!' Then he passed on, but a few paces farther aft, he stopped again, and held his lamp near to the mould-hidden deck.

" 'Lord bless me, Doctor!' he called out, in a low voice. 'Did you ever see the like of that? Why, it's a foot long, if it's a hinch!'

"I stooped over his shoulder, and saw what he meant; it was a clear, colorless creature, about a foot long, and about eight inches high, with a curved back that was extraordinary narrow. As we stared, all in a group, it gave a queer little flick, and was gone.

" 'Jumped!' said the captain. 'Well, if that ain't a giant of all the sea-lice that I've ever seen! I guess it jumped twenty foot clear.' He straightened his back, and scratched his head a moment, swinging the lantern this way and that with the other hand, and staring about us. 'Wot are *they* doin' aboard 'ere!' he said. 'You'll see 'em (little things) on fat cod, an' such like. . . . I'm blowed, Doctor, if I understand.'

"He held his lamp towards a big mound of the mould, that occupied part of the after portion of the low poop-deck, a little foreside of where there came a two-foot high 'break' to a kind of second and loftier poop, that ran away aft to the taffrail. The mound was pretty big, several feet across, and more than a yard high. Captain Gannington walked up to it.

" 'I reckon this's the scuttle,' he remarked, and gave it a heavy kick. The only result was a deep indentation into the huge, whitish hump of mould, as if he had driven his foot into a mass of some doughy substance. Yet, I am not altogether correct in saying that this was the only result; for a certain other thing happened—from a place made by the captain's foot, there came a little gush of purplish fluid, accompanied by a peculiar smell, that was, and was not, half familiar. Some of the mouldlike substance had stuck to the toe of the captain's boot, and from this, likewise, there issued a sweat, as it were, of the same color.

" 'Well!' said Captain Gannington, in surprise, and drew back his foot to make another kick at the hump of mould; but he paused, at an exclamation from the second mate:

" 'Don't sir!' said the second mate.

"I glanced at him, and the light from Captain Gannington's lamp showed me that his face had a bewildered, half-frightened look, as if it were suddenly and unexpectedly half afraid of something, and as if his tongue had given way to his sudden fright, without any intention on his part to speak.

"The captain also turned and stared at him.

" 'Why, mister?' he asked, in a somewhat puzzled voice, through which there sounded just the vaguest hint of annoyance. "We've got to shift this muck, if we're to get below.'

"I looked at the second mate, and it seemed to me that, curiously enough, he was listening less to the captain, than to some other sound.

"Suddenly, he said in a queer voice: 'Listen, everybody!'

"Yet we heard nothing, beyond the faint murmur of the men talking together in the boat alongside.

" 'I don't hear nothin',' said Captain Gannington, after a short pause. 'Do you, Doctor?'

" 'No,' I said.

" 'What was it you thought you heard?' asked the captain, turning again to the second mate. But the second mate shook his head, in a curious, almost irritable way; as if the captain's question interrupted his listening. Captain Gannington stared a moment at him, then held his lantern up, and glanced about him, almost uneasily. I know I felt a queer sense of strain. But the light showed nothing, beyond the grayish, dirty white of the mould in all directions.

" 'Mister Selvern,' said the captain at last, looking at him, 'don't get fancying things. Get hold of your bloomin' self. Ye know ye heard nothin'?'

"I'm quite sure I heard something, sir!' said the second mate. 'I seemed to hear—' He broke off sharply, and appeared to listen, with an almost painful intensity.

" 'What did it sound like?' I asked.

" 'It's all right, Doctor,' said Captain Gannington, laughing gently. 'Ye can give him a tonic when we get back. I'm goin' to shift this stuff.'

"He drew back, and kicked for the second time at the ugly mass, which he took to hide the companion-way. The result of his kick was startling; for the whole thing wobbled sloppily, like a mound of unhealthy-looking jelly.

"He drew his foot out of it quickly, and took a step backwards, staring, and holding his lamp towards it.

" 'By gum!' he said, and it was plain that he was genuinely startled. 'The blessed thing's gone soft!'

"The man had run back several steps from the suddenly flaccid mound, and looked horribly frightened. Though, of what, I am sure he had not the least idea. The second mate stood where he was, and stared. For my part, I know I had a most hideous uneasiness upon me. The captain continued to hold his light towards the wobbling mound, and stare.

" 'It's gone squashy all through!' he said. 'There's no scuttle there. There's no bally woodwork inside that lot! Phoo! What a rum smell!'

"He walked round to the after-side of the strange mound, to see whether there might be some signs of an opening into the hull at the back of the great heap of mould-stuff. And then:

" *'Listen!'* said the second mate, again, and in the strangest sort of voice.

"Captain Gannington straightened himself upright, and there succeeded a pause of the most intense quietness, in which there was not even the hum of talk from the men alongside in the boat. We all heard it—a kind of dull, soft, *Thud! Thud! Thud! Thud!* somewhere in the hull under us, yet so vague that I might have been half doubtful I heard it, only that the others did so, too.

"Captain Gannington turned suddenly to where the man stood:

" 'Tell them—' he began. But the fellow cried out something, and pointed. There had come a strange intensity into his somewhat unemotional face; so that the captain's glance followed his action instantly. I stared, also, as you may think. It was the great mound, at which the man was pointing. I saw what he meant.

"From the two gaps made in the mould-like stuff by Captain Gannington's boot, the purple fluid was jetting out in a queerly regular fashion, almost as if it were being forced out by a pump. My word, but I stared! And even as I stared, a larger jet squirted out, and splashed as far as the man, spattering his boots and trouser-legs.

"The fellow had been pretty nervous before, in a stolid, ignorant way, and his funk had been growing steadily; but, at this, he simply let out a yell, and turned about to run. He paused an instant, as if a sudden fear of the darkness that held the decks between him and the boat had taken him. He snatched at the second mate's lantern, tore it out of his hand, and plunged heavily away over the vile stretch of mould.

"Mr. Selvern, the second mate, said not a word; he was just standing, staring at the strange-smelling twin streams of dull purple that were jetting out from the wobbling mound. Captain Gannington, however, roared an order to the man to come back; but the man plunged on and on across the mould, his feet seeming to be clogged by the stuff, as if it had grown suddenly soft. He zigzagged as he ran, the lantern swaying in wild circles as he wrenched his feet free, with a constant *plop, plop;* and I could hear his frightened gasps, even from where I stood.

" 'Come back with that lamp!' roared the captain again; but still the man took no notice, and Captain Gannington was silent an instant, his lips working in a queer, inarticulate fashion; as if he were stunned momentarily by the very violence of his anger at the man's insubordination. And, in the silence, I heard the sound again: *Thud! Thud! Thud! Thud!* Quite distinctly now, beating, it seemed suddenly to me, right down under my feet, but deep.

"I stared down at the mould on which I was standing, with a quick, disgusting sense of the terrible all about me; then I looked at the captain, and tried to say something, without appearing frightened. I saw that he had turned again to the mound, and all the anger had gone out of his face. He had his lamp out toward the mound, and was listening. There was a further moment of absolute silence; at least, I know that I was not conscious of any sound at all, in all the world, except that extraordinary *Thud! Thud! Thud! Thud!* down somewhere in the huge bulk under us.

"The captain shifted his feet, with a sudden, nervous movement; and as he lifted them, the mould went *plop, plop.* He looked quickly at me, trying to smile, as if he were not thinking anything very much about it. 'What do you make of it, Doctor?' he said.

" 'I think—' I began. But the second mate interrupted with a single word; his voice pitched a little high, in a tone that made us both stare instantly at him.

" 'Look!' he said, and pointed at the mound. The thing was all of a slow quiver. A strange ripple ran outward from it, along the deck, as you will see a ripple run inshore out of a calm sea. It reached a mound a little fore-side of us, which I supposed to be the cabin-skylight; and in a moment the second mound sank nearly level with the surrounding decks, quivering floppily in a most extraordinary fashion. A sudden quick tremor took the mould right under the second mate, and he gave out a hoarse cry, and held his arms out on each side of him, to keep his balance. The tremor in the mould spread, and Captain Gannington swayed, and spread his feet with a sudden curse of fright. The second mate jumped across to him, and caught him by the wrist.

" 'The boat, sir!' he said, saying the very thing that I had lacked the pluck to say. 'For God's sake—'

"But he never finished; for a tremendous hoarse scream cut off his words. They hove themselves round, and looked. I could see without turning. The man who had run from us, was standing in the waist of the ship, about a fathom from the starboard bulwarks.

"He was swaying from side to side and screaming in a dreadful fashion. He appeared to be trying to lift his feet, and the light from his swaying lantern showed an almost incredible sight. All about him the mould was in active movement. His feet had sunk out of sight. The stuff appeared to be *lapping* at his legs; and abruptly his bare flesh showed.

"The hideous stuff had rent his trouser-legs away, as if they were paper. He gave out a simply sickening scream, and, with a vast effort, wrenched one leg free. It was partly destroyed. The next instant he pitched face downward, and the stuff heaped itself upon him, as if it were actually alive, with a dreadful savage life. It was simply infernal. The man had gone from sight. Where he had fallen was now a writhing mound, in constant and horrible increase, as the mould appeared to move toward it in strange ripples from all sides.

"Captain Gannington and the second mate were stone silent, in amazed and incredulous horror; but I had begun to reach towards a grotesque and terrific conclusion, both helped and hindered by my professional training.

"From the men in the boat alongside, there was a loud shouting, and I saw two of their faces appear suddenly above the rail. They showed clearly, a moment, in the light from the lamp which the man had snatched from Mr. Selvern; for strangely enough, this lamp was standing upright and unharmed on the deck, a little way fore-side of that dreadful, elongated, growing mound, that still swayed and writhed with an incredible horror.

The lamp rose and fell on the passing ripples of the mould just— for all the world—as you will see a boat rise and fall on little swells. It is of some interest to me now, psychologically, to remember how that rising and falling lantern brought home to me, more than anything, the incomprehensible, dreadful strangeness of it all.

"The men's faces disappeared, with sudden yells, as if they had slipped or been suddenly hurt; and there was a fresh uproar of shouting from the boat. The men were calling to us to come away; to come away. In the same instant, I felt my left boot drawn suddenly and forcibly downward, with a horrible painful grip. I wrenched it free, with a yell of angry fear. Forrard of us, I saw that the vile surface was all a-move, and abruptly I found myself shouting in a queer frightened voice:

" 'The boat, Captain! The boat, Captain!'

"Captain Gannington stared round at me, over his right shoulder, in a peculiar, dull way that told me he was utterly dazed with bewilderment and the incomprehensibleness of it all. I took a quick, clogged, nervous step towards him, and gripped his arm and shook it fiercely.

" 'The boat!' I shouted at him. 'The boat! For God's sake, tell the men to bring the boat aft!'

"Then the mould must have drawn his feet down; for, abruptly, he bellowed fiercely with terror, his momentary apathy giving place to furious energy. His thick-set, vastly muscular body doubled and whirled with his enormous effort, and he struck out madly, dropping the lantern. He tore his feet free, something ripped as he did so. The *reality* and necessity of the situation had come upon him, brutishly real, and he was roaring to the men in the boat:

" 'Bring the boat aft! Bring 'er aft! Bring 'er aft!'

"The second mate and I were shouting the same thing, madly.

" 'For God's sake be smart, lads!' roared the captain, and he stooped quickly for his lamp, which still burned. His feet were gripped again, and he hove them out, blaspheming breathlessly, and leaping a yard high with his effort. Then he made a run for the side, wrenching his feet free at each step. In the same instant, the second mate cried out something, and grabbed at the captain.

" 'It's got hold of my feet! It's got hold of my feet!' the second mate screamed. His feet had disappeared up to his boot-tops, and Captain Gannington caught him round the waist with his powerful left arm, gave a mighty heave, and the next instant had him free; but both his boot-soles had almost gone.

"For my part, I jumped madly from foot to foot, to avoid the plucking of the mould; and suddenly I made a run for the ship's side. But before I got there, a queer gap came in the mould, between us and the side, at least a couple of feet wide, and how deep I don't know. It closed up in an instant, and all the mould, where the gap had been, went into a sort of flurry of horrible ripplings, so that I ran back from it; for I did not dare to put my foot upon it. Then the captain was shouting at me:

" 'Aft, Doctor! Aft, Doctor! This way, Doctor! Run!' I saw then that he had passed me, and was up on the after raised portion of the poop. He had the second mate thrown like a sack, all loose and quiet, over his left shoulder; for Mr. Selvern had fainted, and his long legs flopped, limp and helpless, against the captain's massive knees as the captain ran. I saw, with a queer, unconscious noting of minor details, how the torn soles of the second mate's boots flapped and jigged, as the captain staggered aft.

" 'Boat ahoy! Boat ahoy! Boat ahoy!' shouted the captain; and then I was beside him, shouting also. The men were answering with loud yells of encouragement, and it was plain they were working desperately to force the boat aft, through the thick scum about the ship.

"We reached the ancient, mould-hid taffrail, and slewed about, breath-lessly, in the half darkness, to see what was happening. Captain Gannington had left his lantern by the big mound, when he picked up the second mate; and as we stood gasping, we discovered suddenly that all the mould between us and the light was full of movement. Yes, the part on which we stood, for about six or eight feet forward of us, was still firm.

"Every couple of seconds, we shouted to the men to hasten, and they kept calling to us that they would be with us in an instant. And all the time, we watched the deck of that dreadful hulk, I felt, for my part, literally sick with mad suspense, and ready to jump overboard into that filthy scum all about us.

"Down somewhere in the huge bulk of the ship, there was all the time the extraordinary, dull, ponderous *Thud! Thud! Thud! Thud!* growing ever louder. I seemed to feel the whole hull of the derelict beginning to quiver and thrill with each dull beat. And to me, with the grotesque and monstrous suspicion of what made that noise, it was, at once, the most dreadful and incredible sound I have ever heard.

"As we waited desperately for the boat, I scanned incessantly so much of the gray-white bulk as the lamp showed. The whole of the decks seemed to be in strange movement. Forrard of the lamp I could see, indistinctly, the moundings of the mould swaying and nodding hideously, beyond the circle of the brightest rays. Nearer, and full in the glow of the lamp, the mound which should have indicated the skylight, was swelling steadily. There were ugly purple veinings on it, and as it swelled, it seemed to me that the veinings and mottling on it were becoming plainer—rising, as though embossed upon it, as you will see the veins stand out on the body of a powerful full-blooded horse. It was most extraordinary. The mound that we had supposed to cover the companion-way had sunk flat with the surrounding mould, and I could not see that it jetted out any more of the purplish fluid.

"A quaking movement of the mould began, away forward of the lamp, and came flurrying away aft towards us; and at the sight of that, I climbed up on to the spongy-feeling taffrail, and yelled afresh for the boat. The men answered with a shout, which told me they were nearer, but the beastly scum was so thick that it was evidently a fight to move the boat at all. Beside me, Captain Gannington was shaking the second mate furiously, and the man stirred and began to moan. The captain shook him awake.

" 'Wake up! Wake up, Mister!' he shouted.

"The second mate staggered out of the captain's arms, and collapsed suddenly, shrieking: 'My feet! Oh, God! My feet!' The captain and I lugged him off the mould, and got him into a sitting position upon the taffrail, where he kept up a continual moaning.

" 'Hold 'em, Doctor,' said the Captain, and whilst I did so, he ran forrard a few yards, and peered down over the starboard quarter rail. 'For God's sake, be smart, lads! Be smart! Be smart!' he shouted down to the men; and they answered him, breathless, from close at hand; yet still too far away for the boat to be any use to us on the instant.

"I was holding the moaning, half-unconscious officer, and staring forrard along the poop decks. The flurrying of the mould was coming aft, slowly and noiselessly. And then, suddenly, I saw something closer:

" 'Look out, Captain!' I shouted; and even as I shouted, the mould near to him gave a sudden peculiar slobber. I had seen a ripple stealing towards him through the horrible stuff. He gave an enormous, clumsy leap, and landed near to us on the sound part of the mould, but the movement followed him. He turned and faced it, swearing fiercely. All about his feet there came abruptly little gapings, which made horrid sucking noises.

" 'Come *back*, Captain!' I yelled. 'Come back, *quick!*' and he stamped insanely at it, and leaped back, his boot torn half off his foot. He swore madly with pain and anger, and jumped swiftly for the taffrail.

" 'Come on, Doctor! Over we go!' he called. Then he remembered the filthy scum, and hesitated, roaring out desperately to the men to hurry. I started down, also.

" 'The second mate?' I said.

" 'I'll take charge, Doctor,' said Captain Gannington, and caught hold of Mr. Selvern. As he spoke, I thought I saw something beneath us, outlined against the scum. I leaned out over the stern, and peered. There was something under the port quarter.

" 'There's something down there, Captain!' I called, and pointed in the darkness.

"He stooped far over, and stared.

" 'A boat, by gum! A *boat!*' he yelled, and began to wriggle swiftly along the taffrail, dragging the second mate after him. I followed.

" 'A boat it is, sure!' he exclaimed, a few moments later, and, picking up the second mate clear of the rail, he hove him down into the boat, where he fell with a crash into the bottom.

" 'Over ye go, Doctor!' he yelled at me, and pulled me bodily off the rail, and dropped me after the officer. As he did so, I felt the whole of the ancient, spongy rail give a peculiar sickening quiver, and begin to wobble. I fell onto the second mate, and the captain came after, almost in the same instant; but fortunately he landed clear of us, on to the fore thwart, which broke under his weight, with a loud crack and splintering of wood.

" 'Thank God!' I heard him mutter. 'Thank God! . . . I guess that was a mighty near thing to goin' to hell.'

"He struck a match, just as I got to my feet, and between us we got the second mate straightened out on one of the after thwarts. We shouted to the men in the boat, telling them where we were, and saw the light of their lantern shining round to tell us they were doing their best, and then, while we waited, Captain Gannington struck another match, and began to overhaul the boat we had dropped into. She was a modern, two-oared boat, and on the stern there was painted *Cyclone Glasgow.* She was in pretty fair condition, and had evidently drifted into the scum and been held by it.

"Captain Gannington struck several matches, and went forrard toward the derelict. Suddenly he called to me, and I jumped over the thwarts to him.

" 'Look, Doctor,' he said; and I saw what he meant—a mass of bones, up in the bow of the boat. I stooped over them and looked. They were the bones of at least three people, all mixed together, in an extraordinary fashion, and quite clean and dry. I had a sudden thought concerning the bones; but I said nothing; for my thought was vague, in some ways, and concerned the grotesque and incredible suggestion that had come to me, as to the cause of that ponderous, dull *Thud! Thud! Thud!* that beat on so infernally within the hull, and was plain to hear even now that we had a sick, horrible, mental picture of that frightful wriggling mound aboard the hulk.

"As Captain Gannington struck a final match I saw something that sickened me, and the captain saw it in the same instant. The match went out, and he fumbled clumsily for another, and struck it. We saw the thing again. We had not been mistaken. . . . A great lip of gray-white was protruding in over the edge of the boat—a great lappet of the mould was coming steadily towards us; a live mess of *the very hull itself.* And suddenly Captain Gannington yelled out, in so many words, the grotesque and incredible thing I was thinking:

" *'She's alive!'*

"I never heard such a sound of *comprehension* and terror in a man's voice. The very horrified assurance of it, made actual to me the thing that, before, had lurked in my subconscious mind. I knew he was right; I knew that the explanation, my reason and my training, both repelled and reached towards, was the true one. . . . I wonder whether anyone can possibly understand our feelings in that moment. . . . The unmitigable horror of it, and the *incredibleness*.

"As the light of the match burned up fully, I saw that the mass of living matter, coming towards us, was streaked and veined with purple, the veins standing out, enormously distended. The whole thing quivered continuously to each ponderous *Thud! Thud! Thud!* of that gargantuan organ that pulsed within the huge gray-white hulk. The flame of the match reached the captain's fingers, and there came to me a little sickly whiff of burned flesh; but he seemed unconscious of any pain. Then the flame went out, in a brief sizzle, yet at the last moment, I had seen an extraordinary raw look become visible upon the end of that monstrous, protruding lappet. It had become dewed with a hideous, purplish sweat. And with the darkness, there came a sudden charnel-like stench.

"I heard the match-box split in Captain Gannington's hands, as he wrenched it open. Then he swore, in a queer frightened voice; for he had come to the end of his matches. He turned clumsily in the darkness, and tumbled over the nearest thwart, in his eagerness to get to the stern of the boat, and I after him; for he knew that thing was coming towards us through the darkness, reaching over that piteous mingled heap of human bones, all jumbled together in the bows. We shouted madly to the men, and for answer saw the bows of the boat emerge dimly into view, round the starboard counter of the derelict.

" 'Thank God!' I gasped out; but Captain Gannington yelled to them to show a light. Yet this they could not do, for the lamp had just been stepped on, in their desperate efforts to force the boat around to us.

" 'Quick! Quick!' I shouted.

" 'For God's sake be smart, men!' roared the captain; and both of us faced the darkness under the port counter, out of which we knew (but could not see) the thing was coming toward us.

" 'An oar! Smart now; pass me an oar!' shouted the captain; and reached out his hand through the gloom toward the oncoming boat. I saw a figure stand up in the bows, and hold something out to us, across the intervening yards of scum. Captain Gannington swept his hands through the darkness, and encountered it.

" 'I've got it. Let go there!' he said, in a quick, tense voice.

"In the same instant, the boat we were in was pressed over suddenly to starboard by some tremendous weight. Then I heard the captain shout: 'Duck y'r head, Doctor,' and directly afterwards he swung the heavy, fourteen-foot ash oar round his head, and struck into the darkness. There came a sudden squelch, and he struck again, with a savage grunt of fierce energy. At the second blow, the boat righted, with a slow movement, and directly afterwards the other boat bumped gently into ours.

"Captain Gannington dropped the oar, and springing across to the second mate, hove him up off the thwart, and pitched him with knee and arms clear in over the bows among the men; then he shouted to me to follow, which I did, and he came after me, bringing the oar with him. We carried the second mate aft, and the captain shouted to the men to back the boat a little; then they got her bows clear of the boat we had just left, and so headed out through the scum for the open sea.

" 'Where's Tom 'Arrison?' gasped one of the men, in the midst of his exertions. He happened to be Tom Harrison's particular chum; and Captain Gannington answered him briefly enough:

" 'Dead! Pull! Don't talk!'

"Now, difficult as it had been to force the boat through the scum to our rescue, the difficulty to get clear seemed tenfold. After some five minutes pulling, the boat seemed hardly to have moved a fathom, if so much; and a quite dreadful fear took me afresh; which one of the panting men put suddenly into words:

" 'It's got us!' he gasped out; 'same as poor Tom!' It was the man who had inquired where Harrison was.

" 'Shut y'r mouth and *pull!*' roared the captain. And so another few minutes passed. Abruptly, it seemed to me that the dull, ponderous *Thud! Thud! Thud!* came more plainly through the dark, and I stared intently over the stern. I sickened a little; for I could almost swear that the dark mass of the monster was actually *nearer* . . . that it was coming nearer to us through the darkness. Captain Gannington must have had the same thought; for after a brief look into the darkness, he made one jump to the stroke-oar, and began to double bank it.

" 'Get forrid under the thwarts, Doctor!' he said to me, rather breathlessly. 'Get in the bows, an' see if you can't free the stuff a bit round the bows.'

"I did as he told me, and a minute later I was in the bows of the boat, puddling the scum from side to side with the boathook, and trying to break up the viscid, clinging muck. A heavy, almost animal-like odor rose off it, and all the air seemed full of the deadening smell. I shall never find words to tell any one the whole horror of it—the threat that seemed to hang in the very air around us; and, but a little astern, that incredible thing, coming, as I firmly believe, nearer, and the scum holding us like half-melted glue.

"The minutes passed in a deadly, eternal fashion, and I kept staring back.

"Abruptly, Captain Gannington sang out:

" 'We're gaining, lads. Pull!' And I felt the boat forge ahead perceptibly, as they gave way, with renewed hope and energy. There was soon no doubt of it; for presently that hideous *Thud! Thud! Thud! Thud!* had grown quite dim and vague somewhat astern, and I could no longer see the derelict, for the night had come down tremendously dark, and all the sky was thick overset with heavy clouds. As we drew nearer and nearer to the edge of the scum, the boat moved more and more freely, until suddenly we emerged with a clean, sweet, fresh sound, into the open sea.

" 'Thank God!' I said aloud, and drew in the boat-hook, and made my way aft again to where Captain Gannington now sat once more at the tiller. I saw him looking anxiously up at the sky, and across to where the lights of our vessel burned, and again he would seem to listen intently; so that I found myself listening also.

" 'What's that, Captain?' I said sharply; for it seemed to me that I heard a sound far astern, something between a queer whine and a low whistling. 'What's that?'

" 'It's the wind, Doctor,' he said, in a low voice. 'I wish to God we were aboard.'

"Then, to the men: 'Pull! Put y'r backs into it, or ye'll never put y'r teeth through good bread again!'

"The men obeyed nobly, and we reached the vessel safely, and had the boat safely stowed, before the storm came, which it did in a furious white smother out of the west. I could see it for some minutes beforehand, tearing the sea, in the gloom, into a wall of phosphorescent foam; and as it came nearer, that peculiar whining, piping sound grew louder and louder, until it was like a vast steam-whistle, rushing towards us across the sea.

"And when it did come, we got it very heavy indeed; so that the morning showed us nothing but a welter of white seas; and that grim derelict was many a score of miles away in the smother, lost as utterly as our hearts could wish to lose her.

When I came to examine the second mate's feet, I found them in a very extraordinary condition. The soles of them had the appearance of having been partly digested. I know of no other word that so exactly describes their condition; and the agony the man suffered must have been dreadful.

"Now," concluded the doctor, "that is what I call a case in point. If we could know exactly what that old vessel had originally been loaded with, and the juxtaposition of the various articles of her cargo, plus the heat and time she had endured, plus one or two other only guessable quantities, we should have solved the chemistry of the Life-Force, gentlemen. Not necessarily the *origin,* mind you; but, at least, we should have taken a big step on the way.

"I've often regretted that gale, you know—in a way, that is, in a way! It was a most amazing discovery; but, at the time, I had nothing but thankfulness to be rid of it. . . . A most amazing chance. I often think of the way the monster woke out of its torpor. And that scum. . . . The dead pigs caught in it. . . . I fancy that was a grim kind of net, gentlemen. . . . It caught many things. . . . It. . . ."

The old doctor sighed and nodded.

"If I could have had her bill of lading," he said, his eyes full of regret. "If—It might have told me something to help. But, anyway. . . ." He began to fill his pipe again. "I suppose," he ended, looking round at us gravely, "I s'pose we humans are an ungrateful lot of beggars, at the best!

"But what a chance! What a chance—eh?"

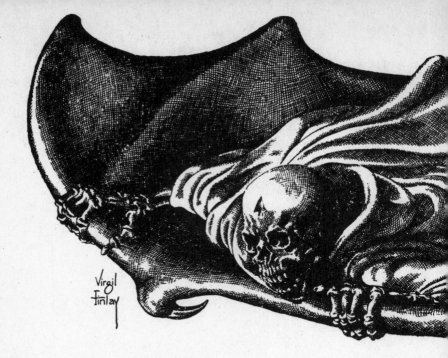

Virgil Finlay

The Novel of the White Powder

ARTHUR MACHEN

The work of Arthur Machen has been unfairly neglected since his death in 1947. Some of the blame can be laid at his own feet, since Machen wrote a vast quantity of fiction and non-fiction that is negligible by any standards. However, his short story "The White People" continually tops lists of the best supernatural fiction and "The Great God Pan" is among the most frequently anthologized horror stories in the English language. Some of Machen's best writing can be found in his episodic 1895 novel The Three Impostors, *segments of which are often reprinted as separate stories.* Famous Fantastic Mysteries *carried three of these stories, including the oft-imitated "The Novel of the White Powder."*

MY NAME is Helen Leicester; my father, Major-General Wyn Leicester, a distinguished officer of artillery, succumbed five years ago to a complicated liver complaint acquired in the deadly climate of India. A year later my only brother, Francis, came home after an exceptionally brilliant career at the University, and settled down with the resolution of a hermit to master what has been well called the great legend of the law. He was a man who seemed to live in utter indifference to everything that is called pleasure; and though he was handsomer than most men, and could talk as merrily and wittily as if he were a mere vagabond, he avoided society, and shut himself up in a large room at the top of the house to make himself a lawyer. Ten hours a day of hard reading was at first his allotted portion; from the first light in the east to the late afternoon he remained shut up with his books, taking a hasty half-hour's lunch with me as if he grudged the wasting of the moments, and going out for a short walk when it began to grow dusk. I thought that such relentless application must be injurious, and tried to cajole him from the crabbed textbooks, but his ardor seemed to grow rather than diminish, and his daily tale of hours increased. I spoke to him seriously, suggesting some occasional relaxation, if it were but an idle afternoon with a harmless novel; but he laughed, and said that he read about feudal tenures when he felt in need of amusement, and scoffed at the notions of theatres, or a month's fresh air. I confessed that he looked well, and seemed not to suffer from his labors, but I knew that such unnatural toil would take revenge at last, and I was not mistaken. A look of anxiety began to lurk about his eyes, and he seemed languid, and at last he avowed that he was no longer in perfect health; he was troubled, he said, with a sensation of dizziness, and awoke now and then of nights from fearful dreams, terrified and cold with icy sweats. "I am taking care of myself," he said, "so you must not trouble; I passed the whole of yesterday afternoon in idleness, leaning back in that comfortable chair you gave me, and scribbling nonsense on a sheet of paper. No, no; I will not overdo my work; I shall be well enough in a week or two depend upon it."

Yet in spite of his assurances I could see that he grew no better, but rather worse; he would enter the drawing-room with a face all miserably wrinkled and despondent, and endeavor to look gaily when my eyes fell on him, and I thought such symptoms of evil omen, and was frightened sometimes at the nervous irritation of his movements, and at glances which I could not decipher. Much against his will, I prevailed on him to have medical advice, and with an ill grace he called in our old doctor.

Dr. Haberden cheered me after examination of his patient.

"There is nothing really much amiss," he said to me. "No doubt he reads too hard and eats hastily, and then goes back again to his books in too great a hurry, and the natural sequence is some digestive trouble and a little mischief in the nervous system. But I think—I do indeed, Miss Leicester—that we shall be able to set this all right. I have written him a prescription which ought to do great things. So you have no cause for anxiety."

My brother insisted on having the prescription made up by a chemist in the neighborhood. It was an odd, old-fashioned shop, devoid of the studied coquetry and calculated glitter that make so gay a show on the counters and shelves of the modern apothecary; but Francis liked the old chemist, and believed in the scrupulous purity of his drugs. The medicine was sent in due course, and I saw that my brother took it regularly after lunch and dinner. It was an innocent-looking white powder, of which a little was dissolved in a glass of cold water; I stirred it in, and it seemed to disappear, leaving the water clear and colorless. At first Francis seemed to benefit greatly; the weariness vanished from his face, and he became more cheerful than he had ever been since the time when he left school; he talked gaily of reforming himself, and avowed to me that he had wasted his time.

"I have given too many hours to law," he said, laughing; "I think you have saved me in the nick of time. Come, I shall be Lord Chancellor yet, but I must not forget life. You and I will have a holiday together before long; we will go to Paris and enjoy ourselves, and keep away from the Bibliothèque Nationale."

I confessed myself delighted with the prospect.

"When shall we go?" I said. "I can start the day after tomorrow if you like."

"Ah! that is perhaps a little too soon; after all, I do not know London yet, and I suppose a man ought to give the pleasures of his own country the first choice. But we will go off together in a week or two, so try and furbish up your French. I only know law French myself, and I am afraid that wouldn't do."

We were just finishing dinner, and he quaffed off his medicine with a parade of carousal as if it had been wine from some choicest bin.

"Has it any particular taste?" I said.

"No; I should not know I was not drinking water," and he got up from his chair and began to pace up and down the room as if he were undecided as to what he should do next.

"Shall we have coffee in the drawing-room?" I said; "or would you like to smoke?"

"No, I think I will take a turn; it seems a pleasant evening. Look at the afterglow; why, it is as if a great city were burning in flames, and down there between the dark houses it is raining blood fast. Yes, I will go out; I may be in soon, but I shall take my key; so goodnight, dear, if I don't see you again."

The door slammed behind him, and I saw him walk lightly down the street, swinging his malacca cane, and I felt grateful to Dr. Haberden for such an improvement.

I believe my brother came home very late that night, but he was in a merry mood the next morning.

"I walked on without thinking where I was going," he said, "enjoying the freshness of the air, and livened by the crowds as I reached more frequented quarters. And then I met an old college friend, Orford, in the press of the pavement, and then—well, we enjoyed ourselves. I have felt what it is to be young and a man; I find I have blood in my veins, as other men have. I made an appointment with Orford for tonight; there will be a little party of us at the restaurant. Yes; I shall enjoy myself for a week or two, and hear the chimes at midnight, and then we will go for our little trip together."

Such was the transmutation of my brother's character that in a few days he became a lover of pleasure, a careless and merry idler of western pavements, a hunter out of snug restaurants, and a fine critic of fantastic dancing; he grew fat before my eyes, and said no more of Paris, for he had clearly found his paradise in London. I rejoiced, and yet wondered a little; for there was, I thought, something in his gaiety that indefinitely displeased me, though I could not have defined my feeling. But by degrees there came a change; he returned still in the cold hours of the morning, but I heard no more about his pleasures, and one morning as we sat at breakfast together I looked suddenly into his eyes and saw a stranger before me.

"Oh, Francis!" I cried. "Oh, Francis, Francis, what have you done?" and rending sobs cut the words short. I went weeping out of the room; for though I knew nothing, yet I knew all, and by some odd play of thought I remembered the evening when he first went abroad, and the picture of the sunset sky glowed before me; the clouds like a city in burning flames, and the rain of blood. Yet I did battle with such thoughts, resolving that perhaps, after all, no great harm had been done, and in the evening at dinner I resolved to press him to fix a day for our holiday in Paris. We had talked easily enough, and my brother had just taken his medicine, which he continued all the while. I was about to begin my topic when the words forming in my mind vanished, and I wondered for a second what icy and intolerable weight oppressed my heart and suffocated me as with the unutterable horror of the coffin-lid nailed down on the living.

We had dined without candles; the room had slowly grown from twilight to gloom and the walls and corners were indistinct in the shadow. But from where I sat I looked out into the street; and as I thought of what I would say to Francis, the sky began to flush and shine, as it had done on a well-remembered evening, and in the gap between two dark masses that were houses an awful pageantry of flame appeared—lurid whorls of writhed cloud, and utter depths burning, grey masses like the fume blown from a smoking city, and an evil glory blazing far above shot with tongues of more ardent fire, and below as if there were a deep pool of blood. I looked down to where my brother sat facing me, and the words were shaped on my lips, when I saw his hand resting on the table. Between the thumb and forefinger of the closed hand there was a mark, a small patch about the size of a sixpence, and somewhat of the color of a bad bruise. Yet, by some sense I cannot define, I knew that what I saw was no bruise at all; oh! if human flesh could burn with flame, and if flame could be black as pitch, such was that before me. Without thought or fashioning of words grey horror shaped within me at the sight, and in an inner cell it was known to be a brand. For the moment the stained sky became dark as midnight, and when the light returned to me I was alone in the silent room, and soon after I heard my brother go out.

Late as it was, I put on my hat and went to Dr. Haberden, and in his great consulting room, ill lighted by a candle which the doctor brought in with him, with stammering lips, and a voice that would break in spite of my resolve, I told him all, from the day on which my brother began to take the medicine down to the dreadful thing I had seen scarcely half an hour before.

When I had done, the doctor looked at me for a minute with an expression of great pity on his face.

"My dear Miss Leicester," he said, "you have evidently been anxious about your brother; you have been worrying over him, I am sure. Come, now, is it not so?"

"I have certainly been anxious," I said. "For the last week or two I have not felt at ease."

"Quite so; you know, of course, what a queer thing the brain is?"

"I understand what you mean; but I was not deceived. I saw what I have told you with my own eyes."

"Yes, yes, of course. But your eyes had been staring at that very curious sunset we had tonight. That is the only explanation. You will see it in the proper light tomorrow, I am sure. But, remember, I am always ready to give any help that is in my power; do not scruple to come to me, or to send for me if you are in any distress."

I went away but little comforted, all confusion and terror and sorrow, not knowing where to turn. When my brother and I met the next day, I looked quickly at him, and noticed, with a sickening at heart, that the right hand, the hand on which I had clearly seen the patch as of a black fire, was wrapped up with a handkerchief.

"What is the matter with your hand, Francis?" I said in a steady voice.

"Nothing of consequence. I cut a finger last night, and it bled rather awkwardly. So I did it up roughly to the best of my ability."

"I will do it neatly for you, if you like."

"No, thank you, dear; this will answer very well. Suppose we have breakfast; I am quite hungry."

We sat down and I watched him. He scarcely ate or drank at all, but tossed his meat to the dog when he thought my eyes were turned away; there was a look in his eyes that I had never yet seen, and the thought flashed across my mind that it was a look that was scarcely human. I was firmly convinced that awful and incredible as was the thing I had seen the night before, yet it was no illusion, no glamor of bewildered sense, and in the course of the evening I went again to the doctor's house.

He shook his head with an air puzzled and incredulous, and seemed to reflect for a few minutes.

"And you say he still keeps up the medicine? But why? As I understand, all the symptoms he complained of have disappeared long ago; why should he go on taking the stuff when he is quite well? And by the by, where did he get it made up? At Sayce's? I never send any one there; the old man is getting careless. Suppose you come with me to the chemist's; I should like to have some talk with him."

We walked together to the shop; old Sayce knew Dr. Haberden, and was quite ready to give any information.

"You have been sending that in to Mr. Leicester for some weeks, I think, on my prescription," said the doctor, giving the old man a pencilled scrap of paper.

The chemist put on his great spectacles with trembling uncertainty, and held up the paper with a shaking hand.

"Oh, yes," he said, "I have very little of it left; it is rather an uncommon drug, and I have had it in stock some time. I must get in some more, if Mr. Leicester goes on with it."

"Kindly let me have a look at the stuff," said Haberden, and the chemist gave him a glass bottle. He took out the stopper and smelt the contents, and looked strangely at the old man.

"Where did you get this?" he said, "and what is it? For one thing, Mr. Sayce, it is not what I prescribed. Yes, yes, I see the label is right enough, but I tell you this is not the drug."

"I have had it a long time," said the old man in feeble terror; "I got it from Burbage's in the usual way. It is not prescribed often, and I have had it on the shelf for some years. You see there is very little left."

"You had better give it to me," said Haberden. "I am afraid something wrong has happened."

We went out of the shop in silence, the doctor carrying the bottle neatly wrapped in paper under his arm.

"Dr. Haberden," I said, when we had walked a little way— "Dr. Haberden."

"Yes," he said, looking at me gloomily enough.

"I should like you to tell me what my brother has been taking twice a day for the last month or so."

"Frankly, Miss Leicester, I don't know. We will speak of this when we get to my house."

We walked on quickly without another word till we reached Dr. Haberden's. He asked me to sit down, and began pacing up and down the room, his face clouded over, as I could see, with no common fears.

"Well," he said at length, "this is all very strange; it is only natural that you should feel alarmed, and I must confess that my mind is far from easy. We will put aside, if you please, what you told me last night and this morning, but the fact remains that for the last few weeks Mr. Leicester has been impregnating his system with a drug which is completely unknown to me. I tell you, it is not what I ordered; and what the stuff in the bottle really is remains to be seen."

He undid the wrapper, and cautiously tilted a few grains of the white powder on to a piece of paper, and peered curiously at it.

"Yes," he said, "it is like the sulphate of quinine, as you say; it is flaky. But smell it."

He held the bottle to me, and I bent over it. It was a strange, sickly smell, vaporous and overpowering like some strong anaesthetic.

"I shall have it analysed," said Haberden; "I have a friend who has devoted his whole life to chemistry as a science. Then we shall have something to go upon. No, no; say no more about the other matter; I cannot listen to that; and take my advice and think no more about it yourself."

That evening my brother did not go out as usual after dinner.

"I have had my fling," he said with a queer laugh, "and I must go back to my old ways. A little law will be quite a relaxation after so sharp a dose of pleasure," and he grinned to himself, and soon after went up to his room. His hand was still all bandaged.

Dr. Haberden called a few days later.

"I have no special news to give you," he said. "Chambers is out of town, so I know no more about that stuff than you do. But I should like to see Mr. Leicester, if he is in."

"He is in his room," I said; "I will tell him you are here."

"No, no, I will go up to him; we will have a little quiet talk together. I dare say that we have made a good deal of fuss about a very little; for, after all, whatever the powder may be, it seems to have done him good."

The doctor went upstairs, and standing in the hall I heard his knock, and the opening and shutting of the door; and then I waited in the silent house for an hour, and the stillness grew more and more intense as the hands of the clock crept round. Then there sounded from above the noise of a door shut sharply, and the doctor was coming down the stairs. His foot-steps crossed the hall, and there was a pause at the door; I drew a long, sick breath with difficulty, and saw my face white in a little mirror, and he came in and stood at the door. There was an unutterable horror shining in his eyes; he steadied himself by holding the back of a chair with one hand, his lower lip trembled like a horse's, and he gulped and stammered unintelligible sounds before he spoke.

"I have seen that man," he began in a dry whisper. "I have been sitting in his presence for the last hour. My God! And I am alive and in my senses! I, who have dealt with death all my life, and have dabbled with the melting ruins of the earthly tabernacle. But not this, oh! not this," and he covered his face with his hands as if to shut out the sight of something before him.

"Do not send for me again, Miss Leicester," he said with more composure. "I can do nothing in this house. Good-bye."

As I watched him totter down the steps, and along the pavement towards his house, it seemed to me that he had aged by ten years since the morning.

My brother remained in his room. He called out to me in a voice I hardly recognized that he was very busy, and would like his meals brought to his door and left there, and I gave the order to the servants. From that day it seemed as if the arbitrary conception we call time had been annihilated for me; I lived in an ever-present sense of horror, going through the routine of the house mechanically, and only speaking a few necessary words to the servants. Now and then I went out and paced the streets for an hour or two and came home again; but whether I were without or within, my spirit delayed before the closed door of the upper room, and, shuddering, waited for it to open. I have said that I scarcely reckoned time; but I suppose it must have been a fortnight after Dr. Haberden's visit that I came home from my stroll a little refreshed and lightened. The air was sweet and pleasant, and the hazy form of green leaves, floating cloud-like in the square, and the smell of blossoms, had charmed my senses, and I felt happier and walked more briskly. As I delayed a moment at the verge of the pavement, waiting for a van to pass by before crossing over to the house, I happened to look up at the windows, and instantly there was the rush and swirl of deep cold waters in my ears, my heart leapt up and fell down, down as into a deep hollow, and I was amazed with a dread and terror without form or shape. I stretched out a hand blindly through the folds of thick darkness, from the black and shadowy valley, and held myself from falling, while the stones beneath my feet rocked and swayed and tilted, and the sense of solid things seemed to sink away from under me. I had glanced up at the window of my brother's study, and at that moment the blind was drawn aside, and something that had life stared out into the world. Nay, I cannot say I saw a face or any human likeness; a living thing, two eyes of burning flame glared at me, and they were in the midst of something as formless as my fear, the symbol and presence of all evil and all hideous corruption. I stood shuddering and quaking as with the grip of ague, sick with unspeakable agonies of fear and loathing, and for five minutes I could not summon force or motion to my limbs. When I was within the door, I ran up the stairs to my brother's room and knocked.

"Francis, Francis," I cried, "for Heaven's sake, answer me. What is the horrible thing in your room? Cast it out, Francis; cast it from you."

I heard a noise as of feet shuffling slowly and awkwardly, and a choking, gurgling sound, as if some one was struggling to find utterance, and then the noise of a voice, broken and stifled, and words that I could scarcely understand.

"There is nothing here," the voice said. "Pray do not disturb me. I am not very well today."

I turned away, horrified, and yet helpless. I could do nothing, and I wondered why Francis had lied to me, for I had seen the appearance beyond the glass too plainly to be deceived, though it was but the sight of a moment. And I sat still, conscious that there had been something else, something I had seen in the first flash of terror, before those burning eyes had looked at me. Suddenly I remembered; as I lifted my face the blind was being drawn back, and I had had an instant's glance of the thing that was moving it, and in my recollection I knew that a hideous image was engraved forever on my brain. It was not a

hand; there were no fingers that held the blind, but a black stump
pushed it aside, the mouldering outline and the clumsy movement as
of a beast's paw had glowed into my senses before the darkling waves
of terror had overwhelmed me as I went down quick into the pit. My
mind was aghast at the thought of this, and of the awful presence that
dwelt with my brother in his room; I went to his door and cried to
him again, but no answer came. That night one of the servants came
up to me and told me in a whisper that for three days food had been
regularly placed at the door and left untouched; the maid had knocked
but had received no answer; she had heard the noise of shuffling feet
that I had noticed. Day after day went by, and still my brother's meals
were brought to his door and left untouched; and though I knocked
and called again and again, I could get no answer. The servants began
to talk to me; it appeared they were as alarmed as I; the cook said
that when my brother first shut himself up in his room she used to
hear him come out at night and go about the house; and once, she
said, the hall door had opened and closed again, but for several nights
she had heard no sound. The climax came at last; it was in the dusk
of the evening, and I was sitting in the darkening dreary room when
a terrible shriek jarred and rang harshly out of the silence, and I heard
a frightened scurry of feet dashing down the stairs. I waited, and
the servant-maid staggered into the room and faced me, white and
trembling.

"Oh, Miss Helen!" she whispered; "oh! for the Lord's sake, Miss
Helen, what has happened? Look at my hand, miss; look at that hand!"

I drew her to the window, and saw there was a black wet stain upon
her hand.

"I do not understand you," I said. "Will you explain to me?"

"I was doing your room just now," she began. "I was turning down
the bedclothes, and all of a sudden there was something fell upon my
hand, wet, and I looked up, and the ceiling was black and dripping
on me."

I looked hard at her and bit my lip.

"Come with me," I said. "Bring your candle with you."

The room I slept in was beneath my brother's, and as I went in I
felt I was trembling. I looked up at the ceiling, and saw a patch, all
black and wet, and a dew of black drops upon it, and a pool of horrible
liquor soaking into the white bedclothes.

I ran upstairs and knocked loudly.

"Oh, Francis, Francis, my dear brother," I cried, "What has happened
to you?"

And I listened. There was a sound of choking, and a noise like water
bubbling and regurgitating, but nothing else, and I called louder, but
no answer came.

In spite of what Dr. Haberden had said, I went to him; with tears
streaming down my cheeks I told him all that had happened, and he
listened to me with a face set hard and grim.

"For your father's sake," he said at last, "I will go with you, though I can do nothing."

We went out together; the streets were dark and silent, and heavy with heat and a drought of many weeks. I saw the doctor's face white under the gas-lamps, and when we reached the house his hand was shaking.

We did not hesitate, but went upstairs directly. I held the lamp, and he called out in a loud, determined voice—

"Mr. Leicester, do you hear me? I insist on seeing you. Answer me at once."

There was no answer, but we both heard that choking noise I have mentioned.

"Mr. Leicester, I am waiting for you. Open the door this instant or I shall break it down." And he called a third time in a voice that rang and echoed from the walls—

"Mr. Leicester! For the last time I order you to open the door."

"Ah!" he said, after a pause of heavy silence, "we are wasting time here. Will you be so kind as to get me a poker, or something of the kind?"

I ran into a little room at the back where odd articles were kept, and found a heavy adze-like tool that I thought might serve the doctor's purpose.

"Very good," he said, "that will do, I dare say. I give you notice, Mr. Leicester," he cried loudly at the keyhole, "that I am now about to break into your room."

Then I heard the wrench of the adze, and the wood-work split and cracked under it; with a loud crash the door suddenly burst open, and for a moment we started back aghast at a fearful screaming cry, no human voice, but as the roar of a monster, that burst forth inarticulate and struck at us out of the darkness.

"Hold the lamp," said the doctor, and we went in and glanced quickly around the room.

"There it is," said Dr. Haberden, drawing a quick breath; "look, in that corner."

I looked, and a pang of horror seized my heart as with a white-hot iron. There upon the floor was a dark and putrid mass, seething with corruption and hideous rottenness, neither liquid nor solid, but melting and changing before our eyes, and bubbling with unctuous oil bubbles like boiling pitch. And out of the midst of it shone two burning points like eyes, and I saw a writhing and stirring as of limbs, and something moved and lifted up what might have been an arm. The doctor took a step forward, raised the iron bar and struck at the burning points; he drove in the weapon, and struck again and again in the fury of loathing.

A week or two later, when I had recovered to some extent from the terrible shock, Dr. Haberden came to see me.

"I have sold my practice," he began, "and tomorrow I am sailing on a long voyage. I do not know whether I shall ever return to England; in all probability I shall buy a little land in California, and settle there for the remainder of my life. I have brought you this packet, which you may open and read when you feel able to do so. It contains the report of Dr. Chambers on what I submitted to him. Good-bye, Miss Leicester, good-bye."

When he was gone I opened the envelope; I could not wait, and proceeded to read the papers within. Here is the manuscript, and if you will allow me, I will read you the astounding story it contains.

"My dear Haberden," the letter began, "I have delayed inexcusably in answering your questions as to the white substance you sent me. To tell you the truth, I have hesitated for some time as to what course I should adopt, for there is a bigotry and orthodox standard in physical science as in theology, and I knew that if I told you the truth I should offend rooted prejudices which I once held dear myself. However, I have determined to be plain with you, and first I must enter into a short personal explanation.

"You have known me, Haberden, for many years as a scientific man; you and I have often talked of our profession together, and discussed the hopeless gulf that opens before the feet of those who think to attain to truth by any means whatsoever except the beaten way of experiment and observation in the sphere of material things. I remember the scorn with which you have spoken to me of men of science who had dabbled a little in the unseen, and have timidly hinted that perhaps the senses are not, after all, the eternal, impenetrable bounds of all knowledge, the everlasting walls beyond which no human being has ever passed. We have laughed together heartily, and I think justly, at the 'occult' follies of the day, disguised under various names—the mesmerisms, spiritualisms, materializations, theosophies, all the rabble rout of imposture, with their machinery of poor tricks and feeble conjuring, the true back-parlor of shabby London streets. Yet, in spite of what I have said, I must confess to you that I am no materialist, taking the word of course in its usual signification. It is now many years since I have convinced myself, a sceptic, remember—that the old ironbound theory is utterly and entirely false. Perhaps this confession will not wound you so sharply as it would have done twenty years ago; for I think you cannot have failed to notice that for some time hypotheses have been advanced by men of pure science which are nothing less than transcendental, and I suspect that most modern chemists and biologists of repute would not hesitate to subscribe the *dictum* of the old Schoolman, *Omnia exeunt in mysterium,* which means, I take it, that every branch of human knowledge if traced up to its source and final principles vanishes into mystery. I need not trouble you now with a detailed account of the painful steps which led me to my conclusions; a few simple experiments suggested a doubt as to my then standpoint, and a train of thought that rose from circumstances comparatively trifling brought me far; my old conception of the universe has been swept away, and I stand in a world that seems as strange and awful to me as the endless waves of the ocean seen for the first time, shining, from a peak in Darien. Now I know that the walls of sense that seemed so impenetrable, that seemed to loom up above the heavens and to be founded below the depths, and to shut us in for evermore, are no such ever-lasting impassable barriers as we fancied, but thinnest and most airy veils that melt away before the seeker, and dissolve as the early mist of the morning about the brooks. I know that you never adopted the extreme materialistic position; you did not go about trying to prove a universal negative, for your logical sense withheld you from that crowning absurdity; but I am sure that you will find all that I am saying strange and repellent to your habits of thought. Yet, Haberden, what I tell you is the truth, nay, to adopt our common language, the sole and scientific truth, verified by experience; and the universe is verily more splendid and more awful than we used to dream. The whole universe, my friend, is a tremendous sacrament; a mystic, ineffable force and energy, veiled by an outward form of matter; and man, and the sun and the other stars, and the flower of the grass, and the crystal in the test-tube are each and every one as spiritual, as material, and subject to an inner working.

"You will perhaps wonder, Haberden, whence all this tends; but I think a little thought will make it clear. You will understand that from such a standpoint the whole view of things is changed, and what we thought incredible and absurd may be possible enough. In short, we must look at legend and belief with other eyes, and be prepared to accept tales that had become mere fables. Indeed this is no such great demand. After all, modern science will concede as much, in a hypocritical manner; you must not, it is true, believe in witchcraft, but you may credit hypnotism; ghosts are out of date, but there is a good deal to be said for the theory of telepathy. Give superstition a Greek name, and believe in it, should almost be a proverb.

"So much for my personal explanation. You sent me, Haberden, a phial, stoppered and sealed, containing a small quantity of flaky white powder, obtained from a chemist who has been dispensing it to one of your patients. I am not surprised to hear that this powder refused to yield any results to your analysis. It is a substance which was known to a few many hundred years ago, but which I never expected to have submitted to me from the shop of a modern apothecary. There seems no reason to doubt the truth of the man's tale; he no doubt got, as he says, the rather uncommon salt you prescribed from the wholesale chemist's; and it has probably remained on his shelf for twenty years, or perhaps longer. Here what we call chance and coincidence begin to work; during all these years the salt in the bottle was exposed to certain recurring variations of temperature, variations probably ranging from 40° to 80°. And, as it happens, such changes, recurring year after year at irregular intervals, and with varying degrees of intensity and duration, have constituted a process, and a process so complicated and so delicate, that I question whether modern scientific apparatus directed with the utmost precision could produce the same result. The white powder you sent me is something very different from the drug you prescribed; it is the powder from which the wine of the Sabbath, the *Vinum Sabbati,* was prepared. No doubt you have read of the Witches' Sabbath, and have laughed at the tales which terrified our ancestors; the black cats, and the broomsticks, and dooms pronounced against some old woman's cow. Since I have known the truth I have often reflected that it is on the whole a happy thing that such burlesque as this is believed, for it serves to conceal much that is better should not be known generally. However, if you care to read the appendix to Payne Knight's monograph, you will find that the true Sabbath was something very different, though the writer has very nicely refrained from printing all he knew. The secrets of the true Sabbath were the secrets of remote times surviving into the Middle Ages, secrets of an evil science which existed long before Aryan man entered Europe. Men and women, seduced from their homes on specious pretences, were met by beings well qualified to assume, as they did assume, the part of devils, and taken by their guides to some desolate and lonely place, known to the initiate by long tradition, and unknown to all else. Perhaps it was a cave in some bare and windswept hill, perhaps some inmost recess of a great forest, and there the Sabbath was held. There, in the blackest hour of night, the *Vinum Sabbati* was prepared, and this evil graal was poured forth and offered to the neophytes, and they partook of an infernal sacrament; *sumentes calicem principis inferorum,* as an old author well expresses it. And suddenly, each one that had drunk found himself attended by a companion, a shape of glamor and unearthly allurement, beckoning him apart, to share in joys more exquisite, more piercing than the thrill of any dream, to the consummation of the marriage of the Sabbath. It is hard to write of such things as these, and chiefly because that shape that allured with loveliness was no hallucination, but, awful as it is to express, the man himself. By the power of that Sabbath wine, a few grains of white powder thrown into a glass of water, the house of life was riven asunder and the human trinity dissolved, and the worm which never dies, that which lies sleeping within us all, was made tangible and an external thing, and clothed with a garment of flesh. And then, in the hour of midnight, the primal fall was repeated and re-presented, and the awful thing veiled in the mythos of the Tree in the Garden was done anew. Such was the *nuptiae Sabbati.*

"I prefer to say no more; you, Haberden, know as well as I do that the most trivial laws of life are not to be broken with impunity; and for so terrible an act as this, in which the very inmost place of the temple was broken open and defiled, a terrible vengeance followed. What began with corruption ended also with corruption."

Underneath is the following in Dr. Haberden's writing:—

"The whole of the above is unfortunately strictly and entirely true. Your brother confessed all to me on that morning when I saw him in his room. My attention was first attracted to the bandaged hand, and I forced him to show it to me. What I saw made me, a medical man of many years' standing, grow sick with loathing, and the story I was forced to listen to was infinitely more frightful than I could have believed possible. It has tempted me to doubt the Eternal Goodness which can permit nature to offer such hideous possibilities; and if you had not with your own eyes seen the end, I should have said to you—disbelieve it all. I have not, I think, many more weeks to live, but you are young, and may forget all this.

"Joseph Haberden, M.D."

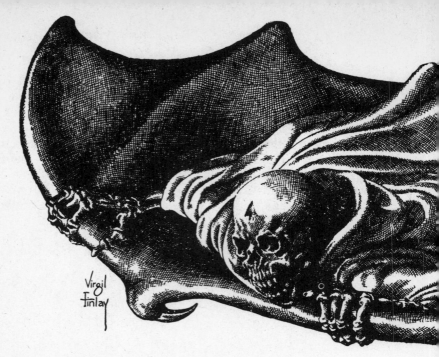

The Highwayman

LORD DUNSANY

No library of fantasy fiction would be complete without The Gods of
Pegana, The Book of Wonder, *and* A Dreamer's Tales, *three collections
of short stories by Lord Dunsany published between 1905 and 1912.
Although many authors have imitated the style of the stories found in
those books, none have ever managed to portray fantasy worlds full of
fallible gods and foolish mortals with the same effortlessness as Dunsany.
Much of the charm of Dunsany's fiction derives from its wit and genuine
understanding of human foibles. "The Highwayman," one of three Dunsany
stories reprinted in* Famous Fantastic Mysteries, *is both a poignant tale
of friendship and a subtle satire.*

TOM O' THE ROADS had ridden his last ride, and was now alone
in the night. From where he was, a man might see the white
recumbent sheep and the black outline of the lonely downs, and the
grey line of the farther and lonelier downs beyond them; or in hollows
far below him, out of the pitiless wind, he might see the grey smoke
of hamlets arising from black valleys. But all alike was black to the
eyes of Tom, and all the sounds were silence in his ears; only his soul
struggled to slip from the iron chains and to pass southwards into
Paradise. And the wind blew and blew.

But the soul of Tom o' the Roads was nipped by the cruel chains,
and whenever it struggled to escape it was beaten backwards into the

iron collar by the wind that blows from Paradise from the south. And swinging there by the neck, there fell away old sneers from off his lips, and scoffs that he had long since scoffed at God fell from his tongue, and there rotted old bad lusts out of his heart, and from his fingers the stains of deeds that were evil; and they all fell to the ground and grew there in pallid rings and clusters. And when these ill things had all fallen away, Tom's soul was clean again, as his early love had found it, a long while since in spring; and it swung up there in the wind with the bones of Tom, and with his old torn coat and rusty chains.

And the wind blew and blew.

And ever and anon the souls of the sepulchred, coming from consecrated acres, would go by beating up wind to Paradise past the Gallows Tree and past the soul of Tom, that might not go free.

Night after night Tom watched the sheep upon the downs with empty hollow sockets, till his dead hair grew and covered his poor dead face, and hid the shame of it from the sheep. And the wind blew and blew.

Sometimes on gusts of the wind came some one's tears, and beat and beat against the iron chains, but could not rust them through. And the wind blew and blew.

And every evening all the thoughts that Tom had ever uttered came flocking in from doing their work in the world, the work that may not cease, and sat along the branches and chirrupped to the soul of Tom, the soul that might not go free. All the thoughts that he had ever uttered! And the evil thoughts rebuked the soul that bore them because they might not die. And all those that he had uttered the most furtively, chirrupped the loudest and the shrillest in the branches all the night.

And all the thoughts that Tom had ever thought about himself now pointed at the wet bones and mocked at the old torn coat. But the thoughts that he had had of others were the only companions that his soul had to soothe it in the night as it swung to and fro. And they twittered to the soul and cheered the poor dumb thing that could have dreams no more, till there came a murderous thought and drove them all away.

And the wind blew and blew.

Paul, Archbishop of Alois and Vayence, lay in his white sepulchre of marble, facing full to the southwards toward Paradise. And over his tomb was sculptured the Cross of Christ, that his soul might have repose. No wind howled here as it howled in lonely tree-tops up upon the downs, but came with gentle breezes, orchard scented, over the low lands from Paradise from the southwards, and played about forget-me-nots and grasses in the consecrated land where lay the Reposeful round the sepulchre of Paul, Archbishop of Alois and Vayence. Easy it was for a man's soul to pass from such a sepulchre, and, flitting low over remembered fields, to come upon the garden lands of Paradise and find eternal ease.

And the wind blew and blew.

In a tavern of foul repute three men were lapping gin. Their names were Joe and Will and the gypsy Puglioni; no other names had they, for of whom their fathers were they had no knowledge, but only dark suspicions.

Sin had carressed and stroked their faces often with its paws, but the face of Puglioni Sin had kissed all over the mouth and chin. Their food was robbery and their pastime murder. All of them had incurred the sorrow of God and the enmity of man. They sat at a table with a pack of cards before them, all greasy with the marks of cheating thumbs. And they whispered to one another over their gin, but so low that the landlord of the tavern at the other end of the room could hear only muffled oaths, and knew not by Whom they swore or what they said.

These three were the staunchest friends that ever God had given unto a man. And he to whom their friendship had been given had nothing else besides, saving some bones that swung in the wind and rain, and an old torn coat and iron chains, and a soul that might not go free.

But as the night wore on the three friends left their gin and stole away, and crept down to that graveyard where rested in his sepulchre Paul, Archbishop of Alois and Vayence. At the edge of the graveyard, but outside the consecrated ground, they dug a hasty grave, two digging while one watched in the wind and rain. And the worms that crept in the unhallowed ground wondered and waited.

And the terrible hour of midnight came upon them with its fears, and found them still beside the place of tombs. And the three friends trembled at the horror of such an hour in such a place, and shivered in the wind and drenching rain, but still worked on. And the wind blew and blew.

Soon they had finished. And at once they left the hungry grave with all its worms unfed, and went away over the wet fields stealthily but in haste, leaving the place of tombs behind them in the midnight. And as they went they shivered, and each man as he shivered cursed the rain aloud. And so they came to the spot where they had hidden a ladder and a lantern. There they held long debate whether they should light the lantern, or whether they should go without it for fear of the King's men. But in the end it seemed to them better that they should have the light of the lantern, and risk being taken by the King's men and hanged, than that they should come suddenly face to face in the darkness with whatever one might come face to face with a little after midnight about the Gallows Tree.

On three roads in England whereon it was not the wont of folks to go their ways in safety, travellers tonight went unmolested. But the three friends, walking several paces wide of the King's highway, approached the Gallows Tree, and Will carried the lantern and Joe the ladder, but Puglioni carried a great sword wherewith to do the work which must be done. When they came close, they saw how bad was the case with Tom, for little remained of that fine figure of a man and nothing at all of his great resolute spirit, only as they came they thought they heard a whimpering cry like the sound of a thing that was caged and unfree.

To and fro, to and fro in the winds swung the bones and the soul of Tom, for the sins that he had sinned on the King's highway against the laws of the King; and with shadows and a lantern through the darkness, at the peril of their lives, came the three friends that his soul had won before it swung in chains. Thus the seeds of Tom's own soul that he had sown all his life had grown into a Gallows Tree that bore in season iron chains in clusters; while the careless seeds that he had strewn here and there, a kindly jest and a few merry words, had grown into the triple friendship that would not desert his bones.

Then the three set the ladder against the tree, and Puglioni went up with his sword in his right hand, and at top of it he reached up and began to hack at the neck below the iron collar. Presently, the bones and the old coat and the soul of Tom fell down with a rattle, and a moment afterwards his head that had watched so long alone swung clear from the swinging chain. These things Will and Joe gathered up, and Puglioni came running down his ladder, and they heaped upon its rungs the terrible remains of their friend, and hastened away wet through with the rain, with the fear of phantoms in their hearts and horror lying before them on the ladder. By two o'clock they were again in the valley out of the bitter wind, but they went on past the open grave into the graveyard all among the tombs, with their lantern and their ladder and the terrible thing upon it, which kept their friendship still. Then these three, that had robbed the Law of its due and proper victim, still sinned on for what was still their friend, and levered out the marble slabs from the sacred sepulchre of Paul, Archbishop of Alois and Vayence. And from it they took the very bones of the Archbishop himself, and carried them away to the eager grave that they had left, and put them in and shovelled back the earth. But all that lay on the ladder they placed, with a few tears, within the great white sepulchre under the Cross of Christ, and put back the marble slabs.

Thence the soul of Tom, arising hallowed out of the sacred ground, went at dawn down the valley, and lingering a little about his mother's cottage and old haunts of childhood, passed on and came to the wide lands beyond the clustered homesteads. There, there met with it all the kindly thoughts that the soul of Tom had ever had, and they flew and sang beside it all the way southwards, until at last, with singing all about it, it came to Paradise.

But Will and Joe and the gypsy Puglioni went back to their gin, and robbed and cheated again in the tavern of foul repute, and knew not that in their sinful lives they had sinned one sin at which the Angels smiled.

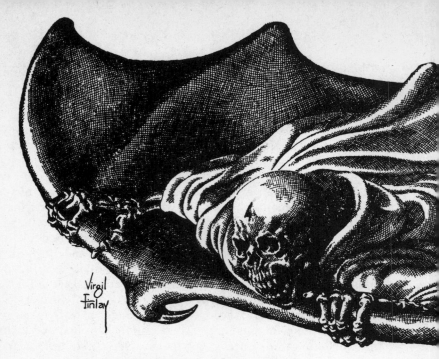

Daemon

C. L. MOORE

Most pulp artists were illustrators in the truest sense: they were given a story in advance of its publication and asked to supply appropriate artwork. Occasionally, though, an editor received a piece of art that was so good he or she commissioned a story to use with it. Such was the case for "Daemon," which editor Mary Gnaedinger asked Catherine L. Moore to write for Famous Fantastic Mysteries *based on a stunning drawing by Virgil Finlay. The excellent results of this pairing were not completely unexpected, as Finlay had proven himself one of Moore's best illustrators in the pages of* Weird Tales *several years before.*

PADRE, the words came slowly. It is a long time now since I have spoken in the Portuguese tongue. For more than a year, my companions here were those who do not speak with the tongues of men. And you must remember, *padre,* that in Rio, where I was born, I was named Luiz *o Bobo,* which is to say, Luiz the Simple. There was something wrong with my head, so that my hands were always clumsy and my feet stumbled over each other. I could not remember very much. But I could see things. Yes, *padre,* I could see things such as other men do not know.

I can see things now. Do you know who stands beside you, *padre,* listening while I talk? Never mind that. I am Luiz *o Bobo* still, though here on this island there were great powers of healing, and I can remember now the things that happened to me years ago. More easily than I remember what happened last week or the week before that. The year has been like a single day, for time on this island is not like time outside. When a man lives with *them,* there is no time.

The *ninfas,* I mean. And the others. . . .

I am not lying. Why should I? I am going to die, quite soon now. You were right to tell me that, *padre.* But I knew. I knew already. Your crucifix is very pretty, *padre.* I like the way it shines in the sun. But that is not for me. You see, I have always known the things that walk beside men—other men. Not me. Perhaps they are souls, and I have no soul, being simple. Or perhaps they are daemons such as only clever men have. Or perhaps they are both these things. I do not know. But I know that I am dying. After the *ninfas* go away, I would not care to live.

Since you ask how I came to this place, I will tell you if the time remains to me. You will not believe. This is the one place on earth, I think, where they lingered still—those things you do not believe.

But before I speak of them, I must go back to an earlier day, when I was young beside the blue bay of Rio, under Sugar Loaf. I remember the docks of Rio, and the children who mocked me. I was big and strong, but I was *o Bobo* with a mind that knew no yesterday or tomorrow.

Minha avó, my grandmother, was kind to me. She was from Ceará, where the yearly droughts kill hope, and she was half blind, with pain in her back always. She worked so that we could eat, and she did not scold me too much. I know that she was good. It was something I could see; I have always had that power.

One morning my grandmother did not waken. She was cold when I touched her hand. That did not frighten me for the—good thing— about her lingered for a while. I closed her eyes and kissed her, and then I went away. I was hungry, and because I was *o Bobo,* I thought that someone might give me food, out of kindness. . . .

In the end, I foraged from the rubbish-heaps.

I did not starve. But I was lost and alone. Have you ever felt that, *padre?* It is like a bitter wind from the mountains and no sheepskin cloak can shut it out. One night I wandered into a sailors' saloon, and I remember that there were many dark shapes with eyes that shone, hovering beside the men who drank there. The men had red, windburned faces and tarry hands. They made me drink *'guardiente* until the room whirled around and went dark.

I woke in a dirty bunk. I heard planks groaning and the floor rocked under me.

Yes, *padre,* I had been shanghaied. I stumbled on deck, half blind in the dazzling sunlight, and there I found a man who had a strange and shining daemon. He was the captain of the ship, though I did not know it then. I scarcely saw the man at all. I was looking at the daemon.

Now, most men have shapes that walk behind them, *padre*. Perhaps you know that, too. Some of them are dark, like the shapes I saw in the saloon. Some of them are bright, like that which followed my grandmother. Some of them are colored, pale colors like ashes or rainbows. But this man had a scarlet daemon. And it was a scarlet beside which blood itself is ashen. The color blinded me. And yet it drew me, too. I could not take my eyes away, nor could I look at it long without pain. I never saw a color more beautiful, nor more frightening. It made my heart shrink within me, and quiver like a dog that fears the whip. If I have a soul, perhaps it was my soul that quivered. And I feared the beauty of the color as much as I feared the terror it awoke in me. It is not good to see beauty in that which is evil.

Other men upon the deck had daemons too. Dark shapes and pale shapes that followed them like their shadows. But I saw all the daemons waver away from the red, beautiful thing that hung above the captain of the ship.

The other daemons watched out of burning eyes. The red daemon had no eyes. Its beautiful, blind face was turned always toward the captain, as if it saw only through his vision. I could see the lines of its closed lids. And my terror of its beauty, and my terror of its evil, were nothing to my terror of the moment when the red daemon might lift those lids and look out upon the world.

The captain's name was Jonah Stryker. He was a cruel man, dangerous to be near. The men hated him. They were at his mercy while we were at sea, and the captain was at the mercy of his daemon. That was why I could not hate him as the others did. Perhaps it was pity I felt for Jonah Stryker. And you, who know men better than I, will understand that the pity I had for him made the captain hate me more bitterly than even his crew hated him.

When I came on deck that first morning, because I was blinded by the sun and by the redness of the scarlet daemon, and because I was ignorant and bewildered, I broke a shipboard rule. What it was, I do not know. There were so many, and I never could remember very clearly in those days. Perhaps I walked between him and the wind. Would that be wrong on a clipper ship, *padre?* I never understood.

The captain shouted at me, in the Yankee tongue, evil words whose meaning I did not know, but the daemon glowed redder when he spoke them. And he struck me with his fist, so that I fell. There was a look of secret bliss on the blind crimson face hovering above his, because of the anger that rose in him. I thought that through the captain's eyes the closed eyes of the daemon were watching me.

I wept. In that moment, for the first time, I knew how truly alone a man like me must be. For I had no daemon. It was not the simple loneliness for my grandmother or for human companionship that brought the tears to my eyes. That I could endure. But I saw the look of joy upon the blind daemon-face because of the captain's evil, and I remembered the look of joy that a bright shape sometimes wears who follows a good man. And I knew that no deed of mine would ever bring joy or sorrow to that which moves behind a man with a soul.

I lay upon the bright, hot deck and wept, not because of the blow, but because I knew suddenly, for the first time, that I was alone. No daemon for good or evil would ever follow me. Perhaps because I have no soul. *That* loneliness, father, is something not even you could understand.

The captain seized my arm and pulled me roughly to my feet. I did not understand, then, the words he spoke in his Yankee tongue, though later I picked up enough of that speech to know what men were saying around me. You may think it strange that *o Bobo* could learn a foreign tongue. It was easy for me. Easier, perhaps, than for a wiser man. Much I read upon the faces of their daemons, and there were many words whose real sounds I did not know, but whose meaning I found in the hum of thoughts about a man's head.

The captain shouted for a man named Barton, and the first mate hurried up, looking frightened. The captain pushed me back against the rail so that I staggered, seeing him and the deck and the watching daemons through the rainbows that tears cast before one's eyes.

There was loud talk, and many gestures toward me and the other two men who had been shanghaied from the port of Rio. The first mate tapped his head when he pointed to me, and the captain cursed again in the tongue of the foreigners, so that his daemon smiled very sweetly at his shoulder.

I think that was the first time I let the captain see pity on my face when I looked at him.

That was the one thing he could not bear. He snatched a belaying pin from the rail and struck me in the face with it, so that I felt the teeth break in my mouth. The blood I spat upon the deck was a beautiful color, but it looked paler than water beside the color of the captain's daemon. I remember all the daemons but the red one leaned a little forward when they saw blood running, snuffing up the smell and the brightness of it like incense. The red one did not even turn his blind face.

The captain struck me again because I had soiled his deck. My first task aboard the *Dancing Martha* was to scrub up my own blood from the planking.

Afterward they dragged me to the galley and threw me into the narrow alley at the cook's feet. I burned my hands on the stove. The captain laughed to see me jump back from it. It is a terrible thing that, though I heard his laughter many times a day, I never heard mirth in it. But there was mirth on his daemon's face.

Pain was with me for many days thereafter, because of the beating and the burns, but I was glad in a way. Pain kept my mind from the loneliness I had just discovered in myself. Those were bad days, *padre.* The worst days of my life. Afterward, when I was no longer lonely,

I looked back upon them as a soul in paradise might look back on purgatory.

No, I am still alone. Nothing follows me as things follow other men. But here on the island I found the *ninfas,* and I was content.

I found them because of the Shaughnessy. I can understand him today in a way I could not do just then. He was a wise man and I am *o Bobo,* but I think I know some of his thoughts now, because today I, too, know I am going to die.

The Shaughnessy lived many days with death. I do not know how long. It was weeks and months in coming to him, though it lived in his lungs and his heart as a child lives within its mother, biding its time to be born. The Shaughnessy was a passenger. He had much money, so that he could do what he willed with his last days of living. Also he came of a great family in a foreign land called Ireland. The captain hated him for many reasons. He scorned him because of his weakness, and he feared him because he was ill. Perhaps he envied him too, because his people had once been kings and because the Shaughnessy was not afraid to die. The captain, I know, feared death. He feared it most terribly. He was right to fear it. He could not know that a daemon rode upon his shoulder, smiling its sweet, secret smile, but some instinct must have warned him that it was there, biding its time like the death in the Shaughnessy's lungs.

I saw the captain die. I know he was right to fear the hour of his daemon. . . .

Those were bad days on the ship. They were worse because of the great beauty all around us. I had never been at sea before, and the motion of the ship was a wonder to me, the clouds of straining sail above us and the sea all about, streaked with the colors of the currents and dazzling where the sun-track lay. White gulls followed us with their yellow feet tucked up as they soared over the deck, and porpoises followed too, playing in great arcs about the ship and dripping diamonds in the sun.

I worked hard, for no more wages than freedom from blows when I did well, and the scraps that were left from the table after the cook had eaten his fill. The cook was not a bad man like the captain, but he was not a good man, either. He did not care. His daemon was smoky, asleep, indifferent to the cook and the world.

It was the Shaughnessy who made my life worth the trouble of living. If it had not been for him, I might have surrendered life and gone into the breathing sea some night when no one was looking. It would not have been a sin for me, as it would be for a man with a soul.

But because of the Shaughnessy I did not. He had a strange sort of daemon himself, mother-of-pearl in the light, with gleams of darker colors when the shadows of night came on. He may have been a bad man in his day. I do not know. The presence of death in him opened his eyes, perhaps. I know only that to me he was very kind. His daemon grew brighter as the man himself grew weak with the oncoming of death.

He told me many tales. I have never seen the foreign country of Ireland, but I walked there often in my dreams because of the tales he told. The foreign isles called Greece grew clear to me too, because the Shaughnessy had dwelt there and loved them.

And he told me of things which he said were not really true, but I thought he said that with only half his mind, because I saw them so clearly while he talked. Great Odysseus was a man of flesh and blood to me, with a shining daemon on his shoulder, and the voyage that took so many enchanted years was a voyage I almost remembered, as if I myself had toiled among the crew.

He told me of burning Sappho, and I knew why the poet used that word for her, and I think the Shaughnessy knew too, though we did not speak of it. I knew how dazzling the thing must have been that followed her through the white streets of Lesbos and leaned upon her shoulder while she sang.

He told me of the nereids and the oceanids, and once I think I saw, far away in the sun-track that blinded my eyes, a mighty head rise dripping from the water, and heard the music of a wreathed horn as Triton called to his fishtailed girls.

The *Dancing Martha* stopped at Jamaica for a cargo of sugar and rum. Then we struck out across the blue water toward a country called England. But our luck was bad. Nothing was right about the ship on that voyage. Our water-casks had not been cleaned as they should be, and the drinking water became foul. A man can pick the maggots out of his salt pork if he must, but bad water is a thing he cannot mend.

So the captain ordered our course changed for a little island he knew in these waters. It was too tiny to be inhabited, a rock rising out of the great blue deeps with a fresh spring bubbling high up in a cup of the forested crags.

I saw it rising in the dawn like a green cloud on the horizon. Then it was a jewel of green as we drew nearer, floating on the blue water. And my heart was a bubble in my chest, shining with rainbow colors, lighter than the air around me. Part of my mind thought that the island was an isle in Rio Bay, and somehow I felt that I had come home again and would find my grandmother waiting on the shore. I forgot so much in those days. I forgot that she was dead. I thought we would circle the island and come in across the dancing Bay to the foot of the Rua d'Oporto, with the lovely city rising on its hills above the water.

I felt so sure of all this that I ran to tell the Shaughnessy of my delight in homecoming. And because I was hurrying, and blind to all on deck with the vision of Rio in my eyes, I blundered into the captain himself. He staggered and caught my arm to save his footing, and we were so close together that for a moment the crimson daemon swayed above my own head, its eyeless face turned down to mine.

I looked up at that beautiful, smiling face, so near that I could touch it and yet, I knew, farther away than the farthest star. I looked at it and screamed in terror. I had never been so near a daemon before, and I could feel its breath on my face, sweet-smelling, burning my skin with its scorching cold.

The captain was white with his anger and his—his envy? Perhaps it was envy he felt even of me, *o Bobo,* for a man with a daemon like that one hanging on his shoulder may well envy the man without a soul. He hated me bitterly, because he knew I pitied him, and to receive the pity of *o Bobo* must be a very humbling thing. Also he knew that I could not look at him for more than a moment or two, because of the blinding color of his daemon. I think he did not know why I blinked and looked away, shuddering inside, whenever he crossed my path. But he knew it was not the angry fear which other men felt for him which made me avert my eyes. I think he sensed that because he was damned I could not gaze upon him long, and that too made him hate and fear and envy the lowliest man in his crew.

All the color went out of his face as he looked at me, and the daemon above him flushed a deeper and lovelier scarlet, and the captain reached for a belaying pin with a hand that trembled. That which looked out of his eyes was not a man at all, but a daemon, and a daemon that quivered with joy as I was quivering with terror.

I heard the bone crack when the club came down upon my skull. I saw lightning dazzle across my eyes and my head was filled with brightness. I remember almost nothing more of that bad time. A little night closed around me and I saw through it only when the lightning of the captain's blows illumined the dark. I heard his daemon laughing.

When the day came back to me, I was lying on the deck with the Shaughnessy kneeling beside me bathing my face with something that stung. His daemon watched me over his shoulder, bright mother-of-pearl colors, its face compassionate. I did not look at it. The loneliness in me was sharper than the pain of my body, because no daemon of my own hung shining over my hurts, and no daemon ever would.

The Shaughnessy spoke in the soft, hushing Portuguese of Lisboa, that always sounded so strange to me.

"Lie still, Luiz," he was saying. "Don't cry. I'll see that he never touches you again."

I did not know until then that I was weeping. It was not for pain. It was for the look on his daemon's face, and for loneliness.

The Shaughnessy said, "When he comes back from the island, I'll have it out with him." He said more than that, but I was not listening. I was struggling with a thought, and thoughts came hard through the sleepiness that always clouded my brain.

The Shaughnessy meant kindly, but I knew the captain was master upon the ship. And it still seemed to me that we were anchored in the Bay of Rio and my grandmother awaited me on the shore.

I sat up. Beyond the rail the high green island was bright, sunshine winking from the water all around it, and from the leaves that clothed its slopes. I knew what I was going to do.

When the Shaughnessy went away for more water, I got to my feet. There was much pain in my head, and all my body ached from the captain's blows, and the deck was reeling underfoot with a motion the waves could not give it. When I got to the rail, I fell across it before I could jump, and slid into the sea very quietly.

I remember only flashes after that. Salt water burning me, and great waves lifting and falling all around me, and the breath hot in my lungs when the water did not burn even hotter there. Then there was sand under my knees, and I crawled up a little beach and I think I fell asleep in the shelter of a clump of palms.

Then I dreamed that it was dark, with stars hanging overhead almost near enough to touch, and so bright they burned my eyes. I dreamed I heard men calling me through the trees, and I did not answer. I dreamed I heard voices quarreling, the captain's voice loud and angry, the Shaughnessy's tight and thin. I dreamed of oarlocks creaking and water splashing from dipping blades, and the sound if it receding into the warmth and darkness.

I put up a hand to touch a star cluster that hung above my head, and the cluster was bright and tingling to feel. Then I saw that it was the Shaughnessy's face.

I said, "Oh, s'nhor," in a whisper, because I remembered that the captain had spoken from very close by.

The Shaughnessy smiled at me in the starlight. "Don't whisper, Luiz. We're alone now."

I was happy on the island. The Shaughnessy was kind to me, and the days were long and bright, and the island itself was friendly. One knows that of a place. And I thought, in those days, that I would never see the captain again or his beautiful scarlet daemon smiling its blind, secret smile above his shoulder. He had left us to die upon the island, and one of us did die.

The Shaughnessy said that another man might have perished of the blows the captain gave me. But I think because my brain is such a simple thing it mended easily, and perhaps the blow that made my skull crack let in a little more of wit than I had owned before. Or perhaps happiness did it, plenty of food to eat, and the Shaughnessy's tales of the things that—that you do not believe, *meu padre.*

The Shaughnessy grew weak as I grew strong. He lay all day in the shade of a broad tree by the shore, and as his strength failed him, his daemon grew brighter and more remote, as if it were already halfway through the veil of another world.

When I was well again, the Shaughnessy showed me how to build a thatched lean-to that would withstand the rain.

"There may be hurricanes, Luiz," he said to me. "This *barraca* will be blown down. Will you remember how to build another?"

"Sim," I said. "I shall remember. You will show me."

"No, Luiz. I shall not be here. You must remember."

He told me many things, over and over again, very patiently. How to find the shellfish on the rocks when the tide was out, how to trap fish in the stream, what fruit I might eat and what I must never touch. It was not easy for me. When I tried to remember too much it made my head hurt.

I explored the island, coming back to tell him all I had found. At first I was sure that when I had crossed the high hills and stood upon their peaks I would see the beautiful slopes of Rio shining across the water. My heart sank when I stood for the first time upon the heights and saw only more ocean, empty, heaving between me and the horizon.

But I soon forgot again, and Rio and the past faded from my mind. I found the pool cupped high in a hollow of the crags, where clear sweet water bubbled up in the shadow of the trees and the streamlet dropped away in a series of pools and falls toward the levels far below. I found groves of pale trees with leaves like streaming hair, rustling with the noise of the waterfall. I found no people here, and yet I felt always that there were watchers among the leaves, and it seemed to me that laughter sounded sometimes behind me, smothered when I turned my head.

When I told the Shaughnessy this he smiled at me.

"I've told you too many tales," he said. "But if anyone could see them, I think it would be you, Luiz."

"Sim, s'nhor," I said. "Tell me again of the forest-women. Could they be here, do you think, *s'nhor?*"

He let sand trickle through his fingers, watching it as if the fall of sand had some meaning to his mind that I could not fathom.

"Ah, well," he said. "they might be. They like the olive groves of Greece best, and the tall trees on Olympus. But every mountain has its oread. Here, too, perhaps. The Little People left Ireland years ago and for all I know the oreads have fled from civilization too, and found such places as this to put them in mind of home. . . .

"There was one who turned into a fountain once, long ago. I saw that fountain in Greece. I drank from it. There must have been a sort of magic in the waters, for I always went back to Greece after that. I'd leave, but I couldn't stay long away." He smiled at me. "Maybe now, because I can't go back again, the oreads have come to me here."

I looked hard at him to see if he meant what he said, but he shook his head and smiled again. "I think they haven't come for me. Maybe for you, Luiz. Belief is what they want. If you believe, perhaps you'll really see them. I'd be the last man to deny a thing like that. You'll need something like them to keep you company, my friend—afterward." And he trickled sand through his fingers again, watching it fall with a look upon his face I did not understand.

The night came swiftly on that island. It was a lovely place. The Shaughnessy said islands have a magic all their own, for they are the place where earth and ocean meet. We used to lie on the shore watching the fire that burned upon the edges of the waves lap up the beach and breathe away again, and the Shaughnessy told me many tales. His voice was growing weaker, and he did not trouble so much any more to test my memory for the lessons he had taught. But he spoke of ancient magic, and more and more in these last days, his mind turned back to the wonders of the country called Ireland.

He told me of the little green people with their lanterns low down among the ferns. He told me of the *unicórnio,* swift as the swiftest bird, a magical stag with one horn upon its forehead as long as the shaft of a spear and as sharp as whatever is sharpest. And he told me of Pan, goat-footed, moving through the woodland with laughter running before him and panic behind, the same panic terror which my language and the Shaughnessy's get from his name. *Pânico,* we Brazilians call it.

One evening he called to me and held up a wooden cross. "Luiz, look at this," he said. I saw that upon the arms of the cross he had made deep carvings with his knife. "This is my name," he told me. "If anyone ever comes here asking for me, you must show them this cross."

I looked at it closely. I knew what he meant about the name—it is that sort of enchantment in which markings can speak with a voice too tiny for the ears to hear. I am *o Bobo* and I never learned to read, so that I do not understand how this may be done.

"Some day," the Shaughnessy went on, "I think someone will come. My people at home may not be satisfied with whatever story Captain Stryker invents for them. Or a drunken sailor may talk. If they do find this island, Luiz, I want this cross above my grave to tell them who I was. And for another reason," he said thoughtfully. "For another reason too. But that need not worry you, *meu amigo.*"

He told me where to dig the bed for him. He did not tell me to put in the leaves and the flowers. I thought of that myself, three days later, when the time came. . . .

Because he had wished it, I put him in the earth. I did not like doing it. But in a way I feared not to carry out his commands, for the daemon of the Shaughnessy still hovered above him, very bright, very bright—so bright I could not look it in the face. I thought there was music coming from it, but I could not be sure.

I put the flowers over him and then the earth. There was more to go back in the grave than I had taken out, so I made a mound above him, as long as the Shaughnessy was long, and I drove in the stake of the wooden cross, above where his head was, as he had told me. Then for a moment I laid my ear to the markings to see if I could hear what they were saying, for it seemed to me that the sound of his name, whispered to me by the marks his hands had made, would lighten my loneliness a little. But I heard nothing.

When I looked up, I saw his daemon glow like the sun at noon, a light so bright I could not bear it upon my eyes. I put my hands before them. When I took them down again, there was no daemon.

You will not believe me when I tell you this, *padre,* but in that moment the—the feel of the island changed. All the leaves, I think, turned the other way on the trees, once, with a rustle like one vast syllable whispered for that time only, and never again.

I think I know what the syllable was. Perhaps I will tell you, later— if you let me.

And the island breathed. It was like a man who has held his breath for a long while, in fear or pain, and let it run out deeply when the fear or the pain departed.

I did not know, then, what it was. But I thought it would go up the steep rocks to the pool, because I wanted a place that would not remind me of the Shaughnessy. So I climbed the crags among the hanging trees. And it seemed to me that I heard laughter when the wind rustled among them. Once I saw what I thought must be a *ninfa,* brown and green in the forest. But she was too shy. I turned my head, and the brown and green stilled into the bark and foliage of the tree.

When I came to the pool, the unicorn was drinking. He was very beautiful, whiter than foam, whiter than cloud, and his mane lay upon his great shoulders like spray upon the shoulder of a wave. The tip of his long, spiraled horn just touched the water as he drank, so that the ripples ran outward in circles all around it. He tossed his head when he scented me, and I saw the glittering diamonds of the water sparkling from his velvet muzzle. He had eyes as green as a pool with leaves reflecting in it, and a spot of bright gold in the center of each eye.

Very slowly, with the greatest stateliness, he turned from the water and moved away into the forest. I know I heard a singing where he disappeared.

I was still *o Bobo* then. I drank where he had drunk, thinking there was a strange, sweet taste to the water now, and then I went down to the *barraca* on the beach, for I had forgotten already and thought perhaps the Shaughnessy might be there. . . .

Night came, and I slept. Dawn came, and I woke again. I bathed in the ocean. I gathered shellfish and fruit, and drank of the little stream that fell from the mountain pool. And as I leaned to drink, two white dripping arms rose up to clasp my neck, and a mouth as wet and cold as the water pressed mine. It was the kiss of acceptance.

After that the *ninfas* of the island no longer hid their faces from me.

My hair and beard grew long. My garments tore upon the bushes and became the rags you see now. I did not care. It did not matter. It was not my face they saw. They saw my simpleness. And I was one with the *ninfas* and the others.

The oread of the mountain came out to me often, beside the pool where the unicorn came to drink. She was wise and strange, being immortal. The eyes slanted upward in her head, and her hair was a shower of green leaves blowing always backward in a wind that moved about her when no other breezes blew. She used to sit beside the pool in the hot, still afternoons, the unicorn lying beside her and her brown fingers combing out his silver mane. Her wise slanting eyes, the color of shadows in the forest, and his round green eyes the color of the pool, with the flecks of gold in each, used to watch me as we talked.

The oread told me many things. Many things I could never tell you, *padre*. But it was as the Shaughnessy had guessed. Because I believed, they were glad of my presence there. While the Shaughnessy lived, they could not come out into the plane of being, but they watched from the other side. . . . They had been afraid. But they were afraid no longer.

For many years they have been homeless now, blowing about the world in search of some spot of land where no disbelief dwells, and where one other thing has not taken footing. . . . They told me of the isles of Greece, with love and longing upon their tongues, and it seemed to me that I heard the Shaughnessy speak again in their words.

They told me of the One I had not yet seen, or more than glimpsed. That happened when I chanced to pass near the Shaughnessy's grave in the dimness of the evening, and I saw the cross that bore his name had fallen. I took it up and held it to my ear again, hoping the tiny voices of the markings would whisper. But that is a mystery which has never been given me.

I saw the—the One—loitering by that grave. But when I put up the cross, he went away, slowly, sauntering into the dark woods, and a thin piping floated back to me from the spot where he had vanished.

Perhaps the One did not care for my presence there. The others welcomed me. It was not often any more, they said, that men like me were free to move among them. Since the hour of their banishment, they told me, and wept when they spoke of that hour, there had been too few among mankind who really knew them.

I asked about the banishment, and they said that it had happened long ago, very long ago. A great star had stood still in the sky over a stable in a town whose name I do not know. Once I knew it. I do not remember now. It was a town with a beautiful name.

The skies opened and there was singing in the heavens, and after that the gods of Greece had to flee. They have been fleeing ever since.

They were glad I had come to join them. And I was doubly glad. For the first time since my grandmother died, I knew I was not alone. Even the Shaughnessy had not been as close to me as these *ninfas* were. For the Shaughnessy had a daemon. The *ninfas* are immortal, but they have no souls. That, I think, is why they welcomed me so warmly. We without souls are glad of companionship among others of our kind. There is a loneliness among our kind that can only be assuaged by huddling together. The *ninfas* knew it, who must live forever, and I shared it with them, who may die before this night is over.

Well, it was good to live upon the island. The days and the months went by beautifully, full of clear colors and the smell of the sea and the stars at night as bright as lanterns just above us. I even grew less *Bobo,* because the *ninfas* spoke wisdom of a kind I never heard among men. They were good months.

And then, one day, Jonah Stryker came back to the island.

You know, *padre,* why he came. The Shaughnessy in his wisdom had guessed that in Ireland men of the Shaughnessy's family might ask questions of Captain Stryker—questions the captain could not answer. But it had not been guessed that the captain might return to the island, swiftly, before the Shaughnessy's people could discover the truth, with the thought in his evil mind of wiping out all traces of the two he had left to die.

I was sitting on the shore that day, listening to the songs of two *ninfas* of the nereid kind as they lay in the edge of the surf, with the waves breaking over them when the water lapped up the slopes of sand. They were swaying their beautiful rainbow-colored fish-bodies as they sang, and I heard the whisper of the surf in their voices, and the long rhythms of the undersea.

But suddenly there came a break in their song, and I saw upon one face before me, and then the other, a look of terror come. The green blood in their veins sank back with fear, and they looked at me, white with pallor and strangely transparent, as if they had halfway ceased to be. With one motion they turned their heads and stared out to sea.

I stared too. I think the first thing I saw was that flash of burning crimson, far out over the waves. And my heart quivered within me like a dog that fears the whip. I knew that beautiful, terrible color too well.

It was only then that I saw the *Dancing Martha,* lying at anchor beyond a ridge of rock. Between the ship and the shore a small boat rocked upon the waves, light flashing from oar-blades as the one man in the boat bent and rose and bent to his work. Above him, hanging like a crimson cloud, the terrible scarlet glowed.

When I looked back, the *ninfas* had vanished. Whether they slid back into the sea, or whether they melted away into nothingness before me I shall never know now. I did not see them again.

I went back a little way into the forest, and watched from among the trees. No dryads spoke to me, but I could hear their quick breathing and the leaves trembled all about me. I could not look at the scarlet daemon coming nearer and nearer over the blue water, but I could not look away long, either. It was so beautiful and so evil.

The captain was alone in the boat. I was not quite so *Bobo* then and I understood why. He beached the boat and climbed up the slope of sand, the daemon swaying behind him like a crimson shadow. I could see its blind eyes and the beautiful, quiet face shut up with bliss because of the thing the captain had come to do. He was carrying in his hand a long shining pistol, and he walked carefully, looking to left and right. His face was anxious, and his mouth had grown more cruel in the months since I saw him last.

I was sorry for him, but I was very frightened, too. I knew he meant to kill whomever he found alive upon the island, so that no tongue could tell the Shaughnessy's people of his wicked deed.

He found my thatched *barraca* at the edge of the shore, and kicked it to pieces with his heavy boots. Then he went on until he saw the long mound above the Shaughnessy's bed, with the cross standing where his head lay. He bent over the cross, and the markings upon it spoke to him as they would never speak to me. I heard nothing, but he heard and knew. He put out his hand and pulled up the cross from the Shaughnessy's grave.

Then he went to the ruins of my *barraca* and to the embers of the fire I kept smouldering there. He broke the cross upon his knee and fed the pieces into the hot coals. The wood was dry. I saw it catch flame and burn. I saw, too, the faint stirring of wind that sprang up with the flames, and I heard the sighing that ran through the trees around me. Now there was nothing here to tell the searchers who might come afterward that the Shaughnessy lay in the island earth. Nothing— except myself.

He saw my footprints around the ruined *barraca*. He stooped to look. When he rose again and peered around the shore and forest, I could see his eyes shine, and it was the daemon who looked out of them, not the man.

Following my tracks, he began to move slowly toward the forest where I was hiding.

Then I was very frightened. I rose and fled through the trees, and I heard the dryads whimpering about me as I ran. They drew back their boughs to let me pass and swept them back after me to bar the way. I ran and ran, upward among the rocks, until I came to the pool of the unicorn, and the oread of the mountain stood there waiting for me, her arm across the unicorn's neck.

There was a rising wind upon the island. The leaves threshed and talked among themselves, and the oread's leafy hair blew backward from her face with its wise slanting eyes. The unicorn's silver mane tossed in that wind and the water ruffled in the pool.

"There is trouble coming, Luiz," the oread told me.

"The daemon. I know." I nodded to her, and then blinked, because it seemed to me that she and the unicorn, like the sea-*ninfas,* were growing so pale I could see the trees behind them through their bodies. But perhaps that was because the scarlet of the daemon had hurt my eyes.

"There is a man with a soul again upon our island," the oread said. "A man who does not believe. Perhaps we will have to go, Luiz."

"The Shaughnessy had a daemon too," I told her. "Yet you were here before his daemon left him to the earth. Why must you go now?"

"His was a good daemon. Even so, we were not fully here while he lived. You must remember, Luiz, that hour I told you of when a star stood above a stable where a child lay, and all our power went from us. Where the souls of men dwell, we cannot stay. This new man has brought a very evil soul with him. It frightens us. Yet since he had burned the cross, perhaps the Master can fight. . . ."

"The Master?" I asked.

"The One we serve. The One you serve, Luiz. The One I think the Shaughnessy served, though he did not know it. The Lord of the opened eyes and the far places. He could not come until the Sign was taken down. Once you had a glimpse of him, when the Sign fell by accident from the grave, but perhaps you have forgotten that."

"I have not forgotten. I am not so *Bobo* now."

She smiled at me, and I could see the tree behind her through the smile.

"Then perhaps you can help the Master when the time comes. We cannot help. We are too weak already, because of the presence of the unbeliever, the man with the daemon. See?" She touched my hand, and I felt not the firm, soft brush of fingers but only a coolness like mist blowing across my skin.

"Perhaps the Master can fight him," the oread said, and her voice was very faint, like a voice from far away, though she spoke from so near to me. "I do not know about that. We must go, Luiz. We may not meet again. Good-bye, *caro bobo,* while I can still say good-by. . . ." The last of it was faint as the hushing of the leaves, and the oread and the unicorn together looked like smoke blowing from a campfire across the glade.

The knowledge of my loneliness came over me then more painfully than I had felt it since that hour when I first looked upon the captain's daemon and knew at last what my own sorrow was. But I had no time to grieve, for there was a sudden frightened whispering among the leaves behind me, and then the crackle of feet in boots, and then a flicker of terrible crimson among the trees.

I ran. I did not know where I ran. I heard the dryads crying, so it must have been among trees. But at last I came out upon the shore again and I saw the Shaughnessy's long grave without a cross above it. And I stopped short, and a thrill of terror went through me. For there was a Something that crouched upon the grave.

The fear in me then was a new thing. A monstrous, dim fear that moves like a cloud about the Master. I knew he meant me no harm, but the fear was heavy upon me, making my head spin with panic. *Pânico.* . . .

The Master rose upon the grave, and he stamped his goat-hoofed foot twice and set the pipes to his bearded lips. I heard a thin, strange wailing music that made the blood chill inside me. And at the first sound of it there came again what I had heard once before upon the island.

The leaves upon all the trees turned over once, with a great single whispering of one syllable. The syllable was the Master's name. I fled from it in the *pânico* all men have felt who hear that name pronounced. I fled to the edge of the beach, and I could flee no farther. So I crouched behind a hillock of rock on the wet sand, and watched what came after me from the trees.

It was the captain, with his daemon swaying like smoke above his head. He carried the long pistol ready, and his eyes moved from left to right along the beach, seeking like a wild beast for his quarry.

He saw the Master, standing upon the Shaughnessy's grave.

I saw how he stopped, rigid, like a man of stone. The daemon swayed forward above his head, he stopped so suddenly. I saw how he stared. And such was his disbelief, that for an instant I thought even the outlines of the Master grew hazy. There is great power in the men with souls.

I stood up behind my rock. I cried above the noises of the surf, "Master—Great Pan—I believe!"

He heard me. He tossed his horned head and his bulk was solid again. He set the pipes to his lips.

Captain Stryker whirled when he heard me. The long pistol swung up and there was a flash and a roar, and something went by me with a whine of anger. It did not touch me.

Then the music of the pipes began. A terrible music, thin and high, like the ringing in the ears that has no source. It seized the captain as if with thin, strong fingers, making him turn back to the sound. He stood rigid again, staring, straining. The daemon above him turned uneasily from side to side, like a snake swaying.

Then Captain Stryker ran. I saw the sand fly up from under his boots as he fled southward along the shore. His daemon went after him, a red shadow with its eyes still closed, and after them both went Pan, moving delicately on the goat-hoofs, the pipes to his lips and his horns shining golden in the sun.

And that midday terror I think was greater than any terror that can stalk a man by dark.

I waited beside my rock. The sea was empty behind me except for the *Dancing Martha* waiting the captain's orders at its anchor. But no *ninfas* came in on the foam to keep me company; no heads rose wreathed with seaweed out of the water. The sea was empty and the island was empty too, except for a man and a daemon and the Piper who followed at their heels.

Myself I do not count. I have no soul.

It was nearly dark when they came back along the beach. I think the Piper had hunted them clear around the island, going slowly on his delicate hoofs, never hurrying, never faltering, and that dreadful thin music always in the captain's ears.

I saw the captain's face when he came back in the twilight. It was an old man's face, haggard, white, with deep lines in it and eyes as wild as Pan's. His clothing was torn to ribbons and his hands bled,

but he still held the pistol and the red daemon still hung swaying
above him.

I think the captain did not know that he had come back to his
starting place. By that time, all places must have looked alike to him.
He came wavering toward me blindly. I rose up behind my rock.

When he saw me he lifted the pistol again and gasped some Yankee
words. He was a strong man, Captain Stryker. With all he had endured
in that long chase, he still had the power to remember he must kill
me. I did not think he had reloaded the pistol, and I stood up facing
him across the sand.

Behind him Pan's pipes shrilled a warning, but the Master did not
draw nearer to come between us. The red daemon swayed at the
captain's back, and I knew why Pan did not come to my aid. Those
who lost their power when the Child was born can never lay hands
upon men who possess a soul. Even a soul as evil as the captain's
stood like a rock between him and the touch of Pan. Only the pipes
could reach a human's ears, but there was that in the sound of the
pipes which did all Pan needed to do.

It could not save me. I heard the captain laugh, without breath, a
strange, hoarse sound, and I saw the lightning dazzle from the pistol's
mouth. The crash it made was like a blow that struck me here, in the
chest. I almost fell. That blow was heavy, but I scarcely noticed it
then. There was too much to do.

The captain was laughing, and I thought of the Shaughnessy, and I
stumbled forward and took the pistol by its hot muzzle with my hand.
I am strong. I tore it from the captain's fist and he stood there gaping
at me, not believing anything he saw. He breathed in dreadful, deep
gasps, and I found I was gasping too, but I did not know why
just then.

The captain's eyes met mine, and I think he saw that even now I
had no hate for him—only pity. For the man behind the eyes vanished
and the crimson daemon of his rage looked out, because I dared to
feel sorrow for him. I looked into the eyes that were not his, but the
eyes behind the closed lids of the beautiful, blind face above him. It
I hated, not him. And it was it I struck. I lifted the pistol and smashed
it into the captain's face.

I was not very clear in my head just then. I struck the daemon with
my blow, but it was the captain who reeled backward three steps and
then fell. I am very strong. One blow was all I needed.

For a moment there was no sound in all the island. Even the waves
kept their peace. The captain shuddered and gave one sigh, like that
of a man who comes back to living reluctantly. He got his hands
beneath him and rose upon them, peering at me through the hair that
had fallen across his forehead. He was snarling like an animal.

I do not know what he intended then. I think he would have fought
me until one of us was dead. But above him just then I saw the
daemon stir. It was the first time I had ever seen it move except in

answer to the captain's motion. All his life it had followed him, blind, silent, a shadow that echoed his gait and gestures. Now for the first time it did not obey him.

Now it rose up to a great, shining height above his head, and its color was suddenly very deep, very bright and deep, a blinding thing that hung above him too hot in color to look at. Over the beautiful blind face a look of triumph came. I saw ecstasy dawn over that face in all its glory and its evil.

I knew that this was the hour of the daemon.

Some knowledge deeper than any wisdom warned me to cover my eyes. For I saw its lids flicker, and I knew it would not be good to watch when that terrible gaze looked out at last upon a world it had never seen except through the captain's eyes.

I fell to my knees and covered my face. And the captain, seeing that, must have known at long last what it was I saw behind him. I think now that in the hour of a man's death, he knows. I think in that last moment he knows, and turns, and for the first time and the last, looks his daemon in the face.

I did not see him do it. I did not see anything. But I heard a great, resonant cry, like the mighty music that beats through paradise, a cry full of triumph and thanksgiving, and joy at the end of a long, long, weary road. There was mirth in it, and beauty, and all the evil the mind can compass.

Then fire glowed through my fingers and through my eyelids and into my brain. I could not shut it out. I did not even need to lift my head to see, for that sight would have blazed through my very bones.

I saw the daemon fall upon its master.

The captain sprang to his feet with a howl like a beast's howl, no mind or soul in it. He threw back his head and his arms went up to beat that swooping, beautiful, crimson thing away.

No flesh could oppose it. This was its hour. What sets that hour I do not know, but the daemon knew, and nothing could stop it now.

I saw the flaming thing descend upon the captain like a falling star. Through his defending arms it swept, and through his flesh and his bones and into the hollows where the soul dwells.

He stood for an instant transfixed, motionless, glowing with that bath of crimson light. Then I saw the crimson begin to shine *through* him, so that the shadows of his bones stood out upon the skin. And then fire shot up, wreathing from his eyes and mouth and nostrils. He was a lantern of flesh for that fire of the burning spirit. But he was a lantern that is consumed by the flame it carries. . . .

When the color became too bright for the eyes to bear it, I tried to turn away. I could not. The pain in my chest was too great. I thought of the Shaughnessy in that moment, who knew, too, what pain in the chest was like. I think that was the first moment when it came to me that, like the Shaughnessy, I too was going to die.

Before my eyes, the captain burned in the fire of his daemon, burned and burned, his living eyes looking out at me through the crimson glory, and the laughter of the daemon very sweet above the sound of the whining flame. I could not watch and I could not turn away.

But at last the whine began to die. Then the laughter roared out in one great peal of triumph, and the beautiful crimson color, so dreadfully more crimson than blood, flared in a great burst of light that turned to blackness against my eyeballs.

When I could see again, the captain's body lay flat upon the sand. I know death when I see it. He was not burned at all. He looked as any dead man looks, flat and silent. It was his soul I had watched burning, not his body.

The daemon had gone back again to its own place. I knew that, for I could feel my aloneness on the island.

The Others had gone too. The presence of that fiery daemon was more, in the end, than their power could endure. Perhaps they shun an evil soul more fearfully than a good one, knowing themselves nothing of good and evil, but fearing what they do not understand.

You know, *padre,* what came after. The men from the *Dancing Martha* took their captain away next morning. They were frightened of the island. They looked for that which had killed him, but they did not look far, and I hid in the empty forest until they went away.

I do not remember their going. There was a burning in my chest, and this blood I breathe out ran from time to time, as it does now. I do not like the sight of it. Blood is a beautiful color, but it reminds me of too much that was beautiful also, and much redder. . . .

Then you came, *padre.* I do not know how long thereafter. I know the Shaughnessy's people brought you with their ship, to find him or his grave. You know now. And I am glad you came. It is good to have a man like you beside me at this time. I wish I had a daemon of my own, to grow very bright and vanish when I die, but that is not for *o Bobo* and I am used to that kind of loneliness.

I would not live, you see, now that the *ninfas* are gone. To be with them was good, and we comforted one another in our loneliness but, *padre,* I will tell you this much. It was a chilly comfort we gave each other, at the best. I am a man, though *bobo,* and I know. They are *ninfas,* and will never guess how warm and wonderful it must be to own a soul. I would not tell them if I could. I was sorry for the *ninfas, padre.* They are, you see, immortal.

As for me, I will forget loneliness in a little while. I will forget everything. I would not want to be a *ninfa* and live forever.

There is one behind you, *padre.* It is very bright. It watches me across your shoulder, and its eyes are wise and sad. No, daemon, this is no time for sadness. Be sorry for the *ninfas,* daemon, and for men like him who burned upon this beach. But not for me. I am well content.

I will go now.

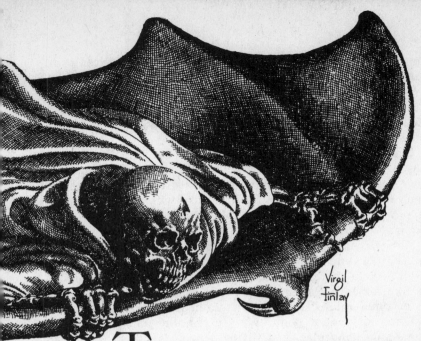

The Burial of the Rats

BRAM STOKER

For every person who knows the name of the world's most famous vampire,
Count Dracula, there are many who know nothing of the fictional Dracula's
creator, Bram Stoker. Fewer still are aware that Stoker, who died in 1912,
left a considerable legacy of supernatural horror fiction, including the
novels Jewel of the Seven Stars *and* The Lair of the White Worm *and*
a slim collection of stories entitled Dracula's Guest. *The latter contains*
Stoker's frequently reprinted horror stories "The Squaw" and "The Judge's
House," and two others published in Famous Fantastic Mysteries, *"The*
Secret of Growing Gold" and "The Burial of the Rats."

LEAVING PARIS by the Orleans road, cross the Enciente, and, turning to the right, you find yourself in a somewhat wild and not at all savory district. Right and left, before and behind, on every side rise great heaps of dust and waste accumulated by the process of time.

Paris has its night as well as its day life, and the sojourner who enters his hotel in the Rue de Rivoli or the Rue St. Honore late at night or leaves it early in the morning, can guess, in coming near Montrouge—if he has not done so already—the purpose of those great wagons that look like boilers on wheels which he finds halting every-where as he passes.

Every city has its peculiar institutions created out of its own needs; and one of the most notable institutions of Paris is its rag-picking population. In the early morning—and Parisian life commences at an early hour—may be seen in most streets standing on the pathway opposite every court and alley and between every few houses, as still in some American cities, even in parts of New York, large wooden boxes into which the domestics or tenement-holders empty the accumulated dust of the past day.

Round these boxes gather and pass on, when the work is done, to fresh fields of labor and pastures new, squalid, hungry-looking men and women, the implements of whose craft consist of a coarse bag or basket slung over the shoulder and a little rake with which they turn over and probe and examine in the minutest manner the dustbins. They pick up and deposit in their baskets, by aid of their rakes, whatever they may find, with the same facility as a Chinaman uses his chopsticks.

Paris is a city of centralization—and centralization and classification are closely allied. In the early times, when centralization is becoming a fact, its forerunner is classification. All things which are similar or analogous become grouped together, and from the grouping of groups rises one whole or central point. We see radiating many long arms with innumerable tentaculae, and in the center rises a gigantic head with a comprehensive brain and keen eyes to look on every side and ears sensitive to hear—and a voracious mouth to swallow.

Other cities resemble all the birds and beasts and fishes whose appetites and digestions are normal. Paris alone is the analogical apotheosis of the octopus. Product of centralization carried along *ad absurdum,* it fairly represents the devil fish; and in no respects is the resemblance more curious than in the similarity of the digestive apparatus.

Those intelligent tourists who, having surrendered their individuality into the hands of Messrs. Cook or Gaze, "do" Paris in three days, are often puzzled to know how it is that the dinner which in London would cost about six shillings, can be had for three francs in a café in the Palais Royal. They need have no more wonder if they will but consider the classification which is a theoretic specialty of Parisian life, and adopt all round the fact from which the chiffonier has his genesis.

The Paris of 1850 was not like the Paris of today, and those who see the Paris of Napoleon and Baron Hausseman can hardly realize the existence of the state of things forty-five years ago.

Amongst other things, however, which have not changed are those districts where the waste is gathered. Dust is dust all the world over, in every age, and the family likeness of dust-heaps is perfect. The traveler, therefore, who visits the environs of Montrouge can go back in fancy without difficulty to the year 1850.

In this year I was making a prolonged stay in Paris. I was very much in love with a young lady who, though she returned my passion, so far yielded to the wishes of her parents that she had promised not to see me or to correspond with me for a year. I, too, had been compelled to accede to these conditions under a vague hope of parental approval.

During the term of probation I had promised to remain out of the country and not to write to my dear one until the expiration of the year.

Naturally the time went heavily with me. There was no one of my own family or circle who could tell me of Alice, and none of her own folk had, I am sorry to say, sufficient generosity to send me even an occasional word of comfort regarding her health and well-being. I spent six months wandering about Europe, but as I could find no satisfactory distraction in travel, I determined to come to Paris, where, at least, I would be within easy hail of London in case any good fortune should call me thither before the appointed time.

That "hope deferred maketh the heart sick" was never better exemplified than in my case, for in addition to the perpetual longing to see the face I loved there was always with me a harrowing anxiety lest some accident should prevent me showing Alice in due time that I had, throughout the long period of probation, been faithful to her trust and my own love.

Thus, every adventure which I undertook had a fierce pleasure of its own, for it was fraught with possible consequences greater than it would have ordinarily borne.

Like all travelers I exhausted the places of most interest in the first month of my stay, and was driven in the second month to look for amusement whithersoever I might. Having made sundry journeys to the better-known suburbs, I began to see that there was a *terra incognita,* in so far as the guide book was concerned, in the social wilderness lying between these attractive points. Accordingly I began to systemize my researches, and each day took up the thread of my exploration at the place where I had on the previous day dropped it.

In process of time my wanderings led near Montrouge, and I saw that hereabouts lay the Ultima Thule of social exploration—a country as little known as that round the source of the White Nile. And so I determined to investigate philosophically the chiffonier—his habitat, his life, and his means of life.

The job was an unsavory one, difficult of accomplishment, and with little hope of adequate reward. However, despite reason, obstinacy prevailed, and I entered into my new investigation with a keener energy than I could have summoned to aid me in any investigation leading to any end valuable or worthy.

One day, late in a fine afternoon, toward the end of September, I entered the holy of holies of the city of dust. The place was evidently the recognized abode of a number of chiffoniers, for some sort of arrangement was manifested in the formation of the dust-heaps near the road. I passed amongst these heaps, which stood like orderly sentries, determined to penetrate further and trace dust to its ultimate location.

As I passed I saw behind the dust-heaps a few forms that flitted to and fro, evidently watching with interest the advent of any stranger in such a place. The district was like a small Switzerland, and as I went forward my tortuous course shut out the path behind me.

Presently I got into what seemed a small city or community of chiffoniers. There were a number of shanties or huts, such as may be met with in the remote parts of the Bog of Allan—rude places with wattled walls, plastered with mud and roofs of rude thatch made from stable refuse—such places as one would not like to enter for any consideration, and which even in water-color could only look pictur-esque if judiciously treated.

In the midst of these huts was one of the strangest adaptations—I cannot say habitations—I had ever seen. An immense old wardrobe, the colossal remnant of some boudoir of Charles VII, or Henry II, had been converted into a dwelling-house. The double doors lay open, so that the entire menage was open to public view. In the open half of the wardrobe was a common sitting-room of some four feet by six, in which sat, smoking their pipes round a charcoal brazier, no fewer than six old soldiers of the First Republic, with their uniforms torn and threadbare. Evidently they were of a *mauvais sujet* class; their bleary eyes and limp jaws told plainly of a common love of absinthe; and their eyes had that haggard, worn look which stamps the drunkard at his worst, and that look of slumbering ferocity which follows in the wake of drink. The other side stood as of old, with its shelves intact, save that they were cut to half their depth, and in each shelf of which there were six, was a bed made with rags and straw.

The half-dozen worthies who inhabited this structure looked at me curiously as I passed; and when I looked back after going a little way I saw their heads together in a whispered conference. I did not like the look of this at all, for the place was very lonely, and the men looked very, very villainous. However, I did not see any cause for fear, and went on my way, penetrating further and further into the Sahara. The way was tortuous to a degree, and from going round in a series of semicircles, as one goes in skating with the Dutch roll, I got rather confused with regard to the points of the compass.

When I had penetrated a little way I saw, as I turned the corner of a half-made heap, sitting on a heap of straw an old soldier with threadbare coat.

"Hallo!" said I to myself; "the First Republic is well represented here in its soldiery."

As I passed him the old man never even looked up at me, but gazed on the ground with stolid persistency. Again I remarked to myself; "See what a life of rude warfare can do! This old man's curiosity is a thing of the past."

When I had gone a few steps, however, I looked back suddenly, and saw that curiosity was not dead, for the veteran had raised his head and was regarding me with a queer expression. He seemed to me to look like one of the six worthies in the press. When he saw me looking he lowered his head; and without thinking further of him I went on my way, satisfied that there was a strange likeness between these old warriors.

Presently I met another old solider in a similar manner. He, too, did not notice me while I was passing.

By this time it was getting late in the afternoon, and I began to think of retracing my steps. Accordingly I turned to go back, but could see a number of tracks leading between different mounds and could not ascertain which of them I should take. In my perplexity I wanted to see someone of whom to ask the way, but could see no one. I determined to go on a few mounds further and so try to see someone—not a veteran.

I gained my object, for after going a couple of hundred yards I saw before me a single shanty such as I had seen before—with, however, the difference that this was not one for living in, but merely a roof with three walls open in front. From the evidence which the neighborhood exhibited I took it to be a place for sorting. Within it was an old woman wrinkled and bent with age; I approached her to ask the way.

She rose as I came close and I asked her my way. She immediately commenced a conversation; and it occurred to me that here in the very center of the Kingdom of Dust was the place to gather details of the history of Parisian rag-picking—particularly as I could do so from the lips of one who looked like the oldest inhabitant.

I began my inquiries, and the old woman gave me most interesting answers—she had been one of the ceteuces who sat daily before the guillotine and had taken an active part among the women who signalized themselves by their violence in the revolution. While we were talking she said suddenly: "But m'sieur must be tired standing," and dusted a rickety old stool for me to sit down. I hardly liked to do so for many reasons; but the poor old woman was so civil that I did not like to run the risk of hurting her by refusing, and moreover the conversation of one who had been at the taking of the Bastille was so interesting that I sat down and so our conversation went on.

While we were talking an old man—older and more bent and wrinkled even than the woman—appeared from behind the shanty. "Here is Pierre," said she. "M'sieur can hear stories now if he wishes, for Pierre was in everything, from the Bastille to Waterloo." The old man took another stool at my request and we plunged into a sea of revolutionary reminiscenses. This old man, albeit clothed like a scarecrow, was like any one of the six veterans.

I was now sitting in the center of the low hut with the woman on my left hand and the man on my right, each of them being somewhat in front of me. The place was full of all sorts of curious objects of lumber, and of many things that I wished far away. In one corner was a heap of rags which seemed to move from the number of vermin it contained, and in the other a heap of bones whose odor was something shocking. Every now and then, glancing at the heaps, I could see the gleaming eyes of some of the rats which infested the place.

These loathsome objects were bad enough, but what looked even more dreadful was an old butcher's ax with an iron handle stained with clots of blood leaning up against the wall on the right-hand side. Still these things did not give me much concern. The talk of the two old people was so fascinating that I stayed on and on, till evening came and the dust heaps threw dark shadows over the vales between them.

After a time I began to grow uneasy, I couldn't tell how or why, but somehow I did not feel satisfied. Uneasiness is an instinct and means warning. The psychic faculties are often the sentries of the intellect; and when they sound alarm the reason begins to act, although perhaps not consciously.

This was so with me. I began to bethink me where I was and by what surrounded, and to wonder how I should fare in case I should be attacked; and then the thought suddenly burst upon me, although without any overt cause, that I was in danger. Prudence whispered: "Be still and make no sign," and so I was still and made no sign, for I knew that four cunning eyes were upon me. Four eyes—if not more. My God, what a horrible thought! The whole shanty might be surrounded on three sides with villains! I might be in the midst of a band of such desperadoes as only half a century of periodic revolution can produce.

With a sense of danger my intellect and observation quickened, and I grew more watchful than was my wont. I noticed that the old woman's eyes were constantly wandering toward my hands. I looked at them too, and saw the cause—my rings. On my left little finger I had a large signet and on the right a good diamond.

I thought that if there was any danger my first care was to avert suspicion. Accordingly I began to work the conversation round to rag-picking—to the drains—of the things found there; and so by easy stages to jewels. Then, seizing a favorable opportunity, I asked the old woman if she knew anything of such things. She answered that she did, a little. I held out my right hand, and, showing her the diamond, asked her what she thought of that. She answered that her eyes were bad, and stooped over my hand. I said as nonchalantly as I could: "Pardon me! You will see better thus!" and taking it off handed it to her. An unholy light came into her withered old face, as she touched it. She stole one glance at me swift and keen as a flash of lightning.

She bent over the ring for a moment, her face quite concealed as though examining it. The old man looked straight out of the front of the shanty before him, at the same time fumbling in his pockets and producing a screw of tobacco in a paper and a pipe, which he proceeded to fill. I took advantage of the pause and the momentary rest from the searching eyes on my face to look carefully round the place, now dim and shadowy in the gloaming.

There still lay all the heaps of varied reeking foulness; there the terrible blood-stained ax leaning against the wall in the right-hand corner, and everywhere, despite the gloom, the baleful glitter of the eyes of the rats. I could see them even through some of the chinks of the boards at the back low down close to the ground. But stay! these latter eyes seemed more than usually large and bright and baleful!

For an instant my heart stood still, and I felt in that whirling condition of mind in which one feels a sort of spiritual drunkenness, and as though the body is only maintained erect in that there is no time for it to fall before recovery. Then, in another second, I was calm—coldly calm, with all my energies in full vigor, with a self-control which I felt to be perfect and with all my feeling and instincts alert.

Now I knew the full extent of my danger: I was watched and surrounded by desperate people! I could not even guess at how many of them were lying there on the ground behind the shanty, waiting for the moment to strike. I knew that I was big and strong, and they knew it, too. They knew also, as I did, that I was an Englishman and would make a fight for it; and so we waited. I had, I felt, gained an advantage in the last few seconds, for I knew my danger and understood the situation. Now, I thought, is the test of my courage—the enduring test: the fighting test may come later!

The old woman raised her head and said to me in a satisfied kind of way:

"A very fine ring, indeed—a beautiful ring! Oh, me! I once had such rings, plenty of them, and bracelets and earrings! Oh! for in those fine days I led the town a dance! But they've forgotten me now! They've forgotten me! They? Why they never heard of me! Perhaps their grandfathers remember me, some of them!" and she laughed a harsh, croaking laugh. And then I am bound to say that she astonished me, for she handed me back the ring with a certain suggestion of old-fashioned grace which was not without its pathos.

The old man eyed her with a sort of sudden ferocity, half rising from his stool, and said to me suddenly and hoarsely:

"Let me see!"

I was about to hand the ring over when the old woman said:

"No! no, do not give it to Pierre! Pierre is eccentric. He loses things; and such a pretty ring!"

"Cat!" said the old man, savagely. Suddenly the old woman said, rather more loudly than was necessary:

"Wait! I shall tell you something about a ring." There was something in the sound of her voice that jarred upon me. Perhaps it was my hypersensitiveness, wrought up as I was to such a pitch of nervous excitement, but I seemed to think that she was not addressing me. As I stole a glance round the place I saw the eyes of the rats in the bone heaps, but missed the eyes along the back. But even as I looked I saw them again appear. The old woman's "Wait!" had given me a respite from attack, and the men had sunk back to their reclining posture.

"I once lost a ring—a beautiful diamond hoop that had belonged to a queen, and which was given to me by a farmer of the taxes, who afterwards cut his throat because I sent him away. I thought it must have been stolen, and taxed my people; but I could get no trace. The police came and suggested that it had found its way to the drain. We descended—I in my fine clothes, for I would not trust them with my beautiful ring! I know more of the drains since then, and of rats, too! but I shall never forget the horror of that place—alive with blazing eyes, a wall of them just outside the light of our torches. Well, we got beneath my house. We searched the outlet of the drain, and there in the filth found my ring, and we came out.

"But we found something else also before we came! As we were coming toward the opening a lot of sewer rats—human ones this time—came toward us. They told the police that one of their number had gone into the drain, but had not returned. He had gone in only shortly before we did, and, if lost, could hardly be far off. They asked help to seek him, so we turned back. They tried to prevent me going, but I insisted. It was a new excitement, and had I not recovered my ring?

"Not far did we go till we came on something. There was but little water, and the bottom of the drain was raised with brick, rubbish, and much matter of the kind. He had made a fight for it, even when his torch had gone out. But they were too many for him! They had not been long about it! The bones were still warm; but they were picked clean. They had even eaten their own dead ones and there were bones of rats as well as of the man. They took it cool enough those others—the human ones—and joked of their comrade when they found him dead, though they would have helped him living. Bah! what matters it—life or death?"

"And had you no fear?" I asked her.

"Fear!" she said with a laugh. "Me have fear? Ask Pierre! But I was younger then, and, as I came through that horrible drain with its wall of greedy eyes, always moving with the circle of the light from the torches, I did not feel uneasy. I kept on before the men, though! It is a way I have! I never let the men get before me. All I want is a chance and a means! And they ate him up—took every trace away except the bones; and no one knew it, nor no sound of him was ever heard!" Here she broke into a chuckling fit of the ghastliest merriment which it was ever my lot to hear and see. A great poetess describes her heroine singing: "Oh! to see or hear her singing! Scarce I know which is the divinest."

And I can apply the same idea to the old crone—in all save the dignity, for I scarce could tell which was the most hellish—the harsh, malicious, satisfied, cruel laugh, or the leering grin, and the horrible square opening of the mouth like a tragic mask, and the yellow gleam of the few discolored teeth in the shapeless gums. In that laugh and with that grin and the chuckling satisfaction I knew as well as if it had been spoken to me in words of thunder that my murder was settled, and the murderers only bided the proper time for its accomplishment. I could read between the lines of her gruesome story the commands to her accomplices. "Wait," she seemed to say, "bide your time. I shall strike the first blow. Find the weapon for me, and I shall make the opportunity! He shall not escape! Keep him quiet, and then no one will be the wiser. There will be no outcry, and the rats will do their work!"

It was growing darker and darker; the night was coming. I stole a glance round the shanty, still all the same! The bloody ax in the corner, the heaps of filth, and the eyes on the bone heaps and the crannies of the floor.

Pierre had been still ostensibly filling his pipe; he now struck a light and began to puff away at it. The old woman said:

"Dear heart, how dark it is! Pierre, like a good lad, light the lamp!"

Pierre got up and with the lighted match in his hand touched the wick of a lamp which hung at one side of the entrance to the shanty, and which had a reflector that threw light all over the place. It was evidently that which was used for their sorting at night.

"Not that, stupid! Not that! The lantern!" she called out to him.

He immediately blew it out, saying: "All right, mother, I'll find it," and he hustled about the left corner of the room—the old woman saying through the darkness:

"The lantern! the lantern! Oh! That is the light that is most useful to us poor folks. The lantern was the friend of the revolution! It is the friend of the chiffonier! It helps us when all else fails."

Hardly had she said the word when there was a kind of creaking of the whole place, and something was steadily dragging over the roof.

Again I seemed to read between the lines of her words. I knew the lesson of the lantern.

"One of you get on the roof with a noose and strangle him as he passes out if we fail within."

As I looked out of the opening I saw a loop of rope outlined black against the lurid sky. I was now, indeed, beset!

Pierre was not long in finding the lantern. I kept my eyes fixed through the darkness on the old woman. Pierre struck his light, and by its flash I saw the old woman raise from the ground beside her where it had mysteriously appeared, and then hide in the folds of her gown, a long sharp knife or dagger. It seemed to be like a butcher's sharpening iron fixed to a keen point.

The lantern was lit.

"Bring it here, Pierre," she said. "Place it in the doorway where we can see it. See how nice it is! It shuts out the darkness from us; it is just right!"

Just right for her and her purposes! It threw all of its light on my face, leaving in gloom the faces of both Pierre and the old woman, who sat outside of me on each side.

I felt that the time of action was approaching; but I knew now that the first signal and movement would come from the woman, and so watched her.

I was unarmed, but I had made up my mind what to do. At the first movement I would seize the butcher's ax in the right-hand corner and fight my way out. At least, I would die hard. I stole a glance round to fix its exact locality so that I could not fail to seize it at the first effort, for then, if ever, time and accuracy would be precious.

Good God! It was gone! All the horror of the situation burst upon me; but the bitterest thought of all was that if the issue of the terrible position should be against me Alice would infallibly suffer. Either she would believe me false—and any lover, or any one who has ever been one, can imagine the bitterness of the thought—or else she would go on loving long after I had been lost to her and to the world, so that her life would be broken and embittered, shattered with disappointment and despair. The very magnitude of the pain braced me up and nerved me to bear the dread scrutiny of the plotters.

I think I did not betray myself. The old woman was watching me as a cat does a mouse; she had her right hand hidden in the folds of her gown, clutching, I knew, that long, cruel-looking dagger. Had she seen any disappointment in my face she would, I felt, have known that the moment had come, and would have sprung on me like a tigress, certain of taking me unprepared.

I looked out into the night, and there I saw new cause for danger. Before and around the hut were at a little distance some shadowy forms; they were quite still, but I knew that they were all alert and on guard. Small chance for me now in that direction.

Again I stole a glance round the place. In moments of great excitement and of great danger, which is excitement, the mind works very quickly, and the keenness of the faculties which depend on the mind grows in proportion. I now felt this. In an instant I took in the whole situation. I saw that the ax had been taken through a small hole in one of the rotten boards. How rotten they must be to allow such a thing being done without a particle of noise.

The hut was a regular murder-trap, and was guarded all around. A garroter lay on the roof ready to entangle me with his noose if I should escape the dagger of the old hag. In front the way was guarded by I know not how many watchers. And at the back was a row of desperate men—I had seen their eyes still through the crack in the boards of the floor, when last I looked—as they lay prone waiting for the signal to start erect. If it was to be ever, now for it!

As nonchalantly as I could I turned slightly on my stool so as to get my right leg well under me. Then with a sudden jump, turning my head, and guarding it with my hands, and with the fighting instinct of the knights of old, I breathed my lady's name and hurled myself against the back wall of the hut.

Watchful as they were, the suddenness of my movement surprised both Pierre and the old woman. As I crashed through the rotten timbers

I saw the old woman rise with a leap like a tiger and heard her low gasp of baffled rage. My feet lit on something that moved, and as I jumped away I knew that I had stepped on the back of one of the row of men lying on their faces outside the hut. I was torn with nails and splinters, but otherwise unhurt. Breathless I rushed up the mound in front of me, hearing as I went the dull crash of the shanty as it collapsed into a mass.

It was a nightmare climb. The mound, though but low, was awfully steep, and with each step I took the mass of dust and cinders tore down with me and gave way under my feet. The dust choked me; it was sickening, foetid, awful; but my climb was, I felt, for life or death, and I struggled on. The seconds seemed hours; but the few moments I had in starting, combined with my youth and strength, gave me a great advantage, and though several forms struggled after me in deadly silence which was more dreadful than any sound, I easily reached the top. Since then I have climbed the cone of Vesuvius, and as I struggled up that dreary steep amid the sulphurous fumes the memory of that awful night at Montrouge came back to me so vividly that I almost grew faint.

The mound was one of the tallest in the region of dust, and as I struggled to the top, panting for breath and with my heart beating like a sledge hammer, I saw away to my left the dull red gleam of the sky, and nearer still the flashing of lights. Thank God! I knew where I was now and where lay the road to Paris!

For two or three seconds I paused and looked back. My pursuers were still well behind me, but struggling up resolutely, and in deadly silence. Beyond, the shanty was a wreck—a mass of timber and moving forms. I could see it well, for flames were already bursting out; the rags and straw had evidently caught fire from the lantern. Still silence there! Not a sound! These old wretches could die game, anyhow.

I had no time for more than a passing glance, for as I cast an eye round the mound preparatory to making my descent I saw several dark forms rushing round on either side to cut me off on my way. It was now a race for life. They were trying to head me on my way to Paris, and with the instinct of the moment I dashed down to the right-hand side. I was just in time, for, though I came as it seemed to me down the steep in a very few steps, the wary old men who were watching me turned back, and one, as I rushed by into the opening between the two mounds in front, almost struck me a blow with that terrible butcher's ax. There could surely not be two such weapons about!

Then began a really horrible chase. I easily ran ahead of the old men, and even when some younger ones and a few women joined in the hunt I easily distanced them. But I did not know the way, and I could not even guide myself by the light in the sky, for I was running away from it.

I had heard that, unless of conscious purpose, hunted men turn always to the left, and so I found it now; and so, I suppose knew also

my pursuers, who were more animals than men, and with cunning or
instinct had found out such secrets for themselves: for on finishing a
quick spurt, after which I intended to take a moment's breathing space,
I suddenly saw ahead of me two or three forms swiftly passing behind
a mound to the right.

I was in the spider's web now indeed! But with the thought of this
new danger came the resource of the hunted, and so I darted down
the next turning to the right. I continued in this direction for some
hundred yards, and then, making a turn to the left again, felt certain
that I had, at any rate, avoided the danger of being surrounded.

But not of pursuit, for on came the rabble after me, steady, dogged,
relentless, and still in grim silence.

In the greater darkness the mounds seemed now to be somewhat
smaller than before, although—for the night was closing—they looked
bigger in proportion. I was now well ahead of my pursuers, so I made
a dart up the mound in front.

Oh joy of joys! I was close to the edge of this inferno of dustheaps.
Away behind me the red light of Paris in the sky, and towering up
behind rose the heights of Montmartre—a dim light, with here and
there brilliant points like stars.

Restored to vigor in a moment, I ran over the few remaining mounds
of decreasing size, and found myself on the level land beyond. Even
then, however, the prospect was not inviting. All before me was dark
and dismal, and I had evidently come to one of those dank, low-lying
waste places which are found here and there in the neighborhood of
great cities. Places of waste and desolation, where the space is required
for the ultimate agglomeration of all that is noxious, and the ground
is so poor as to create no desire of occupancy even in the lowest
squatter.

With eyes accustomed to the gloom of the evening, and away now
from the shadows of those dreadful dust-heaps, I could see much more
easily than I could a little while ago. It might have been, of course,
that the glare in the sky of the lights of Paris, though the city was
some miles away, was reflected here. Howsoever it was, I saw
well enough to take my bearings for certainty some little distance
around me.

In front was a bleak, flat waste that seemed almost dead level, with
here and there the dark shimmering of stagnant pools. Seemingly far
off on the right, amid a small cluster of scattered lights, rose a dark
mass of Fort Montrouge, and away to the left in the dim distance,
pointed with stray gleams from cottage windows, the lights in the sky
showed the locality of Bicêtre. A moment's thought decided me to take
the right and try to reach Montrouge. There at least would be some
sort of safety, and I might possibly long before come on some of the
cross roads which I knew. Somewhere, not far off, must lie the strategic
road made to connect the outlying chain of forts circling the city.

Then I looked back. Coming over the mounds, and outlined black against the glare of the Parisian horizon, I saw several moving figures, and still away to the right several more deploying out between me and my destination. They evidently meant to cut me off in this direction, and so my choice became constricted; it lay now between going straight ahead or turning to the left. Stooping to the ground, so as to get the advantage of the horizon as a line of sight, I looked carefully in this direction, but could detect no sign of my enemies. I argued that as they had not guarded or were not trying to guard that point, there was evidently danger to me there already. So I made up my mind to go straight on before me.

It was not an inviting prospect, and as I went on the reality grew worse. The ground became soft and oozy, and now and again gave way beneath me in a sickening kind of way. I seemed somehow to be going down, for I saw around me places seemingly more elevated than where I was, and this in a place which from a little way back seemed dead level. I looked around, but could see none of my pursuers. This was strange, for all along these birds of the night had been following me through the darkness as well as though it were now daylight. How I blamed myself for coming out in my light-colored tourist suit of tweed.

The silence, and my not being able to see my enemies, while I felt that they were watching me, grew appalling, and in the hope of some one not of this ghastly crew hearing me I raised my voice and shouted several times. There was not the slightest response; not even an echo rewarded my efforts. For a while I stood stock still and kept my eyes in one direction. On one of the rising places around me I saw something dark move along, then another, and another. This was to my left, and seemingly moving to head me off.

I thought that again I might with my skill as a runner elude my enemies at this game, and so with all my speed darted forward.

Splash!

My feet had given way in a mass of slimy rubbish, and I had fallen headlong into a reeking, stagnant pool. The water and the mud in which my arms sank up to the elbows were filthy and nauseous beyond description, and in the suddenness of my fall I had actually swallowed some of the filthy stuff, which nearly choked me, and made me gasp for breath. Never shall I forget the moments during which I stood trying to recover myself, almost fainting from the foetid odor of the filthy pool, whose white mist rose ghostlike around. Worst of all, with the acute despair of the hunted animal when he sees the pursuing pack closing on him, I saw before my eyes while I stood helpless the dark forms of my pursuers moving swiftly to surround me.

It is curious how our minds work on odd matters even when the energies of thought are seemingly concentrated on some terrible and pressing need. I was in momentary peril of my life: my safety depended on my action, and my choice of alternatives coming now with almost every step I took, and yet I could not but think of the strange dogged persistency of these old men. Their silent resolution, their steadfast, grim persistency even in such a cause commanded, as well as fear, even a measure of respect. What must they have been in the vigor of their youth? I could understand now that whirlwind rush on the bridge of Arcola, that scornful exclamation of the Old Guard at Waterloo! Unconscious cerebration has its own pleasures, even at such moments; but fortunately it does not in any way clash with the thought from which action springs.

I realized at a glance that so far I was defeated in my object, my enemies as yet had won. They had succeeded in surrounding me on three sides, and were bent on driving me off to the left-hand, where there was already some danger ahead of me, for they had left no guard. I accepted the alternative—it was a case of Hobson's choice and run. I had to keep to the lower ground, for my pursuers were on the higher places.

However, though the ooze and broken ground impeded me, my youth and training made me able to hold my ground, and by keeping a diagonal line I not only kept them from gaining on me, but even began to distance them. This gave me new heart and strength, and by this time habitual training was beginning to tell and my second wind had come.

Before me the ground rose slightly. I rushed up the slope and found before me a waste of watery slime, with a low dyke or bank looking black and grim beyond. I felt that if I could but reach that dyke in safety I could there, with solid ground under my feet and some kind of path to guide me, find with comparative ease a way out of my troubles. After a glance right and left and seeing no one near, I kept my eyes for a few minutes to their rightful work of aiding my feet while I crossed the swamp. It was rough, hard work, but there was little danger, merely toil; and a short time took me to the dyke. I rushed up the slope exulting; but here again I met a new shock. On either side of me rose a number of crouching figures. From right and left they rushed at me. Each body held a rope.

The cordon was nearly complete. I could pass on neither side, and the end was near.

There was only one chance, and I took it. I hurled myself across the dyke, and escaping out of the very clutches of my foes, threw myself into the stream.

At any other time I should have thought that water foul and filthy, but now it was as welcome as the most crystal stream to the parched traveler. It was a highway of safety!

My pursuers rushed after me. Had only one of them held the rope it would have been all up with me, for he could have entangled me before I had time to swim a stroke; but the many hands holding it embarrassed and delayed them, and when the rope struck the water I heard a splash well behind me. A few minutes' hard swimming took me across the stream. Refreshed with the immersion and encouraged by the escape, I climbed the dyke in comparative gaiety of spirits.

From the top I looked back. Through the darkness I saw my assailants scattering up and down along the dyke. The pursuit was evidently not ended, and again I had to choose my course. Beyond the dyke where I stood was a wild, swampy space very similar to that which I had crossed. I determined to shun such a place, and thought for a moment whether I would take up or down the dyke. I thought I heard a sound— the muffled sound of oars, so I listened, and then shouted.

No response; but the sound ceased. My enemies had evidently got a boat of some kind. As they were on the up side of me I took the down path and began to run. As I passed to the left of where I had entered the water I heard several splashes, soft and stealthy, like the sound a rat makes as he plunges into the stream, but vastly greater; and as I looked I saw the dark sheen of the water broken by the ripples of several advancing heads. Some of my enemies were swimming the stream also.

And now behind me, up the stream, the silence was broken by the quick rattle and creak of oars; my enemies were in hot pursuit. I put my best leg foremost and ran on. After a break of a couple of minutes I looked back, and by a gleam of light through the ragged clouds I saw several dark forms climbing the bank behind me. The wind had now begun to rise, and the water beside me was ruffled and beginning to break in tiny waves on the bank. I had to keep my eyes pretty well on the ground before me, lest I should stumble, for I knew that to stumble was death. After a few minutes I looked back behind me. On the dyke were only a few dark figures, but crossing the waste, swampy ground were many more. What new danger this portended I did not know—could only guess. Then as I ran it seemed to me that my track kept ever sloping away to the right. I looked up ahead and saw that the river was much wider than before, and that the dyke on which I stood fell quite away, and beyond it was another stream on whose near bank I saw some of the dark forms now across the marsh. I was on an island of some kind.

My situation was now indeed terrible, for my enemies had hemmed me in on every side. Behind came the quickening roll of oars, as though my pursuers knew that the end was close. Around me on every side was desolation; there was not a roof or light, as far as I could see. Far off to the right rose some dark mass, but what it was I knew not.

For a moment I paused to think what I should do, not for more, for my pursuers were drawing closer. Then my mind was made up. I slipped down the bank and took to the water. I struck out striaght ahead, so as to gain the current by clearing the backwater of the island for such I presume it was, when I had passed into the stream. I waited till a cloud came driving across the moon and leaving all in darkness. Then I took off my hat and laid it softly on the water floating with the stream, and a second after dived to the right and struck out under water with all my might. I was, I suppose, half a minute under water, and when I rose came up as softly as I could, and turning, looked back. There went my light brown hat floating merrily away. Close behind it came a rickety old boat, driven furiously by a pair of oars. The moon was still partly obscured by the drifting clouds, but in the partial light I could see a man in the bows holding aloft ready to strike what appeared to me to be that same dreadful pole-ax which I had before escaped.

As I looked the boat drew closer, closer, and the man struck savagely. The hat disappeared. The man fell forward, almost out of the boat. His comrades dragged him in but without the ax, and then as I turned with all my energies bent on reaching the further bank, I heard the fierce whirr of the muttered *"Sacré!"* which marked the anger of my baffled pursuers.

That was the first sound I had heard from human lips during all this dreadful chase, and full as it was of menace and danger to me it was a welcome sound for it broke that awful silence which shrouded and appalled me. It was as an overt sign that my opponents were men and not ghosts, and that with them I had, at least, the chance of a man, though but one against many.

But now that the spell of silence was broken the sounds came thick and fast. From boat to shore and back from shore to boat came quick question and answer, all in the fiercest whispers. I looked back—a fatal thing to do—for in the instant someone caught sight of my face, which showed white on the dark water, and shouted. Hands pointed to me, and in a moment or two the rowboat was under way, and following hard after me. I had but a little way to go, but quicker and quicker came the boat after me. A few more strokes and I would be on the shore, but I felt the oncoming of the boat, and expected each second to feel the crash of an oar or other weapon on my head. Had I not seen that dreadful ax disappear in the water I do not think that I could have won the shore.

I heard the muttered curses of those not rowing and the labored breath of the rowers. With one supreme effort for life or liberty I touched the bank and sprang up it. There was not a single second to spare, for hard behind me the boat grounded and several dark forms sprang after me. I gained the top of the dyke, and keeping to the left ran on again. The boat put off and followed down the stream. Seeing this I feared danger in this direction, and quickly turning, ran down the dyke on the other side, and after passing a short stretch of marshy ground gained a wild, open flat country and sped on.

Still behind me came on my relentless pursuers. Far away, below me, I saw the same dark mass as before, but now grown closer and greater. My heart gave a great thrill of delight, for I knew that it must be the fortress of Bicêtre, and with new courage I ran on. I had heard that between each and all of the protecting forts of Paris there are strategic ways, deep sunk roads, where soldiers marching should be sheltered from the enemy. I knew that if I could gain this road I would be safe, but in the darkness I could not see any sign of it, so, in blind hope of striking it, I ran on.

Presently I came to the edge of a deep cut, and found that down below me ran a road guarded on each side by a ditch of water fenced on either side by a straight, high wall.

Getting fainter and dizzier, I ran on; the ground got more broken— more and more still, till I staggered and fell, and rose again, and ran on in the blind anguish of the hunted. Again the thought of Alice nerved me. I would not be lost and wreck her life: I would fight and struggle for life to the bitter end. With a great effort I caught the top of the wall. As, scrambling like a catamount, I drew myself up, I actually felt a hand touch the sole of my foot. I was now on a sort of causeway, and before me I saw a dim light. Blind and dizzy, I ran on, staggered, and fell, rising covered with dust.

"Halt *là!*"

The words sounded like a voice from heaven. A blaze of light seemed to enwrap me, and I shouted with joy.

"*Qui va là?*" The rattle of musketry, the flash of steel before my eyes. Instinctively I stopped, though close behind me came a rush of my pursuers.

Another word or two, and out from a gateway poured, as it seemed to me, a tide of red and blue, as the guard turned out. All around seemed blazing with light, and the flash of steel, the clink and rattle of arms, and the loud, harsh voices of command. As I fell forward, utterly exhausted, a soldier caught me. I looked back in dreadful expectation, and saw the mass of dark forms disappearing into the night. Then I must have fainted.

When I recovered my senses I was in the guard room. They gave me brandy, and after a while I was able to tell them something of what had passed. Then a commissary of police appeared, apparently out of the empty air, as is the way of the Parisian police officer. He listened attentively, and then had a moment's consultation with the officer in command. Apparently they were agreed, for they asked me if I were ready now to come with them.

"Where to?" I asked, rising to go.

"Back to the dust heaps. We shall, perhaps, catch them yet!"

"I shall try!" said I.

He eyed me for a moment keenly, and said suddenly:

"Would you like to wait a while or till tomorrow, young Englishman?" This touched me to the quick, as perhaps he intended, and I jumped to my feet.

"Come now!" I said: "Now! Now! An Englishman is always ready for his duty!"

The commissary was a good fellow, as well as a shrewd one; he slapped my shoulder kindly. "Brave *garçon!*" he said. "Forgive me, but I knew what would do you most good. The guard is ready. Come!"

And so, passing right through the guard room, and through a long vaulted passage, we were out into the night. A few of the men in front had powerful lanterns. Through courtyards and down a sloping way we passed out through a low archway to a sunken road, the same that I had seen in my flight. The order was given to get at the double, and with a quick, springing stride, half run, half walk, the soldiers went swiftly along.

I felt my strength renewed again—such is the difference between hunter and hunted. A very short distance took us to a low-lying pontoon bridge across the stream, and evidently very little higher up than I had struck it. Some effort had evidently been made to damage it, for the ropes had all been cut, and one of the chains had been broken. I heard the officer say to the commissary:

"We are just in time! A few more minutes, and they would have destroyed the bridge. Forward, quicker still!" and on we went. Again we reached a pontoon on the winding stream; as we came up we heard the hollow boom of the metal drums as the efforts to destroy the bridge were again renewed. A word of command was given, and several men raised their rifles.

"Fire!" A volley rang out. There was a muffled cry, and the dark forms dispersed. But the evil was done, and we saw the far end of the pontoon swing into the stream. This was a serious delay, and it was nearly an hour before we had renewed ropes and restored the bridge sufficiently to allow us to cross.

We renewed the chase. Quicker, quicker we went towards the dust heaps.

After a time we came to a place that I knew. There were the remains of a fire—a few smoldering wood ashes still cast a red glow, but the bulk of the ashes were cold. I knew the site of the hut and the hill behind it up which I had rushed, and in the flickering glow the eyes of the rats still shone with a sort of phosphorescence. The commissary spoke a word to the officer, and he cried:

"Halt!"

The soldiers were ordered to spread around and watch, and then we commenced to examine the ruins. The commissary himself began to lift away the charred boards and rubbish. These the soldiers took and piled together. Presently he started back, then bent down and rising beckoned me.

"See!" he said.

It was a gruesome sight. There lay a skeleton face downwards, a woman by the lines—an old woman by the coarse fiber of the bone. Between the ribs rose a long spike-like dagger made from a butcher's sharpening knife, its keen point buried in the spine.

"You will observe," said the commissary to the officer and to me as he took out his note book, "that the woman must have fallen on her dagger. The rats are many here—see their eyes glistening among that heap of bones—and you will also notice"—I shuddered as he placed his hand on the skeleton—"that but little time was lost by them, for the bones are scarcely cold!"

There was no other sign of any one near, living or dead; and so deploying again into line the soldiers passed on. Presently we came to the hut made of the old wardrobe. We approached. In five of the six compartments were sleeping old men—sleeping so soundly that even the glare of the lanterns did not wake them. Old and grim and grizzled they looked, with their gaunt, wrinkled bronzed faces and their white mustaches.

The officer called out harshly and loudly a word of command, and in an instant each one of them was on his feet before us and standing at "attention"!

"What do you here?"

"We sleep," was the answer.

"Where are the other chiffoniers?" asked the commissary.

"Gone to work."

"And you?"

"We are on guard!"

"Peste!" laughed the officer grimly, as he looked at the old men one after the other in the face and added with cool deliberate cruelty, "Asleep on duty! Is this the manner of the Old Guard! No wonder, then, a Waterloo!"

By the gleam of the lantern I saw the grim old faces grow deadly pale, and almost shuddered at the look in the eyes of the old men as the laugh of the soldiers echoed the grim pleasantry of the officer.

I felt in that moment that I was in some measure avenged.

For a moment they looked as if they would throw themselves on the taunter, but years of their life had schooled them and they remained still.

"You are but five," said the commissary; "where is the sixth?" The answer came with a grim chuckle.

"He is there!" and the speaker pointed to the bottom of the wardrobe. "He died last night. You won't find much of him. The burial of the rats is quick!"

The commissary stooped and looked in. Then he turned to the officer and said calmly:

"We may as well go back. No trace here now; nothing to prove that man was the one wounded by your soldiers' bullets! Probably they murdered him to cover up the trace. See!" Again he stooped and placed his hands on the skeleton. "The rats work quickly and they are many. These bones are warm!"

I shuddered, and so did many more of those around me.

"Form!" said the officer, and so in marching order, with the lanterns swinging in front and the manacled veterans in the midst, with steady

tramp we took ourselves out of the dust-heaps and turned backward
to the fortress of Bicêtre.

My year of probation has long since ended, and Alice is my wife.
But when I look back upon that trying twelvemonth one of the most
vivid incidents that memory recalls is that associated with my visit to
the City of Dust.

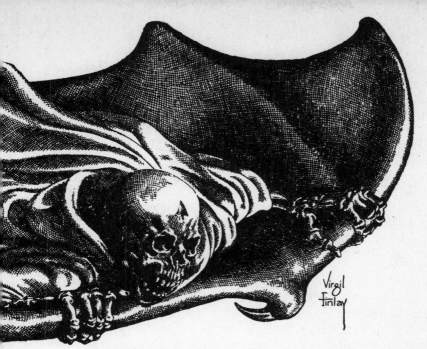

The Day of the Deepies

MURRAY LEINSTER

Many authors who wrote science fiction and fantasy for the early Munsey magazines found it difficult to adapt to the specialized demands of the genre pulps. Not so Murray Leinster (the best-known pseudonym of Will F. Jenkins). Although Leinster's first story, "The Runaway Sky-scraper," appeared in a 1919 issue of Argosy, *he eventually became a regular writer for* Astounding Science-Fiction *as well as a presence in the original paperback market that flourished after the war years.* Famous Fantastic Mysteries *published three original submissions from Leinster, including "The Day of the Deepies," a harbinger of the paranoid invasion stories that would dominate science fiction in the postwar era.*

K ENIE WAKED with all the shivering ecstasy one feels at the age of thirteen on a morning when excitement looms deliciously ahead. She lay still for a moment, listening to the noises that told her the house was awake. Her brother Tom, down the hall, was doggedly enduring the squawks and howls of the television set he'd put together from wreckage their father had brought back from what used to be Camden. Then there was the whooshing roar of the tractor, pulling past the front of the house with its monstrous wood-gas generator on the back and the squeak that Bub Taylor said was metal-fatigue setting in. But it couldn't be dismantled, for youthening, until the fall wheat had been planted.

Her mother's voice came out of what had been the air-conditioning duct when air conditioners still worked.

"Kenie! It's late!"

"I'm up and practically dressed," said Kenie, anticipating the fact by seconds. "Right down, Mother!"

She slid out of bed. She almost danced across the room to look at herself in the mirror.

The mirror was a trifle leprous, in spots, where the silver had tarnished through, but she found her own eyes bright and anticipating. She beamed at her reflection. She didn't know how things would turn out, but excitement was sure. Her very best boy friend, Bub, had told her in strict confidence that the neighbors were coming over today to warn her father that Tom had to stop fiddling with science. And that ghastly deepie, Mr. Wedderson, was coming to receive the family's answer to his proposal for Aunt Sarah's hand. And Kenie was practically certain that Roland—whom her sister Cissie used to be in love with—was hiding out somewhere in the woods. So it would be a full day.

She went blithely down the stairs in work-stained shorts and jumper. It was just as exciting to be thirteen in the year 2096 as it had been when Kenie's great-great-grandmother watched soldiers march off to some war or other, back in the days when they had wars. Now, of course, war was just a word. There couldn't be a war when there was nothing to fight with and you didn't know whom to fight.

Anyhow, Kenie doubted that a war would be as exciting as knowing that Bub was secretly working on an electric generator in the cellar he'd dug under his father's barn, or having a delicious suspicion that Roland was hiding near-by and that Cissie had seen him at least once.

Roland would be hung as a matter of public safety if he were discovered, because he was a scientist. And if she merely hinted her suspicion of his presence to her brother Tom, he'd go crazy trying to find Roland to pump scientific information out of him, because Tom meant to be a scientist, too.

She felt that she could burst, but she seemed completely demure as she went into the kitchen. The great electric range and storage cabinet, off to one side, was used as a cupboard and working space for the preparation of meals. Her mother said it was wonderful, before a bomb fell over at Westport and then there wasn't any more electricity. Kenie'd always thought vaguely that it wasn't scrapped because they hoped that some day there might be electricity again. But she was not sure.

"Stay close to the house, Kenie," said her mother, as she put breakfast before her. "I may need you. Some of the neighbors are coming over to your father and we'll have to offer refreshments."

Kenie said mildly, "Does Tom know yet?"

Her mother looked at her sharply.

"What do you mean by that, Kenie?"

"Aren't they coming over to tell father that Tom has to stop messing with science? I told him not to get so confidential with that revolting

Mr. Wedderson. I'll bet he's the one who passed the word that Tom was experimenting."

Her mother pressed her lips together.

"Kenie—"

"He's a deepie," said Kenie scornfully. "Oh, I know, Mother! Deepies are just displaced persons, and some of them are quite nice. They are people who've never settled down or who are afraid to settle down even if people would let them. They think if they keep moving, they'll be safe. 'Fraidy-cats! But some deepies are snoopers, too, and you know it!"

"Kenie!" said her mother. "Mr. Wedderson wants to marry your Aunt Sarah! He's quite a good blacksmith, he says, and with a family connection so he'd be allowed to settle down here—"

Kenie started to stuff her mouth full, and remembered that she was growing up, and took a dainty mouthful instead. She said with a vast calmness:

"Darling Mother, you don't fool me. You don't like him any more than I do. You're just as afraid he's a snooper. And with Roland—"

Her mother went white. Kenie's heart turned one complete somersault. Then it was true! Roland was back, and hiding out! Her mother knew it, as well as Cissie! Kenie's hand shook with the thrill as she gulped her milk in outward composure.

"Don't worry, Mother," she said calmly. "I won't say that to anyone else. But I notice things. I'm thirteen, now."

"I don't know where you get silly ideas about Roland," her mother began. But there were footsteps in the hall and she stopped short. She went on in an even, unhurried tone, "I think that if you took over the new calf this morning, since your father is so busy—Good morning, Sarah!"

Kenie's Aunt Sarah came into the kitchen. Kenie spoke to her politely. Aunt Sarah looked thrilled and haggard and defiant and sorrowful all at once, with a hint of tragedy queen thrown in. Kenie used to feel sorry for her because she'd never gotten married—Kenie intended to marry Bub when they both grew up—but Mr. Wedderson had ended her sympathy. He couldn't be anybody's ideal! He was untidy with a hint of greasiness. He wore thick eyeglasses and a smug air which wasn't suitable to a deepie, and he petted Kenie. With the pretense of treating her as a child, he patted her. Kenie frankly despised him— with an uneasy feeling underneath.

"Good morning, Martha," said Aunt Sarah. "Where is John? I simply must have a talk with him! Mr. Wedderson is coming—"

Kenie's mother said vaguely, "He's running the tractor, Sarah. I think he's been asking the neighbors if they object—"

"What have they to do with it?" demanded Aunt Sarah sharply. "My brother John is a leading citizen! If I choose to marry, why should the neighbors have anything to say?"

"You know how it is," said Kenie's mother soothingly. "People resent newcomers settling—"

"Would John send his own sister wandering?" demanded Aunt Sarah fiercely. "Must I wander through the woods and forests to be with the man I love, when he is a good blacksmith and one is needed here?"

Kenie choked on her milk. Aunt Sarah always managed to mess things up when she tried to be dramatic. Her mother said:

"Kenie! The calf—"

"Yes, Mother," said Kenie.

She drained the mug and managed not giggle until she got out of doors. Then she went down to the barn. It was a good barn, very old and with the wires for electric lights still in place. There were iron stalls for the cows and there had been an electric milking machine. It would be nice to have electricity to do things for you, Kenie reflected.

She milked an anxious cow who was bitterly indignant because her calf was muzzled. She led the calf into another stall and set to work to teach him to drink. It was rather fun, but she felt all churned up inside herself.

Roland was nice. He'd been gone for two years, now, because of course, when he practically said he was a scientist he couldn't stay around. It wouldn't have mattered before things happened and the big cities were either abandoned or destroyed, and before the railroads stopped running, and all that. But since the world had got to be as it was, scientists weren't good neighbors. Everybody knew that. When scientists set to work to find out things, sooner or later a bomb fell from the sky. Then there was an empty place three or four miles across where people had lived, and things wouldn't grow there for a long time because the ground was all baked to a bricky, glassy kind of stuff that Kenie had never seen but had heard about. Only eight years ago a bomb had fallen on a locality only fifty miles away. And people said it was because there was a scientist there.

It wasn't his fault directly, though. It was because of the deepies. There were always deepies coming around—bright-eyed, usually skinny people who worked awhile and got a store of food and moved on. Lots of deepies were very respectable and nice, but there were some snoopers among them, and if a snooper found out that there was a scientist around, somehow or other they got word to whoever had planes and bombs—and then a bomb fell. So one must always be careful not to say anything nice about science. Bub was especially bitter because one mustn't even have electricity, and he was making a generator down in a secret cellar he'd dug. *He* was going to have electricity and keep it a secret.

The trouble with Roland was that he talked. As long as he just kept machinery in repair and made funny stuff that made welding easier, he was all right. He was crazy about Cissie, too, and she about him. But one day somebody said that people were better off nowadays than back when cities had millions of people in them, and Roland got mad.

Right in front of everybody he said that people lived like pigs, now, compared to the old days. Running tractors on wood-gas and burning tallow lamps wasn't his idea of living, he said.

Science had made a world fit to live in, and fools had smashed it, Roland said. And then he declared defiantly that some day science would come back and the world would be better than ever, with electricity and airplanes and great cities and universities and books and television everywhere. And he said it where everybody could hear him!

Deepies were listening, so the neighbors had to act at once. They tried him right on the spot for advocating science, after what it had done to the world, and they ordered him to leave the locality and said they'd hang him if he came back. And they made sure all the deepies knew it. Kenie's own father was the sternest of Roland's judges, though he liked Roland a lot. Cissie'd cried for weeks, too, because she'd been going to marry him. But of course being ordered away from home made Roland a deepie, and nobody would let a deepie settle anywhere. Everybody was afraid that almost any deepie might be a snooper, reporting to whoever had bombs and planes. So naturally Cissie couldn't marry Roland.

Teaching the calf to drink, Kenie's anticipations rose. Roland's return was exciting. And Mr. Wedderson wanting to marry Aunt Sarah. He was a deepie who pretended to be enormously smitten with Aunt Sarah's charms. Now she was hounding Kenie's father to stand sponsor for him and get him permission to settle down here. Otherwise, of course, she'd have to go off and be a deepie, too, if she married him. But Kenie was scornfully sure that Mr. Wedderson was a snooper, and if he found out that Roland was back. . . .

That was something to shiver about! Cissie'd seen Roland. Kenie knew it. She used to be in love with him and still must be or she wouldn't have risked seeing him.

There was a trampling of many hoofs in front of the house. The far-away tractor stopped. Kenie looked out of the barn and saw her father walking across the fields. She heard Tom's television set still squawking. When he got it to work, it only brought silly things like talks on farming and how to keep well. But her father said that whoever was visicasting was very brave. They might be safe if they talked only about crop rotation and sanitation, but he warned Tom to tell him if they ever started to 'cast about science. Tom probably wouldn't tell him, though. Tom was always mooning around, trying out things and trying to find old books with science in them, but not talking.

Kenie watched, wide-eyed, as the neighbors rode up to the house. They were going to remind father that there were nearly five thousand people in this locality, and they couldn't have their lives jeopardized by a boy working on science. Tom could either give up his experiments or leave. They didn't want any bombs falling from a seemingly empty sky.

There was a rustling in the barn. There was Cissie; she put her arm around Kenie and hugged her a little. That wasn't unheard of, but it was unusual. Kenie wriggled.

"They've come to talk to father about Tom, Cissie!" Kenie was thrilled. "It's going to be awful! Maybe he'll get mad—"

"He won't," said Cissie. "He promised me he wouldn't."

They heard their father's voice inside the house. He was calling Tom. Then a great stillness settled on everything. The neighbors were gathered in the front parlor. They'd be grim. Just as grim as when they told Roland to leave or be hanged. Tom would be white and stricken. But their father would do what he could. He'd probably tell how Tom helped him in metal recovery—smelting down iron rust for fresh metal to make things that had to be made new. He'd been the first one to do that, with charcoal from the woods for fuel. The neighbors respected Kenie's father, and they wouldn't be mean. Just firm. Anyhow, they knew how Kenie's father felt about science. He'd been the first one to say that Roland had to go away, even though Roland and Cissie were planning to get married.

"Darling," said Cissie, and she hugged Kenie. "You like me, don't you? I want to tell you something."

"About Roland?" asked Kenie quickly.

Cissie seemed not to realize what she meant.

"Partly," she said softly. "But not altogether. I'm not sorry about Roland, you know. There used to be a wonderful world, and it got spoiled. But there's going to be a wonderful world again, and Roland will help to make it. That's worth while, isn't it?"

"The world's all right now," said Kenie blithely. "It's fun. But it might be nice to have electricity. Bub says so."

Cissie laughed a little.

"That's what I want to tell you. Not about electricity, but about Bub. I used to watch you tagging after him, and now he tags after you, Kenie. And as your older sister—"

Kenie said matter-of-factly, "Bub's going to marry me when we grow up. He doesn't know it yet, but I can make him do almost anything I want to."

Cissie's arm tightened about her.

"I—just want to say something serious, for once," she said quite gravely. "It's nice, loving someone, Kenie. And if you—grow up and marry Bub—you won't want to regret it. If he wants to be like everybody else, he'll be safe and so will you. But if he doesn't, Kenie—let him be different! Like Roland. Make him be careful, of course! Make him be terribly careful! But it will be worth it if he—risks his life and yours, too, to try to build back to a better world than the one that got smashed. Even for a little thing like electricity! Remember it, Kenie! Please!"

Kenie almost started to tell her that Bub was already building an electric generator in his secret cellar—Cissie could be trusted—but just then Mr. Wedderson came in view. He was marching toward the house, and he was fat and smug and revolting.

"That," said Kenie scornfully, "is Aunt Sarah's ideal! She wants us to call him Uncle! He'll want me to sit on his lap! I despise him!"

Cissie drew a quick breath. She looked oddly at Kenie, as if what she'd just said was a very special admonition that she might not be able to give again, but Kenie was sticking out her tongue at the waddling, stocky figure. Then she turned.

"We'd better go to the house," she said resentfully. "Mother's going to serve refreshments. I'd like to put a bug in Mr. Wedderson's mug. Or something worse!"

Cissie followed silently. Their mother was moving about the kitchen. She nodded when they came in.

"Just in time," she told them. "You take in the coffee, Cissie, and Kenie, you carry the cakes."

Cissie was grown-up and calm, and Kenie envied her a little. Her own elbows seemed to get in the way going through doors. But she got to the parlor without mishap. Then she thrilled.

It was dreadful in there. Her brother Tom stood ashen-faced at one side of the room. The neighbors were unsmiling and grim. Not unkindly, of course. That made it worse. Kenie saw twin wet streaks on Tom's cheeks. He was seventeen, but the tears had come when he met the unalterable ultimatum of the neighbors and found that his own father backed it.

"It ain't," said a heavy voice doggedly, "that we're against anybody doin' what they want to, Tom. You got a life to live. If you want to go off and study science, you got a right to an' we ain't stoppin' you. But we got our families to think of. Where there's science and people know of it, bombs fall. You can go, an' you'll have no spite go with you. But you can't come back. You'll do a lot better by your family and friends if you stay amongst us an' be a good neighbor—"

Tom's hands were clenched tightly. He was the very picture of stunned grief. But suddenly he said in a choked voice:

"I'll bet it was Mr. Wedderson who told you! He started talking about science! He s-seemed to know a lot and I g-got interested and t-told him too much—"

The faces in the parlor hardened. There were thumpings outside. Kenie's mother went to the door. Cissie moved among the neighbors, offering them dandelion root coffee. Kenie's mother said:

"Why, yes, Mr. Wedderson! Quite a gathering! Come in!"

Eyes turned to the door. Mr. Wedderson entered. His eyes glittered behind their thick lenses. He swaggered a little.

"Gentlemen," he said pompously, "as a mere poor deepie, I have come to do you a service. Did you know that a plane landed near here two days ago?"

It had been quiet in the parlor, before. The only sounds had been the small clickings of the coffee mugs. But then the stillness became absolute. Kenie's breath stopped. A plane landed here! That was science at its worst! She had never seen a plane in her life. They were deadly. Bub said they could have electricity again if it wasn't for snoopers, but nothing was more sure to bring a bomb from empty sky than a plane. . . .

"It has not taken off," added Mr. Wedderson blandly. "It is still here. I have seen it. Does it surprise you?"

Kenie saw the faces of the neighbors. Every one was stony. A plane landed here—and known to a deepie! A bomb might fall at any instant. It might be falling now. . . . For a moment Kenie tried to imagine a bomb falling. She tried to picture this house, the barn, the fields yonder and the new-ploughed land, all gone and nothing but glassy, baked-hard emptiness in its place. She tried to imagine herself, Kenie, completely obliterated. But her imagination boggled at the last. She could not imagine a world without Kenie in it. She found herself licking her lips.

"We know nothing of it!" said her father fiercely. "You gentlemen have your horses here! We'll see if this is true! And if it is, Mr. Wedderson, you'll see what we do when people bring science into this locality!"

Mr. Wedderson said, blinking in a sort of smug meekness, "I had hoped to form a family connection and be allowed to settle here, but even we deepies do not like localities where science is favored. Here, even the young boys—"

"Tom!" said Kenie's father harshly. "Saddle three horses. One for Mr. Wedderson. Right away!"

Tom stumbled from the room. Kenie boiled. Mr. Wedderson had persuaded Tom to talk about science, and then told the neighbors on him! Now he told about a plane landing, and mentioned what deepies would think about it. And if deepies knew about it, sooner or later a snooper would know! He was threatening! He was telling them they'd better be nice to him! It was things like this that made people not let anybody stay in a locality unless he had kinfolk and relatives who'd share any danger he brought on the rest.

"Come, Kenie," said Cissie in her ear.

Kenie followed to the kitchen and shook with a murderous rage.

"I hate him!" she said furiously. "He told on Tom! If he's ever my uncle I'll—I'll—"

Cissie pushed her firmly out of doors. She followed. But her tone was shaky rather than indignant as she said:

"You mustn't talk like that, Kenie! Aunt Sarah thinks she's in love with him! If she heard you—"

Kenie grumbled, "You were in love with Roland, but it didn't make you crazy!"

"That," said Cissie quietly, "was real. Not just desperation. She isn't like—you and Bub, either, is she?"

"Huh!" said Kenie. "I can make Bub do almost anything I want!"

Tom rode blindly past them, leading two horses. One for his father and one for Mr. Wedderson. Tom was seventeen, and Kenie normally admired him with a trace of female condescension. But even she could see something close to dignity in his grief-stricken look.

"Poor Tom!" said Cissie.

Her voice was soft enough, but her eyes were oddly hard as she looked back at the house. There was a clattering of hoofs and the neighbors rode off with Mr. Wedderson in their midst. He said a plane had landed—and a plane was sure to bring a bomb. He was going to show them where it was. Most deepies would simply run. There was something—

Kenie watched breathlessly. She would have liked to go, but she was a girl, and if they found out who had landed the plane there'd be a hanging. A sudden thought struck her. Roland! Suppose it was Roland who came in the plane! Suppose her father helped to hang Roland because he was a scientist and he'd come back after being warned not to. . . .

Kenie jerked her head to stare at Cissie. If it was Roland, Cissie knew it. She knew that they were going to hunt for whoever had landed the plane. Cissie looked quite pale, though entirely composed. Entirely. She looked startlingly grown up.

There was a yell, and a gangling horse jumped the fence behind the barn. Bub waved to Kenie. He always arrived that way. He was sixteen. And Kenie squealed at sight of him and dashed to meet him. Speculations were unimportant now. She poured out an almost incoherent account of the morning's happenings, from the formal warning to Tom, to Mr. Wedderson's notification of the incredible fact that a plane had landed near-by and they might all be blown up any second.

Bub simply wheeled his horse about, his lips set. Kenie jumped in front of him.

"You've got to take me!" she cried fiercely. "I told you about it! You've got to take me! You won't dare show yourself anyhow—"

He thrust down a bony hand. She caught it and scrambled up. He dug his heels into the horse's sides and they went off at a shambling gallop, Kenie astride behind him and clinging to his waist. She was filled with an ecstasy amounting almost to delirium. This was excitement! She and Bub trailing the neighbors on the way to destroy an airplane! Perhaps to hang Roland! Nothing so deliciously thrilling had ever happened in the world before!

Bub said tragically, "All my life I've wanted to see a plane, and the only chance I'll ever get is to see the neighbors smash one!"

Kenie was abashed by such grief, but nothing could make her unhappy while such thrilling events went forward. They sighted the cavalcade a long distance ahead. They trailed it. It swung aside into the woods. Bub dared close up until he could see the thrashing of branches as the horsemen forced their way through low-hanging trees.

A long time later the cavalcade halted. Kenie could feel the tension in Bub's body. He reined aside.

"Come on!" he said feverishly. "We'll hide the horse and sneak up to see before it's all smashed—"

It was a matter only of seconds before he and Kenie were dashing, hand in hand, from one thick patch of brushwood to another to get where they could see what impended.

It was Kenie who jerked him aside and pointed.

"There!"

They saw perfectly through a gap among the trees. There were the horses, stamping and snuffling in an uneasy group. The men advanced silently toward a silvery white object on the ground. The plane wasn't big, and somehow it looked awkward. It looked as if it had been built of inadequate materials, by men who'd made ingenuity take the place of equipment. There were little pipes sticking out of it astern. There were fins—not wings—and there was a folded-up contrivance which Kenie guessed excitedly was a helicopter screw. She'd seen pictures.

"Rocket-drive," said Bub in a broken, mourning whisper. "Atmospheric rocket, Kenie. Not like the ones men went to the evening star with, once. But, oh, isn't it beautiful!"

It wasn't. Kenie stared with all her eyes, but to her it was not beautiful. It was merely extraordinarily thrilling. Her eyes went to the human figures. Mr. Wedderson looked brisk and shrewd and very different from the way he usually did. He stood back while the others went grimly to the plane and pulled open its door and went in. They went over it in every possible fashion, looking for some clue to who had brought it. Kenie's father said harshly:

"Anyhow, we can pile brush on it and set it afire!"

Then he stopped. Mr. Wedderson stood composedly with something like a little switch in his hand, only it had a cup on it and he held that to his mouth. He seemed to be talking into it.

There was a dreadful stillness. Then Mr. Wedderson grinned.

"This," he told the neighbors, still holding the cup near his mouth, "is a radio and I am talking to the people who have planes and bombs. They can hear everything I say. They do not want the plane destroyed. So you will not destroy the plane."

Men made a concerted small noise like a growl.

"I brought you here and had you go into it and handle it," said Mr. Wedderson with an infuriating smugness, "because it was possible that whoever left it had mined it—set explosives to destroy meddlers. But you are not destroyed. So I shall fly it to where I came from, and we shall examine it. Our radar said that it was even faster than our planes! But you will let me take it because your whole community will be bombed within minutes if you do not."

He grinned at them. Enragingly. But there was absolute dead silence save for the stamping and snorting of the horses. Mr. Wedderson walked over to the plane. The neighbors made way for him, their hands clenched. He got in and touched something. The folded-up thing reached up and expanded. It began to move, at first slowly and then more swiftly. A little puff of vapor came from one of the pipes at the stern.

All this in dead silence.

The plane shifted itself around bodily. It slid forward over fallen leaves until it was no longer under a tree, but under open sky. Mr. Wedderson grinned at the neighbors.

"You are very docile," he said blandly, "so I have reported that you need not be bombed. And your funny sister—" He looked at Kenie's father—"was very amusing. Tell her I laugh."

The whirring thing speeded up. The plane rose, and hovered, and rose swiftly again. It danced lightly up above the treetops.

Up and up and up. . . . It was a bare speck when vapor streamed from behind it.

It moved forward. The blurred disk of the lift-screw vanished suddenly and it was merely a mote which moved so fast that the eye lost trace of it. Then it was gone.

Bub was crying almost happily, "B-beautiful!" he gasped. "Oh, b-beautiful! B-but he took it away. . . ."

Then he sobbed. And then Kenie's father loomed up sternly. He'd seen her. He opened his mouth to ask how she'd gotten there, and saw Bub. He said nothing.

He waved his hand, and Tom came numbly over with the three horses from home.

They went to Bub's tethered horse. Kenie mounted the now spare animal. They went back toward home. The neighbors were riding off singly, every man's face like stone.

"And now," said Kenie's father tiredly, "we ought to hang Roland."

Then Tom spoke thickly, "I'm—I'm sorry, Dad," he said, "but if— if this is—what you have to do—not to have bombs fall, I—I'm going away. Maybe I'll only be a deepie, but—if there's science anywhere on earth—"

Bub gulped and said uncertainly, "I—guess I'll go too, Tom."

For an instant Kenie was fiercely proud of her brother and of Bub. She, too, felt the bitter scorn of youth for the compromises older people make for the sake of youth. But then she realized that their going away would mean they'd be like Roland.

They couldn't come back. They'd be hanged, if they did.

She made no sound. She rode on stoically, a small figure in shorts and jumper, with her hair hanging in a pigtail down her back. But tears flowed down her cheeks. She licked them furtively from the corners of her mouth.

"Eh? Desperate?" said her father. Then he grunted. "I forgot. You boys have thought science was play. It's not. You had to learn a lesson, and I think Tom has. You'll never talk too much to a deepie again, Tom!"

"I'm—going to be one," said Tom, doggedly.

"Being careful gets to be a habit," said Kenie's father, dryly. "It's one you'd better learn, Tom. But Roland won't be hung. Of course! We'll all say so—all the neighbors. But actually he's going to be married. To Cissie. Kenie's to be bridesmaid. It will all happen after supper tonight. They'll be off before morning."

Then he added, "Roland flew that plane here."

Kenie's eyes opened wide. She felt a complete topsy-turviness in all the world. She blinked incredulously up at her father.

"The idea," said her father deliberately, "is that the people who've dropped bombs have had things their way too long. If they find we can hit back, they'll pull in their horns a bit. We're planning to use electricity again. They have to have a lesson."

Kenie rode on in a dream. She heard her father's voice. Tom and Bub babbled questions—eager, thirsty questions. Kenie heard her father say, ". . . don't have to rebuild the old generators. Simpler ways to make electricity have turned up . . ." and "couldn't conquer anybody with bombs, of course . . ." and incomprehensible things like, ". . . of course all the neighbors have known all along, but we've had to be careful. . . ."

But Kenie was wrestling with a desperate problem of her own.

She barely heard Bub say in a tone of anguish:

"But he carried off the plane!" And then her father again, in a tone she'd never heard before—amused without any laughter in it:

"What do you think Roland flew it here for?"

Kenie's problem was unsolvable. They were coming out of the woods, and she turned appealingly to her father, but the boys had his attention. She couldn't get it. He said quietly:

"There's no secret about the bombs, but you can't fight a war with them, and who wants a war, anyhow? We want electricity—to start with. So Roland flew that plane until he knew a radar beam had touched it, and noted its speed, so they'd want to capture it instead of simply blowing it up. Then he landed it. It was risky, but it had to be done. Fortunately, it worked."

They were on the road toward home. The boys begged simultaneously:

"Was there a bomb in the plane? To go off when—"

"The plane," said Kenie's father softly, "*was* a bomb. Which will go off when they investigate its high-speed drive. When they look at it. That'll be in the middle of their workshops and laboratories, wherever they may be. There may not be many of them left.

"But anyhow there will be two hundred localities like ours all starting to use electricity on the same day, and they won't quite dare to bomb any of them because then they'll know we can now strike back."

The two boys rocked and whooped in their saddles. They shouted. Kenie's plaintive, "But what am I going to *do?*" went unheard.

They reached home, and as they dismounted in the barnyard there was a momentary feeling of insecurity underfoot. The ground seemed to tremble just a little. The barn-joists creaked and groaned. Then everything was still again. Kenie's father nodded as young faces turned quickly to him.

"Probably," he said softly. "Quite likely that was it. A few hundred miles away. They'll never know how we did it, but they won't risk trying to find out by bombing us for trying to use electricity again!"

Aloud, he said in a tired, natural voice, "Tom, I'm going to ask you to put up the horses."

Tom moved joyfully to obey. Bub leaped to help.

Kenie caught hold of her father's hand.

A great feat had been accomplished and the world had moved a step nearer to something more spacious and more sane. Universities and cities and television were closer.

Dread was now pushed a little farther back. The new climb of humanity was really begun.

But Kenie had a terrific problem all her own.

"Daddy!" she wailed desperately. "What can I *do*? You say I'm going to be Cissie's bridesmaid! And I haven't a thing to wear!"

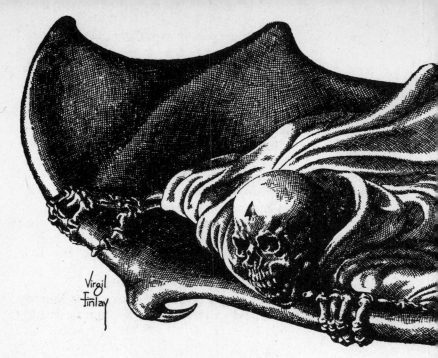

Virgil Finlay

The Horror of the Heights

ARTHUR CONAN DOYLE

Were one to assemble the collected works of Sir Arthur Conan Doyle, his tales of Sherlock Holmes would comprise a significant but small percentage of the whole. In addition to historical novels, treatises on psychic research, and tales of the medical profession, Doyle wrote the popular Professor Challenger science fiction novels and several collections of horror and science fiction stories, two of which were reprinted in Famous Fantastic Mysteries. *"The Horror of the Heights" was first published in 1913 for an era that did not yet know air travel as a popular form of transportation. At that time, it was not unreasonable for a fantasy writer to ponder the unknown mysteries of the upper atmosphere and think, "Here Be Monsters."*

THE IDEA that the extraordinary narrative which has been called the Joyce-Armstrong Fragment is an elaborate practical joke evolved by some unknown person, cursed by a perverted and sinister sense of humor, has now been abandoned by all who have examined the matter. The most *macabre* and imaginative of plotters would hesitate before linking his morbid fancies with the unquestioned and tragic facts which reinforced the statement. Though the assertations contained in it are amazing and even monstrous, it is none the less forcing itself upon the general intelligence that they are true, and that we must readjust our ideas to the new situation.

This world of ours appears to be separated by a slight and precarious margin of safety from a most singular and unexpected danger. I will endeavor in this narrative, which reproduces the original document in its necessarily somewhat fragmentary form, to lay before the reader the whole of the facts up to date, prefacing my statement by saying that, if there be any who doubt the narrative of Joyce-Armstrong, there can be no question at all as to the facts concerning Lieutenant Myrtle, R.N., and Mr. Hay Connor, who undoubtedly met their end in the manner described.

The Joyce-Armstrong Fragment was found in the field which is called Lower Haycock, lying one mile to the westward of the village of Withyham, upon the Kent and Sussex border. It was on the fifteenth of September last that an agricultural laborer, James Flynn, in the employment of Mathew Dodd, farmer, of the Chauntry Farm, Withyham, perceived a briar pipe lying near the footpath which skirts the hedge in Lower Haycock.

A few paces farther on he picked up a pair of broken binocular glasses. Finally, among some nettles in the ditch, he caught sight of a flat, canvas-backed book, which proved to be a note-book with detachable leaves, some of which had come loose and were fluttering along the base of the hedge. These he collected, but some, including the first, were never recovered, and leave a deplorable hiatus in this all-important statement. The note-book was taken by the laborer to his master, who in turn showed it to Dr. J. H. Atherton, of Hartfield. This gentleman at once recognized the need for an expert examination, and the manuscript was forwarded to the Aero Club in London, where it now lies.

The first two pages of the manuscript are missing. There is also one torn away at the end of the narrative, though none of these affect the general coherence of the story. It is conjectured that the missing opening is concerned with the record of Mr. Joyce-Armstrong's qualifications as an aeronaut, which can be gathered from other sources and are admitted to be unsurpassed among the air pilots of England. For many years he has been looked upon as among the most daring and the most intellectual of flying men, a combination which has enabled him to both invent and test several new devices, including the common gyroscopic attachment which is known by his name. The main body of the manuscript is written neatly in ink, but the last few lines are in pencil and are so ragged as to be hardly legible—exactly, in fact, as they might be expected to appear if they were scribbled off hurriedly from the seat of a moving plane.

There are, it may be added, several stains, both on the last page and on the inside cover which have been pronounced by the home office experts to be blood—probably human and certainly mammalian. The fact that something closely resembling the organism of malaria was discovered in this blood, and that Joyce-Armstrong is known to have suffered from intermittent fever, is a remarkable example of the new weapons which modern science has placed in the hands of our detectives.

And now a word as to the personality of the author of this epoch-making statement. Joyce-Armstrong, according to the few friends who really knew something of the man, was a poet and a dreamer, as well as a mechanic and an inventor. He was a man of considerable wealth, much of which he had spent in the pursuit of his aeronautical hobby. He had four private aeroplanes in his hangars near Devizes, and is said to have made no fewer than one hundred and seventy ascents in the course of last year.

He was a retiring man with dark moods, in which he would avoid the society of his fellows. Captain Dangerfield, who knew him better than anyone, says that there were times when his eccentricity threatened to develop into something more serious. His habit of carrying a shot-gun with him in his aeroplane was one manifestation of it.

Another was the morbid effect which the fall of Lieutenant Myrtle had upon his mind. Myrtle, who was attempting the height record, fell from an altitude of something over thirty thousand feet. Horrible to narrate, his head was entirely obliterated, though his body and limbs preserved their configuration. At every gathering of airmen Joyce-Armstrong, according to Dangerfield, would ask, with an enigmatic smile: "And where, pray, is Myrtle's head?"

On another occasion after dinner, at the mess of the flying school on Salisbury Plain, he started a debate as to what will be the most permanent danger which airman will have to encounter. Having listened to successive opinions as to air-pockets, faulty construction, and overbanking, he ended by shrugging his shoulders and refusing to put forward his own views, though he gave the impression that they differed from any advanced by his companions.

It is worth remarking that after his own complete disappearance it was found that his private affairs were arranged with a precision which may show that he had a strong premonition of disaster. With these essential explanations I will now give the narrative exactly as it stands, beginning at page three of the blood-soaked note-book:—

"Nevertheless, when I dined at Rheims with Coselli and Gustave Raymond I found that neither of them was aware of any particular danger in the higher layers of the atmosphere. I did not actually say what was in my thoughts, but I got so near to it that if they had any corresponding idea they could not have failed to express it. But then they are two empty, vainglorious fellows with no thought beyond seeing their silly names in the newspaper. It is interesting to note that neither of them had ever been much beyond the twenty-thousand-foot level. Of course, men have been higher than this both in balloons and in the ascent of mountains. It must be well above that point that the aeroplane enters the danger zone—always presuming that my premon-itions are really correct.

"Aeroplaning has been with us now for more than twenty years, and one might well ask: Why should this peril be only revealing itself in our day? The answer is obvious. In the old days of weak engines, when a hundred horse-power Gnome or Green was considered ample for every need, the flights were very restricted. Now that three hundred horse-power is the rule rather than the exception, visits to the upper layers have become easier and more common. Some of us can remember how, in our youth, Garros made a world-wide reputation by attaining nineteen thousand feet, and it was considered a remarkable achievement to fly over the Alps. Our standard now has been immeasurably raised, and there are twenty high flights for one in former years. Many of them have been undertaken with impunity. The thirty-thousand-foot level has been reached time after time with no discomfort beyond cold and asthma.

"What does this prove? A visitor might descend upon this planet a thousand times and never see a tiger. Yet tigers exist, and if he chanced to come down into a jungle he might be devoured. There are jungles of the upper air, and there are worse things than tigers which inhabit them. I believe in time they will map these jungles accurately out. Even at the present moment I could name two of them. One of them lies over the Pau-Biarritz district of France. Another is just over my head as I write here in my house in Wiltshire. I rather think there is a third in the Homburg-Wiesbaden district.

"It was the disappearance of the airmen that first set me thinking. Of course, everyone said that they had fallen into the sea, but that did not satisfy me at all. First there was Verrier in France; his machine was found near Bayonne, but they never got his body. There was the case of Baxter also, who vanished, though his engine and some of the iron fixings were found in a wood in Leicestershire. In that case, Dr. Middleton, of Amesbury, who was just watching the flight with a telescope, declares that just before the clouds obscured the view he saw the machine, which had an enormous height, suddenly rise perpendicularly upwards in a succession of jerks in a manner that he would have thought to be impossible. That was the last seen of Baxter. There was a correspondence in the papers, but it never led to anything.

"There were several other similar cases, and there was the death of Hay Connor. What a cackle there was about an unsolved mystery of the air, and what columns in the half-penny papers, and yet how little was done to get to the bottom of the business! He came down in a tremendous volplane from an unknown height. He never got off his machine and died in his pilot's seat. Died of what? 'Heart disease,' said the doctors. Rubbish! Hay Connor's heart was as sound as mine is. What did Venables say? Venables was the only man who was at his side when he died. He said that he was shivering and looked like a man who had been badly scared. 'Died of fright,' said Venables, who could not imagine what he was frightened about. Only said one word to Venables, which sounded like 'Monstrous.' They could make nothing of that at the inquest. But I could make something of it. Monsters! That was the last word of poor Harry Hay Connor. And he did die of fright, just as Venables thought.

"And then there was Myrtle's head. Do you really believe—does anybody really believe—that a man's head could be driven clean into his body by the force of a fall? Well, perhaps it may be possible, but I, for one, have never believed it was so with Myrtle. And the grease upon his clothes—'all slimy with grease,' said somebody at the inquest. Queer that nobody got thinking after that! I did—but, then, I had been thinking for a good long time.

"I've made three ascents—how Dangerfield used to chaff me about my shot-gun—but I've never been high enough. Now, with this light Paul Veroner machine and its one hundred and seventy-five Robur, I should easily touch the thirty thousand tomorrow. I'll have a shot at the record. Maybe I shall have a shot at something else as well. Of course, it's dangerous. If a fellow wants to avoid danger he had best keep out of flying altogether and subside finally into flannel slippers and a dressing-gown. But I'll visit the air-jungle tomorrow—and if there's anything there I shall know it. If I return, I'll find myself a bit of a celebrity. If I don't, this note-book may explain what I am trying to do, and how I lost my life in doing it. But no drivel about accidents or mysteries, if *you* please.

"I chose my Paul Veroner monoplane for the job. There's nothing like a monoplane when real work is to be done. Beaumont found that out in very early days. For one thing, it doesn't mind damp, and the weather looks as if it should be in the clouds all the time. It's a bonny little model and answers my hand like a tender-mouthed horse. The engine is a ten-cylinder rotary Robur working up to one hundred and seventy-five. It has all the modern improvements—enclosed fuselage, high-curved landing skids, brakes, gyroscopic steadiers, and three speeds, worked by an alteration of the angle of the planes upon the Venetian Blind principle. I took a shot-gun with me and a dozen cartridges filled with buck-shot.

"You should have seen the face of Perkins, my old mechanic, when I directed him to put them in. I was dressed like an Arctic explorer, with two jerseys under my overalls, thick socks inside my padded boots, a storm cap with flaps, and my talc goggles. It was stifling outside the hangars, but I was going for the summit of the Himalayas, and had to dress for the part. Perkins knew there was something on and implored me to take him with me. Perhaps I should if I were using a biplane, but a monoplane is a one-man show—if you want to get the last foot of lift out of it. Of course, I took an oxygen bag; the man who goes for the altitude record without one will either be frozen or smothered—or both.

"I had a good look at the planes, the rudder-bar, and the elevating lever before I got in. Everything was in order so far as I could see. Then I switched on my engine and found that she was running sweetly. When they let her go she rose almost at once upon the lowest speed. I circled my home field once or twice just to warm her up, and then, with a wave to Perkins and the others, I flattened out my planes and put her on her highest. She skimmed like a swallow down wind for eight or ten miles until I turned her nose up a little and she began to climb in a great spiral for the cloud bank above me. It's all-important to rise slowly and adapt yourself to the pressure as you go.

It was a close, warm day for an English September, and there was the hush and heaviness of impending rain. Now and then there came sudden puffs of wind from the south-west—one of them so gusty and unexpected that it caught me napping and turned me half-round for an instant. I remember the time when gusts and whirls and air-pockets used to be things of danger—before we learned to put an over-mastering power into our engines. Just as I reached the cloud banks, with the altimeter marking three thousand, down came the rain. My word, how it poured! It drummed upon my wings and lashed against my face, blurring my glasses so that I could hardly see. I got down on to a low speed, for it was painful to travel against it. As I got higher it became hail, and I had to turn tail to it. One of my cylinders was out of action—a dirty plug, I should imagine, but still I was rising steadily with plenty of power. After a bit the trouble passed, whatever it was, and I heard the full deep-throated purr—the ten singing as one. That's where the beauty of our modern silencers come in. We can at last control our engines by ear. How they squeal and squeak and sob when they are in trouble! All those cries for help were wasted in the old days, when every sound was swallowed up by the monstrous racket of the machine. If only the earlier aviators could come back and see the beauty and perfection of the mechanism which had been brought at the cost of their lives!

"About nine-thirty I was nearing the clouds. Down below me, all blurred and shadowed with rain, lay the vast expanse of Salisbury Plain. Half-a-dozen flying machines were doing hack-work at the thousand-foot level, looking like little black swallows against the green background. I dare say they were wondering what I was doing up in cloud-land. Suddenly a grey curtain drew across beneath me and the wet folds of vapor were swirling round my face. I was clammily cold and miserable. But I was above the hailstorm, and that was something gained. The cloud was as dark and thick as a London fog. In my anxiety to get clear, I cocked her nose up until the automatic alarm-bell rang, and I actually began to slide backwards.

"My sopped, dripping wings made me heavier than I thought, but presently I was in higher clouds, and soon had cleared the first layer. There was a second—opal-colored and fleecy—at a great height above my head, a white unbroken ceiling above, and a dark unbroken floor below, with the monoplane labouring upwards upon a vast spiral between them. It is deadly lonely in these cloud-spaces. Once a great flight of some small water-birds went past me, flying very fast to the westwards. The quick whirr of their wings and their musical cry were cheery to my ear. I fancy that they were teal, but I am a wretched zoologist. Now that we humans have become birds we must really learn to know our brethren by sight.

"The wind down beneath me whirled and swayed the broad cloud-plain. Once a great eddy formed in it, a whirlpool of vapor, and through it, as down a funnel, I caught sight of the distant world. A large white biplane was passing at a vast depth beneath me. I fancy it was the morning mail service betwixt Bristol and London. Then the drift swirled inwards again and the great solitude was unbroken.

"Just after ten I touched the lower edge of the upper cloud-stratum. It consisted of fine diaphanous vapor drifting swiftly from the westward. The wind had been steadily rising all this time and it was now blowing a sharp breeze—twenty-eight an hour by my gauge. Already it was very cold, though my altimeter only marked nine thousand. The engines were working beautifully, and we went droning steadily upwards. The cloud-bank was thicker than I had expected, but at last it thinned out to a golden mist before me, and then in an instant I had shot out from it, and there was an unclouded sky and a brilliant sun above my head—all blue and gold above, all shining silver below, one vast glimmering plain as far as my eyes could reach.

"It was a quarter past ten o'clock. The barograph needle pointed to twelve thousand eight hundred. Up I went and up, my ears concentrated upon the deep purring of my motor, my eyes busy always with the watch, the revolution indicator, the petrol lever, and the oil pump. No wonder aviators are said to be a fearless race. With so many things to think of there is no time to trouble about oneself. About this time I noted how unreliable is the compass when above a certain height from earth. At fifteen thousand feet mine was pointing east and a point south. The sun and the wind gave me my true bearings.

"I had hoped to reach an eternal stillness in these high altitudes, but with every thousand feet of ascent the gale grew stronger. My machine groaned and trembled in every joint and rivet as she faced it, and swept away like a sheet of paper when I banked her on the turn, skimming down at a greater pace, perhaps, than ever mortal man has moved. Yet I had always to turn again and tack up in the wind's eye, for it was not merely a height record that I was after. By all my calculations it was above little Wiltshire that my air-jungle lay and all my labor might be lost if I struck the outer layers at some farther point.

"When I reached the nineteen-thousand-foot level, which was about midday, the wind was so severe that I looked with some anxiety to the stays of my wings, expecting momentarily to see them snap or slacken. I even cast loose the parachute behind me, and fastened its hook into the ring of my leathern belt, so as to be ready for the worst. Now was the time when a bit of scamped work by the mechanic is paid for by the life of the aeronaut. But she held together bravely. Every cord and strut was humming and vibrating like so many harp-strings, but it was glorious to see how, for all the beating and the buffeting, she was still the conqueror of Nature and the mistress of the sky.

"There is surely something divine in man himself that he should rise so superior to the limitations which Creation seemed to impose— rise, too, by such unselfish, heroic devotion as this air-conquest has shown. Talk of human degeneration! When has such a story as this been written in the annals of our race?

"These were the thoughts in my head as I climbed that monstrous inclined plane with the wind sometimes beating in my face and sometimes whistling behind my ears, while the cloud-land beneath me fell away to such a distance that the folds and hummocks of silver had all smoothed out into one flat, shining plain. But suddenly I had a horrible and unprecedented experience. I have known before what it is to be in what our neighbors have called a *tourbillon,* but never on such a scale as this. That huge, sweeping river of wind of which I had spoken had, as it appears, whirlpools within it which were as monstrous as itself. Without a moment's warning I was dragged suddenly into the heart of one. I spun around for a minute or two with such velocity that I almost lost my senses, and then fell suddenly, left wing foremost, down the vacuum funnel in the center. I dropped like a stone, and lost nearly a thousand feet.

"It was only my belt that kept me in my seat, and the shock and breathlessness left me hanging half insensible over the side of the fuselage. But I am always capable of a supreme effort—it is my one great merit as an aviator. I was conscious that the descent was slower. The whirlpool was a cone rather than a funnel, and I had come to the apex. With a terrific wrench, throwing my weight all to one side, I levelled my planes and brought her head away from the wind. In an instant I had shot out from the eddies and was skimming down the sky. Then, shaken but victorious, I turned her nose up and began once more my steady grind on the upward spiral. I took a large sweep to avoid the dangerspot of the whirlpool, and soon I was safely above it. Just after one o'clock I was twenty-one thousand feet above the sealevel. To my great joy I had topped the gale, and with every hundred feet of ascent the air grew stiller. On the other hand, it was very cold, and I was conscious of the peculiar nausea which goes with rarefication of the air. For the first time I unscrewed the mouth of my oxygen bag and took an occasional whiff of the glorious gas. I could feel it running like a cordial through my veins, and I was exhilarated almost to the point of drunkenness. I shouted and sang as I roared upwards into the cold, still outer world.

"It is very clear to me that the insensibility which came upon Glaisher, and in a lesser degree upon Coxwell, when, in 1862, they ascended in a balloon to the height of thirty thousand feet, was due to the extreme speed with which a perpendicular ascent is made. Doing it at an easy gradient and accustoming oneself to the lessened barometric pressure by slow degrees, there are no such dreadful symptoms. At the same great height I found that even without my oxygen inhaler I could breathe without undue distress. It was bitterly cold, however, and my thermometer was at zero, Fahrenheit.

"At one-thirty I was nearly seven miles above the earth, and still ascending steadily. I found, however, that the rarefied air was giving markedly less support to my wings, and that my angle of ascent had to be considerably lowered in consequence. It was already clear that even with my light weight and strong engine-power there was a point in front of me where I should be held. To make matters worse, one of my sparking-plugs was in trouble again and there was intermittent misfiring in the engine. My heart was heavy with the fear of failure.

"It was about that time that I had a most extraordinary experience. Something wizzed past me in a trail of smoke and exploded with a loud, hissing sound, sending forth a cloud of steam. For the instant I could not imagine what had happened. Then I remembered that the earth is forever being bombarded by meteor stones, and would be hardly inhabitable were they not in nearly every case turned to vapor in the outer layers of the atmosphere. Here is a new danger for the high-altitude man, for two others passed me when I was nearing the forty-thousand-foot mark. I cannot doubt that at the edge of the earth's envelope the risk would be a very real one.

"My barograph needle marked forty-one thousand three hundred when I became aware that I could go no further. Physically, the strain was not as yet greater than I could bear, but my machine had reached its limit. The attentuated air gave no firm support to the wings, and the least tilt developed into side-slip, while she seemed sluggish on her controls. Possibly, had the engine been at its best, another thousand feet might have been within our capacity, but it was still misfiring, and two out of the ten cylinders appeared to be out of action.

"If I'd not already reached the zone for which I was searching then I should never see it upon this journey. But was it not possible that I had attained it? Soaring into circles like a monstrous hawk upon the forty-thousand-foot level I let the monoplane guide herself, and with my Mannheim glass I made a careful observation of my surroundings. The heavens were perfectly clear; there was no indication of those dangers I had imagined.

"I have said that I was soaring in circles. It struck me suddenly that I would do well to take a wider sweep and open up a new air-tract. If the hunter entered an earth-jungle he would drive through it if he wished to find his game. My reasoning had led me to believe that the air-jungle which I had imagined lay somewhere over Wiltshire. This should be to the south and west of me. I took my bearings from the sun, for the compass was hopeless and no trace of earth was to be seen—nothing but the distant silver cloud-plain. However, I got my direction as best I might and kept her head straight to the mark. I reckoned that my petrol supply would not last for another hour or so, but I could afford to use it to the last drop, since a single magnificent volplane could at any time take me to the earth.

"Suddenly I was aware of something new. The air in front of me had lost its crystal clearness. It was full of long, ragged wisps of something which I can only compare to fine cigarette smoke. It hung about in wreaths and coils, turning and twisting slowly in the sunlight. As the monoplane shot through it, I was aware of a faint taste of oil on my lips, and there was a greasy scum upon the woodwork of the machine. Some infinitely fine organic matter appeared to be suspended in the atmosphere. There was no life there. It was inchoate and diffuse, extending for many square acres and then fringing off into the void. No, it was not life. But might it not be the remains of life? Above all, might it not be the food of life, of monstrous life, even as the humble grease of the ocean is the food for the mighty whale? The thought was in my mind when my eyes looked upwards and I saw the most wonderful vision that man has even seen. Can I hope to convey it to you even as I saw it myself last Thursday?

"Conceive a jelly-fish such as sails our summer seas, bell-shaped and of enormous size—far larger, I should judge, than the dome of St. Paul's. It was of a light pink color veined with a delicate green, but the whole huge fabric so tenuous that it was but a fairy outline against the dark blue sky. It pulsated with a delicate and regular rhythm. From it there depended two long, dripping green tentacles, which swayed slowly backwards and forwards. This gorgeous vision passed gently with noiseless dignity over my head, as light and fragile as a soap-bubble, and drifted upon its stately way.

"I had half turned my monoplane, that I might look after this beautiful creature, when, in a moment, I found myself amidst a perfect fleet of them, of all sizes, but none so large as the first. Some were quite small, but the majority about as big as an average balloon, and with much the same curvature at the top. There was in them a delicacy of texture and coloring which reminded me of the finest Venetian glass. Pale shades of pink and green were the prevailing tints, but all had a lovely irridescence where the sun shimmered through their dainty forms. Some hundreds of them drifted past me, a wonderful fairy squadron of strange, unknown argosies of the sky—creatures whose forms and substance were so attuned to these pure heights that one could not conceive anything so delicate within actual sight or sound of earth.

"But soon my attention was drawn to a new phenomenon—the serpents of the outer air. These were long, thin, fantastic coils of vapor-like material, which turned and twisted with great speed, flying round and round at such a pace that the eyes could hardly follow them. Some of these ghost-like creatures were twenty or thirty feet long, but it was difficult to tell their girth, for their outline was so hazy that it seemed to fade away into the air around them.

"These air-snakes were of a very light grey or smoke color, with some darker lines within, which gave the impression of a definite organism. One of them whisked past my very face, and I was conscious of a cold, clammy contact, but their composition was so unsubstantial that I could not connect them with any thought of physical danger, any more than the beautiful bell-like creatures which had preceded them. There was no more solidity in their frames than in the floating spume from a broken wave.

"But a more terrible experience was in store for me. Floating downwards from a great height there came a purplish patch of vapor, small as I saw it first, but rapidly enlarging as it approached me, until it appeared to be hundreds of square feet in size. Though fashioned of some transparent, jelly-like substance, it was none the less of much more definite outline and solid consistence than anything which I had seen before. There were more traces, too, of a physical organization, especially two vast shadowy, circular plates upon either side, which may have been eyes, and a perfectly solid white projection between them which was as curved and cruel as the beak of a vulture.

"The whole aspect of this monster was formidable and threatening, and it kept changing its color from a very light mauve to a dark, angry purple so thick that it cast a shadow as it drifted between my monoplane and the sun. On the upper curve of its huge body there were three great projections which I can only describe as enormous bubbles and I was convinced as I looked at them that they were charged with some extremely light gas which served to buoy up the misshapen and semi-solid mass in the rarefied air. The creature moved swiftly along, keeping pace easily with the monoplane, and for twenty miles or more it formed my horrible escort, hovering over me like a bird of prey which was waiting to pounce.

"Its method of progression—done so swiftly that it was not easy to follow—was to throw out a long, glutinous streamer in front of it, which in turn seemed to draw forward the rest of the writhing body. So elastic and gelatinous was it that never for two successive minutes was it the same shape, and yet each change made it more threatening and loathsome than the last.

"I knew that it meant mischief. Every purple flush of its hideous body told me so. The vague, goggling eyes which were turned always upon me were cold and merciless in their viscid hatred. I dipped the nose of my monoplane downwards to escape it. As I did so, as quick as a flash there shot out a long tentacle from this mass of floating blubber, and it fell as light and sinuous as a whip-lash across the front of my machine. There was a loud hiss as it lay for a moment across the hot engine, and it whisked itself into the air again, while the huge flat body drew itself together as if in sudden pain. I dipped to a volpiqué, but again a tentacle fell over the monoplane and was shorn off by the propeller as easily as it might have cut through a smoke wreath. A long, gliding, sticky, serpent-like coil came from behind and caught me round the waist, dragging me out of the fuselage. I tore at it, my fingers sinking into the smooth, gluelike surface, and for an instant I disengaged myself, but only to be caught around the boot by another coil, which gave me a jerk that tilted me almost on my back.

"As I fell over I blazed both barrels of my gun, though, indeed, it was like attacking an elephant with a pea-shooter to imagine that any human weapon could cripple that bulk. And yet I aimed better than I knew, for, with a loud report, one of the great blisters upon the creature's back exploded with the puncture of the buck-shot. It was very clear that my conjecture was right, and that these vast clear bladders were distended with some lifting gas, for in an instant the huge cloud-like body turned sideways, writhing desperately to find its balance, while the white beak snapped and gaped in horrible fury. But already I had shot away on the steepest glide that I dared attempt, my engine was on full, the flying propeller and the force of gravity shooting me downwards like an aerolite. Far behind me I saw a dull, purplish smudge growing swiftly smaller and merging into the blue sky behind it. I was safe out of the deadly jungle of the outer air.

"Once out of danger I throttled my engine, for nothing tears a machine to pieces quicker than running on full power from a height. It was a glorious spiral volplane from nearly eight miles of altitude—first, to the level of the silver cloud-bank, then to that of the storm-cloud beneath it, and finally, in beating rain, to the surface of the earth. I saw the Bristol Channel beneath me, as I broke from the clouds, but, having still some petrol in my tanks, I got twenty miles inland before I found myself stranded in a field half a mile from Ashcombe. There I got three tins of petrol from a passing motor-car, and at ten minutes past six that evening I alighted gently in my own home meadow at Devizes, after such a journey as no mortal on earth has ever yet taken and lived to tell the tale. I have seen the beauty and I have seen the horror of the heights—and greater beauty or greater horror than that is not within the ken of man.

"And now it is my plan to go once again before I give my results to the world. My reason for this is that I must surely have something to show by way of proof before I lay such a tale before my fellow-men. It is true that others will soon follow and confirm what I have said, and yet I should wish to carry conviction from the first. Those lovely iridescent bubbles of the air should not be hard to capture. They drift slowly upon their way, and the swift monoplane could intercept their leisurely course. It is likely enough that they would dissolve in the heavier layers of the atmosphere, and that some small heap of amorphous jelly might be all that I should bring to earth with me. And yet something there would surely be by which I could substantiate my story. Yes, I will go, even if I run a risk by doing so. These purple horrors would not seem to be numerous. It is probable that I shall not see one. If I do I shall dive at once. At the worst there is always the shot-gun and my knowledge of. . . ."

Here a page of manuscript is unfortunately missing. On the next page is written, in large, straggling writing:—

Forty-three thousand feet. I shall never see earth again. They are beneath me, three of them. God help me; it is a dreadful death to die!

Such in its entirety is the Joyce-Armstrong Statement. Of the man nothing has since been seen. Pieces of his shattered monoplane have been picked up in the preserves of Mr. Budd-Lushington, upon the borders of Kent and Sussex, within a few miles of the spot where the notebook was discovered. If the unfortunate aviator's theory is correct that this air-jungle, as he called it, existed only over the south-west of England, then it would seem that he had fled from it at the full speed of his monoplane, but had been overtaken and devoured by these horrible creatures in some spot in the outer atmosphere above the place where the grim relics were found.

There are many, I am aware, who still jeer at the facts which I have here set down, but even they must admit that Joyce-Armstrong has oddly disappeared.

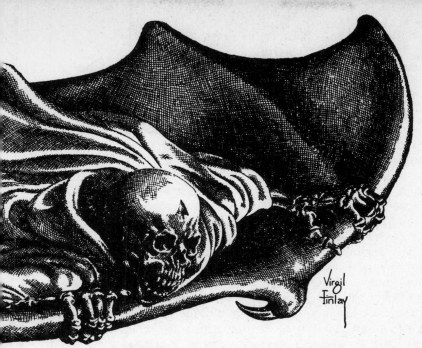

The Lonesome Place

AUGUST DERLETH

The idea that children are sensitive to impressions and insights not accessible to adults gained philosophical acceptance in the late eighteenth century. In the twentieth century, it has served as the basis for a great deal of horror fiction. A book of fantasy variations on this theme might include tales by Saki, John Collier, Ray Bradbury, Henry Kuttner, David H. Keller, and Anthony Boucher, as well as August Derleth's "The Lonesome Place." Written originally for Famous Fantastic Mysteries *in 1948, the story invites comparison to "Mr. George," another tale of an unusually perceptive child that appeared in* Weird Tales *in 1947 under Derleth's Stephen Grendon pseudonym.*

YOU WHO sit in your houses of nights, you who sit in the theaters, you who are gay at dances and parties—all you who are enclosed by four walls—you have no conception of what goes on outside in the dark. In the lonesome places. And there are so many of them, all over—in the country, in the small towns, in the cities. If you were out in the evenings, in the night, you would know about them, you would pass them and wonder, perhaps, and if you were a small boy you might be frightened. Frightened the way Johnny Newell and I were frightened, the way thousands of small boys from one end of the country to the other are being frightened when they have to go out

alone at night, past lonesome places, dark and lightless, somber and
haunted. . . .

I want you to understand that if it had not been for the lonesome
place at the grain elevator, the place with the big old trees and the
sheds up close to the sidewalk, and the piles of lumber—if it had not
been for that place Johnny Newell and I would never have been guilty
of murder. I say it even if there is nothing the law can do about it.
They cannot touch us, but it is true, and I know, and Johnny knows,
but we never talk about it, we never say anything. It is just something
we keep here, behind our eyes, deep in our thoughts where it is a fact
which is lost among thousands of others, but no less there, something
we know beyond cavil.

It goes back a long way. But as time goes, perhaps it's not long. We
were young, we were little boys in a small town. Johnny lived three
houses away and across the street from me, and both of us lived in
the block west of the grain elevator. We were never afraid to go past
the lonesome place together. But we were not often together. Sometimes
one of us had to go that way alone, sometimes the other. I went that
way most of the time—there was no other, except to go far around,
because that was the straight way down town, and I had to walk there,
when my father was too tired to go.

In the evenings it would happen like this. My mother would discover
that she had no sugar or salt or bologna, and she would say, "Steve,
you go down town and get it. Your father's too tired."

I would say, "I don't wanna."

She would say, "You go."

I would say, "I can go in the morning before school."

She would say, "You go now. I don't want to hear another word
out of you. Here's the money."

And I would have to go.

Going down was never quite so bad, because most of the time there
was still some afterglow in the west, and a kind of pale light lay there,
a luminousness, like part of the day lingering there, and all around
town you could hear the kids hollering in the last hour they had to
play, and you felt somehow not alone. You could go down into that
dark place under the trees and you would never think of being lonesome.
But when you came back—that was different. When you came back
the afterglow was gone; if the stars were out, you could never see them
for the trees, and though the streetlights were on—the old fashioned
lights arched over the cross-roads—not a ray of them penetrated the
lonesome place near to the elevator. There it was, half a block long,
black as black could be, dark as the deepest night, with the shadows
of the trees making it a solid place of darkness, with the faint glow of
light where a streetlight pooled at the end of the street. Far away it
seemed, and that other glow behind, where the other corner light lay.

And when you came that way you walked slower and slower. Behind
you lay the brightly lit stores; all along the way there had been houses,

with lights in the windows and music playing and voices of people sitting to talk on their porches. But up there, ahead of you, there was the lonesome place, with no house nearby, and up beyond it the tall, dark grain elevator, gaunt and forbidding. The lonesome place of trees and sheds and lumber, in which anything might be lurking, anything at all. The lonesome place where you were sure that something haunted the darkness waiting for the moment and the hour and the night when you came through to burst forth from its secret place and leap upon you, tearing you and rending you and doing the unmentionable things before it had done for you.

That was the lonesome place. By day it was oak and maple trees over a hundred years old, low enough so that you could almost touch the big spreading limbs; it was sheds and lumber piles which were seldom disturbed; it was a sidewalk and long grass, never mowed or kept down until late fall, when somebody burned it off; it was a shady place in the hot summer days where some cool air always lingered. You were never afraid of it by day, but by night it was a different place.

For, then, it was lonesome, away from sight or sound, a place of darkness and strangeness, a place of terror for little boys haunted by a thousand fears.

And every night, coming home from town, it happened like this. I would walk slower and slower, the closer I got to the lonesome place. I would think of every way around it. I would keep hoping somebody would come along, so that I could walk with him, Mr. Newell, maybe, or old Mrs. Potter, who lived farther up the street, or Reverend Bislor, who lived at the end of the block beyond the grain elevator. But nobody ever came. At this hour it was too soon after supper for them to go out, or, already out, too soon for them to return. So I walked slower and slower, until I got to the edge of the lonesome place—and then I ran as fast as I could, sometimes with my eyes closed.

Oh, I knew what was there, all right. I knew there was something in that dark, lonesome place. Perhaps it was the bogeyman. Sometimes my grandmother spoke of him, of how he waited in dark places for bad boys and girls. Perhaps it was an ogre. I knew about ogres in the books of fairy tales. Perhaps it was something else, something worse. I ran. I ran hard. Every blade of grass, every leaf, every twig that touched me was *its* hand reaching for me. The sound of my footsteps slapping the sidewalk were *its* steps pursuing. The hard breathing which was my own became *its* breathing in its frantic struggle to reach me, to rend and tear me, to imbue my soul with terror.

I would burst out of that place like a flurry of wind, fly past the gaunt elevator, and not pause until I was safe in the yellow glow of the familiar streetlight. And then, in a few steps, I was home.

And mother would say, "For the Lord's sake, have you been running on a hot night like this?"

I would say, "I hurried."

"You didn't have to hurry that much. I don't need it till breakfast time."

And I would say, "I coulda got it in the morning. I coulda run down before breakfast. Next time, that's what I'm gonna do."

Nobody would pay any attention.

Some nights Johnny had to go down town, too. Things then weren't the way they are today, when every woman makes a ritual of afternoon shopping and seldom forgets anything.

In those days, they didn't go down town so often, and when they did, they had such lists they usually forgot something. And after Johnny and I had been through the lonesome place on the same night, we compared notes next day.

"Did you see anything?" he would ask.

"No, but I heard it," I would say.

"I felt it," he would whisper tensely. "It's got big, flat clawed feet. You know what has got the ugliest feet around?"

"Sure, one of those stinking yellow soft-shell turtles."

"It's got feet like that. Oh, ugly, and soft, and sharp claws! I saw one out of the corner of my eye," he would say.

"Did you see its face?" I would ask.

"It ain't got no face. Cross my heart an' hope to die, there ain't no face. That's worse'n if there was one."

Oh, it was a horrible beast—not an animal, not a man—that lurked in the lonesome place and came forth predatorily at night, waiting there for us to pass. It grew like this, out of our mutual experiences. We discovered that it had scales, and a great long tail, like a dragon. It breathed from somewhere, hot as fire, but it had no face and no mouth in it, just a horrible opening in its throat. It was as big as an elephant, but it did not look like anything so friendly. It belonged there in the lonesome place; it would never go away; that was its home, and it had to wait for its food to come to it—the unwary boys and girls who had to pass through the lonesome place at night.

How I tried to keep from going near the lonesome place after dark!

"Why can't Mady go?" I would ask.

"Mady's too little," mother would answer.

"I'm not so big."

"Oh, shush! You're a big boy now. You're going to be seven years old. Just think of it."

"I don't think seven is old," I would say. I didn't, either. Seven wasn't nearly old enough to stand up against what was in the lonesome place.

"Your Sears-Roebuck pants are long ones," she would say.

"I don't care about any old Sears-Roebuck pants. I don't wanna go."

"I want you to go. You never get up early enough in the morning."

"But I will. I promise I will. I promise, Ma!" I would cry out.

"Tomorrow morning it will be a different story. No, you go."

That was the way it went every time. I had to go. And Mady was

the only one who guessed. "Fraidycat," she would whisper. Even she
never really knew. She never had to go through the lonesome place
after dark. They kept her at home. She never knew how something
could lie up in those old trees, lie right along those old limbs across
the sidewalk and drop down without a sound, clawing and tearing,
something without a face, with ugly clawed feet like a softshell turtle's,
with scales and a tail like a dragon, something as big as a house, all
black, like the darkness in that place.

But Johnny and I knew.

"It almost got me last night," he would say, his voice low, looking
anxiously out of the woodshed where we sat, as if it might hear us.

"Gee, I'm glad it didn't," I would say. "What was it like?"

"Big and black. Awful black. I looked around when I was running,
and all of a sudden there wasn't any light way back at the other end.
Then I knew it was coming. I ran like everything to get out of there.
It was almost on me when I got away. Look there!"

And he would show me a rip in his shirt where a claw had come
down.

"And you?" he would ask excitedly, big-eyed. "What about you?"

"It was back behind the lumber piles when I came through," I said.
"I could just feel it waiting. I was running, but it got right up—you
look, there's a pile of lumber tipped over there."

And we would walk down into the lonesome place in midday and
look. Sure enough, there would be a pile of lumber tipped over, and
we would look to where something had been lying down, the grass all
pressed down. Sometimes we would find a handkerchief and wonder
whether *it* had caught somebody.

Then we would go home and wait to hear if anyone was missing,
speculating apprehensively all the way home whether *it* had got Mady
or Christine or Helen, or any one of the girls in our class or Sunday
School. Or, whether maybe *it* had got Miss Doyle, the young primary
grades teacher who had to walk that way sometimes after supper. But
no one was ever reported missing, and the mystery grew. Maybe *it*
had got some stranger who happened to be passing by and didn't know
about the Thing that lived there in the lonesome place. We were sure
it had got somebody.

"Some night I won't come back, you'll see," I would say.

"Oh, don't be silly," my mother would say.

What do grown-up people know about the things boys are afraid of?
Oh, hickory switches and such like, they know that. But what about
what goes on in their minds when they have to come home alone at
night through the lonesome places? What do they know about lonesome
places where no light from the street-corner ever comes? What do they
know about a place and time when a boy is very small and very alone,
and the night is as big as the town, and the darkness is the whole
world? When grown-ups are big, old people who cannot understand
anything, no matter how plain?

A boy looks up and out, but he can't look very far when the trees bend down over and press close, when the sheds rear up along one side and the trees on the other, when the darkness lies like a cloud along the sidewalk and the arc-lights are far, far away. No wonder, then, that Things grow in the darkness of lonesome places the way *it* grew in that dark place near the grain elevator. No wonder a boy runs like the wind until his heartbeats sound like a drum and push up to suffocate him.

"You're white as a sheet," Mother would say sometimes. "You've been running again."

"You don't have to run," my father would say. "Take it easy."

"I ran," I would say. I wanted the worst way to say I had to run and to tell them why I had to. But I knew they wouldn't believe me any more than Johnny's parents believed him when he told them, as he did once.

He got a licking with a strap and had to go to bed.

I never got licked. I never told them.

But now it must be told, now it must be set down.

For a long time we forgot about the lonesome place. We grew older and we grew bigger. We went on through school into high school, and somehow we forgot about the Thing in the lonesome place. That place never changed. The trees grew older. Sometimes the lumber piles were bigger or smaller. Once the sheds were painted—red, like blood. Seeing them that way the first time, I remembered. Then I forgot again. We took to playing baseball and basketball and football. We began to swim in the river and to date the girls. We never talked about the Thing in the lonesome place any more, and when we went through there at night it was like something forgotten that lurked back in a corner of the mind. We thought of something we ought to remember, but never could quite remember; that was the way it seemed—like a memory locked away, far away in childhood. We never ran through that place, and sometimes it was even a good place to walk through with a girl, because she always snuggled up close and said how spooky it was there under the overhanging trees. But even then we never lingered there, not exactly lingered; we didn't run through there, but we walked without faltering or loitering, no matter how pretty a girl she was.

The years went past, and we never thought about the lonesome place again.

We never thought how there would be other little boys going through it at night, running with fast-beating hearts, breathless with terror, anxious for the safety of the arc-light beyond the margin of the shadow which confined the dweller in that place, the light-fearing creature that haunted the dark, like so many terrors dwelling in similar lonesome places in the cities and small towns and countrysides all over the world, waiting to frighten little boys and girls, waiting to invade them with horror and unshakable fear—waiting for something more. . . .

Three nights ago little Bobby Jeffers was killed in the lonesome place.

He was all mauled and torn and partly crushed, as if something big had fallen on him. Johnny, who was on the Village Board, went to look at the place, and after he had been there, he telephoned me to go, too, before other people walked there.

I went down and saw the marks, too. It was just as the coroner said, only not an "animal of some kind," as he put it. Something with a dragging tail, with scales, with great clawed feet—and I knew it had no face.

I knew, too, that Johnny and I were guilty. We had murdered Bobby Jeffers because the thing that killed him was the thing Johnny and I had created out of our childhood fears and left in that lonesome place to wait for some scared little boy at some minute in some hour during some dark night, a little boy who, like fat Bobby Jeffers, couldn't run as fast as Johnny and I could run.

And the worst is not that there is nothing to do, but that the lonesome place is being changed. The village is cutting down some of the trees now, removing the sheds, and putting up a streetlight in the middle of that place; it will not be dark and lonesome any longer, and the Thing that lives there will have to go somewhere else, where people are unsuspecting, to some other lonesome place in some other small town or city or countryside, where it will wait as it did here, for some frightened little boy or girl to come along, waiting in the dark and the lonesomeness. . . .

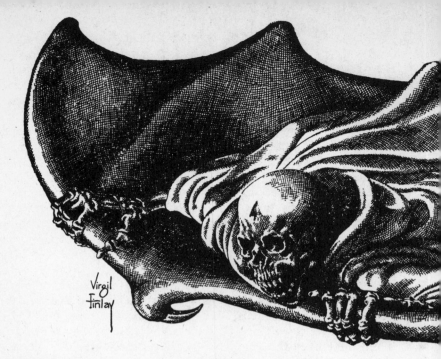

The Shadow and the Flash

JACK LONDON

Jack London is one of those authors whose work demonstrates the futility of distinguishing popular fiction from literature and genre stories from mainstream fiction. At the same time that he penned such literary classics as The Call of the Wild, The Sea-Wolf, *and a gripping chronicle of alcoholism,* John Barleycorn, *London wrote a good deal of fantasy and science fiction for the popular fiction magazines. Famous Fantastic Mysteries reprinted his disaster story "The Scarlet Plague" and scientific romance* The Star Rover, *as well as the short tale "The Shadow and the Flash." The story's extrapolations on optics are pure pseudoscience, but they set up an inventive climax for an otherwise conventional love story.*

WHEN I look back, I realize what a peculiar friendship it was. First, there was Lloyd Inwood, tall, slender, and finely knit, nervous and dark. And then Paul Tichlorne, tall, slender, and finely knit, nervous and blond. Each was the replica of the other in everything except color. Lloyd's eyes were black; Paul's were blue. Under stress of excitement, the blood coursed olive in the face of Lloyd, crimson in the face of Paul. But outside this matter of coloring they were as like as two peas. Both were high-strung, prone to excessive tension and endurance, and they lived at concert pitch.

But there was a trio involved in this remarkable friendship, and the third was short, and fat, and chunky, and lazy, and, loath to say, it

288

was I. Paul and Lloyd seemed born to rivalry with each other, and I to be peacemaker between them. We grew up together, the three of us, and full often have I received the angry blows each intended for the other. They were always competing, striving to outdo each other, and when entered upon some such struggle there was no limit either to their endeavors or passions.

This intense spirit of rivalry obtained in their studies and their games. If Paul memorized one canto of "Marmion," Lloyd memorized two cantos, Paul came back with three, and Lloyd again with four, till each knew the whole poem by heart. I remember an incident that occurred at the swimming hole—an incident tragically significant of the life-struggle between them. The boys had a game of diving to the bottom of a ten-foot pool and holding on by submerged roots to see who could stay under the longest. Paul and Lloyd allowed themselves to be bantered into making the descent together. When I saw their faces, set and determined, disappear in the water as they sank swiftly down, I felt a foreboding of something dreadful.

The moments sped, the ripples died away, the face of the pool grew placid and untroubled, and neither black nor golden head broke surface in quest of air. We above grew anxious. The longest record of the longest-winded boy had been exceeded, and still there was no sign. Air bubbles trickled slowly upward, showing that the breath had been expelled from their lungs, and after that the bubbles ceased to trickle upward. Each second became interminable, and, unable longer to endure the suspense, I plunged into the water.

I found them down at the bottom, clutching tight to the roots, their heads not a foot apart, their eyes wide open, each glaring fixedly at the other. They were suffering frightful torment, writhing and twisting in the pangs of voluntary suffocation; for neither would let go and acknowledge himself beaten. I tried to break Paul's hold on the root, but he resisted me fiercely. Then I lost my breath and came to the surface, badly scared. I quickly explained the situation, and half a dozen of us went down and by main strength tore them loose. By the time we got them out, both were unconscious, and it was only after much barrel-rolling and rubbing and pounding that they finally came to their senses. They would have drowned there, had no one rescued them.

When Paul Tichlorne entered college, he let it be generally understood that he was going in for the social sciences. Lloyd Inwood, entering at the same time, elected to take the same course. But Paul had had it secretly in mind all the time to study the natural sciences, specializing on chemistry, and at the last moment he switched over. Though Lloyd had already arranged his year's work and attended the first lectures, he at once followed Paul's lead and went in for the natural sciences and especially for chemistry.

Their rivalry soon became a noted thing throughout the university. Each was a spur to the other, and they went into chemistry deeper than did ever students before—so deep, in fact, that ere they took their sheepskins they could have stumped any chemistry or "cow college" professor in the institution, save "old" Moss, head of the department, and even him they puzzled and edified more than once. Lloyd's discovery of the "death Bacillus" of the sea toad, and his experiments on it with potassium cyanide, sent his name and that of his university ringing round the world; nor was Paul a whit behind when he succeeded in producing laboratory colloids exhibiting amoeba-like activities, and when he cast new light upon the processes of fertilization through his startling experiments with simple sodium chlorides and magnesium solutions on low forms of marine life.

It was in their undergraduate days, however, in the midst of their profoundest plunges into the mysteries of organic chemistry, that Doris Van Benschoten entered into their lives. Lloyd met her first, but within twenty-four hours Paul saw to it that he also made her acquaintance. Of course, they fell in love with her, and she became the only thing in life worth living for.

They wooed her with equal ardor and fire, and so intense became their struggle for her that half the student-body took to wagering wildly on the result. Even "old" Moss, one day, after an astounding demonstration in his private laboratory by Paul, was guilty to the extent of a month's salary of backing him to become the bridegroom of Doris Van Benschoten.

In the end she solved the problem in her own way, to everybody's satisfaction except Paul's and Lloyd's. Getting them together, she said that she really could not choose between them because she loved them both equally well; and that, unfortunately, since polyandry was not permitted in the United States she would be compelled to forego the honor and happiness of marrying either of them. Each blamed the other for this lamentable outcome, and the bitterness between them grew more bitter.

But things came to a head soon enough. It was at my home, after they had taken their degrees and dropped out of the world's sight, that the beginning of the end came to pass. Both were men of means, with little inclination and no necessity for professional life. My friendship and their mutual animosity were the two things that linked them in any way together. While they were very often at my place, they made it a fastidious point to avoid each other on such visits, though it was inevitable, under the circumstances, that they should come upon each other occasionally.

On the day I have in recollection, Paul Tichlorne had been mooning all morning in my study over a current scientific review. This left me free to my own affairs, and I was out among my roses when Lloyd Inwood arrived. Clipping and pruning and tacking the climbers on the porch, with my mouth full of nails, and Lloyd following me about and lending a hand now and again, we fell to discussing the mythical race of invisible people, that strange and vagrant people the traditions of which have come down to us. Lloyd warmed to the talk in his nervous, jerky fashion, and was soon interrogating the physical properties and possibilities of invisibility. A perfectly black object, he contended, would elude and defy the acutest vision.

"Color is a sensation," he was saying. "It has no objective reality. Without light, we can see neither colors nor objects themselves. All objects are black in the dark, and in the dark it is impossible to see them. If no light strikes upon them, then no light is flung back from them to the eye, and so we have no vision-evidence of their being."

"But we see black objects in daylight," I objected.

"Very true," he went on warmly. "And that is because they are not perfectly black. Were they perfectly black, absolutely black, as it were, we could not see them—ay, not in the blaze of a thousand suns could we see them! And so I say, with the right pigments, properly compounded, an absolutely black paint could be produced which would render invisible whatever it was applied to."

"It would be a remarkable discovery," I said noncommittally, for the whole thing seemed too fantastic for aught but speculative purposes.

"Remarkable!" Lloyd slapped me on the shoulder. "I should say so! Why, old chap, to coat myself with such a paint would be to put the world at my feet. The secrets of kings and courts would be mine, the machinations of diplomats and politicians, the play of stock-gamblers, the plans of trusts and corporations. I could keep my hand on the inner pulse of things and become the greatest power in the world. And I—" He broke off shortly, then added, "Well, I have begun my experiments, and I don't mind telling you that I'm right in line for it."

A laugh from the doorway startled us. Paul Tichlorne was standing there, a smile of mockery on his lips.

"You forget, my dear Lloyd," he said.

"Forget what?"

"You forget," Paul went on—"ah, you forget the shadow."

I saw Lloyd's face drop, but he answered sneeringly, "I can carry a sunshade, you know." Then he turned suddenly and fiercely upon him. "Look here, Paul, you'll keep out of this if you know what's good for you."

A rupture seemed imminent, but Paul laughed good-naturedly. "I wouldn't lay fingers on your dirty pigments. Succeed beyond your most sanguine expectations, yet you will always fetch up against the shadow. You can't get away from it. Now I shall go on the very opposite tack. In the very nature of my proposition the shadow will be eliminated—"

"Transparency!" ejaculated Lloyd, instantly. "But it can't be achieved."

"Oh, no; of course not." And Paul shrugged his shoulders and strolled off.

This was the beginning of it. Both men attacked the problem with all the tremendous energy for which they were noted, and with a rancor and bitterness that made me tremble for the success of either. Each trusted me to the utmost, and in the long weeks of experimentation that followed I was made a party to both sides, listening to their theorizings and witnessing their demonstrations. Never, by word or sign, did I convey to either the slightest hint of the other's progress, and they respected me for the seal which I always put upon my lips.

Lloyd Inwood, after prolonged and unintermittent application, when the tension upon his mind and body became too great to bear, had a strange way of obtaining relief. He attended prize fights. It was at one of these brutal exhibitions, whither he had dragged me in order to tell his latest results, that his theory received striking confirmation.

"Do you see that red-whiskered man?" he asked, pointing across the ring to the fifth tier of seats on the opposite side. "And do you see the next man to him, the one in the white hat? Well, there is quite a gap between them, is there not?"

"Certainly," I answered. "They are a seat apart. The gap is the unoccupied seat."

He leaned over to me and spoke seriously. "Between the red-whiskered man and the white-hatted man sits Ben Wasson. You have heard me speak of him. He is the cleverest pugilist of his weight in the country. He is also a Caribbean Negro, full-blooded, and the blackest in the United States. He has on a black overcoat buttoned up. I saw him when he came in and took that seat. As soon as he sat down he disappeared. Watch closely; he may smile."

I was for crossing over to verify Lloyd's statement, but he restrained me. "Wait," he said.

I waited and watched, till the red-whiskered man turned his head as though addressing the unoccupied seat; and then, in that empty space, I saw the rolling whites of a pair of eyes and the white double-crescent of two rows of teeth, and for the instant I could make out a Negro's face. But with the passing of the smile his visibility passed, and the chair seemed vacant as before.

"Were he perfectly black, you could sit alongside him and not see him," Lloyd said; and I confess the illustration was apt enough to make me well-nigh convinced.

I visited Lloyd's laboratory a number of times after that, and found him always deep in his search after the absolute black. His experiments covered all sorts of pigments, such as lamp-blacks, tars, carbonized vegetable matters, soots of oils and fats, and the various carbonized animal substances.

"White light is composed of the seven primary colors," he argued to me. "But it is itself, of itself, invisible. Only by being reflected from objects do it and the objects become visible. But only that portion of it that is reflected becomes visible. For instance, here is a blue tobacco-box. The white light strikes against it, and, with one exception, all its component colors—violet, indigo, green, yellow, orange, and red—are absorbed. The one exception is *blue*. It is not absorbed, but reflected. Wherefore the tobacco-box gives us a sensation of blueness. We do not see the other colors because they are absorbed. We see only the blue. For the same reason grass is *green*. The green waves of white light are thrown upon our eyes."

"When we paint our houses, we do not apply color to them," he said at another time. "What we do is to apply certain substances that have the property of absorbing from white light all the colors except those that we would have our houses appear. When a substance reflects all the colors to the eye, it seems to us white. When it absorbs all the colors, it is black. But, as I said before, we have as yet no perfect black. *All* the colors are not absorbed. The perfect black, guarding against high lights, will be utterly and absolutely invisible. Look at that, for example."

He pointed to the palette lying on his work-table. Different shades of black pigments were brushed on it. One, in particular, I could hardly see. It gave my eyes a blurring sensation, and I rubbed them and looked again.

"That," he said impressively, "is the blackest black you or any mortal man ever looked upon. But just you wait, and I'll have a black so black that no mortal man will be able to look upon it—*and see it!*"

On the other hand, I used to find Paul Tichlorne plunged as deeply into the study of light polarization, diffraction, and interference, single and double refraction and all manner of strange organic compounds.

"Transparency: a state or quality of body which permits all rays of light to pass through," he defined for me. "That is what I am seeking. Lloyd blunders up against the shadow with her perfect opaqueness. But I escape it. A transparent body casts no shadow; neither does it reflect light-waves—that is, the perfectly transparent does not. So, avoiding high lights, not only will such a body cast no shadow, but, since it reflects no light, it will also be invisible."

We were standing by the window at another time. Paul was engaged in polishing a number of lenses, which were ranged along the sill. Suddenly, after a pause in the conversation, he said, "Oh! I've dropped a lens. Stick your head out, old man, and see where it went to."

Out I started to thrust my head, but a sharp blow on the forehead caused me to recoil. I rubbed my bruised brow and gazed with reproachful inquiry at Paul, who was laughing in gleeful, boyish fashion.

"Well?" he said.

"Well?" I echoed.

"Why don't you investigate?" he demanded. And investigate I did. Before thrusting out my head, my senses, active, had told me there was nothing there, that nothing intervened between me and out-of-doors, that the aperture of the window opening was utterly empty. I stretched forth my hand and felt a hard object, smooth and cool and flat, which my touch, out of its experience, told me to be glass. I looked again, but could see positively nothing.

"White quartzose sand," Paul rattled off, "sodic carbonate, slaked lime, cullet, manganese peroxide—there you have it, the finest French plate glass, made by the great St. Gobain Company, who made the finest plate glass in the world, and this is the finest piece they ever made. It cost a king's ransom. But look at it! You can't see it. You don't know it's there till you run your head against it.

"Eh, old boy! That's merely an object-lesson—certain elements, in themselves opaque, yet so compounded as to give a resultant body which is transparent. But that is a matter of inorganic chemistry, you say. Very true. But I dare to assert, standing here on my two feet, that in the organic I can duplicate whatever occurs in the inorganic.

"Here!" He held a test-tube between me and the light, and I noted the cloudy or muddy liquid it contained. He emptied the contents of another test-tube into it, and almost instantly it became clear and sparkling.

"Or here!" With quick, nervous movements among his array of test-tubes, he turned a white solution to a wine color, and a light yellow solution to a dark brown. He dropped a piece of litmus paper into an acid, when it changed instantly to red, and on floating it in an alkali it turned as quickly to blue.

"The litmus paper is still the litmus paper," he enunciated in the formal manner of the lecturer. "I have not changed it into something else. Then what did I do? I merely changed the arrangement of its molecules. Where, at first, it absorbed all colors from the light but red, its molecular structure was so changed that it absorbed red and all colors except blue. And so it goes, *ad infinitum.* Now, what I propose to do is this."

He paused for a space.

"I propose to seek—ay, and to find—the proper reagents, which, acting upon the living organism, will bring about molecular changes analogous to those you have just witnessed. But these reagents, which I shall find, and for that matter, upon which I already have my hands, will not turn the living body to blue or red or black, but they will turn it to transparency. All light will pass through it. It will be invisible. It will cast no shadow."

A few weeks later I went hunting with Paul. He had been promising me for some time that I should have the pleasure of shooting over a wonderful dog—the most wonderful dog, in fact, that ever man shot over, so he averred, and continued to aver till my curiosity was aroused. But on the morning in question I was disappointed, for there was no dog in evidence.

"Don't see him about," Paul remarked, unconcernedly, and we set off across the fields.

I could not imagine, at the time, what was ailing me, but I had a feeling of some impending and deadly illness. My nerves were all awry, and, from the astounding tricks they played me, my senses seemed to have run riot. Strange sounds disturbed me. At times I heard the swish-swish of grass being shoved aside, and once the patter of feet across a patch of stony ground.

"Did you hear anything, Paul?" I asked once.

But he shook his head, and thrust his feet steadily forward.

While climbing a fence, I heard the low, eager whine of a dog, apparently from within a couple of feet of me; but on looking about me I saw nothing.

I dropped to the ground, limp and trembling.

"Paul," I said, "we had better return to the house. I am afraid I am going to be sick."

"Nonsense, old man," he answered. "The sunshine has gone to your head like wine. You'll be all right. It's famous weather."

But, passing along a narrow path through a clump of cottonwoods, some object brushed against my legs and I stumbled and nearly fell. I looked with sudden anxiety at Paul.

"What's the matter?" he asked. "Tripping over your own feet?"

I kept my tongue between my teeth and plodded on, though sore perplexed and thoroughly satisfied that some acute and mysterious malady had attacked my nerves. So far my eyes had escaped; but, when we got to the open fields again, even my vision went back on me. Strange flashes of vari-colored, rainbow light began to appear and disappear on the path before me. Still, I managed to keep myself in hand, till the vari-colored lights persisted for a space of fully twenty seconds, dancing and flashing in continuous play. Then I sat down, weak and shaky.

"It's all up with me," I gasped, covering my eyes with my hands. "It has attacked my eyes. Paul, take me home."

But Paul laughed long and loud. "What did I tell you?—the most wonderful dog, eh? Well, what do you think?"

He turned partly from me and began to whistle. I heard the patter of feet, the panting of a heated animal, and the unmistakable yelp of a dog. Then Paul stooped down and apparently fondled the empty air.

"Here! Give me your fist."

And he rubbed my hand over the cold nose and jowls of a dog. A dog it certainly was, with the shape and the smooth, short coat of a pointer.

Suffice to say, I speedily recovered my spirits and control. Paul put a collar about the animal's neck and tied his handkerchief to its tail. And then was vouchsafed us the remarkable sight of an empty collar and a waving handkerchief cavorting over the fields. It was something to see that collar and handkerchief pin a bevy of quail in a clump of locusts and remain rigid and immovable till we had flushed the birds.

Now and again the dog emitted the vari-colored light-flashes I have mentioned. The one thing, Paul explained, which he had not anticipated and which he doubted could be overcome.

"They're a large family," he said, "these sun dogs, wind dogs, rainbows, halos, and parhelia. They are produced by refraction of light from mineral and ice crystals, from mist, rain, spray, and no end of things; and I am afraid they are the penalty I must pay for transparency. I escaped Lloyd's shadow only to fetch up against the rainbow flash."

A couple of days later, before the entrance to Paul's laboratory, I encountered a terrible stench. So overpowering was it that it was easy to discover the source—a mass of putrescent matter on the doorstep which in general outlines resembled a dog.

Paul was startled when he investigated my find. It was his invisible dog, or rather, what had been his invisible dog, for it was now plainly visible. It had been playing about but a few minutes before in all health and strength. Closer examination revealed that the skull had been crushed by some heavy blow. While it was strange that the animal should have been killed, the inexplicable thing was that it should decay so quickly.

"The reagents I injected into its system were harmless," Paul explained. "Yet they were powerful, and it appears that when death comes they force practically instantaneous disintegration. Remarkable! Most remarkable! Well, the only thing is not to die. They do not harm so long as one lives. But I do wonder who smashed in that dog's head."

Light, however, was thrown upon this when a frightened housemaid brought the news that Gaffer Bedshaw had that very morning, not more than an hour back, gone violently insane, and was strapped down at home, in the huntsman's lodge, where he raved of a battle with a ferocious and gigantic beast that he had encountered in the Tichlorne pasture. He claimed that the thing, whatever it was, was invisible, that with his own eyes he had seen that it was invisible; wherefore his tearful wife and daughters shook their heads, and wherefore he but waxed the more violent, and the gardener and the coachman tightened the straps by another hole.

Nor, while Paul Tichlorne was thus successfully mastering the problem of invisibility, was Lloyd Inwood a whit behind. I went over in answer to a message of his to come and see how he was getting on. Now his laboratory occupied an isolated situation in the midst of his vast grounds. It was built in a pleasant little glade, surrounded on all sides by a dense forest growth, and was to be gained by way of a winding and erratic path. But I had travelled that path so often as to know every foot of it, and conceive my surprise when I came upon the glade and found no laboratory. The quaint shed structure with its red sandstone chimney was not. Nor did it look as if it ever had been. There were no signs of ruin, or débris, nothing.

I started to walk across what had once been the site of the laboratory. "This," I said to myself, "should be where the step went up to the door." Barely were the words out of my mouth when I stubbed my toe on some obstacle, pitched forward, and butted my head into something that *felt* very much like a door. I reached out my hand. It *was* a door. I found the knob and turned it. And at once, as the door swung inward on its hinges, the whole interior of the laboratory impinged upon my vision.

Greeting Lloyd, I closed the door and backed up the path a few paces. I could see nothing of the building. Returning and opening the door, at once all the furniture and every detail of the interior were visible. It was indeed startling, the sudden transition from void to light and form and color.

"What do you think of it, eh?" Lloyd asked, wringing my hand. "I slapped a couple of coats of absolute black on the outside yesterday afternoon to see how it worked. How's your head? You bumped it pretty solidly, I imagine."

"Never mind that," he interrupted my congratulations. "I've something better for you to do."

While he talked he began to strip, and when he stood naked before me he thrust a pot and brush into my hand and said, "Here, give me a coat of this."

It was an oily, shellac-like stuff, which spread quickly and easily over the skin and dried immediately.

"Merely preliminary and precautionary," he explained when I had finished; "but now for the real stuff."

I picked up another pot he indicated, and glanced inside, but could see nothing.

"It's empty," I said.

"Stick your finger in it."

I obeyed, and was aware of a sensation of cool moistness. On withdrawing my hand I glanced at the forefinger, the one I had immersed, but it had disappeared. I moved it, and knew from the alternate tension and relaxation of the muscles that I moved it, but it defied my sense of sight. To all appearances I had been shorn of a finger; nor could I get any visual impression of it till I extended it under the skylight and saw its shadow plainly blotted on the floor.

Lloyd chuckled. "Now spread it on, and keep your eyes open."

I dipped the brush into the seemingly empty pot, and gave him a long stroke across his chest. With the passage of the brush the living flesh disappeared from beneath. I covered his right leg, and he was a one-legged man defying all laws of gravitation. And so, stroke by stroke, member by member, I painted Lloyd Inwood into nothingness. It was a creepy experience, and I was glad when naught remained in sight but his burning black eyes, poised apparently unsupported in mid-air.

"I have a refined and harmless solution for them," he said. "A fine spray with an air-brush, and presto! I am not."

This deftly accomplished, he said, "Now I shall move about, and do you tell me what sensations you experience."

"In the first place, I cannot see you," I said, and I could hear his gleeful laugh from the midst of the emptiness. "Of course," I continued, "you cannot escape your shadow, but that was to be expected. When you pass between my eye and an object, the object disappears, but so unusual and incomprehensible is its disappearance that it seems to me as though my eyes had blurred. When you move rapidly, I experience a bewildering succession of blurs. The blurring sensation makes my eyes ache and my brain tired.

"Have you any other warnings of my presence?" he asked.

"No, and yes," I answered. "When you are near me I have feelings similar to those produced by dank warehouses, gloomy crypts, and deep mines. And as sailors feel the loom of the land on dark nights, so I think I feel the loom of your body. But it is all very vague and intangible."

Long we talked that last morning in his laboratory; and when I turned to go, he put his unseen hand in mine with nervous grip, and said, "Now I shall conquer the world!" And I could not dare to tell him of Paul Tichlorne's equal success.

At home I found a note from Paul, asking me to come up immediately, and it was high noon when I came spinning up the driveway on my wheel. Paul called me from the tennis court, and I dismounted and went over. But the court was empty. As I stood there, gaping open-mouthed, a tennis ball struck me on the arm, and another whizzed past my ear.

For aught I could see of my assailant, they came whirling at me from out of space, and right well was I peppered with them. But when the balls already flung at me began to come back for the second whack, I realized the situation. Seizing a racquet and keeping my eyes open, I quickly saw a rainbow flash appearing and disappearing and darting over the ground. I took out after it, and when I laid the racquet upon it for a half-dozen stout blows, Paul's voice rang out:

"Enough! Enough! Oh! Ouch! Stop! You're landing on my naked skin, you know! Ow! O-w-w! I'll be good! I'll be good! I only wanted you to see my metamorphosis," he said ruefully, and I imagined that he was rubbing his hurts.

A few minutes later we were playing tennis—a handicap on my part, for I could have no knowledge of his position save when all the angles between himself, the sun, and me, were in proper conjunction. Then he flashed, and only then. But the flashes were more brilliant than the rainbow—purest blue, most delicate violet, brightest yellow, and all the intermediary shades, with the scintillant brilliancy of the diamond, dazzling, blinding, iridescent.

But in the midst of our play I felt a sudden cold chill, reminding me of deep mines and gloomy crypts, such a chill as I had experienced that very morning. The next moment, close to the net, I saw a ball rebound in mid-air and empty space, and at the same instant, a score of feet away, Paul Tichlorne emitted a rainbow flash. It could not be he from whom the ball rebounded, and with sickening dread I realized that Lloyd Inwood had come upon the scene. To make sure, I looked for his shadow, and there it was, a shapeless blotch the girth of his body, (the sun was overhead), moving along the ground. I remembered his threat, and felt sure that all the long years of rivalry were about to culminate in an uncanny battle.

I cried a warning to Paul, and heard a snarl as of a wild beast, and an answering snarl. I saw the dark blotch move swiftly across the court, and a brilliant burst of vari-colored light moving with equal swiftness to meet it; and then shadow and flash came together and there was the sound of unseen blows. The net went down before my frightened eyes. I sprang toward the fighters, crying:

"For God's sake!"

But their locked bodies smote against my knees, and I was overthrown.

"You keep out of this, old man!" I heard the voice of Lloyd Inwood from out of the emptiness. And then Paul's voice crying, "Yes, we've had enough of peacemaking."

From the sound of their voices I knew they had separated. I could not locate Paul, and so approached the shadow that represented Lloyd. But from the other side came a stunning blow on the point of my jaw, and I heard Paul scream angrily, "Now will you keep away?"

Then they came together again, the impact of their blows, their groans and gasps, and the swift flashings and shadow-movings telling plainly of the deadliness of the struggle.

I shouted for help, and Gaffer Bedshaw came running into the court. I could see, as he approached, that he was looking at me strangely, but he collided with the combatants and was hurled headlong to the ground. With despairing shriek and a cry of "O Lord, I've got 'em!" he sprang to his feet and tore madly out of the court.

I could do nothing, so I sat up, fascinated and powerless, and watched the struggle. The noonday sun beat down with dazzling brightness on the naked tennis court. And it *was* naked. All I could see was the blotch of shadow and the rainbow flashes, the dust rising from the invisible feet, the earth tearing up from beneath the straining footgrips, and the wire screen bulge once or twice as their bodies hurled against it. That was all, and after a time even that ceased. There were no more flashes, and the shadow had become long and stationary; and I remembered their set boyish faces when they clung to the roots in the deep coolness of the pool.

They found me an hour afterward. Some inkling of what had happened got to the servants and they quitted the Tichlorne service in a body. Gaffer Bedshaw never recovered from the second shock he received, and is confined in a madhouse, hopelessly incurable. The secrets of their marvelous discoveries died with Paul and Lloyd, both laboratories being destroyed by grief-stricken relatives. As for myself, I no longer care for chemical research, and science is a tabooed topic in my household. I have returned to my roses. Nature's colors are good enough for me.

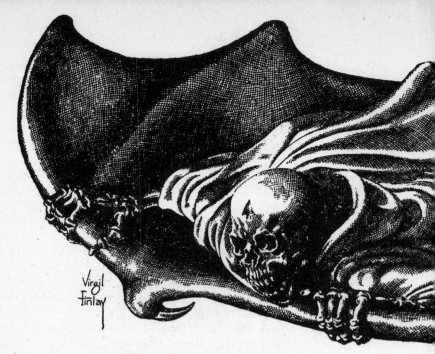

That Low

THEODORE STURGEON

Theodore Sturgeon was that rare writer who could move easily back and forth between fantasy, horror, and science fiction. The secret to his success was his skill at characterization: most Sturgeon protagonists are regular guys, some are downright losers, but all earn the reader's sympathy and respect through their believable responses to the incredible situations they find themselves in. "That Low," an original contribution to Famous Fantastic Mysteries, *calls to mind Sturgeon's little-known fantasy "He Shuttles," in which a character discovers that the desperate measures circumstance has forced him to take are only the beginning of his problems.*

T HERE WAS a "psychic" operating on Vine Street. Fowler went to see her. Not that he had any faith in mumbo-jumbo; far from it. He had been told that this Mrs. Hallowell worked along strict logical lines. That's why he went. He liked the sound of that, being what he was. He went to her and asked her if there were any good reason for not killing himself. She said he couldn't do it. Not "You won't." She said, "You can't."

This Fowler was a failure specialist, in the sense that a man is a carburetor specialist or a drainage specialist or a nerve specialist. You don't get to be that kind of specialist without spending a lot of time with carburetors or drainage layouts or nerves. You don't stay nice and objective about it, either. You get in it up to the elbows, up to

300

the eyeballs. Fowler was a man who knew all that one man could know about failure. He knew all of the techniques, from the small social failure of letting his language forget what room of the house he was in, through a declaration of war on the clock and the calendar (every appointment and schedule in his life was a battle lost) to the crowning stupidity of regarding his opinions as right purely because they were his opinions. So he had fallen and floundered through life, never following through, jumping when he should have crept, and lying down at sprinting-time. He could have written a book on the subject of failure, except for the fact that if he had, it might have been a success . . . and he hated failure. Well, you don't have to love your specialty to be a specialist. You just have to live with it.

It was understandable, therefore, that he should be impressed by Mrs. Hallowell's reputation for clarity and logic, for he truly believed that here was a kindred spirit. He brought his large features and his flaccid handshake to her and her office, which were cool. The office was Swedish modern and blond. Mrs. Hallowell was dark, and said, "Sit down. Your name?"

"Maxwell Fowler."

"Occupation?"

"Engineer."

She glanced up. She had aluminum eyes. "Not a graduate engineer." It was not a question.

"I would have been," said Fowler, "except for a penny-ante political situation in the school. There was a fellow—"

"Yes," she said. "Married?"

"I was. You know, the kind that will kick a man when he's down. She was a—"

"Now, Mr. Fowler. What was it you wanted here?"

"I hear you can foretell the future."

"I'm not interested in gossip," she said, and it was the only cautionary thing she said in the entire interview. "I know about people, that's all."

He said, "Ever since I could walk and talk, people have been against me. I can whip one or two or sometimes a half dozen or more, but by and large I'm outnumbered. I'm tired. Sometimes I think I'll check out."

"Are you going to ask me if you should?"

"No. If I will."

She said, "All right. I don't give advice. I just tell about what's going to happen."

"What's going to happen?"

"Fill out a check. Leave the amount blank and don't sign it. Give it to me."

"But—"

"You wouldn't pay me afterward."

"My word's as good as—" and then he looked into the eyes. He got out his checkbook. When he had done as she asked, she took a pen and wrote on the check.

"That's foolish," he said.

"You have it, though."

"Yes, I have, but—"

"Sign it," she said casually, "or go away."

He signed it. "Well?"

She hesitated. There was something—

"Well?" he rapped again. "What will I do? I'm tired of all this persecution."

"Your tenses are mixed up." She smiled. "Do you want to know what you should do? Or what you shall do?"

"What shall I do?"

She wet her lips. "You shall live a long and unhappy life."

"It can't be any unhappier than it is."

"I said nothing comparative."

"Then I don't want to live a long life."

"You shall, however."

"Not if I don't want to," he said grimly. "I'm tired, I tell you."

She shook her head. "You've gone too far," she said, not unkindly. "You can't change it."

"Any time I don't like it, I can kill myself."

That was when she told him he couldn't. He was very angry, but she did not give him back his check. By the time he thought of stopping payment on it, it had cleared the bank. He went on living his life.

But Mrs. Hallowell had one bad moment over the matter. She started up out of her sleep one night, thinking about Fowler.

"Oh, how awful," she said. "I made a mistake!"

She phoned in the morning. Fowler was not there. He had just decided to kill himself. The amount he had paid Mrs. Hallowell made it impossible for him to meet a certain vital obligation, and since his efforts to borrow failed, he had no choice but to face his creditor. Or to kill himself. So he got a piece of rope and made a noose and put it around his neck. He tied the other end to the leg of the radiator and jumped out the window. He was a big man. The rope held, but the leg broke off the radiator. He fell six stories, struck the canvas marquee, tore through it and fell heavily to the sidewalk. There was quite a crowd there to listen to the noises he made because of what was broken.

Mrs. Hallowell called and called until someone answered who could tell her what had happened. The someone said, "Is there any message I could send to him?" And Mrs. Hallowell said, "No. No, there isn't. He'll find out when the time comes."

Fowler took a while to mend, during which he developed a scheme to clear himself with his creditors. Some money was entrusted to him and he stole it, and before he could sink it into his new plan, he was billed for the hospital expenses and threatened with a suit. He could not handle the suit. He paid the money to the hospital and his money-making scheme fell through. He determined to kill himself.

While he was bleeding in the bathroom from his opened wrists, the tenant in the next apartment, who had a bad cold, lit a match in a gas-filled kitchen and blew the end of the building out. Fowler was picked up from the wreckage, still bleeding. They saved him that time, too. It was a lot of trouble. They had to take this and that off, and the other out. He was put, finally, in a very short bed with a mass of equipment beside him, which hummed and clicked all the time. The equipment circulated fluids, and another part of it dripped into a tube, and another part pressured him gently to hold his breathing. It was all highly efficient.

That was the trouble with Mrs. Hallowell's talent. It lay in such broad lines. No details. A mistake could cover a lot of territory. Her mistake showed up after Fowler had been in that short bed for two months.

People came by and clucked their tongues when they saw him. There was a bright-eyed, dry-faced old lady who put flowers near him every couple of weeks. Everybody was sorry for him, and everybody always would be, as long as he lived, which would be very nearly as long as the equipment could be kept running. A long time. A long life. Mrs. Hallowell had been perfectly right, there. Where she made her mistake was in thinking that he would be unhappy. He didn't work. He didn't move very much. He just lay and was served and people were sorry. Maxwell Fowler was quite happy.

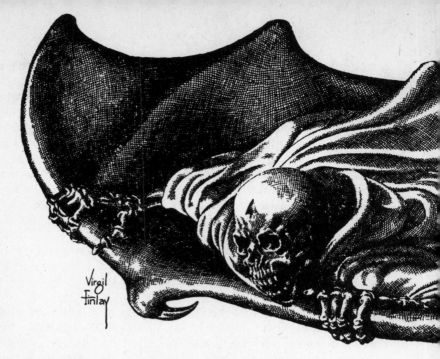

The Human Angle

WILLIAM TENN

Any representative collection of postwar fantasy and science fiction would be obliged to include at least one story by William Tenn (a pseudonym for Philip J. Klass). Memorable for their wit and often satiric portrayal of humanity, Tenn's stories fill six volumes and include his classic tale of the biggest con artist of all time, "Bernie the Faust." Although Tenn usually wrote for magazines such as Galaxy *and* Astounding, *occasionally he contributed to fantasy magazines like* Weird Tales *and* Famous Fantastic Mysteries. *"The Human Angle," a variation on the vampire theme, became the title of his second story collection.*

WHAT A ROAD! What filthy, dismal, blinding rain! And, by the ghost of old Horace Greeley, what an idiotic, impossible assignment!

John Shellinger cursed the steamy windshield from which a monotonous wiper flipped raindrops. He stared through the dripping, half-clear triangle of glass and tried to guess which was broken country road and which was the overgrown brown vegetation of autumn. He might have passed the slowly moving line of murderous men stretching to right and left across country and road; he might have angled off into a side-road and be heading off into completely forsaken land. But he didn't think he had.

What an assignment!

"Get the human angle on this vampire hunt," Randall had ordered. "All the other news services will be giving it the hillbilly twist, medieval superstition messing up the atomic world. What dumb jerks these dumb jerks are! You stay off that line. Find yourself a weepy individual slant on bloodsucking and sob me about three thousand words. And keep your expense account down—you just can't work a big swindle sheet out of that kind of agricultural slum."

So I saddles my convertible, Shellinger thought morosely, and I tools off to the pappy-mammy country where nobody speaks to strangers nohow "specially now, 'cause the vampire done got to three young 'uns already." And nobody will tell me the names of those three kids or whether any of them are still alive; and Randall's wires keep asking when I'll start sending usable copy; and I still can't find one loquacious Louise in the whole country. Wouldn't even have known of this cross-country hunt if I hadn't begun to wonder where all the men in town had disappeared to on such an unappetizing, rainy evening.

The road was bad in second, but it was impossible in almost any other gear. The ruts weren't doing the springs any good, either. Shellinger rubbed moisture off the glass with his handkerchief and wished he had another pair of headlights. He could hardly see.

That dark patch ahead, for instance. Might be one of the vampire posse. Might be some beast driven out of cover by the brush-beating. Might even be a little girl.

He ground into his brake. It was a girl. A little girl with dark hair and blue jeans. He twirled the crank and stuck his head out into the falling rain.

"Hey, kid. Want a lift?"

The child stooped slightly against the somber background of night and decaying, damp countryside. Her eyes scanned the car, came back to his face and considered it. The kid had probably not known that this chromium-plated kind of postwar auto existed. She'd certainly never dreamed of riding in one. It would give her a chance to crow over the other kids in the 'tater patch.

Evidently deciding that he wasn't the kind of stranger her mother had warned her about and that it would be less uncomfortable in the car than walking in the rain and mud, she nodded. Very slowly, she came around the front and climbed in at his right.

"Thanks, mister," she said.

Shellinger started again and took a quick, sidewise glance at the girl. Her blue jeans were raggedy and wet. She must be terribly cold and uncomfortable, but she wasn't going to let him know. She would bear up under it with the stoicism of the hill people.

But she was frightened. She sat hunched up, her hands folded neatly in her lap, at the far side of the seat right up against the door. What was the kid afraid of? Of course, the vampire!

"How far up do you go?" he asked her gently.

"'Bout a mile and a half. But that way." She pointed over her shoulder with a pudgy thumb. She was plump, much more flesh on her than most of these scrawny, share-cropped kids. She'd be beautiful, too, some day, if some illiterate lummox didn't cart her off to matrimony and hard work in a drafty cabin.

Regretfully, he maneuvered around on the road, got the car turned and started back. He'd miss the hunters, but you couldn't drag an impressionable child into that sort of grim nonsense. He might as well take her home first. Besides, he wouldn't get anything out of those uncommunicative farmers with their sharpened stakes and silver bullets in their squirrel rifles.

"What kind of crops do your folks raise—tobacco or cotton?"

"They don't raise nothing yet. We just came here."

"Oh." That was right: she didn't have a mountain accent. Come to think of it, she was a little more dignified than most of the children he'd met in this neighborhood. "Isn't it a little late to go for a stroll? Aren't your folks afraid to let you out this late with a vampire around?"

She shivered. "I—I'm careful," she said at last.

Hey! Shellinger thought. Here was the human angle. Here was what Randall was bleating about. A frightened little girl with enough curiosity to swallow her big lump of fear and go out exploring on this night of all others. He didn't know how it fitted, just yet—but his journalistic nose was twitching. There was copy here; the basic, colorful human angle was sitting fearfully on his red leather seat.

"Do you know what a vampire is?"

She looked at him, startled, dropped her eyes and studied her folded hands for words. "It's—it's like someone who needs people instead of meals." A hesitant pause. "Isn't it?"

"Ye-es." That was good. Trust a child to give you a fresh viewpoint, unspoiled by textbook superstition. He'd use that—"People instead of meals." "A vampire is supposed to be a person who will be immortal— not die, that is—so long as he or she gets blood and life from living people. The only way you can kill a vampire—"

"You turn right here, mister."

He pointed the car into the little branchlet of side road. It was annoyingly narrow; surprised wet boughs tapped the windshield, ran their leaves lazily across the car's fabric top. Once in a while, a tree top sneezed collected rain water down.

Shellinger pressed his face close to the windshield and tried to decipher the picture of brown mud amid weeds that his headlights gave him. "What a road! Your folks are really starting from scratch. Well, the only way to kill a vampire is with a silver bullet. Or you can drive a stake through the heart and bury it in a crossroads at midnight. That's what those men are going to do tonight if they catch it." He turned his head as he heard her gasp. "What's the matter—don't you like the idea?"

"I think it's horrid," she told him emphatically.

"Why? How do you feel—live and let live?"

She thought it over, nodded, smiled. "Yes. Live and let live. Live and let live. After all—" She was having difficulty finding the right words again. "After all, some people can't help what they are. I mean," very slowly, very thoughtfully, "like if a person's a vampire, what can they do about it?"

"You've got a good point there, kid." He went back to studying what there was of the road. "The only trouble's this: if you believe in things like vampires, well, you don't believe in them good—you believe in them nasty. Those people back in the village who claim three children have been killed or whatever it was by the vampire, they hate it and want to destroy it. If there are such things as vampires—mind you, I said 'if'—then, by nature, they do such horrible things that any way of getting rid of them is right. See?"

"No. You shouldn't drive stakes through people."

Shellinger laughed. "I'll say you shouldn't. Never could like that deal myself. However, if it were a matter of a vampire to me or mine, I think I could overcome my squeamishness long enough to do a little roustabout work on the stroke of twelve."

He paused and considered that this child was a little too intelligent for her environment. She didn't seem to be bollixed with superstitions as yet, and he was feeding her *Shellinger on Black Magic*. That was vicious. He continued soberly, "The difficulty with those beliefs is that a bunch of grown men who hold them are spread across the countryside tonight because they think a vampire is on the loose. And they're likely to flush some poor hobo and finish him off gruesomely for no other reason than that he can't give a satisfactory explanation for his presence in the fields on a night like this."

Silence. She was considering his statement. Shellinger liked her dignified, thoughtful attitude. She was a bit more at ease, he noticed, and was sitting closer to him. Funny how a kid could sense that you wouldn't do her any harm. Even a country kid. Especially a country kid, come to think of it, because they lived closer to nature or something.

He had won her confidence, though, and consequently rewon his. A week of living among thin-lipped ignoramuses who had been not at all diffident in showing *their* disdain had made him a little uncertain. This was better. And he'd finally gotten a line on the basis of a story.

Only, he'd have to dress it up. In the story, she'd be an ordinary hillbilly kid, much thinner, much more unapproachable; and the quotes would all be in "mountain" dialect.

Yes, he had the human interest stuff now.

She had moved closer to him again, right against his side. Poor kid! His body warmth made the wet coldness of her jeans a little less uncomfortable. He wished he had a heater in the car.

The road disappeared entirely into tangled bushes and gnarly trees. He stopped the car, flipped the emergency back.

"You don't live here? This place looks as if nothing human's been around for years."

He was astonished at the uncultivated desolation.

"Sure I live here, mister," her warm voice said at his ear. "I live in that little house over there."

"Where?" He rubbed at the windshield and strained his vision over the sweep of headlights. "I don't see any house. Where is it?"

"There." A plump hand came up and waved at the night ahead. "Over there."

"I still can't see—" The corner of his right eye had casually noticed that the palm of her hand was covered with fine brown hair.

Strange, that.

Was covered with fine brown hair. Her palm!

"What *was* that you remembered about the shape of her teeth?" his mind shrieked. He started to whip his head around, to get another look at her teeth. But he couldn't.

Because her teeth were in his throat.

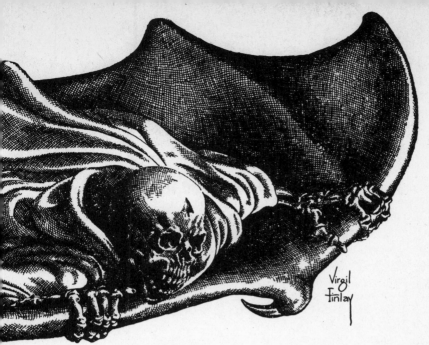

The Toys of Fate

TOD ROBBINS

Expatriate American author Tod Robbins is yet another writer whose legacy has outlasted his name. His short story "Spurs," about the terrible revenge a group of sideshow freaks takes on a pair of circus stars, was adapted for the screen in 1932 as Freaks, *a Tod Browning (the director of* Dracula*) film considered so outside the boundaries of taste that it was banned for decades. The stories and novels that Robbins contributed to* The Thrill Book *and the Munsey magazines tended to focus more on the grotesque than the supernatural. An exception is "The Toys of Fate," reprinted in a 1948 issue of* Fantastic Novels, *which presents one of the cruelest personifications of Fate in literature.*

THERE WAS a raucous screaming of brakes, and the train, which had been gliding along smoothly through the night, came to an abrupt, shivering halt. I was violently precipitated against the man who sat opposite me, and he was thrown to the floor.

"I beg your pardon," I said. "I hope you're not hurt."

He was a stout, middle-aged man in a light woolly overcoat. Lying on the floor of the smoking-compartment, his large and melancholy brown eyes staring up at me from his unexpressive face, he closely resembled a sheep awaiting the attentions of the butcher. There was an irritating passivity about his inert figure which was galling in the extreme. My right toe tingled to stir him into a more upright and dignified position.

"I hope you're not hurt," I repeated, but this time there was no sympathy in my tone.

His hands fluttered uncertainly about his plump person.

"No, I'm not hurt," he said at last, rising slowly to his feet. "For a moment I thought that he'd finally taken me out of his pocket; but—"

He broke off and regarded me mournfully with his head on one side.

"I beg your pardon," I said, making no sense out of his words. "You were saying—"

But at this point I was interrupted by the conductor who bustled in with an air of importance. The somber pride of the tragedian was mirrored on the official's face as he picked up a lantern and lighted it.

"What's the trouble?" I asked.

"A man's been run over," he answered tersely. "Got his foot caught in the switch, and couldn't get away in time."

"Poor devil! Is he dead?"

"I should say so! They tell me he's torn to rags. I'm going up there now. Want to go along?"

"No," I answered hastily. "That kind of thing makes me sick."

The conductor smiled rather contemptuously and strode out into the passageway. A moment later I could see his lantern, one among a dozen or more, gliding past the window like a large, luminous bubble. We had come to a standstill in a deserted tract of swampland. The black, brooding night seemed to hang heavily over the earth like a threatening hand. Not a light glimmered anywhere, except those gay bobbing lanterns which flowed on merrily to the feet of tragedy; not a sound broke the silence, except the faraway murmur of voices and the dismal croaking of frogs.

"He would have chosen such a night!"

I started involuntarily. For the moment I had forgotten the existence of the man in the woolly overcoat. He now sat facing me in his old seat near the window, looking particularly docile, stupid, and altogether aggravating.

"I'm sure I haven't the slightest idea what you're talking about," I said rather irritably. "Will you kindly explain?"

"Naturally you wouldn't," he murmured sadly. "And you won't believe me if I tell you the story. You'll think me mad."

"Oh, no, I won't," I hastened to assure him.

I had realized at the first glance that this fellow with the muddy brown eyes was too stupid to be threatened with insanity. Madness, after all, is a mental fungus dependent on right soil for its growth—the disease of a vivid imagination. Looking at my traveling companion with the trained eyes of a physiognomist, I said with conviction:

"I would never consider you insane!"

At this he brightened visibly, as if I had paid him a compliment.

"That's a satisfaction," he said, crossing his plump legs. "To be quite candid with you, Mr.—"

"Burton's my name," said I.

"To be quite candid, Mr. Burton," he continued, "I've been called mad more times than once. And when I haven't been called mad, I've been called a good liar, which is just as insulting."

"Neither is insulting," I replied; "but let that pass. You were about to tell me your story."

"So I was, sir," said he, with a mournful shake of the head. "It all happened a long time ago, when I was living in Prestonville. Perhaps, you've heard of Prestonville, Mr. Burton?"

"Prestonville?" I murmured. "Prestonville?" And then memory flashed up in me. "Why, that's the town that was destroyed by an earthquake!" I cried, in the tone of a man making a happy discovery. "There was a great loss of life, wasn't there?"

"A frightful loss of life, Mr. Burton! It came after midnight, when people were in their beds, and the houses were bowled over as if they were made of cardboard. There was no warning. All at once the earth began to shake, and then—"

He made a sweeping gesture with his hand.

"It was a thriving town, I understand?"

"Yes, indeed, sir—a progressive town. By this time it would have been a large city. There were enterprising business men who had made their homes there—clean-living, ambitious men, who would have been the pride of the country if they had survived; but most of them were buried under their own roofs. They died with the town."

He broke off and rubbed the bald spot just above his right temple, which was glistening with perspiration. "And there was no reason for it all!" he finished, almost fiercely. "If it had been a vicious growth like some towns in this State, one could call it a visitation of Providence, and explain it that way."

"Can one ever satisfactorily explain what happens?" I broke in. "Fate is a blindfolded baby attempting to play chess for the first time."

"No, he isn't!" the man in the woolly overcoat cried excitedly. "I'll tell you what he is. He's an old fellow—a little mad, you understand, but not so mad as not to be vicious."

"You seem positive that you're right," I said with a smile. "Why?"

Before he answered, he drew out a cigar and lighted it with a hand that shook oddly.

"I'll tell you why," he answered very calmly between puffs. "I have met Fate."

"You have met Fate?" I said slowly, trying to figure out his meaning.

"Exactly," he replied with a half-hearted chuckle. "He's a dirty old man with a face white and wrinkled as a paper bag—an untidy old man who drops crumbs in his beard and soup on his vest—an old man who neighs when he laughs, like a frightened horse."

In spite of his stupid look this man is quite mad, was my thought. But aloud I said, "How did you know that the old fellow was Fate? Tell me about it."

"Willingly," he said. "It unburdens my mind to tell what I know, even though people think me mad. Living and remaining silent is unendurable. I feel that I am hidden away from the world in some black recesses—a recess from which I cannot escape, and in which I must wait patiently. Some day his hand will grope about in that recess, touch me, and then—" He broke off and passed his handkerchief across his perspiring forehead. "And when I am finally plucked out into the light of day, what will happen to me? I do not know, nor can I guess. Perhaps he has forgotten me; perhaps I may be overlooked for years. He has so many playthings, that mad old man!"

"You were about to tell me your story," I ventured.

"To be sure," the man said in a somewhat calmer tone. "It all happened ten years ago in Prestonville. I was in the toy business then, and had a large shop on Main Street. My show-windows were the delight of every child in town. They would stop on their way to school and stare in, with their noses pressed tight against the glass. And often grown people would stop. You see, I had an artistic temperament, and it found expression in my show-windows."

"How?" I asked.

"Well, I arranged scenes like a stage-director. For instance, there was my tobogganing scene. Through the show-window one caught a glimpse of a hill covered with snow and children sliding down it on gaily painted sleds. And then there was my hunting scene in the forest. One saw a miniature bear at bay, surrounded by miniature sportsmen with leveled rifles. The bear growled, opened its cavernous mouth, and struck at the hunters with its heavy forepaws. It was all quite realistic, I assure you."

"No wonder your windows drew a crowd!"

"Yes, one can perform miracles with mechanical toys," he said. "But perhaps my greatest success was my replica in miniature of Prestonville itself. That, indeed, was a work of art. Every street, every house, every tree, was an exact counterpart of one in the town. When I finally put it on exhibition, it interested not only the children but the grown people as well. It was a drawing card which helped my business and quite eclipsed the efforts of my rival across the street.

"Every day hundreds of people would stop to see what was happening in this tiny town of Prestonville; for with great skill I arranged scenes for them—scenes which parodied the happenings of yesterday. It was a clever joke on the town—a harmless joke at which all could laugh, and at which none could take offense. And I was extremely happy in my ability to amuse, when one dark, rainy evening in October he came and peered solemnly through my show-window."

"He?" I asked.

"Yes, that untidy old man I told you of—the old man who dropped crumbs in his beard and soup on his vest—the mad old man whom later I grew to fear worse than death.

"On account of the weather the streets were deserted; and, as there seemed to be little or no prospect of business on such an evening, I had allowed my two assistants to leave before their usual time. I was standing by the counter, staring absently at the rain-splashed windows, when I suddenly saw a dingy coat-sleeve rubbing against the plate glass. A moment later a white, wrinkled face appeared through the space which had been wiped dry, and a pair of small grey eyes stared solemnly down on my miniature of Prestonville.

"On first seeing it thus, Mr. Burton, I experienced an involuntary tremor of fear. I had an odd fancy that there was a face out there in the night and nothing more—a face drifting about quite independent of a body—a thin mask with a tangle of wild, disreputable beard hanging from it, and shark's eyes staring coldly through the slits above the cheek-bones. But it wasn't what this face held that troubled me, Mr. Burton. No, it was what it lacked—the thinness of it—a feeling that behind its flat, wrinkled surface there was nothing but vacancy. A thin mask of flesh, it had blown off its owner's real face and come floating to my window—or, at least, such was my vague, disquieting thought of it.

"For some time I stared stupidly at the face; and it, in turn, stared down on the toy town. From where I stood the scene suggested a picture. The town no longer seemed a group of miniature houses at my elbow, but the real Prestonville at a great distance; and the face, surrounded as it was by the gray mist which had formed on the window-pane, resembled the face of a cruel divinity looking down from the clouds on what it might presently destroy. It suggested one of those religious pictures of old times when man believed God to be capable of an implacable hatred and desire for vengeance. As I stood there, motionless and staring, I actually trembled for my toy town, which by some mysterious flight of the imagination had also become Prestonville."

The shopkeeper paused and blew a ring of smoke thoughtfully ceilingward.

"All this must sound absurd to you," he resumed after a moment. "In fact, on looking back on it later that night, it seemed absurd to me that an old man's face should have filled me with such wild notions. You see, Mr. Burton, I'm not ordinarily an imaginative man. I've always prided myself on my practicality."

"How long did he stare through the window?" I asked with growing interest.

"I don't know exactly. It might have been only a minute, but it seemed an age. I remember that my eyes, which have always been weak, winked shut for an instant. When I opened them again, the face had gone. I might have thought I had dreamed the whole thing if it hadn't been for the clean patch on the window-pane."

"Did you see the face again?"

"Yes, many times; but always when I was alone in the store, or at night. Sometimes I saw it surrounded by other faces, but it was usually by itself. It seemed to pick stormy nights to stare in at the toy town."

"Were you always affected in the same way?" I asked.

"Yes, always. I could not rid myself of the unhealthy feeling that this face was only a mask, like those I sold to children on Hallowe'en. If it had mirrored any human emotion or thought, it would not have affected me so. There was a sickening thinness about it, if you can understand me. It hung over my toy town like an evil moon. Soon I began to dream about it. It was a great relief when the old man finally came into my shop."

"So he came in!" I cried. "That's rather unusual, isn't it? Faces such as you describe seldom trust themselves under the glare of electric lights."

"I knew you wouldn't believe me," the shopkeeper said wistfully. "Nobody does."

"So far I believe you," I answered truthfully enough. "Go ahead."

"Well, as I was saying, he finally came in. It was a great relief to see that the face had a body to it; but what a body it was! Here were old bones, Mr. Burton—the oldest bones I've ever seen outside a graveyard. I give you my word, the man was a walking mummy. I felt the great age of those bones as they moved slowly beneath the parchment-like skin, and they filled me with a kind of awe; but there was nothing to command respect in his shuffling gait, or in his tangle of beard, where bread-crumbs were sticking like currants in a bush, or in his clothes, which were dingy beyond belief, or in his silly senile smile, which set the wrinkles on his face all aquiver, like ripples on a bowl of milk when you stir it with a spoon. All in all, he was as disreputable-looking an old man as the town could boast of—and half-witted as well, if his wagging lower lip did not belie him. But, as I was saying, there was something awe-inspiring in his slow-moving bones—something which filled me with an unaccountable reverence.

"Well, he shuffled up to the counter and leaned on it for a space mumbling to himself, like a man rehearsing a speech. His pale gray eyes were fixed on me, but they didn't seem to see me. He ran his fingers through his beard in a nervous fashion, so that several stray crumbs rolled down his soup-stained vest and fell on the floor.

" 'Well, sir,' I finally said, speaking pleasantly and even respectfully, for I couldn't forget the age of his bones, 'what can I do for you?'

"At that he winked one eye at me and snickered. It wasn't a laugh at all, rightly speaking, but more like the neigh of a frightened horse.

" 'Tut, tut!' says he with a reproving roll of his head. 'Don't ask silly questions, young man. You know what I want. Why, I've come for your town!'

" 'My town?' I cried in astonishment. 'You mean you want to buy it?'

" 'Isn't it for sale?' he asked, cocking his beard at me. 'I'll tell you what it is, sir. I've found everything for sale in this world but myself—myself!' He smirked and bowed like a dancing-master in his dotage. 'The prices that have been offered me just for a nod or a smile! Ha, they would turn your head, young man! You'd sell your soul for a hundredth part of them; but I? Ah, no! I may not be intelligent, but I'm essentially honest—yes, essentially honest. What do you want for your town?'

" 'I hadn't intended to sell it,' I replied weakly, for his torrent of wild words had played havoc with my wits. 'You see, it's a good advertisement for the shop.'

" 'Come, come, young man!' he says, tapping his nose slyly with a shriveled forefinger. 'None of your tradesman's tricks with me! Everything has a price, you know. Out with it!'

"At that, Mr. Burton, I took a careful survey of this old man from top to toe, from the dingy felt hat set awry on his head to his mud-splashed boots rich with the red clay of the countryside. I had no intention of selling my toy town, and I meant to ask a price far beyond his ability to pay.

" 'Well, young man?' he cried.

" 'Five thousand dollars is the price of that town,' I answered, thinking that now I would be rid of him.

"You may well imagine my surprise, Mr. Burton, when he pulled out an old leather wallet fairly bursting with bills, and counted five thousand-dollar notes into my palm. One would as soon expect to find a scarecrow stuffed with banknotes. Here he was, a very beggar of a man in appearance, with a purse whose contents would have done credit to any millionaire! It made my head swim.

" 'There you have it,' he said with one of his snickers. 'A very moderate price, I'd say, for such a thriving town. I'm afraid you've cheated yourself, young man.' He turned his back on me and stepped over to the show-window. 'You shouldn't have kept it so long!' he cried sharply. 'You're hopelessly old-fashioned!

" 'Yes, old-fashioned,' he said sourly. 'You show nothing here except what happened yesterday. What sort of business is that? Now I'm abreast of the times, and sometimes a step or so in advance of them. I may look antiquated, but I'm not. See here!'

"As quick as thought, Mr. Burton, this strange old man put his hand in his pocket and drew out a match. Striking it on the heel of his boot, he bent forward and applied the flame carefully to one of the tiny cardboard houses in the town.

" 'Look out!' I cried. 'You'll set it on fire! It's only made of paper!'

" 'It is on fire,' he answered with evident satisfaction, slowly straightening his aged back. 'It gives quite a blaze for such a small house.' He broke off and regarded me with a strange look of childish innocence on his wrinkled old face. 'I love fires!' he said. 'Don't you?'

"I made him no answer. My eyes were on the toy town and on the tiny cardboard house which was going up in flames and smoke. Instantly I knew which one this old mad man had picked out to destroy—it was the miniature of my own house on Sanford Avenue. There it blazed merrily; and I was moved by the sight of it. Hot anger surged through me against this old fool at my elbow—an anger which was tinged with fear. I felt regret, too, that I had sold my toy town to this destroyer of miniature homes.

"At last the toy house crumbled into red-hot ashes, Mr. Burton; and the old man, who all this time had been stretching his hands over the blaze, once more turned to me with an air of great triumph.

"'You see I'm not old-fashioned!' he cried with a high, neighing laugh. 'No—I keep abreast of the times, although I'm so dingy. Who cares about yesterday's doings? We want a peep into the minute ahead, not the minute behind. Do the little figures of wood go with the town?'

"'Yes,' I answered sourly. 'As perhaps you know, each is supposed to represent some one in Prestonville.'

"'And are you included?' he asked, half closing his dull, fishy eyes. 'Did you sell yourself as well as the others?'

"'I suppose you'll find the wooden manikin of me in the collection.' I muttered, 'unless it was burned up in that little house.'

"'How could that happen?' he said pleasantly. 'You've been in this shop all the time. No, not a soul was burned but your mother-in-law. Here she is, sir,' he continued with a grin, holding up for my inspection a tiny charred figure of wood. 'Burned to a cinder, you see! Well, you won't miss her much.'

"And then I smiled weakly, Mr. Burton. I was very much attached to Sally's mother, but I smiled, as almost any man smiles when his mother-in-law's name is coupled with tragedy.

"'Of course, I won't miss her much,' I answered, with quite the conventional air of gay unconcern.

"'Well, that's lucky,' he went on, stroking some more crumbs out of his beard; 'for, as you can see for yourself, she's well toasted. Not that it makes one iota of difference to me whether you miss her or not,' he added fiercely. 'To be quite candid, young man, I'm neither very intelligent nor very kind-hearted, and I don't pretend to be, although there are optimistic fools in this world who call me both.'

"'Indeed?' I said politely.

"'Yes,' he continued, 'they think I sit up at night trying to better the human race—I, who have so many amusing things to do. There are people who imagine I'm a cousin of Santa Claus.'

"'Once removed or far removed?' I said.

"At that he began to snicker, Mr. Burton, in a most unpleasant way.

"'I wish I could think up bright things like that,' he said after a time. 'Far removed, I'd call it. But seriously, young man, I often kick those fools in the face just to see what they'll do; and, bless me, if they don't come crawling back on all fours to lick my boots!'

" 'You're a stranger to me,' I broke in. 'I thought I knew by sight every soul in town. Where are you staying?'

"For answer he bent over the toy town and touched with his finger a house which stood a little apart from the others.

" 'Preston Mansion!' I cried in surprise. 'Why, that hasn't been lived in for twenty years—not since old Colonel Preston cut his throat.'

" 'I live in it,' he said simply.

" 'But it's in a deplorable state of disrepair,' I ventured.

" 'So am I,' he rejoined. 'We're good company for each other.'

" 'But the roof's never been shingled since it got hit by lightning two summers back. It can't keep out the rain.'

" 'I'm living under that roof, not you!' he replied sharply. 'It suits me.'

" 'I'm sure I didn't mean any offense,' I said. 'Shall I have the toy town sent there tomorrow morning?'

" 'No, no!' he cried irritably. 'I'll call for it when I want it. None of your impudence, young man!'

"And at that he shuffled out of my shop, Mr. Burton, without so much as a good night, leaving me fairly dumbfounded. Nothing that I had said could possibly have given offense to the most sensitive person; yet he had left me in high dudgeon. Later I came to learn that he was always like that toward the end of our talks. It wasn't anything that had passed between us, but just a natural weariness of my society— the same irritability that a child shows when he is forced to stay indoors with his nurse. Indeed, that terrible old man was very much like a spoiled child in a great many ways—his love of excitement; his pure joy in destroying objects of value; his fickleness; and, lastly, his down-right fury if he was opposed in anything."

"Possibly," I assented. "But why do you call such a harmless old lunatic terrible?"

"I'm coming to that, Mr. Burton," the shopkeeper replied, with a calm which I could see was forced for my benefit.

"Let me get on in my own way, and then you can judge for yourself. As I have said, he left me with all my wits all astray, gaping behind the counter; and it was there one of the neighbors found me a few minutes later.

" 'Come, come!' he cried, shaking me by the arm. 'There's been a fire up at your place. Your wife wants you.'

" 'A fire!' I cried, coming to myself with a start. 'My house?'

" 'Burned to the ground,' he answered shortly. 'But that isn't the worst of it. Your wife's all broken up, and you must go to her at once. She needs you!'

" 'And Sally's mother?' I cried weakly. 'She's safe?'

"The man shook his head sadly.

" 'Lost, I'm afraid,' he murmured. 'She was the only one in the house when it caught fire, and they think the smoke must have suffocated her, for she hasn't been seen since. Your place was insured, I hope?'

"I made him no answer. Stepping to the show-window, I bent down and looked long and curiously at the ashes where once had stood my miniature house.

" 'It all happened here,' I muttered dully. 'It happened here before my eyes!'

" 'Come, come!' my neighbor said bruskly. 'Don't break down. Play the manly part. Your wife's the real sufferer, you know. After all, a mother-in-law is only a mother-in-law.'

" 'It all happened here,' I repeated stupidly, pointing at the toy town. 'Everything!'

"But he did not even so much as glance at the show-window. His eyes were on my right hand, which still grasped what the old man had given me.

" 'You're drunk!' he cried after a moment. 'Perhaps you'd better not go back to your wife in this condition.'

"All that I had gone through that evening, added to this final affront, made me see red.

" 'Drunk!' I cried, stepping forward. 'Why, you fool, I—'

"Unconsciously my right hand opened. From it dropped—not crisp thousand-dollar bills, but half a dozen chocolate creams wrapped up in a piece of tissue paper. The money that the old man gave me had all disappeared."

The shopkeeper regarded me wistfully. Evidently he still hoped that I might believe his improbable story. The train was once more slipping through the night, only now at a faster pace, to make up for the enforced delay. I could see nothing through the window but a curtain of moving blackness, could hear nothing but the monotonous lullaby of the revolving wheels; but I was vaguely conscious of the sky which overhung us, somber and threatening, like an immense, hovering hand.

"Well, what do you think?" he said at last, a trifle timidly.

"I think that you were badly frightened by a coincidence," I answered. "Of course, it was strange that the old man should have burned your house in miniature; but those things happen. I remember once—"

"How about my mother-in-law?" he broke in.

"Another strange coincidence—startling enough, I grant you."

"But can you explain how the money turned to chocolate creams?" he demanded.

"Well, as for that," I answered, "probably it was a sleight-of-hand trick. No doubt your mad old man was a practical joker with some knowledge of parlor legerdemain. Those fellows can fool even the brightest eyes, and you acknowledge that yours are weak."

"You have common sense," he said bitterly, "and all that I told you is an affront to it. You argue very much as I used to argue before I met that terrible old man for the second time and learned the truth."

"He came into your shop again?"

"Yes, a week after my mother-in-law's funeral. He came in just as my nephew went out. They must have met each other at the door. I can still remember the old man's first words as he hobbled up to the counter.

" 'I don't like that boy,' he said peevishly, his cold gray eyes fixed on my face. 'He aggravates me.'

" 'That's a pity,' I answered ironically.

"You must know that I was very fond of my sister's son, Mr. Burton. There wasn't a cheerier, better-natured boy in Prestonville than Charlie, though I say it myself. He was a bit mischievous, perhaps, but there was no malice in it. He was a real boy who showed that he was glad to be alive.

" 'No, I don't like him,' the old man continued, plucking irritably at his tangled beard. 'He's happy—entirely too happy. Why, the little fool goes hopping about this town like a canary! When he isn't whistling he's grinning like an idiot. The way he acts, you wouldn't think that I existed. He ignores me, and that's the truth of the matter—me, whom nobody should ignore.' He paused and twitched a gray hair savagely out of his beard. 'Besides,' he finished, 'I can't abide round-eyed, apple cheeked boys! Can you?'

" 'I'm very fond of Charlie,' I answered warmly. 'Of course, he's happy. Why shouldn't he be? He's strong and healthy.'

" 'Strong and healthy, eh?' the old man cried, with one of his unpleasant snickers. 'Well, that can be mended. Have you any toy trolley-cars in your shop—the kind that you wind up and run?'

" 'Yes, I have several,' I answered; 'but what do you want with one?'

" 'Never you mind,' he said with a sly wink. 'Never you mind, sir. Perhaps I'm buying it for Charlie. When I don't like children, I buy them toys—not at all like Santa Claus, you see!'

"Now, Mr. Burton, he was grinning at me so slyly, with his beard ruffled out like the tail of a turkey-cock, and his eyes shifting from side to side, that, in spite of the strange fear I had of him, it was all I could do to keep from bursting out into a laugh. Here was this mummy of a man puttering about my shop like a child of ten. A toy trolley-car, indeed!

"And yet there was a childish sincerity about him, an eager curiosity to see the stock of toys, which stroked my business pride the right way. There he stood as I brought out my supply of cars, bending forward in wonder, and actually sucking his thumb.

" 'Here they are,' I said from between twitching lips.

" 'A nice assortment,' he said gravely; 'a very pretty lot of trolley-cars. Now I wonder which would be best suited for Charlie. Let's see!' He bent lower still, so that his gray beard brushed the counter. 'I rather fancy this one without a fender,' he muttered. 'It looks more businesslike than the others. Do you wind it up with a key?'

" 'Yes, here's the key,' I answered, holding it out to him. 'And there's where it winds up, right behind the rear seat. Do you want to see it run?'

" 'Indeed I do,' he said eagerly. As he spoke, he picked up the toy and began to wind it. His beard twitched with excitement, and he hopped about as nimbly as a goat. 'This is what I call fun!' he cried.

" 'Put it on the counter,' I suggested. 'It'll run about there all right.'

"He shook his head.

" 'No, no,' he said. 'That's silly. Who ever heard of a trolley-car running on a counter? There's just one place for it. Look here!'

"And as quick as thought, Mr. Burton, he skipped over to the window and placed the trolley-car on one of the streets of my toy town.

" 'Here's the place for it—right on Main Street!' he cried joyously. 'Now I'll let her go. Ding dong! All aboard!'

" 'It will do damage there,' I told him, stepping forward. 'There are people on that street. It will break all my manikins. Stop it!'

"But I was too late. Before I reached the window, the toy trolley-car had bowled over one of the little wooden figures and had smashed both its tiny legs.

" 'Now see what you've done!' I cried angrily, as the old man picked up the manikin in the palm of his hand. 'I must ask you to leave my show-window alone in the future. That's no way to treat toys!'

" 'They're mine, aren't they?' he demanded innocently. 'Didn't I buy your town, with everything in it?'

" 'No, you didn't,' I retorted. 'If you think a handful of chocolate creams paid for this artistic miniature of Prestonville, you've got another guess coming.'

" 'Chocolate creams?' he said, with a puckered brow. 'Chocolate creams? Did I pay you with chocolate creams?'

" 'You did!' I answered hotly. 'What good are they?'

" 'Why, chocolate creams are good to eat,' he answered solemnly, staring at me like an owl. 'You should consider yourself lucky, young man. There are people who would pay more than five thousand dollars for a handful of chocolate creams.'

" 'Nonsense!' I cried, quite out of temper. 'If you think—'

"But he cut me short with a wave of his hand.

" 'Now you speak about it,' he said blandly, 'I do remember about the chocolate creams. You must know that it was one of my little jokes. I'm not very intelligent, but I've a keen sense of humor. It happened that there was a young man who got lost in the Maine woods last week. He had five thousand dollars and six chocolate creams in his pocket. For days he wandered about in a circle, till his provisions were all gone. He grew very hungry. The five thousand dollars were no good to him; but the chocolate creams!' The old man broke off to snicker, while his cold shifty eyes wandered here, there, and everywhere. 'Those chocolate creams would have kept life in his bones till his friends found him,' he finished with a grin.

" 'Well?' I demanded.

" 'Well, sir,' he replied, 'I took those chocolate creams out of his pocket while he slept, and gave them to you in place of the five thousand dollars. You see, they were very precious chocolate creams—

to him. That poor man died of starvation four days ago. Now doesn't that prove that I have a keen sense of humor, sir?'

"It was an extremely warm day; and yet, in spite of the heat, I felt cold. For the first time, Mr. Burton, a real tangible terror of that old man took possession of me. As I have told you, he was not so mad as not to be vicious; and now his white, wrinkled face was convulsed with a malicious merriment. Once more, in my imagination, it had become the mask of flesh which had stared through my show-window— that thin mask without human substance behind it, which might be worn in turn by all evil emotions.

" 'If you really did such a thing,' I said at last, 'it shows a strange kind of humor!'

" 'Strange it may be,' he answered sourly, 'but it's mine.' He drew out his bulging wallet and put five thousand dollars on the counter. 'It seems that you were not satisfied with chocolate creams,' he added. 'Well, there's no suiting everybody. Here's the money. You'd better count it carefully this time, for I've come to carry the toy town away with me.'

"It is needless to tell you, Mr. Burton, that I acted on his suggestion. I counted the bills three times, and then locked them in my safe. Next, at his bidding, I packed up the toy town in a large leather case and helped him carry it to the door; but here I paused.

" 'How about the trolley-car?' I asked. 'Don't you want that, too?'

" 'No, young man,' he answered, with a solemn shake of his head. 'I have no further use for trolley-cars at present. Perhaps some other day. We'll see, we'll see. Meanwhile you can give this one to Charlie, with my compliments. It will make him remember me in the future. A souvenir of our meeting in your shop, eh? Good evening, sir.'

"Frail as he looked, he picked up the leather case as easily as if it were filled with feathers. Indeed, he was surprisingly strong for a man of his age.

" 'I find you rather amusing company, young man,' were his final words to me. 'Drop in some evening at Preston Mansion. You'll always find me at home.'

" 'Whom shall I ask for?' I inquired.

" 'Mr. Fate,' he said, grinning up at me from beneath his ragged hat-brim. 'Mr. L. P. D. Fate, at your service.'

"For some time after he had left me I stood on the door-sill, following his bent, crooked figure with my eyes. Finally it vanished in a crowd that had gathered on the corner of Main Street and Sanford Avenue. Then I heard the clatter of horses' feet and the brazen clanging of a bell. A moment later the Prestonville ambulance swept past my shop, the horses' shoes striking sparks on the pavement.

"An accident, I thought, not without a sensation of personal fear.

"Snatching my hat from the rack, I hurried up the street and was soon in the midst of a horrified group. Not a dozen yards further on a trolley-car had been deserted by both motorman and conductor, and stood motionless on the tracks. Contrary to the law, the car had no fender.

" 'Who's been hurt?' I asked an acquaintance who stood on the outskirts of the crowd.

"For a moment, Mr. Burton, this man didn't recognize me. When he did his face took on a frightened look.

" 'Push your way through, Jim,' he told me. 'You've got a right to see. It's your nephew, Charlie Carey. He was hit by that trolley. The poor kid. Both his legs are smashed to a pulp.'

"I waited to hear no more. Pushing my way through the crowd, quite overmastered by horror and grief, I would have been by Charlie's side in another moment, had not a long, thin hand reached out and plucked me by the sleeve.

" 'It's Mr. Fate,' a low, insinuating voice whispered in my ear. 'Mr. L. P. D. Fate, at your service. Don't you forget him, young man. It doesn't pay to forget Mr. Fate!'

"And then I saw that terrible old man at my elbow. There he stood, grinning up at me, his cold gray eyes fixed on my face, his left hand outstretched and holding in its palm a little broken figure of wood.

"Suddenly he pocketed his toy and turned away.

" 'Don't you forget Mr. Fate, young man,' he called back over his shoulder. 'Home every evening—Preston Mansion—Mr. L. P. D. Fate!'

"His voice died away; he was gone. And I? Why, a new horror had overmastered me—a horror of the old man's tangled beard; a horror of his cold, fishy eyes; and, worst of all, a horror of his shriveled, claw-like hands. Yes, I feared his hands the most. What were they not capable of, those hands? Guided by a brain—a little mad, you understand, but not so mad as not to be vicious—surely they gripped the world and spun it at their pleasure. This old man's talons held the throat of strangling humanity in their grasp. Only twice had I seen them at their work, but I wanted no more proof. I was convinced of their power, Mr. Burton!"

The shopkeeper paused to light his cigar, which had gone out. Once again I noticed the uncertainty of his every movement. I had seen drunken men, or men heavy with sleep, fumble with a match before striking it in just such a fashion.

Indeed, there was something of the somnambulist about my traveling companion. His acts did not seem to spring from the promptings of his own brain; it was as if he obeyed another's orders. He reminded me forcibly of a famous murderer whom I had interviewed a month before for my paper. Yes, that condemned poisoner had had exactly the same manner—the irresolute gestures, the trick of yawning unexpectedly, the terror and weariness of the eyes.

"I suppose you think me mad?" he said at last.

"Not yet," I answered. "Of course, what you've told me seems unbelievable; but there may be some simple solution to the affair which we've both overlooked."

"No, no!" he cried impatiently. "There isn't any solution. Hear me out, and you'll see that for yourself."

"I'm all attention," I assured him.

"You can well imagine," he resumed, "that this second tragedy, coming hard on the heels of the first, shattered my peace of mind. From that time on I lived in constant fear of the old man; and yet, much as I feared him, much as I dreaded to see his face or hear his name, he exerted a peculiar fascination over me. Like many another fool, I longed to look into the eyes of the future. Preston Mansion beckoned my imagination.

"At first downright fear held this unhealthy curiosity in check; but gradually, as the days went by, the first horror of what I had seen wore off slightly, giving place to a burning desire to prove the mystery. Soon I began to haunt the streets at night."

"You visited Preston Mansion?" I broke in.

"Yes, frequently. I couldn't stay away, Mr. Burton. Night after night I stole out to the outskirts of town, where that old brick building stood somber and solitary. At first it would seem dark and deserted as I took my stand in the garden among the nodding weeds; but always, after I had been there a short time, one of the windows on the topmost floor would light up on a sudden, and a thin black shadow would pass back and forth across its glowing surface. Often this shadow would pause for an instant and bend down eagerly; and then I knew that something of moment was about to happen in Prestonville. It was terrible to stand there, Mr. Burton, and not know for certain what was happening behind that fire-flecked pane of glass."

"Didn't you ever go inside the house?" I inquired.

"Not until the old man called me. You see, I was afraid; but one night, as I stood in the garden, the front door swung open on its rusty hinges, and I saw him waiting for me in the hall. He held an old-fashioned taper above his head. Its light showed me that he wore a yellow nightcap and a disreputable velvet robe with rents in it.

" 'Don't be afraid, young man,' he called softly. 'Come in!'

" 'I'm not afraid,' I replied, stepping forward bravely, although my knees were fairly knocking together from fright. 'I'm cold from standing so long in your garden.'

" 'You've been patient, young man,' said he. 'There's no gain-saying that; but one has to be patient with L. P. D. Fate.'

"By this time, Mr. Burton, I was standing beside him in the hallway. The mansion was in a pitiable state of neglect. Cobwebs hung in long festoons from the rafters overhead; dust covered the floors and powdered the broad, winding staircase, lying nearly an inch deep on the carved mahogany balustrades; and behind the walls an army of rats scampered back and forth. A dismal odor of damp and decay filled my nostrils.

" 'The house seems a little old-fashioned, like me,' the old man said, giving me a suspicious sidelong look; 'but we're not old-fashioned—

neither of us. Ah, no—we keep abreast of the times. Come up to my room, young man.'

"He led the way up the staircase, while I followed close at his heels. Up and up he went, three flights or more, till we came to the attic. Here he ushered me into a large, bare room, lit dimly by two wax tapers and by the rays of the moon, which peeped in timidly through a hole in the roof; but I had eyes for nothing but the toy town.

"There it stood, Mr. Burton, on a large straw mat in the center of the room. Many changes had taken place since I had seen it last— changes, of course, which corresponded with the actual changes in Prestonville. For instance, there was the foundation of my new house standing where there had been a heap of ashes. Then there was the new public library, which had been built in record time; and, lastly, standing outside my sister's home, was the miniature of the wheel-chair in which poor Charlie managed to get about after his legs had been amputated. These were the details that caught my immediate attention.

" 'I haven't played very much with this town,' the old man said, sitting down on the dusty floor. 'Other matters have taken up nearly all my time. There was a steamer to be sunk in the Baltic Sea, an uprising to be arranged in China, some emperor to be assassinated— I can't think of his name now—and a thousand other amusing things to do. They kept me hopping about, I can tell you! But I mustn't grow lazy. I must amuse you.'

" 'Don't bother about me,' I said quickly. 'I don't need to be amused.'

" 'You are my guest,' he said rather sternly, 'and I always try to amuse my guests. Now how would a flood suit you, young man? The river seemed very high tonight. Floods are rather commonplace, of course; but still'—he rose and picked up a glass of water which stood on a table within arm's reach—'they're amusing. Don't you think so?' he finished, seating himself in front of the toy town and regarding me with childish solemnity.

" 'Don't,' I cried in horror, stretching out a detaining hand. 'Don't!' And then, seeing that he was tipping the glass in spite of my protests, I shouted, 'Floods are old-fashioned! Why, they date back to Noah's ark! Surely you wouldn't be as old-fashioned as that?'

" 'One grows tired of the new things,' he replied, with a sad shake of the head. 'I've had enough of trolley-cars and trains and steamers. Come, a flood isn't so bad!'

"And then, without another word to say on the matter, he tipped the tumbler more and more till the water spilled out of it in a thin stream and flowed straight toward the miniature town of Prestonville. In a moment more it was dashing down Main Street, sweeping one or two of the cardboard stores with it, threatening all. Fortunately the glass was only half-full, otherwise the inhabitants might very well have been drowned in their beds.

" 'Not enough water!' the old man cried peevishly. 'Well, that's a disappointment! Better luck next time. I'd go down and fill this tumbler at the pump, if the steps weren't so confoundedly steep. I'm not so spry as I was, young man.'

" 'I'm afraid I've got to be going,' I said, glancing up at the moon, which had grown gray and ghostly. 'It is morning.'

" 'So it is!' he cried angrily, as if I had insulted him. 'It's time you went home. Some guests fairly have to be turned out of doors! Get along now, you humbug, or I'll set my dogs on you!'

" 'You have dogs?' I cried in surprise, snatching up my hat.

" 'Hell-hounds,' he told me, 'that eat sulfur. Get along with you! Come later next time, and don't stay so early. I can't abide guests who think me old-fashioned.'

"Well, I hurried out of that house as fast as I could, keeping a wary lookout for any such beasts as he described; but I didn't see any. After a time I came to Main Street, which was a good two feet under water. Here it was that I found Charlie's wheel-chair floating peacefully along on its back; so I pushed it home ahead of me, to show my wife that I hadn't wasted the whole night. For the first of that week, we citizens of Prestonville wore rubber boots."

The shopkeeper broke off, and yawned prodigiously. I could see that he would be fast asleep in another moment if I didn't prod him out of it. As you may well guess, I was anxious to hear the rest of his strange story, and I lost no time in keeping him at it.

"Did you go back to Preston Mansion again?" I asked.

"What's that?" said he, coming out of his doze with a start. "I was almost asleep, sir. I've been like that lately. I simply can't keep awake. What were you saying, sir? Oh, yes, I visited Preston Mansion many times. Indeed, I couldn't seem to keep away from it. That large room on the top floor—that bare, dusty room where the moon peeped through a hole in the roof—drew me as a magnet draws steel. Night after night I sat on the floor beside the mad old man, and, sitting thus, watched him play with his toys.

"It was here that I saw the murder of Molly Adams in miniature— a crime which horrified the entire State. It was in this room that I witnessed the robbing of the Prestonville Bank, when one of the clerks was killed, the burning of the schoolhouse, the explosion at the gasworks which froze me with horror. But what could I do, Mr. Burton? I was powerless to turn him from his grim jests. Any word from me only drove him to a more brutal mishandling of his toys.

"And yet, in spite of Fate's cruelty, in spite of his wanton destruction of people and objects I held dear, there were times when I pitied him. Boredom sat heavy on his shoulders. You see, Mr. Burton, there was no game under the sun which he hadn't played a million times before. For centuries, no doubt, he had been playing the same savage tricks on his toys. To them, his vagaries were always new; but to him, they were as old as the stars. I knew that he felt the age and mustiness of all he did, and that it filled him with a kind of blind fury against the world. The savor of his brutal jests was gone; nothing remained but the dregs of laughter, which are even more bitter than the dregs of tears. And it was because he knew himself to be a decrepit, toothless tiger, unable to masticate with enjoyment the stale tidbits beneath his claws, that he rent so terribly cruelly whatever crossed his path.

" 'I'm not old-fashioned!' he was wont to say over and over again, as if to convince himself rather than me.

"Yes, relentless as he was, I often pitied Fate."

"But did he pity you?" I asked.

"No, pity was denied him. He lacked the imagination from which pity springs. I remember that last terrible night we spent together— the night when I knelt on the floor with tears gushing from my eyes.

" 'Pretty, pretty!' he gurgled like a baby, touching my cheek with an inquiring forefinger. 'Pretty, pretty—like diamonds!'

"You see, he simply didn't know the meaning of tears."

"Tell me about that last night," I said eagerly.

"Well, sir, it was a beautiful summer evening when I reached Preston Mansion. A full moon rode the heavens, casting its pale, silvery light on the dilapidated old house and the weed-choked garden. Not a breath of wind stirred the languid leaves of the maples. From the broad veranda I could see the roofs of Prestonville, faintly luminous in the distance. Never did the earth feel firmer underfoot; never did the well-being of the town seem so assured.

"On this last night, Mr. Burton, I hadn't long to wait. Hardly had I rapped gently on the door before it swung open and my host confronted me.

"At first glance I saw that trouble was brewing. For days he had been sulky and out of sorts, taking no interest in his toys, and sitting silently in a dark corner; but now this sullen brooding had given place to a forced gaiety, which was a sure sign of coming danger. Evidently he was contemplating some new atrocity.

" 'Come in, young man!' he cried, capering about in his ragged velvet robe like some kind of mad marionette. 'I've got a surprise for you. Come in!'

" 'What is it?' I asked, with the gloomiest apprehensions.

"But he gave me no answer—just skipped nimbly up the winding stairway, waving the taper gaily above his head. Soon he had ushered me into that bare attic room where, as I have told you, he kept the toy town spread out in perfect order on a straw mat. The moonlight streamed down upon it through the broken roof.

" 'I am tired of all these playthings,' the old man cried, pointing at the miniature of Prestonville with a wrathful forefinger. 'For days they have bored me to distraction. Never have I been so bored since I looked down on Pompeii. Those old Italians! Ah, I served them out for tiring me with their stupid arts and pompous pageantry! It seems only yesterday that I destroyed them and their city, yet it was many centuries ago.'

" 'What are you going to do to Prestonville?' I cried; and all the blood seemed to flow away from my heart, leaving it cold and dead.

"For answer he stooped painfully, so that his crooked back curved like a bent bow and his long, tangled beard brushed the floor. Following his every movement with dread and horror, I saw him pick up the corner of the straw mat between finger and thumb.

" 'What are you going to do to Prestonville?' I repeated dully.

" 'This, young man,' he murmured, shaking the mat very gently. 'This!'

"You can imagine what happened then, Mr. Burton. No sooner had he taken the corner of that mat between his fingers than I felt the solid floor shake beneath my feet. The whole room swayed dizzily from side to side, and the moon swung back and forth across the opening in the roof like the pendulum of a clock.

" 'Don't!' I cried, sinking on the floor and covering my eyes. 'Don't!'

When I looked again, Mr. Burton, the room was once more stationary; but the toy town of Prestonville! Ah, that had changed in those few brief moments beyond belief! Half the tiny houses were in ruins, and the rest were tottering on their foundations. My new home was still standing, but it was heavily listed to one side.

" 'Don't!' I cried, holding my clasped hands toward him in entreaty. 'Everything that I love is in that town!'

" 'An earthquake is both unusual and amusing,' he murmured, still holding one corner of the mat between finger and thumb. 'Don't be selfish, young man. I simply must be amused!'

" 'I pray you be merciful, Fate!' I cried in a breaking voice.

" 'Ah, yes!' he broke in hurriedly. 'Pray to me! I love to have people pray to me. Some of them have done it so well—Mark Antony, for instance. Let me hear you pray to Mr. Fate, young man!'

"And then a strange eloquence was vouchsafed me, Mr. Burton. Words, melodious and rich with feeling, flowed from my lips. It was as if the floodgates of restraint that bottle up a man's emotional outbursts had suddenly opened in my breast. To this day, I don't know what I said, or with what fine poetic imagery I clothed it all; but I do know that it pleased that terrible old man and made him wag his beard at me and smile.

" 'Very well put!' he cried when I had done. 'Mark Antony himself could hardly have improved it. You have gifts, young man!'

" 'I pray you be merciful, Fate!' I repeated.

" 'Merciful?' he cried irritably, with a sudden change of mood. 'Tut, tut, young man! How should I know what mercy is? No one has ever shown me any. Certainly my playthings haven't had mercy on me. No, they have bored me to distraction by their sameness. I can't die, remember, and I've got to live on endlessly in an immense shop through which millions of toys pass daily. Do you wonder that I destroy them when I find time? Mercy? Tut, young man!'

"And then, Mr. Burton, he gave the mat such a savage shake that the walls and the moon spun round and round like a top. When the room finally righted itself again, I saw that my worst fears had been realized. The miniature Prestonville had been destroyed. Not a house was left standing, with the single exception of Preston Mansion, which was lurching drunkenly to one side. It was as I looked at this desolate waste of ruin which so shortly before had been a thriving town, at my own home toppled over on the sidewalk, that tears arose up into my eyes and fairly blinded me—weak, womanly tears at my own impotency.

" 'Pretty, pretty!' muttered Fate, touching my wet cheeks with his callous forefinger. 'Pretty—like diamonds!'

"It was not until many days later that I came to realize that this terrible old man did not know the meaning of tears; that he took delight in them, like a baby, because they were bright and shining. At the time I thought he was mocking me, and I cursed him from my heart. I cursed him, Mr. Burton, as I don't believe any other man has ever cursed Fate. My tongue fairly flamed with invectives. I cursed his cold, fishy eyes, his beard all gritty with bread-crumbs, his vibrating, claw-like hands. I cursed his youth in the days when the world was young, and his old age when the world would be dying. I cursed him by all his names together—Luck, Providence, Destiny, Fate—and by each one singly. And when I had done, Mr. Burton, when my throat had gone dry of words, I found him grinning.

" 'Well done, young man!' he said, with his head on one side. 'You curse even better than you pray. I can't think of anybody who has so spoken up to me since Judas Iscariot on the day when he hanged himself. He had a scorpion for a tongue, did Judas! You did very creditably, young man. You actually succeeded in amusing me. I feel that I should reward you. What would you have of me, young man?'

" 'Nothing!' I cried, half out of my mind from grief. 'Treat me as you do the rest of mankind—carry me around in your pocket.'

" 'Not a bad idea!' said he, once more bending his crooked back over the ruins of the town. 'So that's what you want, is it?'

" 'I want nothing from you,' I told him coldly.

"He paid me no heed—just began to grope about with his long, thin fingers in the only house that still was standing. At last, with a shrill, neighing laugh, he pulled through one of the open windows a tiny wooden figure and held it toward me in the palm of his hand.

" 'Here you are!' said he. 'You came out of this business without a scratch. So you want to go into old Fate's pocket, do you? Well, I must warn you that it's dark in there. Your ambition may fall asleep.'

" 'Ambition?' I cried in despair. 'My ambition is buried under this town!'

" 'Very well,' said he, cocking his beard at me whimsically. 'You're safe in my pocket—at least, for a time.' He paused and regarded me steadily with his cold gray eyes. 'I'm essentially honest,' he continued, 'and so I'm going to warn you again. Good-by until then, young man!' "

The shopkeeper again yawned, and his chin sank down on his breast.

Evidently he was on the very brink of sleep; but I had no intention of letting him doze off until he had told me the rest of his story. I bent forward and touched him on the arm.

"And then what happened?" I asked.

"Why, then he slipped the little wooden figure into his pocket and went out through the open door. I've never seen him again since that night, Mr. Burton."

"But what did you do?"

"I knelt on the dusty floor of that attic for a long, long time, quite alone with the ruins of my toy town. Nothing seemed to matter very much any more, Mr. Burton. It was as if I had been suddenly plucked out of life, as if its happiness and suffering were as remote as the stars. Later, even the real town of Prestonville failed to move me—that tragic heap of shattered masonry beneath the paling moon. Everything had died in my breast but fear—fear of the mental darkness which now enshrouded me, fear of that terrible old man whom I could no longer see, fear of that future time when Fate would drag me out of his pocket into the light of a relentless day. And so I have lived ever since—without love or ambition or hope. Only fear has remained, Mr. Burton!"

Once more the shopkeeper's chin sank on his breast and his brown eyes closed.

"I'm so tired!" I heard him mutter fretfully.

Far ahead, around a distant bend, I saw a glow in the murky sky which informed me that I should soon reach my destination. A few minutes more and the train would pull into Fairview. The light came from a factory on the brow of the hill above the town.

Turning from the window, I started picking up my belongings. Suddenly I saw something which caused a cold thrill to run up my spine. While I had been staring out at the landscape, an old man had noiselessly entered the smoking-compartment. He now sat beside the sleeping shopkeeper, peering into a large cardboard box that rested on his bony knees. I noticed, with an involuntary shudder, that this old man's long, tangled beard was sprinkled with bread-crumbs, which dangled from it like berries in a bush.

"What have you got there?" I asked.

"Toys," he said with a snicker. "Do you want to see them?"

Not waiting for my response, he put his hand into the box and pulled out a toy train. Next he drew forth a coil of tin tracks, and placed them on the floor.

"Do you want to see it work?" he asked, winding the engine as he spoke. "I love toy trains! Don't you?"

"Yes, of course," I answered, glancing hastily at the shopkeeper, who was still sleeping peacefully; "but I'm leaving at the next station and I'm afraid I won't have time to see it work."

"Yes, you will, young man!" he cried excitedly. "Oh, yes, you will! I'm going to start it now!"

In spite of my common sense, I felt a sudden flicker of fear as he got painfully down on his hands and knees and placed the toy train on the tracks. A moment later it started off. Faster and faster it went.

"It's going to smash!" I heard him mutter in a strange sing-song voice. "It's going to smash!"

But it didn't—not that time, at least. Slowing down at the last vicious curve, even as the train which carried us was doing now, it came to a shivering halt.

Before it had fairly stopped, the old man seized the engine and began winding it savagely. Then, glancing slyly at the sleeping shopkeeper, he felt in his pocket and pulled out a little wooden figure. This he carefully inserted through a window of the first toy car, and replaced the engine on the tracks.

By now we had reached Fairview. Pushing past the old man, I hurried out of the smoking-compartment.

I have little more to add. All of you, no doubt, still remember the glaring headlines in the morning papers, telling of the most disastrous railroad wreck that this country had ever known—how that ill-fated train, while making up time between Fairview and Forest Point, was derailed by a tree-trunk which had fallen across the tracks, and pitched over a hundred-foot embankment; and how every man, woman, and child aboard met an almost instantaneous death.

But the old man—what of him? He was not among the charred bodies taken from the burning train.

Of late I have been thinking that perhaps that unfortunate shopkeeper was not so mad; that Fate may indeed wear a human guise while he stalks someone among us. If this is so, surely it was he whom I met that night as the train drew into Fairview! Fate, an old man playing with toys like a child of ten—a mad old man who is not so mad as not to be vicious! Truly a terrible thought!

But there is another thought, more terrible still, which of late has plagued me sorely. How was it that I came to escape that night? Yet did I actually escape? Perhaps, after all, I have not slipped through those eager, groping fingers—perhaps that merciless old man has merely dropped me into a ragged pocket, to play with me at his leisure. Yes, I feel that he can still hold me at will in the hollow of his hand.

Long ago, like the shopkeeper, I lost love and hope and ambition. Now, of all human emotions, only fear remains—the fear of a rat in a trap when it hears its jailer's footsteps approaching—the fear of a fly in the threatening shadow of a descending hand.

And yet, as I draw back with a shudder, as I look about hopelessly for some means of escape, a merciful drowsiness descends upon me, calming the wild, tumultuous beating of my heart. Yes, all my senses are engulfed in a sea of tranquil dreams. Yawning, I stretch my arms above my head and yawn again. Surely this must mean the beginning of the end. I, too, am in Fate's pocket!

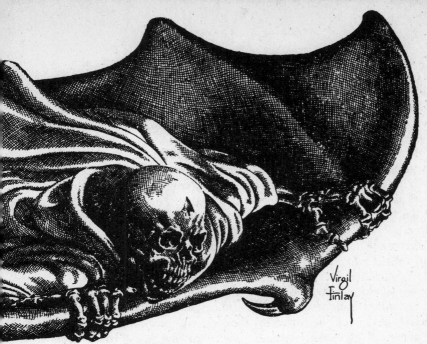

The Counter Charm

MARGARET ST. CLAIR

Margaret St. Clair led a double life in fantasy. Under her own name, she was known as a frequent contributor to Startling Stories, Fantastic Adventures, *and the last issues of* Weird Tales. *Under the alias Idris Seabright, she published a number of droll and literate fantasies in* The Magazine of Fantasy and Science Fiction, *including an excellent homage to Lord Dunsany, "The Man Who Sold Rope to the Gnoles." "The Counter Charm" was one of three stories she sold to* Famous Fantastic Mysteries, *and one can only wonder if its portrayal of the bad blood between a pulp editor and an illustrator was based in fact.*

LOUSY MONSTERS, Sanderson said critically. He leafed once more through the latest issue of *Glowing Skull Magazine.* "The backgrounds are no good, either. I don't say it just because they're our competitors, but this new artist of theirs stinks."

Mopsa Hansen, his assistant, stretched out her plump hand for the magazine. She studied it, twisting absently at her wedding ring. "Oh, I don't know," she said after a minute. "He can't draw, of course, and his composition is no good, but you've got to admit he has a sort of talent for weird atmosphere. Those trees like mushrooms, and the way the grass or whatever it is looks half-alive. I bet most of the fantasy fans go for him. And the teeth on his monsters really frighten me."

Sanderson sneered. His Adam's apple bobbed up and down. "He not only can't draw, has no sense of composition, and adopts a fiendishly repulsive tonality," he said with relish, "he has a general lack of taste that would sicken a billy goat. He's not just inept, he's bad on purpose. Poisonously, viciously bad. I don't know when I've seen work I dislike so much. If he ever has the crust to submit a picture to *Unearthly Tales,* I'll send it back to him so fast his art gum eraser will hurt."

"Poor old Sandy," Mopsa said indulgently, "you're too aesthetic for your own good." She opened a tin of butterscotch and popped three or four of the candies into her mouth. "You can't seem to realize," she said in muffled tones, "that being art editor of a weird fiction magazine isn't Art. Sit on your ideals, boy. You're only here to please the customers."

Sanderson made no reply. After a moment he picked up the copy of *Glowing Skull Magazine* and flipped through it once more. And once more he sneered.

Some two weeks later George Blades, Editor-in-Chief of Publex Publications, called Sanderson into his office.

"Sanderson, old chap," he said after the requisite preliminary remarks had been made, "I want you to meet Jabez Ordway. Mr. Ordway, this is Angus Sanderson, our art editor."

Sanderson shook hands with Ordway gingerly. He disliked the man on sight. Ordway had light, piggish eyes, a flabby handclasp, and a form which reminded Sanderson of mashed potatoes which have been made into rosettes by being forced through a pastry tube. As a final touch the man was wearing dark green knee breeches. Where did Blades pick up these people, anyhow?

"Ordway is the new chap who's been doing those splendid drawings for *Glowing Skull,*" Blades went on. "No doubt you've noticed them." Sanderson stared.

"You'll be pleased to know, Sanderson, that as of today Ordway is doing all the art work for *Unearthly Tales.* It's an experiment which I am sure will be a satisfactory one. You and he will work very closely together."

Sanderson's jaw dropped. He turned red and made noises like strangling. His Adam's apple was throbbing incoherently.

Ordway gave a faint, pursy smile. He got a box from the pocket of his Norfolk jacket, opened it, and put something from it with his thumb in either side of his nose. After a moment he sneezed.

Sanderson found his voice. "Listen, George, could I speak privately to you for a minute?"

"If it's necessary, yes." George Blades did not look pleased.

"What's the big idea?" Sanderson demanded hotly when they were alone. "Who ever heard of one artist doing all the art work for a book?"

"It's an experiment, I told you."

"But he's lousy! I know his work, and it's terrible. He can't draw anything right except monsters' teeth."

Blades shrugged. "Frankly, Angus, I'm acting on orders from above. You know how Publex is and who owns it. I got a note from her today, couched in what you might call vigorous terms, telling me what to do with Ordway. She's a pretty shrewd business woman, so I don't suppose it'll hurt the circulation. The note said he was a cousin of hers, but my private opinion is that he's got something on her."

"But—am I Art Editor of *Unearthly Tales,* or not?"

"Today you're the art editor. Tomorrow—who can say?"

Sanderson winced. He knew he could get another job, probably a good one, but it might take time. Last week he had made a down payment on a choice wooded cabin site in Marina, and he had been planning to see an architect soon. If he resigned, he didn't know how long he'd have to wait.

"O.K.?" Blades asked, watching him.

"O.K."

Ordway proved unexpectedly easy to work with. Sanderson, who had decided to handle him with kid gloves, made his suggestions with laborious tact; Ordway listened, smiling faintly and taking snuff from time to time. The drawings, when he submitted them, were perhaps a shade less disgusting than those he had done for *Glowing Skull Magazine,* and in the matter of monsters, which were Sanderson's particular aversion, Ordway had been remarkably restrained. There were only two in the entire batch.

Sanderson was not as pleased by Ordway's tractability as he might have been. He disliked the man more for each time he set eyes on him. And the thought of the pages of *Unearthly Tales—his Unearthly Tales*—being defaced by Ordway's abominable drawings made him miserable. His stomach began bothering him. He got a bottle of anti-acid pills from the drug store, but they didn't help much. His depression increased as press time drew near. By the time the first copies of the December issue were coming off, his mood was so noticeable that Mopsa commented on it.

"What's the matter, Sandy? Ulcers getting started again? Or are knee breeches' drawings getting you down?"

"Mainly the drawings. Need you ask?"

Mopsa's smile vanished slowly. "He *is* nasty," she said as if to herself. "As nasty as his disgusting drawings are. A nasty, nasty little man." She gave her girdle a downward jerk.

"Has he been bothering you?" Sanderson asked suspiciously. He liked Mopsa, and had always had a brotherly attitude toward her.

"No—unh—" Mopsa hesitated. "I suppose I might as well tell you," she said. "He did make what you might call overtures. I pushed him away, and he said, 'My dear, you had better be careful. Have you ever hear of what Cagliostro did to women who displeased him? And his powers were nothing compared to mine. Now and then a fancy for plumpness takes me. I should advise you to be nice to me.' "

"Why, the nasty little squirt! I'll—"

"Take it easy, Sandy. I fixed him. I made the Horns at him, and told him if he bothered me again I'd sick grandmother on him." Mopsa's maternal grandmother was an Italian whose herbs, charms, and poultices were the wonder of her neighborhood. From what Mopsa had told him about the old lady, Sanderson had gathered that she was a white witch. "So now he gives me a wide berth. But he still bothers the other girls."

"Bothers them, does he?" Sanderson's face wore an expression of dour triumph. "Why, Mopsa, we've got him on toast. Even Mrs. Conner would fire him for that." Mrs. Conner was Publex Publishing Company's owner.

Mopsa shook her blond curls. "The girls are lots too scared to complain," she said. "He's got them all sold on the idea that he has some horrid occult power. They just try to keep out of his way."

"I'll beat up on him."

Again Mopsa shook her head. "Don't," she advised. "Most of us are married, and anyway, what I've been telling you would sound awfully, awfully queer in police court."

There was a defeated silence. Mopsa helped herself to a gum drop. Sanderson spoke at last. "Let's hope the readers don't like his work. If enough of them complain, Conner might transfer him to the staff of *Range Dreams*."

"Maybe. *If* enough of them complain."

Time passed. Ordway began work on the drawings for the issue after next, the April one. And the usual letters from the readers began coming in.

Sanderson's heart sank when the fiction editor gave the tabulation to him. Almost every letter this month had mentioned the new art work. About one person out of five had disliked it vehemently. The other four expressed attitudes ranging from tepid liking to actual enthusiasm.

It wasn't good enough. Sanderson went over to the window, raised it, and stood looking out and thinking. It wasn't good enough. Madeleine Conner would never transfer Ordway on the weight of such conflicting evidence. Knee breeches, occult powers, snuff and all, he was here to stay.

Of course Sanderson could resign. But the architect had already started on the plans for his cabin, and anyway resigning wouldn't solve the problem for Mopsa and the other girls. Ordway would still be around to pester and threaten them.

It began to get dark. The sky looked as if it might rain. Quitting time came. The office force left in the elevator. Sanderson stayed at the window, frowning and considering.

He had just decided that he might as well see about getting some dinner before it was too late, when the door opened and Ordway came in. He was carrying a portfolio under one arm. The knee breeches he was wearing were dull yellow ones.

"Hello, Sanderson," he said. "I happened to be in this part of town, and took a chance you wouldn't have left. I want you to O.K. these."

He handed the portfolio to Sanderson. Mechanically, the latter accepted and opened it.

His first reaction was of outrage. These drawings were terrible, worse than the worst Ordway had done for *Glowing Skull*. The backgrounds insulted the nose, the tonality had that gritty lack of contrast Sanderson found so maddening, and there was a monster in every one.

"But—but—" he stammered, too astonished to remember tact, "you've put monsters in all of them!"

"So I have," Ordway replied. "I like monsters. Mrs. Conner and I had a most interesting talk last week." He took the sheaf of drawings back from Sanderson and walked over to the window.

"But—Ordway, these monsters aren't well done. Their teeth are good, of course." Sanderson swallowed. Even this limited compliment was painful to him. "But their wings are too big, way out of scale. And their bodies don't articulate."

"What do you know about monsters?" Ordway asked in his high, insolent voice. "Have you ever seen one?" He was looking out the open window.

"No."

"Well, then, be quiet," Ordway said without turning. "As I told you, I've been talking to Mrs. Conner. Besides that, Sanderson, you'd better understand that it's not wise to vex me. I know some things to do with drawings and cut-out paper scraps. Unpleasant things. Unpleasant for you."

Sanderson inhaled. He had always hated Ordway. Now he was so angry he was trembling. Even then it might have been all right; he had every intention of leaving the room. But Ordway, still arrogantly keeping his back turned, spoke. "Take these, Sanderson. See that they get to the photoengraver tomorrow the first thing. Here." He flapped the sheaf of drawings at him.

The drawing on top featured a particularly badly drawn monster, an outsized lizard with pipestem legs and bat wings. It was standing in a dark and gritty landscape of exceptional repellency. At the sight of it, Sanderson felt a whir in his brain like that of an automatic calculating machine. Before he was even aware that he had moved, he had taken Ordway below the waist, lifted him up, and pitched him out over the window sill. The office was on the sixteenth floor. If Sanderson had had super acute hearing he might have heard, several seconds later, a squelchy plop.

The art editor sank down in a chair. After two or three minutes it occurred to him that he was a murderer. Shakily he put on his hat and coat and went out in the hall toward the emergency stairway. For obvious reasons he did not care to use the elevator.

The inquest went off beautifully. An elevator operator remembered bringing Ordway up. A key to the office door was found in the dead

man's pocket. Mopsa, without any prompting, testified that she and
Sanderson had gone down in the elevator together, about half past five.
Sanderson, doggedly perjuring himself, testified the same. Several witnesses spoke of Ordway's peculiar mannerisms, nervousness, eccentricity. The verdict of the coroner's jury included the words, "while of
unsound mind."

For a week or so Sanderson felt an enormous relief. He burned the
drawings Ordway had left, got in touch with his favorite artists, and
began happily planning the three full-page spreads for the next issue
of *Unearthly Tales*. His nervous indigestion stopped. Then he began
to have the dreams.

At first they were not so bad. Ordway's figure was unsubstantial and
tenuous, and it appeared only once in every two or three nights. But
as time went on he took to appearing more and more frequently, always
wearing his abominable yellow knee breeches, until Sanderson's dreams
were full of him. Sanderson began to drink coffee late at night, to
avoid his bed.

He thought of going to a psychiatrist. It must be his sense of guilt
over the murder which was causing the dreams. (If it could be considered
murder to kill a dirty, snuff-taking, breeches-wearing blackmailer like
Ordway.) But would a psychiatrist's professional ethics prevent his
turning a patient who admitted he was a murderer over to the police?
Sanderson felt it was too big a chance to take. He'd have to figure this
one out by himself.

The dreams went on. The dark circles under Sanderson's eyes turned
into pouchy brownish bags. Mopsa watched him with growing solicitude.
Late one Thursday afternoon, despite his resistance, she got him in a
corner and questioned him until she found out all about the dreams.

"We'll go see grandmother," she said briskly when he had finished.
"She's just wonderful at things like that."

"You don't think a psychiatrist—" Sanderson began hopefully.

"No, I don't. These dreams aren't caused by guilt for anything you've,
uh, done, Sandy. They're something else. Ordway was a nasty man,
and it's my belief he had some rather nasty powers."

Mopsa's grandmother lived at the end of the street car line in a
suburb where all the houses were alike. The old lady herself, though
she had a heavy moustache and a figure from which too much *pasta*
had eliminated the waistline, had retained such attractions of youth as
a velvety olive skin and fine dark eyes. Sanderson took to her and
trusted her at once.

"You no shoulda keel him," she said when the art editor had finished
his halting tale. "Falla like that more dangerous dead."

Sanderson jumped. He looked reproachfully at Mopsa. She shook
her blond head. "Grandmother always knows things," she said.

"Yes, yes," Mrs. Straglini replied emphatically. She spoke to Mopsa
in Italian for a moment. "Is not so bad," she said, addressing Sanderson
again. "Lotsa things worse than dreams."

The art editor quivered. "You mean you can't do anything to stop my dreams?" he asked.

Mrs. Straglini shrugged. "Coulda do things," she answered. "Notta good idea. Dreams no can hurt you. You getta use' to them."

There was a silence. Sanderson studied his fingernails. He was thinking of Ordway as he had seen him last night—pale faced, heavy jowled, obscenely ladling snuff into his nose with the flat of his thumb. And the look of malicious, hateful triumph in his little, piggish eyes—no, it wasn't possible. Sanderson couldn't get used to it.

"I—" he said. He halted to control his voice. "I haven't had any real sleep for three weeks. I've got to sleep some time. But I feel that I—that I'd rather die than go to sleep and see him standing there."

Mrs. Straglini looked at him keenly. After a moment, she nodded. "Ho Kay," she said. "Isa your funeral." She got up and walked out in the kitchen. In a few moments a very odd smell—burned, feathery, dusty and cloyingly sweet—began to float upon the air.

"What's she doing?" Sanderson asked Mopsa. A belated caution was stirring in him.

"Making a counter charm."

"Is that dangerous?"

"Not usually." Mopsa twisted the wedding ring on her plump left hand. "But you see, Sandy, Ordway got in on the ground floor. Grandmother's trying to make a barrier against him, and it'll be all right unless he's able to sort of short circuit it. In that case, he'd have all the power that was in the counter charm to draw upon. Magic is a little like judo—you use your opponent's power to disable him."

"Um. I see."

"But don't use the charm unless you have to, Sandy."

"I won't."

Mopsa's grandmother came back from the kitchen. She carried a very small bottle in one hand and a red flannel bag in the other. She put the bottle in the bag, tied it up, and handed it to Sanderson. He examined it wonderingly.

"Poot ina pocket of da night shirt," Mrs. Straglini explained. "No more dream."

Sanderson got out his billfold. She repulsed him with a magnificent gesture. "For frandship I do," she said. "Isa no charge."

"Will it really work?" Sanderson asked Mopsa when they were standing on the corner waiting for the street car. Freed of Mrs. Straglini's rather overwhelming presence, the likelihood of the charm's having any effect whatever had begun to seem remote to him.

"Oh, sure. If grandmother says no more dreams, no more dreams. But like I told you, it's dangerous. You never can tell with things like that. Don't use it unless you're really right at the end of your rope, Sandy."

Sanderson went to bed that night at about eight. He was too tired to eat, too tired even to mix himself a drink. He took a big dose of bicarbonate of soda and then put the red flannel bag carefully on the night stand beside his bed. He fell asleep almost at once.

He woke about twenty minutes later, covered with sweat. Ordway had been standing by the head of his bed grinning at him. Unhesitatingly Sanderson picked up the charm and put it in the breast pocket of his pajamas. He turned out the light.

This time, he slept wonderfully well. He awoke feeling fully rested and refreshed, with the consciousness that many hours had passed.

It was still dark, with only a faint light in the sky. Sanderson yawned and stretched and began to get out of bed. It was then that he realized that something was wrong.

He was not in his bed, he was not even in his bedroom. Though it was still too dark to make out details, he seemed to be standing on a sort of springy turf. Over his head was a lusterless and somehow gritty sky.

Divided between panic and disbelief, Sanderson looked about him. He was indubitably awake, and equally indubitably not where he usually woke up. Where was he, then?

With a haunting sense of familiarity he studied the sky, the turf, the bloated, spongy trees. That gritty, sooty texture, that deliberately taste-less arrangement of objects and planes—where had he seen them before? In—in—

No. Wait. It wasn't possible. He had seen them before in . . . in that last picture of Ordway's. The picture Ordway had been waving at him just before he . . . died. Somehow, Sanderson had got inside the picture.

Mopsa's grandmother's charm had backfired.

It *must* be a dream. Sanderson was still trying to convince himself of this when there came a sinister rustling in the brush behind him. Without a moment's hesitation, dream or no dream, Sanderson took to his heels. He stopped running only when he came up against a sort of glassy, invisible barrier which, he realized almost immediately, must be the picture's edge. He knew only too well what was chasing him.

It was the miserable sharp-toothed monster Ordway had drawn.

He had just begun to get his breath back when the rustle came again. Once more Sanderson ran. His heart was knocking against his ribs. Running, in the disgusting world that Ordway had limned, was an oddly exhausting feat. The clumps of spongy vegetation sucked at Sanderson's heels, and his body felt heavy and drawn-out. Ordway must have endowed his odious picture with greater than normal gravity.

How long would Sanderson be able to keep running? How much longer could he keep it up?

If day would only come! If he could see better he might be able to think what to do, how to get out of here. But as the rustle in the brush came time after time and the invisible monster continued its tireless pursuit of him, minutes lengthened into what must have been hours without any lightening of the sky. Sanderson realized with a dreadful sinking feeling that dawn would never come. The picture would stay as Ordway had created it, sunk in its leaden gritty gloom, forever and ever. World without end.

He was tiring now. The slithering noise in the bushes no longer roused him to instant activity. Pretty soon the monster—Sanderson tried to swallow with his dry throat—pretty soon the monster, the most hateful object in the hateful world Ordway had created, would overtake him at its leisure. Badly drawn as it was, it had a set of cruelly competent long white teeth.

There might be some way of getting out of the picture. But he was too thirsty, frightened and tired to even think of it.

He came at last to a brook, a sluggish sheet of ambiguous liquid Ordway had created with many scratches of the pen. No longer greatly caring whether the monster was gaining on him or not, Sanderson stooped to drink. He halted, terrified—more terrified than he had yet been. From the dim surface of the water a huge horned head was staring up at him.

Sanderson wheeled about with a hoarse cry. At first he did not understand. Trailing behind him in the sooty light were a long, scaly lizardlike tail, two wobbling pipestem legs. And on the back were folded ribbed, repulsive, rusty bat wings. His wings.

Sanderson began to run. He ran with the last of his strength, desperately, his tail trailing behind him, through the pulpy, bulbous hell Ordway had created for him. He stopped at last, shuddering with exhaustion. It was no use. He could not run away from himself. *He* was the monster in the picture. And he was in the picture to stay.

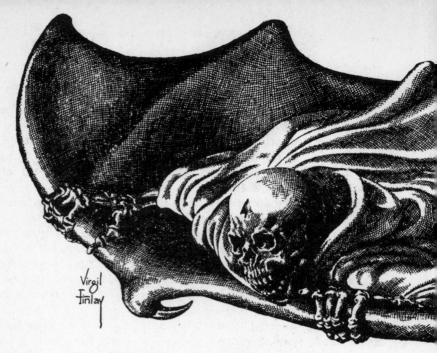

Virgil
Finlay

Guardian Angel

ARTHUR C. CLARKE

Arthur C. Clarke is one of that small group of science fiction writers who are actually scientists. His early work on radar and telecommunications satellites is reflected in novels like The Sands of Mars, Against the Fall of Night, *and* The Fountains of Paradise, *and the short stories "Dial F for Frankenstein" and "A Meeting with Medusa," all of which anchor their human dramas to hard scientific concepts. "Guardian Angel," which appeared in the April 1950 issue of* Famous Fantastic Mysteries, *was later published in Britain's* New Worlds, *one of the most important postwar science fiction magazines. In 1953, Clarke developed "Guardian Angel" into* Childhood's End, *the novel whose concepts ultimately gave birth to the 1968 blockbuster film* 2001: A Space Odyssey.

PIETER VAN RYBERG shivered, as he always did, when he came into Stormgren's room. He looked at the thermostat and shrugged his shoulders in mock resignation.

"You know, Chief," he said, "although we'll be sorry to lose you, it's nice to feel that the pneumonia death-rate will soon be falling."

"How do you know?" smiled Stormgren. "The next Secretary-General may be an Eskimo. The fuss some people make over a few degrees centigrade!"

Van Ryberg laughed and walked over to the curving double window.

He stood in silence for a moment, staring along the avenue of great white buildings, still only partly finished.

"Well," he said, with a sudden change of tone, "are you going to see them?"

"Yes, I think so. It usually saves trouble in the long run."

Van Ryberg suddenly stiffened and pressed his face against the glass.

"Here they are!" he said. "They're coming up Wilson Avenue. Not as many as I expected, though—about two thousand, I'd say."

Stormgren walked over to the Assistant-Secretary's side. Half a mile away, a small but determined crowd carried banners along the avenue towards Headquarters Building. Presently he could hear, even through the insulation, the ominous sound of chanting voices. He felt a sudden wave of disgust sweep over him. Surely the world had had enough of marching mobs and angry slogans!

The crowd had now come abreast of the building: it must know that he was watching, for here and there fists were being shaken in the air. They were not defying him, though the gesture was meant for him to see. As pygmies may threaten a giant, those angry fists were directed against the sky some fifty miles above his head.

And as likely as not, thought Stormgren, Karellen was looking down at the whole thing and enjoying himself hugely.

This was the first time that Stormgren had ever met the head of the Freedom League. He still wondered if the action was wise: in the final analysis he had only taken it because the League would employ any refusal as ammunition against him. He knew that the gulf was far too wide for any agreement to come from this meeting.

Alexander Wainwright was a tall but slightly stooping man in the late fifties. He seemed inclined to apologize for his more boisterous followers, and Stormgren was rather taken aback by his obvious sincerity and also by his considerable personal charm.

"I suppose," Stormgren began, "the chief object of your visit is to register a formal protest against the Federation Scheme. Am I correct?"

"That is my main purpose, Mr. Secretary. As you know, for the last five years we have tried to awaken the human race to the danger that confronts it. I must admit that, from our point of view, the response has been disappointing. The great majority of people seem content to let the Overlords run the world as they please. But this European Federation is as intolerable as it will be unworkable. Even Karellen can't wipe out two thousand years of the world's history at the stroke of a pen."

"Then do you consider," interjected Stormgren, "that Europe, and the whole world, must continue indefinitely to be divided into scores of sovereign states, each with its own currency, armed forces, customs, frontiers, and all the rest of that—that medieval paraphernalia?"

"I don't quarrel with Federation as an *ultimate* objective, though some of my supporters might not agree. My point is that it must come from within, not be superimposed from without. We must work out our own destiny—we have a right to independence. There must be no more interference in human affairs!"

Stormgren sighed. All this he had heard a hundred times before, and he knew that he could only give the old answers that the Freedom League had refused to accept. He had faith in Karellen, and they had not. That was the fundamental difference, and there was nothing he could do about it. Luckily, there was nothing that the Freedom League could do either.

"Let me ask you a few questions," he said. "Can you deny that the Overlords have brought security, peace and prosperity to the world?"

"That is true. But they have taken our freedom. Man does not live—"

"By bread alone. Yes, I know—but this is the first age in which every man was sure of getting even that. In any case, what freedom have we lost compared with that which the Overlords have given us for the first time in human history?"

"Freedom to control our own lives, under God's guidance."

Stormgren shook his head.

"Last month, five hundred bishops, cardinals and rabbis signed a joint declaration pledging support for the Supervisor's policy. The world's religions are against you."

"Because so few people realize the danger. When they do, it may be too late. Humanity will have lost its initiative and will have become a subject race."

Stormgren did not seem to hear. He was watching the crowd below, milling aimlessly, now that it had lost its leader. How long, he wondered, would it be before men ceased to abandon their reason and identity when more than a few of them were gathered together? Wainwright might be a sincere and honest man, but the same could not be said of many of his followers.

Stormgren turned back to his visitor.

"In three days I shall be meeting the Supervisor again. I shall explain your objections to him, since it is my duty to represent the views of the world. But it will alter nothing."

Rather slowly, Wainwright began again.

"That brings me to another point. One of our main objections to the Overlords, as you know, is their secretiveness. You are the only human being who has ever spoken with Karellen—and even you have never seen him. Is it surprising that many of us are suspicious of his motives?"

"You have heard his speeches. Aren't they convincing enough?"

"Frankly, words are not sufficient. I do not know which we resent more—Karellen's omnipotence, or his secrecy."

Stormgren was silent. There was nothing he could say to this—nothing, at any rate, that would convince the other. He sometimes wondered if he had really convinced himself.

It was, of course, only a very small operation from their point of view, but to Earth it was the biggest thing that had ever happened. There had been no warning, but a sudden shadow had fallen across a score of the world's greatest cities. Looking up from their work, a million men saw in that heart-freezing instant that the human race was no longer alone.

The twenty great ships were unmistakable symbols of a science Man could not hope to match for centuries. For seven days they floated motionless above his cities, giving no hint that they knew of his existence. But none was needed—not by chance alone could those mighty ships have come to rest so precisely over New York, London, Moscow, Canberra, Rome, Capetown, Tokyo. . . .

Even before the ending of those unforgettable days, some men had guessed the truth. This was not a first tentative contact by a race which knew nothing of Man. Within those silent, unmoving ships, master psychologists were studying humanity's reactions. When the curve of tension had reached its peak, they would reveal themselves.

And on the eighth day, Karellen, Supervisor for Earth, made himself known to the world; in perfect English. But the content of the speech was more staggering even than its delivery. By any standards, it was a work of superlative genius, showing a complete and absolute mastery of human affairs.

There was little doubt but that its scholarship and virtuosity, its tantalizing glimpses of knowledge still untapped, were deliberately designed to convince Mankind that it was in the presence of overwhelming intellectual power. When Karellen had finished, the nations of Earth knew that their days of precarious sovereignty were ending. Local, internal governments would still retain their powers, but in the wider field of international affairs the supreme decisions had passed out of human hands. Arguments, protests—all were futile. No weapon could touch those brooding giants, and even if it could, their downfall would utterly destroy the cities beneath. Overnight, Earth had become a protectorate in some shadowy, star-strewn empire beyond the knowledge of Man.

In a little while the tumult had subsided, and the world went about its business again. The only change a suddenly awakened Rip Van Winkle would have noticed was a hushed expectancy, a mental glancing-over-the-shoulder, as Mankind waited for the Overlords to show themselves and to step down from their gleaming ships.

Five years later, it was still waiting.

* * *

The room was small and, save for the single chair and the table beneath the vision-screen, unfurnished. As was intended, it told nothing of the creatures who had built it. There was only the one entrance, and that led directly to the airlock in the curving flank of the great ship. Through that lock only Stormgren, alone of living men, had ever come to meet Karellen, Supervisor for Earth.

The vision screen was empty now, as it had always been. Behind that rectangle of darkness lay utter mystery—but there too lay affection and an immense and tolerant understanding of mankind. An understanding which, Stormgren knew, could only have been acquired through centuries of study.

From the hidden grille came that calm, never-hurried voice with its undercurrent of humor—the voice which Stormgren knew so well though the world had heard it only thrice in history.

"Yes, Rikki, I was listening. What did you make of Mr. Wainwright?"

"He's an honest man, whatever his supporters may be. What are we going to do about him? The League itself isn't dangerous, but some of its more extreme supporters are openly advocating violence. I've been wondering for some time if I should put a guard on my house. But I hope it isn't necessary."

Karellen evaded the point in the annoying way he sometimes had.

"The details of the European Federation have been out for a month now. Has there been a substantial increase in the seven percent who disapprove of me, or the nine percent who Don't Know?"

"Not yet, despite the press reactions. What I'm worried about is a general feeling, even among your supporters, that it's time this secrecy came to an end."

Karellen's sigh was technically perfect, yet somehow lacked conviction.

"That's your feeling, too, isn't it?"

The question was so rhetorical that Stormgren didn't bother to answer it.

"Do you really appreciate," he continued earnestly, "how difficult this state of affairs makes my job?"

"It doesn't exactly help mine," replied Karellen with some spirit. "I wish people would stop thinking of me as a world dictator and remember that I'm only a civil servant trying to administer a somewhat idealistic colonial policy."

"Then can't you at least give us some reason for your concealment? Because we don't understand it; it annoys us and gives rise to all sorts of rumors."

Karellen gave that deep, rich laugh of his, just too musical to be altogether human.

"What am I supposed to be now? Does the robot theory still hold the field? I'd rather be a mass of cogwheels than crawl around the floor like a centipede, as some of the tabloids seem to imagine."

Stormgren let out a Finnish oath he was fairly sure Karellen wouldn't know—though one could never be quite certain in these matters.

"Can't you ever be serious?"

"My dear Rikki," said Karellen, "it's only by not taking the human race seriously that I retain those fragments of my once considerable mental powers that I still possess."

Despite himself, Stormgren smiled.

"That doesn't help me a great deal, does it? I have to go down there and convince my fellow men that although you won't show yourself, you've got nothing to hide. It's not an easy job. Curiosity is one of the most dominant human characteristics. You can't defy it forever."

"Of all the problems that faced us when we came to Earth, this was the most difficult," admitted Karellen. "You have trusted our wisdom in other things—surely you can trust us in this!"

"*I* trust you," said Stormgren, "but Wainwright doesn't, nor do his supporters. Can you really blame them if they put a bad interpretation upon your unwillingness to show yourself?"

"Listen, Rikki," Karellen answered at length. "These matters are beyond my control. Believe me, I regret the need for this concealment, but the reasons are—sufficient. However, I will try to get a statement from my superior which may satisfy you and perhaps placate the Freedom League. Now, please, can we return to the agenda and start recording again? We've only reached Item 23, and I want to make a better job of settling the middle question than my predecessors for the last few thousand years. . . ."

* * *

"Any luck, Chief?" asked van Ryberg anxiously.

"I don't know," Stormgren replied wearily as he threw the files down on his desk and collapsed into the seat. "Karellen's consulting his superior now, whoever or whatever he may be. He won't make any promises."

"Listen," said Pieter abruptly. "I've just thought of something. What reason have we for believing that there *is* anyone beyond Karellen? The Overlords may be a myth—you know how he hates the word."

Tired though he was, Stormgren sat up with a start.

"It's an ingenious theory. But it clashes with what little I do know about Karellen's background."

"And how much is that?"

"Well, he was a professor of astropolitics on a world he calls Skyrondel, and he put up a terrific fight before they made him take this job. He pretends to hate it, but he's really enjoying himself."

Stormgren paused for a moment, and a smile of amusement softened his rugged features.

"At any rate, he once remarked that running a private zoo is rather good fun."

"H'm-m—a somewhat dubious compliment. He's immortal, isn't he?"

"Yes, after a fashion, though there's something thousands of years ahead of him which he seems to fear: I can't imagine what it is. And that's really all I know."

"He could easily have made it up. My theory is that his little fleet's lost in space and looking for a new home. He doesn't want us to know how few he and his comrades are. Perhaps all those other ships are automatic, and there's no one in any of them. They're just an imposing facade."

"You," said Stormgren with great severity, "have been reading science-fiction in office hours."

Van Ryberg grinned.

"The 'Invasion from Space' didn't turn out quite as expected, did it? My theory would certainly explain why Karellen never shows himself. He doesn't want us to learn that there are no Overlords."

Stormgren shook his head in amused disagreement.

"Your explanation, as usual, is much too ingenious to be true. Though we can only infer its existence, there must be a great civilization behind the Supervisor—and one that's known about Man for a very long time. Karellen himself must have been studying us for centuries. Look at his command of English, for example. He taught me how to speak it idiomatically!"

"I sometimes think he went a little too far," laughed van Ryberg. "Have you ever discovered anything he *doesn't* know?"

"Oh, yes, quite often—but only on trivial points. Yet, taken one at a time, I don't think his mental gifts are quite outside the range of human achievement. But no man could possibly do all the things he does."

"That's more or less what I'd decided already," agreed van Ryberg. "We can argue around Karellen forever, but in the end we always come back to the same question—why the devil won't he show himself? Until he does, I'll go on theorizing and the Freedom League will go on fulminating."

He cocked a rebellious eye at the ceiling.

"One dark night, Mr. Supervisor, I'm going to take a rocket up to your ship and climb in through the back door with my camera. What a scoop *that* would be!"

If Karellen was listening, he gave no sign of it. But, of course, he never did give any sign.

*   *   *

It was completely dark when Stormgren awoke. How strange that was, he was for a moment too sleepy to realize. Then, as full consciousness dawned, he sat up with a start and felt for the light-switch beside his bed.

In the darkness his hand encountered a bare stone wall, cold to the touch. He froze instantly, mind and body paralyzed by the impact of the unexpected. Then, scarcely believing his senses, he kneeled on the bed and began to explore with his finger tips that shockingly unfamiliar wall.

He had been doing this for only a moment when there was a sudden 'click' and a section of the darkness slid aside. He caught a glimpse of a man silhouetted against a dimly lit background: then the door closed again and the darkness returned. It happened so swiftly that he saw nothing of the room in which he was lying.

An instant later, he was dazzled by the light of a powerful electric torch. The beam flickered across his face, held him steadily for a moment, then dipped to illuminate the whole bed—which was, he now saw, nothing more than a mattress supported on rough planks.

Out of the darkness a soft voice spoke to him in excellent English but with an accent which at first Stormgren could not identify.

"Ah, Mr. Secretary, I'm glad to see you're awake. I hope you feel all right."

The angry questions he was about to ask died upon his lips. He stared back into the darkness, then replied calmly, "How long have I been unconscious?"

"Several days. We were promised that there would be no after-effects. I'm glad to see it's true."

Partly to gain time, partly to test his own reactions, Stormgren swung his legs over the side of the bed. He was still wearing his night-clothes, but they were badly crumpled and seemed to have gathered considerable dirt. As he moved he felt a slight dizziness—not enough to be troublesome, but sufficient to convince him that he had indeed been drugged.

The oval of light slipped across the room and for the first time Stormgren had an idea of its dimensions. He realized that he was underground, possibly at a great depth. If he had been unconscious for several days he might be anywhere on Earth.

The torch-light illuminated a pile of clothes draped over a packing case.

"This should be enough for you," said the voice from the darkness. "Laundry's rather a problem here, so we grabbed a couple of your suits and half a dozen shirts."

"That," said Stormgren without humor, "was considerate of you."

"We're sorry about the absence of furniture and electric light. This place is convenient in some ways, but it rather lacks amenities."

"Convenient for what?" asked Stormgren as he climbed into a shirt. The feel of the familiar cloth beneath his fingers was strangely reassuring.

"Just—convenient," said the voice. "And by the way, since we're likely to spend a good deal of time together, you'd better call me Joe."

"Despite your nationality," retorted Stormgren, "I think I could pronounce your real name. It won't be worse than many Finnish ones."

There was a slight pause and the light flickered for an instant.

"Well, I should have expected it," said Joe resignedly. "You must have plenty of practice at this sort of thing."

"It's a useful hobby for a man in my position. I suppose you were born in Poland, and picked up your English in Britain during the War?

I should think you were stationed quite a while in Scotland, from your r's."

"That," said the other very firmly, "is quite enough. As you seem to have finished dressing—thank you."

The walls around them, though occasionally faced with concrete, were mostly bare rock. It was clear to Stormgren that he was in some disused mine, and he could think of few more effective prisons. Until now the thought that he had been kidnapped had somehow failed to worry him greatly. He felt that, whatever happened, the immense resources of the Supervisor would soon locate and rescue him. Now he was not so sure—there must be a limit even to Karellen's powers, and if he was indeed buried in some remote continent all the science of the Overlords might be unable to trace him.

There were three other men round the table in the bare but brightly lit room. They looked up with interest and more than a little awe as Stormgren entered. Joe was by far the most outstanding character—not merely in physical bulk. The others were nondescript individuals, probably Europeans also. He would be able to place them when he heard them talk.

"Well," he said evenly, "now perhaps you'll tell me what this is all about, and what you hope to get out of it."

Joe cleared his throat.

"I'd like to make one thing clear," he said. "This has nothing to do with Wainwright. He'll be as surprised as anyone else."

Stormgren had rather expected this. It gave him relatively little satisfaction to confirm the existence of an extremist movement inside the Freedom League.

"As a matter of interest," he said, "how did you kidnap me?"

He hardly expected a reply, and was taken aback by the other's readiness—even eagerness—to answer. Only slowly did he guess the reason.

"It was all rather like one of those old Fritz Lang films," said Joe cheerfully. "We weren't sure if Karellen had a watch on you, so we took somewhat elaborate precautions. You were knocked out by gas in the air-conditioner—that was easy. Then we carried you out into the car and drove off—no trouble at all. All this, I might say, wasn't done by any of our people. We hired—er—professionals for the job. Karellen may get them—in fact, he's supposed to—but he'll be no wiser. When it left your house, the car drove into a long road tunnel not a thousand kilometers from New York. It came out again on schedule at the other end, still carrying a drugged man extraordinarily like the Secretary-General. About the same time a large truck loaded with metal cases emerged in the opposite direction and drove to a certain airfield where one of the cases was loaded aboard a freighter. Meanwhile the car that had done the job continued elaborate evasive action in the general direction of Canada. Perhaps Karellen's caught it by now: I don't know.

"As you'll see—I do hope you appreciate my frankness—our whole plan depended on one thing. We're pretty sure that Karellen can see and hear everything that happens on the surface of the Earth—but unless he uses magic, not science, he can't see underneath it. So he won't know about that transfer in the tunnel. Naturally we've taken a risk, but there were also one or two other stages in your removal which I won't go into now. We may have to use them again one day, and it would be a pity to give them away."

Joe had related the whole story with such obvious gusto that Stormgren found it difficult to be appropriately furious. Yet he felt very disturbed. The plan was an ingenious one, and it seemed more than likely that whatever watch Karellen kept on him, he would have been tricked by this ruse.

The Pole was watching Stormgren's reactions closely. He would have to appear confident, whatever his real feelings.

"You must be a lot of fools," said Stormgren scornfully, "if you think you can trick the Overlords like this. In any case, what conceivable good would it do?"

Joe offered him a cigarette, which Stormgren refused, then lit one himself.

"Our motives," he began, "should be pretty obvious. We've found that argument's useless, so we have to take other measures. Whatever powers he's got, Karellen won't find it easy to deal with us. We're out to fight for our independence. Don't misunderstand me. There'll be nothing violent—at first, anyway. But the Overlords have to use human agents, and we can make it mighty uncomfortable for them."

Starting with me, I suppose, thought Stormgren.

"What do you intend to do with me?" asked Stormgren at length. "Am I a hostage, or what?"

"Don't worry—we'll look after you. We expect some visitors in a day or two, and until then we'll entertain you as well as we can."

He added some words in his own language, and one of the others produced a brand-new pack of cards.

"We got these especially for you," explained Joe. His voice suddenly became grave. "I hope you've got plenty of cash," he said anxiously. "After all, we can hardly accept checks."

Quite overcome, Stormgren stared blankly at his captors. Then it suddenly seemed to him that all the cares and worries of office had lifted from his shoulders. Whatever happened, there was absolutely nothing he could do about it—and now these fantastic criminals wanted to play poker with him.

Abruptly, he threw back his head and laughed as he had not done for years.

During the next three days Stormgren analyzed his captors with some thoroughness. Joe was the only one of any importance, the others were nonentities—the riffraff one would expect any illegal movement to gather round itself.

Joe was an altogether more complex individual, though sometimes he reminded Stormgren of an overgrown baby. Their interminable poker games were punctuated with violent political arguments, but it became obvious to Stormgren that the big Pole had never thought seriously about the cause for which he was fighting. Emotion and extreme conservatism clouded all his judgments. His country's long struggle for independence had conditioned him so completely that he still lived in the past. He was a picturesque survival, one of those who had no use for an ordered way of life. When his type had vanished, if it ever did, the world would be a safer but less interesting place.

There was little doubt, as far as Stormgren was concerned, that Karellen had failed to locate him. He was not surprised when, five or six days after his capture, Joe told him to expect visitors. For some time the little group had shown increasing nervousness, and the prisoner guessed that the leaders of the movement, having seen that the coast was clear, were at last coming to collect him.

They were already waiting, gathered round the rickety table, when Joe waved him politely into the living room. The three thugs had vanished, and even Joe seemed somewhat restrained. Stormgren could see at once that he was now confronted by men of a much higher caliber. There was intellectual force, iron determination, and ruthlessness in these six men. Joe and his like were harmless—here were the real brains behind the organization.

With a curt nod, Stormgren moved over to the seat and tried to look self-possessed. As he approached, the elderly, thick-set man on the far side of the table leaned forward and stared at him with piercing gray eyes. They made Stormgren so uncomfortable that he spoke first— something he had not intended to do.

"I suppose you've come to discuss terms. What's my ransom?"

He noticed that in the background someone was taking down his words in a shorthand notebook. It was all very businesslike.

The leader replied in a musical Welsh accent.

"You could put it that way, Mr. Secretary-General. But we're interested in information, not cash. You know what our motives are. Call us a resistance movement, if you like. We believe that sooner or later Earth will have to fight for its independence. We kidnaped you partly to show Karellen that we mean business and are well organized, but largely because you are the only man who can tell us anything of the Overlords. You're a reasonable man, Mr. Stormgren. Give us your cooperation, and you can have your freedom."

"Exactly what do you wish to know?" asked Stormgren cautiously.

"Do you know who, or what, the Overlords really are?"

Stormgren almost smiled.

"Believe me," he said, "I'm quite as anxious as you to discover that."

"Then you'll answer our questions?"

"I make no promises. But I may."

There was a slight sigh of relief from Joe and a rustle of anticipation went round the room.

"We have a general idea," continued the other, "of the circumstances in which you meet Karellen. Would you go through them carefully, leaving out nothing of importance?"

That was harmless enough, thought Stormgren. He had done it scores of times before, and it would give the appearance of co-operation.

He felt in his pockets and produced a pencil and an old envelope. Sketching rapidly while he conversed, he began:

"You know, of course, that a small flying machine, with no obvious means of propulsion, calls for me at regular intervals and takes me up to Karellen's ship. There is only one small room in that machine, and it's quite bare apart from a couch and table. The layout is something like this." As Stormgren talked, it seemed to him that his mind was operating on two levels simultaneously. On the one hand he was trying to defy the men who had captured him, yet on the other he was hoping that they might help him to unravel Karellen's secret. He did not feel that he was betraying the Supervisor, for there was nothing here that he had not told many times before. Moreover, the thought that these men could harm Karellen in any way was fantastic.

The Welshman conducted most of the interrogation. It was fascinating to watch that agile mind trying one opening after another, testing and rejecting all the theories that Stormgren himself had abandoned long ago. Presently he leaned back with a sigh and the shorthand writer laid down his stylus.

"We're getting nowhere," he said resignedly. "We want more facts, and that means action—not argument." The piercing eyes stared thoughtfully at Stormgren. For a moment he tapped nervously on the table—the first sign of uncertainty that Stormgren had noticed. Then he continued:

"I'm a little surprised, Mr. Secretary, that you've never made an effort to learn more about the Overlords."

"What do you suggest?" asked Stormgren coldly. "I've told you that there's only one way out of the room in which I've had my talks with Karellen—and that leads straight to the airlock."

"It might be possible," mused the other, "to devise instruments which could teach us something. I'm no scientist, but we can look into the matter. If we give you your freedom, would you be willing to assist with such a plan?"

"Once and for all," said Stormgren angrily, "let me make my position perfectly clear. Karellen is working for a united world, and I'll do nothing to help his enemies. What his ultimate plans may be, I don't know, but I believe that they are good. You may annoy him, you may even delay the achievement of his aims, but it will make no difference in the end. You may be sincere in believing as you do: I can understand your fear that the traditions and cultures of little countries will be overwhelmed when the World State arrives. But you are wrong: it is useless to cling to the past. Even before the Overlords came to Earth, the sovereign state was dying. No one can save it now, and no one should try."

There was no reply: the man opposite neither moved nor spoke. He sat with lips half open, his eyes now lifeless and blind. Around him the others were equally motionless, frozen in strained, unnatural attitudes. With a little gasp of pure horror, Stormgren rose to his feet and backed away toward the door. As he did so the silence was suddenly broken.

"That was a nice speech, Rikki. Now I think we can go."

"Karellen! Thank God—but what have you done?"

"Don't worry. They're all right. You can call it a paralysis, but it's much subtler than that. They're simply living a few thousand times more slowly than normal. When we're gone, they'll never know what happened."

"You'll leave them here until the police come?"

"No: I've a much better plan. I'm letting them go."

Stormgren felt an illogical sense of relief which he did not care to analyze. He gave a last valedictory glance at the little room and its frozen occupants. Joe was standing on one foot, staring very stupidly at nothing. Suddenly Stormgren laughed and fumbled in his pockets.

"Thanks for the hospitality, Joe," he said. "I think I'll leave a souvenir."

On a reasonably clean sheet of paper he wrote carefully:

BANK OF MANHATTAN
Pay "Joe" the sum of Fifteen Dollars
Thirty-five Cents ($15.35).
                              R. Stormgren.

As he laid the strip of paper beside the Pole, Karellen's voice inquired: "Exactly what are you up to?"

"Paying a debt of honor," explained Stormgren. "The other two cheated, but I think Joe played fair."

He felt very gay and light-headed as he walked to the door. Hanging just outside it was a large, featureless metal sphere that moved aside to let him pass. He guessed that it was some kind of robot, and it explained how Karellen had been able to reach him through the unknown layers of rock overhead.

"Carry on for a hundred yards," said the sphere, speaking in Karellen's voice. "Then turn to the left until I give you further instructions."

He ran forward eagerly, though he realized that there was no need for hurry. The sphere remained hanging in the corridor, and Stormgren guessed that it was the generator of the paralysis field.

A minute later he came across a second sphere, waiting for him at a fork in the corridor.

"You've half a mile to go," it said. "Keep to the left until we meet again."

Six times he encountered the spheres on his way to the open. At first he wondered if somehow the first robot had slipped ahead of him; then he guessed that there must be a chain of them maintaining a complete circuit down into the depths of the mine. At the entrance a group of guards formed a piece of improbable still life, watched over by yet another of the ubiquitous spheres. On the hillside a few yards away lay the little flying machine in which Stormgren had made all his journeys to Karellen.

He stood for a moment blinking in the fierce sunlight. As he climbed into the little ship, he had a last glimpse of the mine entrance and the men frozen round it. Quite suddenly a line of metal spheres raced out of the opening like silver cannon balls. Then the door closed behind him and with a sigh of relief he sank back upon the familiar couch.

For a while Stormgren waited until he had recovered his breath, then he uttered a single, heartfelt syllable:

"Well?"

"I'm sorry I couldn't rescue you before. But you'll see how very important it was to wait until all the leaders had gathered here."

"Do you mean to say," spluttered Stormgren, "that you knew where I was all the time? If I thought—"

"Don't be so hasty," answered Karellen, "or at any rate, let me finish explaining."

"It had better be good," said Stormgren darkly. He was beginning to suspect that he had been no more than the bait in an elaborate trap.

"I've had a tracer on you for some time," began Karellen, "and though your late friends were correct in thinking that I couldn't follow you underground, I was able to keep track until they brought you to the mine. That transfer in the tunnel was ingenious, but when the first car ceased to react, it gave the show away and I soon located you again. Then it was merely a matter of waiting. I knew that once they were certain I'd lost you, the leaders would come here and I'd be able to trap them all."

"But you're letting them go!"

"Until now," said Karellen, "I did not know which of the two billion men on this planet were the heads of the organization. Now that they're located, I can trace their movements anywhere on Earth. That's far better than locking them up. They're effectively neutralized, and they know it."

That rich laugh echoed round the tiny room.

"In some ways the whole affair was a comedy, but it had a serious purpose. It will be a valuable object lesson for any other plotters."

Stormgren was silent for a while. He was not altogether satisfied, but he could see Karellen's point of view and some of his anger had evaporated.

"Yes."

"It's rather small. Will you get one at least ten centimeters deep, and use it from now on so that he becomes used to seeing it?"

"Very well," said Stormgren doubtfully. "Do you want me to carry a concealed X-ray set?"

The physicist grinned.

"I don't know yet, but we'll think of something. I'll let you know what it is in about a month's time."

He gave a little laugh.

"Do you know what this all reminds me of?"

"Yes," said Stormgren promptly, "the time you were building illegal radio sets during the German occupation."

Duval looked disappointed.

"Well, I suppose I *have* mentioned that once or twice before."

*   *   *

Stormgren laid down the thick folder of typescript with a sigh of relief. "Thank heavens that's settled at last," he said. "It's strange to think that those few hundred pages hold the future of Europe."

Stormgren dropped the file into his brief-case, the back of which was now only six inches from the dark rectangle of the screen. From time to time his fingers played across the locks in a half-conscious nervous reaction, but he had no intention of pressing the concealed switch until the meeting was over. There was a chance that something might go wrong—though Duval had sworn that Karellen would detect nothing, one could never be sure.

"Now, you said you'd some news for me," Stormgren continued, with scarcely concealed eagerness. "Is it about—"

"Yes," said Karellen. "I received the Policy Board's decision a few hours ago, and am authorized to make an important statement. I don't think that the Freedom League will be very satisfied, but it should help to reduce the tension. We won't record this, by the way.

"You've often told me, Rikki, that no matter how unlike you we are physically, the human race will soon grow accustomed to us. That shows a lack of imagination on your part. It would probably be true in your case, but you must remember that most of the world is still uneducated by any reasonable standards, and is riddled with prejudices and superstitions that may take another hundred years to eradicate.

"You will grant us that we know something of human psychology. We know rather accurately what would happen if we revealed ourselves to the world in its present state of development. I can't go into details, even with you, so you must accept my analysis on trust. We can, however, make this definite promise, which should give you some satisfaction. *In fifty years—two generations from now—we shall come down from our ships and humanity will at last see us as we are.*"

Stormgren was silent for a while. He felt little of the satisfaction that

Karellen's statement would have once given him. Indeed, he was somewhat confused by his partial success, and for a moment his resolution faltered. The truth would come with the passage of time, and all his plotting was unnecessary and perhaps unwise. If he still went ahead, it would only be for the selfish reason that he would not be alive fifty years from now.

Karellen must have seen his irresolution, for he continued:

"I'm sorry if this disappoints you, but at least the political problems of the near future won't be your responsibility. Perhaps you still think that our fears are unfounded, but believe me, we've had convincing proof of the dangers of any other course."

Stormgren leaned forward, breathing heavily.

"I always thought so! You *have* been seen by Man!"

"I didn't say that," Karellen answered after a short pause. "Your world isn't the only planet we've supervised."

Stormgren was not to be shaken off so easily.

"There have been many legends suggesting that Earth has been visited in the past by other races."

"I know. I've read the Historical Research Section's report. It makes Earth look like the crossroads of the Universe."

"There may have been visits about which you know nothing," said Stormgren, still angling hopefully. "Though since you must have been observing us for thousands of years, I suppose that's rather unlikely."

"I suppose it is," said Karellen in his most unhelpful manner. And at that moment Stormgren made up his mind.

"Karellen," he said abruptly, "I'll draft out the statement and send it up to you for approval. But I reserve the right to continue pestering you, and if I see any opportunity, I'll do my best to learn your secret."

"I'm perfectly well aware of that," replied the Supervisor, with a suspicion of a chuckle.

"And you don't mind?"

"Not in the slightest—though I draw the line at atomic bombs, poison gas, or anything else that might strain our friendship."

Stormgren wondered what, if anything, Karellen had guessed. Behind the Supervisor's banter he had recognized the note of understanding, perhaps—who could tell?—even of encouragement.

"I'm glad to know it," Stormgren replied in as level a voice as he could manage. He rose to his feet, bringing down the cover of his case as he did so. His thumb slid along the catch.

"I'll draft that statement at once," he repeated, "and send it up on the teletype later today."

While he was speaking, he pressed the button—and knew that all his fears had been groundless. Karellen's senses were no finer than Man's. The Supervisor could have detected nothing, for there was no change in his voice as he said good-by and spoke the familiar code-words that opened the door of the chamber.

Yet Stormgren still felt like a shoplifter leaving a department store under the eyes of the house detective, and breathed a sigh of relief when the airlock doors had finally closed behind him.

*   *   *

"I admit," said van Ryberg, "that some of my theories haven't been very bright. But tell me what you think of this one."

"Must I?"

Pieter didn't seem to notice.

"It isn't really my idea," he said modestly. "I got it from a story of Chesterton's. Suppose that the Overlords are hiding the fact that they've got nothing to hide?"

"That sounds a little complicated to me," said Stormgren, interestedly.

"What I mean is this," van Ryberg continued eagerly. "*I* think that physically they're human beings like us. They realize that we'll tolerate being ruled by creatures we imagine to be—well, alien and super-intelligent. But the human race being what it is, it just won't be bossed around by creatures of the same species."

"Very ingenious, like all your theories," said Stormgren. "I wish you'd give them Opus numbers so that I could keep up with them. The objections to this one—"

But at that moment Alexander Wainwright was ushered in.

Stormgren wondered what he was thinking. He wondered, too, if Wainwright had made any contact with the men who had kidnaped him. He doubted it, for he believed Wainwright's disapproval of violent methods to be perfectly genuine. The extremists in his movement had discredited themselves thoroughly, and it would be a long time before the world heard of them again.

The head of the Freedom League listened in silence while the draft was read to him. Stormgren hoped that he appreciated this gesture, which had been Karellen's idea. Not for another twelve hours would the rest of the world know of the promise that had been made to its grandchildren.

"Fifty years," said Wainwright thoughtfully. "That is a long time to wait."

"Not for Karellen, nor for humanity," Stormgren answered. Only now was he beginning to realize the neatness of the Overlords' solution. It had given them the breathing space they believed they needed, and it had cut the ground from beneath the Freedom League's feet. He did not imagine that the League would capitulate, but its position would be seriously weakened.

Certainly Wainwright realized this as well, as he must also have realized that Karellen would be watching him. For he said very little and left as quickly as he could; Stormgren knew that he would not see him again in his term of office. The Freedom League might still be a nuisance, but that was a problem for his successor.

There were some things that only time could cure. Evil men could be destroyed, but nothing could be done about good men who were deluded.

* * *

"Here's your case," said Duval. "It's as good as new."

"Thanks," Stormgren answered, inspecting it carefully none the less. "Now perhaps you can tell me what it was all about—and what we are going to do next."

The physicist seemed more interested in his own thoughts.

"What I can't understand," he said, "is the ease with which we've got away with it. Now if *I'd* been Kar—"

"But you're not. Get to the point, man. What *did* we discover?"

Duval pushed forward a photographic record which to Stormgren looked rather like the autograph of a mild earthquake.

"See that little kink?"

"Yes. What is it?"

"Only Karellen."

"Good Lord! Are you sure?"

"It's a pretty safe guess. He's sitting, or standing, or whatever he does, about two meters on the other side of the screen. If the resolution had been better, we might even have calculated his size."

Stormgren's feelings were very mixed as he stared at the scarcely visible deflexion of the trace. Until now, there had been no proof that Karellen even had a material body. The evidence was still indirect, but he accepted it with little question.

Duval's voice cut into his reverie.

"You'll realize," he said, "that there's no such thing as a truly one-way glass. Karellen's screen, we found when we analyzed our results, transmits light about a hundred times as easily in one direction as the other." With the air of a conjuror producing a whole litter of rabbits, he reached into his desk and pulled out a pistol-like object with a flexible bell-mouth. It reminded Stormgren of a rubber blunderbuss, and he couldn't imagine what it was supposed to be.

Duval grinned at his perplexity.

"It isn't as dangerous as it looks. All you have to do is to ram the muzzle against the screen and press the trigger. It gives out a very powerful flash lasting five seconds, and in that time you'll be able to swing it around the room. Enough light will come back to give you a good view."

"It won't hurt Karellen?"

"Not if you aim low and sweep it upward. That will give him time to accommodate—I suppose he has reflexes like ours, and we don't want to blind him."

Stormgren looked at the weapon doubtfully and hefted it in his hand. For the last few weeks his conscience had been pricking him. Karellen had always treated him with unmistakable affection, despite his occasional devastating frankness, and now that their time together was drawing to its close he did not wish to do anything that might spoil that relationship. But the Supervisor had received due warning, and Stormgren had the conviction that if the choice had been his, Karellen would long ago have shown himself. Now the decision would be made for him—when their last meeting came to its end, Stormgren would gaze upon Karellen's face.

If, of course, Karellen had a face.

*   *   *

The nervousness that Stormgren had first felt had long since passed away. Karellen was doing almost all the talking, weaving the long, intricate sentences of which he was so fond. Once this had seemed to Stormgren the most wonderful and certainly the most unexpected of all Karellen's gifts. Now it no longer appeared quite so marvelous, for he knew that like most of the Supervisor's abilities it was the result of sheer intellectual power and not of any special talent.

Karellen had time for any amount of literary composition when he slowed his thoughts down to the pace of human speech.

"Do not worry," he said, "about the Freedom League. It has been very quiet for the past month, and though it will revive again, it is no longer a real danger. Indeed, since it's always valuable to know what your opponents are doing, the League is a very useful institution. Should it ever get into financial difficulties I might even subsidize it."

Stormgren had often found it difficult to tell when Karellen was joking. He kept his face impassive.

"Very soon the League will lose another of its strongest arguments. There's been a good deal of criticism, mostly rather childish, of the special position you have held for the past few years. I found it very valuable in the early days of my administration, but now that the world is moving along the lines that I planned, it can cease. In the future, all my dealings with Earth will be indirect and the office of Secretary-General can once again become what it was originally intended to be.

"During the next fifty years there will be many crises, but they will pass. Almost a generation from now, I shall reach the nadir of my popularity, for plans must be put into operation which cannot be fully explained at the time. Attempts may even be made to destroy me. But the pattern of the future is clear enough, and one day all these difficulties will be forgotten—even to a race with memories as long as yours."

The last words were spoken with such a peculiar emphasis that Stormgren immediately froze in his seat. Karellen never made accidental slips and even his indiscretions were calculated to many decimal places. But there was no time to ask questions—which certainly would not be answered—before the Supervisor had changed the subject again.

"You've often asked me about our long-term plans," he continued. "The foundation of the World State is of course only the first step.

You will live to see its completion—but the change will be so imperceptible that few will notice it when it comes. After that there will be a pause for thirty years while the next generation reaches maturity. And then will come the day which we have promised. I am sorry that you will not be there."

Stormgren's eyes were open, but his gaze was fixed far beyond the dark barrier of the screen. He was looking into the future, imagining the day he would never see.

"On that day," continued Karellen, "the human mind will experience one of its very rare psychological discontinuities. But no permanent harm will be done—the men of that age will be more stable than their grandfathers. We will always have been part of their lives, and when they meet us, we will not seem so—strange—as we would do to you."

Stormgren had never known Karellen in so contemplative a mood, but this gave him no surprise. He did not believe that he had ever seen more than a few facets of the Supervisor's personality—the real Karellen was unknown and perhaps unknowable to human beings. And once again Stormgren had the feeling that the Supervisor's real interests were elsewhere.

"Then there will be another pause, only a short one this time, for the world will be growing impatient. Men will wish to go out to the stars, to see the other worlds of the Universe and to join us in our work. For it is only beginning—not a thousandth of the suns in the Galaxy have ever been visited by the races of which we know. One day, Rikki, your descendants in their own ships will be bringing civilization to the worlds that are ripe to receive it—just as we are doing now."

Karellen had fallen silent and Stormgren had the impression that the Supervisor was watching him intently.

"It is a great vision," he said softly. "Do you bring it to all your worlds?"

"Yes," said Karellen, "all that can understand it."

Out of nowhere, a strangely disturbing thought came into Stormgren's mind.

"Suppose, after all, your experiment fails with Man? We have known such things in our own dealings with other races. Surely you have had your failures too?"

"Yes," said Karellen, so softly that Stormgren could scarcely hear him. "We have had our failures."

"And what do you do then?"

"We wait—and try again."

There was a pause lasting perhaps ten seconds. When Karellen spoke again, his words were muffled and so unexpected that for a moment Stormgren did not react.

"Good-by, Rikki!"

Karellen had tricked him—probably it was too late. Stormgren's paralysis lasted only for a moment. Then he whipped out the flash-gun and jammed it against the screen.

* * *

Was it a lie? What *had* he really seen? No more, he was certain, than Karellen had intended. He was as sure as he could be of anything that the Supervisor had known his plan from the beginning, and had foreseen every moment of it.

Why else had that enormous chair been already empty when the circle of light blazed upon it? In the same moment he had started to swing the beam, but he was too late. The metal door, twice as high as a man, was closing swiftly when he first caught sight of it—closing swiftly, yet not quite swiftly enough.

Karellen had trusted him, had not wished him to go down into the long evening of his life still haunted by a mystery he could never solve. Karellen dared not defy the unknown power above him (was he of that same race, too?) but he had done all that he could. If he had disobeyed Him, He could never prove it.

"We have had our failures."

Yes, Karellen, that was true—and were you the one who failed, before the dawn of human history? Even in fifty years, could you overcome the power of all the myths and legends of the world?

Yet Stormgren knew there would be no second failure. When the two races met again, the Overlords would have won the trust and friendship of Mankind, and not even the shock of recognition could undo that work.

And Stormgren knew also that the last thing he would ever see as he closed his eyes on life, would be that swiftly turning door, and the long black tail disappearing behind it.

A very famous and unexpectedly beautiful tail.

A barbed tail.

". . . and he put up a terrific fight before they made him take this job. He pretends to hate it, but he's really enjoying himself."

". . . immortal, isn't he?"

"Yes, after a fashion, though there's something thousands of years ahead of him which he seems to fear—I can't imagine what it is."

Armageddon?

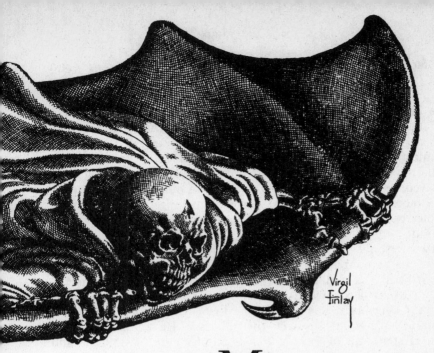

Mimic

DONALD A. WOLLHEIM

As editor of Cosmic Stories *and* Stirring Science Stories *in the 1940s, head of the science fiction division at Ace Books in the postwar years, and publisher of Daw Books up through 1990, Donald A. Wollheim had a strong personal influence on the course science fiction took from its pulp origins to the present day. Wollheim is so well known for his editing that readers tend to overlook the considerable amount of fiction he wrote under his own name and several pseudonyms. "Mimic," reprinted in a 1950 issue of* Fantastic Novels, *was one of the briefest stories to appear in that magazine, but also one of the best.*

IT IS less than five hundred years since an entire half of the world was discovered. It is less than two hundred years since the discovery of the last continent. The sciences of chemistry and physics go back scarce one century. The science of aviation goes back forty years. The science of atomics is being born.

And yet we think we know a lot.

We know little or nothing. Some of the most startling things are unknown to us. When they are discovered they may shock us to the bone.

We search for secrets in the far islands of the Pacific and among the ice fields of the frozen North while under our very noses, rubbing shoulders with us every day, there may walk the undiscovered. It is a curious fact of nature that that which is in plain view is oft best hidden.

I have always known of the man in the black cloak. Since I was a child he has always lived on my street, and his eccentricities are so familiar that they go unmentioned except among casual visitors. Here, in the heart of the largest city in the world, in swarming New York, the eccentric and the odd may flourish unhindered.

As children we had hilarious fun jeering at the man in black when he displayed his fear of women. We watched, in our evil, childish way, for those moments; we tried to get him to show anger. But he ignored us completely, and soon we paid him no further heed, even as our parents did.

We saw him only twice a day. Once in the early morning, when we would see his six-foot figure come out of the grimy dark hallway of the tenement at the end of the street and stride down towards the elevated to work—again when he came back at night. He was always dressed in a long black cloak that came to his ankles, and he wore a wide-brimmed black hat down far over his face. He was a sight from some weird story out of the old lands. But he harmed nobody, and paid attention to nobody.

Nobody—except perhaps women.

When a woman crossed his path, he would stop in his stride and come to a dead halt. We could see that he closed his eyes until she had passed. Then he would snap those wide watery blue eyes open and march on as if nothing had happened.

He was never known to speak to a woman. He would buy some groceries maybe once a week, at Antonio's—but only when there were no other patrons there. Antonio said once that he never talked, he just pointed at things he wanted and paid for them in bills that he pulled out of a pocket somewhere under his cloak. Antonio did not like him, but he never had any trouble with him either.

Now that I think of it, nobody ever did have any trouble with him.

We got used to him. We grew up on the street; we saw him occasionally when he came home and went back into the dark hallway of the house he lived in.

One of the kids on the block lived in that house too. A lot of families did. Antonio said they knew nothing much about him either, though there were one or two funny stories.

He never had visitors, he never spoke to anyone. And he had once built something in his room out of metal.

He had then, years ago, hauled up some long flat metal sheets, sheets of tin or iron, and they had heard a lot of hammering and banging in his room for several days. But that had stopped and that was all there was to that story.

Where he worked I don't know and never found out. He had money, for he was reputed to pay his rent regularly when the janitor asked for it.

Well, people like that inhabit big cities and nobody knows the story of their lives until they're all over. Or until something strange happens.

*   *   *

I grew up, I went to college, I studied. Finally I got a job assisting a museum curator. I spent my days mounting beetles and classifying exhibits of stuffed animals and preserved plants, and hundreds and hundreds of insects from all over.

Nature is a strange thing, I learned. You learn that very clearly when you work in a museum. You realize how nature uses the art of camouflage. There are twig insects that look exactly like a leaf or a branch of a tree. Exactly. Even to having phony vein markings that look just like the real leaf's. You can't tell them apart, unless you look very carefully.

Nature is strange and perfect that way. There is a moth in Central America that looks like a wasp. It even has a fake stinger made of hair, which it twists and curls just like a wasp's stinger. It has the same colorings and, even though its body is soft and not armored like a wasp's, it is colored to appear shiny and armored. It even flies in the daytime when wasps do, and not at night like all the other moths. It moves like a wasp. It knows somehow that it is helpless and that it can survive only by pretending to be as deadly to other insects as wasps are.

I learned about army ants, and their strange imitators.

Army ants travel in huge columns of thousands and hundreds of thousands. They move along in a flowing stream several yards across and they eat everything in their path. Everything in the jungle is afraid of them. Wasps, bees, snakes, other ants, birds, lizards, beetles—even men run away, or get eaten.

But in the midst of the army ants there also travel many other creatures—creatures that aren't ants at all, and that the army ants would kill if they knew of them. But they don't know of them because these other creatures are disguised. Some of them are beetles that look like ants. They have false markings like ant-thoraxes and they run along in imitation of ant speed. There is even one that is so long it is marked like three ants in single file. It moves so fast that the real ants never give it a second glance.

There are weak caterpillars that look like big armored beetles. There are all sorts of things that look like dangerous animals. Animals that are the killers and superior fighters of their groups have no enemies. The army ants and the wasps, the sharks, the hawk and the felines. So there are a host of weak things that try to hide among them—to mimic them.

And man is the greatest killer, the greatest hunter of them all. The whole world of nature knows man for the irresistible master. The roar of his gun, the cunning of his trap, the strength and agility of his arm place all else beneath him.

It was, as often happens to be the case, sheer luck that I happened to be on the street at that dawning hour when the janitor came running out of the tenement on my street shouting for help. I had been working all night mounting new exhibits.

The policeman on the beat and I were the only people besides the janitor to see the things that we found in the two dingy rooms occupied by the stranger of the black cloak.

The janitor explained—as the officer and I dashed up the narrow rickety stairs—that he had been awakened by the sound of heavy thuds and shrill screams in the stranger's rooms. He had gone out in the hallway to listen.

Severe groaning as of someone in terrible pain—the noise of someone thrashing around in agony—was coming from behind the closed door of the stranger's apartment. The janitor had listened, then run for help.

When we got there the place was silent. A faint light shone from under the doorway. The policeman knocked; there was no answer. He put his ear to the door and so did I.

We heard a faint rustling—a continuous slow rustling as of a breeze blowing paper. The cop knocked again but there was still no response.

Then, together, we threw our weight at the door. Two hard blows and the rotten old lock gave way. We burst in.

The room was filthy, the floor covered with scraps of torn paper, bits of detritus and garbage. The room was unfurnished, which I thought was odd.

In one corner there stood a metal box, about four feet square. A tight box, held together with screws and ropes. It had a lid, opening at the top, which was down and fastened with a sort of wax seal.

The stranger of the black cloak lay in the middle of the floor—dead.

He was still wearing the cloak. The big slouch hat was lying on the floor some distance away. From the inside of the box the faint rustling was coming.

We turned over the stranger, took the cloak off. For several instants we saw nothing amiss—

At first we saw a man, dressed in a somber, featureless black suit. He had a coat and skin-tight pants.

His hair was short and curly brown. It stood straight up in its inch-long length. His eyes were open and staring. I noticed first that he had no eyebrows, only a curious dark line in the flesh over each eye.

It was then that I realized that he had no nose. But no one had ever noticed that before. His skin was oddly mottled. Where the nose should have been there were dark shadowings that made the appearance of a nose, if you only just glanced at him. Like the work of a skillful artist in a painting.

His mouth was as it should be, and slightly open—but he had no teeth. His head perched upon a thin neck.

The suit was—not a suit. It was part of him. It was his body.

What we thought was a coat was a huge black wing sheath, like a beetle has. He had a thorax like an insect, only the wing sheath covered it and you couldn't notice it when he wore the cloak. The body bulged out below, tapering off into the two long, thin hind legs. His arms came out from under the top of the "coat." He had a tiny secondary pair of arms folded tightly across his chest. There was a sharp round hole newly pierced in his chest just above these arms still oozing a watery liquid.

The janitor fled gibbering. The officer was pale but standing by his duty. I heard him muttering under his breath an endless stream of *Hail Marys.*

The lower thorax—the "abdomen"—was very long and insectlike. It was crumpled up now like the wreck of an airplane fuselage.

I recalled the appearance of a female wasp that had just laid eggs—her thorax had had that empty appearance.

The sight was a shock such as leaves one in full control. The mind rejects it, and it is only in afterthought that one can feel the dim shudder of horror.

The rustling was still coming from the box. I motioned the white-faced cop and we went over and stood before it. He took his nightstick and knocked away the waxen seal.

Then we heaved and pulled the lid open.

A wave of noxious vapor assailed us. We staggered back as suddenly a stream of flying things shot out of the huge iron container. The window was open, and straight out into the first glow of dawn they flew.

There must have been dozens of them. They were about two or three inches long and they flew on wide gauzy beetle wings. They looked like little men, strangely terrifying as they flew—clad in their black suits, with expressionless faces and their dots of watery blue eyes. And they flew out on transparent wings that came from under their black beetle coats.

I ran to the window, fascinated, almost hypnotized. The horror of it had not reached my mind at once. Afterwards I have had spasms of numbing terror as my mind tries to put the things together. The whole business was so utterly unexpected.

We knew of army ants and their imitators, yet it never occurred to us that we too were army ants of a sort. We knew of stick insects and it never occurred to us that there might be others that disguise themselves to fool, not other animals, but the supreme animal himself—man.

We found some bones in the bottom of that iron case afterwards. But we couldn't identify them.

Perhaps we did not try hard. They might have been human—

I suppose the stranger of the black cloak did not fear women so much as it distrusted them. Women notice men, perhaps, more closely then other men do. Women might become suspicious sooner of the inhumanity, the deception. And then there might perhaps have been some touch of instinctive feminine jealousy. The stranger was disguised as a man, but its sex was surely female. The things in the iron box were its young.

But it is the other thing I saw when I ran to the window that has shaken me most. The policeman did not see it. Nobody else saw it but me, and I only for an instant.

Nature practices deceptions in every angle. Evolution will create a being for any niche, no matter how unlikely.

When I went to the window, I saw the small cloud of flying things rising up into the sky and sailing away into the purple distance. The dawn was breaking and the first rays of the sun were just striking over the housetops.

Shaken, I looked away from that fourth floor tenement room over the roofs of the lower buildings. Chimneys and walls and empty clotheslines made the scenery over which the tiny mass of horror passed.

And then I saw a chimney, not thirty feet away on the next roof. It was squat and red brick and had two black pipe ends flush with its top. I saw it suddenly vibrate, oddly. And its red brick surface seem to peel away, and the black pipe openings turn suddenly white.

I saw two big eyes staring up into the sky.

A great, flat-winged thing detached itself silently from the surface of the real chimney and darted hungrily after the cloud of flying things.

I watched until all had lost themselves in the sky.

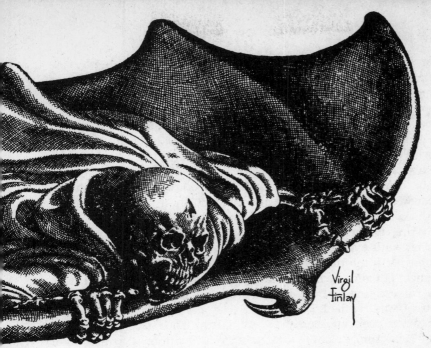

The Music of Erich Zann

H. P. LOVECRAFT

H. P. Lovecraft's only appearance in the original Munsey magazines was as an avid letter writer. By the time Famous Fantastic Mysteries *came into existence, he had become one of the best living writers of supernatural horror fiction and had had an enormous influence on many authors writing for the weird fiction pulps. In recognition of Lovecraft's talents,* Famous Fantastic Mysteries *reprinted his classic science fiction horror story "The Colour out of Space" from* Amazing Stories, *the only non-Munsey pulp story so honored before the magazine was sold to Popular Publications. Four more of Lovecraft's stories were to appear in* Famous Fantastic Mysteries *and* Fantastic Novels, *including his tale of cosmic horror, "The Music of Erich Zann."*

I HAVE EXAMINED maps of the city with the greatest care, yet have never again found the Rue d'Auseil. These maps have not been modern maps alone, for I know that names change. I have, on the contrary, delved deeply into all the antiquities of the place, and have personally explored every region, of whatever name, which could possibly answer to the street I knew as the Rue d'Auseil. But despite all I have done, it remains a humiliating fact that I cannot find the house, the street, or even the locality, where, during the last months of my impoverished life as a student of metaphysics at the university, I heard the music of Erich Zann.

That my memory is broken, I do not wonder; for my health, physical and mental, was gravely disturbed throughout the period of my residence in the Rue d'Auseil, and I recall that I took none of my few acquaintances there. But that I cannot find the place again is both singular and perplexing; for it was within a half-hour's walk of the university and was distinguished by peculiarities which could hardly be forgotten by anyone who had been there. I have never met a person who has seen the Rue d'Auseil.

The Rue d'Auseil lay across a dark river bordered by precipitous brick blear-windowed warehouses and spanned by a ponderous bridge of dark stone. It was always shadowy along that river, as if the smoke of neighboring factories shut out the sun perpetually. The river was also odorous with evil stenches which I have never smelled elsewhere, and which may some day help me to find it, since I should recognize them at once. Beyond the bridge were narrow cobbled streets with rails; and then came the ascent, at first gradual, but incredibly steep as the Rue d'Auseil was reached.

I have never seen another street as narrow and steep as the Rue d'Auseil. It was almost a cliff, closed to all vehicles, consisting in several places of flights of steps, and ending at the top in a lofty ivied wall. Its paving was irregular, sometimes stone slabs, sometimes cobblestones, and sometimes bare earth with struggling greenish-grey vegetation. The houses were tall, peaked-roofed, incredibly old, and crazily leaning backward, forward, and sidewise. Occasionally an opposite pair, both leaning forward, almost met across the street like an arch; and certainly they kept most of the light from the ground below. There were a few overhead bridges from house to house across the street.

The inhabitants of that street impressed me peculiarly. At first I thought it was because they were all silent and reticent; but later decided it was because they were all very old. I do not know how I came to live on such a street, but I was not myself when I moved there. I had been living in many poor places, always evicted for want of money; until at last I came upon that tottering house in the Rue d'Auseil kept by the paralytic Blandot. It was the third house from the top of the street, and by far the tallest of them all.

My room was on the fifth story; the only inhabited room there, since the house was almost empty. On the night I arrived I heard strange music from the peaked garret overhead, and the next day asked old Blandot about it. He told me it was an old German viol-player, a strange dumb man who signed his name as Erich Zann, and who played evenings in a cheap theater orchestra; adding that Zann's desire to play in the night after his return from the theater was the reason he had chosen this lofty and isolated garret room, whose single gable window was the only point on the street from which one could look over the terminating wall at the declivity and panorama beyond.

Thereafter I heard Zann every night, and although he kept me awake, I was haunted by the weirdness of his music. Knowing little of the art myself, I was yet certain that none of his harmonies had any relation to music I had heard before; and concluded that he was a composer of highly original genius. The longer I listened, the more I was fascinated, until after a week I resolved to make the old man's acquaintance.

One night as he was returning from his work, I intercepted Zann in the hallway and told him that I would like to know him and be with him when he played. He was a small, lean, bent person, with shabby clothes, blue eyes, grotesque, satyr-like face, and nearly bald head; and at my first words seemed both angered and frightened. My obvious friendliness, however, finally melted him; and he grudgingly motioned me to follow him up the dark, creaking and rickety attic stairs.

His room, one of only two in the steeply pitched garret, was on the west side, toward the high wall that formed the upper end of the street. Its size was very great, and seemed the greater because of its extraordinary barrenness and neglect. Of furniture there was only a narrow iron bedstead, a dingy wash-stand, a small table, a large bookcase, an iron music-rack, and three old-fashioned chairs. Sheets of music were piled in disorder about the floor. Evidently Erich Zann's world of beauty lay in some far cosmos of the imagination.

Motioning me to sit down, the dumb man closed the door, turned the large wooden bolt, and lighted a candle to augment the one he had brought with him. He now removed his viol from its moth-eaten covering, and taking it, seated himself in the least uncomfortable of the chairs. He did not employ the music-rack, but, offering no choice and playing from memory, enchanted me for over an hour with strains I had never heard before; strains which must have been of his own devising. To describe their exact nature is impossible for one unversed in music. They were a kind of fugue, with recurrent passage of the most captivating quality, but to me were notable for the absence of any of the weird notes I had overheard from my room below on other occasions.

Those haunting notes I had remembered, and had often hummed and whistled inaccurately to myself, so when the player at length laid down his bow I asked him if he would render some of them. As I began my request the wrinkled satyr-like face lost the bored placidity it had possessed during the playing, and seemed to show the same curious mixture of anger and fright which I had noticed when first I accosted the old man. For a moment I was inclined to use persuasion, regarding rather lightly the whims of senility; and even tried to awaken my host's weirder mood by whistling a few of the strains to which I had listened the night before.

But I did not pursue this course for more than a moment; for when the dumb musician recognized the whistled air his face grew suddenly distorted with an expression wholly beyond analysis, and his long, cold, bony right hand reached out to stop my mouth and silence the crude imitation. As he did this he further demonstrated his eccentricity by casting a startled glance toward the lone curtained window, as if fearful of some intruder—a glance doubly absurd, since the garret stood high and inaccessible above all the adjacent roofs, this window being the only point on the steep street, as the concierge had told me, from which one could see over the wall at the summit.

The old man's glance brought Blandot's remark to my mind, and with a certain capriciousness I felt a wish to look out over the wide and dizzying panorama of moonlit roofs and city lights beyond the hilltop, which of all the dwellers in the Rue d'Auseil, only this crabbed musician could see. I moved toward the window and would have drawn aside the nondescript curtains, when with a frightened rage even greater than before, the dumb lodger was upon me again; this time motioning with his head toward the door as he nervously strove to drag me thither with both hands. Now thoroughly disgusted with my host, I ordered him to release me, and told him I would go at once. His clutch relaxed, and as he saw my disgust and offense, his own anger seemed to subside. He tightened his relaxing grip, but this time in a friendly manner, forcing me into a chair; then with an appearance of wistfulness crossing to the littered table, where he wrote many words with a pencil, in the labored French of a foreigner.

The note which he finally handed me was an appeal for tolerance and forgiveness. Zann said that he was old, lonely, and afflicted with strange fears and nervous disorders connected with his music and with other things. He had enjoyed my listening to his music, and wished I would come again and not mind his eccentricities. But he could not play to another his weird harmonies, and could not bear hearing them from another; nor could he bear having anything in his room touched by another. He had not known until our hallway conversation that I could overhear his playing in my room, and now asked me if I would arrange with Blandot to take a lower room where I could not hear him in the night. He would defray the difference in rent.

As I sat deciphering the execrable French, I felt more lenient toward the old man. So when I had finished reading, I shook my host by the hand, and departed as a friend.

The next day Blandot gave me a more expensive room on the third floor.

There was no one on the fourth floor.

It was not long before I found that Zann's eagerness for my company was not as great as it had seemed while he was persuading me to move down from the fifth story. He did not ask me to call on him, and when I did call he appeared uneasy and played listlessly. This was always at night—in the day he slept and would admit no one. My liking for him did not grow, though the attic room and the weird music seemed to hold an odd fascination for me. I had a curious desire to look out of that window, over the wall and down the unseen slope.

What I did succeed in doing was to overhear the nocturnal playing of the dumb old man. At first I would tip-toe up to my old fifth floor, then I grew bold enough to climb the last creaking staircase to the peaked garret. There in the narrow hall, outside the bolted door with the covered keyhole, I often heard sounds which filled me with an indefinable dread—the dread of vague wonder and brooding mystery. It was not that the sounds were hideous, for they were not; but that they held vibrations suggesting nothing on this globe of earth, and that at certain intervals they assumed a symphonic quality which I could hardly conceive as produced by one player.

Then one night as I listened at the door, I heard the shrieking viol swell into a chaotic babel of sound; a pandemonium which would have led me to doubt my own shaking sanity had there not come from behind that barred portal a piteous proof that the horror was real—the awful, inarticulate cry which only a mute can utter, and which rises only in moments of the most terrible fear or anguish. I knocked repeatedly at the door, but received no response. Afterward I waited in the black hallway, shivering with cold and fear, till I heard the poor musician's feeble effort to rise from the floor by the aid of a chair. Believing him just conscious after a fainting fit, I renewed my rapping, at the same time calling out my name reassuringly. I heard Zann stumble to the window and close both shutter and sash, then stumble to the door, which he falteringly unfastened to admit me. This time his delight at having me present was real.

Shaking pathetically, the old man forced me into a chair whilst he sank into another, beside which his viol and bow lay carelessly on the floor. He sat for some time inactive, nodding oddly, but having a paradoxical suggestion of intense and frightened listening. Subsequently he seemed to be satisfied, and crossing to a chair by the table wrote a brief note, handed it to me, and returning to the table, where he began to write rapidly and incessantly. The note implored me in the name of mercy, to wait where I was while he prepared a full account in German of all the marvels and terrors which beset him. I waited, and the dumb man's pencil flew.

It was perhaps an hour later, while I still waited and while the old musician's feverishly written sheets still continued to pile up, that I saw Zann start as from the hint of a horrible shock. Unmistakably he was looking at the curtained window and listening shudderingly. Then I half fancied I heard a sound myself; though it was not a horrible sound, but rather an exquisitely low and infinitely distant musical note, suggesting a player in one of the neighboring houses, or in some abode beyond the lofty wall over which I had never been able to look. Upon Zann the effect was terrible, for, dropping his pencil, suddenly he rose, seized his viol, and commenced to rend the night with the wildest playing I had ever heard from his bow save when listening at the barred door.

It would be useless to describe the playing of Erich Zann on that dreadful night. It was more horrible than anything I had ever overheard, because I could not see the expression of his face, and could realize that this time the motive was stark fear. He was trying to make a noise; to ward something off or drown something out—what, I could not imagine, awesome though I felt it must be. The playing grew fantastic, delirious, and hysterical, yet kept to the last the qualities of supreme genius which I know this strange old man possessed. I recognized the air—it was a wild Hungarian dance popular in the theaters.

Louder and louder, wilder and wilder, mounted the shrieking and whining of that desperate viol. The player was dripping with an uncanny perspiration and twisted like a monkey, always looking frantically at the curtained window. In his frenzied strains I could almost see shadowy satyrs and bacchanals dancing and whirling insanely through seething abysses of clouds and smoke and lightning. And then I thought I heard a shriller, steadier note that was not from the viol; a calm, deliberate, purposeful, mocking note from far away in the west.

At this juncture the shutter began to rattle in a howling night wind which had sprung up outside as if in answer to the mad playing within. Zann's screaming viol now outdid itself emitting sound I had never thought a viol could emit. The shutter rattled more loudly, unfastened, and commenced slamming against the window. Then the glass broke shiveringly under the persistent impacts, and the chill wind rushed in, making the candles sputter and rustling the sheets of paper on the table where Zann had begun to write out his horrible secret. I looked at Zann, and saw that he was past conscious observation. His blue eyes were bulging, glassy and sightless, and the frantic playing had become a blind, mechanical unrecognizable orgy that no pen could even suggest.

A sudden gust, stronger than the others, caught up the manuscript and bore it toward the window. I followed the flying sheets in desperation, but they were gone before I reached the demolished panes. Then I remembered my old wish to gaze from this window, the only window in the Rue d'Auseil from which one might see the slope beyond the wall, and the city outspread beneath. It was very dark, but the city's lights always burned, and I expected to see them there amidst the rain and wind. Yet when I looked from that highest of all gable windows, looked while the candles sputtered and the insane viol howled with the night-wind, I saw no city spread below, and no friendly lights gleamed from remembered streets, but only the blackness of space illimitable; unimagined space alive with motion and music, and having no semblance of anything on earth. And as I stood there looking in terror, the wind blew out both the candles in that ancient peaked garret, leaving me in savage and impenetrable darkness with chaos and pandemonium before me, and the demon madness of that night-baying viol behind me.

I staggered back in the dark, without the means of striking a light, crashing against the table, overturning a chair, and finally groping my way to the place where the blackness screamed with shocking music. To save myself and Erich Zann I could at least try, whatever the powers opposed to me. Once I thought some chill thing brushed me, and I screamed, but my scream could not be heard above the hideous viol. Suddenly out of the blackness the madly sawing bow struck me, and I knew I was close to the player. I felt ahead, touched the back of Zann's chair, and then found and shook his shoulder.

He did not respond, and still the viol shrieked on without slackening. I moved my hand to his head, whose mechanical nodding I was able to stop, and shouted in his ear that we must both flee from the unknown things of the night. But he neither answered me nor abated the frenzy of his unutterable music, while all through the garret strange currents of wind seemed to dance in the darkness and babel. When my hand touched his ear I shuddered, though I knew not why—knew not why till I felt of the still face; the ice-cold, stiffened, unbreathing face whose glassy eyes bulged uselessly into the void. And then, by some miracle, finding the door and the large wooden bolt, I plunged wildly away from that glassy-eyed thing in the dark, and from the ghoulish howling of that accursed viol whose fury increased even as I plunged.

Leaping, floating, flying down those endless stairs through the dark house; racing mindlessly out into the narrow, steep, and ancient street of steps and tottering houses; clattering down steps and over cobbles to the lower streets and the putrid canyon-walled river; panting across the great dark bridge to the broader, healthier streets and boulevards we know; all these are terrible impressions that linger with me. And I recall that there was no wind, and that the moon was out, and that all the lights of the city twinkled.

Despite my most careful searches and investigations, I have never since been able to find the Rue d'Auseil. But I am not wholly sorry; either for this or for the loss in undreamable abysses of the closely-written sheets which alone could have explained the music of Erich Zann.

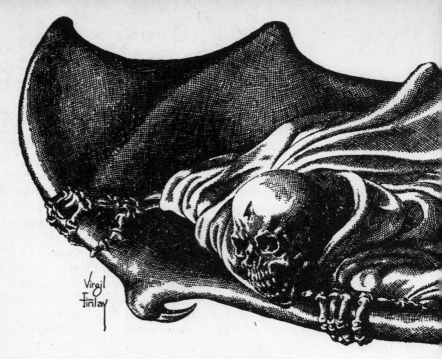

The Dancing Partner

JEROME K. JEROME

*Although Jerome K. Jerome was best known in his day as a playwright,
his comic novel* Three Men in a Boat *established him as a humorist of
the first rank. Jerome extended this talent to the area of weird fiction
when he wrote* Told after Supper, *a collection of humorous fantasies that
lampoon the clichés of the ghost story. "The Dancing Partner," however,
is a serious story that suggests Jerome was familiar with and respected
the fairy tales of the Brothers Grimm and E. T. A. Hoffman's fantasy
classic "The Sandman."*

THIS STORY, commenced MacShaugnassy, "comes from Furtwangen, a small town in the Black Forest. There lived there a very
wonderful old fellow named Nicholaus Geibel. His business was the
making of mechanical toys, at which work he had acquired an almost
European reputation. He made rabbits that would emerge from the
heart of a cabbage, flop their ears, smooth their whiskers, and disappear
again; cats that would wash their faces, and mew so naturally that dogs
would mistake them for real cats, and fly at them; dolls, with phon-
ographs concealed within them, that would raise their hats and say,
'Good morning; how do you do?' and some that would even sing a
song.

"But he was something more than a mere mechanic; he was an artist.
His work was with him a hobby, almost a passion. His shop was filled

with all manner of strange things that never would, or could, be sold—
things he had made for the pure love of making them. He had contrived
a mechanical donkey that would trot for two hours by means of stored
electricity, and trot, too, much faster than the live article, and with
less need for exertion on the part of the driver; a bird that would
shoot up into the air, fly around and around in a circle, and drop to
earth at the exact spot from where it started; a skeleton that, supported
by an upright iron bar, would dance a hornpipe; a life-size lady doll
that could play the fiddle; and a gentleman with a hollow inside who
could smoke a pipe and drink more lager beer than any three average
German students put together, which is saying much.

"Indeed, it was the belief of the town that old Geibel could make
a man capable of doing everything that a respectable man need want
to do. One day he made a man who did too much, and it came about
in this way:

"Young Doctor Follen had a baby, and the baby had a birthday. Its
first birthday put Doctor Follen's household into somewhat of a flurry,
but on the occasion of its second birthday, Mrs. Doctor Follen gave
a ball in honor of the event. Old Geibel and his daughter Olga were
among the guests.

"During the afternoon of the next day some three or four of Olga's
bosom friends, who had also been present at the ball, dropped in to
have a chat about it. They naturally fell to discussing the men, and
to criticizing their dancing. Old Geibel was in the room, but he appeared
to be absorbed in his newspaper, and the girls took no notice of him.

" 'There seem to be fewer men who can dance at every ball you go
to,' said one of the girls.

" 'Yes, and don't the ones who can give themselves airs?' said another.
'They make quite a favor of asking you.'

" 'And how stupidly they talk,' added a third. They always say exactly
the same things: "How charming you are looking tonight." "Do you
often go to Vienna? Oh, you should, it's delightful." "What a charming
dress you have on." "What a warm day it has been." "Do you like
Wagner?" I do wish they'd think of something new.'

" 'Oh, I never mind how they talk,' said a fourth. 'If a man dances
well he may be a fool for all I care.'

" 'He generally is,' slipped in a thin girl, rather spitefully.

" 'I go to a ball to dance,' continued the previous speaker, not noticing
the interruption. 'All I ask of a partner is that he shall hold me firmly,
take me round steadily, and not get tired before I do.'

" 'A clockwork figure would be the thing for you,' said the girl who
had interrupted.

"Bravo!' cried one of the others, clapping her hands, 'what a capital
idea!"

" 'What's a capital idea?' they asked.

" 'Why, a clockwork dancer, or, better still, one that would go by
electricity and never run down.'

"The girls took up the idea with enthusiasm.

" 'Oh, what a lovely partner he would make!' cried one. 'He would never kick you, or tread on your toes.'

" 'Or tear your dress,' said another.

" 'Or get out of step.'

" 'Or get giddy and lean on you.'

" 'And he would never want to mop his face with his handkerchief. I do hate to see a man do that after every dance.'

" 'And wouldn't want to spend the whole evening in the supper room.'

" 'Why, with a phonograph inside him to grind out all the stock remarks, you would not be able to tell him from a real man,' said the girl who had first suggested the idea.

" 'Oh, yes, you would,' said the thin girl. 'He would be so much nicer.'

"Old Geibel had laid down his paper, and was listening with both his ears. On one of the girls glancing in his direction, however, he hurriedly hid himself again behind it.

"After the girls were gone, he went into his workshop, where Olga heard him walking up and down, and every now and then chuckling to himself; and that night he talked to her a good deal about dancing and dancing men—asked what they usually said and did—what dances were most popular—what steps were gone through, with many other such questions.

"Then for a couple of weeks he kept much to his factory, and was very thoughtful and busy, though prone at unexpected moments to break into a quiet low laugh, as if enjoying a joke that nobody else knew of.

"A month later another ball took place in Furtwangen. On this occasion it was given by old Wenzel, the wealthy timber merchant, to celebrate his niece's betrothal, and Geibel and his daughter were again among the invited.

"When the hour arrived to set out, Olga sought her father. Not finding him in the house, she tapped at the door of his workshop. He appeared in his shirtsleeves, looking hot but radiant.

" 'Don't wait for me,' he said, 'you go on. I'll follow you. I've got something to finish.'

"As she turned to obey he called after her, 'Tell them I'm going to bring a young man with me—such a nice young man, and an excellent dancer. All the girls will like him.' Then he laughed and closed the door.

"Her father generally kept his doings secret from everybody, but she had a pretty shrewd suspicion of what he had been planning, and so, to a certain extent, was able to prepare the guests for what was coming. Anticipation ran high, and the arrival of the famous mechanist was eagerly awaited.

"At length the sound of wheels was heard outside, followed by a great commotion in the passage, and old Wenzel himself, his jolly face red with excitement and suppressed laughter, burst into the room and announced in stentorian tones:

" 'Herr Geibel—and a friend.'

"Herr Geibel and his 'friend' entered, greeted with shouts of laughter and applause, and advanced to the center of the room.

" 'Allow me, ladies and gentlemen,' said Herr Geibel, 'to introduce you to my friend, Lieutenant Fritz. Fritz, my dear fellow, bow to the ladies and gentlemen.'

"Geibel placed his hand encouragingly on Fritz's shoulder, and the lieutenant bowed low, accompanying the action with a harsh clicking noise in his throat, unpleasantly suggestive of a death rattle. But that was only a detail.

" 'He walks a little stiffly' (old Geibel took his arm and walked him forward a few steps; he certainly did walk stiffly), 'but then, walking is not his forte. He is essentially a dancing man. I have only been able to teach him the waltz as yet, but at that he is faultless. Come, which of you ladies may I introduce him to as a partner? He keeps perfect time; he never gets tired; he won't kick you or tread on your dress; he will hold you as firmly as you like, and go as quickly or as slowly as you please; he never gets giddy; and he is full of conversation. Come, speak up for yourself, my boy.'

"The old gentleman twisted one of the buttons at the back of his coat, and immediately Fritz opened his mouth, and in thin tones that appeared to proceed from the back of his head, remarked suddenly, 'May I have the pleasure?' and then shut his mouth again with a snap.

"That Lieutenant Fritz had made a strong impression on the company was undoubted, yet none of the girls seemed inclined to dance with him. They looked askance at his waxen face, with his staring eyes and fixed smile, and shuddered. At last old Geibel came to the girl who had conceived the idea.

" 'It is your own suggestion, carried out to the letter,' said Geibel, 'an electric dancer. You owe it to the gentleman to give him a trial.'

"She was a bright, saucy little girl, fond of a frolic. Her host added his entreaties, and she consented.

"Herr Geibel fixed the figure to her. Its right arm was screwed round her waist, and held her firmly; its delicately jointed left hand was made to fasten itself upon her right. The old toymaker showed her how to regulate its speed, and how to stop it, and release herself.

" 'It will take you round in a complete circle,' he explained; 'be careful that no one knocks against you, and alters its course.'

"The music struck up. Old Geibel put the current in motion, and Annette and her strange partner began to dance.

"For a while everyone stood watching them. The figure performed its purpose admirably. Keeping perfect time and step, and holding its little partner tight clasped in an unyielding embrace, it revolved steadily.

" 'How charming you are looking tonight,' it remarked in its thin, far-away voice. 'What a lovely day it has been. Do you like dancing? How well our steps agree. You will give me another, won't you? Oh, don't be so cruel. What a charming gown you have on. Isn't waltzing delightful?'

"As she grew more familiar with the uncanny creature, the girl's nervousness wore off.

" 'Oh, he's just lovely,' she cried, laughing. 'I could go on dancing with him all my life.'

"Couple after couple now joined them, and soon all the dancers in the room were whirling round behind them. Nicholaus Geibel stood looking on, beaming with childish delight at his success.

"Old Wenzel approached him, and whispered something in his ear. Geibel laughed and nodded, and the two worked their way quietly towards the door.

" 'This is the young people's house tonight,' said Wenzel, so soon as they were outside; 'you and I will have a quiet pipe and a glass of hock, over in the counting house.'

"Meanwhile the dancing grew more fast and furious. Little Annette loosened the screw regulating her partner's rate of progress, and the figure flew round with her swifter and swifter. Couple after couple dropped out exhausted, but they only went the faster, till at length they remained dancing alone.

"Madder and madder became the waltz. The music lagged behind: the musicians, unable to keep the pace, ceased, and sat staring. The younger guests applauded, but the older faces began to grow anxious.

" 'Hadn't you better stop, dear?' said one of the women. "You'll make yourself so tired.'

"But Annette did not answer.

" 'I believe she's fainted,' cried out a girl who had caught sight of her face as it was swept by.

"One of the men sprang forward and clutched at the figure, but its impetus threw him down onto the floor, where its steel-cased feet laid bare his cheek. The thing evidently did not intend to part with its prize easily.

"Had anyone retained a cool head, the figure, one cannot help thinking, might easily have been stopped. Two or three men acting in concert might have lifted it bodily off the floor, or have jammed it into a corner. But few human heads are capable of remaining cool under excitement. Those who are not present think how stupid must have been those who were; those who are reflect afterwards how simple it would have been to do this, that, or the other, if only they had thought of it at the time.

"The women grew hysterical. The men shouted contradictory directions to one another. Two of them made a bungling rush at the figure, which had the result of forcing it out of its orbit in the center of the room, and sending it crashing against the walls and furniture. A stream of blood showed itself down the girl's white frock, and followed her along the floor. The affair was becoming horrible. The women rushed screaming from the room. The men followed them.

"One sensible suggestion was made: 'Find Geibel—fetch Geibel.'

"No one had noticed him leave the room, no one knew where he was. A party went in search of him. The others, too unnerved to go back into the ballroom, crowded outside the door and listened. They could hear the steady whir of the wheels upon the polished floor as the thing spun round and round; the dull thud as every now and again it dashed itself and its burden against some opposing object and ricocheted off in a new direction.

"And everlastingly it talked in that thin ghostly voice, repeating over and over the same formula: 'How charming you are looking tonight. What a lovely day it has been. Oh, don't be so cruel. I could go on dancing forever—with you. Have you had supper?'

"Of course they sought for Geibel everywhere but where he was. They looked in every room in the house, then rushed off in a body to his own place, and spent precious minutes in waking up his deaf old housekeeper. At last it occurred to one of the party that Wenzel was missing also, and then the idea of the counting house across the yard presented itself to them, and there they found him.

"He rose up, very pale, and followed them; and he and old Wenzel forced their way through the crowd of guests gathered outside, and entered the room, and locked the door behind them.

"From within there came the muffled sound of low voices and quick steps, followed by a confused scuffling noise, then silence, then the low voices again.

"After a time the door opened, and those near it pressed forward to enter, but old Wenzel barred the way.

" 'I want you—and you, Bekler,' he said, addressing a couple of the elder men. His voice was calm, but his face was deadly white. 'The rest of you, please go—get the women away as quickly as you can.'

"From that day old Nicholaus Geibel confined himself to the making of mechanical rabbits, and cats that mewed and washed their faces."

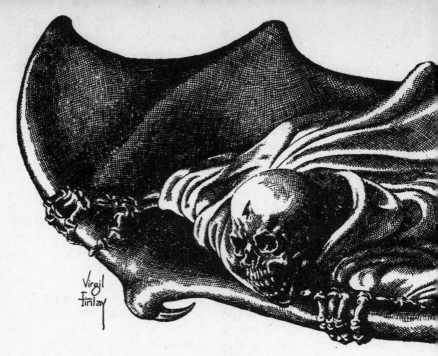

Virgil
Finlay

Lukundoo

EDWARD LUCAS WHITE

One of the most hackneyed ideas in horror fiction is the native curse, but Edward Lucas White's 1925 story "Lukundoo" breathes new life into the theme through its account of the peculiar fate visited upon a transgressor. The tale eventually became the title of White's first collection of fantasy stories, all of which he claimed had been based on dreams. He singled out "Lukundoo" in particular as having been inspired by a nightmare he had after reading H. G. Wells' "Pollock and the Poroh Man."

I T STANDS to reason, said Twombly, "that a man must accept the evidence of his own eyes, and when eyes and ears agree, there can be no doubt. He has to believe what he has both seen and heard."

"Not always," put in Singleton, softly.

Every man turned toward Singleton. Twombly was standing on the hearth-rug, his back to the grate, his legs spread out, with his habitual air of dominating the room. Singleton, as usual, was as much as possible effaced in a corner. But when Singleton spoke he said something. We faced him in that flattering spontaneity of expectant silence which invites utterance.

"I was thinking," he said, after an interval, "of something I both saw and heard in Africa."

Now, if there was one thing we had found impossible it had been to elicit from Singleton anything definite about his African experiences.

As with the Alpinist in the story, who could tell only that he went up and came down, the sum of Singleton's revelations had been that he went there and came away. His words now riveted our attention at once. Twombly faded from the hearth-rug, but not one of us could ever recall having seen him go. The room readjusted itself, focused on Singleton, and there was some hasty and furtive lighting of fresh cigars. Singleton lit one also, but it went out immediately, and he never relit it.

*   *   *

We were in the Great Forest, exploring for pigmies. Van Rieten had a theory that the dwarfs found by Stanley and others were a mere cross-breed between ordinary natives and the real pigmies. He hoped to discover a race of men three feet tall at most, or shorter. We had found no trace of any such beings.

Natives were few, game scarce; food, except game, there was none; and the deepest, dankest, drippingest forest all about. We were the only novelty in the country, no native we met had even seen a white man before, most had never heard of white men. All of a sudden, late one afternoon, there came into our camp an Englishman, and pretty well used up he was, too. We had heard no rumor of him; he had not only heard of us but had made an amazing five-day march to reach us. His guide and two bearers were nearly as done up as he. Even though he was in tatters and had five days' beard on, you could see he was naturally dapper and neat and the sort of man to shave daily. He was small, but wiry. His face was the sort of British face from which emotion has been so carefully banished that a foreigner is apt to think the wearer of the face incapable of any sort of feeling; the kind of face which, if it has any expression at all, expresses principally the resolution to go through the world decorously, without intruding upon or annoying anyone.

His name was Etcham. He introduced himself modestly, and ate with us so deliberately that we should never have suspected, if our bearers had not had it from his bearers, that he had had but three meals in the five days, and those small. After we had lit up he told us why he had come.

"My chief is ve'y seedy," he said between puffs. "He is bound to go out if he keeps this way. I thought perhaps. . . ."

He spoke quietly in a soft, even tone, but I could see little beads of sweat oozing out on his upper lip under his stubby mustache, and there was a tingle of repressed emotion in his tone, a veiled eagerness in his eye, a palpitating inward solicitude in his demeanor that moved me at once. Van Rieten had no sentiment in him; if he was moved he did not show it. But he listened. I was surprised at that. He was just the man to refuse at once. But he listened to Etcham's halting, diffident hints. He even asked questions.

"Who is your chief?"

"Stone," Etcham lisped.

That electrified both of us.

"Ralph Stone?" we ejaculated together.

Etcham nodded.

For some minutes Van Rieten and I were silent. Van Rieten had never seen him, but I had been a classmate of Stone's, and Van Rieten and I had discussed him over many a camp-fire. We had heard of him two years before, south of Luebo in the Balunda country, which had been ringing with his theatrical strife against a Balunda witch-doctor, ending in the sorcerer's complete discomfiture and the abasement of his tribe before Stone. They had even broken the fetish-man's whistle and given Stone the pieces. It had been like the triumph of Elijah over the prophets of Baal, only more real to the Balunda.

We had thought of Stone as far off, if still in Africa at all, and here he turned up ahead of us and probably forestalling our quest.

Etcham's naming of Stone brought back to us all his tantalizing story, his fascinating parents, their tragic death; the brilliance of his college days; the dazzle of his millions; the promise of his young manhood; his wide notoriety, so nearly real fame; his romantic elopement with the meteoric authoress whose sudden cascade of fiction had made her so great a name so young, whose beauty and charm were so much heralded; the frightful scandal of the breach-of-promise suit that followed; his bride's devotion through it all; their sudden quarrel after it was all over; their divorce; the too much advertised announcement of his approaching marriage to the plaintiff in the breach-of-promise suit; his precipitate remarriage to his divorced bride; their second quarrel and second divorce; his departure from his native land; his advent in the dark continent. The sense of all this rushed over me and I believe Van Rieten felt it, too, as he sat silent.

Then he asked:

"Where is Werner?"

"Dead," said Etcham. "He died before I joined Stone."

"You were not with Stone above Luebo?"

"No," said Etcham. "I joined him at Stanley Falls."

"Who is with him?" Van Rieten asked.

"Only his Zanzibar servants and the bearers," Etcham replied.

"What sort of bearers?" Van Rieten demanded.

"Mang-Battu men," Etcham responded simply.

Now that impressed both Van Rieten and myself greatly. It bore out Stone's reputation as a notable leader of men. For up to that time no one had been able to use Mang-Battu as bearers outside of their own country, or to hold them for long or difficult expeditions.

"Were you long among the Mang-Battu?" was Van Rieten's next question.

"Some weeks," said Etcham. "Stone was interested in them and made up a fair-sized vocabulary of their words and phrases. He had a theory that they are an offshoot of the Balunda and he found much confirmation in their customs."

"What do you live on?" Van Rieten enquired.

"Game, mostly," Etcham lisped.

"How long has Stone been laid up?" Van Rieten next asked.

"More than a month," Etcham answered.

"And you have been hunting for the camp?" Van Rieten exclaimed.

Etcham's face, burnt and flayed as it was, showed a flush.

"I missed some easy shots," he admitted ruefully. "I've not felt ve'y fit myself."

"What's the matter with your chief?" Van Rieten enquired.

"Something like carbuncles," Etcham replied.

"He ought to get over a carbuncle or two," Van Rieten declared.

"They are not carbuncles," Etcham explained. "Nor one or two. He has had dozens, sometimes five at once. If they had been carbuncles he would have been dead long ago. But in some ways they are not so bad, though in others they are worse."

"How do you mean?" Van Rieten queried.

"Well," Etcham hesitated, "they do not seem to inflame so deep nor so wide as carbuncles, nor to be so painful, nor to cause so much fever. But then they seem to be part of a disease that affects his mind. He let me help him dress the first, but the others he has hidden most carefully, from me and from the men. He keeps to his tent when they puff up, and will not let me change the dressings or be with him at all."

"Have you plenty of dressings?" Van Rieten asked.

"We have some," said Etcham doubtfully. "But he won't use them; he washes out the dressings and uses them over and over."

"How is he treating the swellings?" Van Rieten enquired.

"He slices them off clear down to flesh level, with his razor."

"What?" Van Rieten shouted.

Etcham made no answer but looked him steadily in the eyes.

"I beg your pardon," Van Rieten hastened to say. "You startled me. They can't be carbuncles. He'd have been dead long ago."

"I thought I had said they are not carbuncles," Etcham lisped.

"But the man must be crazy!" Van Rieten exclaimed.

"Just so, " said Etcham. "He is beyond my advice or control."

"How many has he treated that way?" Van Rieten demanded.

"Two, to my knowledge," Etcham said.

"Two?" Van Rieten queried.

Etcham flushed again.

"I saw him," he confessed, "through a crack in the hut. I felt impelled to keep a watch on him, as if he was not responsible."

"I should think not," Van Rieten agreed. "And you saw him do that twice?"

"I conjecture," said Etcham, "that he did the like with all the rest."

"How many has he had?" Van Rieten asked.

"Dozens," Etcham lisped.

"Does he eat?" Van Rieten enquired.

"Like a wolf," said Etcham. "More than any two bearers."

"Can he walk?" Van Rieten asked.

"He crawls a bit, groaning," said Etcham simply.

"Little fever, you say," Van Rieten ruminated.

"Enough and too much," Etcham declared.

"Has he been delirious?" Van Rieten asked.

"Only twice," Etcham replied; "once when the first swelling broke, and once later. He would not let anyone come near him then. But we could hear him talking, talking steadily, and it scared the natives."

"Was he talking their patter in delirium?" Van Rieten demanded.

"No," said Etcham, "but he was talking some similar lingo. Hamed Burghash said he was talking Balunda. I know too little Balunda. I do not learn languages readily. Stone learned more Mang-Battu in a week than I could have learned in a year. But I seemed to hear words like Mang-Battu words. Anyhow the Mang-Battu bearers were scared."

"Scared?" Van Rieten repeated, questioningly.

"So were the Zanzibar men, even Hamed Burghash, and so was I," said Etcham, "only for a different reason. He talked in two voices."

"In two voices," Van Rieten reflected.

"Yes," said Etcham, more excitedly than he had yet spoken. "In two voices, like a conversation. One was his own, one a small, thin, bleaty voice like nothing I ever heard. I seemed to make out, among the sounds the deep voice made, something like Mang-Battu words I knew, as *nedru, metababa,* and *nedo,* their terms for 'head,' 'shoulder,' 'thigh,' and perhaps *kudra* and *nekere* ('speak' and 'whistle'); and among the noises of the shrill voice *matompia, angunzi,* and *kamomami* ('kill,' 'death,' and 'hate'). Hamed Burghash said he also heard those words. He knew Mang-Battu far better than I."

"What did the bearers say?"

"They said, *'Lukundoo, Lukundoo!'*" Etcham replied. "I did not know that word; Hamed Burghash said it was Mang-Battu for 'leopard.'"

"It's Mang-Battu for 'witchcraft,'" said Van Rieten.

"I don't wonder they thought so," said Etcham. "It was enough to make one believe in sorcery to listen to those two voices."

"One voice answering the other?" Van Rieten asked perfunctorily.

Etcham's face went gray under his tan.

"Sometimes both at once," he answered huskily.

"Both at once!" Van Rieten ejaculated.

"It sounded that way to the men, too," Etcham told him. "And that was not all."

He stopped and looked helplessly at us for a moment.

"Could a man talk and whistle at the same time?" he asked.

"How do you mean?" Van Rieten queried.

"We could hear Stone talking away, his big, deep-chested baritone rumbling along, and through it all we could hear a high, shrill whistle, the oddest, wheezy sound. You know, no matter how shrilly a grown man may whistle, the note has a different quality from the whistle of a boy or a woman or a little girl. They sound more treble, somehow. Well, if you can imagine the smallest girl who could whistle keeping it up tunelessly right along, that whistle was like that, only even more piercing, and it sounded right through Stone's bass tones."

"And you didn't go to him?" Van Rieten cried.

"He is not given to threats," Etcham disclaimed. "But he had threatened, not volubly, nor like a sick man, but quietly and firmly, that if any man of us (he lumped me in with the men) came near him while he was in his trouble, that man should die. And it was not so much his words as his manner. It was like a monarch commanding respected privacy for a death-bed. One simply could not transgress."

"I see," said Van Rieten shortly.

"He's ve'y seedy," Etcham repeated helplessly. "I thought perhaps. . . ."

His absorbing affection for Stone, his real love for him, shone out through his envelope of conventional training. Worship of Stone was plainly his master passion.

Like many competent men, Van Rieten had a streak of hard selfishness in him. It came to the surface then. He said we carried our lives in our hands from day to day just as genuinely as Stone; that he did not forget the ties of blood and calling between any two explorers, but that there was no sense in imperiling one party for a very problematical benefit to a man probably beyond any help; that it was enough of a task to hunt for one party; that if two were united, providing food would be more than doubly difficult; that the risk of starvation was too great. Deflecting our march seven full days' journey (he complimented Etcham on his marching powers) might ruin our expedition entirely.

Van Rieten had logic on his side and he had a way with him. Etcham sat there, apologetic and deferential, like a fourth-form schoolboy before a head master. Van Rieten wound up.

"I am after pigmies, at the risk of my life. After pigmies I go."

"Perhaps, then, these will interest you," said Etcham, very quietly.

He took two objects out of the side-pocket of his blouse, and handed them to Van Rieten. They were round, bigger than big plums, and smaller than small peaches, about the right size to enclose in an average hand. They were black, and at first I did not see clearly what they were.

"Pigmies!" Van Rieten exclaimed. "Pigmies, indeed! Why, they wouldn't be two feet high! Do you mean to claim that these are adult heads?"

"I claim nothing," Etcham answered evenly. "You can see for yourself."

Van Rieten passed one of the heads to me. The sun was just setting and I examined it closely. A dried head it was, perfectly preserved, and the flesh as hard as Argentine jerked beef. A bit of a vertebra stuck out where the muscles of the vanished neck had shriveled into folds. The puny chin was sharp on a projecting jaw, the minute teeth white and even between the retracted lips, the tiny nose was flat, the little forehead retreating, there were inconsiderable clumps of stunted wool on the Lilliputian cranium. There was nothing babyish, childish or youthful about the head, rather it was mature to senility.

"Where did these come from?" Van Rieten enquired.

"I do not know," Etcham replied precisely. "I found them among Stone's effects while rummaging for medicines or drugs or anything that could help me to help him. I do not know where he got them. But I'll swear he did not have them when we entered this district."

"Are you sure?" Van Rieten queried his eyes big and fixed on Etcham's.

"Ve'y sure," lisped Etcham.

"But how could he have come by them without your knowledge?"

"Sometimes we were apart ten days at a time, hunting," said Etcham. "Stone is not a talking man. He gave me no account of his doings and Hamed Burghash keeps a still tongue and a tight hold on the men.

"You have examined these heads?" Van Rieten asked.

"Minutely," said Etcham.

Van Rieten took out his notebook. He was a methodical chap. He tore out a leaf, folded it and divided it equally into three pieces. He gave one to me and one to Etcham.

"Just for a test of my impressions," he said, "I want each of us to write separately just what he is most reminded of by these heads. Then I want to compare the writings."

I handed Etcham a pencil and he wrote. Then he handed the pencil back to me and I wrote.

"Read the three," said Van Rieten, handing me his piece.

Van Rieten had written:

"An old Balunda witch-doctor."

Etcham had written:

"An old Mang-Battu fetish-man."

I had written:

"An old Katongo magician."

"There!" Van Rieten exclaimed. "Look at that! There is nothing Wagabi or Batwa or Wambuttu or Wabotu about these heads. Nor anything pigmy either."

"I thought as much," said Etcham.

"And you say he did not have them before?"

"To a certainty he did not," Etcham asserted.

"It is worth following up," said Van Rieten. "I'll go with you. And first of all, I'll do my best to save Stone."

He put out his hand and Etcham clasped it silently. He was grateful all over.

Nothing but Etcham's fever of solicitude could have taken him in
five days over the track. It took him eight days to retrace with full
knowledge of it and our party to help. We could not have done it in
seven, and Etcham urged us on, in a repressed fury of anxiety, no
mere fever of duty to his chief, but a real ardor of devotion, a glow
of personal adoration for Stone which blazed under his dry conventional
exterior and showed in spite of him.

We found Stone well cared for. Etcham had seen to a good, high
thorn *zareba* round the camp, the huts were well built and thatched,
and Stone's was as good as their resources would permit. Hamed
Burghash was not named after two Seyyids for nothing. He had in him
the making of a sultan. He had kept the Mang-Battu together, not a
man had slipped off, and he had kept them in order. Also he was a
deft nurse and a faithful servant.

The two other Zanzibaris had done some creditable hunting. Though
all were hungry, the camp was far from starvation.

Stone was on a canvas cot and there was a sort of collapsible camp-
stool-table, like a Turkish tabouret, by the cot. It had a water-bottle
and some vials on it and Stone's watch, also his razor in its case.

Stone was clean and not emaciated, but he was far gone; not unconscious, but in a daze; past commanding or resisting anyone. He did
not seem to see us enter or to know we were there. I should have
recognized him anywhere. His boyish dash and grace had vanished
utterly, of course. But his head was even more leonine; his hair was
still abundant, yellow and wavy; the close, crisped blond beard he had
grown during his illness did not alter him. He was big and big-chested
yet. His eyes were dull and he mumbled and babbled mere meaningless
syllables, not words.

Etcham helped Van Rieten to uncover him and look him over. He
was in good muscle for a man so long bedridden. There were no scars
on him except about his knees, shoulders and chest. On each knee and
above it he had a full score of roundish cicatrices, and a dozen or
more on each shoulder, all in front. Two or three were open wounds
and four or five barely healed. He had no fresh swellings, except two,
one on each side, on his pectoral muscles, the one on the left being
higher up and farther out than the other. They did not look like boils
or carbuncles, but as if something blunt and hard were being pushed
up through the fairly healthy flesh and skin, not much inflamed.

"I should not lance those," said Van Rieten, and Etcham assented.

They made Stone as comfortable as they could, and just before sunset
we looked in at him again. He was lying on his back, and his chest
showed big and massive yet, but he lay as if in a stupor. We left
Etcham with him and went into the next hut, which Etcham had
resigned to us. The jungle noises were no different there than anywhere
else for months past, and I was soon fast asleep.

Some time in the pitch dark I found myself awake and listening. I
could hear two voices, one Stone's, the other sibilant and wheezy. I

knew Stone's voice after all the years that had passed since I heard it last. The other was like nothing I remembered. It had less volume than the wail of a new-born baby, yet there was an insistent carrying power to it, like the shrilling of an insect. As I listened I heard Van Rieten breathing near me in the dark, then he heard me and realized that I was listening, too. Like Etcham I knew little Balunda, but I could make out a word or two. The voices alternated with intervals of silence between.

Then suddenly both sounded at once and fast. Stone's baritone basso, full as if he were in perfect health, and that incredibly stridulous falsetto, both jabbering at once like the voices of two people quarreling and trying to talk each other down.

"I can't stand this," said Van Rieten. "Let's have a look at him."

He had one of those cylindrical electric night-candles. He fumbled about for it, touched the button and beckoned me to come with him. Outside of the hut he motioned me to stand still, and instinctively turned off the light, as if seeing made listening difficult.

Except for a faint glow from the embers of the bearers' fire we were in complete darkness; little starlight struggled through the trees; the river made but a faint murmur. We could hear the two voices together and then suddenly the creaking voice changed into a razor-edged, slicing whistle, indescribably cutting, continuing right through Stone's grumbling torrent of croaking words.

"Good God!" exclaimed Van Rieten.

Abruptly he turned on the light.

We found Etcham utterly asleep, exhausted by his long anxiety and the exertions of his phenomenal march and relaxed completely now that the load was in a sense shifted from his shoulders to Van Rieten's. Even the light on his face did not wake him.

The whistle had ceased and the two voices now sounded together. Both came from Stone's cot, where the concentrated white ray showed him lying just as we had left him, except that he had tossed his arms above his head and had torn the coverings and bandages from his chest.

The swelling on his right breast had broken. Van Rieten aimed the center line of the light at it and we saw it plainly. From his flesh, grown out of it, there protruded a head, such a head as the dried specimens Etcham had shown us, as if it were a miniature of the head of a Balunda fetish-man. It rolled the whites of its wicked, wee eyes and showed its microscopic teeth between lips repulsive in their red fullness, even in so diminutive a face. It had crisp, fuzzy wool on its minikin skull, it turned malignantly from side to side and chittered incessantly in that inconceivable falsetto. Stone babbled brokenly against its patter.

Van Rieten turned from Stone and waked Etcham, with some difficulty. When he was awake and saw it all, Etcham stared and said not one word.

"You saw him slice off two swellings?" Van Rieten asked.

Etcham nodded, chokingly.

"Did he bleed much?" Van Rieten demanded.

"Ve'y little," Etcham replied.

"You hold his arms," said Van Rieten to Etcham.

He took up Stone's razor and handed me the light. Stone showed no sign of seeing the light or of knowing we were there. But the little head mewled and screeched at us.

Van Rieten's hand was steady, and the sweep of the razor even and true. Stone bled amazingly little and Van Rieten dressed the wound as if it had been a bruise or scrape.

Stone had stopped talking the instant the excrescent head was severed. Van Rieten did all that could be done for Stone and then fairly grabbed the light from me. Snatching up a gun he scanned the ground by the cot and brought the butt down once and twice, viciously.

We went back to our hut, but I doubt if I slept.

Next day, near noon, in broad daylight, we heard the two voices from Stone's hut. We found Etcham dropped asleep by his charge. The swelling on the left had broken, and just such another head was there miauling and spluttering. Etcham woke up and the three of us stood there and glared. Stone interjected hoarse vocables into the tinkling gurgle of the portent's utterance.

Van Rieten stepped forward, took up Stone's razor and knelt down by the cot. The atomy of a head squealed a wheezy snarl at him.

Then suddenly Stone spoke English.

"Who are you with my razor?"

Van Rieten started back and stood up.

Stone's eyes were clear now and bright, as they moved restlessly about the hut.

"The end," he said; "I recognize the end. I seem to see Etcham, as if in life. But Singleton! Ah, Singleton! Ghosts of my boyhood come to watch me pass! And you, strange specter with the black beard and my razor! Aroint ye all!"

"I'm no ghost, Stone," I managed to say. "I'm alive. So are Etcham and Van Rieten. We have come here to help you."

"Van Rieten!" he exclaimed. "My work passes on to a better man. Luck go with you, Van Rieten."

Van Rieten went nearer to him.

"Just hold still a moment, old man," he said soothingly. "It will be only one twinge."

"I've held still for many such twinges," Stone answered quite distinctly. "Let me be. Let me die in my own way. The hydra was nothing to this. You can cut off ten, a hundred, a thousand heads, but the curse you cannot cut off, or take off. What's soaked into the bone won't come out of the flesh, any more than what's bred there. Don't hack me any more. Promise!"

His voice had all the old commanding tone of his boyhood and it swayed Van Rieten as it always had swayed everybody he knew.

"I promise," said Van Rieten.

Almost as he said the word Stone's eyes filmed again.

Then we three sat about Stone and watched that hideous, gibbering prodigy grow up out of Stone's flesh, till two horrid, spindling little black arms disengaged themselves. The infinitesimal nails were perfect to the barely perceptible moon at the quick, the pink spot on the palm was horridly natural. These arms gesticulated and the right plucked toward Stone's blond beard.

"I can't stand this," Van Rieten exclaimed and took hold of the razor again.

Instantly Stone's eyes opened.

"Van Rieten break his word?" he enunciated slowly. "Never!"

"But we must help you," Van Rieten gasped.

"I am past all help and all hurting," said Stone. "This is my hour. This curse is not put on me; it grew out of me, like this horror here. Even now I am going."

His eyes closed and we stood helpless, the adherent figure spouting shrill sentences.

In a moment Stone broke the terrible silence.

"You speak all tongues?" he said quickly.

And the emergent minikin replied in sudden English:

"Yea, verily, all that you speak," putting out its microscopic tongue, writhing its lips and wagging its head from side to side.

We could now see the thready ribs on its exiguous flanks heave as if the thing breathed.

"Has she forgiven me?" Stone asked in a muffled strangle.

"Not while the moss hangs from the cypresses," the head squeaked. "Not while the stars shine on Lake Ponchartrain will she forgive."

And then Stone, all with one motion, wrenched himself over on his side. The next instant he was dead.

*   *   *

When Singleton's voice ceased the room was hushed for a space. We could hear each other breathing.

Twombly, the tactless, suddenly broke the silence.

"I presume," he said, "you cut off the little miniken and brought it home in alcohol."

Singleton turned on him a stern countenance.

"We buried Stone," he said, "unmutilated as he died."

"But," said the unconscionable Twombly, "the whole thing is simply incredible."

Singleton stiffened.

"I did not expect you to believe it," he said; "I began by saying that although I heard and saw it, when I look back on it I cannot credit it myself."

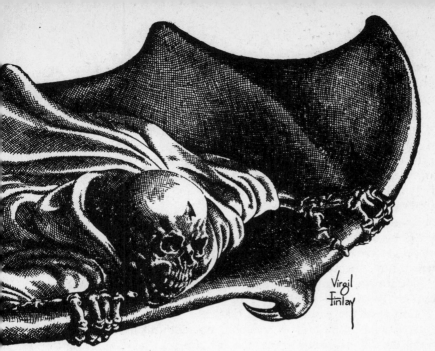

The Man Who Collected Poe

ROBERT BLOCH

Most of the writers who number among the best in horror fiction appeared in Famous Fantastic Mysteries, *except for Edgar Allan Poe—that is, if one excludes his presence in Robert Bloch's "The Man Who Collected Poe." Although Bloch is more often associated with his mentor, H. P. Lovecraft, this story shows great familiarity with the work of Lovecraft's own mentor as well as insight into what might best be called the pathology of avid fandom. In 1953, two years after "The Man Who Collected Poe" was published, Bloch was given the honor of completing Poe's unfinished tale "The Lighthouse" for* Fantastic.

DURING THE whole of a dull, dark and soundless day in the autumn of the year, when the clouds hung oppressively low in the heavens, I had been passing alone, by automobile, through a singularly dreary tract of country, and at length found myself, as the shades of the evening drew on, within view of my destination.

I looked upon the scene before me—upon the mere house, and the simple landscape features of the domain—upon the bleak walls—upon the vacant eye-like windows—upon a few rank sedges—and upon a few white trunks of decayed trees—with a feeling of utter confusion commingled with dismay. For it seemed to me as though I had visited this scene once before, or read of it, perhaps, in some frequently re-scanned tale. And yet assuredly it could not be, for only three days

had passed since I had made the acquaintance of Launcelot Canning
and received an invitation to visit him at his Maryland residence.

The circumstances under which I met Canning were simple; I happened to attend a bibliophilic meeting in Washington and was introduced to him by a mutual friend. Casual conversation gave place to
absorbed and interested discussion when he discovered my preoccupation with works of fantasy. Upon learning that I was traveling upon
a vacation with no set itinerary, Canning urged me to become his guest
for a day and to examine, at my leisure, his unusual display of
memorabilia.

"I feel, from our conversation, that we have much in common," he
told me. "For you see, sir, in my love of fantasy I bow to no man.
It is a taste I have perhaps inherited from my father and from his
father before him, together with their considerable acquisitions in the
genre. No doubt you would be gratified with what I am prepared to
show you, for in all due modesty, I beg to style myself the world's
leading collector of the works of Edgar Allen Poe."

I confess that his invitation as such did not enthrall me, for I hold
no brief for the literary hero-worshipper or the scholarly collector as
a type. I own to a more than passing interest in the tales of Poe, but
my interest does not extend to the point of ferreting out the exact date
upon which Mr. Poe first decided to raise a mustache, nor would I be
unduly intrigued by the opportunity to examine several hairs preserved
from that hirsute appendage.

So it was rather the person and personality of Launcelot Canning
himself which caused me to accept his proferred hospitality. For the
man who proposed to become my host might have himself stepped
from the pages of a Poe tale. His speech, as I have endeavored to
indicate, was characterized by a courtly rodomontade so often exemplified in Poe's heroes—and beyond certainty, his appearance bore out
the resemblance.

Launcelot Canning had the cadaverousness of complexion, the large,
liquid, luminous eye, the thin, curved lips, the delicately modelled
nose, finely moulded chin, and dark, web-like hair of a typical Poe
protagonist.

It was this phenomenon which prompted my acceptance and led me
to journey to his Maryland estate which, as I now perceived, in itself
manifested a Poe-etic quality of its own, intrinsic in the images of the
gray sedge, the ghastly tree-stems, and the vacant and eye-like windows
of the mansion of gloom. All that was lacking was a tarn and a moat—
and as I prepared to enter the dwelling I half expected to encounter
therein the carved ceilings, the sombre tapestries, the ebon floors and
the phantasmagoric armorial trophies so vividly described by the author
of *Tales of the Grotesque and Arabesque.*

Nor, upon entering Launcelot Canning's home, was I too greatly
disappointed in my expectations. True to both the atmospheric quality
of the decrepit mansion and to my own fanciful presentiments, the

door was opened in response to my knock by a valet who conducted me, in silence, through dark and intricate passages to the study of his master.

The room in which I found myself was very large and lofty. The windows were long, narrow, and pointed, and at so vast a distance from the black oaken floor as to be altogether inaccessible from within. Feeble gleams of encrimsoned light made their way through the trellised panes, and served to render sufficiently distinct the more prominent objects around; the eye, however, struggled in vain to reach the remoter angles of the chamber or the recesses of the vaulted and fretted ceiling. Dark draperies hung upon the walls. The general furniture was profuse, comfortless, antique, and tattered. Many books and musical instruments lay scattered about, but failed to give any vitality to the scene.

Instead they rendered more distinct that peculiar quality of quasi-recollection; it was as though I found myself once again, after a protracted absence, in a familiar setting. I had read, I had imagined, I had dreamed, or I had actually beheld this setting before.

Upon my entrance, Launcelot Canning arose from a sofa on which he had been lying at full length, and greeted me with a vivacious warmth which had much in it, I at first thought, of an overdone cordiality.

Yet his tone, as he spoke of the object of my visit, of his earnest desire to see me, and of the solace he expected me to afford him in a mutual discussion of our interests, soon alleviated my initial misapprehension.

Launcelot Canning welcomed me with the rapt enthusiasm of the born collector—and I came to realize that he was indeed just that. For the Poe collection he shortly proposed to unveil before me was actually his birthright.

Initially, he disclosed, the nucleus of the present accumulation had begun with his grandfather, Christopher Canning, a respected merchant of Baltimore. Almost eighty years ago he had been one of the leading patrons of the arts in his community and as such was partially instrumental in arranging for the removal of Poe's body to the south-eastern corner of the Presbyterian Cemetery at Fayette and Green Streets, where a suitable monument might be erected. This event occurred in the year 1875, and it was a few years prior to that time that Canning laid the foundation of the Poe collection.

"Thanks to his zeal," his grandson informed me, "I am today the fortunate possessor of a copy of virtually every existing specimen of Poe's published works. If you will step over here"—and he led me to a remote corner of the vaulted study, past the dark draperies, to a bookshelf which rose remotely to the shadowy ceiling—"I shall be pleased to corroborate that claim. Here is a copy of *Al Aaraaf, Tamerlane and other Poems* in the eighteen twenty-nine edition, and here is the still earlier *Tamerlane and other Poems* of eighteen twenty-seven. The Boston edition, which, as you doubtless know, is valued today at fifteen thousand dollars. I can assure you that Grandfather Canning parted with no such sum in order to gain possession of this rarity."

He displayed the volumes with an air of commingled pride and cupidity which is oft-times characteristic of the collector and is by no means to be confused with either literary snobbery or ordinary greed. Realizing this, I remained patient as he exhibited further treasures—copies of the *Philadelphia Saturday Courier* containing early tales, bound volumes of *The Messenger* during the period of Poe's editorship, *Graham's Magazine,* editions of the *New York Sun* and the *New York Mirror* boasting, respectively, of *The Balloon Hoax* and *The Raven,* and files of *The Gentleman's Magazine.* Ascending a short library ladder, he handed down to me the Lea and Blanchard edition of *Tales of the Grotesque and Arabesque,* the *Conchologist's First Book,* the Putnam *Eureka,* and, finally, the little paper booklet, published in 1843 and sold for 12½¢, entitled *The Prose Romances of Edgar A. Poe;* an insignificant trifle containing two tales which is valued by present-day collectors at $50,000.

Canning informed me of this last fact, and, indeed, kept up a running commentary upon each item he presented. There was no doubt but that he was a Poe scholar as well as a Poe collector, and his words informed tattered specimens of the *Broadway Journal* and *Godey's Lady's Book* with a singular fascination not necessarily inherent in the flimsy sheets or their contents.

"I owe a great debt to Grandfather Canning's obsession," he observed, descending the ladder and joining me before the bookshelves. "It is not altogether a breach of confidence to admit that his interest in Poe did reach the point of an obsession, and perhaps eventually of an absolute mania. The knowledge, alas, is public property, I fear.

"In the early seventies he built this house, and I am quite sure that you have been observant enough to note that it in itself is almost a replica of a typical Poeesque mansion. This was his study, and it was here that he was wont to pore over the books, the letters, and the numerous mementoes of Poe's life.

"What prompted a retired merchant to devote himself so fanatically to the pursuit of a hobby, I cannot say. Let it suffice that he virtually withdrew from the world and from all other normal interests. He conducted a voluminous and lengthy correspondence with aging men and women who had known Poe in their lifetime—made pilgrimages to Fordham, sent his agents to West Point, to England and Scotland, to virtually every locale in which Poe had set foot during his lifetime. He acquired letters and souvenirs as gifts, he bought them, and—I fear—stole them, if no other means of acquisition proved feasible."

Launcelot Canning smiled and nodded. "Does all this sound strange to you? I confess that once I, too, found it almost incredible, a fragment of romance. Now, after years spent here, I have lost my own objectivity."

"Yes, it is strange," I replied. "But are you quite sure that there was not some obscure personal reason for your grandfather's interest? Had he met Poe as a boy, or been closely associated with one of his friends? Was there, perhaps, a distant, undisclosed relationship?"

At the mention of the last word, Canning started visibly, and a tremor of agitation overspread his countenance.

"Ah!" he exclaimed. "There you voice my own inmost conviction. A relationship—assuredly there must have been one—I am morally, instinctively certain that Grandfather Canning felt or knew himself to be linked to Edgar Poe by ties of blood. Nothing else could account for his strong initial interest, his continuing defense of Poe in the literary controversies of the day, and his final melancholy lapse into a world of delusion and illusion.

"Yet he never voiced a statement or put an allegation upon paper—and I have searched the collection of letters in vain for the slightest clue.

"It is curious that you so promptly divine a suspicion held not only by myself but by my father. He was only a child at the time of my Grandfather Canning's death, but the attendant circumstances left a profound impression upon his sensitive nature. Although he was immediately removed from this house to the home of his mother's people in Baltimore, he lost no time in returning upon assuming his inheritance in early manhood.

"Fortunately being in possession of a considerable income, he was able to devote his entire lifetime to further research. The name of Arthur Canning is still well known in the world of literary criticism, but for some reason he preferred to pursue his scholarly examination of Poe's career in privacy. I believe this preference was dictated by an inner sensibility; that he was endeavoring to unearth some information which would prove his father's, his, and for that matter, my own, kinship to Edgar Poe."

"You say your father was also a collector?" I prompted.

"A statement I am prepared to substantiate," replied my host, as he led me to yet another corner of the shadow-shrouded study. "But first, if you would accept a glass of wine?"

He filled, not glasses, but veritable beakers from a large carafe, and we toasted one another in silent appreciation. It is perhaps unnecessary for me to observe that the wine was a fine old Amontillado.

"Now, then," said Launcelot Canning. "My father's special province in Poe research consisted of the accumulation and study of letters."

Opening a series of large trays or drawers beneath the bookshelves, he drew out file after file of glassined folios, and for the space of the next half hour I examined Edgar Poe's correspondence—letters to Henry Herring, to Doctor Snodgrass, Sarah Shelton, James P. Moss, Elizabeth Poe—missives to Mrs. Rockwood, Helen Whitman, Anne Lynch, John Pendleton Kennedy—notes to Mrs. Richmond, to John Allan, to Annie, to his brother, Henry—a profusion of documents, a veritable epistolary cornucopia.

During the course of my perusal my host took occasion to refill our beakers with wine, and the heady draught began to take effect—for we had not eaten, and I own I gave no thought to food, so absorbed was I in the yellowed pages illumining Poe's past.

Here was wit, erudition, literary criticism; here were the muddled, maudlin outpourings of a mind gone in drink and despair; here was the draft of a projected story, the fragments of a poem; here was a pitiful cry for deliverance and a paean to living beauty; here was a dignified response to a dunning letter and an editorial pronunciamento to an admirer; here was love, hate, pride, anger, celestial serenity, abject penitence, authority, wonder, resolution, indecision, joy, and soul-sickening melancholia.

Here was the gifted elocutionist, the stammering drunkard, the adoring husband, the frantic lover, the proud editor; the indigent pauper, the grandiose dreamer, the shabby realist, the scientific inquirer, the gullible metaphysician, the dependent stepson, the free and untrammeled spirit, the hack, the poet, the enigma that was Edgar Allan Poe.

Again the beakers were filled and emptied.

I drank deeply with my lips, and with my eyes more deeply still.

For the first time the true enthusiasm of Launcelot Canning was communicated to my own sensibilities—I divined the eternal fascination found in a consideration of Poe the writer and Poe the man; he who wrote Tragedy, lived Tragedy, was Tragedy; he who penned Mystery, lived and died in Mystery, and who today looms on the literary scene as Mystery incarnate.

And Mystery Poe remained, despite Arthur Canning's careful study of the letters. "My father learned nothing." my host confided, "even though he assembled, as you see here, a collection to delight the heart of a Mabbott or a Quinn. So his search ranged further. By this time I was old enough to share both his interest and his inquiries. Come," and he led me to an ornate chest which rested beneath the windows against the west wall of the study.

Kneeling, he unlocked the repository, and then drew forth, in rapid and marvelous succession, a series of objects each of which boasted of intimate connection with Poe's life.

There were souvenirs of his youth and his schooling abroad—a book he had used during his sojourn at West Point—mementoes of his days as a theatrical critic in the form of playbills, a pen used during his editorial period, a fan once owned by his girl-wife, Virginia, a brooch of Mrs. Clemm's; a profusion of objects including such diverse articles as a cravat-stock and—curiously enough—Poe's battered and tarnished flute.

Again we drank, and I own the wine was potent. Canning's countenance remained cadaverously wan—but, moreover, there was a species of mad hilarity in his eye—an evident restrained hysteria in his whole demeanor. At length, from the scattered heap of curiosa, I happened to draw forth and examine a little box of no remarkable character, whereupon I was constrained to inquire its history and what part it had played in the life of Poe.

"In the *life* of Poe?" A visible tremor convulsed the features of my host, then rapidly passed in transformation to a grimace, a rictus of amusement. "This little box—and you will note how, by some fateful design or contrived coincidence it bears a resemblance to the box he himself conceived of and described in his tale, *Berenice*—this little box is concerned with his death, rather than his life. It is, in fact, the self-same box my grandfather Christopher Canning clutched to his bosom when they found him down there."

Again the tremor, again the grimace. "But stay, I have not yet told you of the details. Perhaps you would be interested in seeing the spot where Christopher Canning was stricken; I have already told you of his madness, but I did no more than hint at the character of his delusions. You have been patient with me, and more than patient. Your understanding shall be rewarded, for I perceive you can be fully entrusted with the facts."

What further revelations Canning was prepared to make I could not say, but his manner was such as to inspire a vague disquiet and trepidation in my breast.

Upon perceiving my unease he laughed shortly and laid a hand upon my shoulder. "Come, this should interest you as an *aficionado* of fantasy," he said. "But first, another drink to speed our journey."

He poured, we drank, and then he led the way from that vaulted chamber, down the silent halls, down the staircase, and into the lowest recesses of the building until we reached what resembled a donjon-keep, its floor and the interior of a long archway carefully sheathed in copper. We paused before a door of massive iron. Again I felt in the aspect of this scene an element evocative of recognition or recollection.

Canning's intoxication was such that he misinterpreted, or chose to misinterpret, my reaction.

"You need not be afraid," he assured me. "Nothing has happened down here since that day, almost seventy years ago, when his servants discovered him stretched out before this door, the little box clutched to his bosom; collapsed, and in a state of delirium from which he never emerged. For six months he lingered, a hopeless maniac—raving as wildly from the very moment of his discovery as at the moment he died—babbling his visions of the giant horse, the fissured house collapsing into the tarn, the black cat, the pit, the pendulum, the raven on the pallid bust, the beating heart, the pearly teeth, and the nearly liquid mass of loathsome—of detestable putridity from which a voice emanated.

"Nor was that all he babbled," Canning confided, and here his voice sank to a whisper that reverberated through the copper-sheathed hall and against the iron door. "He hinted other things far worse than fantasy; of a ghastly reality surpassing all of the phantasms of Poe.

"For the first time my father and the servants learned the purpose of the room he had built beyond this iron door, and learned too what Christopher Canning had done to establish his title as the world's foremost collector of Poe.

"For he babbled again of Poe's death, thirty years earlier, in eighteen forty-nine—of the burial in the Presbyterian Cemetery—and of the removal of the coffin in eighteen seventy-four to the corner where the monument was raised. As I told you, and as was known then, my grandfather had played a public part in instigating that removal. But now we learned of the private part—learned that there was a monument and a grave, but no coffin in the earth beneath Poe's alleged resting place. The coffin now rested in the secret room at the end of this passage. That is why the room, the house itself, had been built.

"I tell you, he had stolen the body of Edgar Allan Poe—and as he shrieked aloud in his final madness, did not this indeed make him the greatest collector of Poe?

"His ultimate intent was never divined, but my father made one significant discovery—the little box clutched to Christopher Canning's bosom contained a portion of the crumbled bones, the veritable dust that was all that remained of Poe's corpse."

My host shuddered and turned away. He led me back along that hall of horror, up the stairs, into the study. Silently, he filled our beakers and I drank as hastily, as deeply, as desperately as he.

"What could my father do? To own the truth was to create a public scandal. He chose instead to keep silence; to devote his own life to study in retirement.

"Naturally the shock affected him profoundly; to my knowledge he never entered the room beyond the iron door and, indeed, I did not know of the room or its contents until the hour of his death—and it was not until some years later that I myself found the key among his effects.

"But find the key I did, and the story was immediately and completely corroborated. Today I am the greatest collector of Poe—for he lies in the keep below, my eternal trophy!"

This time I poured the wine. As I did so, I noted for the first time the imminence of a storm; the impetuous fury of its gusts shaking the casements, and the echoes of its thunder rolling and rumbling down the time-corroded corridors of the old house.

The wild, overstrained vivacity with which my host hearkened, or apparently hearkened, to these sounds did nothing to reassure me— for his recent revelation led me to suspect his sanity.

That the body of Edgar Allan Poe had been stolen—that this mansion had been built to house it—that it was indeed enshrined in a crypt below—that grandsire, son, and grandson had dwelt here alone, apart, enslaved to a sepulchral secret—was beyond sane belief.

And yet, surrounded now by the night and the storm, in a setting torn from Poe's own frenzied fancies, I could not be sure. Here the past was still alive, the very spirit of Poe's tales breathed forth its corruption upon the scene.

As thunder boomed, Launcelot Canning took up Poe's flute, and, whether in defiance of the storm without or as a mocking accompaniment, he played; blowing upon it with drunken persistence, with eery atonality, with nerve-shattering shrillness. To the shrieking of that infernal instrument the thunder added a braying counterpoint.

Uneasy, uncertain and unnerved, I retreated into the shadows of the bookshelves at the farther end of the room, and idly scanned the titles of a row of ancient tomes. Here was the *Chiromancy* of Robert Flud, the *Directorium Inquisitorum,* a rare and curious book in quarto Gothic that was the manual of a forgotten church; and betwixt and between the volumes of pseudo-scientific inquiry, theological speculation, and sundry incunabula I found titles that arrested and appalled me. *De Vermis Mysteriis* and the *Liber Eibon,* treatises on demonology, on witchcraft, on sorcery mouldered in crumbling binding. The books were old, but the books were not dusty. They had been read—

"Read them?" It was as though Canning divined my inmost thoughts. He had put aside his flute and now approached me, tittering as though in continued drunken defiance of the storm. Odd echoes and boomings now sounded through the long halls of the house, and curious grating sounds threatened to drown out his words and his laughter.

"Read them?" said Canning. "I study them. Yes, I have gone beyond grandfather and father, too. It was I who procured the books that held the key, and it was I who found the key. A key more difficult to discover, and more important, than the key to the vaults below. I often wonder if Poe himself had access to these selfsame tomes, knew the selfsame secrets. The secrets of the grave and what lies beyond, and what can be summoned forth if one but holds the key."

He stumbled away and returned with wine. "Drink," he said. "Drink to the night and the storm."

I brushed the proferred glass aside. "Enough," I said. "I must be on my way."

Was it fancy or did I find fear frozen on his features? Canning clutched my arm and cried, "No, stay with me! This is no night on which to be alone; I swear I cannot abide the thought of being alone, I can bear to be alone no more!"

His incoherent babble mingled with the thunder and the echoes; I drew back and confronted him. "Control yourself," I counseled. "Confess that this is a hoax, an elaborate imposture arranged to please your fancy."

"Hoax? Imposture? Stay, and I shall prove to you beyond all doubt"— and so saying, Launcelot Canning stooped and opened a small drawer set in the wall beneath and beside the bookshelves. "This should repay you for your interest in my story, and in Poe," he murmured. "Know that you are the first, other person than myself, to glimpse these treasures."

He handed me a sheaf of manuscripts on plain white paper; documents written in ink curiously similar to that I had noted while perusing Poe's letters. Pages were clipped together in groups, and for a moment I scanned titles alone.

"The Worm of Midnight, by Edgar Poe," I read, aloud. *"The Crypt,"* I breathed. And here, *"The Further Adventures of Arthur Gordon Pym"* —and in my agitation I came close to dropping the precious pages. "Are these what they appear to be—the unpublished tales of Poe?"

My host bowed.

Unpublished, undiscovered, unknown, save to me—and to you."

"But this cannot be," I protested. "Surely there would have been a mention of them somewhere, in Poe's own letters or those of his contemporaries. There would have been a clue, an indication, somewhere, some place, somehow."

Thunder mingled with my words, and thunder echoed in Canning's shouted reply.

"You dare to presume an imposture? Then compare!" He stooped again and brought out a glassined folio of letters. "Here—is this not the veritable script of Edgar Poe? Look at the calligraphy of the letter, then at the manuscripts. Can you say they are not penned by the selfsame hand?"

I looked at the handwriting, wondered at the possibilities of a monomaniac's forgery. Could Launcelot Canning, a victim of mental disorder, thus painstakingly simulate Poe's hand?

"Read, then!" Canning screamed through the thunder. "Read, and dare to say that these tales were written by any other than Edgar Poe, whose genius defies the corruption of Time and the Conqueror Worm!"

I read but a line or two, holding the topmost manuscript close to eyes that strained beneath wavering candlelight; but even in the flickering illumination I noted that which told me the only, the incontestable truth. For the paper, the curiously *unyellowed* paper, bore a visible watermark; the name of a firm of well-known modern stationers, and the date—1949.

Putting the sheaf aside, I endeavored to compose myself as I moved away from Launcelot Canning. For now I knew the truth; knew that, one hundred years after Poe's death, a semblance of his spirit still lived in the distorted and disordered soul of Canning. Incarnation, reincarnation, call it what you will; Canning was, in his own irrational mind, Edgar Allan Poe.

Stifled and dull echoes of thunder from a remote portion of the mansion now commingled with the soundless seething of my own inner turmoil, as I turned and rashly addressed my host.

"Confess!" I cried. "Is it not true that you have written these tales, fancying yourself the embodiment of Poe? Is it not true that you suffer from a singular delusion born of solitude and everlasting brooding upon the past; that you have reached a stage characterized by the conviction that Poe still lives on in your own person?"

A strong shudder came over him and a sickly smile quivered about his lips as he replied. "Fool! I say to you that I have spoken the truth. Can you doubt the evidence of your senses? This house is real, the Poe collection exists, and the stories exist—they exist, I swear, as truly as the body lying in the crypt below!"

I took up the little box from the table and removed the lid. "Not so," I answered. "You said your grandfather was found with this box clutched to his breast, before the door of the vault, and that it contained Poe's dust. Yet you cannot escape the fact that the box is empty." I faced him furiously. "Admit it, the story is a fabrication, a romance. Poe's body does not lie beneath this house, nor are these his unpublished works, written during his lifetime and concealed."

"True enough." Canning's smile was ghastly beyond belief. "The dust is gone because I took it and used it—because in the works of wizardry I found the formulae, the arcana whereby I could raise the flesh, recreate the body from the essential salts of the grave. Poe does not *lie* beneath this house—he *lives!* And the tales are *his posthumous works!*"

Accented by thunder, his words crashed against my consciousness.

"That was the end-all and the be-all of my planning, of my studies, of my work, of my life! To raise, by sorcery, the veritable spirit of Edgar Poe from the grave—reclothed and animate in flesh—set him to dwell and dream and do his work again in the private chambers I built in the vaults below—and this I have done! To steal a corpse is but a ghoulish prank; mine is the achievement of true genius!"

The distinct, hollow, metallic, and clangorous, yet apparently muffled reverberation accompanying his words caused him to turn in his seat and face the door of the study, so that I could not see the workings of his countenance—nor could he read my own reaction to his ravings.

His words came but faintly to my ears through the thunder that now shook the house in a relentless grip; the wind rattling the casements and flickering the candle-flame from the great silver candelabra sent a soaring sighing in an anguished accompaniment to his speech.

"I would show him to you, but I dare not; for he hates me as he hates life. I have locked him in the vault, alone, for the resurrected have no need of food nor drink. And he sits there, pen moving over paper, endlessly moving, endlessly pouring out the evil essence of all he guessed and hinted at in life and which he learned in death.

"Do you not see the tragic pity of my plight? I sought to raise his spirit from the dead, to give the world anew of his genius—and yet these tales, these works, are filled and fraught with a terror not to be endured. They cannot be shown to the world, he cannot be shown to the world; in bringing back the dead I have brought back the fruits of death!"

*   *   *

Echoes sounded anew as I moved toward the door—moved, I confess, to flee this accursed house and its accursed owner.

Canning clutched my hand, my arm, my shoulder. "You cannot go!" he shouted above the storm. "I spoke of his escaping, but did you not guess? Did you not hear it through the thunder—the grating of the door?"

I pushed him aside and he blundered backward upsetting the candelabra, so that flames licked now across the carpeting.

"Wait!" he cried. "Have you not heard his footstep on the stair? *Madman, I tell you that he now stands without the door!*"

A rush of wind, a roar of flame, a shroud of smoke rose all about us. Throwing open the huge, antique panels to which Canning pointed, I staggered into the hall.

I speak of wind, of flame, of smoke—enough to obscure all vision. I speak of Canning's screams, and of thunder loud enough to drown all sound. I speak of terror born of loathing and of desperation enough to shatter all my sanity.

Despite these things, I can never erase from my consciousness that which I beheld as I fled past the doorway and down the hall.

There without the doors there *did* stand a lofty and enshrouded figure; a figure all too familiar, with pallid features, high, domed forehead, mustache set above a mouth. My glimpse lasted but an instant, an instant during which the man—the corpse—the apparition—the hallucination, call it what you will—moved forward into the chamber and clasped Canning to his breast in an unbreakable embrace. Together, the two figures tottered toward the flames, which now rose to blot out vision forevermore.

From that chamber, and from that mansion, I fled aghast. The storm was still abroad in all its wrath, and now fire came to claim the house of Canning for its own.

Suddenly there shot along the path before me a wild light, and I turned to see whence a gleam so unusual could have issued—but it was only the flames, rising in supernatural splendor to consume the mansion, and the secrets, of the man who collected Poe.

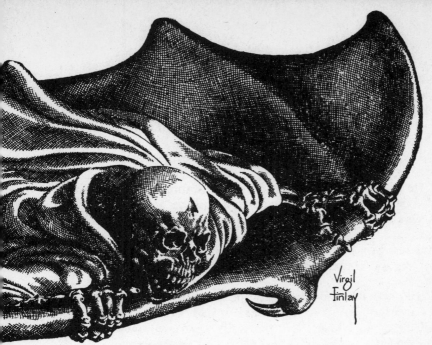

Thus I Refute Beelzy

JOHN COLLIER

Along with colleagues Shirley Jackson, Roald Dahl, and Jack Finney, John Collier proved that the macabre had a place in the literary main-stream. His sardonic tales of murderous plants, vengeful wives, and people who masquerade as department store mannequins appeared not in the pulps, but in magazines such as The New Yorker, The Atlantic Monthly, *and* Playboy. *Many of these stories were collected into his International Fantasy Award-winning 1951 book* Fancies and Goodnights. *"Thus I Refute Beelzy," reprinted in the October 1952* Famous Fantastic Mysteries, *is considered one of the best horror stories to deal with the theme of the imaginary playmate.*

"THERE GOES the tea bell," said Mrs. Carter. "I hope Simon hears it."

They looked out from the window of the drawing-room. The long garden, agreeably neglected, ended in a waste plot. Here a little summer-house was passing close by beauty on its way to complete decay. This was Simon's retreat. It was almost completely screened by the tangled branches of the apple tree and the pear tree, planted too close together, as they always are in the suburbs. They caught a glimpse of him now and then, as he strutted up and down, mouthing and gesticulating, performing all the solemn mumbo-jumbo of small boys who spend long afternoons at the forgotten ends of long gardens.

"There he is, bless him!" said Betty.

"Playing his game," said Mrs. Carter. "He won't play with the other children any more. And if I go down there—the temper! And comes in tired out!"

"He doesn't have his sleep in the afternoons?" asked Betty.

"You know what Big Simon's ideas are," said Mrs. Carter. " 'Let him choose for himself,' he says. That's what he chooses, and he comes in as white as a sheet."

"Look! He's heard the bell," said Betty. The expression was justified, though the bell had ceased ringing a full minute ago. Small Simon stopped in his parade exactly as if its tinny dingle had at that moment reached his ear.

They watched him perform certain ritual sweeps and scratchings with his little stick, and come lagging over the hot and flaggy grass toward the house.

Mrs. Carter led the way down to the playroom, or garden-room, which was also the tearoom for hot days. It had been the huge scullery of this tall Georgian house. Now the walls were cream-washed, there was coarse blue net in the windows, canvas-covered armchairs on the stone floor, and a reproduction of Van Gogh's *Sunflowers* over the mantelpiece.

Small Simon came drifting in, and accorded Betty a perfunctory greeting. His face was an almost perfect triangle, pointed at the chin, and he was paler than he should have been. "The little elf-child!" cried Betty.

Simon looked at her. "No," said he.

At that moment the door opened, and Mr. Carter came in, rubbing his hands. He was a dentist, and washed them before and after everything he did. "You!" said his wife, "Home already!"

"Not unwelcome, I hope," said Mr. Carter, nodding to Betty. "Two people cancelled their appointments; I decided to come home. I said, I hope I am not unwelcome."

"Silly!" said his wife. "Of course not."

"Small Simon seems doubtful," continued Mr. Carter. "Small Simon, are you sorry to see me at tea with you?"

"No, Daddy."

"No, what?"

"No, Big Simon."

"That's right. Big Simon and Small Simon. That sounds more like friends, doesn't it? At one time little boys had to call their father 'sir.' If they forgot—a good spanking. On the bottom, Small Simon! On the bottom!" said Mr. Carter, washing his hands once more with his invisible soap and water.

The little boy turned crimson with shame or rage.

"But now, you see," said Betty, to help, "you can call your father whatever you like."

"And what," asked Mr. Carter, "has Small Simon been doing this afternoon? While Big Simon has been at work?"

"Nothing," muttered his son.

"Then you have been bored," said Mr. Carter. "Learn from experience, Small Simon. Tomorrow, do something amusing, and you will not be bored. I want him to learn from experience, Betty. That is my way, the new way."

"I have learned," said the boy, speaking like an old, tired man, as little boys so often do.

"It would hardly seem so," said Mr. Carter, "if you sit on your behind all the afternoon, doing nothing. Had *my* father caught me doing nothing, I should not have sat very comfortably."

"He played," said Mrs. Carter.

"A bit," said the boy, shifting on his chair.

"Too much," said Mrs. Carter. "He comes in all nervy and dazed. He ought to have his rest."

"He is six," said her husband. "He is a reasonable being. He must choose for himself. But what game is this, Small Simon, that is worth getting nervy and dazed over? There are very few games that are as good as all of that."

"It's nothing," said the boy.

"Oh, come," said his father. "We are friends, are we not? You can tell me. I was a Small Simon once, just like you, and played the same games you play. Of course there were no aeroplanes in those days. With whom do you play this fine game? Come on, we must all answer civil questions, or the world would never go round. With whom do you play?"

"Mr. Beelzy," answered the boy, unable to resist.

"Mr. Beelzy?" said his father, raising his eyebrows inquiringly at his wife.

"It's a game he makes up," said she.

"Not makes up!" cried the boy. "Fool!"

"That is telling stories," said his mother. "And rude as well. We had better talk of something different."

"No wonder he is rude," said Mr. Carter, "if you say he tells lies, and then insist on changing the subject. He tells you his fantasy: you implant a guilt feeling. What can you expect? A defense mechanism. Then you get a real lie."

"Like in *These Three*," said Betty. "Only different, of course. *She* was an unblushing little liar."

"I would have made her blush," said Mr. Carter, "in the proper part of her anatomy. But Small Simon is in the fantasy stage. Are you not, Small Simon? You just make things up."

"No, I don't," said the boy.

"You do," said his father. "And because you do, it is not too late to reason with you. There is no harm in a fantasy, old chap. There is no harm in a bit of make-believe. Only you have to know the difference between day-dreams and real things, or your brain will never grow. It will never be the brain of a Big Simon. So come on. Let us hear about this Mr. Beelzy of yours. Come on. What is he like?"

"He isn't like any thing," said the boy.

"Like nothing on earth?" said his father. "That's a terrible fellow."

"I'm not frightened of him," said the child, smiling. "Not a bit."

"I should hope not," said his father. "If you were, you would be frightening yourself. I am always telling people, older people than you are, that they are just frightening themselves. Is he a funny man? Is he a giant?"

"Sometimes he is," said the little boy.

"Sometimes one thing, sometimes another," said his father. "Sounds pretty vague. Why can't you tell us just what he's like?"

"I love him," said the small boy. "He loves me."

"That's a big word," said Mr. Carter. "That might be better kept for real things, like Big Simon and Small Simon."

"He is real," said the boy, passionately. "He's not a fool. He's real."

"Listen," said his father. "When you go down the garden there's nobody there. Is there?"

"No," said the boy.

"Then you think of him, inside your head, and he comes."

"No," said Small Simon. "I have to make marks. On the ground. With my stick."

"That doesn't matter."

"Yes, it does."

"Small Simon, you are being obstinate," said Mr. Carter. "I am trying to explain something to you. I have been longer in the world than you have, so naturally I am older and wiser. I am explaining that Mr. Beelzy is a fantasy of yours. Do you hear? Do you understand?"

"Yes, Daddy."

"He is a game. He is a let's pretend."

The little boy looked down at his plate, smiling resignedly.

"I hope you are listening to me," said his father. "All you have to do is to say, 'I have been playing a game of let's-pretend. With someone I make up, called Mr. Beelzy.' Then no one will say you tell lies, and you will know the difference between dreams and reality. Mr. Beelzy is a daydream."

The little boy stared down steadfastly at his plate.

"He is sometimes there and sometimes not there," pursued Mr. Carter. "Sometimes he's like one thing, sometimes another. You can't really see him. Not as you see me. I am real. You can't touch him. You can touch me. I can touch you." Mr. Carter stretched out his big, white, dentist's hand, and took his little son by the nape of the neck. He stopped speaking for a moment and tightened his hand.

The little boy sank his head still lower.

"Now you know the difference," said Mr. Carter, "between a pretend and a real thing. You and I are one thing; he is another. Which is the pretend? Come on. Answer me. What is the pretend?"

"Big Simon and Small Simon," said the little boy.

"Don't!" cried Betty, and at once put her hand over her mouth, for why should a visitor cry "Don't!" when a father is explaining things in a scientific and modern way? Besides, it annoys the father.

"Well, my boy," said Mr. Carter, "I have said you must be allowed to learn from experience. Go upstairs. Right up to your room. You shall learn whether it is better to reason, or to be perverse and obstinate. Go up. I shall follow you."

"You are not going to beat the child?" cried Mrs. Carter.

"No," said the little boy. "Mr. Beelzy won't let him."

"Go on up with you!" shouted his father.

Small Simon stopped at the door. "He said he wouldn't let anyone hurt me," he whimpered. "He said he'd come like a lion, with wings on, and eat them up."

"You'll learn how real he is!" shouted his father after him. "If you can't learn it at one end, you shall learn it at the other. I'll have your breeches down. I shall finish my cup of tea first, however," said he to the two women.

Neither of them spoke. Mr. Carter finished his tea, and unhurriedly left the room, washing his hands with his invisible soap and water.

Mrs. Carter said nothing. Betty could think of nothing to say. She wanted to be talking for she was so afraid of what they might hear.

Suddenly it came. It seemed to tear the air apart. "Good God!" she cried. "What was that? He's hurt him." She sprang out of her chair, her silly eyes flashing behind her glasses. "I'm going up there!" she cried, trembling.

"Yes, let us go up," said Mrs. Carter. "Let us go up. That was not Small Simon."

It was on the second-floor landing that they found the shoe, with the man's foot still in it, like that last morsel of a mouse which sometimes falls unnoticed from the side of the jaws of the cat.

Homecoming

RAY BRADBURY

The supernatural creatures in Ray Bradbury's "The Homecoming" first made their appearance in stories written for Weird Tales. *They did not seem out of place when "The Homecoming" was published in* Mademoiselle *in 1946, because Bradbury portrayed their feelings of love and loneliness as no different from those of characters found in more realistic fiction. Indeed, it is Bradbury's concern with the emotional lives of both his mortal and fantastic characters that raised his work out of the pulps and earned him recognition as a representative twentieth-century author. The only one of Bradbury's three contributions to* Famous Fantastic Mysteries *not written especially for the magazine, "Homecoming" is a poignant variation on the theme of the misfit child.*

HERE THEY COME, said Cecy, lying there flat in her bed.

"Where are they?" cried Timothy from the doorway.

"Some of them are over Europe, some over Asia, some of them over the Islands, some over South America!" said Cecy, her eyes closed, the lashes long, brown, and quivering, her mouth opening to let the words whisper out swiftly.

Timothy came forward upon the bare plankings of the upstairs room. "*Who* are they?"

"Uncle Einar and Uncle Fry, and there's Cousin William, and I see

Frulda and Helgar and Aunt Morgianna, and Cousin Vivian, and I see Uncle Johann! They're all coming fast."

"Are they up in the sky?" cried Timothy, his little grey eyes flashing. Standing by the bed, he looked no more than his fourteen years. The wind blew outside, the house was dark and lit only by starlight.

"They're coming through the air and traveling along the ground, in many forms," said Cecy, in her sleeping. She did not move on the bed; she thought inward upon herself and told what she saw. "I see a wolf-like thing coming over a dark river—at the shallows—just above a waterfall, the starlight shining up his pelt. I see a brown oak leaf blowing far up in the sky. I see a small bat flying. I see many other things, running under the forest trees and slipping through the highest branches; and they're *all* coming this way!"

"Will they be here by tomorrow night?" Timothy clutched the bed-clothes. The spider on his lapel swung like a black pendulum, excitedly dancing. He leaned over his sister. "Will they all be here in time for the Homecoming?"

"Yes, yes, Timothy, yes," sighed Cecy. She stiffened. "Ask no more of me. Go away now. Let me travel in the places I like best."

"Thanks, Cecy," he said. Out in the hall, he ran to his room. He hurriedly made his bed. He had just awakened a few minutes ago, at sunset, and as the first stars had risen, he had gone to let his excitement about the party run with Cecy. Now she slept so quietly there was not a sound.

The spider hung on a silvery lasso about his slender neck as he washed his face. "Just think, Spid, tomorrow night is All Hallows' Eve!"

He lifted his face and looked into the mirror. His was the only mirror allowed in the house. It was his mother's concession to his "illness." Oh, if only he were not so afflicted! He opened his mouth, surveyed the poor, inadequate teeth nature had given him. No more than so many bean kernels, round, soft and pale in his jaws. The canines were nothing at all! Some of the high spirit died in him.

It was now totally dark and he lit a candle to see by. He felt exhausted. This past week the whole family had lived in the fashion of the old country. Sleeping by day, rousing at sunset to move about. There were blue hollows under his eyes. "Spid, I'm no good," he said quietly, to the little creature. "Can't even get used to sleeping days like the others."

He took up the candle. Oh, to have *strong* teeth, with incisors like spikes. Or strong hands, even; or a strong mind. To have the power to send one's mind out, free, as Cecy did, while lying on her soft bed—sleeping. But, no; he was the imperfect one, the sick one. He was even—he shivered and drew the candle flame closer—afraid of the dark. His brothers snorted at him. Bion and Leonard and Sam. They laughed because he slept in a *bed*. With Cecy it was different; her bed was part of her comfort for the composure necessary to send her mind abroad to hunt. But Timothy, did *he* sleep in the wonderful polished boxes like the others? He did *not!* Mother allowed him his own bed, his own room, his own *mirror!* No wonder the family skirted him like a holy man's crucifix. If only the wings would sprout from his shoulder blades. He bared his back, stared at it. He sighed again. No chance. Never.

Downstairs were exciting and mysterious sounds. The slithering sound of black crepe going up in all the halls and on the ceilings and doors. The smell of burning black tapers crept up the banistered stair-well.

Mother's voice, high and firm. Father's voice, echoing from the damp cellar. Bion walking from outside the old country house, lugging vast two gallon jugs of liquid that gurgled as he moved.

"I've just got to go to the party, Spid," said Timothy. The spider whirled at the end of its silk, and Timothy felt alone. He would polish cases, fetch toadstools and spiders, hang crepe, but when the party started he'd be ignored. The less seen or said of the imperfect son the better.

All through the house below, Laura ran. "The Homecoming!" she shouted gaily. "The Homecoming!" her footsteps everywhere at once.

Timothy passed Cecy's room again, and she slept soundly. Once in a great while she went below stairs. Mostly she stayed in bed. Lovely Cecy. He felt like asking her, "Where are you now, Cecy? And *in* who? And what's happening? Are you beyond the hills? And what goes on there?" But he walked on to Ellen's room instead.

Ellen sat at her desk, sorting out all kinds of blonde, red and dark hair and little clips of fingernail gathered from her manicurist job at the Mellin Town beauty parlor five miles over. A sturdy mahogany case lay in one corner with her name on it.

"Go away," she said, not even looking up at him. "I can't work with you gawking."

"All Hallows' Eve, Ellen!" he said, trying to be friendly. "Just think!"

"Huh!" She put fingernail clippings in small white sacks and labeled them. "What's it mean to you? It'll scare the hell out of you. Go back to bed."

His cheeks burned. "I'm needed to polish and work and help serve."

"If you don't go you'll find a dozen raw oysters in your bed tomorrow," said Ellen, matter-of-factly. "Good-by, Timothy."

In his anger, rushing downstairs, he bumped into Laura.

"Watch where you're going!" she shrieked from clenched teeth, out of which stuck tiny flat-headed nails. She hammered them into doors and upon them hung—what a joke!—imitation wolfsbane! "Won't this give Uncle Einar a fright!" she shouted to everybody.

She swept away. He ran to the open cellar door, smelled the channel of moist earthy air rising from below. "Father?"

"It's about time," father shouted up the steps. "Hurry down, or they'll be here before we're ready!"

Timothy hesitated only long enough to hear the million other house sounds. Brothers came and went like trains in a station, talking and arguing. If you stood in one spot long enough the entire household passed with their pale hands full of things. Leonard with his little black medical case, Samuel with his large, dusty, ebon-bound book under his arm, bearing more black crepe, and Bion excursioning to the wagon outside and bringing in many more gallons of liquid.

Father stopped polishing to give Timothy a rag and a scowl. He thumped the huge mahogany box. "Come on, shine this up, so we can start on another. Sleep your life away."

While waxing it, Timothy looked inside.

"Uncle Einar's a big man, isn't he, papa?"

"Umm."

"How big?"

"The size of the box'll tell you."

"Seven feet tall?"

"You talk a lot."

Timothy made the box shine. "And he weighs two hundred and five."

Father blew. "Two hundred and *fifteen*."

"And space for wings!"

Father elbowed him. "You're doing that wrong. *This* way. Watch!"

About nine o'clock Timothy ran out into the October weather. For two hours in the now-warm, now-cold wind he walked the meadows collecting toadstools and spiders.

He passed a farm house. "If only you knew what's happening at *our* house!" he said to the glowing windows. He climbed a hill and looked at the town, miles away, settling into sleep, the church clock high and round and white in the distance. The town didn't know, either.

He brought home many jars of toadstools and spiders.

In the cellar chapel a brief ceremony was celebrated with father incanting the dark lines, mother's beautiful white ivory hands moving in the reverse blessings, and all the children gathered except Cecy, who lay upstairs in bed. But Cecy was present. You saw her peering from now Bion's eyes, now Samuel's, now mother's, and you felt a movement and now she was in you, fleetingly, and gone.

Timothy prayed to the Dark One with a tightened stomach.

"Please, please, help me grow up, help me be like my brothers and sisters. Don't let me be different. If only I could put the hair in the plastic images as Ellen does, or make people fall in love with me, as Laura does with people, or read strange old books as Sam does, or work in a fine job like Leonard and Bion do. Or even raise a family some day, like mother and father've done. . . ."

At midnight the first relatives arrived! Grandmother and grandfather, all the way from the old country; cheery and talkative.

There was much greeting!

After that, people arrived every hour. There were flutters at side windows, raps on the front door, knocks at the back. Noises from the

cellar and rustlings from the attic, and the chimney whistled with
autumn wind. Mother filled the large crystal punch bowl with a fluid.
Father hurried from room to room lighting more tapers. Laura and
Ellen hammered up more imitation wolfsbane. And Timothy stood in
the center of the excitement, no expression on his face, his hands
trembling a little at his sides, gazing now here, now there, quickly,
quickly! See everything! Banging of doors, laughter, darkness, the sound
of wine fluidly poured, sound of wind, the rush of feet, the welcoming
bursts of talk at the doors, the transparent rattlings of windows, the
shadows passing, re-passing, whirling, vanishing.

The party was begun!

Five, ten, fifteen, thirty people! And sixty more to come!

"Well, and this *must* be Timothy!"

"What?"

A chilly hand took his hand. A long beardy face leaned down over
Timothy's brow. "A good lad, a good lad," said the man.

"Timothy," said mother. "This is your Uncle Jason."

"Hello, Uncle Jason."

"My, my, you don't sound very happy, Nephew Timothy."

"I'm all right."

"Thanks for telling me, my boy. Perk up." The man buffed Timothy's
chin with his cold fist, gently.

"And over *here*—" Mother drifted Uncle Jason away. Uncle Jason
glanced over his caped shoulder, winked at Timothy glassily.

Timothy stood alone.

From off a thousand miles in the candled dark, he heard a high
fluting voice; that was Ellen. "And my brothers, they *are* clever. Can
you guess their occupations, Aunt Morgianna?"

"I have no *idea*."

"They operate a mortuary in town."

"What!" A gasp.

"Yes!" Shrill laughter. "Isn't that *priceless!*"

"Wonderful!"

They all roared.

Timothy stood very still.

The laughter quieted. "They bring home sustenance for us all, you
know."

Laura cried. "Oh, yes! Are you familiar with how a mortician works,
Auntie darling?"

Aunt Morgianna was uncertain of the details.

"Well," began Laura, scientifically. "They push little silver needles
attached to red rubber tubing into the bodies, draw out the blood.
They inject preservative. Most morticians flush the blood down the
drain. But not Leonard and Bion, ah no! They carry it home in gallon
casques for mama and papa and all of us. Of course—Timothy. . . ."

Timothy jerked his mouth, softly.

"No, no," cried mother in a swift whisper to Laura.

"Timothy," drawled Laura, reluctant to leave the word alone.

An uneasy silence. Uncle Jason's voice demanded. "Well? Come on. What *about* Timothy?"

"Oh, Laura, your tongue," sighed mother.

Laura went on with it. Timothy shut his eyes. "Timothy doesn't—well—he doesn't *like* blood. He's—delicate."

"He'll learn," explained mother. "Given a little time," she said very firmly. "He's my son, and he'll learn. He's only fourteen."

"But I was *raised* on the stuff," said Uncle Jason, his voice passing from one room to another. The wind played the trees outside like harps. A little rain spattered on the window. "Raised on the stuff. . . ." passing away into faintness.

Timothy bit his lips and opened his eyes.

"Well, it was all *my* fault." Mother was showing them into the kitchen now. "I tried forcing him. You can't force children; you only make them sick and then they never get a taste for things. Look at Bion, now, he was thirteen before he'd drink b—"

The last word was lost in a rise of wind.

"I understand," murmured Uncle Jason. "Timothy'll come around."

"I'm *sure* he will," said mother, defiantly.

Candles flamed as shadows crossed and recrossed the dozen musty rooms. Timothy was cold. He smelled the hot tallow in his nostrils and instinctively he grabbed at a candle and walked with it around and about the house, pretending to straighten the crepe.

"Timothy." Someone whispered behind a patterned wall, hissing and sizzling and sighing the words. "Tim-o-thy-iss-a-fraid-of-thee-dark." Leonard's voice. Hateful Leonard! "So—mother sometimes—let's him take—a candle. You see them up and down the stairs together—the candle and Timothy's two grey eyes just behind the flame—close to it for warmth and color—shining."

"I *like* the candle, that's all," said Timothy, in a reproachful whisper.

"He'll be all right. Children are children," said an aunt's voice way over in the dining room blacknesses.

More noise, more laughter, more thunder! Cascades of wild laughter! Bangings and clickings and shouts and whisperings of clothing and capes! Moist fog swept through the front door like powder from exploded cannons! Out of the fog, settling his wings, stalked a tall man.

"Uncle Einar!"

Timothy propelled himself on his thin legs, straight through the fog, under the green webbing shadows. He threw himself into Uncle Einar's arms. Einar lifted him!

"You've wings, Timothy!" Light as thistles, he tossed the boy. "Wings, Timothy, fly!" Faces wheeled under. Darkness rotated. The house blew away. Timothy felt breezelike. He flopped his arms. Einar's fingers caught and threw him again to the ceiling. The ceiling fell like a charred wall. "Fly! Fly!" shouted Einar, loud and deep. "Fly with wings! Wings!"

He felt exquisite agonies in his shoulder blades, as if roots grew, burst to explode and blossom into fresh long moist membranes! He babbled wild stuff; again Einar hurled him high!

Autumn wind broke in a tide on the house, rain crashed down, shaking the beams, causing chandeliers to tilt their enraged candles. And the one hundred relatives stared out from each black enchanted niche and room, circling inward, all forms and sizes, to where Einar balanced the child like a puppet in the roaring spaces. "Beat your wings! Take off!"

"Enough!" cried Einar, at last.

Timothy, deposited gently to the floor timbers, exaltedly, fell against Uncle Einar, sobbing happily, "Uncle, uncle, uncle!"

"Good flying, eh, Timothy?"

Einar patted Timothy's head. "Good, good."

It was almost dawn. Most had arrived and were ready to bed down for the daylight, sleep motionlessly with no sound until the following sunset, when they'd jump out of their mahogany boxes for the revel.

Uncle Einar, followed by round dozens of others, moved toward the cellar. Mother directed them downward to the crowded row on row of highly polished boxes. Einar, his wings like sea green tarpaulins tented behind him, moved with a curious whistling and sussurus through the passageway. Where his wings touched they made a sound of drum heads gently beaten.

Upstairs, Timothy lay wearily, thinking, trying to *like* the darkness. There was so much you could do in darkness that people couldn't criticise you for, because they never saw you. He *did* like the night, but it was a qualified liking; some times there was so much night he cried out in rebellion.

In the cellar, mahogany lids sealed downward, drawn in upon gesturing pale hands. In corners, certain relatives circled three times to lie down, heads on paws, eyelids shut.

The sun rose. There was a sleeping with no snores in it.

*   *   *

Sunset. The revel exploded like a bat nest struck full, shrieking out, fluttering, spreading! Box lids banged wide! Steps rushed up from cellar damp! More late guests, kicking on front and back portals, were admitted, and apologized.

It rained, and sodden visitors flung their capes, their water-pelleted hats, their sprinkled veils over Timothy who bore them to a closet, where they hung like mummified bats to dry. The rooms were crowd-packed. The laughter of one cousin shot from the hall, angled off the parlor wall, riccocheted, banked and returned to Timothy's ears from a fourth room, accurate and cynical. It was followed by a volley of laughs!

A mouse ran across the floor.

"I know *you,* Niece Leibersrouter!" exclaimed father.

The mouse spiraled three women's feet and vanished in a corner. Moments later a beautiful woman rose up out of nothing, stood in the corner, smiling her white smile at them all.

Something huddled against the flooded pane of the kitchen window. It sighed and wept and tapped continually, pressed against the glass, but Timothy could make nothing of it, he saw nothing there. In imagination he was outside, staring in. The rain was on him, the wind at him, and the taper-dotted darkness inside was inviting. Waltzes were being waltzed; tall thin figures pirouetted and glided to outlandish music. Stars of light flickered off lifted bottles; small earth clods crumbled from the handled casques, and a spider fell and went silently legging over the floor.

Timothy shivered. He was inside the house again. Mother called him to run here, run there, help, serve, out to the kitchen, fetch this, fetch that, bring plates, heap the food, be careful, don't stumble, here now, and here—on and on—the party happened around him but not *to* him. Dozens of towering black shapes pressed by him, elbowed him, ignored him.

Finally, he turned and slipped away up the stairs.

*   *   *

He stood by Cecy's bed. There was not a tremor in her long narrow white face; it was completely calm. Her bosom did not rise or descend. Yet if you touched her, you felt warmth.

"Cecy," he called, softly.

There was no response until the third call, when her lips parted a little. "Yes." She sounded very tired and happy and dreaming, and remote.

"This is Timothy," he whispered.

"I know," she said, after a long wait.

"Where are you tonight, Cecy?"

After he had repeated the question twice, she said:

"Far west of here. In California. In the Imperial Valley, beside the Salten Sea, near the Mud Pots and the steam and the quiet. I'm a farmer's wife, and I'm sitting on a wooden porch. The sun's going slowly down."

"What's it like, Cecy?"

"You can hear the mud pots talking," she said, slowly, as if talking in church. "The mud pots lift little gray heads of steam, pushing up the mud like bald men rising in the thick syrup, head first, out in the broiling channels, and the grey heads rip like rubber fabric and collapse with a noise like wet lips moving. And little plumes of steam escape from the ripped tissue. And there is a smell of sulphur and deep burning and old time. The dinosaur had been a-broiling here ten million years."

"Is he done yet, Cecy?"

Cecy's calm sleeper's lips turned up. "Yes, he's done. Quite done."

about. "Look, Uncle Einar! I'll fly, at last!" Beat! went his hands. Up, down, pumped his feet! Faces flashed by him!

At the top of the stairs before knowing it, flapping, Timothy heard his mother cry, "Stop, Timothy!" far below.

"Hey!" shouted Timothy, and leaped off the top of the well, thrashing! Halfway down, the wings he thought he owned dissolved. He screamed. Uncle Einar caught him.

Timothy flailed whitely in the receiving arms. A voice burst from his lips, unbidden:

"This is Cecy! This is Cecy!" it announced, shrilly. "Cecy! Come see me, all of you! Upstairs, first room on the left!" Followed by a long trill of laughter. Timothy tried to cut it off with his tongue, his lips.

Everybody laughed. Einar set him down. Running through the crowded blackness as the relatives flowed upstairs toward Cecy's room to congratulate her. Timothy kicked the front door open. Mother called out behind him, anxiously.

Flap! went his dinner, straight down upon the cold earth.

*   *   *

"Cecy, I hate you, I hate you!"

Inside the barn, in deep shadow, Timothy sobbed bitterly and threshed in a stack of odorous hay. Then he lay still. From his blouse-pocket, from the protection of the match-box he used for his retreat, the spider crawled forth. Spid walked along Timothy's arm. Spid explored up his neck to his ear and climbed in the ear to tickle it.

Timothy shook his head. "Don't, Spid. Don't."

The feathery touch of a tentative feeler probing his eardrum set Timothy shivering. "Don't, Spid!" He sobbed somewhat less.

The spider traveled down his cheek, took a station under the boy's nose, looked up into the nostrils as if to see the brain, and then clambered softly up over the rim of the nose to sit, to squat there peering at Timothy with green gem eyes until Timothy filled with ridiculous laughter.

"Go away, Spid!"

In answer, the spider floated down to his lips and with sixteen delicate movements tacked silver strands back and forth, zigzag, over Timothy's mouth.

"Mmmm," cried Timothy.

Timothy sat up, rustling the hay. The land was very bright with moon now that the rain had retired. In the big house he could hear the faint ribaldry as MIRROR, MIRROR was played. In that game, a huge mirror was set against one wall. Celebrants shouted, dimly muffled as they tried to identify those of themselves whose reflections did not, had not ever, and *never would* appear in a mirror!

"What'll we do, Spid?" The mouth-web broke.

Falling to the floor, Spid scuttled swiftly toward the house, until Timothy caught him and returned him to his blouse pocket. "Okay, Spid. Back in it is. We'll have fun, no matter what."

Outside, a green tarpaulin fell from the sycamore as Timothy passed and pinned him down with the yards of silken goods. "Uncle Einar!"

"Timothy." The wings spread and twitched and came in with a sound like kettledrums. Timothy felt himself plucked up like a thimble and set on Einar's shoulder. "Don't feel badly, Nephew Timothy. Each to his own, each in his own way. How much better things are for you. How rich. The world's dead for us. We've seen so much of it, believe me. It's all one color; grey. Life's best to those who live the least of it. It's worth more per ounce."

From midnight on, Uncle Einar bore him about the house, from room to room, weaving, singing. Late arrivals by the horde set hilarities off afresh. Great-great-great-great and a thousand more greats grandmother was there, wrapped in Egyptian cerements, roll on roll of linen bandage coiled about her fragile dark brown bird bones. She said not a word, but lay stiff as a burnt ironing board against one wall, her eye hollows cupping a distant, wise, silent glimmering. At the four a.m. breakfast, one-thousand-odd greats grandma stiffly seated at the head of the longest table and red toasts were pantomimed to her.

Grandfather Tom wandered about through the throng at all hours, tickling young nieces, holding them, gumming their necks, a look of unbearable desperation flushing his features as time passed. Poor grandpa, in *his* profession, and no teeth!

The numerous young cousins caroused at the crystal punch bowl. Their shiny olive-pit eyes, their conical, devilish faces and curly bronze hair hovered over the drinking table, their hard-soft, half-girl, half-boy bodies wrestling against each other as they got unpleasantly, sullenly drunk.

Laura and Ellen, over and above the wine-sated tumult, produced a parlor drama with Uncle Fry. They represented innocent maidens strolling, when the Vampire (Uncle Fry) stepped from behind a tree (Cousin Anna). The Vampire smiled upon the innocents.

Where were they going?

Oh, just down to the river path.

Could he escort them along the way?

He might if he were pleasant.

He walked with them, grinning secretly, from time to time licking his lips.

He was just preparing to attack one of them (at the river) when the Innocents, whirling eagerly, knocked him flat and drained him vacuum-dry of his blood. They sat down on his carcass as on a bench, and laughed and laughed.

So did everybody at the Homecoming.

The wind got higher, the stars burned with fiery intensity, the noises redoubled, the dances quickened, the drinking became more positive.

To Timothy there were thousands of things to hear and watch. The many darknesses roiled, bubbled, the many faces mixed, vanished, reappeared, passed on. Mother moved everywhere, gracious and tall and beautiful, bowing and gliding, and father made sure that all the chalices were kept full.

The children played COFFINS. Coffins, set in a row, surrounded by marching children. Timothy with them. A flute kept them marching. One by one coffins were removed. The scramble for their polished interiors eliminated two, four, six, eight, contestants, until only one coffin remained. Timothy circled it cautiously, pitted against his fey cousin, Roby. The flute notes stopped. Like gopher to hole, Timothy made it, popped into the coffin, while everyone applauded.

Once more the wine cups were full.

"How is Lotte?"

"Lotte? Did you not hear? Oh, it is too good to tell!"

"Who's Lotte, Mama?"

"Hush. Uncle Einar's sister. She of the wings. Go on, Paul."

"Lotte flew over Berlin not long ago and was shot for a British plane."

"Shot for a plane!"

Cheeks blew out, lungs bulged and sank, hands slapped thighs. The laughter was like a cave of winds.

"And what of Carl?"

"The little one who lives under bridges? Ah, poor Carl. Where is there a place for Carl in all Europe? Each bridge has been devastated. Carl is either dead or homeless. There are more refugees in Europe tonight than meet mortal eyes."

"True, true. *All* the bridges, eh? Poor Carl."

"Listen!"

The party held its breath. Far away the town clock struck its chimes, saying six o'clock. The party was ending. As if at a cue, in time to the rhythm of the clock striking, their one hundred voices began to sing songs that were four hundred years old, songs Timothy could not know. They twined their arms around each other, circling slowly, and sang, and somewhere in the cold distance of morning the town clock finished out its chimes and quieted.

Timothy sang. He knew no words, no tune, yet he sang and the words and tune came correctly.

At the verse end, he gazed at the stairs and the closed door at the top of the stairs.

"Thanks, Cecy," he whispered. He listened.

Then he said, "That's all right, Cecy. You're forgiven. I know you."

Then he just relaxed and let his mouth move as it wished, and words came out rhythmically, purely, melodiously.

Good-bys were said, there was a great rustling. Mother and father and the brothers and sisters lined up in grave happiness at the door to shake each hand firmly and kiss each departing cheek in turn. The sky beyond the open door, colored and shone in the east. A cold wind entered.

Again Timothy was forced to listen to a voice talking and when it finished he nodded and said, "Yes, Cecy, I would like to do that. Thanks."

And Cecy helped him into one body after another. Instantly, he felt himself inside Uncle Fry's body at the door, bowing and pressing lips to mother's pale fingers, looking out from the wrinkled leather face at her. Then he side-stepped out into the wind, the draft seized him, took him in a flurry of leaves away up over the house and awakening hills. The Town flashed under. With a snap, Timothy was in another body, at the door, saying farewell. It was Cousin William's body.

Within Cousin William, swift as a smoke puff, he loped down the dirt road, red eyes burning, fur pelt rimed with morning, padded feet rising, falling with silent sureness, panting easily, again over the hill and into a hollow, and then dissolving away. . . .

Only to well up in the tall cold hollows of Uncle Einar and look out from his tolerant, amused eyes. And he was picking up the tiny pale body of Timothy. Picking up himself, through Einar! "Be a good boy, Timothy. I'll see you again, from time to time."

Swifter than the bourne leaves, with a webbed thunder of wings, faster than the lupine thing of the country's road, going so swiftly the earth's features blurred and the last stars rotated to one side, like a pebble in Uncle Einar's mouth. Timothy flew, accompanied him on half his startling journey.

He came back to his own body.

The shouting and the laughing bit by bit faded and went away. Dawn grew more apparent. Everybody was embracing and crying and thinking how the world was becoming less a place for them. There had been a time when they had met every year, but now decades passed with no reconciliation. "Don't forget, we meet in Salem in nineteen seventy!" someone cried.

Salem. Timothy's numbed mind turned the word over. Salem—1970. And there would be Uncle Fry and grandma and grandfather and a thousand-times-great grandmother in her withered cere-clothes. And mother and father and Ellen and Laura and Cecy and Leonard and Bion and Sam and all the rest. But would he be there? Would *he* be alive that long?

With one last withering wind blast, away they all shot, so many scarves, so many fluttery mammals, so many sered leaves, so many wolves loping, so many whinings and clustering noises, so many midnights and ideas and insanities.

Mother shut the door. Laura picked up a broom. "No," said mother. "We'll clean up tonight. We need sleep, first."

Father walked down into the cellar, followed by Laura and Bion and Sam. Ellen walked upstairs, as did Leonard.

Timothy walked across the crepe-littered hall. His head was down, and in passing the party mirror he saw himself, the pale mortality of his face. He was cold and trembling.

"Timothy," said mother.

He stopped at the stairwell. She came to him, laid a hand on his face. "Son," she said. "We love you. Remember that. We all love you. No matter how different you are, no matter if you leave us one day," she said. She kissed his cheek. "And if and when you die your bones will lie undisturbed, we'll see to that. You'll lie at ease forever, and I'll come see you every Hallows' Eve and tuck you in more secure."

The house echoed to polished wooden doors creaking and slamming hollowly shut.

The house was silent. Far away, the wind went over a hill with its last cargo of small dark bats, echoing, chittering.

He walked up the steps, one by one, crying to himself all the way.

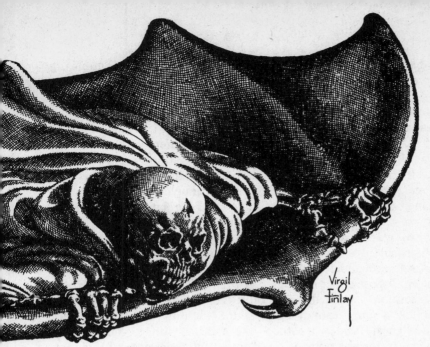

Worms of the Earth

ROBERT E. HOWARD

The brand of heroic fantasy known as sword-and-sorcery is generally considered to have originated with the work of Robert E. Howard, particularly in his tales of Conan the Barbarian. Howard's stories of Bran Mak Morn, King of the Picts, preceded his Conan tales into print by several years, and many readers find their fallible anti-hero a more complex and intriguing figure than the ever-victorious Conan. "Worms of the Earth" is a rare sword-and-sorcery story that is more a tale of horror than fantasy. It was originally published in Weird Tales, *and its appearance in the last issue of* Famous Fantastic Mysteries *can be seen as a tribute to the magazine that helped make* Famous Fantastic Mysteries, Fantastic Novels, *and all other fantasy fiction pulps possible.*

CHAPTER I

"STRIKE IN the nails, soldiers, and let our guest see the reality of our good Roman justice!"

The speaker wrapped his purple cloak closer about his powerful frame and settled back into his official chair, much as he might have settled back in his seat at the Circus Maximus to enjoy the clash of gladiatorial swords. Realization of power colored his every move. Whetted pride was necessary to Roman satisfaction, and Titus Sulla was justly proud; for he was military governor of Ebbracum and answerable only to the emperor of Rome. He was a strongly built man of medium height, with the hawk-like features of the pure-bred Roman. Now a mocking smile curved his full lips, increasing the arrogance of his haughty aspect. Distinctly military in appearance, he wore the golden-scaled corselet and chased breastplate of his rank, with the short stabbing sword at his belt, and he held on his knee the silvered helmet with its plumed crest. Behind him stood a clump of impassive soldiers with shield and spear—blond titans from the Rhineland.

Before him was taking place the scene which apparently gave him so much real gratification—a scene common enough wherever stretched the far-flung boundaries of Rome. A rude cross lay flat upon the barren earth and on it was bound a man—half naked, wild of aspect with his corded limbs, glaring eyes and shock of tangled hair. His executioners were Roman soldiers, and with heavy hammers they prepared to pin the victim's hands and feet to the wood with iron spikes.

Only a small group of men watched this ghastly scene in the dread place of execution beyond the city walls: the governor and his watchful guards; a few young Roman officers; the man to whom Sulla had referred as "guest" and who stood like a bronze image, unspeaking. Beside the gleaming splendor of the Roman, the quiet garb of this man seemed drab, almost somber.

He was dark, but did not resemble the Latins around him. There was about him none of the warm, almost Oriental sensuality of the Mediterranean which colored their features. The blond barbarians behind Sulla's chair were less unlike the man in facial outline than were the Romans. Not his were the full curving red lips, nor the rich waving locks suggestive of the Greek. Nor was his dark complexion the rich olive of the south; rather it was the bleak darkness of the north. The whole aspect of the man vaguely suggested the shadowed mists, the gloom, the cold and the icy winds of the naked northern lands. Even his black eyes were savagely cold, like black fires burning through fathoms of ice.

His height was only medium but there was something about him which transcended mere physical bulk—a certain fierce innate vitality, comparable only to that of a wolf or a panther. In every line of his supple, compact body, as well as in his coarse straight hair and thin lips, this was evident—in the hawk-like set of the head on the corded neck, in the broad square shoulders, in the deep chest, the lean loins, the narrow feet. Built with the savage economy of a panther, he was an image of dynamic potentialities, pent in with iron self-control.

At his feet crouched one like him in complexion—but there the resemblance ended. This other was a stunted giant, with gnarly limbs, thick body, a low sloping brow and an expression of dull ferocity, now clearly mixed with fear. If the man on the cross resembled, in a tribal way, the man Titus Sulla called guest, he far more resembled the stunted crouching giant.

"Well, Partha Mac Othna," said the governor with studied effrontery, "when you return to your tribe, you will have a tale to tell of the justice of Rome, who rules the south."

"I will have a tale," answered the other in a voice which betrayed no emotion, just as his dark face, schooled to immobility, showed no evidence of the maelstrom in his soul.

"Justice to all under the rule of Rome," said Sulla. "Pax Romana! Reward for virtue, punishment for wrong!" He laughed inwardly at his own black hypocrisy, then continued: "You see, emissary of Pictland, how swiftly Rome punishes the transgressor."

"I see," answered the Pict in a voice which strongly-curbed anger made deep with menace, "that the subject of a foreign king is dealt with as though he were a Roman slave."

"He has been tried and condemned in an unbiased court," retorted Sulla.

"Aye! and the accuser was a Roman, the witnesses Roman, the judge Roman! He committed murder? In a moment of fury he struck down a Roman merchant who cheated, tricked and robbed him, and to injury added insult—aye, and a blow! Is his king but a dog, that Rome crucifies his subjects at will, condemned by Roman courts? Is his king too weak or foolish to do justice, were he informed and formal charges brought against the offender?"

"Well," said Sulla cynically, "you may inform Bran Mak Morn yourself. Rome, my friend, makes no account of her actions to barbarian kings. When savages come among us, let them act with discretion or suffer the consequences."

The Pict shut his iron jaws with a snap that told Sulla further badgering would elicit no reply. The Roman made a gesture to the executioners. One of them seized a spike and placing it against the thick wrist of the victim, smote heavily. The iron point sank deep through the flesh, crunching against the bones. The lips of the man on the cross writhed, though no moan escaped him. As a trapped wolf fights against his cage, the bound victim instinctively wrenched and struggled. The veins swelled in his temples, sweat beaded his low forehead, the muscles in arms and legs writhed and knotted. The hammers fell in inexorable strokes, driving the cruel points deeper and deeper, through wrists and ankles; blood flowed in a black river over the hands that held the spikes, staining the wood of the cross, and the splintering of bones was distinctly heard. Yet the sufferer made no outcry, though his blackened lips writhed back until the gums were visible, and his shaggy head jerked involuntarily from side to side.

The man called Partha Mac Othna stood like an iron image, eyes burning from an inscrutable face, his whole body hard as iron from the tension of his control. At his feet crouched his misshapen servant, hiding his face from the grim sight, his arms locked about his master's knees. Those arms gripped like steel and under his breath the fellow mumbled ceaselessly as if in invocation.

The last stroke fell; the cords were cut from arm and leg, so that the man would hang supported by the nails alone. He had ceased his struggling that only twisted the spikes in his agonizing wounds. His bright black eyes, unglazed, had not left the face of the man called Partha Mac Othna; in them lingered a desperate shadow of hope. Now the soldiers lifted the cross and set the end of it in the hole prepared, stamped the dirt about it to hold it erect. The Pict hung in midair, suspended by the nails in his flesh, but still no sound escaped his lips. His eyes still hung on the somber face of the emissary, but the shadow of hope was fading.

"He'll live for days" said Sulla cheerfully. "These Picts are harder than cats to kill; I'll keep a guard of ten soldiers watching night and day to see that no one takes him down before he dies. Ho, there, Valerius, in honor of our esteemed neighbor, King Bran Mak Morn, give him a cup of wine!"

With a laugh the young officer came forward, holding a brimming wine-cup, and rising on his toes, lifted it to the parched lips of the sufferer. In the black eyes flared a red wave of unquenchable hatred; writhing his head aside to avoid even touching the cup, he spat full into the young Roman's eyes. With a curse Valerius dashed the cup to the ground, and before any could halt him, wrenched out his sword and sheathed it in the man's body.

Sulla rose with an imperious exclamation of anger; the man called Partha Mac Othna had started violently, but he bit his lip and said nothing. Valerius seemed somewhat surprised at him, as he sullenly cleansed his sword. The act had been instinctive, following the insult to Roman pride, the one thing unbearable.

"Give up your sword, young sir!" exclaimed Sulla. "Centurion Publius, place him under arrest. A few days in a cell with stale bread and water will teach you to curb your patrician pride, in matters dealing with the will of the empire. What, you young fool, do you not realize that you could not have made the dog a more kindly gift? Who would not rather desire a quick death on the sword than the slow agony on the cross? Take him away. And you, centurion, see that guards remain at the cross so that the body is not cut down until the ravens pick bare the bones. Partha Mac Othna, I go to a banquet at the house of Demetrius—will you not accompany me?"

Chapter II

THE EMISSARY shook his head, his eyes fixed on the limp form which sagged on the black-stained cross. He made no reply. Sulla smiled sardonically, then rose and strode away, followed by his secretary who bore the gilded chair ceremoniously, and by the stolid soldiers, with whom walked Valerius, head sunken.

The man called Partha Mac Othna flung a wide fold of his cloak about his shoulder, halted a moment to gaze at the grim cross with its burden, darkly etched against the crimson sky, where the clouds of night were gathering. Then he stalked away, followed by his silent servant.

In an inner chamber of Ebbracum, the man called Partha Mac Othna paced tigerishly to and fro. His sandalled feet made no sound on the marble tiles.

"Grom!" he turned to the gnarled servant, "well I know why you held my knees so tightly—why you muttered aid of the Moon-Woman— you feared I would lose my self-control and make a mad attempt to succor that poor wretch. By the gods, I believe that was what that dog Roman wished—his iron-cased watchdogs watched me narrowly, I know, and his baiting was harder to bear than ordinarily.

"Gods black and white, dark and light!" he shook his clenched fists above his head in the black gust of his passion. "That I should stand by and see a man of mine butchered on a Roman cross—without justice and with no more trial than that farce! Black gods of R'lyeh, even you would I invoke to the ruin and destruction of those butchers! I swear by the Nameless Ones, men shall die howling for that deed, and Rome shall cry out as a woman in the dark who treads upon an adder!"

"He knew you, master," said Grom.

The other dropped his head and covered his eyes with a gesture of savage pain.

"His eyes will haunt me when I lie dying. Aye, he knew me, and almost until the last, I read in his eyes the hope that I might aid him. Gods and devils, is Rome to butcher my people beneath my very eyes? Then I am not king but dog!"

"Not so loud, in the name of all the gods!" exclaimed Grom in affright. "Did these Romans suspect you were Bran Mak Morn, they nail you on a cross beside that other."

"They will know it ere long," grimly answered the king. "Too long I have lingered here in the guise of an emissary, spying upon mine enemies. They have thought to play with me, these Romans, masking their contempt and scorn only under polished satire. Rome is courteous to barbarian ambassadors, they give us fine houses to live in, offer us slaves, pander to our lusts with women and gold and wine and games, but all the while they laugh at us; their very courtesy is an insult, and sometimes—as today—their contempt discards all veneer. Bah! I've seen through their baitings—have remained imperturbably serene and swallowed their studied insults. But this—by the fiends of Hell, this is beyond human endurance! My people look to me; if I fail them—if I fail even one—even the lowest of my people, who will aid them? To whom shall they turn? By the gods, I'll answer the gibes of these Roman dogs with black shaft and trenchant steel!"

"And the chief with the plumes?" Grom meant the governor and his gutturals thrummed with the blood-lust. "He dies?" He flicked out a length of steel.

Bran scowled. "Easier said than done. He dies—but how may I reach him? By day his German guards keep at his back; by night they stand at door and window. He has many enemies, Romans as well as barbarians. Many a Briton would gladly slit his throat."

Grom seized Bran's garment, stammering as fierce eagerness broke the bonds of his inarticulate nature.

"Let me go, master! My life is worth nothing. I will cut him down in the midst of his warriors!"

Bran smiled fiercely and clapped his hand on the stunted giant's shoulder with a force that would have felled a lesser man.

"Nay, old war-dog, I have too much need of thee! You shall not throw your life away uselessly. Sulla would read the intent in your eyes, besides, and the javelins of his Teutons would be through you ere you could reach him. Not by dagger in the dark will we strike this Roman, not by the venom in the cup nor the shaft from the ambush."

The king turned and paced the floor a moment, his head bent in thought. Slowly his eyes grew murky with a thought so fearful he did not speak it aloud to the waiting warrior.

"I have become somewhat familiar with the maze of Roman politics during my stay in this accursed waste of mud and marble," said he. "During a war on the Wall, Titus Sulla, as governor of this province, is supposed to hasten thither with his centurions. But this Sulla does not do; he is no coward, but the bravest avoid certain things—to each man, however bold, his own particular fear. So he sends in his place Caius Camillus, who in times of peace patrols the fens of the west, lest the Britons break over the border. And Sulla takes his place in the Tower of Trajan. Ha!"

He whirled and gripped Grom with steely fingers.

"Grom, take the red stallion and ride north! Let no grass grow under the stallion's hoofs! Ride to Cormac na Connacht and tell him to sweep the frontier with sword and torch! Let his wild Gaels feast their fill of slaughter. After a time I will be with him. But for a time I have affairs in the west."

Grom's black eyes gleamed and he made a passionate gesture with his crooked hand—an instinctive move of savagery.

Bran drew a heavy bronze seal from beneath his tunic.

"This is my safe-conduct as an emissary to Roman courts," he said grimly. "It will open all gates between this house and Baal-dor. If any official questions you too closely—here!"

Lifting the lid of an iron-bound chest, Bran took out a small, heavy leather bag which he gave into the hands of the warrior.

"When all keys fail at a gate," said he, "try a golden key. Go now!"

There were no ceremonious farewells between the barbarian king and his barbarian vassal. Grom flung up his arm in a gesture of salute; then turning he hurried out.

Bran stepped to a barred window and gazed out into the moonlit streets.

"Wait until the moon sets," he muttered grimly. "Then I'll take the road to—Hell! But before I go I have a debt to pay."

The stealthy clink of a hoof on the flags reached him.

"With the safe-conduct and gold, not even Rome can hold a Pictish reaver," muttered the king. "Now I'll sleep until the moon sets."

With a snarl at the marble frieze-work and fluted columns, as symbols of Rome, he flung himself down on a couch, from which he had long impatiently torn the cushions and silk stuffs, as too soft for his hard body. Hate and the black passion of vengeance seethed in him, yet he went instantly to sleep. The first lesson he had learned in his bitter hard life was to snatch sleep any time he could, like a wolf that snatches sleep on the hunting trail. Generally his slumber was as light and dreamless as a panther's, but tonight it was otherwise.

He sank into fleecy gray fathoms of slumber and in a timeless, misty realm of shadows he met the tall, lean, white-bearded figure of old Gonar, the priest of the Moon, high counsellor to the king. And Bran stood aghast, for Gonar's face was white as driven snow and he shook as with ague. Well might Bran stand appalled, for in all the years of his life he had never before seen Gonar the Wise show any sign of fear.

"What now, old one?" asked the king. "Goes all well in Baal-dor?"

"All is well in Baal-dor where my body lies sleeping," answered old Gonar. "Across the void I have come to battle with you for your soul. King, are you mad, this thought you have thought in your brain?"

"Gonar," answered Bran somberly, "this day I stood still and watched a man of mine die on the cross of Rome. What his name or his rank, I do not know. I do not care. He might have been a faithful unknown warrior of mine, he might have been an outlaw. I only know that he was mine; the first scents he knew were the scents of the heather; the first light he saw was the sunrise on the Pictish hills. He belonged to me, not to Rome. If punishment was just, then none but me should have dealt it. If he were to be tried, none but me should have been his judge. The same blood in our veins; the same fire maddened our brains; in infancy we listened to the same old tales, and in youth we sang the same old songs. He was bound to my heart-strings, as every man and every woman and every child of Pictland is bound. It was mine to protect him; now it is mine to avenge him."

"But in the name of the gods, Bran," expostulated the wizard, "take your vengeance in another way! Return to the heather—mass your warriors—join with Cormac and his Gaels, and spread a sea of blood and flame the length of the great Wall!"

"All that I will do," grimly answered Bran. "But now—*now*—I will have a vengeance such as no Roman ever dreamed of! Ha, what do they know of the mysteries of this ancient isle, which sheltered strange life long before Rome rose from the marshes of the Tiber?"

"Bran, there are weapons too foul to use, even against Rome!"

Bran barked short and sharp as a jackal.

"Ha! There are no weapons I would not use against Rome! My back is at the wall. By the blood of the fiends, has Rome fought me fair? Bah! I am a barbarian king with a wolfskin mantle and an iron crown, fighting with my handful of bows and broken pikes against the queen of the world. What have I? The heather hills, the wattle huts, the spears of my shock-headed tribesmen! And I fight Rome—with her armored legions, her broad fertile plains and rich seas—her mountains and her rivers and her gleaming cities—her wealth, her steel, her gold, her mastery and her wrath. By steel and fire I will fight her—and by subtlety and treachery—by the thorn in the foot, the adder in the path, the venom in the cup, the dagger in the dark; aye," his voice sank somberly, "and by the worms of the earth!"

"But it is madness!" cried Gonar. "You will perish in the attempt you plan—you will go down to Hell and you will not return! What of your people then?"

"If I cannot serve them I had better die," growled the king.

"But you cannot even reach the beings you seek," cried Gonar. "For untold centuries they have dwelt *apart*. There is no door by which you can come to them. Long ago they severed the bonds that bound them to the world we know."

"Long ago," answered Bran somberly, "you told me that nothing in the universe was separated from the stream of Life—a saying the truth of which I have often seen evident. No race, no form of life but is close-knit somehow, by some manner, to the rest of Life and the world. Somewhere there is a thin link connecting *those* I seek to the world I know. Somewhere there is a Door. And somewhere among the bleak fens of the west I will find it."

Stark horror flooded Gonar's eyes and he gave back crying, "Wo! Wo! Wo! Wo! to Pictdom! Wo to the unborn kingdom! Wo, black wo to the sons of men! Wo, wo, wo, wo!"

Bran awoke to a shadowed room and the starlight on the window-bars. The moon had sunk from sight though its glow was still faint above the house tops. Memory of his dream shook him and he swore beneath his breath.

Rising, he flung off cloak and mantle, donning a light shirt of black meshmail, and girding on sword and dirk. Going again to the iron-bound chest he lifted several compact bags and emptied the clinking contents into the leathern pouch of his girdle. Then wrapping his wide cloak about him, he silently left the house. No servants there were to spy on him—he had impatiently refused the offer of slaves which it was Rome's policy to furnish her barbarian emissaries. Gnarled Grom had attended to all Bran's simple needs.

The stables fronted on the courtyard. A moment's groping in the dark and he placed his hand over a great stallion's nose, checking the nicker of recognition. Working without a light he swiftly bridled and saddled the great brute, and went through the courtyard into a shadowy side-street, leading him. The moon was setting, the border of floating shadows widening along the western wall. Silence lay on the marble palaces and mud hovels of Ebbracum under the cold stars.

Bran touched the pouch at his girdle, which was heavy with minted gold that bore the stamp of Rome. He had come to Ebbracum posing as an emissary of Pictdom, to act the spy. But being a barbarian, he had not been able to play his part in aloof formality and sedate dignity. He retained a crowded memory of wild feasts where wine flowed in fountains; of white-bosomed Roman women, who, sated with civilized lovers, looked with something more than favor on a virile barbarian; of gladiatorial games; and of other games where dice clicked and spun and tall stacks of gold changed hands. He had drunk deeply and gambled recklessly, after the manner of barbarians, and he had had a remarkable run of luck, due possibly to the indifference with which he won or lost. Gold to the Pict was so much dust, flowing through his fingers. In his land there was no need of it. But he had learned its power in the boundaries of civilization.

Almost under the shadow of the northwestern wall he saw ahead of him loom the great watch-tower which was connected with and reared above the outer wall. One corner of the castle-like fortress, farthest from the wall, served as a dungeon. Bran left his horse standing in a dark alley, with the reins hanging on the ground, and stole like a prowling wolf into the shadows of the fortress.

The young officer Valerius was awakened from a light, unquiet sleep by a stealthy sound at the barred window. He sat up, cursing softly under his breath as the faint starlight which etched the window-bars fell across the bare stone floor and reminded him of his disgrace. Well, in a few days he ruminated, he'd be well out of it; Sulla would not be too harsh on a man with hush high connections; then let any man or woman gibe at him! Damn that insolent Pict! But wait, he thought suddenly, remembering: what of the sound which had roused him?

"Hsssst!" it was a voice from the window.

Why so much secrecy? It could hardly be a foe—yet, why should it be a friend? Valerius rose and crossed his cell, coming close to the window. Outside all was dim in the starlight and he made out but a shadowy form close to the window.

"Who are you?" he leaned close against the bars, straining his eyes into the gloom.

His answer was a snarl of wolfish laughter, a long flicker of steel in the starlight. Valerius reeled away from the window and crashed to the floor, clutching his throat, gurgling horribly as he tried to scream. Blood gushed through his fingers, forming about his twitching body a pool that reflected the dim starlight dully and redly.

Outside Bran glided away like a shadow, without pausing to peer into the cell. In another minute the guards would round the corner on their regular routine. Even now he heard the measured tramp of their iron-clad feet. Before they came in sight he had vanished and they clumped stolidly by the cell-windows with no intimation of the corpse that lay on the floor within.

Bran rode to the small gate in the western wall, unchallenged by the sleepy watch. What fear of foreign invasion in Ebbracum?—and certain well organized thieves and women-stealers made it profitable for the watchmen not to be too vigilant. But the single guardsman at the western gate—his fellows lay drunk in a nearby brothel—lifted his spear and bawled for Bran to halt and give an account of himself. Silently the Pict reined closer. Masked in the dark cloak, he seemed dim and indistinct to the Roman, who was only aware of the glitter of his cold eyes in the gloom. But Bran held up his hand against the starlight and the soldier caught the gleam of gold; in the other he saw a long sheen of steel. The soldier understood, and he did not hesitate between the choice of a golden bribe or a battle to the death with this unknown rider who apparently a barbarian of some sort. With a grunt he lowered his spear and swung the gate open. Bran rode through, casting a handful of coins to the Roman. They fell about his feet in a golden shower, clinking against the flags. He bent in greedy haste to retrieve them and Bran Mak Morn rode westward like a flying ghost in the night.

Into the dim fens of the west came Bran Mak Morn. A cold wind breathed across the gloomy waste and against the gray sky a few herons flapped heavily. The long reeds and marsh-grass waved in broken undulations and out across the desolation of the wastes a few still meres reflected the dull light. Here and there rose curiously regular hillocks above the general levels, and gaunt against the somber sky Bran saw a marching line of upright monoliths—menhirs, reared by what nameless hands?

A faint blue line to the west lay the foothills that beyond the horizon grew to the wild mountains of Wales where dwelt still wild Celtic tribes—fierce blue-eyed men that knew not the yoke of Rome. A row of well-garrisoned watch-towers held them in check. Even now, far away across the moors, Bran glimpsed the unassailable keep men called the Tower of Trajan.

These barren wastes seemed the dreary accomplishment of desolation, yet human life was not utterly lacking. Bran met the silent men of the fen, reticent, dark of eye and hair; speaking a strange mixed tongue whose long-blended elements had forgotten their pristine separate sources. Bran recognized a certain kinship in these people to himself, but he looked on them with the scorn of a pure-blooded patrician for men of mixed strains.

Not that the common people of Caledonia were altogether pure-blooded; they got their stocky bodies and massive limbs from a primitive Teutonic race which had found its way into the northern tip of the isle even before the Celtic conquest of Britain was completed, and had been absorbed by the Picts. But the chiefs of Bran's folk had kept their blood from foreign taint since the beginnings of time, and he himself was a pure-bred Pict of the Old Race. But these fenmen, overrun repeatedly by British, Gaelic and Roman conquerors, had assimilated blood of each, and in the process almost forgotten their original language and lineage.

For Bran came of a race that was very old, which had spread over western Europe in one vast Dark Empire, before the coming of the Aryans, when the ancestors of the Celts, the Hellenes and the Germans were one primal people, before the days of tribal splitting-off and westward drift.

Only in Caledonia, Bran brooded, had his people resisted the flood of Aryan conquest. He had heard of a Pictish people called Basques, who in the crags of the Pyrenees called themselves an unconquered race; but he knew that they had paid tribute for centuries to the ancestors of the Gaels, before these Celtic conquerors abandoned their mountain-realm and set sail for Ireland. Only the Picts of Caledonia had remained free, and they had been scattered into small feuding tribes—he was the first acknowledged king in five hundred years—the beginning of a new dynasty under a new name. In the very teeth of Rome he dreamed his dreams of empire.

He wandered through the fens, seeking a Door. Of his quest he said nothing to the dark-eyed fenmen. They told him news that drifted from mouth to mouth—a tale of war in the north, the skirl of war-pipes along the winding Wall, of gathering-fires in the heather, of flame and smoke and rapine and the glutting of Gaelic swords in the crimson sea of slaughter. The eagles of the legions were moving northward and the ancient road resounded to the measured tramp of the iron-clad feet. And Bran, in the fens of the west, laughed, well pleased.

In Ebbracum Titus Sulla gave secret word to seek out the Pictish emissary with the Gaelic name who had been under suspicion, and who had vanished the night young Valerius was found dead in his cell with his throat ripped out. Sulla felt that this sudden bursting flame of war on the Wall was connected closely with his execution of a condemned Pictish criminal, and he set his spy system to work, though he felt sure that Partha Mac Othna was by this time far beyond his reach. He prepared to march from Ebbracum, but he did not accompany the considerable force of legionairies which he sent north. Sulla was a brave man, but each man has his own dread, and Sulla's was Cormac na Connacht, the black-haired prince of the Gaels, who had sworn to cut out the governors' heart and eat it raw. So Sulla rode with his ever-present bodyguard, westward, where lay the Tower of Trajan with its war-like commander, Caius Camillus, who enjoyed nothing more than taking his superior's place when the red waves of war washed at the foot of the Wall. Devious politics, but the legate of Rome seldom visited this far isle, and what with his wealth and intrigues, Titus Sulla was the highest power in Britain.

And Bran, knowing all this, patiently waited his coming, in the deserted hut in which he had taken up his abode.

One gray evening he strode on foot across the moors, a stark figure, blackly etched against the dim crimson fire of the sunset. He felt the incredible antiquity of the slumbering land, as he walked like the last man on the day after the end of the world. Yet at last he saw a token of human life—a drab hut of wattle and mud, set in the reedy breast of the fen.

A woman greeted him from the open door and Bran's somber eyes narrowed with a dark suspicion. The woman was not old, yet the evil wisdom of ages was in her eyes; her garments were ragged and scanty, her black locks tangled and unkempt, lending her an aspect of wildness well in keeping with her grim surroundings. Her red lips laughed but there was no mirth in her laughter, only a hint of mockery, and under the lips her teeth showed sharp and pointed like fangs.

"Enter, master," said she, "if you do not fear to share the roof of the witch-woman of Dagon-moor!"

Bran entered silently and sat him down on a broken bench while the woman busied herself with the scanty meal cooking over an open fire on the squalid hearth. He studied her lithe, almost serpentine motions, the ears which were almost pointed, the yellow eyes which slanted curiously.

"What do you seek in the fens, my lord?" she asked, turning toward him with a supple twist of her whole body.

"I seek a Door," he answered, chin resting on his fist. "I have a song to sing to the worms of the earth!"

She started upright, a jar falling from her hands to shatter on the hearth.

"This is an ill saying, even spoken in chance," she stammered.

"I speak not by chance but by intent," he answered.

She shook her head. "I know not what you mean."

"Well you know," he returned. "Aye, you know well! My race is very old—they reigned in Britain before the nations of the Celts and the Hellenes were born out of the womb of peoples. But my people were not first in Britain. By the mottles on your skin, by the slanting of your eyes, by the taint in your veins, I speak with full knowledge and meaning."

A while she stood silent, her lips smiling but her face inscrutable.

"Man, are you mad?" she asked, "that in your madness you come seeking that from which strong men fled screaming in old times?"

"I seek a vengeance," he answered, "that can be accomplished only by Them I seek."

She shook her head.

"You have listened to a bird singing; you have dreamed empty dreams."

"I have heard a viper hiss," he growled, "and I do not dream. Enough of this weaving of words. I came seeking a link between two worlds; I have found it."

"I need lie to you no more, man of the North," answered the woman.

"They you seek still dwell beneath the sleeping hills. They have drawn *apart*, farther and farther from the world you know."

"But they still steal forth in the night to grip women straying on the moors," said he, his gaze on her slanted eyes. She laughed wickedly.

"What would you of me?"

"That you bring me to Them."

She flung back her head with a scornful laugh. His left hand locked like iron in the breast of her scanty garment and his right closed on his hilt. She laughed in his face.

"Strike and be damned, my northern wolf! Do you think that such life as mine is so sweet that I could cling to it as a babe to the breast?"

His hand fell away.

"You are right. Threats are foolish. I will buy your aid."

"How?" the laughing voice hummed with mockery.

Bran opened his pouch and poured into his cupped palm a stream of gold.

"More wealth than the men of the fen ever dreamed of."

Again she laughed. "What is this rusty metal to me? Save it for some white-breasted Roman woman who will play the traitor for you!"

"Name me a price!" he urged. "The head of an enemy—"

"By the blood in my veins, with its heritage of ancient hate, who is mine enemy but thee?" she laughed and springing, struck cat-like. But her dagger splintered on the mail beneath his cloak and he flung her off with a loathsome flirt of his wrist which tossed her sprawling across her grass-strewn bunk. Lying there she laughed up at him.

"I will name you a price, then, my wolf, and it may be in days to come you will curse the armor that broke Atla's dagger!" She rose and came close to him, her disquietingly long hands fastened fiercely into his cloak. "I will tell you, Black Bran, king of Caledon! Oh, I knew you when you came into my hut with your black hair and your cold eyes! I will lead you to the doors of Hell if you wish—and the price shall be the kisses of a king!

"What of my blasted and bitter life, I, whom mortal men loathe and fear? I have not known the love of men, the clasp of a strong arm, the sting of human kisses, I, Atla, the were-woman of the moors! What have I known but the lone winds of the fens, the dreary fire of cold sunsets, the whispering of the marsh grasses?—the faces that blink up at me in the waters of the meres, the foot-pad of night—things in the gloom, the glimmer of red eyes, the grisly murmur of nameless beings in the night!

"I am half-human, at least! Have I not known sorrow and yearning and crying wistfulness, and the drear ache of loneliness? Give to me, king—give me your fierce kisses and your hurtful barbarian's embrace. Then in the long dear years to come I shall not utterly eat out my heart in vain envy of the white-bosomed women of men; for I shall have a memory few of them can boast—the kisses of a king! One night of love, oh king, and I will guide you to the gates of Hell!"

Bran eyed her somberly; he reached forth and gripped her arm in his iron fingers. An involuntary shudder shook him at the feel of her sleek skin. He nodded slowly and drawing her close to him, forced his head down to meet her lifted lips.

CHAPTER III

THE COLD gray mists of dawn wrapped King Bran like a clammy cloak. He turned to the woman whose slanted eyes gleamed in the gray gloom.

"Make good your part of the contract," he said roughly. "I sought a link between worlds and in you I found it. I seek the one thing sacred to Them. It shall be the Key opening the Door that lies unseen between me and Them. Tell me how I can reach it."

"I will, " the red lips smiled terribly. "Go to the mound men call Dagon's Barrow. Draw aside the stone that blocks the entrance and go under the dome of the mound. The floor of the chamber is made of seven great stones, six grouped about the seventh. Lift out the center stone—and you will see!"

"Will I find the Black Stone?" he asked.

"Dagon's Barrow is the Door to the Black Stone," she answered, "if you dare follow the Road."

"Will the symbol be well guarded?" He unconsciously loosened his blade in its sheath. The red lips curled mockingly.

"If you meet any on the Road you will die as no mortal man has died for long centuries. The Stone is not guarded, as men guard their treasures. Why should They guard what man has never sought? Perhaps They will be near, perhaps not. It is a chance you must take, if you wish the Stone. Beware, king of Pictdom! Remember it was your folk who, so long ago, cut the thread that bound Them to human life. They were almost human then—they overspread the land and knew the sunlight. Now they have drawn *apart*. They know not the sunlight and they shun the light of the moon. Even the starlight they hate. Far, far apart have they drawn, who might have been men in time, but for the spears of your ancestors."

The sky was overcast with misty gray, through which the sun shone coldly yellow when Bran came to Dagon's Barrow, a round hillock overgrown with rank grass of a curious fungoid appearance. On the eastern side of the mound showed the entrance of a crudely built stone tunnel which evidently penetrated the barrow. One great stone blocked the entrance to the tomb. Bran laid hold of the sharp edges and exerted all his strength. It held fast. He drew his sword and worked the blade between the blocking stone and the sill. Using the sword as a lever, he worked carefully, and managed to loosen the great stone and wrench it out. A foul charnel-house scent flowed out of the aperture and the dim sunlight seemed less to illuminate the cavern-like opening than to be fouled by the rank darkness which clung there.

Sword in hand, ready for he knew not what, Bran groped his way into the tunnel, which was long and narrow, built up of heavy joined stones, and was too low for him to stand erect. Either his eyes became somewhat accustomed to the gloom, or the darkness was, after all, somewhat lightened by the sunlight filtering in through the entrance. At any rate he came into a round low chamber and was able to make out its general dome-like outline. Here, no doubt, in old times, had reposed the bones of him for whom the stones of the tomb had been joined and the earth heaped high above them; but now of those bones no vestige remained on the stone floor. And bending close and straining his eyes, Bran made out the strange, startlingly regular pattern of that floor: six well-cut slabs clustered about a seventh, six-sided stone.

He drove his sword-point into a crack and pried carefully. The edge of the central stone tilted slightly upward. A little work and he lifted it out and leaned it against the curving wall. Straining his eyes downward he saw only the gaping blackness of a dark well, with small, worn steps that led downward and out of sight. He did not hesitate. Though the skin between his shoulders crawled curiously, he swung himself into the abyss and felt the clinging blackness swallow him.

Groping downward, he felt his feet slip and stumble on steps too small for human feet. With one hand pressed hard against the side of the well he steadied himself, fearing a fall into unknown and unlighted depths. The steps were cut into solid rock, yet they were greatly worn away. The farther he progressed, the less like steps they became, mere bumps of worn stone. Then the direction of the shaft changed sharply. It still led down, but at a shallow slant down which he could walk, elbows braced against the hollowed sides, head bent low beneath the curved roof. The steps had ceased altogether and the stone felt slimy to the touch, like a serpent's lair. What beings, Bran wondered, had slithered up and down this slanting shaft, for how many centuries?

The tunnel narrowed until Bran found it rather difficult to shove through. He lay on his back and pushed himself along with his hands, feet first. Still he knew he was sinking deeper and deeper into the very guts of the earth; how far below the surface he was, he dared not contemplate. Then ahead a faint witch-fire gleam tinged the abysmal blackness. He grinned savagely and without mirth. If They he sought came suddenly upon him, how could he fight in that narrow shaft? But he had put the thought of personal fear behind him when he began this hellish quest. He crawled on, thoughtless of all else but his goal.

And he came at last into a vast space where he could stand upright. He could not see the roof of the place, but he got an impression of dizzying vastness. The blackness pressed in on all sides and behind him he could see the entrance to the shaft from which he had just emerged—a black well in the darkness. But in front of him a strange grisly radiance glowed about a grim altar built of human skulls. The source of that light he could not determine, but on the altar lay a sullen night-black object—the Black Stone!

Bran wasted no time in giving thanks that the guardians of the grim relic were nowhere near. He caught up the Stone, and gripping it under his left arm, crawled into the shaft. When a man turns his back on peril its clammy menace looms more grisly than when he advances upon it. So Bran, crawling back up the nighted shaft with his grisly prize, felt the darkness turn on him and slink behind him, grinning with dripping fangs. Clammy sweat beaded his flesh and he hastened to the best of his ability, ears strained for some stealthy sound to betray that fell shapes were at his heels. Strong shudders shook him, despite himself, and the short hair on his neck prickled as if a cold wind blew at his back.

When he reached the first of the tiny steps he felt as if he had attained to the outer boundaries of the mortal world. Up them he went, stumbling and slipping, and with a deep gasp of relief, came out into the tomb, whose spectral grayness seemed like the blaze of noon in comparison to the stygian depths he had just traversed. He replaced the central stone and strode into the light of the outer day, and never was the cold yellow light of the sun more grateful as it dispelled the shadows of black-winged nightmares of fear and madness that seemed to have ridden him up out of the black deeps. He shoved the great blocking stone back into place, and picking up the cloak he had left at the mouth of the tomb, he wrapped it about the Black Stone and hurried away, a strong revulsion and loathing shaking his soul and lending wings to his strides.

A gray silence brooded over the land. It was desolate as the blind side of the moon, yet Bran felt the potentialities of life—under his feet, in the brown earth—sleeping, but how soon to waken, and in what horrific fashion?

He came through the tall masking reeds to the still deep men called Dagon's Mere. No slightest ripple ruffled the cold blue water to give evidence of the grisly monster legend said dwelt beneath. Bran closely scanned the breathless landscape. He saw no hint of life, human or unhuman. He sought the instincts of his savage soul to know if any unseen eyes fixed their lethal gaze upon him, and found no response. He was alone as if he were the last man alive on earth.

Swiftly he unwrapped the Black Stone, and as it lay in his hands like a solid sullen block of darkness, he did not seek to learn the secret of its material nor scan the cryptic characters carved thereon. Weighing it in his hands and calculating the distance, he flung it far out, so that it fell almost exactly in the middle of the lake. A sullen splash and the waters closed over it. There was a moment of shimmering flashes on the bosom of the lake; then the blue surface stretched placid and unrippled again.

CHAPTER IV

THE WERE-WOMAN turned swiftly as Bran approached her door. Her slant eyes widened.

"You! And alive! And sane!"

"I have been into Hell and I have returned," he growled. "What is more, I have that which I sought."

"The Black Stone?" she cried. "You really dared steal it? Where is it?"

"No matter; but last night my stallion screamed in his stall and I heard something crunch beneath his thundering hoofs which was not the wall of the stable—and there was blood on his hoofs when I came to see, and blood on the floor of the stall. And I have heard stealthy sounds in the night, and noises beneath my dirt floor, as if worms burrowed deep in the earth. They know I have stolen their Stone. Have you betrayed me?"

She shook her head.

"I keep your secret; they do not need my word to know you. The farther they have retreated from the world of men, the greater have grown their powers in other uncanny ways. Some dawn your hut will stand empty and if men dare investigate they will find nothing—except crumbling bits of earth on the dirt floor."

Bran smiled terribly.

"I have not planned and toiled thus far to fall prey to the talons of vermin. If They strike me down in the night, They will never know what became of their idol—or whatever it be to Them. I would speak with Them."

"Dare you come with me and meet them in the night?" she asked.

"Thunder of all gods!" he snarled. "Who are you to ask me if I dare? Lead me to Them and let me bargain for a vengeance this night. The hour of retribution draws nigh. This day I saw silvered helmets and bright shields gleam across the fens—the new commander has arrived at the Tower of Trajan and Caius Camillus has marched to the Wall."

That night the king went across the dark desolation of the moors with the silent were-woman. The night was thick and still as if the land lay in ancient slumber. The stars blinked vaguely, mere points of red struggling through the unbreathing gloom. Their gleam was dimmer than the glitter in the eyes of the woman who glided beside the king. Strange thoughts shook Bran, vague, titanic, primeval. Tonight ancestral linkings with these slumbering fens stirred in his soul and troubled him with the fantasmal, eon-veiled shapes of monstrous dreams. The vast age of his race was borne upon him; where now he walked an outlaw and an alien, dark-eyed kings in whose mold he was cast, had reigned in old times. The Celtic and Roman invaders were as strangers to this ancient isle beside his people. Yet his race likewise had been

441

invaders, and there was an older race than his—a race whose beginnings lay lost and hidden back beyond the dark oblivion of antiquity.

Ahead of them loomed a low range of hills, which formed the easternmost extremity of those straying chains which far away climbed at last to the mountains of Wales. The woman led the way up what might have been a sheep-path, and halted before a wide black gaping cave.

"A door to those you seek, oh king!" her laughter rang hateful in the gloom. "Dare ye enter?"

His fingers closed in her tangled locks and he shook her viciously.

"Ask me but once more if I dare," he grated, "and your head and shoulders part company! Lead on."

Her laughter was like sweet deadly venom. They passed into the cave and Bran struck flint and steel. The flicker of the tinder showed him a wide dusty cavern, on the roof of which hung clusters of bats. Lighting a torch, he lifted it and scanned the shadowy recesses, seeing nothing but dust and emptiness.

"Where are They?" he growled.

She beckoned him to the back of the cave and leaned against the rough wall, as if casually. But the king's keen eyes caught the motion of her hand pressing hard against a projecting ledge. He recoiled as a round black well gaped suddenly at his feet. Again her laughter slashed him like a keen silver knife. He held the torch to the opening and again saw small worn steps leading down.

"They do not need those steps," said Atla. "Once they did, before your people drove them into the darkness. But you will need them."

She thrust the torch into a niche above the well; it shed a faint red light into the darkness below. She gestured into the well and Bran loosened his sword and stepped into the shaft. As he went down into the mystery of the darkness, the light was blotted out above him, and he thought for an instant Atla had covered the opening again. Then he realized that she was descending after him.

The descent was not a long one. Abruptly Bran felt his feet on a solid floor. Atla swung down beside him and stood in the dim circle of light that drifted down the shaft. Bran could not see the limits of the place into which he had come.

"Many caves in these hills," said Atla, her voice sounding small and strangely brittle in the vastness, "are but doors to the greater caves which lie beneath, even as a man's words and deeds are but small indications of the dark caverns of murky thought lying behind and beneath."

And now Bran was aware of movement in the gloom. The darkness was filled with stealthy noises not like those made by any human foot. Abruptly sparks began to flash and float in the blackness, like flickering fireflies. Closer they came until they girdled him in a wide half-moon. And beyond the ring gleamed other sparks, a solid sea of them, fading away in the gloom until the farthest were mere tiny pin-points of light.

And Bran knew they were the slanted eyes of the beings who had come upon him in such numbers that his brain reeled at the contemplation—and at the vastness of the cavern.

Now that he faced his ancient foes, Bran knew no fear. He felt the waves of terrible menace emanating from them, the grisly hate, the inhuman threat to body, mind and soul. More than a member of a less ancient race, he realized the horror of his position, but he did not fear, though he confronted the ultimate Horror of the dreams and legends of his race. His blood raced fiercely but it was with the hot excitement of the hazard, not the drive of terror.

"They know you have the Stone, oh king," said Atla, and though he knew she feared, though he felt her physical efforts to control her trembling limbs, there was no quiver of fright in her voice. "You are in deadly peril; they know your breed of old—oh, they remember the days when their ancestors were men! I cannot save you; both of us will die as no human has died for ten centuries. Speak to them, if you will; they can understand your speech, though you may not understand theirs. But it will avail not—you are human—and a Pict."

Bran laughed and the closing ring of fire shrank back at the savagery in his laughter. Drawing his sword with a soul-chilling rasp of steel, he set his back against what he hoped was a solid stone wall. Facing the glittering eyes with his sword gripped in his right hand and his dirk in his left, he laughed as a blood-hungry wolf snarls.

"Aye," he growled, "I am a Pict, a son of those warriors who drove your brutish ancestors before them like chaff before the storm!—who flooded the land with your blood and heaped high your skulls for a sacrifice to the Moon-Woman! You who fled of old before my race, dare ye now snarl at your master? Roll on me like a flood, now, if ye dare! Before your viper fangs drink my life I will reap your multitudes like ripened barley—of your severed heads will I build a tower and of your mangled corpses will I rear up a wall! Dogs of the dark, vermin of Hell, worms of the earth, rush in and try my steel! When Death finds me in this dark cavern, your living will howl for the scores of your dead and your Black Stone will be lost to you forever—for only I know where it is hidden and not all the tortures of all the Hells can wring the secret from my lips!"

Then followed a tense silence; Bran faced the fire-lit darkness, tensed like a wolf at bay, waiting the charge; at his side the woman cowered, her eyes ablaze. Then from the silent ring that hovered beyond the dim torchlight rose a vague abhorrent murmur. Bran, prepared as he was for anything, started. Gods, was *that* the speech of creatures which had once been called men?

Atla straightened, listening intently. From her lips came the same hideous soft sibilances, and Bran, though he had already known the grisly secret of her being, knew that never again could he touch her save with soul-shaken loathing.

She turned to him, a strange smile curving her red lips dimly in the ghostly light.

"They fear you, oh king! By the black secrets of R'lyeh, who are you that Hell itself quails before you? Not your steel, but the stark ferocity of your soul has driven unused fear into their strange minds. They will buy back the Black Stone at any price."

"Good," Bran sheathed his weapons. "They shall promise not to molest you because of your aid of me. And," his voice hummed like the purr of a hunting tiger, "they shall deliver into my hands Titus Sulla, governor of Ebbracum, now commanding the Tower of Trajan. This They can do—how, I know not. But I know that in the old days, when my people warred with these Children of the Night, babes disappeared from guarded huts and none saw the stealers come or go. Do They understand?"

Again rose the low frightful sounds and Bran, who feared not their wrath, shuddered at their voices.

"They understand," said Atla. "Bring the Black Stone to Dagon's Ring tomorrow night when the earth is veiled with the blackness that foreruns the dawn. Lay the Stone on the altar. There They will bring Titus Sulla to you. Trust Them; They have not interfered in human affairs for many centuries, but They will keep their word."

Bran nodded and turning, climbed up the stair with Atla close behind him. At the top he turned and looked down once more. As far as he could see floated a glittering ocean of slanted yellow eyes upturned. But the owners of those eyes kept carefully beyond the dim circle of torchlight and of their bodies he could see nothing. Their low hissing speech floated up to him and he shuddered as his imagination visualized, not a throng of biped creatures, but a swarming, swaying myriad of serpents, gazing up at him with their glittering unwinking eyes.

He swung into the upper cave and Atla thrust the blocking stone back in place. It fitted into the entrance of the well with uncanny precision; Bran was unable to discern any crack in the apparently solid floor of the cavern. Atla made a motion to extinguish the torch, but the king stayed her.

"Keep it so until we are out of the cave," he grunted. "We might tread on an adder in the dark."

Atla's sweetly hateful laughter rose maddeningly in the flickering gloom.

CHAPTER V

IT WAS not long before sunset when Bran came again to the reed-grown marge of Dagon's Mere. Casting cloak and sword-belt on the ground, he stripped himself of his short leathern breeches. Then gripping his naked dirk in his teeth, he went into the water with the smooth ease of a diving seal. Swimming strongly, he gained the center of the small lake, and turning, drove himself downward.

The mere was deeper than he had thought. It seemed he would never reach the bottom, and when he did, his groping hands failed to find what he sought. A roaring in his ears warned him and he swam to the surface.

Gulping deep of the refreshing air, he dived again, and again his quest was fruitless. A third time he sought the depth, and this time his groping hands met a familiar object in the silt of the bottom. Grasping it, he swam up to the surface.

The Stone was not particularly bulky, but it was heavy. He swam leisurely, and suddenly was aware of a curious stir in the waters about him which was not caused by his own exertions. Thrusting his face below the surface, he tried to pierce the blue depths with his eyes and thought to see a dim gigantic shadow hovering there.

He swam faster, not frightened, but wary. His feet struck the shallows and he waded up on the shelving shore. Looking back he saw the waters swirl and subside. He shook his head, swearing. He had discounted the ancient legend which made Dagon's Mere the lair of a nameless water-monster, but now he had a feeling as if his escape had been narrow. The time-worn myths of the ancient land were taking form and coming to life before his eyes. What primeval shape lurked below the surface of that treacherous mere, Bran could not guess, but he felt that the fenmen had good reason for shunning the spot, after all.

Bran donned his garments, mounted the black stallion and rode across the fens in the desolate crimson of the sunset's afterglow, with the Black Stone wrapped in his cloak. He rode, not to his hut, but to the west, in the direction of the Tower of Trajan and the Ring of Dagon. As he covered the miles that lay between the red stars winked out. Midnight passed him in the moonless night and still Bran rode on. His heart was hot for his meeting with Titus Sulla. Atla had gloated over the anticipation of watching the Roman writhe under torture, but no such thought was in the Pict's mind. The governor should have his chance with weapons—with Bran's own sword he should face the Pictish king's dirk, and live or die according to his prowess. And though Sulla was famed throughout the provinces as a swordsman, Bran felt no doubt as to the outcome.

Dagon's Ring lay some distance from the Tower—a sullen circle of tall gaunt stones planted upright, with a rough-hewn stone altar in the center. The Romans looked on these menhirs with aversion; they thought the Druids had reared them; but the Celts supposed Bran's people, the Picts, had planted them—and Bran well knew what hands reared those grim monoliths in lost ages, though for what reasons, he but dimly guessed.

The king did not ride straight to the Ring. He was consumed with curiosity as to how his grim allies intended carrying out their promise. That They could snatch Titus Sulla from the very midst of his men, he felt sure, and he believed he knew how They would do it. He felt the gnawings of a strange misgiving, as if he had tampered with powers of unknown breadth and depth, and had loosed forces which he could not control. Each time he remembered that reptilian murmur, those slanted eyes of the night before, a cold breath passed over him. They had been abhorrent enough when his people drove Them into the caverns under the hills, ages ago, what had long centuries of retrogression made of them? In their nighted, subterranean life, had They retained any of the attributes of humanity at all?

Some instinct prompted him to ride toward the Tower. He knew he was near; but for the thick darkness he could have plainly seen its stark outline tusking the horizon. Even now he should be able to make it out dimly. An obscure, shuddersome premonition shook him and he spurred the stallion into swift canter.

And suddenly Bran staggered in his saddle as from a physical impact, so stunning was the surprise of what met his gaze. The impregnable Tower of Trajan was no more! Bran's astounded gaze rested on a gigantic pile of ruins—of shattered stone and crumbled granite, from which jutted the jagged and splintered ends of broken beams. At one corner of the tumbled heap one tower rose out of the waste of crumpled masonry, and it leaned drunkenly as if its foundations had been half cut away.

Bran dismounted and walked forward, dazed by bewilderment. The moat was filled in places by fallen stones and broken pieces of mortared wall. He crossed over and came among the ruins. Where, he knew, only a few hours before the flags had resounded to the martial tramp of iron-clad feet, and the walls had echoed to the clang of shields and the blast of the loud-throated trumpets, an horrific silence reigned.

Almost under Bran's feet, a broken shape writhed and groaned. The king bent down to the legionary who lay in a sticky red pool of his own blood. A single glance showed the Pict that the man, horribly crushed and shattered, was dying.

Lifting the bloody head, Bran placed his flask to the pulped lips and the Roman instinctively drank deep, gulping through splintered teeth. In the dim starlight Bran saw his glazed eyes roll.

"The walls fell," muttered the dying man. "They crashed down like the skies falling on the day of doom. Ah Jove, the skies rained shards of granite and hailstones of marble!"

"I have felt no earthquake shock," Bran scowled, puzzled.

"It was no earthquake," muttered the Roman. "Before last dawn it began, the faint dim scratching and clawing far below the earth. We of the guard heard it—like rats burrowing, or like worms hollowing out the earth. Titus laughed at us, but all day long we heard it. Then at midnight the Tower quivered and seemed to settle—as if the foundations were being dug away—"

A shudder shook Bran Mak Morn. The worms of the earth! Thousands of vermin digging like moles far below the castle, burrowing away the foundations—gods, the land must be honeycombed with tunnels and caverns—these creatures were even less human than he had thought—what ghastly shapes of darkness had he invoked to his aid?

"What of Titus Sulla?" he asked, again holding the flask to the legionary's lips; in that moment the dying Roman seemed to him almost like a brother.

"Even as the Tower shuddered we heard a fearful scream from the governor's chamber," muttered the soldier. "We rushed there—as we broke down the door we heard his shrieks—they seemed to recede—*into the bowels of the earth!* We rushed in; the chamber was empty. His blood-stained sword lay on the floor; in the stone flags of the floor a black hole gaped. Then—the—towers—reeled—the—roof—broke;—through—a—storm—of—crashing—walls—I—crawled—"

A strong convulsion shook the broken figure.

"Lay me down, friend," whispered the Roman, "I die."

He had ceased to breathe before Bran could comply. The Pict rose, mechanically cleansing his hands. He hastened from the spot, and as he galloped over the darkened fens, the weight of the accursed Black Stone under his cloak was as the weight of a foul nightmare on a mortal breast.

As he approached the Ring, he saw an eery glow within, so that the gaunt stone stood etched like the ribs of a skeleton in which a witch-fire burns. The stallion snorted and reared as Bran tied him to one of the menhirs. Carrying the Stone he strode into the grisly circle and saw Atla standing beside the altar, one hand on her hip, her sinuous body swaying in a serpentine manner. The altar glowed all over with ghastly light and Bran knew some one, probably Atla, had rubbed it with phosphorus from some dank swamp or quagmire.

He strode forward and whipping his cloak from about the Stone, flung the accursed thing on to the altar.

"I have fulfilled my part of the contract," he growled.

"And They, theirs," she retorted. "Look!—they come!"

He wheeled, his hand instinctively dropping to his sword. Outside the Ring the great stallion screamed savagely and reared against his tether. The night wind moaned through the waving grass and an abhorrent soft hissing mingled with it. Between the menhirs flowed a dark tide of shadows, unstable and chaotic. The Ring filled with glittering eyes which hovered beyond the dim illusive circle of illumination cast by the phosphorescent altar. Somewhere in the darkness a human voice tittered and gibbered idiotically. Bran stiffened, the shadows of a horror clawing at his soul.

He strained his eyes, trying to make out the shapes of those who ringed him. But he glimpsed only billowing masses of shadow which heaved and writhed and squirmed with almost fluid consistency.

"Let them make good their bargain!" he exclaimed angrily.

"Then see, oh king!" cried Atla in a voice of piercing mockery.

There was a stir, a seething in the writhing shadows, and from the darkness crept, like a four-legged animal, a human shape that fell down and groveled at Bran's feet and writhed and mowed, and lifting a death's-head, howled like a dying dog. In the ghastly light, Bran, soul-shaken, saw the blank glassy eyes, the bloodless features, the loose, writhing, froth-covered lips of sheer lunacy—gods, was this Titus Sulla, the proud lord of life and death in Ebbracum's proud city?

Bran bared his sword.

"I had thought to give this stroke in vengeance," he said somberly. "I give it in mercy—*Vale Caesar!*"

The steel flashed in the eery light and Sulla's head rolled to the foot of the glowing altar, where it lay staring up at the shadowed sky.

"They harmed him not!" Atla's hateful laugh slashed the sick silence. "It was what he saw and came to know that broke his brain! Like all his heavy-footed race, he knew nothing of the secrets of this ancient land. This night he has been dragged through the deepest pits of Hell, where even you might have blenched!"

"Well for the Romans that they know not the secrets of this accursed land!" Bran roared, maddened, "with its monster-haunted meres, its foul witch-women, and its lost caverns and subterranean realms where spawn in the darkness shapes of Hell!"

"Are they more foul than a mortal who seeks their aid?" cried Atla with a shriek of fearful mirth. "Give them their Black Stone!"

A cataclysmic loathing shook Bran's soul with red fury.

"Aye, take your cursed Stone!" he roared, snatching it from the altar and dashing it among the shadows with such savagery that bones snapped under its impact. A hurried babel of grisly tongues rose and the shadows heaved in turmoil. One segment of the mass detached itself for an instant and Bran cried out in fierce revulsion, though he caught only a fleeting glimpse of the thing, had only a brief impression of a broad strangely flattened head, pendulous writhing lips that bared curved pointed fangs, and a hideously misshapen, dwarfish body that seemed *mottled*—all set off by those unwinking reptilian eyes. Gods!—the myths had prepared him for horror in human aspect, horror induced by bestial visage and stunted deformity—but this was the horror of nightmare and the night.

"Go back to Hell and take your idol with you!" he yelled, brandishing his clenched fists to the skies, as the thick shadows receded, flowing back and away from him like the foul waters of some black flood. "Your ancestors were men, though strange and monstrous—but gods, ye have become in ghastly fact what my people called ye in scorn! Worms of the earth, back into your holes and burrows! Ye foul the air and leave on the clean earth the slime of the serpents ye have become! Gonar was right—there are shapes too foul to use even against Rome!"

He sprang from the Ring as a man flees the touch of a coiling snake, and tore the stallion free. At his elbow Atla was shrieking with fearful laughter, all human attributes dropped from her like a cloak in the night.

"King of Pictland!" she cried, "King of fools! Do you blench at so small a thing? Stay and let me show you real fruits of the pits! Ha! ha! ha! Run, fool, run! But you are stained with the taint—you have called them forth and they will remember! And in their own time they will come to you again!"

He yelled a wordless curse and struck her savagely in the mouth with his open hand. She staggered, blood starting from her lips, but her fiendish laughter only rose higher.

Bran leaped into the saddle, wild for the clean heather and the cold blue hills of the north where he could plunge his sword into clean slaughter and his sickened soul into the red maelstrom of battle, and forget the horror which lurked below the fens of the west. He gave the frantic stallion the rein, and rode through the night like a hunted ghost, until the hellish laughter of the howling were-woman died out in the darkness behind.

About the Editors

STEFAN R. DZIEMIANOWICZ is a contributing editor of *Crypt of Cthulhu* and the author of *The Annotated Guide to "Unknown" and "Unknown Worlds."*

ROBERT WEINBERG, one of the foremost authorities on weird fiction pulp magazines, is the author of *The Weird Tales Story,* for which he won the World Fantasy Award.

MARTIN H. GREENBERG has more than three hundred anthologies to his credit. He is professor of regional analysis and political science at the University of Wisconsin—Green Bay.